I0586394

From Rabbi to Messiah

A Holistic Approach to the Johannine Christology

From Rabbi to Messiah

A Holistic Approach to the Johannine Christology

Michael Raj

2018

From Rabbi to Messiah: A Holistic Approach to the Johannine Christology—
Published by the Rev. Dr. Ashish Amos of the Indian Society for Promoting
Christian Knowledge (ISPCK), Post Box 1585, 1654, Madarsa Road, Kashmere
Gate, Delhi-110006.

© Author, 2018

*All rights reserved. No part of this book may be reproduced or transmitted in any form
or by any means, electronic, mechanical, photocopying, recording, or by any information
storage and retrieval system, without the prior permission in writing from the publisher.*

*The views expressed in the book are those of the author and the publisher takes no
responsibility for any of the statements.*

Online Order: http://ispck.org.in/book.php

Also available on amazon.in

ISBN: 978-81-8465-666-4

Cover credit: Internet sources

Laser typeset by

ISPCK, Post Box 1585, 1654, Madarsa Road, Kashmere Gate, Delhi-110006
• *Tel:* 23866323/22

e-mail: ashish@ispck.org.in • ella@ispck.org.in
website: www.ispck.org.in

Contents

PART - II

PART - III

Acknowledgement

A research study on the biblical concept of discipleship is due to the inspiration that I received from the hundreds of committed and convinced lay volunteers who have real thirst to learn and to spread the Gospel in my home diocese of Sivagangai in the region of Tamil Nadu in India. This exegetical and historical critical study also is an examination of my own priestly identity as a disciple and servant of the Word. I am happy to see this work on the Johannine understanding of discipleship as the fruit of my effort to synthesise my biblical studies with my choice of life and commitment.

Before entering into this doctoral thesis, let me gratefully remember all those who have made this study a success. This work is the outcome of the able and masterly guidance of my promoters Dr. Reimund Bieringer of Catholic University in Leuven, Belgium and Miss. Bernadette Escaffre of Catholic University of Toulouse, France in whom I see indeed an edifying master-disciple relationship. Starting from the beginning of my first meeting, their method and guidance was always to challenge the student to work both exegetically and argumentatively so that it might bring the best of its fruits in my studies. I am sure that their challenging guidance has shaped me as a better exegete and a committed theologian.

I wish to express my sincere gratitude here to my diocesan late Bishop Dr. Edward Francis who sent me abroad for my higher studies in Biblical Theology and the present Bishop Dr. J. Susaimanickam who until today continues to encourage me with his love and blessings. I am greatly indebted to the Missionary Society of Paris for their great financial support to pursue my studies both in Belgium and France.

My sincere thanks also go to all my professors in the Faculty of Theology and the staff of the Library who have contributed a lot to help me reach my goal in the Universities of Leuven and Toulouse. I wish to express my sentiments of gratitude to all my friends here who have extended a tremendous support to the publication of this masterpiece. Thanks a lot to them both for their valuable contribution and brotherly support. I also wish to remember with gratitude my parents and family members, friends and relatives, near and dear ones for their continued love and encouragement. Thanks to all of them and may God bless you!

Rev. Dr. Michael Raj S

Felicitation - 1

I am indeed delighted to felicitate Rev. Dr. S. Michael Raj, a Priest of the Diocese of Sivagangai and a Teaching Faculty at St. Paul's Seminary, Tiruchirappalli, on the occasion of the release of the book *From Rabbi to Messiah. A Holistic Approach to the Johannine Christology,* the fruit of his hard-laboured doctoral research presented at the Catholic University of Toulouse, France.

The Scholars of the Fourth Gospel by and large agree that John the Evangelist has woven his Gospel in a concentric pattern of movements from the centre to the periphery or from the particular to the universal. One such movement of moving from Jews to the Gentiles is vivid in Jesus' meeting of different persons: (1) a Jew - Nicodemus (Jn 3:1-21); (2) a Samaritan - Woman at the Well (4:1-42); (3) a Galilean - an Official (4:43-54); (4) a Greek - the Greeks at the Feast (12:20-22); and (5) a Roman - Pontius Pilate (18:19-16). As the Gospel unfolds one sees a movement from exclusive to inclusive, from Jew to Gentile. Understanding this concentric pattern helps one see the Gospel in a holistic way.

Dr. S. Michael Raj takes the two titles attributed to Jesus in the Fourth Gospel, i.e., 'Rabbi' and 'Messiah,' and through the lexical, historical, historical-critical, socio-religious, and intertextual reading of these terms and their texts, the author comprehends the entire Christology portrayed in John. Hence, the current study stands as a unique contribution to the present scholarship on the Gospel of John and on Christology. At the end of the study the reader is challenged to ask what type of type s/he would attribute to Jesus and what type of relationship it would entail with 'Jesus of History' and 'Christ of Faith.'

As I congratulate Rev. Dr. S. Michael Raj for this voluminous and in-depth study I wish him all the best in his future endeavours as en erudite scholar.

+ Most Rev. Dr. Antony Pappusamy

Archbishop, Archdiocese of Madurai

President, TNBC/TNLBC

Chairman of the Board of Administration, St. Paul's Seminary

Given in Madurai on 27 March 2018

Foreword

We learn from the Gospels that the disciples of Jesus called him 'Rabbi' (cf. Mk 9:5; 11:21; 14:45; Jn 1:38,49; 3:2; 4:31) or its variant 'Rabbouni' (Jn 20:16). This Hebrew term is a honorific title which means 'my master' and corresponded to the Greek διδασκαλος (teacher). The term conveyed respect and bestowed on Jesus a similar rank as that of the Scribes (Mt 13:52; cf. 23:2,7). Jesus' style of preaching and teaching  resembled the rabbinic style and he communicated his message through parables.

The terms 'Rabbi' and 'teacher' are used interchangeably, though they do not denote the same meaning. The author of the Fourth Gospel uses both the terms 'master' and 'teacher' trying to make a link between them. It is used by Martha of Bethany in 11:28 and by Jesus himself after the foot-washing at the Last Supper: "You call me Teacher and Lord – and you are right, for that is what I am. So if I, your Lord and Teacher, have washed your feet, you also ought to wash one another's feet" (13:13-14).

The designation of Jesus as 'Rabbi' in the Fourth Gospel may be a genuine historical reminiscence that dates back to the life of Jesus himself. The followers of Jesus must have attributed an authoritative status to Jesus when they called him 'Rabbi'. But looking at the 'Rabbi' statements of the Fourth Gospel at a deeper level, one notices Christological perspective in most of the occurrences of the term. Andrew, one of the first two disciples who called Jesus 'Rabbi,' proclaims him as the Messiah when he speaks to his brother Simon Peter (1:41). Then Nathanael proclaims this 'Rabbi' to be the Son of God and King of Israel (1:49). This Christological journey continues through Nicodemus who calls Jesus 'Rabbi', a teacher who has come from God (3:2). The Johannine Christological journey concludes in 20:16 when Mary of Magdala recognizes Jesus as the Risen Lord and acknowledges him as 'Rabbouni' – a variant form 'Rabbi' – which, as the author explains, also means Teacher!

Thus the author of the Gospel is trying to persuade his readers so that they may come to believe that the historical Jesus is the Messiah, the Son of God, and that through believing they may have life in his name (20:31). The Gospel aims at playing a crucial role in the lives of its readers, as the foundation for their faith in Jesus as the Messiah and Son of God and therefore the basis of their hope for eternal life.

The book From Rabbi to Messiah: A Holistic Approach to the Johannine Christology in the Fourth Gospel is a biblical and theological presentation by Rev. Dr. S. Michael Raj, Professor of Biblical Theology in St. Paul's Seminary, Tiruchirapalli, and it covers the gradual development of Johannine Christology from addressing Jesus as Rabbi referring to the earthly life and ministry of Jesus to the acclamation of the glorified Messiah as Lord and God (20:28). This significant study includes evaluating the meaning of the term 'Rabbi' attributed to Jesus and deals with its significant position in understanding the ascending Christology of John.

I am sure that this book will be useful to all those who are interested in Johannine Christology. The author deserves our appreciation and hearty congratulations for his scholarly research.

J. Susaimanickam
Bishop of Sivagangai
Chairman, CCBI Commission for Bible

Felicitation - 2

‘ From Rabbi to Messiah: A Holistic Approach to the Johannine Christology' is the title of the thesis presented by Dr. S. Michael Raj, to the Catholic University of Toulouse, France for his Doctoral title. Dr. Michael Raj who belongs to the diocese of Sivagangai is a student of mine. He is very intelligent and articulate. With a synthetic mind he can present any subject in an intelligible and convincing manner.

Dr. Michael Raj has taken the Gospel of St. John as the area of his study. In the Johannine Gospel he has chosen the title 'Rabbi' as the focus of his research. This title given to Jesus in all the Gospels but Luke, is found more frequently in the Gospel of John. The title Rabbi although is one among the many titles given to Jesus shows him as a typical first century sage or Jewish teacher. The historical Jesus was mostly understood by his contemporaries as a Rabbi which means teacher or master. While the Evangelists' portrayal of Jesus transcends that of Rabbi / teacher / master, enlarging the scope of his Christology to include terms such as son of God, son of Man, Christ, etc., it is to be accepted for the contemporaries of Jesus, he was primarily a Rabbi – teacher – master.

Dr. Michael Raj studies the gradual development of Johannine Christology from Jesus being called a Rabbi (earthly ministry) to his being acclaimed as glorified Messiah (Lord and God). Thus Jesus' role as Rabbi constitutes the historical starting point for the John's presentation of Jesus. The role of teacher (Rabbi), prophet and miracle worker are not in conflict with each other; rather they complement each other.

Dr. Michael Raj studies the concept of Rabbi against its historical background. He shows the meaning of Rabbi prior to the historical Jesus. Then he proceeds to show the significance of the title Rabbi at the time when the Gospels were composed. He studies in detail the use the title Rabbi in the Gospels. At the end he deals with the Johannine perception of the title Rabbi. He focuses attention on the questions of relevance and significance of addressing Jesus as Rabbi in the presentation of Johannine Christology. In fact the title Rabbi is a historical starting point of Johannine ascending Christology. In this way John by calling Jesus 'Rabbi' primarily shows that his high Christology is rooted in the earthy life and ministry of Jesus. Thus the Johannine Gospel that starts calling Jesus as the 'Rabbi' (In 1:38b) ends by calling him Messiah (In 1:41) and Lord and God' (In 20:28)

Dr. Michael Raj has done an excellent study of the Gospel of John. He has studied in depth most the Johannine Scholars and made sure that his views are supported by them. I really appreciate and congratulate him on this excellent study. It is definitely a contribution on the study of the title 'Rabbi' in its relation to the Johannine Christology. I wish that many read his work and get deeper insight into the title of Rabbi for Jesus and the Johannine Christology itself.

Rev. Dr. Prof. Cruz M. Hieronymus
Vellamadam
Kanyakumari District

A Historical-Critical Analysis of the Attribution of the Title 'Ραββί to Jesus in the Gospels:

The Role of the Title 'Ραββί, in the Presentation of John's High Christology and Holistic Theology

General Introduction

In biblical times, a name or a title had a significant meaning, often denoting a characteristic or something related to the history of the person or his time. Scripture shows that many titles were used to describe and address Jesus during his lifetime. These names or titles occur in different ways, at different occasions, in confessions, acclamations, formulae of faith, and even as praise and hymns. A complete understanding of Jesus has to take into account these various titles and names. Generally a complete understanding of any person requires a number of descriptions and a variety of terms. The same thing holds true for Jesus. In the NT there are more than fifty different ways of naming the earthly Jesus or the Risen Lord. The complex nature and mission of Jesus Christ is revealed in the many names and titles that are attributed to him. Each of these reveals a particular attribute and tells us something about the person of Jesus.

A summary of Jesus' names and titles can be found in five attributions: The Son of God, the Son of Man, the Messiah, the Prophet, and the Teacher. The words "Messiah" and "Christ" both mean the same thing and refer to the same person. Each is used to identify "The Anointed One." Messiah is the Hebrew word while Christ is the Greek translation. Christ is not a name but a theological title, which comes from the Greek Χριστος (*Christos*) via Latin, which means anointed *with Chrism*. The Greek form Χριστος is a literal translation of *Messiah,* a word which occurs often in the OT and typically signifies "high priest" or "King" or a man, chosen by, or descended from, a man chosen by God, to serve as a religious, civil and/or military authority. In the Old Testament, it is the word used for both priests and kings who were anointed to their office just as David was anointed by Samuel as King of Israel.

An understanding of Jesus as "The Son of God", "the Son of Man," "The Messiah", and "The Prophet" is a beginning toward realizing who he is. The attribute "Son of Joseph of Nazareth" clearly acknowledges Jesus' full humanity. As in the Synoptic Gospels, there are many different names for Jesus in the Gospel of John. John starts by saying that, 'The word was God' θεὸς ἦν ὁ λόγος (Jn 1:1), and he ends with Thomas crying 'My Lord and my God' Ὁ κύριός μου καὶ ὁ θεός μου (Jn 20:28). The various titles for Jesus start at the very beginning of chapter 1. In fact in the first chapter, Jesus is seen as the Word, the Light, the Life, the Lamb, the Baptiser with the Spirit, the Son of God. Also, Jesus is called the Creator (Jn 1:3): "Through him all things were made; without him nothing was made that has been made." Since Jesus is God, and the Living Word, he is the originator of everything. The book of John starts by calling Jesus God, "In the beginning was the Word, and the Word was with God, and the Word was God." The λόγος existed and had His hand in creation long before he was born a human child. Jesus is also called Messiah, King of Israel, and calls himself 'Son of Man', all in this first chapter. Jesus is the "Truth" (Jn 1:14) and the "True Light" (Jn 1:9). He is the "King of Israel" (Jn 1:49), the "Lamb of God" (Jn 1:29), the "Son of God" (Jn 1:49) and the "Only Begotten Son of God" (Jn 1:18). Jn 6:33 says, "For the Bread of God is he who comes down from heaven and gives life to the world". Then, just two verses later in Jn 6:35, Jesus declares, "I am the Bread of Life. He who comes to me will never go hungry, and he who believes in me will never be thirsty." In Jn 6:48 Jesus says, "I am the bread of life." He is the Gate: just as one walks through a gate to reach a destination, one enters God's family through Jesus (Jn 10:9 "Jesus as Gate"). He is our good shepherd. "I am the good shepherd. The good shepherd lays down his life for the sheep" (Jn 10:11). "I am the good shepherd; I know my sheep and my sheep know me (Jn 10:14). In Jn 8:58, he tells us that He is the great "I Am." He is called the "Light of the World" (John 8:12), the "True Bread"

(Jn 6:32). Jesus is also called the "True Vine" (Jn 15:1), the "Truth" (Jn 14:6), and the "Way" (Jn 14:6) and Jesus is the "Resurrection and Life" (Jn 11:25). In addition to all these, Jesus is called ῥαββί, a title which is at the very core of this book.

The Purpose of the Study

Although ῥαββί is only one among the many titles given to Jesus in the Gospels, it cannot be glossed over. In the Gospel accounts, the title "Rabbi" ascribed to Jesus illustrates that, among the various images, Jesus was also considered a typical first-century sage or Jewish teacher. Gerhard Schneider[1] asserts that the title ῥαββί belongs to the pre-Markan tradition, but he also agrees that there is no single utterance in the logia source (Q). It is noted that, whereas the Synoptic writers use the term ῥαββί only a few times, John's constitutes over half the references in all four Gospels combined. Matthew uses it twice (Mt 26:25; 26:49); Mark, four times (9:5; 10:51; 11:21; 14:45), and Luke not at all. The author of the Fourth Gospel uses the term ῥαββί eight times (Jn 1:38, 49; 3:2; 4:31; 6:25; 9:2; 11:8 and in 20:16, it is ῥαββουνί), of which seven times are by the disciples of Jesus. The one remaining reference is addressed to John the Baptist in Jn 3:26. The address ῥαββί in the Gospel of John 1:38 is attributed to the first followers and in Jn 1:49 to Nathanael. Then comes Nicodemus the Pharisee in Jn 3:2 who uses the same title ῥαββί for Jesus. On three occasions 4:31; 9:2; 11:8, it is attributed to the disciples. In 6:25, after the multiplication of the loaves and fish, it is the multitudes which call him ῥαββί. And in the post- Easter narratives of Jn 20:16, Mary Magdalene addresses Jesus as ῥαββουνί. Hence, the first insight is that the title ῥαββί occurs both in the earliest canonical Gospel of Mark and the later Gospel of John. This is the background for this study of the meaning of the title Rabbi for Jesus in the Gospels, and in particular in the gospel of John. Johannine scholarship has paid little attention to the role of Jesus as ῥαββί, which is translated as Teacher. It is noted that in their first encounter with Jesus, the disciples address him as Rabbi. Becoming aware of their following him, Jesus turns and asks, "What do you seek?" They answer,"Rabbi (meaning teacher) where do you live?" (Cf. Jn 1:38). Τί ζητεῖτε; οἱ δὲ εἶπαν αὐτῷ, Ῥαββί (ὃ λέγεται μεθερμηνευόμενον Διδάσκαλε), ποῦ μένεις; Here the question is why the disciples do not use the title that John the Baptist gave to Jesus while introducing him to them. While John the Baptist says Ἴδε ὁ ἀμνὸς τοῦ θεοῦ, the disciples say Ῥαββί (ὃ λέγεται μεθερμηνευόμενον Διδάσκαλε), an address or title that is entirely different from the one that came from the mouth of John. To read and better understand the Johannine Jesus, it is necessary to ask another question; that is, whether it is correct to translate "Rabbi" as teacher or master. What did the two disciples mean by calling Jesus 'Rabbi' at that moment? Did it mean, for example, that the two disciples in Jn 1:38 saw Jesus as a Rabbi similar to any of the many Rabbis in Jerusalem or did the disciples assume Jesus must be a Rabbi because of the exalted way John the Baptist had spoken about him? Could there be some other reason altogether?

The Basic concerns or issues of the Study

In fact, the meaning of the term 'Rabbi' in the context of John forms the basis of this book. A threefold approach has been introduced in this study. First looking at the historical antecedents of the term: secondly, observing the contemporary use of the term during the public ministry of Jesus and thirdly, concluding with the particular way the evangelist John uses the term in the Fourth Gospel.

Jesus must, first of all, be understood in terms of his Jewish cultural context, a conclusion which is aided decisively by the terminological and theological affinity between the Fourth Gospel and the Qumran writings. In this debate, with its matrices of Jewish/Greek and the human/divine, one important aspect of John's presentation of Jesus has been neglected in recent scholarly discussion: the evangelist's portrayal of Jesus as a Jewish Rabbi. This may in part be due to the influence of authors like M. Hengel who, in his significant work *The Charismatic Leader and His Followers*, flatly states that "Jesus was not a Rabbi." While acknowledging that Jesus was doubtless addressed as 'Rabbi,' Hengel contends that this expression did not necessarily carry the connotation of teacher but may merely have functioned as a term of respect. He himself considers Jesus primarily as an "eschatological charismatic," the focus of whose message was no longer the Old Testament. For Hengel, Jesus "stood outside any discoverable uniform teaching tradition of Judaism," so that he concludes, with G. Friedrich, that "there was between him [Jesus] and the rabbis not a difference in degree as between two different teachers, but a difference in principle. He taught as someone specially authorized by God, so that his Word was God's Word, which men could not evade." For this reason Hengel suggests that "we should desist altogether from the description of Jesus as a 'rabbi.'"

In recent years, however, Hengel's analysis has been eclipsed by the magisterial work of R. Riesner on Jesus as a teacher.[2] But Riesner focuses primarily on the Synoptic Gospels, though his argument remains valid that Jesus operated within the Palestinian framework of a Jewish religious teacher. Nevertheless, Riesner's work remains to be supplemented by an equivalent study on Jesus as a Rabbi in the Fourth Gospel. C. Evans' discussion of rabbinic terms and methods as well as Targumic and Midrashic traditions in John likewise is most helpful but is conducted primarily above the fourth evangelist rather than Jesus. In general, Johannine scholarship has paid little attention on Jesus' role of rabbi or teacher. It is not argued here that this is the major, or even a major aspect of Johannine Christology which is comprised of Jesus as the Son Sent; Jesus as the one who came into the world and returned to the Father (descent-ascent); and Jesus as the eschatological Shepherd- teacher. A survey of the history of interpretation of John's Gospel shows that while the first two aspects of Johannine Christology have been adequately recognized, the third role has often reflected the common perception of Jesus among his contemporaries: that Jesus was, perhaps more, but certainly no less, than a Rabbi.

The present study is thus designed to provide a corrective to the current debate regarding the historical Jesus as well as a modest supplement to Riesner's work by studying John's presentation of Jesus as a teacher in the Fourth Gospel. While the evangelist's portrayal of Jesus transcends that of Rabbi/Teacher/Master, enlarging the scope of his Christology to include terms such as Son of God, Son of Man, or Christ, his account makes clear that Jesus' contemporaries perceived and addressed Jesus primarily as a religious teacher, a Rabbi. The present study thus seeks to establish this one thesis: John's Gospel bears witness that Jesus was perceived by his contemporaries primarily as a Jewish teacher.

The validity of this assertion will be established by a demonstration of the following: first, "Rabbi" or "teacher" is the customary way to address Jesus in the Fourth Gospel; and second, John portrays the relationship between Jesus and his closest followers in terms of the customary teacher-disciple relationship in the first-century Judaism. From Rudolf Bultmann, to C. H. Dodd, to the Jesus Seminar, Johannine scholarship has emphasized the Greek background of the Fourth Gospel. Even R. Bultmann's own comment, "Yet in face of the entire content of the Tradition it can hardly be doubted that Jesus did teach as a Rabbi, gathers disciples and engages in disputations."[3] The Johannine Jesus, on the other hand, is often understood in terms of the Fourth Gospel's emphasis on Christ's deity, especially as portrayed in the Prologue. Works such as Marianne Thompson's *The Humanity of Jesus in the Fourth Gospel*, however, have countered the arguments of Käsemann and others that John portrays Jesus in docetic terms, that is, as a divine rather than an earthly human figure.[4] In one of his recent works, Andreas Köstenberger in his *Studies on John and Gender: A Decade of Scholarship*, speaks of "*Jesus as Rabbi in the Fourth Gospel*", stating that "John's "high Christology" is rooted in Jesus' earthly life and ministry."[5] D. Moody Smith in his *The Theology of the Gospel of John* says "Among traditional Jewish titles applied to Jesus in John we find also rabbi."[6] He holds that the term ῥαββί, when applied to the Johannine Jesus, ought to be understood as a Christological title. But J. Ashton's work on "*Understanding the Fourth Gospel*" has paid much attention to the aspects of Messiah, Son of God, Son of Man and the Christ, but not to Jesus as Rabbi. Schnackenburg,[8] for example in his "*Jesus in the Gospels*"[7] has given no attention to the aspect of Jesus as a Jewish teacher. Thus, the study on Christology has never taken this aspect of ῥαββί very seriously, precisely because it was thought that the aspect of Jesus as a religious teacher is not co-related to the notion of Johannine high Christology.

This study will cover the gradual development of Johannine Christology from addressing Jesus as Rabbi (earthly life and ministry) to the acclamation of glorified Messiah (Lord and God). This will include evaluating the meaning of the term 'Rabbi' attributed to Jesus and will deal with its significant position in understanding the ascending Christology of John. Questions will include trying to find whether John understands the term ῥαββί as being a Christological category. Also, when persons address Jesus as ῥαββί in the Fourth Gospel, do they qualify themselves as believers by doing so?

In Johannine studies, Jesus' role as a Rabbi constitutes the historical starting point for the fourth evangelist's presentation of Jesus. But, this aspect has generally been minimized owing to a focus on John's "high" Christology and on Johannine theology rather than on the historical Jesus. It is not argued here that Rabbi is the *only* Johannine category for Jesus, or even the most important. Rather, it is merely contended that John reflects the fact that this was the way Jesus was primarily perceived by his contemporaries. To be sure, on the basis of this common perception, speculation arose whether Jesus was the prophet like Moses or the Messianic king. But if the historical starting point for John's presentation of Jesus is lost, there no longer remains any common ground on the basis of which the historical Jesus conducted the interchange with his Jewish interlocutors and the focus from which the evangelist seeks to lead his readers into a deeper understanding of Jesus' full and true identity.

The present essay's focus on John's presentation of Jesus as a rabbi should in no way be viewed as an effort to diminish John's portrayal of Jesus in apocalyptic-prophetic terms, including Jesus' working of miracles. But there is no implication that these elements are incompatible with John's basic presentation of Jesus as a religious teacher. As Riesner contends, a "high Christology" need not necessarily conflict with a portrayal of Jesus as a teacher, and the role of teacher and the working of miracles may complement each other rather than stand in conflict. Hengel likewise notes that "prophet" and "teacher" should in no way be regarded as opposites. The scholarly tension in this case may rather be the result of an unduly narrow concept of "teacher" that excludes prophetic, miracle-working, or messianic notions and is incompatible with scriptural and Jewish notions in Jesus' day.

Plans and Methodology

The methodology in this study of the meaning of ῥαββί as addressed to Jesus in John will use the historical-critical method of exegesis. This methodology, through examining the context in which rabbi is used will achieve and present a proper understanding of the terminology, enshrined in the notion of the word ῥαββί, as used in the perspective of the Gospel writers and especially in the context of the Fourth Evangelist. This will include discussing whether it was proper to call Jesus a Rabbi. The goal is to understand the full significance of Jesus being addressed as Rabbi and to know what being a Rabbi of the first century entailed, and how he functioned. *Rabbi*, meaning *teacher*, was, and is, a dignified title given to experts of the religious law and distinguished teachers. This book consists of three parts for the systematic study of this particular issue.

Part I will study the concept of Rabbi against its historical background. Thus, it will explore the significance of the title ῥαββί at different historical stages. It will begin with the meaning of the term ῥαββί prior to the time of the historical Jesus. It will include what ῥαββί means historically and how it was interpreted or used. Also, the historical influence of the Rabbi-Disciple relationship, both in the Jewish and Hellenistic contexts, will be given special attention. This includes how this title evolved during the time of transition to Hellenism. For whom and under what conditions was the title ῥαββί conferred? To this end, the cultural level will be reviewed to see how the term was used in the society into which Jesus was born. Beyond this, the significance of the title ῥαββί in the post-resurrection era will be analysed, especially from the time of the destruction of the Temple in 70 AD. Further, the point, put forward by many scholars, that the title may be a gloss used retrospectively only after the destruction of the second Temple in 70 A.D. will not be ignored. It is evidently accepted by most scholars that the use of the title Rabbi for ordained scholars does not appear in any of the Jewish sources before 70 A.D. Thus, using observations on the occurrence of the term ῥαββί in the gospels, a detailed study will be made as to whether the use of the title ῥαββί in the gospels is anachronistic. With this background established, this study will further discuss understanding Jesus as a Rabbi in the Palestinian Jewish context. This will form the focus of this study in Part II.

The significance of the title ῥαββί at the time when the Gospels were written or composed will be evaluated in the context of particular communities. This will lead to the question: In what sense do the different authors of the NT use the term ῥαββί for Jesus? This will include studying the distinction between the office of Rabbi and the exact mission that Jesus had. Though this study's focus is Johannine, it will first adopt a synoptic perspective as a general backdrop for the Jewish context of Jesus and his role as a Jewish teacher. This provides a credible first-century Jewish framework for John's portrayal of Jesus as a Rabbi. In summary, Part II will embrace the synoptic perspective.

The final part, Part III will deal with the Johannine perspective of Rabbi as applied to Jesus. Jn 1:38b says: Τί ζητεῖτε; οἱ δὲ εἶπαν αὐτῷ, Ῥαββί (ὃ λέγεται μεθερμηνευόμενον Διδάσκαλε), ποῦ μένεις; While John the Baptist says, Ἴδε ὁ ἀμνὸς τοῦ θεοῦ ; the disciples say, Ῥαββί (ὃ λέγεται μεθερμηνευόμενον Διδάσκαλε), an address or title that is entirely different from the one that came from the mouth of John the Baptist. John then translates ῥαββί as Διδάσκαλος which means teacher. If John, the author of the Fourth Gospel intends the term ῥαββί to mean teacher, then what it means outside that connotation must also be addressed. If Jesus is addressed as ῥαββί, in the sense of a teacher, in John, does that reflect the use of the term in the time of Jesus or John the Baptist? Thus this historical analysis will focus attention on the question of the relevance and significance of addressing Jesus as ῥαββί in the presentation of Johannine Christology. Consider that when persons address Jesus as ῥαββί in the Fourth Gospel, they may be qualifying themselves as believers. Is using the term ῥαββί in the Fourth Gospel a sufficient qualification for Jesus?

Does John understand the term ῥαββί as a Christological category? Does the Johannine use of the term ῥαββί refer only to the earthly Jesus? If Jesus is perceived as ῥαββί, in the sense of a teacher, what is the significant role it may play in Johannine Christology? In a nutshell, what is the place of 'Jesus the Ραββί in the presentation of the Johannine Theology? This book, in three parts, addresses all these and other questions in presenting a historical analysis of the title ῥαββί for Jesus in the Gospel of John.

Endnotes

[1] Gerhard SCHNEIDER, ῥαββί and ῥαββουνί, in *EDNT* 3 (1990) 205-206, p. 206.

[2] Rainer RIESNER, *Jesus als Lehrer,* WUNT 2/7, 3d ed., Tübingen, J. C. B. Mohr, Paul Siebeck, 1988.

[3] Rudolf BULTMANN, *The History of the Synoptic Tradition,* (trans.) J. MARSH, Oxford, Basil Blackwell, 1963, p. 50.

[4] Cf. Marianne Meye THOMPSON, "The Historical Jesus and the Johannine Christ", in *Exploring the Gospel of John. In Honor of D. Moody Smith,* (ed). R. A. CULPEPPER and C. C. BLACK, Louisville, KY, Westminster/ John Knox, 1996, p. 21.

[5] Andreas J. KÖSTENBERGER, *Studies on John and Gender: A Decade of Scholarship*, New York- Washington D.C. et al., Peter Lang, 2001, p. 96.

[6] Dwight MOODY SMITH, *New Testament Theology, The Theology of the Gospel of John*, Cambridge, NY, Cambridge University Press, 1995, p. 125.

[7] John ASHTON, *Understanding the Fourth Gospel*, Oxford, Clarendon, 1991.

[8] Rudolf SCHNACKENBURG, *Jesus in the Gospels*, Louisville - Westminster, John Knox, 1995.

Part - I

Historical Antecedents and Jesus as Rabbi in the New Testament Gospels

The complex nature and mission of Jesus Christ is revealed in the many names and titles by which he is referred to throughout Scripture. Some of them were intended as attributes, but they came to be used as if they were names. "Christ" is a theological title, a transliteration of the Greek Χριστος, in turn a translation derived from the Hebrew "Messiah", meaning "the anointed." The Greek form occurs often in the Hebrew Bible and typically refers to a "high priest" or "King" but was also reserved for the awaited, God's "Anointed One." An understanding of Jesus as "The Son of God", "The Son of Man", "The Messiah" and "The Prophet" serves as a beginning toward understanding who he is. The title "Son of Joseph of Nazareth" acknowledges Jesus' full humanity, that he was one of them. In the time of Jesus, "Lord"[1] was a title of deepest respect.

Originally, the name that was given to Christ was Jesus ('Ιησοῦς), which means "God saves" (cf. Mt 1:21).[2] The earliest use of 'Ιησοῦς is found in the Septuagint, where it is a transliteration of the Hebrew name Yehoshua known more commonly in English as Joshua. Even today, in the cultural and social arena, to distinguish similarly people with different names from each other, individuals are sometimes identified by their geographical origin. Such a case can be applied to Jesus, for example, when he is called 'Jesus of Nazareth' (Mk 1:24; 10:47) or 'Jesus the Galilean' (Mt 26:69).

John P. Meier says that, "So current was the name, Jesus, that some descriptive phrases like "of Nazareth" or "the Christ (Messiah)" had to be added to distinguish him from the many other bearers of at name."[3] In another context, Jesus is referred to by occupation: 'the carpenter'

(Mk 6:3); by family connection with his father as "Jesus, the son of Joseph" (Lk 3:24; Jn 1:45; 6:42); or 'the carpenter's son' (Mt 13:55). Sometimes, he is identified with his brothers, 'the brother of James[4] and Joses and Judas and Simon' (Mk 6:3), and also with his mother ("Jesus, son of Mary" - Mk 6:3; cf. Mt 13:55). However, the titles that were given to Jesus are significantly different from the name. Although more than one title is attributed to the person of Jesus, each title has a particular and specific origin and a distinct meaning.

The history of Jesus' titles is the result of a detailed examination of the Christological traditions which led to the use of names for Jesus that were long embedded in the life of Judaism, the Palestinian primitive Church, and in pre-Pauline Christianity.[5] The titles of Jesus found in the earliest layer of tradition are hard to interpret and are not always part of self-proclamation by Jesus. Rather, they are the voice of the community, statements about what people around Jesus thought of him. This is because of the mixture of history and kerygma in the Gospels.[6] The New Testament communities used the names and titles as they tried to comprehend Jesus' life and ministry.

While there are various names and titles given or attributed to Jesus, there is no doubt that Jesus was also called ῥαββί, in the Gospels, and more specifically in the Gospel of John. Part I of this book will look into the earliest occurrence of this title in different literatures and in different contexts in Jewish history to know exactly who and what a ῾Ραββί, was in that society. Then, the Rabbi-disciple relationship that existed both in the Jewish and Hellenistic contexts before and at the time of Jesus will be studied. The significance of the title ῾Ραββί, in the post-resurrection era will also be analysed, especially from the time of the destruction of the Temple in A.D. 70. But before proceeding, it is necessary to address possible objections or problem areas. First, a word must be said with regard to the dating of Jewish sources. Judaism did not compile its traditions systematically in written form until the end of the second century A.D. Pre-A.D.70, Judaism was characterized by a comparatively greater variety of traditions than its later counterpart, Rabbinic Judaism (post- A.D.70). Most scholars agree that the use of the title ῾Ραββί, for ordained scholars does not appear in any Jewish sources before 70 A.D. Based on observations made on the occurrences of the term ῾Ραββί, in the Gospels, a detailed study will be made whether the use of the title Rabbi, in the Gospels is anachronistic.

Endnotes

[1] Cf. Oscar CULLMANN, "'Kyrios' as Designation for the Oral Traditions Concerning Jesus", Scottish Journal of Theology 3 (1950) 180ff; F. F. BRUCE, Jesus: Lord and Saviour, Downers Grove, IL, InterVarsity Press, 1986. The Gospels and Acts frequently use "Lord" as a title for Jesus. Jesus himself never seems to have claimed the title and it is only ascribed to him by others, which has led to various interpretations. Different scholars have come up with various explanations: some believe that Jesus' disciples called him Lord, but not because he was divine; this was merely a title used when students addressed their teachers. Some believe that the New Testament uses the term "Lord" to mean divine, but that it was only after Jesus' death and resurrection that his followers ascribed divinity to him. See, Walter L. LIEFELD, "The Hellenistic 'Divine Man' and the Figure of Jesus in the Gospels", Journal of the Evangelical Theological Society 16.4 (1973) 195-205. Others argue that neither Jesus nor his disciples used the Aramaic term for Lord, *mara*, and that the Greek term κύριος meaning, "The Lord" was borrowed from pagan Hellenic usage by early Gentile converts to Christianity. The Hebrew Bible distinguishes between "Lord" (*adon*) and "God"; the word "Lord" does not necessarily imply divinity, although God is often described as "the Lord." Surviving inter-testamental Aramaic texts frequently use the Aramaic *mara* to mean "the Lord", that is, God – but they also provide evidence of people using *mara* and *kyrios* as personal titles, used to address a husband, father, or king. There is little evidence that either term was used specifically to mean "teacher" but there is much evidence of students using the term "mar" to refer to their teachers respectfully, or to refer to an especially respected and authoritative teacher. A close reading of the Gospels suggests to historians that most people addressed Jesus as Lord as a sign of respect for a teacher. See, Ralph MARTIN, "The New Quest of the Historical Jesus", Carl F. H. HENRY, ed., Jesus of Nazareth: Savior and Lord, Grand Rapids, Eerdmans, 1966, pp. 31-45; F. F. BRUCE, "Jesus is Lord", J. McDowell RICHARDS, ed., Soli Deo Gloria: New Testament Essays in Honor of William Childs Robinson, Richmond, VA, John Knox Press, 1968, pp. 23-36; Morris INCH, "Jesus Is Lord!", Journal of the Evangelical Theological Society 15.3 (1972) 173-180; James H. CHARLESWORTH, ed., The Messiah: Developments in Earliest Judaism and Christianity, Princeton Symposium on Judaism and Christian Origins, Augsburg, Fortress Publishers, 1992; E. EARLE ELLIS, Christ and the Future in New Testament History, Novum Testamentum Supplements Series, Vol. 97, Leiden, Brill, 1999; Joel B. GREEN & Max TURNER, eds., Jesus of Nazareth, Lord and Christ, Carlisle, Paternoster Press / Grand Rapids, Eerdmans, 1994, pp. 367-383, Reprinted, Eugene, OR, Wipf & Stock Publishers, 1999; Larry W. HURTADO, Lord Jesus Christ: Devotion to Jesus in Earliest Christianity, Grand Rapids, Eerdmans, 2003.

[2] The name Ἰησοῦς in Mt 1:21 is communicated to Joseph by the angel whereas in Lk 1:31, the name occurs in the story of the annunciation where

the angel asks Mary to name the child "Jesus". The giving of name Ἰησοῦς occurs only in the Infancy Narratives of Matthew and Luke. This does not take place in the other two Gospels of Mark and John. Though neither Mark nor John use the title Ἰησοῦς in their gospels, it is presupposed that the name Ἰησοῦς is known to both of them. Vincent Taylor puts forward the view that, "in general, we may say that the name 'Jesus' is used in the New Testament where the narrative interest is uppermost or where it is desired to emphasize the humanity of the Lord." See, Vincent TAYLOR, The Names of Jesus, London, Macmillan, 1954, pp. 5-8. According to Vincent Taylor, in the first century, the name Ἰησοῦς was by no means uncommon. Taylor quotes from Josephus who speaks about twenty persons named Ἰησοῦς ten of whom were contemporaries of Jesus himself. Walter Bauer observes several persons with this name Ἰησοῦς in biblical history and he points out certain important persons such as Joshua, successor of Moses (Jos 1:1) and another person with the same name in 1 Mac 2:55; 2 Mac 12: 15. In the NT, he mentions Jesus, son of Eliezer, who appears in the genealogy of Jesus in Lk 3:29. Then comes Jesus Barabbas who has also another name Justus. Jesus of Nazareth is mostly addressed as Jesus Christ designated as Χριστός (Mt 1: 1, 21, 25). See, Walter BAUER, Ἰησοῦς in BDAG (2000) 471-472. For more details on the name Ἰησοῦς, see, John P. MEIER, A Marginal Jew: Rethinking the Historical Jesus, Vol. 1: The Roots of the Problem and the Person, The Anchor Bible Reference Library, Bantam Doubleday Dell Publishing Group Inc., 1991, pp. 205-208. Meier opines that among the Jews after the Babylonian exile, "Jesus" became the common form of the name. "Jesus" remained a popular name among Jews until the beginning of the second century A.D. After that period "Jesus" became a rare name among Jews due to a possible factor of Christian veneration to the personal name either as "Jesus" or "Jesus Christ." Read also, John P. MEIER, A Marginal Jew: Rethinking the Historical Jesus, Vol. 2: Mentor, Message, and Miracles, The Anchor Bible Reference Library, Bantam Doubleday Dell Publishing Group Inc., 1994; John P. MEIER, A Marginal Jew: Rethinking the Historical Jesus, Vol. 3: Companions and Competitors, The Anchor Bible Reference Library, Bantam Doubleday Dell Publishing Group Inc., 2001. Read also, F. F. BRUCE, Jesus and Christian Origins Outside the New Testament, London, Hodder & Stoughton / Grand Rapids, Eerdmans, 1974; Ivan H. FRENCH, "The Man Christ Jesus", Grace Theological Journal 1.2 (1980) 185-194; Joel B. GREEN, Scot MCKNIGHT & I. HOWARD MARSHALL, eds., Dictionary of Jesus and the Gospels, Leicester / Downers Grove, Illinois, IVP, 1992; Carl F. H. HENRY, "The Identity of Jesus of Nazareth", Criswell Theological Review 6.1 (1992) 91-130.

[3] J. P. MEIER, A Marginal Jew, Rethinking the Historical Jesus, Vol. 1., p. 206. See also, Leander E. KECK, Jesus in New Testament Christology in ABR (1980) 1-21, p.1. Keck states that it is by no means easy to designate precisely and properly the content of the name of "Jesus." Essentially, however, what is meant is the man from Nazareth who bears the name "Jesus." See also, Allan

BARR, "More Quests of the Historical Jesus", Scottish Journal of Theology 13 (1960) 394; Charles C. ANDERSON, Critical Quests of Jesus, Grand Rapids, Eerdmans, 1969; Leland Jennings WHITE, Jesus the Christ: A Bibliography, Wilmington, Glazier, 1987; Craig E. EVANS, Jesus, IBR Bibliographies 5, Grand Rapids, Baker, 1992; Craig A. EVANS, Life of Jesus Research; An Annotated Bibliography, New Testament Tools and Studies 24, Leiden, Brill, 1996; Dale C. ALLISON, "The Contemporary Quest for the Historical Jesus", Irish Biblical Studies 18 (1996) 174-194; Margaret BARKER, "The Risen Lord: Jesus of History as the Christ of Faith", Scottish Journal of Theology, Current Issues in Theology, Edinburgh, Continuum International Publishing Group, T & T Clark Ltd., 1996; Dale C. ALLISON, Jesus of Nazareth: Millenarian Prophet, Augsburg Fortress, 1999; Darrell L. BOCK, Studying the Historical Jesus: A Guide to Sources and Methods, Grand Rapids / Leicester, Baker book House / IVP, 2002.

[4] An ossuary was recently discovered in Jerusalem on which there is an extraordinary inscription, in Aramaic letters: "James, son of Joseph, brother of Jesus." The authenticity of this discovery of the ossuary is in question and is still discussed in the biblical and archaeological world. For more details, see, André LEMAIRE, "Earliest Archaeological Evidence of Jesus Found in Jerusalem", in Biblical Archaeology 28/6 (2002) 24-33, 70-71. In the beginning of his article, Lemaire André poses a very serious question; Is this the same James who was the brother of Jesus of Nazareth, or was this another James, whose father happened to be called Joseph and who happened coincidentally also to have a brother named Jesus?" (p. 25). Lemaire concludes that this ossuary held the bones of the James who was the brother of Jesus of Nazareth. "On the other hand, nothing in this ossuary inscription clearly confirms the identification.... Jesus is not called 'Jesus of Nazareth' or 'Jesus the Messiah.'" (p. 33). After several examinations to determine the authenticity of this archaeological discovery, many scholars have decided that it is not authentic. Hence, the authenticity of the above propositions of Lemaire is put in doubt. See, Joseph A. FITZMYER, "Whose Name is This?", in America 187 (2002) 9-13, p. 10. Fitzmyer raises the same concern here: "If the Jesus mentioned here is Jesus of Nazareth, then this is further extrabiblical evidence, dating from about A. D. 62-63, of his historical existence. But does the name on the ossuary refer to Jesus of Nazareth?" See also, R. P. NETTELHORST, "The Genealogy of Jesus", Journal of the Evangelical Theological Society 31.2 (1988) 169-172; Richard BAUCKHAM, "The Relatives of Jesus", Themelios 21.2 (January 1996) 18-21; John PAINTER, Just James: The Brother of Jesus in History and Tradition, Personalities of the New Testament, Columbia, SC, Augsburg Fortress Publishers, 1999; Bruce CHILTON & Jacob NEUSNER, eds., The Brother of Jesus: James the Just and His Mission, Louisville, Westminster John Knox Press, 2001; Craig A. Evans, "Jesus and the Ossuaries", Bulletin for Biblical Research 13.1 (2003) 21-46.

[5] Cf. Ferdinand HAHN, The Titles of Jesus in Christology: Their History in Early Christianity, Cambridge, James Clark, 2003; Leon MORRIS, The Lord From Heaven, Inter-Varsity Press, 1974; I. Howard MARSHALL, The Origins of New Testament Christology, Inter- Varsity Press, 1976.

[6] Gerhard Ludwig MÜLLER, "Christological Titles", in Wolfgang BEINERT & Francis Schüssler FIORENZA (ed.), Handbook of Catholic Theology, New York, NY, Herder & Herder, 1995, pp. 82-85. In the NT, the most frequent titles used for Jesus are Christ/Messiah 500 times, Kyrios 350 times, Son of Man 80 times, Son of God 20 times, followed by servant of God, teacher and prophet. The statistics for each title is given in the presentation of G. L. Muller. Among these different titles, attention will be focused on ῥαββί, which brings out the sense of a teacher. For a detailed study on the Christological Titles, see, Oscar CULLMAN, The Christology of the New Testament, Philadelphia, Westminster, 1963; Ferdinand HAHN, The Titles of Jesus in Christology, Their History in Early Christianity, London, Lutterworth, 1969; Graham N. STANTON, Jesus of Nazareth in New Testament Preaching, Cambridge, Cambridge University Press, 1974. In their work, Cullman and Hahn do not believe that these titles go back to the disciples but originated with the later church.

Chapter - 1

Historical Background of the Title ʿΡαββί

Introduction

The title that the disciples gave to Jesus in the Gospel of John in their first encounter with Jesus was ῥαββί (ὃ λέγεται μεθερμηνευόμενον Διδάσκαλε) Teacher. The question of whether there was any significant connection between the titles ῥαββί and διδάσκαλος at that time will have to be examined. To read and understand the history and to understand the Johannine Jesus, another question needs to be raised as to whether it is correct to translate ῥαββί as teacher or master. These questions form the basis for the first part of this study. Because of the important role it plays in this study, this book will present an historical background of the meaning of the title ῥαββί and from there enter into the NT understanding of the term. In this context, the etymological meaning of the root word רב will be analysed to better understand the meaning of the title ῥαββί at different stages of history.

1. Exploring the meaning of the word ʿΡαββί

A ῥαββί in general is defined to be a scholar with authority over the Jewish community to adjudicate, to teach, and to direct the religious life of the community. Jacob Neusner notes that "all the great saints and heroes of Israel, both in the times of ancient Israel and later on, were regarded as Rabbis."[1] However, today ῥαββί is a title given to a Jewish religious teacher and it is applied to Jewish scholars and spiritual leaders. That is, a person qualified by academic studies of the Hebrew Bible and the Talmud to act as a spiritual leader or a religious teacher is given the title ῥαββί[2] in the Jewish community or congregation. J. C. Turro opines that today the word Rabbi designates the spiritual leader of a Jewish community, Orthodox, Conservative, or Reform. "The office of Rabbi reached its present development through stages that are not always easy to pinpoint in history."[3] R. F. Collins notices that the use of the title ῥαββί has undergone a change as follows: "The Hebrew term literally means "my master" and was often used of an esteemed teacher by his students. Later, of course, the term came simply to mean "teacher", and it is commonly used in this sense today."[4] To better understand the meaning of this title ῥαββί, one needs to look back into history to see the evolution of this title at different stages.

1.1 Etymological Meaning of the term Ῥαββί

First, the term Rabbi derived from the Hebrew רִב"(my great one"),expressed considerable respect. This Hebrew[5] term is derived from the Aramaic[6] noun *rav*, which in Hebrew means great or distinguished. R. Laird Harris notes that *rab* is the common Hebrew adjective meaning "much," or "many." The term *rav* in biblical Hebrew meant "much, many, numerous, great" or "distinguished," and in post-biblical Hebrew, "master" in opposition to "slave" or "pupil". The root, *rab*, is cognate both philologically and semantically to Ugaritic *rb* and Akkadian *rabu*."[7] However, Harris also makes another observation that rab has a common Hebrew adjective meaning; "Captain", "Chief." "Rab is a title of Babylonian origin which appears in both Hebrew and Ugaritic. It also designates the chief or executive of a group such as a military detachment (II Kgs 25:8 et al.)."[8] Thus in each language the term denotes different persons of different standings.

Gordon H. Johnston[9] also notes that in its noun form רַב it stands for captain, chief, commander and ruler. The verb form *rbh* means either 'to multiply' or 'to be great'. When it is used as an adjective, it points out to something great and important. Johnston further shows that the term רַב, appears in construct, in the form of genitive, to designate authority in five areas.[10] The five areas are classified as vocational, cultic, judicial, military, and governmental. Among the five, the vocational area stands for a supervisor, foreman or chief. In the cultic area, it points out to the chief priest and in the judicial area it designates the authority of chief magistrate. In the military arena the title designates an officer, captain or commander and finally in government circles, it stands for a royal official or for a ruler. In the observation of Lapin, "In extracanonical sources, both

Aramaic and Phoenician, *rab* has the sense of "officer" or "chief," and it appears most often in the construct form."[11] Hence in its origin, *Rav* meant any one who was considered to be 'great'. It is interesting to see the broader adaptation of this title to various persons with a variety of offices or functions.

Hershel Shanks,[12] in his writings on the *"Origins of the Title 'Rabbi'"*, accepts the adjectival root meaning of the word רב as great or distinguished. Shanks adds that some form of the word *Rab* (possessive, *Rabbi*) was used in most of the Semitic dialects from the earliest times. Rab is a Hebrew term used as a title for those who are distinguished for learning, who are the authoritative teachers of the Law, and who are the appointed spiritual heads of the community. H. Shanks in his detailed study of the origin of this term in different dialects observes a broader usage of the title *Rab*. He gives considerable illustrations to explain the variant use of the title *Rab* in history. "In a large number of Semitic languages or dialects, from Akkadian to Hebrew and Aramaic, we have examples of some form of *Rab* being used as a title or as a part of a title."[13] In Akkadian, the word *Rab* forms the first part of very many titles to denote chief astrologer, chief physician, chief herder, chief cupbearer and chief overseer of the vineyards. In Ugaritic, besides denoting the secular terms such as captain, corporal, chief of the town, it also meant religious titles like Chief of the Priests and High Priest. In early Aramaic, *Rab* was part of the title for the commander of the army. In Syriac, besides denoting the secular terms such as Chief Justice, it also stands for religious titles such as the Leader of the Faithful, the High Priest and the Ruler of the Synagogue. Shmuel Himelstein observes that "the word *rav* from which Rabbi is derived means 'great or distinguished' in biblical Hebrew and was later used to mean master."[14] Hence, it is clear that in the semitic languages, the title *rab* had the sense of 'officer' or 'chief,' more than a 'teacher' and it is only later that it came to mean a teacher or a master.

In Mishnaic Hebrew, *rab* was used by a servant of his master and especially by "a student (*talmid*) of his master or teacher."[15]

In Rabbinic literature, the term *rab* describes someone who occupied a high and respected position in that society or community. The Encyclopaedia Judaica adds that, in the mishnaic Hebrew, the term *rav* stood for "a master as opposed to a slave."[16] Ephraim Kanarfogel opines that "within Talmudic literature, the title "Rabbi" sometimes referred to those with high standing in the community who were not religious authorities, such as individuals of great wealth or lay leaders."[17] Thus, in Hebrew, *rab* also stands for "great" in the sense of "one in a high or distinguished position." In the first century A.D. in the Palestinian schools, the sages were addressed as "Rabbi" (my master).[18]

McKenzie, in his Dictionary of the Bible gives the etymology of ῥαββί as follows. Rabbi is of "Aramaic *rab*, 'master' + first person pronominal suffix, 'my master.'[19] This term of respectful address gradually came to be used as a title, the pronominal suffix 'i' "my" losing its significance with the frequent use of the term. The (i,) termination in the word Rabbi means (my), and it brings a sense of belonging of the disciples to their lord or master. J. C. Turro opines that originally the Hebrew word Rabbi had the sense of "my master" but "in time the force of the possessive adjective fell away and the word came to be used as title in the third person."[20]Johnston concludes that "from the middle of the first century A.D. the suffix increasingly lost its pronominal significance, and examples of rabbî as a general title begin to appear."[21] 'Ραββί thus becomes a title of respect signifying *master, teacher*, given by the Jews to their doctors and teachers.[22] Another form of the title was 'Ραββουνί.

J. C. Turro explains 'Ραββουνί as follows; "a heightened form of Semitic *rab* (chief, master) is Aramaic *rabban*. Hebrew *rabbon*, and the latter with the suffix – "i" (my) is *rabboni*."[23] According to McKenzie, *rabbônî* is an emphatic form[24] of Rabbi. The different titles with the same root of "*Rab*" were used with different degrees of honour; the lowest being rab, *master* then Rabbi, *my master*; next *rabban, our master*; and greatest of all, *Rabboni, my great master*.[25] Thus, 'Ραββουνί was applied to teachers and others in exalted and revered positions.

According to the Jews, the gradations of honour rose from Rab to Rabbi, and thence to Rabban or Rabboni.[26] Samuel Byrskog[27] states that in Rabbinic writings, the titles "Rabbi", "Rab" or "Rabban" are prominent, and are used to a large extent merely as a title for a qualified scholar. Apart from the presidents of the Sanhedrin, no one is called *Rabban*. The title "Rabbi" was borne by the sages of ancient Israel, who were ordained by the Sanhedrin in accordance with the custom handed down by the elders. They were titled ῥαββί and received authority to judge penal cases. 'Ραβ was the title of the Babylonian sages who received their ordination in colleges. In Babylonia, the amora, who headed the academy bore the title of *Rabbah* and was called the senior teacher.

In Talmudic times, the term rab was used in Babylonia. Ephraim Kanarfogel notes that "In Mishnaic parlance, the term *rav* (which means "great" or "distinguished" in biblical Hebrew) connotes a teacher of students and this is its primary usage during the Talmudic period in Babylonia."[28] Gutstein admits that, "In the Talmudic period in Babylonia, the form Rab was used"[29] which is the same period the title of ῥαββί was conferred by the Sanhedrin or by the Talmudic academies, on those qualified by their scholarship to render decisions in Jewish law. Hence, it seems that the term Rabbi was first used in reference to the Rabbis of the Sanhedrin during the first century A.D. The Rabbis of Talmudic times were the sole authority on the Torah. This was before Torah was written, and no one had the opportunity to study the law for themselves.

Jacob Neusner, speaking about Rabbinic Judaism summarises the definition of Rabbis in history as follows: in Rabbinic Judaism, Rabbi is the principal kind of leader and supernatural sage. However, he goes on to say, "The definition of Rabbi shifts in ancient times. The title itself was originally quite neutral and not unique to Jews...Accordingly, through the centuries the title *Rabbi* has come to refer solely to a distinctive amalgam, within the Jewish nation, of learning, piety and holiness or supernatural power, associated with the sages of the Talmud and related writings."[30] In modern times the term "Rabbi" and in Judæo-German, "Rab" is used as a word of courtesy similar to the English "Mister."[31] Thus, in the beginning the term demanded certain authority and, by the first century C.E., it became a title as well as a mode of address for the great teachers or interpreters of Law and Scriptures. The following pages will deal further with the different stages of Jewish history to see what it means to be a "Rabbi."

2.   The Use of the Title "Rab" in the Old Testament

The following sections on the use of the title ῥαββί in OT and Jewish history will shed light on the usage of the title Rabbi in various contexts. The concept of רב, to designate someone as teacher or master, is not often found in the O.T. Yet the title *Rab* appears frequently in the relatively early books, as well as the later books of the Old Testament. Lapin[32] notes that in the OT the word *rab*, as in "big" or "great" occurs only in constructs with other nouns and never used as an independent title.

R. Laird Harris[33] notes that *rab* occurs 420 times in the OT. The primary meaning is "many", which occurs initially in Gen 21:34. KJV finds "many" in 190 occurrences, most dealing with objects (Gen 30:43), days

(Gen 37:24), times (Ps 106:43), and similar subjects. The root is often used in contexts referring to "many" people, as "many evildoers" (Ex 23:2), "Gentiles" (Deut 9:14), and "multitude" at the Exodus (Ex 12:38). Harris also observes that *rab* has also the usage in the sense of "great", which is seen in the translations of KJV and in most parts of RSV in 128 occurrences, among which it denotes "goodness" (Ps 31:20), "evil" (Gen 6:5), "a Person" (Ps 48:3). In the colloquial translation, *rab* means "greater than" (Deut 7:1 et al. and in some other places *rab* is translated as "enough" (Gen 45:28) and "too much for" (1 Kgs 12:28). For Harris, *rab* is often a prefix as it is in Akkadian: cf. Jer 39: 9-10. The term was adopted by the Neo-Babylonians (Dan 1:3), to signify "his Chief-eunuch," and by the Persians who succeeded them (Est 1:8), in the phrase "all the Captains of his house." There is no evidence that the term was ever used except as a rank of foreign origin as in Isa 36:2. 4. 11. 12. 13. 22; 37:4. 8. Thus *rab* in the OT has been used as an adjective with different meanings in different contexts. The chart below gives some of the OT references[34] where the title רַב has been used as a prefix to denote various jobs and offices.

רַב־שָׁקֵה	Chief or Head of the officers	2Kgs18: 17, 19, 27, 28, 37; 19:4, 8.
		Is36:2, 4, 11, 12, 13, 22; 37:4, 8.
רַב־סָרִיס	Chief Eunuch, a high military or diplomatic official	2Kgs 18:17
רַב־מָג	Chief Sooth-sayer	Jer 39:13
רַבֵּי מֶלֶךְ־בָּבֶל	Chief Officers of the King	Jer 39:13
רַב הַחֹבֵל	Chief of the sailors or ship-master	Jon 1:6
רַב בֵּיתוֹ	Officer of the House	Esth 1:8
רַב סָרִיסָיו	Chief Officer	Dan 1:3

M. R. Wilson agrees with many scholars that "in OT times, *rab* was used as a term of respect for an officer, captain, or chief by those under his authority (e.g., Jer 39:13; Dan 1:3; Jonah 1:6)."[35] For Ellison, in OT times, the title Rabbi in the Semitic sense of 'great' was found both inside and outside Israel "as a designation for some chief officers (e.g. Jer. 41:1; 39:13; Dan 1:3; Est. 1:8; Jon. 1:6, of a sea captain), and it has come down to us in the titles of certain Assyrian and Babylonian officials (e.g. 2Kgs. 18:17; Jer 39:18)."[36] The above references from the OT show that the title Rabbi is used in most of the texts as a designation for someone with authority, perhaps to indicate a chief or an officer but nothing referring to a master-disciple connotation. In sum, it is clear: Rabbi in the sense of teacher does not occur in the OT.

Are the Prophets of Israel the "Rabbis" of the OT?

In searching for the concept of master-disciple relationships in the OT, certain characters are found to be the leaders and learners of the will of God (cf. Dt 6:10-12) and who, in turn, appear to have had followers/disciples (e.g. The prophet Elijah). The word 'disciple(s)' appears over 275 times in the New Testament but rarely in the Old Testament. The obligation of the father to teach his son at home is found in the OT.[37] Deut 4:9f; 6:7. 20f; 11:18f; and 32:7.46 speak about such a responsibility. However, the relationship between a father and his son is not a master and pupil relationship. The relationship between Elijah and Elisha, and Moses and Joshua are examples of master and disciple relationships (Ex 24:12; Nu 11:28; 1 Kgs 19:19ff), but they are never called רב. Byrskog notes that, "Joshua appears in some Jewish writings as the pupil of Moses."[38] Lapin observes some special mention of *rab* for the biblical personalities. "Biblical figures (Moses, Elijah, Elisha) are described in terms of the relationship of *rab* and disciple."[39] Though this relationship between these men of God is described as master and servant, it is not purely a discipline of learning from the master, for God was always considered as their Master and authority.

In the OT, certain texts such as 1Kgs 19:19-21; 2Kgs 2:1-18 portray Elijah's relationship with Elisha. The initial interaction between Elijah and Elisha is described in 1Kgs 19:19-21. Just as Moses appointed Joshua as his successor in Num 27:18-23, Elijah chose Elisha to succeed him in his ministry (1Kgs 19:19) by casting his mantle over Elisha as a sign of transferring his power.[40] This also expresses the acceptance by the master of his disciple. According to Byrskog, "a pupil of a prophetic teacher could not separate teacher and teaching to the same degree."[41] This is because, between the prophetic teacher and the pupil there existed a personal involvement and relationship. Note the address of Elisha in 2Kgs 2:12, calling Elijah his "father" as Elijah rises into heaven in a chariot. In the ancient Israelite community, "father" was the figure who represented authority, and a father was also respected as a teacher.[42] When Elisha calls Elijah "father", it is certainly possible that Elisha considered Elijah as his master and teacher, and so Elisha is crying out for his master and teacher as Elijah is taken away from him. Elisha the prophet is associated with bands of the followers called "sons of the prophets." As Byrskog opines, "The possibility that prophetic disciples formed a kind of school has for a

long time been a matter of debate."[43] Old Testament prophets spent much
of their time travelling throughout the country to announce the word of God
and to exercise their prophetic roles. In the northern kingdom of the Old
Testament some prophets travelled with bands of followers called "Sons of
the Prophets" (e.g., II Kings 2:3, 5, 7, and 15). These groups of "Sons of
the Prophets" are often found at ancient cult centres, such as Bethel (2Kgs
2:3), Gilgal (2 Kgs 4:38) and Jericho (2 Kgs 2:5.15) and appear between
the reign of Ahab (c. 869-850 B.C.E.) and the time of Amos. This would
confine the existence of these groups to approximately 870-750 B.C.
Williams[44] believes that Elijah was instrumental in organising the fellowship
and formation of the "Sons of the Prophets." Elijah's relationship with this
group is explained mainly in 2 Kgs 2:1-18.

Byrskog opines that, "Several scholars claim today that the writings
attributed to prophets reflect more or less extensive work within prophetic
schools. In particular, modern scholars use the label of a school to
explain (parts of) the formation of Amos, Hosea, Isaiah and Ezekiel."[45]
In the books of the prophets, Isaiah is also considered a teacher[46] and a
leader of a circle of young literate men. Isaiah also is believed to come
from an aristocratic family, which might have paved the way for his early
education in wisdom circles. There is evidence in the book of Isaiah for
the existence of prophetic disciples who functioned as transmitters of the
tradition. Thus, scholars[47] like D. Jones, Eaton and Gevaryahu assume
the existence of an Isaianic school.

According to Byrskog, "Jeremiah also appears as a teacher."[48] The
Book of Jeremiah indicates that the prophets have groups of followers.
Baruch, who is thought to have been a scribe, gives the impression that
he was a close follower of the prophet Jeremiah, who was his teacher and
master. The Book of Jeremiah, according to Mallau,[49] presents Baruch as
the follower of Jeremiah. Besides being a follower, Baruch also functions
as the scribe of the prophet. According to Byrskog, "whatever the exact
historicity of the accounts, the texts themselves picture Baruch as the
faithful follower of Jeremiah."[50] In the history of the prophets, Jeremiah
also functioned as a teacher, both by his office and mission.

Byrskog presents the prophet Ezekiel also as a teacher. Ezek 3:17;
33:2-6f uses the image of a watchman for the prophet, and Byrskog opines
that, "Ezekiel is not only a watchman of warning, but also of teaching and
interpretation. Second, Ezekiel's priestly background (1:3) might imply
a teaching activity."[51] The book of Ezekiel also contains accounts about

prophetic followers. In their surveys of research into the tradition and redaction history of Ezekiel, scholars like Zimmerli[52] hold that the book, although appearing to be uniform and coherent, depicts a growing process, which would result from more than one author having been involved in the process of redaction and unification. While the texts themselves reveal the possibility of the existence and importance of Ezekiel's followers, it seems that the prophets of the OT also functioned in various capacities as teachers, masters and instructors.

Certain explicit traces for the school of Amos are found in the book of Amos, though there are no explicit statements to show that the prophet functioned like a teacher surrounded by a number of pupils forming a kind of school. Amos 3:13-14 portrays the existence of disciples around Amos when the prophet summons the alleged disciples and explains to them how God can punish Israel's crimes. In the opinion of Byrskog, "there are no explicit references indicating that Hosea had pupils."[53] Certain writers remain sceptical as to whether Hosea was the master or teacher of a school of disciples. Scholars like Wolff[54] place Hosea within the context of pre-Deuteronomic and prophetic-levitical groups in the northern kingdom. This presupposes a faithful group of followers who learnt from Hosea and transmitted this learning to others. Wolff attempts to define the schools of Amos and Hosea, considering the disciples of Hosea as experts in the transmission of Hosea's words.

Teaching of Wisdom and Existence of Schools in the OT

Today scholars argue about the redactional character of the prophetic books and propose of the existence of schools which preserved and elaborated the traditions of each prophet respectively. Byrskog gives a valid explanation for the theory of the existence of the prophetic schools, "if elementary and scribal schools existed in ancient Israel from early on, it is not inconceivable that the brief accounts about a teacher-pupil relationship present in some prophetic texts actually was manifested in the form of schools. The possibility that the transmitters of the prophetic teaching thought of themselves as members of a school identifying itself by reference to a certain prophet should not be rejected altogether."[55] Though the existence of the prophetic schools is not to be rejected, there are always difficulties in determining the nature of these schools. The meager explicit evidence forces a circular way of reasoning. Certain writers like Shupak advocate the existence of scribal schools during the pre-exilic period. Shupak also speaks about Egyptian parallels[56] and acknowledge the epigraphical data, which reveal the terms associated with Egyptian schools. According to Shupak, "the first Hebrew schools were founded as early as the time of Solomon, and that the origins of these schools may be traced back to the educational tradition of Egypt."[57] In sum, that time, there was a need for educated officials and Scribes, and wisdom literature could be a result of the work of this professional class of wise men.

The Book of Sirach speaks of a person who is commonly called Jesus Ben Sira who was very active in Jerusalem in the second century B.C.E. Jesus Ben Sira is considered to be the writer of the Book of Sirach and seems to be a devout scholar of wisdom. Byrskog states that, "many scholars regard Sir. 51:23.29 as references to the school of Ben Sira."[58] Sir 39:8 makes it clear that Jesus Ben Sira is a teacher and Sir. 24:30-34 states that his knowledge became so vast and overflowing that all who were seeking wisdom came to him. Sir. 51:23-29 describes Ben Sira as striving for wisdom and that his teaching activity was connected with a priestly profession. According to Baumgartner,[59] some of the lyric forms used in the Book of Sirach derive from cultic settings and priestly functions, of which Ben Sira was well informed. Hence it is possible that he was also closely linked to priestly office and Temple responsibilities, which were close to educational duties in the post-exilic period. Byrskog in his research finds that "Sir 51:23.29 thus indicate rather clearly that the account about a teacher-pupil relationship corresponded to the educational setting in a school. It is probable that this was the place where the pupils, Ben Sira's 'sons', initially learned and transmitted the teaching of their authoritative teacher."[60] Ben Sira's teaching activity, which is considered to be of wisdom studies, includes both scriptural and moral instructions. In the words of Byrskog, "Ben Sira's ethical admonitions further convey the impression that the teaching is directed to persons able to make moral responsibility."[61] Thus, Ben Sira is projecting a picture of himself both as a teacher and master for the students who were in the pursuit of wisdom. However, in all this, the term 'rav' or 'rab' was never given to a prophet to denote him either as a teacher or a master. Even the different titles that were used either with a prefix or suffix to the title rab always denoted various meanings in their contexts other than a teacher or a master who imparted knowledge to his pupils and was responsible for their formation.

2.2 The Use of the Title Rabbi in the Literature of the NT Period

As was noted in the general introduction, in the New Testament the word ῥαββί is restricted to the Gospels, in which it was a title sought by Jewish religious leaders (Mt 23:7), was employed in a popular or semi-popular manner by the crowds (Jn 6:25), and even by a religious leader such as Nicodemus (Jn 3:2). Jesus is addressed a number of times as "Rabbi" by his disciples (Mt 26:25; Mk 9:5; 11:21; 14:45; Jn 1:49; 4:31; 9:2; 11:8), and even by women in Jesus' group (Jn 20:16). Even John the Baptist, is called ῥαββί by his followers (Jn 3:26). A caritative form, *rabbouni* (rabboni)[62] is found in Mk 10:517 and Jn 20:16. However, within early Christian writings, it is very hard to find the term Rabbi as a title applied to Jesus. That Josephus does not use the term Rabbi can be explained by observing that this author is writing in defence of his Jewish nation, at least in part from a Roman viewpoint which stresses major military and political matters. Josephus only brings in religious material, as in his discussion of the Pharisees, Sadducees, and Essenes, when necessary explanation is needed. It is noted that this first century A. D. Jewish author does not even mention Hillel, Shammai, or Gamaliel except, as far as the last name is concerned, as father of Simeon[63] and of Jesus the high priest.[64] As a possible equivalent of the term ῥαββί, Josephus uses the term sophists[65] and possibly exegetes.[66] This kind of substitution in terms is not too startling when it is realized that Josephus does the same with the word *sunagoge*[67] and in the latter section the participle *sunagomenon* is employed, yet his normal term for the concept is *proseuche*.[68] Josephus does not employ the term διδάσκαλος *often, but there is an* interesting usage in his reference to Jesus as *dictaskalos*[69] of men. Philo, the Alexandrian Jew, does not use the term Rabbi, but this is no surprise since the word was just coming into use in Palestine in his time, and Philo writes from an Alexandrian and, in part, a Greek philosophical viewpoint. He frequently uses the Septuagint which, of course, was written at a time before the use of the term Rabbi. Philo does, however, show understanding of the ῥαββί διδάσκαλος complex in his use of the word διδάσκαλος with μανθάω[70] and also of *sophists* which has been already used by Josephus (which is an equivalent of διδάσκαλος) with μανθάω as well[71] as the use of *huphegetes*[72] with the same verb.

The Apostolic Fathers do not use the term ῥαββί, which would be expected since the New Testament church, especially after the fall of Jerusalem, was developing in a way distinct from Judaism Διδάσκαλος does occur but rather infrequently, one use being a reference to "Jesus

Christ our only διδᾶσκαλος"[73] in the writings of Ignatius and another to
Polycarp as a διδᾶσκαλος *episemos*[74] famous teacher. Ῥαββί does not
appear in the Dead Sea Scrolls material[75] although there are a number of
references to *rab* a word that, as noted earlier, also occurs in the Old
Testament Hebrew text.[76] The *Syriac Peshitta*[77] of the 5th century A.D.,
although a late testimony, interestingly translates διδᾶσκαλος as ῥαββί[78]
where pronominal suffixes were added. The second Latin recension of
the Apocryphal Gospel of Nicodemus[79] relates that three Galilean Rabbis
witnessed the ascension of Jesus, but this witness is late and proves nothing.
Thus, it is very apparent that the title ῥαββί is not prevalent among the
early Christian writers; each one having ones own reason either to replace
the term or to avoid it.

3.   Concept of a *Rab* (רַב): Mishnaic and Talmudic Period

The term רַב has evolved over Jewish history to include many roles and
meanings. The development of the functioning of Jewish Rabbis in the first
century A.D. is very important for an understanding of the significant role
of Rabbis in Jewish society. According to McKenzie,[80] the word Talmud
is of Aramaic origin, meaning "teaching". Talmud is a collection of Jewish
Rabbinical literature and the name 'Talmud' properly belongs to only
part of the whole collection, but the word is used to designate the whole
collection of Rabbinical literature. The core of the Talmudic literature is
said to be the collection of Rabbinical opinions, which is called *Mishna*,
a collection composed by Rabbi Judah ha-Nasi in AD 200. The Rabbis
whose opinions are collected in the Mishna are called *Tannaim*, which means
"teachers." The original language of Mishna is Hebrew but, at a later
time, the development of its language is called Neo-Hebrew or Mishnic
Hebrew. The Mishna Talmud is described generally as an interpretation of
the law. The object of the interpretation is chiefly to settle problems of
casuistry, in order to determine the obligations of the law as precisely
as possible. The Talmud is distinguishable by its place of origin. The
Palestinian Talmud was prepared in the Rabbinical school of Palestine
and the Babylonian Talmud was prepared by the school of Babylon.
The Jerusalem Talmud was possibly completed before AD 450 and the
Babylonian Talmud was substantially completed by AD 500. J. C. Turro
defines the Talmudic period as roughly from 200 B.C. to 500 A.D., and
distinguishes the functions of Rabbis at that time as follows: "In Talmudic
times (roughly from 200 B.C. to A.D.500) there were two categories of
Rabbi, the Rabbi teachers and the Rabbi judges (dayyanim)."[81] In Talmudic

times, ῥαββί is used to mean a master who demanded respect from the pupils. Most of the Jewish teachers had their own circle of 'disciples' who 'followed' them, literally walking behind them.

In the words of McKenzie, "Talmudic traditions show the absolute respect which the Scribes demanded from their students."[82] In this period, being a ῥαββί was an office, title, or position of "teacher," which was highly honoured by the Jews, so much so, that it became a title of prestige and social respect. Solomon Zeitlin objects to this idea. According to him, "the expression *Rav*, mentioned in the Mishna Abot, is not to be translated "teacher," but elder or superior, hence master."[83] Jewish history maintains that Jews had respect for the *Rav* or *Rabbis* who had a prominent place in that society for their knowledge and authority. History reflects accurately the different forms of רב becoming related to the institutional and official authorities. Walter Bauer notes that *rab* in ancient Palestine of the first century C.E. was "properly a form of address and so throughout our literatures, then an honorary title for outstanding teachers of the law."[84] The NT states that when a man was a ῥαββί he was entitled to the best of seats[85] in social gatherings and the praise of the multitudes. Jacob E. Safra observes that in Judaism, a person qualified by academic studies of the Hebrew Bible and the Talmud acted "as spiritual leader and religious teacher of a Jewish community or congregation."[86] Thus, the title *Rab* developed a specialised nuance to mean master, which is equivalent to teacher. Basically Rabbi was used, at this stage in history, as an expression of honour and deep respect in addressing teachers, masters, and people in scholastic circles. Hayim Lapin notes that, "in origin a title of authority, Heb *Rabbi* became, by the 1st century C.E., a title as well as a mode of address."[87] Thus, the word ῥαββί serves as a designation for persons who held various offices and functions. During the period of Rabbinic writings, according to Johnston,[88] in its noun form, *rab* has threefold level of authority and leadership. The first meaning is for chief or head, the second, is master as an antonym to slave; and the third range is teacher. In the observation of Johnston, the term *rab* has multifarious functions among which is the office of the teacher. Hence, the term *rab* was not purely meant to designate a teacher. With this as background, the section below discusses the position and function of Rabbis in the first century Judaism.

3.1 Categories of Rabbis : Teachers and Judges

Shaye J. D. Cohen opines that "the term 'Rabbi' is ambiguous" and he adds, "this ambiguity is beyond dispute."[89] It may be a popular designation for anyone of high position, notably, but not exclusively, a teacher; but it may also be a technical term for someone who has been ordained and has achieved status and power within the society which produced the Mishnah, the Talmudim and related works. During the Talmudic period, the term *Rabbi* came to be more narrowly applied to one learned in the Law of Moses, without signifying an official office. E. Kanarfogel notes that "the Rabbis of the Talmudic period in both Israel and Babylonia were best known and venerated for their mastery of the Torah and for their devotion to its study and observance."[90] Thus, a gradual development is seen both in the functions and positions of a ραββί in Jewish society. Biblical scholars[91] and archaeologists have often assumed that elementary and scribal schools existed in Israel from the pre- exilic period. According to Byrskog, "the Rabbinic literature contains numerous traces of a developed educational system, on the elementary as well as on the advanced level."[92] With the destruction of the two Temples in Jerusalem, the end of the Jewish monarchy, and the decline of the dual institutions of prophets and the priesthood, the focus of scholarly and spiritual leadership within the Jewish people shifted to the sages of the *Anshe Knesset HaGedolah*, which means Men of the Great Assembly. This assembly was composed of the earliest Rabbis. They began the formulation and explication of what became known as Judaism's *Torah SheBe'al Peh* which is the "Oral Law." This was eventually encoded and codified within the Mishnah and Talmud and subsequent Rabbinical scholarship, producing what is known as Rabbinical Judaism. In the words of Byrskog, "the Rabbinic literature pictures the Rabbis as scholars. They devote themselves entirely to the study of different aspects of Torah. This is their basic and primary task."[93] The person in charge of higher education was probably highly esteemed and the purpose of choosing a teacher was to acquire knowledge and skill. As Neusner says, "what makes a person into a Rabbi, therefore, is study, and one central ritual of the Judaic tradition, therefore, is study...When a disciple memorizes his master's traditions and actions, he participates in that myth."[94]

In the Talmudic era, from about the 1st to the 5th century A.D., the term ραββί was applied to the sages, such as Akiba Ben Joseph. From the time of the return from the Babylonian captivity to 500 B.C, the copyists, who were the interpreters of the Torah, took up a preponderant role in the religious life of Judaism. These copyists then became masters - Rabbis - those who taught law and answered the questions related to it, who settled ritual and liturgical plans and settled family conflicts or disputes between individuals. The Rabbi was both authority and judge, but he was not a priest. His was not an ordained office, and it was only his knowledge which differentiated him from the rest of the community. After the demolition of the Temple of Jerusalem in 70 A.D., Cohanim and Levites lost the authority linked to the service of worship of the shrine, to the advantage of the Rabbis.

Jacob Neusner, speaking about "Rabbinic Judaism in Late Antiquity" observes that "the Rabbis of that period conceived that on earth they studied Torah, just as God, the angels, and "Moses our Rabbi," did in heaven. The heavenly scholars were even aware of Babylonian scholastic discussions. This conception must be interpreted by reference to the belief that the man truly made in the divine image was the Rabbi; he embodied revelation, both oral and written, and all his actions constituted paradigms that were not merely correct but actually heavenly."[95] The ῥαββί of the late antiquity period was considered a holy as well as a supernatural person and the authority on theology, including the structure and order of the supernatural world. The Rabbi in the Talmudic period was unlike the modern official minister, who is elected by the congregation and who is paid a stipulated salary.

The function of the Rabbi of the Talmud was to teach the members of the community the Scriptures and the oral and traditional laws. Judah David Eisenstein puts the functions into three categories[96] or three positions: (1) the Presidency of the community with the title "Nasi,"[97] (2) the head of the judiciary and (3) the ordinary master of civil and ritual laws and exemplar in charitable work and moral conduct. In all cases, power resided in the authority with which one spoke.[98] Thus, the power of the charismatic leader in the Talmudic period was in his speech. The leader influenced God, spirits, humans, even foreign rulers by means of speech and dramatic talent. The religious leader was not necessarily a leader crowned by the establishment but an ascetic personality by virtue of poverty, with ties to the other world; from a certain perspective he can be seen as a mystic though he himself would deny it, just as he would deny that he is a prophet. More than once Talmudic literature states that the sages of the Mishnah and Talmud dealt with magic.[99] It can therefore be said that in general, in ancient times no distinction was made between religious practice and magic, and magic was an integral part of religion.[100] Indeed, among the various matters of magic mentioned in the Talmudic literature, three incidents of exorcism by Rabbis are noted explicitly,[101] though presumably many more incidents of this type occurred among Jews in ancient times.

In the context of Jewish history, being a ῥαββί in the later periods was an office, title, or position of "teacher," which, being so highly honoured by the Jews, became a title of prestige and social respect. In the observation of Lapin, "as the term ῥαββί became an honorific title and a mode of deferential address in general, it was taken up by Rabbinic literature in particular as a special designator for teacher."[102] Safra takes a different stand, saying, "by AD 100 the term Rabbi was in general use to denote a sage, i.e., an interpreter of Jewish law, and in early literature it appears in various forms."[103] Originally therefore, the title *rab* stood for authority but it later became a title, as well as a mode of polite address, to teachers and masters, who were held in high esteem in Jewish society. According to Raphael Patai, the author of the *Jewish Mind*, ῥαββί is "the title of the religious leader of a Jewish community. In modern Israel, the Rabbi is called a rav."[104] The Middle Ages denoted 'Rabbi' as an outstanding scholar. Only in modern times has the Rabbi assumed general, practical religious functions, such as the head of a synagogue or temple.

Need for Torah and Rabbis - Counteraction to Hellenism

Rengstorf[105] observes that the master-disciple relationship came into Judaism as part of the educative process of the Greek and Hellenistic[106] philosophical schools. But at the same time it must be made clear that the principle behind this master-disciple relationship in Rabbinic Judaism is not the same as that of the master-disciple relationship in the Greek philosophical world and concepts. During the history of master-disciple relationship in the Hellenistic period, an equivalent term to Rabbi emerges as διδάσκαλος. In the context of discipleship and teaching, the word ῥαββί seems to be synonymous with the Greek equivalent of "teacher" διδάσκαλος.[107] A. F. Zimmermann notes that διδάσκαλος denoted "a person or a personified item conveying information or skills to others by superior knowledge and ability."[108] Since there existed διδάσκαλος in Greek society who functioned as a master or a teacher, there were also disciples who were called as μαθητής.

In an earlier time, prior to the period of Rabbinical Judaism, the Greek term μαθητής refers generally to any student, pupil, apprentice or adherent[109] as opposed to the word διδάσκαλος that means a teacher or a master, who is referred to as a ῥαββί in a Jewish context.[110] The whole principle of master-disciple relationship differs between these two worlds. Since there were several masters, it is possible to think that there later sprang up several schools of Rabbinical thought, each in competition with the other. The Jewish adherents of great leaders formed a kind of series of 'philosophical' schools, or religious, or political, sects. The leaders of the schools or movements were rightly called ῥαββί.

The Sophists also had this way of training disciples under a great master or a philosopher. As Francis John observes, "in the wide range of ancient Philosophical schools, clearly defined master-pupil relationships grew up where the disciples developed and represented their master's case."[111] In the words of Francis John, "the master-disciple relationship of Rabbinic Judaism is closer to the Hellenistic school, except that the primary focus remained to God's revealed Law, not to the person of the master."[112] Thus, in the Hellenistic arena, the student or disciple is apparently an adherent of some wise teacher or leader, and those masters or teachers were addressed with the title ῥαββί. Thus as has already been noted, there were examples of discipleship referring to people committed to following a great leader, by following his life and passing on his teachings. In these cases, master-disciple relationship meant much more than just the transfer of information. Again, when someone became the disciple of a ῥαββί, it included imitating the teacher's life, inculcating his values, and reproducing his teachings. Commenting on the aspect and content of teaching of a master to a disciple, Müller opines that, "here the תַּלְמִד is someone whose concern is the whole of Jewish tradition."[113] This is reflected in the later period where it was decreed that "a candidate for the office of Rabbi must sit for an examination in Talmud and Codes."[114] As Coulot puts it concretely, "Durant cette période, le sage est l'expert en Torah écrite ou orale."[115] The Rabbi was also revered as being a figure closer to God than anyone else in the community. He was thought to have the ability to curse and bless individuals.

Byrskog affirms that, "the Rabbinic literature shows that the accounts about the teacher-pupil relationship corresponded to the actual existence of schools. The colleges, in particular, were often schools in which the teacher himself provided the circle of disciples with its basic identity and coherence."[116] For the Jewish boy above the age of thirteen this meant not only going to study with a recognised Torah scholar but also emulating his life and faith, concentrating on mastering the Mosaic Law and traditional interpretations of it. Byrskog, in speaking about the influence of the Hellenistic culture in Jewish society, also mentions this. He asserts that "Greek education was, generally speaking, well structured." Although significant variations may have existed due to different geographical and social factors, there were in principle, three stages. After primary education from the age of seven to twelve or fourteen, the ephebate followed. In

addition to literary training, this secondary level consisted of physical
and military training in the gymnasium. In the third stage, the young men
(οἱ νέοι) continued their education by studying subjects such as rhetoric
and philosophy, until they reached the age of nineteen or twenty."[117] Though
the role of teachers in the formation of the boys is vital in all the three
stages, the place of Rabbis in the formation of Jewish boys is very important
in the primary education.

The Authority of a Master over His Disciple

In the Scripture, the word "disciple" is used most often to refer to a follower
of Jesus, and it is in this context that discipleship will be looked at more
closely. Muller opines that "In Homer's writings μανθάνω has the sense
of adapting oneself, preparing for, and growing accustomed to."[118] At the
same time, a person was known as a μαθητής in the Greek world only when
he bound himself to a Master or leader in order to acquire his practical and
theoretical knowledge on philosophical concepts and the 'Sophia' which
was the greatest wisdom. Vernon K. Robbins states that, "The source of
the teacher/disciple pattern and of summons and response as a means of
initiating a teacher/disciple relationship in Mediterranean culture is not
difficult to uncover. The dynamics of summons and response accompanied
the social identity of a teacher from the fifth century B.C.E. onwards in
Greco-Roman literature and culture. The Sophist tradition of the teacher
and his disciples provides the base for development of the cultural and
literary traditions."[119] In the Greek world, μαθητής was most often
associated with people who were devoted followers of a great particular
religious leader or teacher of philosophy. Thus, μαθητής stands for a disciple,
a learner, pupil or a student.

The Greek term μαθητής comes from the verb form μαθητεύω which
in most cases is used in the active sense to denote, 'to make someone
into a disciple' and in some other places μανθάνω, which means "to learn,
become acquainted, come to know."[120] In Greek history, Μαθητής generally
stands for "an apprentice or pupil attached to a teacher or movement; one
whose allegiance is to the instruction and commitments of the teacher or
movement."[121] During the time of transition to Hellenism, there is ample
evidence to suggest that schools had been developed to instruct Jewish
boys to withstand the inroads of Hellenism and safeguard one's Jewish
identity. When a Jewish boy was thirteen, if he wanted further training in
preparation for being a teacher, scribe or head of a synagogue, he might
continue his studies of the Torah in a small group, or seek to study as a

disciple under a certain scholar (ῥαββί) in the Law and Scriptures. The apostle Paul was an example of a Jewish boy who left home to study the Law under Gamaliel,[122] a famous teacher (Cf. Ac 5:34; 22:3). So μαθητής under a Rabbi is both a disciple and learner, and διδάσκαλος (Rabbi) is both a master and teacher. A disciple was a learner. A man was known as a μαθητής or disciple when he bound himself to another in order to acquire his practical and theoretical knowledge. There was never a disciple without a master or teacher.[123] Historically in the Greek language, μαθητής referred to a "student" who would attach himself to a teacher (διδάσκαλος) to acquire theoretical and practical knowledge in a certain discipline (e.g., philosophy, medicine, a trade). Likewise, in the Rabbinic tradition, a *talmid* was a student of Torah who would attach himself to a teacher to learn the Scriptures and the traditions of the Fathers. In both instances the pupil would eventually qualify to become a teacher in his own right, with the authority to establish his own school, often carrying on and developing further the traditions of his master.

Byrskog rightly says, "The scholarly devotion is not an end in itself. It is an integral part of the teaching activity. Numerous texts present the Rabbis as teachers studying and transmitting Torah together with the group of pupils."[124] The most significant obligation of the student was to serve or to minister to his teacher. In the story of Joshua serving his master Moses in Ex 24:13; 33:11; Num 11:28; Josh 1:1, it was of vital importance for a student to attend the needs of his master who is a ῥαββί. Jacob Neusner observes "Honor is due to the learned Rabbi more than to the scroll of the Torah, for through his learning and logic, he may alter the very content of Mosaic revelation. He is Torah, not merely because he lives by it, but because at his best he forms as compelling an embodiment of the heavenly model as does a Torah-scroll itself."[125] The "elder in knowledge" was revered even more than the "elder in years" In the words of Metzger, "the Scribes required of their students the most absolute reverence, surpassing even the honour felt for one's parents."[126] *M. 'Abot* 4:12, in a saying attributed to R. Eleazar b. Shammua (A.D.130–160), student of R. Aqiba, says: "Let the fear of your teacher be as the fear of heaven."[127] Hence, respect for the Rabbi surpasses the respect due to parents and elders, and some times it was equated with the fear of God.

The pupil had great respect for his *rab* and followed him with obedience and respect. When the disciple addressed his master as ῥαββί, meaning 'my master' or 'my teacher', it connoted reverence and great esteem. The teacher demanded greater respect than one's father, because "according to their reasoning, one's father has brought his son only into this world, whereas one's teacher, who instructs a pupil in divine wisdom, brings him into the life of the world to come."[128] Thus the Rabbis commanded great respect and had great authority over the disciples for their great ingenuity in the exegesis of the Scripture and Law.

Torah: The Centre of Master-Disciple Relationship

Byrskog states that, "Discipleship centred consequently on Torah, not on a specific teacher."[129] However, the term ῥαββί in most cases is used to denote someone who had knowledge of the Law and Scriptures with authority to teach and thus to make someone into a disciple. From the original meaning in Hebrew (which is either "my teacher," or "my master" and in Judaism a person qualified by academic studies of the Hebrew Bible and the Talmud), ῥαββί came to mean someone who had the authority to act as spiritual leader and religious teacher of a Jewish community or congregation. Hundreds, and perhaps thousands of Rabbis, circulated in the land of Israel in the first century. These Rabbis did not hesitate to travel to the smallest of villages or the most remote parts of the country. In some instances they would conduct their classes in someone's home, but often classes would be held in the village square or under a tree.

As Metzger has pointed out, "More advanced instruction in the Mosaic law was provided by noted Scribes who gathered about themselves followers, called disciples (literally learners)."[130] The ῥαββί (Master or Teacher) was the most important person in their lives. In Judaism one had to learn not only the *Tanak*, but also the oral traditions, the traditions of the Fathers, under a ῥαββί. One would attach himself to a ῥαββί, who would serve as a kind of mediator between the student and the Scriptures. One dared not interpret the Scriptures independently, and could speak with authority only after years of study under a ῥαββί. There was never a disciple without a master or teacher, which means he who wanted to know the law and interpret that to others could not do that without the prior guidance and constant instruction of a master who was a Rabbi. Neusner observes that the Rabbi required the veneration and reverence owed to the Torah. "The extreme forms of respect that evolved over the centuries constitute the most striking rituals attached to "being a Rabbi."[131] According to Neusner, in the schools of Torah, if study was an act of piety, then the master was partly its object, which means the forms of respect reserved for the divinity or for the Torah were not too different, in appropriate circumstances, from those who owed to the master.

Judah David Eisenstein[132] has noted that the function of the Rabbi of the Talmud was to teach the members of the community the Scriptures and the oral and traditional laws. According to him, for a Rabbi to lead the community he had to be elected for that office by the leaders of the community. The judicial members could elect him for the second position (judge) and the very nature of his office of teacher gave him the obligations for the third position (teacher). In the Talmudic texts and times, when the term Rabbi was borne by the Palestinian sages, the term *rav* refers to any Babylonian sage. After 70 A.D., both in Palestine and Babylon, Rabbis enjoyed popular support. When Donald Senior speaks about the role of Rabbis, he maintains that Rabbis were teachers and "they carefully transmitted to their disciples the religious heritage of Israel - a knowledge of the Torah and the network of the oral traditions that developed in an effort to make the Torah applicable to ordinary life."[133] In the opinion of Senior, the Rabbis were the transmitters of a heritage and the authority of the past.

Development of Rabbinical Schools

According to Metzger, "the obligation of the pupil to reproduce to the next generation exactly what his master taught him extended not only to ideas but even to the manner of expression and the choice of words."[134] In later Rabbinical Judaism, the master becomes the intermediary between the disciples and the Torah and the disciples literally followed their master. Byrskog points out that, "as a matter of course, the advanced Rabbinic teachers exhibited a dominating influence on their pupils."[135] W. D. Davies observes that the Jewish teachers had been the pupils of teachers from whom they had learnt faithfully that which they, in turn, transmitted to their own pupils. "While they exercised great ingenuity in the exegesis of the Scriptures, their greatest respect was reserved for the virtue of faithfulness in handing on what had been received."[136] As early as 110 B.C., even before the time of Jesus, the Jews were familiar with the term *Rav* from which the title *Rabbi* is derived. As one reads from Mishna Abot, *"get a teacher (rab) and find a fellow- student"*[137] was a slogan in the Palestinian community. 'Take to yourself a teacher and acquire a companion' was also a slogan for the Rabbinical discipleship. In the later period, Rabbinical Judaism made much of the concept of ῥαββί. Thus, besides other connotations and interpretations, the title Rabbi in history,[138] has evolved to denote the office of a teacher who was also called a master in that community.

In the words of Neusner, "Learning by Rabbis thus finds a central place in a classical Judaic tradition because of the belief that God had revealed his will to mankind through the medium of a written revelation given to Moses at Mount Sinai, accompanied by oral traditions taught in the Rabbinical schools and preserved in the Talmuds and related literature."[139] Jacob Neusner, while speaking about Rabbinical schools or academies, notes that the Rabbinical academy is, in fact, a law school. However, the Rabbinical school was by no means a centre for merely legal study. Its main duty was to apply Torah to every day life. "The personality traits of ordinary men might vary, but those expected of and inculcated into a sage were of a single fabric. The central human relationship in the schools was between the disciple and the master."[140] The school or *yeshiva* (Heb., session) was a council of Judaism, a holy community. Through the school, classical Judaism transformed the Jewish people into its vision of a true replica of Mosaic revelation. "The schools like other holy communities, imposed their own particular rituals, intended, in the first instance, for the disciples and masters. Later, it was hoped, all Jews would conform to those rituals and so join the circle of master and disciples."[141] Neusner affirms that in those schools or *yeshiva*, the school's discipline transformed other ordinary, natural actions, gestures, and functions into rituals - the rituals of "being a Rabbi." The master exemplified the whole Torah to his disciples.

Scripture and Mishnah, written or oral Torah, meant little without observation and imitation of the sage. "The whole Torah was not in books or in words to be memorized. Torah was to be found in whole and complete form in the master. That is why the forms of respect for the master were both so vital and so unique to the mythic life of the schools. What made a man into a Rabbi was study of the Torah as a disciple with a master of the Torah."[142] Rabbis regarded everything as matters of "Torah" and they expected their disciples to learn and act accordingly. A Rabbi, by being the master of Torah, would demonstrate his mastery to the disciples not only through what he said in his teaching but also how he acted before them. The action of the master was normative and witnessing.

The pupil learnt from his master not only by listening to the words but also by doing what the master commanded him to do. Thus, the pupils had an obligation to show exceptional respect to their masters and witness to the actions of the teachers. In these schools, the master was the father figure who considered his disciple as his son, a father who leads him into the world to come. Although the master was owed all the respect due to one's own father, the master never replaced one's father. The service of the sages' disciples separated the true sage from the merely learned man. This service did not require mere personal attendance but also imitation and study of the master as much as of the Torah. An obvious question; what is important in the learning of a pupil? Is it learning from the Torah or learning from the Master? Byrskog states that the basis of integral study of Torah resided outside of the life and status of the teacher. "Torah in its various forms, not the Rabbi himself, was the focus of attention." However Byrskog concludes and confirms that the teacher was of interest primarily as the embodiment of Torah in words and deeds. Hence the teacher is respected by the pupils not only for his position of authority but also for his ability to transmit the content and knowledge of Torah.

4. The Functions of a Rabbi: Is it a Job or a Service?

The Rabbi of the Talmudic period was expected to be an interpreter and expounder of the biblical texts and the oral Law. Rabbinic literature contains many prohibitions against charging for teaching the Scriptures.[143] A charismatic leader in the Talmudic period laboured for the community without asking for anything for himself; an onlooker would see a great similarity between his character and that of the prophet in the period of the Scriptures. Metzger, speaking of the function of a Rabbi of first century Judaism, says that all the labours "whether educational or judicial, were to be gratuitous."[144] He further says that these Rabbis, in addition to teaching and transmitting the law, had to depend upon other means of obtaining a livelihood. He objects to the idea that the function of a *Rab* was a profession from which to derive one's livelihood. According to Shmuel Himelstein, "Until medieval times, Rabbis received no salary from their congregations, in accordance with the Mishnaic law that prohibits deriving any income or benefits from the Torah."[145] R. Hertz observes, "Originally Rabbis were not paid. The Torah was to be taught free of charge, and it was customary for Rabbis to have another occupation."[146] That occupation would be the profession from which "he derived his livelihood."[147] As the demands on Rabbis' time increased, they were permitted to receive financial remuneration in lieu of the money they might have earned if they had the time to engage in a different occupation. According to Neusner, the Rabbis at the time of late antiquity also held a variety of public responsibilities. He writes: "The variety of public responsibilities carried out by the Rabbi is striking. He had to prevent the collapse of mud buildings during a rainstorm. He had to ensure a constant market by encouraging gardens to provide a steady supply of fresh vegetables. He had to give out medical information, to preserve public health, and to make certain that poor people could benefit from the available remedies. And he had to provide for the poor, so that no one would starve in his town."[148] Neusner's observation is remarkable as it reveals that Rabbis, besides being the teachers of the law and scripture, also had a great many other responsibilities in Jewish society.

Himelstein and Ephraim Kanarfogel speak of *sekhar battalah*[149] which are wages for being prevented from being employed in another occupation. J. C. Turro, speaking of a Rabbi judge, notes that "He was paid a fee for the time he consumed in adjudicating a case." However when he speaks about the Rabbi teachers, Turro says that "They did not receive a salary for their teaching activity, but supported themselves by the pursuit of some trade or profession."[150] After medieval times, according to Himelstein "Rabbis always had private occupations - artisan, doctor, farmer, or even laborer."[151] Raphael Patai has a different version. He notes that in the Talmudic period in general the Rabbi was an expounder or interpreter of the Bible and the oral law and occasionally he was a preacher but the Rabbi derived no income from these activities. A Rabbi "generally had a private, income producing occupation, such as cobbler or smith."[152] Hence "The Rabbi of the Talmud was therefore completely different from the present day holder of the title."[153]

According to Patai, "It was only in the 19th Century, with the beginning of the Jewish Reform movement, that Rabbis became appointed and salaried employees of religious congregations."[154] Judah David Eisenstein[155] observes that modern Rabbis are official ministers who are elected by the congregation and are paid a stipulated salary. As was said above, this practice is contrary to the Rabbi of the Talmudic period, when all their services "were honorary positions, without emolument, save the bare living expenses of the Rabbi when he gave up his occupation for the public welfare."[156] Thus, the function of a Rabbi in the Talmud is mostly that of a noble duty and not as a profession in the material sense.

5. The Ordination of Rabbis in the Jewish History

The ordination of Rabbis testifies to the institutional and official character of the office. H. L. Ellison observes that the title Rabbi gradually became "a technical term for a man who had received ordination, i.e. who had received authority to act as judge in religious matters."[157] Kanarfogel observes that ordination was conferred by sages in the land of Israel throughout the period of the Second Temple, "as means of allowing or authorizing a worthy student to issue judicial rulings or to otherwise decide matters of Jewish law."[158] The act of ordination, which is also closely related to the appointment of Rabbis, was the predominant method to validate the Rabbis of the Talmudic era.

The Validation of Ordination

The term Rabbi was thus used "as a title for those who are distinguished for learning, who are the authoritative teachers of the Law, and who are appointed spiritual heads of the community."[159] Rabbinic ordination is called either *semikhah* or *minnui*.[160] Samuel Byrskog states, "Although minor differences existed in the actual performance of the ordination, several general features testify to its institutional and official character."[161] Since such ordination was not in use in Talmudic times outside Erez Israel, it was not applied to the Babylonian sages. Rather they always adopted or were granted the title *rav*. Hershel Shanks notes the letter of Sherira Gaon written to the community of Kairwan in the tenth century, in which it is possible to find proof either for, or against, the practice of ordination. The letter reads thus; "The title 'Rabbi' is borne by the sages of Palestine, who were ordained by the Sanhedrin in accordance with the custom handed down by the elders and were denominated 'Rabbi' and received authority to judge in penal cases."[162] But according to the letter of Sherira, the Babylonian sages received their title 'Rab' with an ordination in their colleges. The office of Rabbi in the late Rabbinical tradition required a person to be particularly well versed in the scriptures and the Talmud, whereas the office of Priest required certain sacrificial and temple ordinance ceremonies. Hence to be recognised as a Rabbi, a Talmudic student had to be ordained before he could start functioning as a teacher of the Law.

So it appears that ordination, or a kind of official conferring of the title Rabbi by some higher authorities, was in practice both in Palestine and Babylon. It is not clear whether, in the period of Rabbinical Judaism, ordination was necessary to function as a Rabbi in that society. Byrskog observes that "some texts claim even that the ordination was an unconditional prerequisite for transmitting torah."[163] Himelstein notes that "the conferring of ordination was restricted to *Erets Yisra'el*, where it was curtailed in the fourth century, but a limited authorization (*hattarat hora'ah* [permission to teach]) was subsequently introduced."[164] However, Himelstein affirms that "at a later period, it was decreed that a candidate for the office of Rabbi must sit for an examination in Talmud and Codes. "Only men steeped in Talmud and Rabbinic literature after many years of intensive study were admitted to Rabbinic honors."[165] Jacob Neusner maintains that "A sage became Rabbi because he knew Torah in the right way, having learned under proper auspices and having given ample evidence of accurate mastery and correct interpretation of the Torah."[166] Byrskog asserts that "It is evident that those who were chosen to be ordained were the best pupils who had learned Torah thoroughly."[167] Byrskog further states that "Of course, the ordination gave a certain status to the individual teacher."[168] He became a member of the Rabbinic court and could be an elder or Rabbi; and the act of ordination also accorded a formal authority to transmit Torah and the legitimate right to perform a particular function.

According to Broyde,[169] the ordination of Rabbis was performed by one who was already ordained, in front of the witnesses, and here the ordination is a further indication of its official character in Rabbinic Judaism. Jacob E. Safra notes that this "Ordination (certification as a Rabbi) can be conferred by any Rabbi, but one's teacher customarily performs this function by issuing a written statement."[170] Ellison says, "This ordination was practised only in Palestine and ceased in the 4th century AD."[171] After that, the title was conferred on someone by the judgment of three Rabbis when they found someone with adequate knowledge to expound the law. So even the practice of conferring the title "Rabbi" on someone differed greatly from Palestine to Babylon. A Rabbi, even with his Rabbinical ordination, had no actual power under Jewish law. It is notable that ordination carries with it no special religious status.

Rabbis as Ordained Ministers

David B. Ruderman, while speaking about the Rabbis of medieval times using a fixed formula of ordination distinguished by the title *Moreinu ha-rav*, compares this with the ordination that Rabbis received in ancient Palestine. Rabbis, who previously had been ordained in ancient Palestine, received "maximal judicial privileges operative within a framework of a Jewish court system."[172] According to M. R. Wilson, in the Jewish community today the term Rabbi is strictly and properly reserved to, "one who has received ordination from the hands of other recognised scholar-teachers."[173] Thus in the later period the term Rabbi has been attributed to a teacher who had the authority to interpret the law and Scriptures, and that had been officially ordained by other recognised scholar-teachers. Hertz also agrees that in Talmudic times, Rabbis were interpreters and expounders of the scriptures and oral Law, but it was not until the Middle Ages that a Rabbi became the spiritual leader of a particular Jewish community, with teaching, preaching, and administrative functions. Hertz concludes that "Rabbis, however, were not priests. They had no sacramental role, and blessing the people was not an integral part of their duties."[174] It was only in the Middle Ages that this title, besides referring to the interpreters of the Law and Scripture, was also given to one who could make decisions concerning the Law, teacher, preacher or spiritual head of the Jewish congregation or community.

J. C. Turro notes that "In the 12th century there emerged a type of Rabbi comparable in position and function to the modern Rabbi."[175] By the 12th century, the job of Rabbi had become a full-time occupation. Shmuel Himelstein observes the change in the functions of Rabbis during the Middle Ages and especially after the persecutions in Spain during the 14th and 15th centuries. "The refugee Rabbis who fled to countries of asylum found little opportunity for making a outside living, and at the same time, new communities of exiles needed full time professional Rabbis to minister them."[176] J. C. Turro states that "In the wake of salaried Rabbis it came to be customary to stipulate in writing the specific services that a given congregation anticipated from its Rabbi. Among other things, a Rabbi was expected to set up and preside over a community court, organize and supervise a lower school and an academy, and to participate in circumcision, *BAR MITZVAH*, marriage, and other ceremonies."[177]

Safra opines that "a Rabbi also preaches on occasions and counsels and consoles as needs arise. A Rabbi has responsibility for the total religious education of the young, but the extent of his participation, beyond the realm of general supervision is dictated by local circumstances."[178] As Himelstein opines, "The formal conferment of a *morenu* diploma was first introduced in Germany in the fourteenth century; it entitled the recipient to act as a Rabbinical *dayyan* (judge)."[179] According to Patai, "In the Middle Ages some Rabbis functioned as religious judges (dayans), while others were the spiritual and moral leaders of their communities. From the 16th century on, outstanding Rabbis served as heads of yeshivas (Talmudic schools). As a rule, all these activities were carried out with no remuneration."[180] Himelstein affirms that in modern times, Rabbinical emphasis has changed. He opines that "Until the 19th century, preaching was of secondary importance."[181] R. Hertz says that in modern times a Rabbi is expected, as community leader, "to give response on legal problems and ambiguities, and to serve in Jewish courts."[182] David B. Ruderman notes that by the late Middle Ages, the Rabbinate had become a multifaceted office. "Despite the growing responsibilities of his position, the Rabbi's actual hegemony within the Jewish community was increasingly attenuated. Most Rabbis were appointed only for limited terms; government officials and powerful communal leaders often interfered with their decisions, and Rabbinic posts sometimes went to the highest bidder. Nevertheless, the institution of the Rabbinate was still associated with the tradition of sanctity and transcendent scholarship originating in ancient times."[183]

In the 18th and the 19th century a great change[184] took place with regard to the position and requirements of the Rabbi and to the services expected of him, a change which finally amounted to a complete revolution of former ideas. M. A. Gutstein notes that "With the rise of Hasidism in the eighteenth century the leaders of the movement adopted the title "Rabbe."[185] Himelstein notes that "Often the election of a Rabbi was subject to confirmation by the civil authorities."[186] The observation of J. C. Turro that, "On occasion Rabbis have been charged with the performance of civil functions; for example, the collection of taxes for the government."[187] The Rabbi is a communal official whose duties include not only religious activities but also embrace educational, pastoral, social, and interfaith activities. Today many Rabbis are simultaneously doctors, lawyers, psychologists, etc. Himelstein also notes that "In the nineteenth century, Rabbinical seminaries and special theological institutions for the training of Rabbis were founded in western Europe and America. Many of these added a body of secular studies to the traditional Rabbinical requirements."[188]

Ruderman affirms that "Undeniably the Rabbi has suffered some loss of political power to lay groups within the Jewish community; the Rabbi also sees his or her exclusive claim to expertise in Jewish matters somewhat eclipsed by the new breed of Judaic scholars in university and seminary settings."[189] However these changes in the authority and power of Rabbis never became an impediment to effective communal leadership and communication of values. The new theological seminaries and universities were never hostile to the functioning of Rabbis and, moreover, most of the scholars in the Jewish theological seminaries are still Rabbis.

It is very interesting to note the observation of Jacob E. Safra that "differences among Orthodox, Conservative, and Reform Jewish groups are reflected, to some degree, in the functions of their respective Rabbis."[190] According to Hertz, "Nowadays the role of the Rabbi varies from community to community. Among reform congregations he, and since 1972, possibly she,[191] also performs a function analogous to that of a Christian minister. The Rabbi is regarded as a spiritual leader of the community; he is involved in preaching, leading services, educating and counselling."[192] Today, the role of a Rabbi mirrors that of a Christian minister. David B. Ruderman echoes the same idea: "In Christian countries, the Rabbi functioned in a similar capacity, although his sacerdotal roles as chief officiary of the Jewish community were more pronounced. Assuming duties more closely analogous to those of a Christian priest, the Rabbi became more directly associated with a specific synagogue or congregation."[193] Thus, the Rabbi today still has the capacity to be the leader of his society, and he or she leads the congregation by preaching and communicating values. The Rabbi is stimulated by academic issues and provides the means for learning and listening. In short, a Rabbi performs the functions that not all academic scholars can perform, that is, learning to teach and teaching in order that the community may follow him. From the beginning until the present day, Rabbis remain very important in Jewish society as chief protagonists. Today, Rabbis are still responsible for teaching on matters of Judaism in general and law in particular; and are qualified to determine the applicability of Jewish law. Rabbis often work as religious leaders. Rabbis typically speak on behalf of their communities on a wide range of issues, offer spiritual leadership for their congregation, and are usually involved in Jewish lifecycle events. Nevertheless, Rabbis do not play any essential role in Jewish liturgy and ritual, and Jewish congregations can persist indefinitely without a Rabbi assigned to them.

6. Rabbis and Scribes in NT

The following section will review the titles and offices of Rabbis and Scribes to see how they are similar and how they are distinct from one another. In the NT, the Scribes are mostly portrayed either as "teachers or scholars in Law as well as one among the many authorities to transmit the content and knowledge of Torah."[194] "Scribes" were commonly also addressed as "Rabbi." The period after the Restoration, led to the gradually increasing importance of the Temple, and of the priesthood ministering to it. The spirit of Esdras'[195] reform survived in the authority (attached to the Law). This was an authority which overshadowed the prestige of the Temple and of the priesthood itself. It tended to put into prominence the teachers and expounders of the Law, the Scribes. Originally the word *scribe* meant writer but soon it was accepted as a matter of course that the scribe who copies the Law knows the Law best, and is its most qualified expounder. Accordingly the word came to mean more than it implies etymologically. Knowledge of the Law became the primary reason for the Scribes' respect and popularity. The earliest Scribes, like Esdras, who came to be hailed as the model of the "Scribe" in the Law of Moses, were priests. However, in time, a large body of lay teachers came to swell the ranks of the Scribes.

Gradually, the spell of Hellenistic usage fell upon the priesthood (i.e. the Scribes) and the lay teachers found themselves more and more the only guardians and exponents of the Law. When the Pharisees began to be recognized as a distinct sect about 150 B. C, the Scribes as a rule adhered to them as being the most ardent observers of the Law (Cf. Mk 2:16; Lk 5:30, and Ac 23:9). At any rate, from that time onwards the Scribes were accepted as the accredited teachers of the people. Until the fall of Jerusalem, the Scribes chiefly congregated in Judea; but in later times their presence is noted in Northern Palestine, even in Rome, and in every important centre of the Dispersion. While a deep historical study of Scribes is beyond the scope of this research, the question to be addressed is whether the Rabbis mentioned in the Gospels can be identified with the Scribes of NT times. To begin, the narrative in Mt 23:2-15 is addressed. D. E. Orton[196] points out that if both Matthew's work and his independent use of the term γραμματεῦς is taken into account, it becomes evident that Mathew has a clear notion of who the Scribes are and what they should ideally be.

A question arises: why is Jesus shown condemning the Scribes and Pharisees who want to be called ῥαββί in that society? In Mt 23:8, both the equivalent terms ῥαββί and διδάσκαλος have been given in a parallel manner. Jesus issues a direct warning to his disciples, not to seek to be called ῥαββί. John O'Neill thinks that the manuscripts that support the reading of Mt 23:8, "perhaps reflect a time when the Church was breaking away from Judaism and dropping the old semitic title Rabbi for her teachers."[197] In Mt 23:7-8, it seems that the term Rabbi denotes 'teacher' with the connotation of 'teacher of the law.' Though the term ῥαββί mostly signifies a teacher in this context, here the title refers to the Scribes and Pharisees. Jesus condemns the Scribes and Pharisees for their pride in seeking the title Rabbi and, with it, the first places on important occasions. Thus, these two references in Matthew come in the "woe betide" sayings of Jesus. Isaac Broyde observes that it is "Jesus' disapprobation of the ambition of the Jewish doctors who loved to be called by this title, and his admonition to his disciples not to suffer themselves to be so styled."[198] In this context, this study will examine whether the Scribes and the Rabbis are one and the same. Were there any functional differences between these two terms? Are they two different names for the same group of people in Jewish society?

The Function of Scribes as Teachers

Bruce M. Metzger points out that, at the time of Jesus, the Scribes were called Rabbis, but in earlier times the Scribes of the Near East were professionals in performing "a useful service as public secretaries."[199] Of course, this public function is entirely different compared to the duties of the NT Scribes. The Scribes or Rabbis in ancient Israel were employed to take down in writing what another dictated. It was only after the Babylonian exile, Metzger opines, that this secular function of this group of Scribes or Rabbis turned to a religious function as guardians or teachers of the Mosaic Law. In the time of Jesus, Scribes were the ones responsible for the interpretation and teaching of law and scriptures. They were more or less the guardians of the law in that society. They were the authorities for the Sanhedrin, responsible as authoritative interpreters of Law and Scripture. Ellison notes that, "Rabbi was in NT times a title of respect given by the common man to the Scribes and by a student to his teacher."[200] Just as there were masters or teachers in the Greco-Roman world of the first century, so there were people called Rabbi or Scribes in Judaism as well. "The Scribes were also teachers and had pupils תלמידמ whom they instructed in the Scripture and in the traditions of the Fathers."[201] As is known, disciples were always committed to a recognised leader or movement.

From the earliest times the Scribes seem to have conceived an exalted opinion of their own merits.[202] Evidently the Scribe in his own estimation belonged to a higher caste. This was understood by the people who, after the time of Hillel, introduced the custom of saluting them as "Rabbi". The word, derived from the Hebrew *Rab* when it became the distinctive title of the Scribes and the specific force of its pronoun was lost, and "Rabbi" was used very much like our "Doctor."[203] Bruce M. Metzger,[204] in his study of the cultural and religious background of Palestinian Judaism, opines that the most usual title bestowed upon the Scribes is the Hebrew appellation Rabbi, which indicates the extraordinary respect accorded them by the populace. Gerd Theissen and Annette Merz tell us that "a Scribe became a 'Rabbi' as soon as others, and especially disciples, addressed him as such and asked him for advice."[205] Thus, an evolution is seen in progressing from "Scribe" to "Rabbi." When Geza Vermes speaks about Jesus as a Rabbi, he suggests, "The Semitic title might suggest that he was regarded as a 'Scribe', the contemporary equivalent of what later became the office of 'Rabbi.'[206] Thus, in the opinion of the above authors, there is a gradual development from the stage of a 'Scribe' to the office or position of 'Rabbi'.

Similarities and Differences in Functions of Rabbis and Scribes

When the roles of the Scribes in the NT are examined, they are sometimes referred to as lawyers and are considered experts in the sacred Mosaic Law. As lawyers, they had authority over the Jewish law and legislated in both civil and religious matters. Scribes became very important in Jewish society, and they were called teachers of the law or simply teachers by the common people and held in high respect. If the Scribes were teachers or teachers of the law, it is evident that they had pupils – either as their followers or students to whom they expounded the law and Scripture. Hence, for a man to be called a Scribe, he must be skilled in the Law of Moses and have his heart set on studying the law of the Lord and carrying it out, and teaching his statutes and ordinances in Israel (cf. Ez 7:6-10). As has been noted, the role and function of the Rabbi was the same as that of the scribe in that society. In fact, the Scribes had a threefold function. As Metzger has observed, the Scribes were concerned with, " (a) the more careful theoretical development of the law itself; (b) the teaching of the law to their pupils; (c) the practical administration of the law in pronouncing legal decisions."[207]

John P. Meier holds the view that "the Scribes in their capacity as Scribes did not form or belong to any one religious group in Palestinian Judaism at the time of Jesus."[208] For Meier, the image of the Scribes that stems from the synoptics is a popular misconception. He objects to the view presented in the synoptics and some of the later Rabbinic literature where these Scribes are portrayed as those "who had formally studied the Mosaic law in great detail, who were therefore acknowledged experts in religious, moral, and legal questions."[209] For Meier, it is an untenable to say that "all Scribes were Torah scholars (alias wise men, sages, Rabbis, or sophists) and all Torah scholars were Scribes."[210] If such a position is adopted, the basic scribal functions of writing and copying documents is often underplayed or forgotten. Meier is not in favour of considering the Scribes as Rabbis or teachers. Although he does not entirely reject their role as teachers, he considers such a portrayal as "hopelessly simplistic."[211] This study affirms with some degree of certainty that the Scribes held different positions, and had different functions in Jewish society at different stages in Jewish history. In the Jewish tradition, the Scribes and the theologians were once called or identified with the office of Rabbi, but later the title ῥαββί became exclusively a term for those who had completed their studies and been ordained as teachers of the law. In sum, several similarities are found to exist in the functions of Rabbis and Scribes, but it cannot be concluded that the titles are one and the same.

Summary and Conclusions

Chapter one of Part I has attempted to explain in what sense and in what different ways the title ῥαββί has been used historically. This chapter also has attempted to define the term "Rabbi" and its meaning from its origin up to the present day. Hence, this study began with the etymology and the interpretation of the term ῥαββί. How the title ῥαββί was used in different contexts and with different meanings was explored. A separate study was made on the literary understanding of the origin of the word "Rabbi" as well as the use of this term from Mosaic times up to the period of the historical Jesus. It was found that the title ῥαββί was not coined by the New Testament writers. Rather it was a familiar term used both as a title and as a form of address in the earlier writings of scripture and in other literatures. Some of the Old Testament instances were noted in which the term was used for different offices or functions. It was found that it often had a different meaning and a different connotation depending on the context in which it was used.

Next a historical survey was done on the use of the term ῥαββί both in Palestinian and Babylonian contexts. It was found that these two separate traditions had their own basic demands (or pre-requisites) for someone entitled to be called a ῥαββί or to bear the title ῥαββί. The study showed that a remarkable evolutionary stage evolved where this title referred to a 'teacher-disciple' relationship. At that stage in history the term ῥαββί stood for someone who was a teacher of Scripture and/or Law and had a group of disciples who depended on him for knowledge. The next step was to see how this title evolved during the time of transition to Hellenism. To this end, the cultural arena was explored to see how the term was used in the society into which Jesus was born.

In Rabbinic Judaism, ῥαββί denotes an authorized teacher of the classical Jewish tradition after the fall of the second Temple in 70 A.D. Bruce Chilton and other scholars recognise that the work of Rabbis after 70 A.D. were critical for Judaism. It is evident that it is because of the work of Rabbis that Judaism came into existence. Rabbis after 70 A.D. functioned as scholars and skilled practitioners in interpreting the Torah as well as its application in that society. These Rabbis were responsible for the observation of the Torah by the Jews, which meant that Rabbis were the persons who safeguarded and promulgated the Jewish heritage. In first century Judaism, beside the title Rabbi, *Rabban* and *Rabbenu* were also in use. It was observed that Presidents of the Sanhedrin were called *rabban* ("our master"). Thus, ῥαββί stands for a Master, a teacher or a leader of high social esteem.

Traditionally, Rabbis served as the legal and spiritual guides of their congregations and communities. The title ῥαββί was conferred on a person after considerable study of traditional Jewish sources. This conferral and its responsibilities are central to the chain of tradition in Judaism. Rabbis' position and function in society, based on their authoritative interpretation of the Scriptures, and their role as interpreters of the law and scriptures for their communities, resulted in their replacing the priesthood. It was also found that, without exception, Rabbis viewed their roles and standing among other Jews neither as deriving from, nor dependant on, the Jewish community. Though the teaching of Torah had to be free of any fees, Rabbis also had multifarious offices and various functions in society which supported their livelihood. By earning his livelihood from other sources not connected to his religious roles, the Rabbi assumed a relatively independent status in society. A Rabbi, besides being a religious scholar and leader, also functioned as a religious judge.

While reviewing the role of the Rabbi in different periods of Jewish history, it was learnt that the Rabbi of late antiquity functioned unambiguously as a holy man. He was devoted mostly to the study of Torah in both its written and oral forms. When a man had mastered the Torah, he became a scholar as well as a spiritual leader or teacher of that society, and so the Rabbis became distinguished and dominant religious leaders of society. Sometime in the twelfth century in medieval Europe, a new Rabbinic office emerged which led the Jewish society to self-governance. At that time, in the Islamic countries, Rabbis remained as judicial authorities. Rabbis also acted essentially as scholars of Jewish law with the authority to interpret scripture and the norms of Judaism in the contexts of Jewish life in and around Israel.

In Christian countries, it was hard to distinguish the work of Rabbis from Christian ministers as the Rabbis exercised their sacerdotal duties like Christian ministers. Nevertheless, a degree of uncertainty prevailed over the status and position of a Rabbi. This was due to the professionalisation of the Rabbi and the Rabbinate and since the Middle Ages to the subordination of the Rabbi to the communal will of Jewish society.

The growing professionalisation of the Rabbinate in Christian Europe reached a further stage of development some time in the fourteenth and fifteenth centuries. By that time most Rabbis started receiving salaries from the communities they served and various tax exemptions from the states where they served their congregations. This study also showed that, by the late Middle Ages, the Rabbinate had become a more complex and multi-faceted office. As a public figure in Jewish society the Rabbi worked as a communal functionary, as a judge and chief expert on Jewish law, and also as a preacher of the law and scripture. He acted as supervisor of the ritual life in the community, and directed the educational programme for the youth in his society. It was observed that present day Rabbis find themselves in an ever more difficult and paradoxical position compared to the Rabbis of the Medieval period. Autonomy and authority are difficult to maintain because they are now salaried employees. Currently, Rabbis supplement their income by revenue from weddings, divorces, civil litigations, and other such private services. In sum, this study found that the role of ῥαββί has changed considerably in different contexts and throughout the centuries. The study also found that the title 'Rabbi' developed a broader meaning as opposed to that of referring exclusively to a teacher having followers.

Endnotes

[1] Jacob NEUSNER & William Scott GREEN (eds.), "*Rabbi*", in *Dictionary of Judaism in the Biblical Period*, Vol. 2., NY, Simon & Schuster Macmillan, (1996) 516-18, p. 517.

[2] This title appears in Nestle-Aland as ῥαββί whereas in some of the manuscripts this is ῥαββεί. See, Reuben J. SWANSON, *John, New Testament Greek manuscripts, Variant Readings Arranged in Horizontal Lines against Codex Vaticanus*, Sheffield, England, Sheffield Academic press, 1995, p. 15. See also, Philip W. COMFORT & David P. BARRETT, *The Complete Text of the Earliest New Testament Manuscripts*, Grand Rapids, MI, Baker, 1999. Here in this manuscript in page 66, it appears ῥαββεί. Where the form is *rabboni* in the gospels such as "*Rabboni*, which is to say, *didaskalos*." MSS. D Q latt. have *rabooni* Dalman observes that "The interchange of u and o in pronunciation can also be seen in other cases like Sousanna at Lk 8:3 as *shoshannah* and the Palmyrenian *Iakoubos* for the name Jacob." G. DALMAN, *The Words of Jesus*, authorized English version by D. M. KAY, Edinburgh, T. and T. Clark, 1902, p. 324, footnote 3.

[3] James C. TURRO, "*Rabbi*", in Bernard L. MARTHALER et al (ed.), *New Catholic Encyclopedia* (2nd ed.), Pau - Red (Vol. 2), Washington D.C., Thomson Gale in association with the Catholic University of America, (2003) 882-883.

⁴ Raymond F. COLLINS, *John and His Witness*, Zacchaeus Studies, NT, Liturgical Press, Collegeville, Minnesota, 1991, p. 37.

⁵ Francis Brown and others, in their grammatical analysis of the word רַב, observe that it is a masculine noun which means 'chief' and in its adjectival form, *Rab* means 'much, many, great.' In Hebrew, *Rab* is translated as 'great or chief.' See, Francis BROWN & S. R. DRIVER et al., *Rab* in *A Hebrew And English Lexicon of the Old Testament with an Appendix Containing the Biblical Aramaic*, Oxford, Clarendon Press, 1952, p. 912; E. LOHSE, ῥαββί, in *TDNT* 6 (1968) 961-965, p. 961. See also, Ludwig KOEHLER & Walter BAUMGARTNER et al., *Rab*, in *HALOT* 3, Leiden & New York, E. J. Brill, 1996, 1172-1174, p. 1172. See, Gordon H. JOHNSTON, (*rab* II) in *NIDOTTE* 3 (1996) 1028-1033, p. 1028. See also, Louis Isaac RABBINOUITZ, *"Rabbi, Rabbinate"* in *EJ* 13 (1971) 1447-1458, p. 1447. The latter reference from *Encyclopaedia Judaica* tells us that the noun form *rav* does not occur anywhere in the Bible. According to Hartmann, the term רבב goes back to mean "to be many." The adjective רַב, expresses the corresponding plentiness in quantity, but it can also have a qualitative connotation, best translated with "great.". See, T. HARTMANN, רַב, *THAT* 2 (1979) 715-26, p. 715.

⁶ L. KOEHLER & W. BAUMGARTNER, p. 1172. The word ῥαββί is derived from the Aramaic noun *Rab* which means 'master or teacher.' Even if there are many questions about the sources of OT, when it comes to the NT, one must understand the Aramaic sources of the books in the Bible. In the decades between the time of the ministry of Jesus and the composition of the various Gospels, the memory of what Jesus said and did is said to have circulated in the form of an oral tradition. For example, the apostle Paul, writing to the congregation at Corinth in about A.D. 55 reminded them that during his visit a few years before, probably in the early fifties, he had orally "delivered to you as of first importance what I also received" still earlier, thus perhaps in the forties, concerning the death and resurrection of Jesus, (See. 1 Cor. 15:1-7) and the institution of the Lord's Supper (See. 1 Cor. 11:23-26). Chronologically and even logically, therefore, there was a tradition of the church before there was a New Testament, or any book of the New Testament. By the time the materials of the oral tradition found their way into written form, they had passed through the life and experience of the church. The New Testament could have been written in Greek, but the language Jesus and his disciples usually spoke seems to have been Aramaic, a Semitic tongue related to Hebrew but not identical with it. Aramaic words and phrases are scattered throughout the Gospels and other early Christian books, reflecting the language in which various sayings and liturgical formulas had been repeated before the transition to Greek became complete. These include such familiar words as Hosanna, as well as the cry of dereliction of Jesus on the cross, *Eloi, Eloi, lama sabachthani?* (Mk 15:34) "My God, my God, why hast thou forsaken me?" (Which in the Hebrew of Psalm 22 was *Eli, Eli, lama azavtani?*). Also in the Gospels is "Immanuel" which means

"God with us." This is the Hebrew title given to the child in the prophecy of Isaiah (Isa7:14) and applied by Matthew (1:23) to Jesus. When one reads the Gospels, three Aramaic words appear as titles for Jesus: Rabbi, or teacher; *Messias*, or Christ; and *Mar*, or Lord. The most neutral of these words is probably *Rabbi*, along with the related *Rabboni*. Except for two passages, the Gospels apply the Aramaic word *rab* only to Jesus. It was observed that the title Rabbi; "teacher" or "master" (Διδάσκαλος in Greek) was intended as a translation of that Aramaic name, and it seems safe to say that it was as Rabbi that Jesus was known and addressed. Indeed at this stage of this book, it is premature to say anything about addressing Jesus as Rabbi, but better to go ahead with an etymological study of the title "Rab" in history.

[7] R. Laird HARRIS, (ed.), *Theological World book of the Old Testament*, Vol.2., Chicago, Moody Press, 1980, p. 827.

[8] *Ibid.*, This applies to persons occupying respected positions. It also was sometimes used to refer to high government officials or army officers (e.g., Jer 39:3, 13). See, LOHSE, ῥαββί, p. 961 f; HARTMANN, רַב , 720f. רַב in OT is in connection with the officials of the Assyrian-Babylonian army. For further references in this area, see, Hershel SHANKS, "Origins of the Title "Rabbi", in *JQR* 59 (1968) 152-57, p. 154; Solomon ZEITLIN, *"The Title Rabbi in the Gospels is Anachronistic"*, in *JQR* 59 (1968) 158-160. According to S. J. D. Cohen, we have one ossuary inscription where רַב is used as a title for a certain Rab Hana. Cf. Shaye J. D. COHEN, *"Epigraphical Rabbis"*, in *JQR* 72 (1981) 1-17. Various forms of רַב were apparently used in a rather titular manner in other languages throughout the ancient Near East. Cf. H. SHANKS, *Origins of the Title Rabbi*, pp. 153f.

[9] Gordon H. JOHNSTON, rab, in *NIDOTTE* 3 (1996) 1028-1033, p. 1028.

[10] *Ibid.*

11 Hayim LAPIN, *"Rabbi"*, in *ABD*, Vol.5, David Noel FREEDMAN (ed.), (1992)16. 600-602, p. 600.

[12] H. SHANKS, *Origins of the Title Rabbi*, p. 152.

[13] *Ibid.* See also, F. BROWN & S. R. DRIVER et al., p. 913.

[14] Shmuel HIMELSTEIN, "Rabbai and Rabbinate", in R. J. Zwi WERBLOWSKY and Geoffrey WIGODER (eds.), *The Oxford Dictionary of Jewish Religion*, New York, (1997) 567-568, p. 567.

[15] M. R. WILSON, "Rabbi", in *ISBE* 4 (1998) 30, p. 30. The Rabbinic writings use the term רַב in the qualitative sense for the teachers and it becomes very prominent in the writings. Of old, רַב is attributed to Joshua b. Perahia (c. 104-78 B.C.E.) in m.Abot 1:6 and in this text it is also attributed to R. Gamaliel.

[16] L. I. RABBINOUITZ, *Rabbi, Rabbinate*, p. 1447. The Rabbinic literature often expresses a qualitative understanding of רַב as to denote the lord in distinction to the servant or the slave. Cf. e.g. m. Pesah.8:2; Sukk. 2:9; m. Git. 4:4, 5; m.

'Ed. 1:13; m. 'Abot 1:3; t. B.Qam. 11:2; b. Ber. 10a; b. Ta'an. 25b; b. Git. 23b; Mek. On 12: 1; Cant. Rab. On 1:1. Thus the term signifies the subordination under the legitimate authority of various figures.

[17] Ephraim KANARFOGEL, "Rabbinate", in Lindsay JONES et al. (ed.), *Encyclopedia of Religion* (2nd ed.), Vol II. (Pius IX – Rivers), Thomsan Gale, 2005, pp. 7578-7581.

[18] See, Morris A. GUTSTEIN, "Rabbi", in William D. HARSEY et al., (eds.), *Collier's Encyclopedia with Bibliography and Index*, New York, Macmillian Educational Company, (1988) 580, p. 580. Gutstein observes that Rabbi is formed from Hebrew *rab* ("master") and the Hebrew pronominal suffix "i", the term, which came into general use during the first century of the Christian Era, literally means "my master" or "my teacher."

[19] John L. MCKENZIE, "Rabbi", in *Dictionary of the Bible*, London, Geoffrey Chapman, 1978, p. 718. In Jesus' day, *rav* was used to refer to the master of a slave or of a disciple. Thus, *Rabbi* literally meant "my master" and was a term of respect used by slaves in addressing their owners and by disciples in addressing their teachers.

[20] J. C. TURRO, *Rabbi*, p. 882. Turro agrees that this is a title of a Jewish religious teacher and is derived from the Hebrew word Rabbi, which is literally 'my master', which in New Testament times was used only as a term of address.

[21] G. H. JOHNSTON, *Rabbi*, p. 1032.

[22] See, M. A. GUTSTEIN, "*Rabbi*", p. 580. Gutstein notes that Rabbi is a title applied to Jewish scholars and spiritual leaders.

[23] J. C. TURRO, *Rabbi*, p. 882.

[24] J. L. MCKENZIE, "*Rabbi*", p. 718. According to McKenzie, in the Talmudic period, the suffix lost its force and the word became a title instead of an address.

[25] See, Roswell D. HITCHCOCK, "Rabbi", in "*An Interpreting Dictionary of Scripture Proper Names*", New York, N.Y., 1869; William SMITH, "Rabbi", in "*Smith's Bible Dictionary*", 1901. See also, W. W. RAND, "Rabbi and Rabboni", in *American Tract Society Bible Dictionary*, 1859. A different account of the origin and the signification of the titles is given in the Tosefta "He who has disciples and whose disciples again have disciples is called 'Rabbi'; when his disciples are forgotten he is called 'Rabban'; and when the disciples of his disciples are also forgotten he is called simply by his own name." Since the demolition of the temple of Jerusalem, the priests *Cohanim* and *Levites* lost the privileges from which they benefited and that were linked to the service of the shrine. In the Jewish religion the Rabbi is no priest, no apostle; he has no hierarchical power. He is a teacher, one who unfolds and explains religion, teaches the young in the school and the old from the pulpit, and both by his writings. The title "Rabbi" was obtained through merit of learning. Any one might become qualified as a Rabbi, irrespective of his antecedents.

[26] See, M. A. GUTSTEIN, "Rabbi", p. 580. For Gutstein, Rabbon or Rabban (the Aramaic equivalent of *rab*) was considered an especially respectful title and was applied only to the presidents of the Sanhedrin. Rabbenu ("our teacher"), which was originally added to the name of Moses, was applied to Judah Hanasi, who was the compiler of the Mishnah. In Babylonia, where the ordination was not normally practised independent of Palestine, the teachers were granted the title רב and the eminent scholars were given the title "Rabban" which is a form superior to "Rabbi." The disciples of the teachers who were called "Rabban" were not always forgotten. Cf. S. ZEITLIN, *The Title Rabbi in the Gospels is Anachronistic*, p. 159f; H. SHANKS, *Origins of the Title "Rabbi"*, p. 155 n. 15. See also, *Dictionary of Judaism in the Biblical period*, Vol. 2. NY, Simon & Schuster Macmillian, 1996 (516-18) p. 516. When the title Rabbi is explained as "my lord", or "my master", *Rabbenu* is explained as a title of honour, meaning "Our Lord." See also, E. KANARFOGEL, *Rabbinate*, p. 7578. Kanarfogel explains the term *Rabbinate* as follows; the term *Rabbinate* is perhaps derived from the title "Rabban", if not from a form of the titles *rav* or Rabbi.

[27] Samuel BYRSKOG, *Jesus the Only Teacher, Didactic Authority and Transmission in Ancient Israel, Ancient Judaism and the Matthean Community*, CB, New Testament Series 24, Stockholm, Almqvist & Wiksell International, 1994, p. 53. The title 'Rabbi' is borne by the sages of Palestine, who were ordained there by the Sanhedrin in accordance with the custom handed down by the elders, and were denominated 'Rabbi,' and received authority to judge penal cases; while 'Rab' is the title of the Babylonian sages, who received their ordination in their colleges. The more ancient generations, however, which were far superior, had no such titles as 'Rabban,' 'Rabbi,' or 'Rab,' for either the Babylonian or Palestinian sages. This is evident from the fact that Hillel I., who came from Babylon, did not have the title 'Rabban' prefixed to his name. For Prophets, who were very eminent, it is simply said, 'the prophet,' etc., e.g. 'Ezra did not come up from Babylon,' etc., the title 'Rabban' not being used. Indeed, in history, this title is not met with earlier than the time of the patriarchate. It was first used of Rabban Gamaliel the elder, Rabban Simeon his son, and Rabban Johanan ben Zakkai, all of whom were patriarchs or presidents of the Sanhedrin. The title 'Rabbi,' too came into vogue among those who received the laying on of hands at this period, as, for instance, Rabbi Zadok, Rabbi Eliezer ben Jacob, and others, and dates from the time of the disciples of Rabban Johanan ben Zakkai. The purpose here is not to deal with the history of the Sanhedrin, rather to have a detailed study of the development of the title "Rabban" at a later stage of this chapter.

[28] E. KANARFOGEL, "*Rabbinate*", p. 7578.

[29] M. A. GUTSTEIN, "*Rabbi*", p. 580.

[30] Jacob NEUSNER, "*Rabbinic Judaism in Late Antiquity*", in Lindsay JONES et al. (ed.), *Encyclopedia of Religion* (2nd ed.), Vol II. (Pius IX – Rivers), Thomsan Gale, (2005) 7583-90, p.7584. Neusner observes that the title Rabbi originally

means simply "My lord", and hence no more than *Monsieur* or *Mein Herr*. When Jesus was called "Rabbi", the term was equivalent to *teacher* or *master*, *Sir*. Rabbis in the Mishnah, figures of the first and second centuries, generally gave opinions about trivial legal matters; they were considered sages but were never represented as wonder workers. Representations of Rabbis in documents from the third century onward, including discussion of first-and second- century figures in those later documents, by contrast present the Rabbi as a supernatural figure. The *Rabbi* then emerges as a lawyer-magician, or supernatural judge-sage-mystic.

[31] It is interesting to note the gradual change in meaning of terms of address from formal to honorific over the period of time. This is not exclusive to the Jewish culture, it is fairly common in other cultures too. For example, in England, the term 'Esquire' originally referred to a landowner of considerable wealth in Victorian times but today it is given to all untitled males. The same goes for "Mr", "Sir", "Squire" and many more in different cultures.

[32] See, H. LAPIN, "*Rabbi*", p. 600. Ref. 2Kgs 18:17; Isa 36: 2; Jer 39:3, 13; 41:1; Dan 1:3; 2:48; 4:6; 5:1, Jon 1:6; Esth 1:8.

[33] R. L. HARRIS, (ed.), *Theological World book of the Old Testament*, p. 827.

[34] The chart on the occurrences of the Hebrew term br in the OT texts has been prepared with the help of the following sources. F. BROWN & S. R. DRIVER et al., בר , pp. 912-13; E. LOHSE, ραββί and ραββυνί, p. 961; Francis I. ANDERSON & A. Dean FORBES, *The Vocabulary of the Old Testament*, Pontifical Biblical Institute, Rome, 1989, p. 225; L. KOEHLER & W. BAUMGARTNER, p. 1172.

[35] M. R. WILSON, "*Rabbi*", p. 30.

[36] Henry Leopold ELLISON, *Rabbi*, in Colin BROWN (ed.), *NIDNTT* 3 (1978) 115-116, p. 115.

[37] Primary education took place in the home (Dt 4:10; 11:19). The parents together provided this early training of the child (Pro 4:4,11; 31:1; Song 8:2). Leaders of the nation, priests, prophets, psalmists, and the wise contributed to the general education of Israel. In addition, some undoubtedly had the advantage of specialized training in the palace school or in other seats of learning, particularly in the later history of Israel (e.g., Pro 1:1-4; 1Ch 25:7 f.). For example, Daniel attended the royal academy of Babylon and was taught the language and literature of the Chaldeans (Dan 1:4).

[38] S. BYRSKOG, *Jesus the Only Teacher,* p. 53. In Ex 33:11, the young boy Joshua follows Moses. Just as the people obeyed Moses, they now obey Joshua (Josh 1:17). Like Moses (Ex 19:10), Joshua makes the people consecrate themselves before an important event (Josh 3:5; 7:13). Just as Moses (Dt 9:25-29), Joshua intercedes for sinful Israel (Josh 7:6-9). Just as Moses (Dt 31:1-33:29), Joshua gives his last will before his death (Josh 23:1-24:28). Furthermore Joshua repeatedly appears as the servant of Moses (See. Ex. 24:13; 33:11; Num 11:28; Josh 1:1). Sir 46:1 presents Joshua as the servant of Moses. Byrskog opines that it is essential for Joshua to follow the teaching of Moses exactly

(Josh 1:7. 13; 4:10; 8:30-35; 11:15, etc.). Joshua depends on the law of Moses and speaks of the book of the law from Moses as the guide for the people of Israel (Josh 23:6). Joshua is seen with Moses on special occasions like climbing the mountain (Ex 24:13; 32:17) or entering the tent (Ex 33:11; Num 11:28; Dt 31:14). Eventually, in Num 27:12-23; Dt 1:38; 31:7.23; 34:9, Joshua takes over the office from Moses. It is noted that it is not Moses who appoints Joshua to succeed him but it is YHWH who publicly appoints him for this mission (Num 27:15-21). Hence, it is not always possible to consider Joshua as a disciple of Moses. Again certain texts like Josh 24:2, show that Joshua occasionally refers to what YHWH himself said and not what Moses said. However the book of Joshua also conveys the impression that Joshua depended on the person of Moses and on his teaching even after the death of Moses. All the respect that was paid to Moses by the people is also paid to Joshua as the leader and successor of Moses (See. Josh 1:17).

[39] H. LAPIN, "*Rabbi*", p. 601.

[40] To see the similarities between Joshua and Elisha, see, R. P. CARROLL, *The Elijah-Elisha Sagas: Some remarks on Prophetic Succession in Ancient Israel*, VT 19 (1969) 400-15, p. 413. Also see, C. SCHAFER-LICHTENBERGER, *'Josua' und 'Elischa' – eine biblische Argumentation zur Begründung der Autorität und Legitimität des Nachfolgers*, ZAW 101 (1989) 198-222. To learn about the prophetic succession in 2kgs 2:1-18 (from Elijah to Elisha) in its relation to the concept of the Mosaic prophet in Dt18:15-18 (from Moses to Joshua), see, R. P. CAROLL, *The Elijah-Elisha Sagas: Some remarks on Prophetic Succession in Ancient Israel*, pp. 400-415. Read also, C. SCHAFER-LICHTENBERGER, *'Josua' und 'Elischa' – eine biblische Argumentation zur Begründung der Autorität und Legitimität des Nachfolgers*, pp. 213-220. In 1Kgs19;20f Elisha starts following his master as an expression of acknowledging Elijah as his master, and in 1Kgs19:21 Elisha serving his master. To learn more about Elisha as the follower of Elijah, see, C. SCHAFER- LICHTENBERGER, *'Josua' und 'Elischa' – eine biblische Argumentation zur Begründung der Autorität und Legitimität des Nachfolgers*, pp. 210-222. This comes as an expression of fellowship and also explains the master-disciple relationship between Elijah and Elisha. Samuel Byrskog opines that while there is no evidence that Elijah brings Elisha into a larger body of pupils within a school, the text does suggest that Elisha enters into contact with a specific master. Cf. S. BYRSKOG, *Jesus the Only Teacher*, p. 37. The relationship between Elijah and Elisha is depicted as presenting Elisha as the legitimate successor of Elijah.

[41] S. BYRSKOG, *Jesus the Only Teacher*, p.56.

[42] Cf. Ex 10:2; 12:26; 13:8. 14; Dt 4:9; 6:7. 20f; 11:18f; 32:7.46; Josh 4:21f; Jud 6:13; Ps 44:2; 78:3-6. The term "father" is also used for persons acting as teachers or advisers in OT. Cf. Gen 45:8; Jud 17:10; 18:19; 2kgs 2:12. In Proverbs, the father teaches his son. Cf. Prov 1:8. 10. 15; 2:1; 3:1. 11. 21; 4: 1-4. 10. 20; 5:1. 7. 20 etc. All these references could be understood exclusively in the

sense of the teacher instructing his pupil. To read more about teacher addressed as 'father', see, K. KOHLER, *Abba Father, Title of Spiritual Leader and Saint*, *JQR* 13 (1901) 567-580.

[43] S. BYRSKOG, *Jesus the Only Teacher*, p.56. The expression "Sons of the Prophets" implies that each "son" as an individual person belonged to a group of prophets and probably lived together. Ref. 2 Kgs 4:38-44; 6:2. Cf. J. G. WILLIAMS, *The Prophetic "Father", A Brief Explanation of the Term "Sons of the Prophets"*, *JBL* 85 (1966) 344- 348, p. 348. According to Williams, the "sons of the prophets" separated themselves from the society and devoted themselves to the service of the true God -YHWH - under Elijah as their leader and spiritual father. Haag classifies "sons of the prophets" as a professional group in which membership denoted certain social and professional status and exhibited some basic coherence. Cf. H. HAAG, *TWAT* I (1973) 670-682, p. 675. In 1Kgs 20:35; 2Kgs 2:3.5.15; 4:1. 38; 5:22; 6:1; 9:1 the phrase "sons of the Prophets" is always connected with Elisha. Here Elisha is not portrayed as a father but a leader of the other 'sons.' In most of the scenes, the sons of the prophets sit before Elisha, as they are there to learn from the master. It implies that Elisha was instructing others as a master and teacher alike. According to Byrskog, it is possible that the "sons of the prophets" initially formulated some of the narratives about Elisha. See, S. BYRSKOG, *Jesus the Only Teacher*, p. 133. 2Kgs 6:32 refers to the elders sitting with Elisha in his house just like disciples. Certain passages, such as 2Kgs 2:15; 4:1. 38; 9:1; 2Kgs 4:38; 6:1, indicate that Elisha was in the position of a leader for the "sons of the prophets." The fact that Elisha in 2 Kgs 2:16-18; 9:1-10 sent out messengers from the group testifies to the coherence of the groups. The close connection between Elisha and the "sons of the prophets" was important and that association or fellowship was more than a band of admirers. Cf. R. RENDTORFF, *Rewägungen zur Frühgeschichte des Prophetentums in Israel*, *ZTK* 59 (1962) 145-167, pp. 154-158; H.-C. SCHMITT, *Prophetie und Tradition. Beobachtungen zur Frühgeschichte des israelitischen Nabitums*, *ZTK* 74 (1977) 255-272, pp. 269f. These groups of "sons of the prophets", by their close association with Elisha, became capable of transmitting the traditions and miracles of Elisha. 1Sam 10:5-12; 19:20 speaks about Samuel being the leader of a group of prophets who all seem to have a common dwelling place where they probably lived together under the leadership of Samuel. It is not clear whether Samuel was actually a leader of that group in the sense of a teacher. As such, the 'Sons of the Prophets' may be different from this 'group of prophets.'

[44] J. G. WILLIAMS, *The Prophetic "Father." A Brief Explanation of the Term "Sons of the Prophets"*, pp. 345-348.

[45] S. BYRSKOG, *Jesus the Only Teacher*, p.57.

[46] Cf. H. M. I. GEVARYAHU, *The School of Isaiah. Biography and Transmission in the Book of Isaiah*, *JBQ* 18 (1989-90) 62-68, p. 64. In Isa 30:20, God is presented as a teacher. In the early chapters, the prophet Isaiah is projected as a teacher. However in Isaiah, when prophets are also considered as teachers,

passages like Isa 9:14 depict false prophets as false teachers. It seems as if Isa 28:10.13 presents Isaiah as a teacher of children. Samuel Byrskog refers to Isa 8:16 and opines that Isaiah is the one who presents Torah and who binds and seals. The object of sealing here is Torah and the receivers are the pupils who receive the instruction from the prophet. In the words of Byrskog, it is affirmed that the Isaianic disciples receive the instruction on Torah from their teacher who is here the prophet Isaiah. Cf. S. BYRSKOG, *Jesus the Only Teacher,* pp. 40-41.

[47] Cf. D. JONES, *The Traditions of the Oracles of Isaiah of Jerusalem, ZAW* 67 (1955) 226-246; J. EATON, *The Origin of the Book of Isaiah, VT* 9 (1959) 138-157, pp. 151-56; H. M. I. GEVARYAHU, *The School of Isaiah. Biography and Transmission in the Book of Isaiah,* pp. 62- 68. Jones and Eaton also speak of Second Isaiah as a disciple of Isaiah of Jerusalem. However, there is no explicit evidence that he was a disciple. Byrskog maintains that, "some interpreters maintain that he was acquainted with the earlier Isaiah tradition and that he was active within a group of descendents from the incipient Isaianic school." See, S. BYRSKOG, *Jesus the Only Teacher,* p. 59. Scholars like Elliger in their analysis of Isa 56-66 opine that some of the material comes from one or several disciples of Second Isaiah. See, K. ELLIGER, *Der Prophet Tritojesaja, ZAW* 49 (1931) 112-141, p. 138. Thus, there is a probability of the existence of the school of Isaiah with the disciples of Isaiah functioning as transmitters of the message of their master.

[48] S. BYRSKOG, *Jesus the Only Teacher,* p. 42. On the basis of the scribal features of Jeremiah's mission, there is a probability that Jeremiah functioned as a teacher. From Jer 29:1; 30:2; 36:2; 51:60 and from the images that are used in 17:1. 13; 22:30; 31:33 Jeremiah is thought to be skilled in writing.

[49] H. H. MALLAU, *Baruch/Baruchschriften, TRE* 5 (1980) 269-276, pp. 269-271. Read also, J. R. LUNDBOM, *Baruch, Seraiah, and Expanded Colophons in the Book of Jeremiah, JSOT* 36 (1986) 89-114, p. 107.

[50] S. BYRSKOG, *Jesus the Only Teacher,* p. 44. A number of factors point to Baruch's educated skill. Among the followers of Jeremiah, there could have been several persons of scribal profession and Baruch is one among them. Jer 32:12.16; 36; 4-32; 43:3.6; 45:1-5 speak about Baruch, son of Neriah and attached to the prophet Jeremiah. Jer 36:2-4.28-32 depicts that whenever Jeremiah is instructed to write, it is in fact Baruch who writes, and in Jer 36:5f, in the place of Jeremiah, Baruch is summoned to read the scroll. Thus, Baruch appears to be both a close disciple (follower) as well as a companion of Jeremiah in his prophetical mission.

[51] *Ibid.*, p. 45. Ezek 18; 33:1-20 are given as didactic instructions and indicate that Ezekiel has a role as teacher. In 2Kgs 4:38; 6:1 the sons of the prophet sat before the prophet Elisha and in 6:32, the elders sat before Elisha. In the Book of Jeremiah, people attentively gather around the prophet. In Ezek 8:1; 14:1; 20:1 the elders of the people, and in 33:31 the people, are assembled in a formal gathering around the prophet. Also see, H. M. I. GEVARYAHU, *Privathäuser*

als Versammlungsstätten von Meister und Jüngern, ASTI 12 (1983) 5-12, p. 7. In Ezek 11:25, Ezekiel's activity appears to be addressed to larger audiences, whereas there is also indication of a more limited activity, restricted to his own house and directed to a group of attentive listeners gathered in front of him. Cf. W. ZIMMERLI, *Ezechiel/Ezechielbuch, TRE* 10 (1982) 766-781, p. 769.

[52] W. ZIMMERLI, *Ezechiel/Ezechielbuch*, pp. 767-769. Zimmerli, in his analysis of the formation and the redaction of the book of Ezekiel, observes that it includes the activity of a group engaged in a degree of interpretation. It is possible that Ezekiel himself initiated the process of interpretative activity of his own book and after his lifetime, the school was responsible for the exegesis of the older units, which led to the coherent impression of the present book. Hence it implies the existence of a school that was made up of the followers or disciples of Ezekiel.

[53] S. BYRSKOG, *Jesus the Only Teacher,* p. 58.

[54] H. W. WOLFF, *Hoseas geistige Heimat, TLZ* 81 (1956) 83-94. For Wolff, Hos 1-3 contains portions of the prophet's own memorabilia (2:4-17; 3:1-5) with additional biographical notes composed by a disciple (1:2-6. 8f; 2:1-3. 18-25). Hos 4-11 speaks of Hosea's activity which is a nucleus of several kerygmatic units which presuppose that someone in the group of the prophet Hosea wrote them down soon after their actual occurrence. Though Hos 4:1-9:9 and 10:9-15 reflect Hosea's public preaching, passages like 9:10-10:8; 11:1-11 are originally addressed to the inner circle around the prophet. However, Byrskog admits that "it is difficult to say with sufficient certainty that a group of disciples - an incipient school - constituted the original addressee of Hos 9:10-10:8; 11:1-11; 14:2-9." See, S. BYRSKOG, *Jesus the Only Teacher,* p. 61. Eventually Hos 12-14 depicts three similar scenes of which two are from the public 12:8ff; 13; 9ff whereas 14:2-9 is from within the group of Hosea's followers. However, scholars like R. Rendtorff objects to this idea of a group of disciples around Hosea. The outlines of the group around Hosea are not as clear as Wolff claims. See, R. RENDTORFF, *Erwägungen zur Frühgeschichte des Prophetentums in Israel, ZTK* 59 (1962) 145-167, pp. 150-152.

[55] S. BYRSKOG, *Jesus the Only Teacher,* p. 63. Byrskog affirms that "all in all, although the biblical evidence is weak, it does not decisively speak against the assumption of the early existence of schools. The testimony about literate persons is not sufficient by itself, but the possibility that they were trained within a school cannot be rejected." p. 66.

[56] N. SHUPAK, *The 'Sitz im Leben' of the Book of Proverbs in the Light of a Comparison of Biblical and Egyptian Wisdom Literature, RB* 94 (1987) 98-119. According to Byrskog, "the cumulative force of the observations made in epigraphical and extra-biblical areas of research sufficiently accounts, as it seems, for the hypothesis that elementary and scribal schools existed at an early time in ancient Israel." See, S. BYRSKOG, *Jesus the Only Teacher,* p. 66.

[57] *Ibid.*, p. 118.

[58] S. BYRSKOG, *Jesus the Only Teacher*, p. 63. On page 68, Byrskog affirms that there is sufficient reason for regarding Sir 51:23. 29 as part of the original composition from Ben Sira himself.

[59] Cf. W. BAUMGARTNER, *Die Literarischen Gattungen in der Weisheit des Jesus Sirach*, ZAW 34 (1914) 161-198, pp. 169-186. Sir 1:27; 4:17.24; 6:18; 8:8; 16:25; 18:14 are some of the passages that are regarded as didactic activities. The book of Sirach is also presented as a book directed towards those who strive for education and wisdom. Popular education seems to be the key-concept of the book of Sirach. Sira 2:1; 3:1; 3:17; 4:1. 20; 6:18. 32; 10:28; 11:10; 14:11; 18:15; 21:1; 23:7; 37:27; 38:9. 16; 40:28; 41:14 speak about didactic characters and some of these passages also speak about pupils. Hence there is a possibility of master- pupil relationships. "My son" as a designation may suggest that the recipients of the teaching are the young men (pupils) starting their pursuit of wisdom and knowledge. However, in the instructions of Ben Sira, the teacher has to remain independent of teaching and the student has to be attracted to the content of the teaching and never to the person of the teacher. Ben Sira was not attracting students to his own person, only to the right kind of teaching. The teaching in Ben Sira's view remained independent of the teacher. Despite the authority of the teacher, the basic motive of transmission focused on the inherent value of the teaching itself. See, S. BYRSKOG, *Jesus the Only Teacher*, p. 133.

[60] S. BYRSKOG, *Jesus the Only Teacher*, p. 69. From Sir 15:1; 19:20; 21:11; 24:23, Byrskog affirms that the central idea of Ben Sira's teaching implies a strong sense of authority. As the first known Jewish wisdom teacher, he explicitly identifies the object of his teaching with the Torah. The circle that was close to Ben Sira and his teachings reveal that he was a teacher of an unusual rank. Cf. p. 81. Again in p.84 Byrskog states that Ben Sira, it seems, appeared to the ancient transmitters of Sirach as a person who delivered teaching and performed actions amounting to an authority valid by reference to prophetic legitimation. In speaking of Ben Sira in teaching Torah and Wisdom to his own circle of followers, it is interesting to note that he was also acquainted with the Hellenistic culture. In p. 86, Byrskog asserts that, in view of the polemical reflections in Sirach, it is conceivable that Ben Sir's elevated status was a means by which the teacher wanted to set himself over the powerful didactic channels through which Greek-Hellenistic ideas were mediated to the Jews of Jerusalem. From the above statement, Byrskog opines that it is indeed probable that several Jewish wisdom schools existed in Jerusalem. However, the Book of Sirach also reveals the conflicts between the wisdom schools of Greek-Hellenistic influence and Jewish schools in Israel. It is also likely that Ben Sira saw the Greek schools as the primary threat to the faith of Israel. Hence Ben Sira tries to influence the students from turning toward Hellenistic influences and is seen as the first Jewish teacher who wanted to provide teaching in accordance with the Faith of Israel, which was mainly based on Torah.

[61] *Ibid.*, p. 48.

[62] MSS. D it. have *kurie Rabbi*

[63] Cf. *Life*, pp. 190. 191.

[64] Cf. *Ant* XX, pp. 213. 223.

[65] See, J. W. I, pp. 648-650; II, 10: Ant. XVII, 152; XVIII, p. 155. On J.W. I. p. 648, the Loeb note translates *sophistai* "doctors" and comments, "Greek *sophists.*" The Greek term originally free from any sinister associations, for a paid professor of rhetoric, etc. is employed by Josephus as the equivalent of "teacher or "doctor." See, *The XXX Classical Library*, Vol. II, New York, G. P. Putnam's Sons, 1927, pp. 306-307, footnote 2. It is to be observed further that the term *sophistes* would be better understood by Roman audiences.

[66] *Ant* XVII, pp. 214, 149.

[67] JOSEPHUS, *Life* pp. 277 & 280. Josephus uses this term only in this work.

[68] JOSEPHUS, *Life,* p. 293.

[69] It is to be noted, however, that this is a disputed passage. Cf. *Ant.* XVIII, p. 63.

[70] PHILO, *On the change of Names*, pp. 270, 288; *Idem, Special Laws IV,* p. 107; cf. *Idem, Special Laws* I, p. 318.

[71] *Idem., Posterity and Exile of Cain*, p. 150.

[72] *Idem., On the Change of Names*, p. 217.

[73] IGNATIUS, *Mag.*, p. IX.

[74] Cf. *Martyrdom of Polycarp*, XIX, p. 1.

[75] See Karl Georg KUHN, ed., *Konkordanz zu den Qumrantexten,* Gottingen, Vandenhoeck and Ruprecht, 1960.

[76] Francis BROWN, S. R. DRIVER and Charles A. BRIGGS, *"rab"*, *A Hebrew and English Lexicon of the Old Testament*, New York, Houghton Mifflin and Co., 1907.

[77] F. F. BRUCE, *The Books and the Parchments*, rev. edition, Westwood, N.J, Fleming H. Revell, 1963, pp. 194-195.

[78] G. DALMAN, *The Words of Jesus*, authorized English version by D.M. Kay, Edinburgh, T. and T. Clark, 1902, p. 338.

[79] *The Descent of Christ Into Hell*, in *The Apocryphal Gospel of Nicodemus*, E. HENNECKE, *New Testament Apocrypha, The Gospels*, vol. 1, ed. by W. SCHNEEMELCHER, trans. by R. Mc L. WILSON, London, Lutterworth Press, 1963, pp. 478-479; also *Actas de Pilato, red. latina* B, I, 1, 5, in *Los Evangelios Apocrifos*, ed. by AURELIO DE SANTOS OTERO, 2nd edition, Madrid, Biblioteca de Autores Cristianos, 1963, pp. 455-458.

[80] For more details on Talmud, see, J.L. MCKENZIE, "Talmud" in Dictionary of the Bible, p. 866. The Law, of course, must be the main study of a Rabbi.

Hence immense mass of inferential teaching arose in the schools, deduced from the written word according to the rules of a special process of reasoning, handed down for generations in the teaching of the faithful Scribes as the official interpretation of the Law, and finally committed to writing, particularly in the Mishnas and Talmuds. Under this traditional teaching of the Law, every word designating the tradition was calculated to remind the Rabbi of the connexion of this tradition with the Law. Mishna means "repetition of the Law": its sources were the sayings of the Tannaite or "repeating" doctors; a *baraitha* is a saying of some early doctor not included in the Mishna; the *baraithoth* are gathered either into the *Tosephta* (addition) or in the *Ghemara* (complement), the Mishna and the *Ghemara* constituting the *Talmud* or "teaching" (of the Law). This teaching is either *halaka* (way) or "customary law", or *agada*, "information", given by or about the Law. Furthermore, some Rabbis were said to be attempting to prove by the Law itself (Ex.34:37) that oral traditions should be preferred to the written word. This exaggerated the authority of these oral traditions. This voluminous body of exegetical traditions, the logical system according to which inferences are drawn and the theological conceptions upon which this whole oral teaching is grounded, are commonly designated as a whole by the name of Rabbinism.

[81] J. C. TURRO, "*Rabbi*", p. 883. The Rabbi teachers qualified themselves for teaching their disciples by their learning and ability to interpret. Thus the Rabbi of the Talmudic times has the ability to teach and interpret the laws. The Rabbi judge was empowered by the Palestinian authorities on the basis of his understanding of the law and by his personal integrity. At times the function of teaching and judging merged in the person of one Rabbi. The term "*harav*" implied scholarship concerning the law and scripture.

[82] J.L. MCKENZIE, *Rabbi* [P]. 718.

[83] S. ZEITLIN, "Beginnings of Christianity and Judaism" in *JQR*, Vol. 27, (1937) 385-398, p.392.

[84] W. BAUER, ῥαββί, in *BDAG* (2000) 902. David B. Ruderman in his "*Rabbi and Teacher*" observes that the title *Rabbi* first appeared in ancient Palestine around the first century of the Common Era to designate an individual of exceptional learning and expertise in Jewish law. While describing the usage of the title Rabbi in the first century, Ruderman attributes the origin of the title *rav* to later centuries. *Rav* emerged in Babylonia to distinguish a learned sage consecrated by his mastery of the Torah. The professional Rabbinate, however, became visible only in medieval times, although the precise origin and development of this new and distinctive communal institution remain somewhat obscure. See, David B. RUDERMAN, "*Rabbi and Teacher*", in Arthur A. COHEN & Paul MENDES-FLOHR (eds.), *Contemporary Jewish Religious Thought*, NY, The Free Press, 1987 (741-47) p. 741.

[85] Cf. Mt 23:5-8. Jesus warned his disciples to avoid seeking of social prestige, the public honours, and the praiseworthy titles that came with the title "Rabbi". According to Parker, "this name was commonly given to men of high rank or

with any kind of honour." See, J. CALVIN, *St. John*, trans. T. H. L. PARKER, (*Calvin's New Testament Commentaries*), Grand Rapids, MI, Eerdmans, 1961, p. 36.

[86] Jacob E. SAFRA (ed.), "*Rabbi*", in *The New Encyclopaedia Britannica*, Vol. 9, (15th ed.), Chicago, 2002, p. 871.

[87] H. LAPIN, "*Rabbi*", p. 600.

[88] G. H. JOHNSTON, p. 1032.

[89] Shaye J. D. COHEN, *Epigraphical Rabbis*, in *JQR* 72 (1981) 1-17, p. 9.

[90] E. KANARFOGEL, "*Rabbinate*", p. 7578. The Rabbis of the Talmudic period conducted themselves modestly and concerned themselves with communal mores and needs such as the proper burial of the dead, the support of widows and orphans, and the ability of the people to pursue livelihoods that were consonant with Jewish law. Some Rabbis were appointed as *parnasim*, an office that charged them with various charity functions or more general communal leadership. Rabbis were approached with all kinds of religious, economic, and personal questions and requests, ranging from the nullification of oaths to the laws of inheritance, and from Sabbath observance to permitted contact with Gentiles.

[91] Cf. F. W. GOLKA, *Die israelitische Weisheitsschule oder 'des Kaisers neue Kleider'*, *VT* 33 (1983) 257-270; N. LOHFINK, *Glauben lernen in Israel*, *KatBl* 108 (1983) 84-99, pp. 86-97; A. LEMAIRE, *Sagesse et écoles*, *VT* 34 (1984) 270-281; N. LOHFINK, *Gottesvolk als Lerngemeinschaft. Zur Kirchenwirklichkeit im Buch Deuteronominum*, *BK* 39 (1984) 90-100, pp. 90-98; GRENSHAW, *JBL* 104 (1985) 601-615; N. SHUPAK, *The 'Sitz im Leben' of the Book of Proverbs in the Light of a Comparison of Biblical and Egyptian Wisdom Literature*, pp. 98-119; A. LEMAIRE, *Education (Israel) ABD* 2 (1992) 305-312.

[92] S. BYRSKOG, *Jesus the Only Teacher*, p. 75. Though there was a biblical ideal of the father teaching his son, when that was not possible, the custom of hiring private tutors and sending the boys to a more organised school for education began to be in practice at the time of the Rabbinical literature. There was scriptural school, which focused on training the boys in reading the Torah. This became more of an obligation, as every boy had to begin his learning from the Scripture school. Byrskog observes that the teacher during the first stages in a college could be a less distinguished Mishnah teacher. However, there was also a more advanced study under the Rabbis and there one sees the authority and teaching of Rabbis in the history of Israel.

[93] *Ibid.*, p. 52.

[94] J. NEUSNER & W. S. GREEN (eds.), "*Rabbi*", pp. 517-8.

[95] J. NEUSNER, "*Rabbinic Judaism in Late Antiquity*", p. 7587. Neusner explains the supernatural character of Rabbis as follows. Rabbis in late antiquity were believed to have the power to create and destroy people because they were righteous, free of sin, or otherwise holy, and so enjoyed exceptional grace from

heaven. It follows that Torah was held to be a source of supernatural power. The Rabbis controlled the power of Torah because of their mastery of its contents.

[96] Judah David EISENSTEIN, "*Rabbi*", in *JE* 10 (1905) 294-297, p.294. For the first position the Rabbi was elected by the leaders of the community; for the second, by the members of the judiciary; the third position was a matter of duty imposed upon the Rabbi by the very Law he was teaching. All these were honorary positions, without emolument, save the bare living expenses of the Rabbi when he gave up his occupation for the public welfare. The Rabbi as a justice could claim only compensation for loss of time. Rabban Gamaliel III said the study of the Law without employment brings transgression (Ab. ii. 2).

[97] See, E. KANARFOGEL, "*Rabbinate*", p. 7578. The title "*Rabban*" was used at this time to designate singularly important scholar-leaders of the generation, such as the Patriarch who is also called *Nasi*.

[98] See, *Dictionary of Judaism in the Biblical period*, Vol. 2. NY, Simon & Schuster Macmillian, 1996, p. 516. The Rabbi functioned in the Jewish community in ancient times as judge and administrator and sometimes lived in a society in some ways quite separate from that of Jewry as a whole. The Rabbinical academy was a law school. Some of its graduates served as judges and administrators of the law. However, the Rabbinical school was by no means a centre for merely legal study. It was, like the Christian monastery, the locus for a peculiar kind of religious living. Only one of its functions concerned those parts of the Torah to be applied in every-day life through the judiciary.

[99] J. NEUSNER, "*Rabbinic Judaism in Late Antiquity*", p. 7587. The Rabbis were masters of witchcraft, incantations, and amulets. They could issue blessings and curses, create men and animals, and communicate with heaven. Their Torah was sufficiently effective to thwart the action of demons. However much they disapproved of other people's magic, they themselves were expected to do the things magicians did. The lack of boundaries between prophet and magician persisted into the Talmudic era (2nd to 5th c. C.E.) A close look into the acts of the sages of the Mishna and Talmud in this field of relation between prophet and magician reveals more than a little about the type of leadership in ancient times. This is a leadership of charismatic authority and the knowledge of Halacha and Shamanism and included also miraculous deeds and political components. It is thus recognized that in ancient times there was no distinction between religion and magic, and key people in the history of Mishna and Talmud dealt with Torah as well as miraculous deeds. It is told of Rabbi Hanina that he cured the sick with his prayer. Another, the son of Rabbi Yochanan ben Zakai, is reputed to have lived for a week on a measure of carobs. He is said to have heard a heavenly voice that announced that the world was sustained because of his merit. As a consequence of his prayer the rain stopped, and after a second prayer it began raining again; and so various other miracles happened to him. It is clear that his piety and righteousness exceeded his learning and his principal power was in being a man recognized for his supernatural power. See also,

J. BAZAK, *le-Mala min ha-Hushim*, Tel-Aviv, 1968; A. A. URBACH, *The Sages*, Jerusalem, 1967, pp. 82-102. On Sages and magic, see, J. GOLDIN, *The Magic of Magic and Superstition*, Elisabeth SCHUESSLER FIORENZA (ed.), *Aspects of Religious Propaganda in Judaism and Early Christianity*, London, University of Notre Dame Press, 1976, pp. 115-147; J. GOLDIN, *Studies in Midrash and Related Literature*, Philadelphia - New York – Jerusalem, The Jewish Publication Society, 1988, pp. 337-57.

[100] See, P. SCHAEFER, *The Aim and Purpose of Early Jewish Mysticism*, Oxford Center for Postgraduate Studies 1986, citations from pp. 13, 16. Compare P. Schaefer who sees dichotomy between the sages and magic, and for that reason rejects the attribution of the Hekhalot literature to the Talmudic sages. He writes: "The authors of the Hekhalot literature believed in the power of magic and attempted to integrate magic into Judaism. They cannot be the same Rabbis who wrote the Mishnah, Talmud and Midrash." See also, P. SCHAEFER, *Hekhalot-Studien*, Tuebingen, J. C. B. MOHR, 1988, p. 290; C. R. PHILLIPS, *In Search of the Occult: An Annotated Anthology*, Helios, 15/2 (1988), pp. 151-170.

[101] See, Jack N. LIGHTSTONE, *The Commerce of the Sacred*, Scholars Press, Chico, California, 1984, pp. 17 ff. The ancient world believed that sickness is caused by spirits that entered the body, hence removal of the spirits would effect a cure. Thus, medicine and ancient folk wisdom recognized exorcism not necessarily as a magic operation but as a matter of therapy.

[102] H. LAPIN, *Rabbi*, p. 601. For Lapin, this understanding of Rabbi as teacher in the period of Rabbinical Judaism was accompanied in the Mishna and the Tosepta by the casting of primary figures of authority as teachers. Based on Mishna and Tosepta, the two earliest Rabbinic collections, Lapin classifies the use of this title "Rab" as in the Absolute and as a mode of Address. For Lapin, "Rab" in the absolute is used either to designate the master of a slave or to designate a teacher, the more relevant usage for present purposes. Rab also designates a link in the chain of authoritative teaching. Going back to the traditions that speak about R. Gamaliel (II), Lapin observes that he was held to have been the patriarch and one who might be addressed as 'Ραββί by analogy with a king or a judge. Gamaliel was addressed as Rabbenu or Rabbi by members of his circle and is challenged on the basis of the laws, which he taught his disciples or those who were with him.

[103] J. E. SAFRA (ed.), *"Rabbi"*, p. 516. Rabbi is generally associated with a master of the Torah.

[104] Raphael PATAI, in *Encyclopaedia Americana*, Vol. 23 (Pumps to Russell), International Edition, Grolier, Danbury – Connecticut, 2000, p. 108. Patai explains that in Talmudic times the Rabbi or *rav* was an expounder or interpreter of the Bible and the oral law. In Talmudic times, the Rabbi was occasionally a preacher.

[105] K. H. RENGSTORF, Μαθητής, in *TDNT* 4 (1967) 439.

[106] J. L. McKenzie states that Hellenism designates the diffusion of Greek civilisation throughout the East Mediterranean basin and West Asia following the conquests of Alexander in 330 B C. Intellectual Hellenism brought the study of Greek literature and philosophy. Greek civilisation also assimilated something from the various areas in which it was diffused. Judaism was influenced by this development. The Jewish communities in the Diaspora which supported themselves by commercial activities in large Hellenistic cities were scarcely able to resist the impact of Hellenism. But most of the communities retained the law and worship in the Synagogue. In the first half of the 2nd century B.C, Hellenism reached its peak when it was adopted and fostered by the members of the sacerdotal aristocracy such as Antiochus Epiphanes who attempted to unify his scattered empire by imposing Hellenism on all his subjects (cf. 1 Mc 1:41ff). The prohibition of Jewish religion by Epiphanes aroused resistance, which caused the wars of the Maccabees and the zeal for the preservation of Jewish religion. See, J. L. MCKENZIE, '*Hellenism*' in *Dictionary of the Bible*, pp. 351-52. See also, Robert H. STEIN, *The Method and Message of Jesus' Teachings*, Philadelphia, The Westminster Press, 1948, p. 6. When Stein makes an analysis of the languages that Jesus spoke, he states that the third major language besides Aramaic and Hebrew spoken in Palestine at the time of Jesus was Greek. Stein notes that since the time of Alexander the Great, Hellenistic influence was present in Palestine, and by the first century B.C. the Mediterranean was a "Greek sea." In Egypt in the second century B.C. the Jewish community there could no longer read the Hebrew Old Testament and thus it was translated into Greek. The LXX became the Bible of the Diaspora.

[107] According to Samuel Byrskog, for an ancient Greek-speaking person, διδάσκαλος was of course the most natural term to use as a designation for a teacher. In the Greek literature, the term διδάσκαλος carries in itself normally neither a negative implication nor validating significance. The basic meaning is merely "teacher," and the context of each Greek text sometimes gives it various further connotations, sometimes negative and sometimes positive. Διδάσκαλος was in itself neutral in regard to the positive or negative estimation of a person. It did not, on one hand, carry negative implications. This is most evident in its use for Greek gods of different kinds. Byrskog states that διδάσκαλος did not serve in itself as an honorary appellation or title. Yet, in the first century C.E., διδάσκαλος had acquired a connotation relating to religious and philosophical teachers. The Greek-speaking Jews of the first century use the term διδάσκαλος for religious teachers. Philo applies this term διδάσκαλος to Moses not only as a religious teacher, but also as the greatest and most perfect of men in every respect. Josephus applies the title to three different groups of religious teachers or leaders who are Pharisees, Sadducees and the Essenes. The Pharisees in the writings of Josephus are called διδάσκαλοι. To learn more, See, S. BYRSKOG, *Jesus the Only Teacher*, pp. 214.219-220. Lesky notes that the term διδάσκαλος is already in use in the Homeric hymns of the seventh or sixth century B.C.E. The fourth hymn to Hermes (Hymn. Merc. 556) uses

the term διδάσκαλος. See, LESKY, *PWSup* XI, 824-831. See also, HESIOD, *Homeric Hymns*, xxxviii. Diels and Krantz observe that the term διδάσκαλος occurs also in the writings of the re-Socratic philosopher Heraclitus of Ephesus (c. 535- 475 B. C. E.). See, DIELS/KRANTZ (eds.), *Fragmente* I, frags 57. 104, pp. 163. 174; HERACLITUS, *frgs*, 57. 104. In the early Greek texts, even Plato has used the term διδάσκαλος in reference to Greek gods. Cf. PLATO, *Menex*. 238b. In addition, there are examples from the first century C.E. showing that the Greek-speaking people also called the god of the Jews διδάσκαλος. Cf. PHILO, *Congr*. 114; MUT, *Nom*, 270; RER, *Div. Her*, 19; SACR, *AC*. 65; VIT, *Mos*, 1:80. Cf. also RER, *Div. Her*, 102. Many scholars note that διδάσκαλος has been used abundantly in later Greek literature, inscriptions, papyri and the writings of Philo and Josephus. Cf. REISCH, *PW* V, 401-406; PREISGKE, *Papyrusurkunden* I, p. 371; RENGSTORF, *TDNT* II, 148-151; KIESSLING (ed.), *Papyrusurkunden* IV, p. 567f; *idem* (ed.), *Papyrusukunden suppl*. I, p. 73; RENGSTORF (ed.), *Concordance to Flavius Josephus* I, p. 487, MAYER, *Index Philoneus*, p. 77; W. BAUER, *Wörterbuch*, pp. 385f; ZIMMERMANN, *Die urchristlichen Lehrer*, pp. 76-86.

[108] A. F. ZIMMERMANN, *Die urchristlichen Lehrer*, p. 76. While describing the meaning and the use of the title διδάσκαλος in the Greek world and its literatures, Zimmermann distinguishes four important fields of application: to an adviser in both a positive and negative sense, to teachers in the elementary schools, to teachers of a specific art or ability and to religious or philosophical teachers. Discipleship was already well known among the Greeks. Such Greek philosophers as Socrates, Plato, and Aristotle exemplified the practice of instructing disciples. Socrates spent much of his time in public places asking questions and engaging in dialogue. His most famous disciple, Plato, eventually gathered his own disciples around him and even founded a school. Aristotle was Plato's most notable pupil and engaged in philosophical debate while walking with his students.

[109] In Rabbinical Judaism, μαθητής or the talmid is someone whose concern is the whole of Jewish tradition. According to Shammai (Shabbath 31a), this was the written Torah (the biblical writings of the OT) and the oral Torah (the traditions of the fathers), which includes the Mishnah, Midrash, Halachah and Haggadah. The talmid now, as originally the Gk. μαθητής belongs to his teacher, to whom he subordinates himself in almost servile fashion. It was the distinct casuistic form of 'Ραβ. theology, built around emphasis on achievement in the religious thought of developed Judaism, which created the pre-requisites for attributing a value of its own to human authority, which previously was entirely unknown in Israel and Judaism. Since the Rabbi's knowledge gives him direct access to the Scriptures, which facilitates right hearing and right understanding, he becomes a kind of mediator between the talmidim and the Torah. To listen to the Scriptures without the guidance of a teacher is something to be avoided at all costs (cf. B. Berakoth 47b). μανθανω still means to learn,

to occupy oneself with the Torah in order to discover God's will in it. But now learning is determined by the authority of the teacher and his interpretation of the Torah and not by a personal and, as far as possible, unbiased study of the Torah. Therefore, learning means primarily that the disciple appropriates the knowledge of his teacher and examines it critically by comparing it against the Torah. Only one who had studied and served under a Rabbi (a Jewish scholar) for an extensive period, and had thus concluded his essential study, could later become a teacher with authority to teach his own tradition in his own school. The pupil-teacher relationship of Rab. Jud., in contradistinction to the OT, thus became an important institution for detailed study of the Torah." D. MÜLLER, *New International Dictionary of New Testament Theology*, I, pp. 485-486. "One can only be a μαθητής in the company of α διδάσκαλος, a master or teacher, to whom the μαθητής since the days of the Sophists generally had to pay a fee." D. Müller, p. 484. "The Gr. pupil and the Rab. talmid bound themselves personally to their master and looked for objective teaching, with the aim of themselves becoming a master or a Rabbi.

[120] In the Tosefta it is stated: "He who has disciples and whose disciples again have disciples is called 'Rabbi'..." I. BROYDE, *"Rabbi,"* in *The Jewish Encyclopedia*, I. SINGER, ed., vol. X, New York, Funk and Wagnalls, 1912, p. 294.

[121] Francis JOHN, *The Vision of Discipleship According to John*, Rome, Pontifical University of Urbania, 1997, p. 54.

[122] *Ibid.*, p. 55. According to Francis John, the Greek understanding of master-disciple relationship was not only taken into Rabbinic Judaism but it was also fully integrated into the central concern of Judaism. This concern is nothing but the concern over Torah. Though, one may argue, that the Rabbi is important here, it is evident that the Torah is a dominating element without which the authority of the Rabbi is limited. For the concept of being disciple of God in Philo, See, WILKINS, *Concept of Disciple*, pp. 101ff.

[123] D. MÜLLER, μαθητής, p. 485. When the disciples of the Jewish Rabbinical system had to learn the Jewish system or tradition, this tradition was interpreted by Shammai as learning of Torah. The learning of Torah was instructed by the master from both the written and oral traditions.

[124] S. HIMELSTEIN, *Rabbi and Rabbinate*, p. 567.

[125] C. COULOT, *Jésus et le disciple: Etude sur l'autorité messianique de Jésus* (Etudes Bibliques 8), Paris, Librarie Lecoffre, 1987, p. 259.

[126] S. BYRSKOG, *Jesus the Only Teacher*, p. 52.

[127] *Ibid.*, p. 87.

[128] D. MÜLLER, μαθητής, in *NIDNT* (1975) 483-490, p. 483. For Homer the words μανθάνω and μαθητής came to mean "to acquire" or "to adopt" through teaching or experience. Raymond Brown notes that this process of learning was

from the period of Heraclitus and Protagoras and it played an important role in the ideas of Socrates. Then Plato goes further than Socrates in defining this process of learning. In Greek philosophy, μανθάνω was applied to the acquisition of theoretical knowledge.

[129] Vernon K. ROBBINS, *Jesus the Teacher: A Socio-Rhetorical Interpretation of Mark*, Philadelphia, Fortress Press, 1984, p. 88. Robbins observes that the impetus for the teacher/disciple relation is summarised in Plato's Apology 19E when Socrates describes the sophists' habit of seeking young men to join up with them.

[130] P. NEPPER-CHRISTENSEN, μαθητής, in *EDNT 2* (1991) 372-374, p. 372. Μανθάνω occurs in 25 places in the NT. But the occurrence of this verb μανθάνω in the NT is different from μαθητεύω and μαθητής.

[131] Philip L. SHULER, *Disciple*, in *Harper's Bible Dictionary* (1990) 222, p. 222.

[132] In Ac 22:3 Paul says that he learnt the Jewish law at the feet of Gamaliel. The concern here, regarding the statement of Paul is not proving its historicity but emphasising the practice of learning the Torah under the master. Here Paul and Gamaliel are brought into the scene solely to substantiate the master - disciple practice in learning of Torah and Law. Gamaliel in Ac 5:34 is regarded with respect and mentioned as the teacher of the law. Hence this study believes that even in the time of Jesus, the Jewish way of learning the Torah under a teacher or a master was in practice.

[133] For a detailed description of this background to see the relationship between the master and disciple, read, *New International Dictionary of New Testament Theology*, vol. 1, 485-86; *Theological Dictionary of New Testament*, vol. 4, 417-28.) Gk ματηετες who is a "pupil, learner", from the verb μανθανω (*manthano* = "to learn"), is someone attached to a teacher, group or movement, who not only "learns" academically but also lives a prescribed lifestyle, sometimes even in a community setting. In secular Greek, the word meant an apprentice in some trade, a student of some subject or a pupil of some teacher. In New Testament times, the same primary meaning is found with the disciples of Moses, who were students of the Mosaic law; and the disciples of the Pharisees, who were preoccupied with an accurate and detailed knowledge of Jewish tradition as given both in the written Torah and in the oral Torah. These disciples would submit themselves entirely to their Rabbi, and were not to study the scriptures without the interpretation and guidance of their teacher, although they expected to become teachers themselves after extensive training. In the Rabbi- disciple pattern of education, the training a disciple received from his master included much more than academic study, and went beyond the classroom. The disciple spent as much time with the teacher as possible, often living with him in the same house. Disciples were expected not only to study the law, but also to acquaint themselves with the specific way of life, which could be done only through constantly watching the master. The Rabbis taught as much from example as by word, so the disciple needed to take

note of his master's daily conversation and habits, as well as his teaching. Students related to their masters with respect. When accompanying their master, disciples were expected to walk behind them. They also served their master in practical ways ranging from setting up the benches in the room used for instruction to shopping and cooking for him. Helping a master at the bathhouse was a service so commonly associated with discipleship that the saying, "I shall bring his clothes for him to the bathhouse" meant "I shall become his disciple". Despite the subordination and respect that characterized the master-disciple relationship, it was not just a distant or merely formal relationship. The teacher attempted to raise his disciples as sons; he cared for them, provided for them and praised or admonished his disciples as he saw fit. Thus the relationships were intense, based on paternal-filial love. Strack and Billerbeck note that attachment to a recognized Rabbi, including being of service to him, was part of a person's religious education. It was possible for someone to acquire scriptural literacy by way of self-study, but this way of obtaining knowledge did not enjoy the same esteem as formal training. Cf. STRACK and BILLERBECK, 2:486.

[134] S. BYRSKOG, *Jesus the Only Teacher,* p. 52. Byrskog explains the same details in p. 89 where he says that the pupils performed a number of acts, which implicitly validated the teacher. These acts were of uttermost importance. He also confirms the old custom and obligation of a student in serving his teacher more then he does his own father. The student was to do for the Rabbi the same services as an ordinary slave was doing his master. Here one needs to be sure that the obligation of service, in taking precedence over the duties to be carried out even to the father, did not exclude respect for the father in Rabbinic Judaism. It is purely a matter of setting priorities and not of choosing options. Cf. PESCE, *ANRW* II 25:1 (1982) 384, n. 109.

[135] J. NEUSNER & W. S. GREEN (eds.), "*Rabbi*", p. 517. When the *Nasi* enters the assembly the pupils rise, standing till he bids them sit down; when the *ab bet din* enters, they form a row on each side of him, standing till he takes his seat; when a Rabbi enters, each one rises as the wise man passes him. The Rabbi lectured before the Talmud students at the bet ha-midrash or yeshibah. He seldom spoke in public except on the days of Kallah, *i.e.,* during the months of Elul and Adar and on the Sabbaths immediately preceding the holy days, when he informed the people of the laws and customs governing the approaching festivals. The Rabbi who was a *haggadist* or *maggid* preached before a multitude of men, women, and children and he demanded the respect from every one in the assembly.

[136] Bruce M. METZGER, *The New Testament: Its Background, Growth, and Content*, Nashville, TN, Abingdon, 1989, p. 47. According to Byrskog, the integration of ministering acts into the actual study of torah implies that an authoritative status was accorded to the Rabbis because they knew torah in its various forms. Cf. S. BYRSKOG, *Jesus the Only Teacher,* p. 133.

[137] Cf. E. SCHÜRER, *The History of the Jewish People in the Age of Jesus Christ,* rev. and ed. by G. VERMES, F. MILLAR, and M. BLACK, Edinburgh, T. & T. Clark, 1979, 2:325; and LOHSE, *Rabbi,* pp. 961–962.

[138] B. M. METZGER, *The New Testament: Its Background, Growth, and Content,* pp. 47-48.

[139] S. BYRSKOG, *Jesus the Only Teacher,* p. 97. In speaking of discipleship in Jewish society, the primary focus was ultimately to learn Torah. The important duty of discipleship was not to follow a specific teacher, but to study and learn Torah. Byrskog makes it very clear that the validation through the ordination and the attribution of the title "Rabbi" yielded institutional and official support. The pupils were essentially disciples of torah, not of individual teachers. And the teacher was merely a carrier of torah, not its originator. See, S. BYRSKOG, *Jesus the Only Teacher,* p. 133.

[140] B. M. METZGER, *The New Testament,* p. 50. The disciples of the Rabbi were followers in both the literal and figurative sense. It is said that when the Rabbi was walking down the road, the disciples would follow a foot behind him, for it was thought unseemly in that society that the learners should walk side-by-side with their master. Schools were associated with the local synagogue in first century Galilee. Apparently each community would hire a Rabbi for the school. While this teacher was responsible for the education of the village he had no special authority in the synagogue itself. Children began their study at age 4-5 in *Beth Sefer* (elementary school). Most scholars believe both boys and girls attended the class in the synagogue. The teaching focused primarily on the Torah, emphasizing both reading and writing Scripture. Large portions were memorized and it is likely that many students knew the entire Torah by memory by the time this level of education was finished. At this point most students stayed at home to help with the family and in the case of boys to learn the family trade. It is at this point that a boy would participate in his first Passover in Jerusalem, a ceremony that probably forms the background of today's *bar mitzvah* in orthodox Jewish families. The best students continued their study while learning a trade in *Beth Midrash* (secondary school) also taught by a Rabbi of the community. Here they studied the prophets and the writings in addition to Torah and began to learn the interpretations of the Oral Torah. Memorization continued to be important because most people did not have their own copy of the Scripture so they either had to know it by heart or go to the synagogue to consult the village scroll. Memory was enhanced by reciting aloud, a practice still widely used in Middle Eastern education. Constant repetition was considered to be an essential element of learning. A few of the most outstanding *Beth Midrash* students would seek permission to study with a famous Rabbi, often leaving home to travel with him for a lengthy period of time. These students were called *talmidim* in Hebrew, which is translated *disciple.* There is much more to a *talmid* than what is now termed student. A student wants to know what the teacher knows for the grade, to complete the class or the degree or even out of respect for the teacher.

A *talmid* wants to become what the teacher is. That meant that students were passionately devoted to their Rabbi and noted everything he did or said. This meant the Rabbi- *Talmid* relationship was a very intense and personal system of education. As the Rabbi lived and taught his understanding of the Scripture, his students '*talmidim*' listened and watched and imitated so as to become like him. Eventually they would become teachers passing on a lifestyle to their *talmidim*.

[141] J. NEUSNER & W. S. GREEN (eds.), *Rabbi*, p. 516.

[142] Judah David EISENSTEIN, "*Rabbi*", in *JE* 10 (1905) 294-297, p. 294

[143] Donald SENIOR, *A Gospel Portrait of Jesus*, Cincinnati, OH, Pflaum Standard, 1975, p. 98. In the observation of Senior, it is clear that a Rabbinic interpretation had weight if it could be fortified by the support of traditional Rabbinic opinion, which was in fact named as the 'authority of the fathers.'

[144] B. M. METZGER, *The New Testament,* p. 50. For a disciple, learning from a Rabbi meant considerable travelling. One literally had to follow a Rabbi to learn from him. There is a Rabbinic saying, which supports this picture of the Rabbi in the land of Israel: Yose ben Yoezer said, "Let your home be a meeting-house for the sages, and cover yourself with the dust of their feet, and drink in their words thirstily." (Avot 1:4) Yose ben Yoezer, living in the first half of the second century B.C., was one of the earliest of the sages of the *Mishnah*. In the context of his statement, "a meeting-house for the sages" should be understood to mean a place where the sages could hold classes, not a place where the sages themselves could assemble. Note the continuation of Yose ben Yoezer's statement: "and cover yourself with the dust of their feet." A number of translators of the *Mishnah* have rendered this, "and sit amidst the dust of their feet." When people walk along the dusty roads they invariably raise a considerable cloud of dust. Any group of disciples following a Rabbi would be covered with dust at the end of a journey, and if one wanted to travel with a Rabbi one literally had to cover oneself with the dust of his feet.

[145] S. BYRSKOG, *Jesus the Only Teacher,* p. 89.

[146] W. D. DAVIES, *The Setting of the Sermon on the Mount*, Cambridge, Cambridge University Press, 1964, p. 131.

[147] *Mishna Abot* 1:6. Formal education at the Synagogue School consisted of Bet Sefer, which was for an elementary education up to age 12. At age twelve the boys were expected to go to work. The more gifted went to Bet Midrash to continue their higher learning. A few of the most outstanding scholars left home to study with a famous sage (like Hillel). For a description of a normal process by which one became a Rabbi, read, Joachim JEREMIAS, *Jerusalem in the Time of Jesus*, trans. by F. H. CAVE and C. H. CAVE, Fortress Press, 1969, pp. 233-245. Only the most promising students would be accepted, as the family would need to support them and allow them to leave home where they would have been used to work on the land. This seeking of a master (Rabbi) by the student (learner) was the advice of Aboth. But in history there have been instances

of Rabbis choosing their own pupils or encouraging the bright students to sit at their feet. Akiba journeyed all the way from Babylon to Jerusalem to get a disciple like Hillel. Vernon K. Robbins, quoting from G. C. Field and G. W. Bowersock, states that it was a common practise even at the time of the Sophists to travel from city to city in order to gather disciples who would seek to embody wisdom and virtue by associating with them, receiving instruction from them, and imitating them. Vernon K. ROBBINS, *Jesus the Teacher: A Socio-Rhetorical Interpretation of Mark*, Philadelphia, Fortress Press, 1984, p. 88. Robbins adds that from the fifth century B.C.E. through the second century C.E., a wide variety of itinerant teachers was active throughout the Mediterranean world, producing a well-established cultural tradition of the preacher- teacher who gathered disciples. Cynics figure prominently among these itinerant teachers, travelling from city to city, gathering disciples who followed them around. Like the sophists, the philosopher-teacher named Socrates (469-399 B.C.E.) did the same kind of activity in and around Athens. Though he did not travel from city to city, he attracted lot of young people who responded to his call.

[148] Here, a brief observation is necessary about Jewish history with regard to the master-disciple relationship. The Jewish people spent most of their history living under pagan occupation. These outside influences must have had some impact in the way they viewed the world despite the purity which the Jewish religious leaders tried to preserve. This is especially true of the Hellenistic period and the Master - apprentice methodology of the Academy and the Lyceum centres of learning. Of course the dominant figures of Socrates and Plato would have been seen as a contemporary model of Teacher in the mind of many a Jewish scholar.

[149] J. NEUSNER & W. S. GREEN (eds.), *"Rabbi"*, p. 517.

[150] *Ibid.*, p. 516.

[151] *Ibid.*

[152] *Ibid.*

[153] See, E. KANARFOGEL, *"Rabbinate"*, p. 7578. According to Kanarfogel, "He who makes a profit from the words of Torah has brought about his own destruction." Cf. Avot 4:5. "Do not charge for teaching Torah. Accept no remuneration for it." Because of such interdictions, almost all Rabbis practised a trade. Some were Scribes, others sandal makers, leather workers or bakers. Acts 18:3 notes that Paul supported himself by making tents or working leather. Cf. JACKSON & LAKE, *The Acts of the Apostles*, volume IV, p. 223.

[154] B. M. METZGER, *The New Testament,* p. 47. To prove that the Rabbis had to work in order to make a living, Metzger quotes from Ac 18:3 where Paul is presented as a tentmaker. The Rabbis were also stonemasons, leatherworkers, carpenters and the like.

[155] Shmuel HIMELSTEIN, *"Rabbi and Rabbinate"*, in *The Oxford Dictionary of Jewish Religion* (1997) 567-568, p. 567. See also, Jacob E. SAFRA (ed.),

"*Rabbi*", in *The New Encyclopaedia Britannica*, Vol. 9, (15th ed.), Chicago, 2002, p. 871. Safra opines that "gradually, salaried Rabbi-judges and un-salaried Rabbi-teachers (interpreters of Jewish law) came to perform routine services for their communities. From the 14th century, Rabbi-teachers were receiving salaries (as Rabbis generally do today) to free them from other obligations."

[156] R. HERTZ, "*Rabbi, Rabbinate*", in Bowker JOHN (ed.), *The Oxford Dictionary of World Religions*, N.Y., Oxford University Press, 1997, p. 788. Hertz notes that by the 14th century, there is evidence of payment, not for teaching the law, but as compensation for loss of time taken up with Rabbinical duties.

[157] L. I. RABBINOUITZ, "*Rabbi, Rabbinate*", p. 1447. Despite the fact that most Rabbis had professions, however, they were not always able to support themselves as they travelled throughout the land. While travelling, the first-century Rabbi could not easily set up a shop due to the shortness of his stay in any given location. Nor would it have been fair when visiting smaller communities to take work away from a local resident in the same profession. Neither could work be readily found for the large number of disciples who often accompanied a Rabbi. Therefore the Rabbi and his disciples were necessarily dependent upon the hospitality of the communities they visited. A Rabbi's stay in a community might last from a few days to weeks or months. Although Rabbis would not accept payment for teaching Torah, most would accept lodging and usually food as well, for themselves and their students.

[158] J. NEUSNER, "*Rabbinic Judaism in Late Antiquity*", p. 7588. In his multifarious functions, a Rabbi as a judge could order the destruction of dangerous property and as administrator he supervised the market place and used his funds to control supply and prices

[159] S. HIMELSTEIN, "*Rabbi and Rabbinate*", p. 567. See also, E. KANARFOGEL, "*Rabbinate*", p. 7578. According to Kanarfogel, Talmudic literature does endorse the concept of *sekhar battalah*, whereby a Rabbi or judge was permitted to receive monetary compensation for his Rabbinic services in lieu of the money that he could have earned had he been able to devote that time to his regular occupation.

[160] J. C. TURRO, "*Rabbi*", p. 883.

[161] S. HIMELSTEIN, "*Rabbi and Rabbinate*", p. 567. In this period, as the demands increased, the Rabbis were permitted to obtain financial remuneration in lieu of the money they might have earned had they had the time to engage in a different occupation.

[162] R. PATAI, *Rabbi*, p. 108. Also see, M. A. GUTSTEIN, "*Rabbi*", p. 580. Gutstein notes that the Rabbi received no remuneration for Rabbinical services but supported himself by the pursuit of some trade or profession. Only those who spent their full time in the Rabbinic courts or in teaching received public support. Patai adds that the Rabbi of the Talmudic period always had a private, income-producing occupation, such as a cobbler or smith. Hence in Talmudic

times the Rabbis were expounders of the Bible and Law and at the same time they were occasional preachers.

[163] L. I. RABBINOUITZ, "*Rabbi, Rabbinate*", p. 1447. It was only in the middle ages that the title 'Rabbi', besides applying to the interpreters of the Law and Scripture, was also given to the decider of the law, the teacher, preacher and spiritual head of the Jewish congregation or community.

[164] R. PATAI, *Rabbi*, p. 108. Patai adds that from the 19th Century, the Rabbinical duties, especially in Western countries, have undergone radical changes. Rabbis had to give up their juridical functions because their right of jurisdiction in civil law was abolished. Instead, their duties began to approximate those of Christian priests and ministers with regard to the religious and spiritual needs of their congregants.

[165] J. D. EISENSTEIN, *Rabbi*, p. 294.

[166] *Ibid.*

[167] H. L. ELLISON, *Rabbi*, p. 115.

[168] E. KANARFOGEL, *Rabbinate*, p. 7578. According to Kanarfogel, even after the destruction of the Temple, ordination was still conferred (despite attempts by the Roman Emperor Hadrian to prohibit it) at least until the suppression of the patriarchate in 425 CE. However, at some point in the post-Talmudic period, the original chain of Rabbinic ordination was broken. Nonetheless, other means of licensing judges, masters, and religious heads of the communities were developed in both Palestine and Babylonia during the Geonic period. The scope of these forms of quasi-ordination was considered to be more limited than the original semikhah, and there were differing views about who had the right to grant them.

[169] I. BROYDE, *Rabbi*, p. 294. Traditionally, a man obtains semicha, which is Rabbinic ordination after the completion of an arduous learning program in the codes of Jewish law and responsa. Some religious leaders such as Hasidic Sages and Talmudic Rosh Yeshivas may not even have a formal semicha. In any event, the title is a credential and not a particular job. The most general form of *semikha* is *Yorei* "he shall teach." Most Orthodox Rabbis hold this qualification; they are sometimes called a *moreh hora'ah* "a teacher of lessons." A more advanced form of *semikha* is *Yadin* "he shall judge." This enables the recipient to adjudicate cases of monetary law, amongst other responsibilities. He is addressed as a *dayan* "judge." Few Rabbis could earn this ordination. Although not strictly necessary, many Orthodox Rabbis hold that a beth din, which is the court of Jewish law, should be made up of *dayanim*.

[170] *Ibid.* It is said that the title *Rabbi* was given in the later period only to the persons who had been properly ordained in the OT sense of the term. Kanarfogel observes that Rabbinic ordination had its origins in the biblical account of Moses placing his hands on Joshua. Carson opines that the terminology 'Rabbi' as used in the OT is not the same as we find in later Judaism. This is because by the first century A. D. the word became restricted to certain ordained teachers who

had successfully completed an appropriate course of Rabbinical instructions. See, D. A. CARSON, *The Gospel according to John*, Michigan MI, Leicester, Inter-Varsity Press, 1991, p. 155.

[171] S. BYRSKOG, *Jesus the Only Teacher*, p. 89. For Byrskog, the ordination of Rabbis was an official matter and it had an official character. While the early teachers took the initiative to ordain a pupil themselves, later teachers needed the consent of the patriarch - either the patriarch alone or the patriarch together with the Rabbinic Sanhedrin. Byrskog observes that ordination required the presence of three men of whom one is already ordained and the other two as witnesses. Thus ordination became a public affair and an act of demonstration in the presence of witnesses. Byrskog refers to the act of ordination which was performed by laying on of both hands. This refers to the biblical account of Joshua's authorization by Moses (Num 27:18. 23; Dt 34: 9). For the Rabbis, Moses ordained Joshua and this act forms a secure and continual succession of ordination of Rabbis by which the one who was ordained received power and authority from the one who ordained. The Rabbis also believed that the ordination conveyed the abilities of the ordainer to the one ordained. However, in the idea of Byrskog, it was not the teacher himself who was at the centre of attention but the concept of torah. The ordination functioned as an official demonstration and acknowledgement of the teacher's capacity to transmit torah.

[172] Hershel SHANKS, *"Is The Title 'Rabbi' Anachronistic in the Gospels?"*, in *JQR* 53 (1963) 337-344, p. 338.

[173] S. BYRSKOG, *Jesus the Only Teacher*, p. 93.

[174] S. HIMELSTEIN, *"Rabbai and Rabbinate"*, p. 567.

[175] *Ibid.* The examination to be admitted as a Rabbi was administered by individual Rabbis of repute and the candidates were tested on their competence in Talmud and Codes. Safra also agrees that for many generations the education of a Rabbi consisted almost exclusively of Talmudic studies, but since the 19th century the necessity and value of a well-rounded, general education has been recognised. See, J. E. SAFRA, *Rabbi*, p. 871.

[176] J. NEUSNER, *Rabbinic Judaism in Late Antiquity*, p. 7584. Neusner describes the importance of Torah and the adherence of the pupils to the Rabbis as follows: the stress upon Torah is expressed in three ways. First is emphasis upon the doctrine of the dual revelation to Moses at Sinai, a written Torah (the Pentateuch) and an oral Torah. Second, comes belief in the leadership of the sage, or Rabbi (in context, "My lord"). Third, is stress upon doing the will of God through study of Torah under the guidance of sages and upon living the holy way of life laid down in the Torah as interpreted by Rabbis.

[177] S. BYRSKOG, *Jesus the Only Teacher*, p. 93.

[178] *Ibid.*, p. 92.

[179] I. BROYDÉ, *Rabbi*, p. 294.

[180] J. E. SAFRA, *Rabbi*, p. 871.

[181] H. L. ELLISON, *Rabbi*, p. 115. The practice of ordination in its Mosaic form ceased in Palestine in the second half of the 4th century (A.D.) when the Judaean academies were closed. In the 16th century an attempt was made in Palestine by the Sanhedrin, with all the power and authority that it possessed, to revive the ancient ordination. But this attempt resulted in failure.

[182] D. B. RUDERMAN, "*Rabbi and Teacher*", p. 742-743. The Rabbis were supposed to determine the Torah, serve as judges in the Rabbinical court, help ensure a form of social welfare in the community, and try to increase religious observance. Ruderman points out that when the earlier institutionalised system of ordination was abolished, Rabbis personally authorised their most worthy students to function as Rabbis.

[183] M. R. WILSON, *Rabbi*, p. 30.

[184] R. HERTZ, *Rabbi, Rabbinate*, p. 788.

[185] J. C. TURRO, *Rabbi*, p. 883. When Turro observes that the Rabbi of the 12th century is comparable to the present day Rabbi, he speaks of the salaried Rabbi. To permit the Rabbi to devote more time to Rabbinical activity it became common to pay him for his services to the community and thereby free him from the need of working to sustain himself. It is only in the course of the Middle Ages, with the development of local communities "professional" Rabbis came into being. They remained first of all masters, but also decision makers. However, many refused to be dependent on a community and lived, often very sparsely, on a job which left them free time to study and transmit Torah and tradition. They were sometimes at the head of a Talmudic school, called 'Yeshiva', which formed the scholars and the masters of generations to come. To solve the problems which happened between individuals or groups, there were Rabbinical courts, composed at the very least of three masters with a deep knowledge of the Law as it had been transmitted through generations.

[186] S. HIMELSTEIN, *Rabbi and Rabbinate*, p. 567. Himelstein notes that after the persecutions, some Rabbis achieved international reputation and authority beyond the limits of their own communities. See also, M.A. GUTSTEIN, "*Rabbi*", p. 580. Gutstein observes that toward the end of the Middle Ages the scope of Rabbinic activity broadened. Communities elected their own Rabbis and by the end of the fifteenth century it became customary to pay them a regular salary. While the Rabbi still remained the authority and judge in matters pertaining to Jewish law and continued his extensive scholarly activity, he assumed a number of other duties, including, for example, the supervision of education, of kashruth, and of other community affairs.

[187] J. C. TURRO, *Rabbi*, p. 883.

[188] J. E. SAFRA (ed.), *Rabbi*, p. 871. In some cases, Rabbis function on a part-time basis, devoting the major portion of their energies to a secular profession.

The Rabbi is not required to lead the services - any knowledgeable congregant can carry out the service. Because a Rabbi does not have sacerdotal status, many functions that he normally performs may be assumed by others who, although not ordained, are qualified to conduct the religious ceremonies with devotion and exactitude.

[189] S. HIMELSTEIN, *"Rabbai and Rabbinate"*, p. 567. Safra opines that in questions of divorce, a Rabbi's role depends on an appointment to a special court of Jewish law. See, J. E. SAFRA (ed.), *"Rabbi"*, p. 871.

[190] R. PATAI, *Rabbi*, in *Encyclopaedia Americana*, p. 108.

[191] S. HIMELSTEIN, *"Rabbi and Rabbinate"*, p. 568. See also, M. A. GUTSTEIN, *"Rabbi"*, p. 580. Gutstein notes that the main function of the Rabbi was to study, interpret, and teach the law, and to act as judge in any controversies that arose. Preaching to the laity was a secondary function and not all Rabbis engaged in it. Thus, the Rabbis were greatly honoured by the community and enjoyed certain special privileges.

[192] R. HERTZ, *"Rabbi, Rabbinate"* p. 788. As Himelstein observes, very often the Rabbinic courts were permitted to try even criminal cases in which only Jews were involved. The main duties of a Rabbi lay in deciding Jewish legal questions, acting as judge in civil and criminal cases, forming a *beit din* which means a Rabbinical court. The Rabbis also supervised religious institutions such as ritual slaughter and ritual baths. Some Rabbis acted as the heads in the local Talmudic academies. See, S. HIMELSTEIN, *"Rabbai and Rabbinate"*, p. 568.

[193] D. B. RUDERMAN, *"Rabbi and Teacher"*, p. 743. Speaking of the functioning of Rabbis in present times, Ruderman says that individual Rabbis continue to occupy the central religious and cultural role among other constituencies such as economics or politics. They are still respected by virtue of their prodigious learning, personal piety and their own spiritual vocation to shape Jewish society.

[194] See, J. E. SAFRA (ed.), *"Rabbi"*, p. 871. Safra notes that the role of modern Rabbis has greatly changed. Whereas modern Rabbis assist at all religious marriages, their presence at most other ceremonies are not required. The state gives Rabbis the permission to perform the marriages. Technically, it is important to have a Rabbi to make sure that the complicated marriage ceremony is done properly. Valid witnesses are needed to make the marriage official. The criteria constituting a valid witness differ among the sects. In Israel, a Rabbi is needed for the secular legality of the wedding. Nonetheless, they generally conduct religious services and are present at funerals and some times at circumcisions. Besides all this religious activity, modern Rabbis are involved in social and philanthropic works and are expected to lend support to any project sponsored by their congregations. See also, M. A. GUTSTEIN, *"Rabbi"*, p. 580. Gutstein notes that in modern times emphasis is placed on the social and educational

functions of the Rabbi. Preaching, the maintenance of close contact with the congregation, and participation in community affairs are considered of prime importance. See also, J. C. TURRO, *"Rabbi"*, p. 883. Turro speaks of changes in the functions of the Rabbi ranging from religious sciences to secular sciences. Turro notes that in the past the training of a Rabbi consisted almost exclusively of Jewish studies. However, from the 19th century on, considerably more stress has been put upon the secular sciences. This change originated in Germany, the country which, from that time, became the centre for the development of Reform Judaism and for the scientific treatment of Jewish history and Jewish religion. The impetus behind this movement was Moses Mendelssohn. Through his translation of the Bible into pure German, Mendelssohn taught his people to speak the language of Germany. In this way he breathed new life into the sluggish masses and educated the German Jews to take an active part in national literary and social life. After the foundation for a scientific treatment of Jewish history and religion had been laid by Leopold Zunz and his collaborators, a number of enthusiastic young Rabbis, struggling against the most violent opposition, strove to bring about a reconciliation of Rabbinism with the modern scientific spirit. Foremost among these was Abraham Geiger, who devoted his whole life to the battle for religious enlightenment and to the work of placing Judaism in its proper light before the world. Geiger and his associates succeeded in arousing the German Jews to the importance of their duties. By fearlessly uncovering existing evils they cast light upon the proper sphere of Rabbinical activity and showed how the moral and religious influence of the Rabbinical office could be enhanced. One of the results of their labours was that some congregations awoke to the fact that Rabbis ought to be more than merely Jewish scholars, that they should be equipped with a thorough secular education. This tendency was furthered by the circumstance that, first in Austria under Joseph II, next in France, and thereafter in many other European especially German states, the government began to demand evidence of a certain degree of general education from Rabbinical aspirants. For further study see, *Encyclopedic Dictionary of the Bible*, (tr. & adap.) L. HARTMAN, New York, (1963) 1774-1775. See also H. ERHARTER, *Lexikon fur Theologie und Kirche*, J. HOFER and K. RAHNER (ed.), Freiberg, 1957-1965, 8:957. E.L. DIETRICH, *Die Religion in Geschichte und Gegenwart*, Tubingen, 1957-1965, 5:759. M. M. BERMAN, *The Role of the Rabbi*, New York, 1941; A. J. FEDDMAN, *The Rabbi and His Early Ministry*, New York, 1941.

[195] M. A. GUTSTEIN, *Rabbi*, p. 580. Gutstein observes that in communities of Spanish-Portuguese Jews, the spiritual leader is called *Haham* ("sage").

[196] S. HIMELSTEIN, *Rabbi and Rabbinate*, p. 568. In countries in which state supervisors guard or support the interests of religion, the function of the Rabbi or chief Rabbi is defined and prescribed by the government, and accordingly the necessary equipment and fitness are demanded of him. Modern life, with its greater complexity and deeper problems, has produced a new type of Rabbi,

possibly less ascetic and not so well versed in Hebrew lore, but more broad-minded, and more efficient in the direction of manifold activities in a larger field of usefulness.

[197] J. C. TURRO, *Rabbi*, p. 883. This duty of assisting civil functions eventually grew into the office of chief Rabbi maintained at various times in certain countries of Europe, e.g., Spain, Portugal, and England. The chief Rabbi was in effect a government appointee authorized to oversee the taxation of Jews and to represent their interests in the particular country.

[198] S. HIMELSTEIN, *Rabbi and Rabbinate*, p. 567. The foundation of seminaries and special institutions of learning played a great role in the works of Jewish Rabbis in promoting Jewish theology. While these institutions have equipped many Rabbis with a thorough knowledge of Jewish religion and literature, based upon general education previously acquired at colleges and universities, they have by no means abandoned the principle that there is in Judaism no distinction between the clergy and the laity except that given by superior learning and character. Meanwhile some Rabbis of even large congregations remained out of touch with educated Jews. They came into contact with their constituents chiefly in decisions of ritual and ceremonial questions, and in the performance of certain legal acts, especially in connection with the laws of marriage and inheritance. Their literary activity was confined to casuistry, their opinions being rendered only in Hebrew. Some led lives so retired from the world that their influence upon the members of their congregations was scarcely perceptible. Many of them, though very learned in Talmud, had not even the most elementary knowledge of the things essential to a common education. They could hardly make themselves understood in the language of their country. Some, again, addressed their congregations only twice every year, and then on subjects uninteresting to the great majority of their hearers. By the abolition of specific Jewish jurisdiction, the Rabbis' acquaintance with the civil law of the Jewish code, which in former times had been paid the greatest attention, became unnecessary for most practical purposes, and the imperative for a general education became obvious. The *yeshibot,* an uncontrolled instruction by individual Rabbis, were found to be increasingly unsatisfactory. The necessity of preaching in the vernacular and of explaining and defending the Jewish religion in a scientific manner required systematic education and training.

[199] D. B. RUDERMAN, *Rabbi and Teacher*, p. 746

[200] J. E. SAFRA, *Rabbi*, p. 871. The conservative and reform movements began to grant women *semicha* in the last few decades. Orthodox congregations do not ordain women as Rabbis. They follow the stricter interpretation in the Talmud prohibiting women from serving as witnesses or judges. In Judaism, there is no power endowed with the right to bind and to loose as we see in the Catholic Church. In Judaism, Rabbis are teachers who expound the Law and give information thereof. The Rabbi holds among Jews the position of moral influence. He is entitled to interfere in religious affairs. He is furthermore the custodian of

the eternal contents, of the transient history, and of the further development, of Judaism. An Orthodox semikha requires the successful completion of a rigorous program encompassing Jewish law and response in keeping with longstanding tradition. Orthodox Rabbinical students work to gain knowledge in Talmud. They study sections of the *Shulkhan Arukh* which is codified Jewish law and its main commentaries that pertain to daily-life questions such as the laws of keeping kosher, Shabbat, and the laws of sex and family purity. Orthodox Rabbis typically study at yeshivas, which are dedicated religious schools. Modern Orthodox Rabbinical students, such as at Yeshiva University, study some elements of modern theology or philosophy, as well as the classical Rabbinic works on such subjects. The entrance requirements for an Orthodox yeshiva include a strong background within Jewish law, liturgy, Talmudic study, and attendant languages, e.g., Hebrew, Aramaic and in some cases Yiddish. Since Rabbinical studies typically flow from other yeshiva studies, those who seek a semicha are typically not required to have completed a university education. Conservative Judaism holds that one may obtain Rabbinic ordination after the completion of a rigorous program in the codes of Jewish law and response in keeping with Jewish tradition. It adds to these requirements the study of the Hebrew Bible, Mishna and Talmud, the Midrash literature, Jewish ethics and the codes of Jewish law, the Conservative responsa literature, both traditional and modern Jewish works on theology and philosophy. Conservative Judaism has less stringent study requirements for Talmud and responsa study compared to Orthodoxy. Entrance requirements to a Conservative Rabbinical study include a strong background within Jewish law and liturgy, knowledge of Hebrew, familiarity with Rabbinic literature, Talmud, etc. Conservative seminaries are now ordaining female Rabbis. There are still traditional conservative congregations which resist this movement. Reconstructionist Judaism and Reform Judaism do not maintain the traditional requirements for study. To become a Reform or Reconstructionist Rabbi, they need to learn Jewish law, Talmud, and responsa that Orthodox Rabbis generally learn. Emphasis is placed not on Jewish law, but rather on cultural studies and modern Jewish philosophy. The Reform or Reconstructionist Rabbinical seminaries hold that one must first earn a bachelor's degree before entering the Rabbinate. In addition studies are mandated in pastoral care and psychology, the historical development of Judaism. Both men and women may be Rabbis or cantors. Orthodox Judaism generally rejects the validity of non-Orthodox Rabbis. Some within Modern Orthodoxy are willing to accept that non-Orthodox Rabbis have legitimacy although to what extent is argued. All non-Orthodox forms of Judaism generally accept the legitimacy of each other's Rabbis, as well as accepting the legitimacy of Orthodox Rabbis. There are several possibilities for receiving Rabbinic ordination in addition to seminaries maintained by the large Jewish denominations. These include seminaries maintained by smaller denominational movements. Finally, there are nondenominational ones which are also called transdenominational or postdenominational Jewish seminaries. There is no formal requirement to have *semicha* in order to be known as a Rabbi. Hasidic Judaism holds that becoming a Rabbi in and of itself is not important. Rather, they encourage their students and disciples within the Yeshivas they control to become great scholars, so that the students will have an innate knowledge of the Talmud, Halakha, the Tanakh and of course the Torah, combined with a commitment to the highest standards of the Shulkhan Arukh which is "The Code of Jewish Law" that should be the basis and guide for all Jewish life.

[201] Jewish tradition and law does not presume that women have more or less aptitude or the moral standing required of Rabbis. However, it has been a longstanding practice that only men become Rabbis. This practice is continued to this day within the Orthodox community but has been revised within non-Orthodox organizations, including the Reform, Reconstructionist, and Conservative movements, where women are routinely granted semicha on an equal basis with men. The issue of allowing women to become Rabbis is not under active debate within the Orthodox community, though there is widespread agreement that women may often be consulted on matters of Jewish religious law. There are reports that a small number of Orthodox yeshivas have unofficially granted semicha to women, but the prevailing consensus among Orthodox leaders and a small number of Conservative communities is that it is not appropriate for women to become Rabbis. The idea that women could eventually be ordained as Rabbis sparks widespread opposition among the Orthodox Rabbinate. The leaders of Modern Orthodoxy totally oppose giving semicha to women. While Orthodox Judaism prohibits women from being given semikha and serving as Rabbis, several efforts are underway within Orthodox communities to include qualified women in activities traditionally limited to Rabbis.

[202] R. HERTZ, *Rabbi, Rabbinate*, p. 788. Today Rabbi usually refers to those who have received ordination and are educated in matters of *halacka* (Jewish law). They are the ones knowledgeable enough to answer *halackic* questions. Most countries have a chief Rabbi they rely on to settle *halackic* disputes. The purpose of a Rabbi is like that of using a judge or a lawyer in civil matters to ensure that the law is complied with. In today's context, the Aramean word Rabbi which is "my master" is taking the form first of all of teacher and spiritual guide. He teaches law and answers questions in family conflicts or in differences between individuals. He is not a priest. The modern Rabbi, though trained to some extent in the halakic literature, is as a rule no longer expected, except in extraordinary cases and in matters concerning marriage or divorce, to decide ritualistic questions; greater stress is laid upon his work as preacher and expounder of the tenets of Judaism, as supervisor and promoter of the educational and spiritual life of the congregation. In matters concerning ancient traditions and beliefs and the views and aims of modern culture, he is looked at to reconcile the present with the past. As the spiritual head of the congregation, he is on

all public occasions regarded as its representative, and accordingly he is treated as the equal of the dignitaries of other ecclesiastical bodies.

[203] D. B. RUDERMAN, *Rabbi and Teacher*, p. 742. Ruderman explains that the Rabbis assumed greater ecclesiastical prerogatives; in some instances, they even demanded the honorific distinction of being called to the reading of Torah prior to those claiming priestly ancestry, whose normative privilege this would be. In the 19th century, the duties of the Rabbi became increasingly influenced by the duties of the Protestant Christian Minister. Sermons, pastoral counseling, representing the community to the outside, all increased in importance. Non-Orthodox Rabbis, on a day-to-day business basis, now spend more time on these traditionally non-Rabbinic functions than they do teaching, or answering questions on Jewish law and philosophy. Within the Modern Orthodox community, Rabbis still mainly deal with teaching and questions of Jewish law, but are increasingly dealing with these same pastoral functions. Orthodox Judaism and Modern Orthodox Judaism have set up supplemental pastoral training programs for their Rabbis. Traditionally, Rabbis have never been an intermediary between God and man. This idea was traditionally considered outside the bounds of Jewish theology. While Catholic priests are often used as intermediaries between man and God, Rabbis are nothing more than regular people who may be officially recognized through a process of ordination, or informally by virtue of the respect they have earned for their knowledge and righteousness. As a matter of course, the example of the minister in the Church, especially in Protestant countries, exerted a great influence upon the function and position of the Rabbi in the Synagogue. This even applied to his outward appearance, since the vestments of the Christian clergy, or their abandonment, have sometimes been copied by the modern Rabbi. Another function of the modern Rabbi which follows the pastoral practice of the Christian minister is the offering of consolation and sympathy to persons or families in bereavement and distress, in ways perhaps more cheering and elevating than those formerly in use. Here, as well as in his pulpit and educational work, the modern Rabbi has the opportunity of bringing the blessings of religion home to every individual in need of spiritual uplifting. He claims to have infused a new spirit and ardour into the divine service and other religious rites by his active participation therein; and in the communal work of charity and philanthropy he takes a conspicuous share. The orthodox Rabbi has also taken on these duties, but has retained his role as legal consultant and interpreter of the written and oral law. In Israel the Rabbi has a unique role, since the Orthodox Rabbinic courts have jurisdiction over matters of personal status. The chief distinction between the old and the modern Rabbi consists in the functions they severally discharge. The former, if living in Eastern countries under medieval conditions, was expected principally to decide questions of law, ritualistic or judicial, for people who adhere scrupulously to the Rabbinical code. He supervised the religious institutions of the community, as head of the council of Rabbis of the town and performing some of the other Rabbinical functions,

such as preaching, were regarded of secondary importance. It was his example rather than his precept that led the community in the fear of God and in a life of purity and sanctity. However the role of a Rabbi is not the same as a minister of the Church. This differs from the non- Jewish concept of a minister having some necessary mystical connection with God that is required to make the ceremony valid. The Rabbi serves the community as an educator, social worker, preacher, and occasionally conducts prayer services. Catholic priests can give absolution for sins; Rabbis can not unless you are asking forgiveness for something you have done against the Rabbi personally. The main difference is as follows. "In addition, the modern Rabbi acts as spokesman for the Jewish community to the larger society of which it is a part." See, R. PATAI, *Rabbi*, p. 108.

[204] In Mt 23:13, the Scribes are mentioned in Greek as γραμματεῦς whereas in the synoptic passage of Lk 11:52, the Scribes are mentioned as νομικοῖς. See, Kurt ALAND, ed., *Synopsis of the Four Gospels (7ᵗʰ ed.), Greek-English Edition of the Synopsis Quattuor Evangeliorum*, Stuttgart, German Bible Society, p. 178. See also, Frans NEIRYNCK, *Q – Parallels, Q Synopsis and IQP/ CritEd Parallels*, Leuven, Peeters, 2001, pp. 38-39. Mt's γραμματεῦς is translated as Scribes whereas Lk's νομικοῖς is translated as lawyers. At the same time, James M. Robinson's *"The Sayings Gospel Q in Greek and English"*, Mt's γραμματεῦς is translated as exegetes of the law. See, James M. ROBINSON & Paul HOFFMANN et al., *The Sayings Gospel Q in Greek and English with parallels from the Gospels of Mark and Thomas*, Leuven & Paris et al., Peeters, 2001, pp. 114-115. In the Gospel of Thomas 39:1-2, it is γραμματεῦς and it is translated as Scribes (pp. 114-115). From all these variant translations, one may ask whether a Scribe had the function of a teacher, a lawyer and an interpreter of law in Jewish society at the time of Jesus. "Scribes" or "teachers of the law" translates in Greek as γραμματεῦς "a class of professional exponents and teachers of the law" who might belong to either the Sadducee party or the Pharisee party. While any male Jew could read the Scripture in the Synagogue and give an interpretation of the scripture, Scribes were respected teachers who often had pupils who studied the law with them. Scribes were often poor and depended on gifts from their students, funds from the distribution to the poor, or the Temple treasury. It was considered meritorious to show hospitality to a Scribe, to give him a share of one's property, or to run his business for him. In some ways Jesus would have been classified in his day as a Scribe, having students who leave their families to study with him. Jesus, however, did not teach like the Scribes, appealing to tradition; rather he spoke authoritatively from God himself. This term "Scribe" refers to all whose profession involved writing. Village school teachers too would be included in this category. Concerning the saying of Jesus in Mt 23, where it refers to "Rabbi", one wonders whether Jesus referred to the group of Scribes, who had these various duties or functions. J. P. Meier sums up. "That Jesus at times dealt, dialogued, and debated with various types of Jewish Scribes is indeed likely. But that the Jewish Scribes

were a homogeneous religious group with a united theological agenda as well
as with a distinct power base, a homogeneous group that formed a united front
against Jesus, is hopelessly wrong. Hence, given the tendency of the Synoptics
to supply Scribes as stock characters in disputes with Jesus or in plots against
him, one must be very wary of appealing to any particular Gospel pericope
for information about specific historical incidents involving Jesus' interaction
with Jewish Scribes." See, John P. MEIER, in his work *A Marginal Jew*, vol. 3,
pp. 559-560.

[205] Cf. I Esd 7:6.

[206] D. E. ORTON, *The Understanding Scribe, Matthew and the Apocalyptic
Ideal*, *JSNTSup* 25, Sheffield 1989, pp. 23-38. To read more about the estimation
of the Scribes in the NT, read, HUMMEL, *Auseinandersetzung*, pp. 17f. 27f;
WALKER, *Heilsgeschichte*, pp. 17-29; SCHENK, *Sprache des Matthäus*, pp.
66f. Quoting Mt 8:19; 13:52; 23:8-10 and 34, the above authors argue that there
is no positive estimation of the Scribes in Matthew at all.

[207] John O'NEILL, *Jesus as Teacher*, in *Priests and People*, Vol. 13 (1999)
308-312, p. 308.

[208] I. BROYDE, *Rabbi*, p. 294. In the context of Mt 23: 7-8, both the titles ῥαββί
and διδάσκαλος are seen. As mentioned above, it comes as a warning from
Jesus to his disciples that they should not follow the ways of the Scribes and
Pharisees in seeking these titles of honour and respect. It is made explicitly clear
in the sayings of Jesus, which we see in the same chapter Mt 23: 13ff. In Mt 9:11;
12:38; 22:15f. 23f. 34-36, the characters with evident negative traits use διδάσκαλος
in reference to Jesus. They represent the religious leaders of the Jewish people.
In Mt 22:34-36, the Scribes are present together with the Pharisees and reveal
their intention to oppose Jesus. The Scribes in Mt 2:4; 7:29; 17:10; 23:2. 7. 13.
16 constitute the teachers of the people and of Jesus' opponents. The opponents
of Jesus in the Gospel of Matthew are given the collective name of "Religious
leaders." However, as Byrskog opines, Matthew does not subordinate all the
Scribes under the general category of religious leaders. In Mt 13:51f; 23:34 and
to some extent also 8:19, a certain positive estimation of the Scribes is shown.
The warning of Jesus recorded in Mt 23 addresses the dangers of discipleship
as practised by the Jews of Jesus' day. "Then Jesus spoke to the multitudes and
to His disciples, saying 'The Scribes and the Pharisees have seated themselves
in the chair of Moses; therefore all that they tell you, do and observe, but do
not do according to their deeds; for they say things, and do not do them. And
they tie up heavy loads, and lay them on men's shoulders; but they themselves
are unwilling to move them with so much as a finger. But they do all their deeds
to be noticed by men; for they broaden their phylacteries, and lengthen the
tassels of their garments. And they love the place of honour at banquets, and
the chief seats in the synagogues, and respectful greetings in the market places,
and being called by men, Rabbi. But do not be called Rabbi; for One is your
Teacher, and you are all brothers. And do not call anyone on earth your father; for

one is your Father, he who is in heaven. And do not be called leaders; for one is your leader, that is, Christ. But the greatest among you shall be your servant. And whoever exalts himself shall be humbled; and whoever humbles himself shall be exalted" (Mt 23:1-12). At first glance, the direct connection between this warning in Mt 23 and discipleship may not be convincing. However, bear in mind that the meaning of the term disciple implies that the disciple is one who submits himself to a higher authority who will serve as his teacher, guide and leader. This is the way the Jewish leadership regarded themselves and their position of authority. In effect, the whole clash between Jesus and the Jewish leaders was one of authority (cf. Mt 21:23). They were greatly distressed over the fact that the masses appeared to be slipping from their grip, and submitting to the leadership of Jesus (cf. Mt 27:18; Jn 4:1.2; 11:47.48). The warning of Jesus in Matthew 23 is at the heart of the dispute between Judaism and Jesus. The error of the Scribes and Pharisees was that they had exalted themselves to a position higher than that of Moses (verse 2). They had boasted to the man born blind that they were disciples of Moses (John 9:28). Such was not really the case, however. To have been a disciple of Moses would mean that they would have placed themselves under the authority of his teaching and doctrine. In effect, they had ousted Moses or Torah by making the interpretation and application of these sacred writings subject to their own traditions and interpretations (Mt 15:1-9). They had placed themselves in the chair of Moses. They were now over the Scriptures, judging them rather than being judged by them. The Scribes and Pharisees usurped the authority to subject men under them as disciples. In so doing they commanded men to follow the clever system they had created by codifying the Law of Moses into 365 prohibitions and 250 commandments. The effect was to place upon unsuspecting Israelites a burden which no one could bear, and which they did nothing to lighten. While they ingeniously devised ways to circumvent their own regulations, the masses were buried under them. These men desired disciples because they basked in the glory and adulation of men.

[209] B. M. METZGER, *The New Testament*, p. 47.

[210] H. L. ELLISON, *Rabbi*, p. 115.

[211] NEPPER -CHRISTENSEN, μαθητής, p. 372.

[212] Cf. Eccl 38:25-26. "The wisdom of the Scribe cometh by his time of leisure: and he that is less in action shall receive wisdom. With what wisdom shall he be furnished that holds the plough, and that glorifies in the goad, that drives the oxen therewith, and is occupied in their labours, and his whole talk is about the offspring of bulls?"

[213] This title was far from unpleasant in the ears of the Scribes as shown in Mt 23:7. In point of fact, a pupil would never omit it when speaking to or of his teacher, and it became a universal usage never to mention the name of a doctor of the Law without prefixing "Rabbi".

[214] B. M. METZGER, *The New Testament*, p. 47.

[215] Gerd THEISSEN & Annette MERZ, *The Historical Jesus*, London, SCM Press, 1998, p. 355.

[216] Geza VERMES, *Jesus and the World of Judaism*, London, SCM Press, 1983, p. 30.

[217] B. M. METZGER, *The New Testament*, p. 48.

[218] J. P. MEIER, *A Marginal Jew, Rethinking The Historical Jesus*, Vol. 3, p. 550.

[219] *Ibid.*

[220] *Ibid.*

[221] *Ibid.*

Chapter - 2

Jesus as Ῥαββί in the New Testament: Anachronistic?

Introduction

In the Gospel accounts, the title "Rabbi" ascribed to Jesus raises a question as to whether Jesus also was considered a typical first-century sage, or Jewish teacher.[1] Jesus was called ῥαββί, a title of high respect, which meant "master" or a designation of "teacher."[2] J.C.Turro makes the following observation: "although the term Rabbi does not occur in the OT, by the first Christian century it must have become common for the Gospels frequently show the disciples of Jesus (Mt 26: 25, 49; Mk 9:5; 11:21; 14:45; Jn 1: 49; 4:31; 9:2; 11:8) and other people (Jn 3: 2; 6:25) addressing him as "Rabbi."[3] So it is possible to argue that the title *rab* was in use at the time of Jesus. However, it is difficult to secure reliable background information for first- century A.D. Rabbi-disciple relationships. Also taken into consideration is the fact that several scholars have recently issued appropriate cautions[4] against an undiscerning use of Rabbinic materials for the illumination of the background of the NT.

This study will investigate whether the gospels accurately reflect the use of the term ῥαββί in the sense of an ordained and trained scholar. Then the question of whether the use of the title ῥαββί in the Gospels is anachronistic will be explored. Does the term ῥαββί in the gospels reflect the result of an evolution, which sprang from the Rabbinic reconstruction of Judaism at the end of the first century, as a designation for a teacher of Jesus' time? The validity or authenticity of the use of the title ῥαββί before the destruction of the second temple is also discussed. Was the title ραββί used at all in the circle of Jesus and his followers (disciples)? Do the authors of the NT who call Jesus ραββί use the term in the sense it had at Jesus' time or in the sense it had in their own time? Was Jesus considered a Rabbi in the first century Christian communities and during the period in which the Gospels were first committed to the written form?

1.   Non-Existence of the Use of the Title ραββί before 70 A. D.

This discussion will be based primarily on the arguments and counter arguments of two scholars. As is known, the history and use of the title ραββί has been the object of some controversy among many scholars including Hershel Shanks and Solomon Zeitlin. The former argues for the existence of a pre-70 A.D. use while the latter claims the absence of any real evidence for the early use of the title. The following references present the position for some authors other than Shanks and Zeitlin. Joseph Klausner[5] in his work "Jesus of Nazareth" observes that Graetz[6] holds the view that the name ραββί used in the Gospels is an anachronism. Graetz concludes from the work of Goodenough who holds that, "because it does not follow later Rabbinic usage," the anachronism lies "in taking the later Rabbinic usage as valid in the early period since for this period we have only the New Testament to certify. Of course this study does not accept as necessarily valid such a conclusion even if the New Testament were to present the only known evidence, on the grounds that other evidence might be forthcoming."[7] It is to be noted that the different positions of the scholars are often complementary or interchangeable with either position.

Zeitlin states that at the time of Jesus, the title ραββί was not used by the Judeans and therefore all the occurrences of the term ραββί in the Gospels as a title for Jesus are anachronistic.[8] For Zeitlin, there is no Jewish evidence for the prefixing of ραββί, to the name of any sages in the period before 70A.D. He maintains that the title ραββί is of a later origin, and that before 70 A.D. it was neither used nor found in any of the Tannaitic literature. If Zeitlin is correct, the term ραββί came into vogue after the destruction of the second temple and so the title was not used by the Judeans in the time of Jesus. Shanks takes the position that the title ραββί in the Gospels is not anachronistic. In addition, Hershel Shanks states that "neither this position nor the reasoning on which it is based is original with Professor Zeitlin."[9] Thus an evaluation is needed of the opposing views of Zeitlin and Shanks. As no position is conclusive at this stage, an evaluation of Shanks' findings will begin with the letter of Sherira Gaon.

Letter of Sherira Gaon

Hershel Shanks[10] mentions in his article a letter from which scholars like Solomon Zeitlin conclude that the title ῥαββί was not in use before the destruction of the Second Temple in Jerusalem. The letter, which Shanks has cited in his article, is the letter of Sherira Gaon, written to the community of Kairwan in the 10th century AD.[11] Jonathan Smith states that "The title 'Rab' is Babylonian, and that of 'Rabbi' is Palestinian."[12] Some of the Tannaim and Amoraim were called simply by their names without any title. Examples are, Simon the Just, Antigonus of Soko, and Jose ben Johanan. Some bear the title ῥαββί (e.g., Rabbi Akiba, Rabbi Jose.); others have the title 'Mar'; and then there are those with the title 'Rab,' e.g., Rab Huna, Rab Judah, etc.; still others have the title 'Rabban' (e.g., Rabban Gamaliel and Rabban Johanan ben Zakkai). At some stage in history, the titular connotations invaded the qualitative and relational appellation. Samuel Byrskog[13] explains how the adjective of רַב became a proper title to be used in front of the name. A letter, written by R. Sherira (c. 906-1006 A.D.) – the Gaon of the Pumbedithan academy - to the north African community of Kairouan circa 987 C.E., relates the history of the title. The letter dates the earliest occurrence of the title רַב to the time of R. Johanan b. Zakkai. Zakkai, who died about 80 C.E., is mentioned as the first teacher practising ordination to bear this title, making clear that this title was not usually prefixed to the names of the old sages. As a title, רַב came to be in use during the first generation of Tannas, which includes such as R. Zadok, R. Eliezer b. Jacob and R. Hanina b. Dosa.

As was shown, in that letter, Sherira speaks about the Palestinian sages who bore the title Rabbi with the authority to judge in penal cases. Sherira's letter also bears evidence of the title Rab for the Babylonian sages. Both titles, ῥαββί in Palestine and ῥαβ in Babylon, according to Sherira, were conferred on sages after the ceremonial ordination. The problem comes when Sherira says that Hillel, who is said to be the contemporary of Jesus, had no title of this kind and there was no prefix of ῥαββί or ῥαββουί before his name. Sherira's letter also mentions that the title Rabban was first used in Jewish history for Rabban Gamaliel the elder (c. 20-50 A.D). For Zeitlin[14] and others, this leads one to conclude that ῥαββί was not used at the time of Jesus nor until the time of the Jewish revolt, which brought about the destruction of the second Temple, in 70 A.D. In Jewish history, according to Solomon Zeitlin, "the name Rabbi or Rabbanan does not occur in the entire tannaitic literature before the destruction of the Second Temple."[15] For Zeitlin, it is only in the later

Tannaitic literature, which means after the destruction of the Temple, that the name ῥαββί and *Rav* had the meaning teacher. There are many other authors who hold to the argument that the usage of the title *Rav* or ῥαββί in Jewish society only occurs after the destruction of the Second Temple.

Hillel and Shammai - Absence of the Title "Rabban"

According to the letter of Sherira Gaon, "the more ancient generations, however, which were far superior, had no such titles as "Rabban", "Rabbi", or "Rab" for either the Babylonian or Palestinian sages. This is evident from the fact that Hillel I, who came from Babylon, had not the title "Rabban" prefixed to his name."[16] The Encyclopaedia Judaica gives the same version. Based on a history of those times, "it was only during the tannaitic period, in the generation after Hillel, that it was employed as a title for the sages."[17] According to Coulot, when the traces of the title ῥαββί are searched for in Jewish history, one has to bear in mind that the term ῥαββί comes on the scene after the Jewish revolt. Coulot opines, "*Il est difficile de décrire la condition du maître et du disciple dans le Rabbinisme d'avant la révolte juive.*"[18] Coulot does not stop with that but also says that the great Jewish teachers of those times were not addressed with the title ʽΡαββί. He observes, "*De très grands maîtres sont apparus tels Hillel, Gamaliel, Yohanan ben Zakkai dont la tradition a conservé les sentences.*"[19] Zeitlin is convinced that the title was not in use during the time of the second Commonwealth. "The sages were quoted by their names without the prefix of Rabbi, as Jose ben Joezer, Simon ben Shetah, Hillel, Shammai, Nahum and many others."[20] Lapin takes the same view that the mode of addressing someone as Rabbi came later, after 70 A.D. "In Rabbinic literature, personages associated with the period before 70 C.E are not referred to with a title (e.g., Hillel, Shammai), while those associated with the later periods are titled (e.g., Rabbi Aqiba, etc.)."[21] According to Lapin, the use of the term *rab* as a title is not attested before roughly the 1st century AD. In the opinion of Lapin, the term Rabbi as a mode of address and designation for teachers belongs to late tradition. "A corrupt and apparently late tradition, which assumes that *rabbî* and *rabbān* designate teacher."[22] Thus only in the late tradition, the *Tannaim*[23] and Palestinian *Amoriam*,[24] bore the title of ῥαββί and had the function of designating the scholars. Hence, for some modern scholars, the term ῥαββί evolved in the course of Jewish history as a title for the sages only in the later periods after 70 A.D. As Chilton observes, "The Rabbis emerged as the new aristocrats, largely replacing the priesthood."[25] Thus, in the opinion of Chilton, only after 70 A.D. did ῥαββί emerge as a responsible and important office in Judaism.

In order to show the person greater honour, the title Rabbi was intensified into ῥαββάν ῥαββονί, so that, in the course of time, custom established a kind of hierarchy among these various forms. ῥαββί, is more than ῥαββί ῥαββονί more than ῥαββί, and the proper name more than ῥαββονί. The latter part of this traditional regulation is particularly related to the two great Doctors, Hillel and Shammai, who are always designated by their unqualified proper names. The successors of Hillel, such as Gamaliel, were titled Rabban, and so also was, by exception, Johanan ben Zakkai. Palestinian doctors are commonly known as Rabbi So-and-so, yet Rabbi Judas, who composed the Mishna, is not infrequently called merely ῥαββί (*par excellence*). In the same manner, Rab, without the proper name, designates Abba Arika (died A. D. 247), the founder of the School of Sora, while Rab is the title prefixed to the names of the Amoras of Babylon. However there is another reference which testifies that Hillel[26] was addressed as יבר.

The use of ῥαββί for a Jewish religious teacher as an address rather than a title is attested to by R. Eleazar b. Azariah,[27] who addressed his teacher R. Yohanan b. Zakkai (80 A.D. (as יבר when visiting him at the occasion of the death of Yohanan's son.[28] According to Kanarfogel, the term *rav*, in its derivative term *Rabbi*, which means 'my master' "is an honorific used originally to address sages in the Land of Israel following the destruction of the Second Temple."[29] The basic form of Rabbi developed in the Pharisaic and Talmudic Era. Lapin states, "The earliest evidence for "Rabbi" as a title attached to a proper name (e.g., Rab Hana) occurs on Jerusalem ossuaries which apparently date from before 100 A.D. The inscriptions, which date from 100 A.D. to 400 A.D. stem largely from the cemeteries of Joppa and Beth-shearim."[30] W. Dennis Tucker, Jr., notes that "In the 1st- Century Judaism the word maintained a loose designation meaning 'teacher.' The use of ῥαββί as an official term for an ordained scholar actually belongs to the period following the destruction of the temple in 70 C.E."[31]Thus, all the scholars quoted in this section testify that ῥαββί as a title was given to anyone only after the destruction of the temple, which means only after 70 A.D, the year which is accepted by most historians for the destruction of the temple in Jerusalem.

Gamaliel - The First Titled Rabbi

Shmuel Himelstein speaking of the title "Rabbi" says "no titles of this nature were used in ancient times (thus, great sages such as Hillel and

Shamm'ai were never given any such appellation), but in the Mishnaic period, *rabban*, which is a variant form of the more common *Rabbi*, was applied honorifically to leading scholars and more particularly to presidents of the Sanhedrin."[32] The Epistle of Sherira Gaon says that the first person to bear the title "rabban" was Gamaliel around the middle of the first century. This period fits with the evidence that only with the school at Jamnia did "Rabbi" come into any regular use as a title for "ordained scholars." Hence, according to Zeitlin the term ῥαββί came into use as a title only after the destruction of the Second Temple and so was not in use in Jesus' time. The first time the name ῥαββί is mentioned was in relation to Gamaliel the First when he was called Rabbi Gamaliel. As one may find from the letter of Sherira, the title Rabbi is not met with earlier than the time of the patriarchate. "It was first used of rabban Gamaliel the elder, Rabban Simon his son and Rabban Johanan ben Zakkai, all of whom were patriarchs or presidents of the Sanhedrin."[33] Up to that time, all the scholars in Jewish history were simply called by their proper names. Zeitlin says that the first four sages to bear this title are "Gamaliel the Elder, Jochanan ben Zakkai, Simon the son of Gamaliel and his son Gamaliel."[34] It is here that Shanks makes an interesting point, as follows; "in the time of Gamaliel the First, the title Rabbi was affixed to his name while his colleagues were called by their proper names, without any title of Rabbi."[35] This situation changed after the destruction of the temple. The *Nasi* still had the title ῥαββί but other scholars, such as the members of the Sanhedrin who received authorization to decide the laws, were also called Rabbis.

According to Shmuel Himelstein, "Rabbi (my master) is an honorific term that was originally used in *Erets Yisra'el* to address sages, but it has gradually developed into a title for any person qualified to render decisions on Jewish law."[36] According to R. Hertz in his "The Rabbi Yesterday and Today", the title ῥαββί (*Rabbi* as transliteration) at the time of Rabbinic Judaism was given to a "Jewish learned man who has received ordination."[37] Himelstein also stresses that the term ῥαββί was not used as a title until the time of Hillel. In Talmudic times, this was not granted outside *Erez* Israel, so that the Babylonian sages bore the title of 'Rav.' The Rabbi is not an occupation found in the Torah as such. The first time this word is mentioned is in the Mishnah. The more ancient generations had no such titles as *Rabban*, *Rabbi*, or *Rab*, for either the Babylonian sages or the sages in Israel. Similarly, the codifier of the Mishna (c. AD 200), Judah ha-Nasi, was called *rabbenu* ("Our teacher")."[38] This is evident from the fact that Hillel I, who came from Babylon, did not have the title *Rabban* prefixed to his name. The title *Rabban* is not used by the Prophets. The title *Rabbi* also came into vogue among those who received the laying on of hands during this period. For instance, Rabbi Zadok and Ribbi Eliezer ben Jacob had this title which dates from the time of the disciples of Rabban Johanan ben Zakkai onward. Thus Zeitlin and others maintain that it was only after the destruction of the Second Temple in Jerusalem (70 A.D.) that Gamaliel was given the title 'Rabbi', and the earlier attribution of the title 'Rabbi' to anyone is an anachronism.[39] Is Zeitlin's position valid, that calling the historical Jesus a Rabbi in the Gospels is an anachronism?

According to Andreas Köstenberger, "a distinction must be made between ῥαββί as an address for teachers prior to 70 AD and ῥαββί as a fixed title in the period of full-fledged Rabbinism."[40] Köstenberger attempts to establish the exact period of time when the title ῥαββί was formally used for teachers and authorities. In the passage above, Köstenberger also says that a distinction must be made between two periods of time. The question here is whether Köstenberger agrees that in both the periods before and after the destruction of the temple, the title 'Rabbi' was used in various ways. Can one say that even before the destruction of the temple, the title had been attributed to sages and teachers? Köstenberger thinks that the title ῥαββί for teachers could have been in use even before the destruction of the temple, but not in the sense of an 'ordained scholar' as it was after 70 A.D. If that is true, how is one to find a solution to the problem of anachronism? The following section will focus on this historical problem.

2.   Evidence for the Use of the Title 'Rabbi' before 70 A. D.

G. H. Dalman in his book *The Words of Jesus* observes that it is unnecessary to provide proof that in Jesus' time ῥαββί was the "usual form of address with which the learned were greeted."[41] Dalman arrives at his position based on Matthew 23 and opines, "For the time of Jesus, its use is expressly stated."[42] Hence, Dalman believes the term r`abbi, was undoubtedly used at the time of Jesus as the designation for the learned and teachers. In *"The Origin of the Title Rabbi"*,[43] Hershel Shanks asserts that the use of the title Rabbi can be dated to before the destruction of the temple in 70 A.D. For Shanks and others there is both historical and literary proof and evidence in history. To show the earlier use of the title ῥαββί and to prove the development of the use of the title ῥαββί between biblical times and the destruction of the Temple in 70 A.D., Shanks cites a number of literary references as historical evidence. But at the same time, Shanks admits that for Zeitlin and others "with the exception of the Dead Sea Scrolls, there is no original extant Hebrew or Aramaic literature between c.167 B. C. and c. 130 C. E."[44] Later, in 1968, when Zeitlin replied to Shanks' claims, he conceded that "in none of this literature does the word Rabbi occur."[45] Rainer Riesner, following Cohen, asserts that the term Rabbi is confined to Palestine in the first century A.D even at the time of Jesus.[46] Shanks continues to defend his position that the title ραββί was in use in the time of Jesus. The following discusses Shanks' views.

First of all, the letter of Sherira, which leads Zeitlin and others to the conclusion that the title "Rabbi" was not in use before 70 A.D., needs to be explained. Shanks says that, "to rely on the facts in Sherira's letter to prove that the title "Rabbi" was not used at the time of Jesus really proves too much."[47] This is because Sherira is more concerned with the official use of the title "Rabbi." In Sherira, the title Rabbi is bestowed only as an official title of honour and authority. If so, it is also possible that the title ραββί in the Gospels was used as an unofficial title and an unofficial mode of address in the time of Jesus. Shanks quotes the work of A. N. Orenstein[48] who quotes a Tosefta,[49] which refers to Jewish usage of the title ραββί, and which dates before the period of Rabbon Yochanan ben Zakkai who died about 80 A.D. Shanks also mentions the opinion of Saul Lieberman whom he considers to be an unrivalled authority on Tosefta in modern times.[50] For Lieberman, "Tosefta" contains an unquestionably authentic reference to the use of r`abbi, in the pre-destruction period.

For Zeitlin, Tosefta cannot be used as a historical document. For him, "It is a historical fact that the title Rabbi prefixed to the name of a sage is not found in the tannaitic literature before the time of the destruction of the Temple. Due to the clear historical perspective of the spiritual life of the Judeans during the Second Commonwealth the text of the Tosefta cannot be used as a historical document."[51] So, for Zeitlin, "Tosefta" cannot be considered as historical evidence, yet Shanks considers it an important source to prove that the title Rabbi was in use before 70 A.D.

Another observation concerns the common use of the Jewish title Rabban before the destruction of the Temple. The first person to have the title *Rabban* was Gamaliel the Elder who lived before the destruction of the Temple. Zeitlin argues that Gamaliel took, or was given, the title Rabban "when the office of the Ab Bet Din (head of the court) was abolished and Gamaliel became, as Nasi, the sole head of the Sanhedrin."[52] From Jewish history,[53] it is known that Gamaliel the Elder occupied a leading position in the Sanhedrin and that he bore the title *Rabban* even before the destruction of the Temple. Today there is a conflict among the scholars about whether Gamaliel the Elder was even alive before the destruction of the Temple, and whether he bore that title. Another question is whether Gamaliel the Elder survived the war or killed. It is asserted that Gamaliel had the title ῥαββονί before the destruction and, if that is so, one can say that the title was used before 70 A.D. Due to the uncertainty of the time of Gamaliel, Shanks says that, "we shall assume that Gamaliel did not take the title until after the Destruction."[54] But Zeitlin asserts that Gamaliel the Elder and his son Simon lived before the destruction of the Temple. Zeitlin asserts that "To maintain that Gamaliel lived after the destruction of the Temple betrays ignorance of the Talmud."[55] While the historical question of the time period of Gamaliel is significant, this study concludes that Shanks' arguments present the possibility that ῥαββί or ῥαββονί were in use even before 70 A.D.

Occurrence of the Title Rabbi in OT and Extra- biblical Texts

Hershel Shanks in his work on the *"Origins of the Title 'Rabbi'"* notes the earlier uses of *Rab* as titles in OT and extra-biblical texts. Shanks states that this title was widely "used throughout the ancient Near East, both early and late, from Mesopotamia to Egypt, in Jewish as well as non-Jewish languages, in secular titles and in religious titles."[56] He had already taken this position in his previous work in 1963, where he says that the title ῥαββί or ῥαββαν attributed to Gamaliel "was not taken from thin air" and the etymology *rab* "must have had some development between biblical times and the destruction."[57] It is important to note that even Zeitlin has accepted the use of the title ῥαββί at the time of Jesus as an unofficial title. If so, it can be claimed that it was used to address Jesus, if only in an honorific and unofficial sense. Thus, despite the fact that Zeitlin's argument is that the name ῥαββί or ῥαββονί does not occur in the entire tannaitic literature before the destruction of the Temple, he does concede its use as an "unofficial title."

'Ραββί *and* διδάσκαλος *in Archaeological Inscriptions*

According to Harold Mare,[58] the evidence for ῥαββί and διδάσκαλος in archaeological inscriptions can be divided into two groups.[59] First, there are those inscriptions found outside Palestine in Europe. The materials here are basically Greek, but sometimes Aramaic is found up to the third or fourth centuries A. D.[60] when Latin became more and more prominent. The other group[61] consists of inscriptions found on archaeological remains inside Palestine, these being written in Greek, Aramaic, and Hebrew.[62] There are some instances in this group when two of the languages are used together[63] on the same stone remains. The inscriptions in Palestine regarding ῥαββί-διδάσκαλος are more numerous and revealing. One of the latest is an Aramaic inscription from a sixth century synagogue at Beth Alpha in Galilee[64] which, in a broken text, includes the word ῥαββί. Another Aramaic inscription from the fifth century in the synagogue at El Hammeh in Transjordan speaks of a Rabbi Tanhum, the Levite.[65] An Aramaic inscription in a mosaic at Sepphoris in Galilee,[66] dated to the third or fourth centuries A.D., speaks of Rabbi Judan, the son of Tanhum[67] and, in the same area, a funeral inscription[68] also mentions the Rabbi. From Er-Rama in Galilee comes an Aramaic third century grave inscription[69] which speaks of Rabbi Eliezer,[70] son of Tedeor (Theodor).

A considerable number of inscriptions in Greek, Hebrew, Aramaic, and Palmyrene, found in the Jewish necropolis which is dated to the first four centuries A.D. at Beth-Shearim in Galilee, have several references to Rabbi[71] both in Greek and Aramaic from about the third century A. D. Some of these inscriptions contain mixed Aramaic and Greek[72] although the majority are in Greek. The Aramaic inscriptions speak of Rabbi Isaac[73] and of another Rabbi whose name is not preserved in the incomplete inscription.[74] The Greek inscriptions given by Frey speak of Rabbi Isakos[75] Rabbi Paregorios[76] Rabbi Joseph[77] and Samuel, the διδάσκαλος[78] This last inscription in the midst of the others, which in Greek and Aramaic speak of ῥαββί, suggests that at this date the two terms, ῥαββί and διδάσκαλος were equivalents. As a matter of fact, the rather frequent reference to ῥαββί in this grave[79] complex suggests that it consists of a family of scholars. Among the Greek inscriptions, the word ῥαββί[80] is spelled out in two cases. In coastal Palestine, a Joppa Jewish necropolis yields a considerable quantity of inscriptions[81] dated to the first few centuries, a good number appearing to be from the second and third centuries A.D.

It has been shown that a number of the names of Rabbis inscribed here are of those known from Jewish literature.[82] Of the four inscriptions which contain the word ῥαββί, three are in Aramaic and one in Greek, the former speaking of Rabbi Tarphon[83] (or Tryphon), Than(k)oum[84] the son of the Rabbi Hanania, son of Rabbi [Laza]rus, of Alexandria.[85] Actually the inscription in which the Greek form of ῥαββί[86] (rab) is to be found (Rab Juda) is in both Aramaic and Greek. L. H. Vincent[87] argues against Frey and Clermont-Ganneau that at Noarah (Ain Duk) near Jericho there was found an Aramaic inscription with the name of Rabbi Safrah,[88] an inscription which has been variously dated as late as the fourth to sixth centuries A.D. and as early as the time of Herod the Great.

Evidence of the Jerusalem Ossuary

A Jerusalem ossuary (small boxes which contain bones of the deceased) was found with inscriptions, some of which refer to ῥαββί or διδάσκαλος and are dated between 200 B. C. and A. D. 200.[89] Although the title Rabbi is not part of the name, reference to a Gamaliel is made in an Aramaic ossuary inscription,[90] which Sukenik takes to be from around the time of Christ,[91] such a reference possibly being to the Gamaliel who taught Paul (Acts 22:3).[92] Two Greek inscriptions found on ossuaries containing both Greek and Aramaic writing, and discovered on the slopes of the Mount of Olives[93] seem to speak of Theomnas, the Διδάσκαλου[94] and of some other Διδάσκαλος not specifically identified.[95] The Aramaic ones refer to Rabbi Hana[96] and Ben Rabban.[97] Another in the same group[98] is of particular interest because Sukenik[99] dates it to the time of Christ. The fact that the inscriptions on this ossuary are bilingual, Theodotion in Aramaic being on one side and Διδάσκαλου on the other, suggests the possibility that just as the Aramaic Theodotion is equivalent to Greek theodotion, so the Greek διδάσκαλος (which does not seem to have been transcribed into Aramaic) is equivalent to the Aramaic ῥαββί.[100] This is evidence that διδάσκαλος was used in the New Testament period in the same manner as teacher-Rabbi. Of uncertain date are Aramaic inscriptions found in and near Jerusalem with the words R. Kaleb R. Joseph;[101] and Rabbi Jehuda[102] from the northwest of Jerusalem near the way to Jaffa; and a Greek inscription with the words Rabbi Samuel[103] of unknown origin. Also of uncertain date are Aramaic inscriptions found at Naoua on the wall of a mosque, one of which has only a possible questionable reference to Rabbi Judan and Rabbi Levi,[104] and another found on a pillar in front of a synagogue at Thella[105] which speaks of Rabbi Mathiah.

Raymond Brown[106] agrees with Zeitlin and others when he says that there is no Jewish evidence for the prefixing of ῥαββί, to the name of any of the sages in the period before 70 A.D. Brown cites E. L. Sukenik who discovered an ossuary on the Mount of Olives in 1929. On one side he found Διδάσκαλος in Greek characters. Sukenik dates this ossuary as being several generations before the destruction of the Temple. Albright, commenting on ascribing the Aramaic name ῥαββί to Jesus of (literally "my master" or the Greek equivalent Διδάσκαλος, literally "teacher") in John, argues that the number of passages where such terms are so ascribed show the lateness of John's Gospel relative to the Synoptics. Such arguments are negated by Sukenik's discovery of the term Διδάσκαλος inscribed on a pre- A.D. 70 ossuary referring to the person whose bones were interred therein."[107] Albright goes on to say that further study of Διδάσκαλος, both archaeologically and linguistically, needs to be done. This study intends to do such an investigation of both ῥαββί and Διδάσκαλος using evidence such as that set forth by Sukenik.[108] When the results of the Jerusalem ossuaries are examined, they give a different picture of the change of meaning of the term ῥαββί as an honorific title. According to Johnston, the earliest evidence for ῥαββί as a title attached to a proper name is seen in the Jerusalem ossuaries dated before A.D 100.[109] The Jerusalem ossuaries and inscriptions, which apparently date before A.D. 100, indicate that men titled ῥαββί were wealthy, and that many were comfortable with the Greek language and with Greco-Roman artistic and architectural styles. In the words of Lapin, "Overall, the inscriptions indicate that the title *rabbî* should be thought of as an honorific roughly equivalent to "sir," with no explicit connection to either teaching or adjudication (much like the colloquial use of Gk *kyrios*)."[110] From this, one may conclude that the title Rabbi is of little value in arguing that it was in use at the time of Jesus. But, one should not forget to see the occurrence of the titles ῥαββί (Jn 1:38) and ῥαββουνί (Jn 20:16) in the Fourth Gospel, where John in both chapters translates the term as διδάσκαλος (teacher).

Hershel Shanks believes the terms ῥαββί and διδάσκαλος are very nearly interchangeable. Harold Mare has the same belief and presents archaeological[111] findings as evidence to prove that the terms ῥαββί and δίδάσκαλος are interchangeable. Reviewing European Jewish inscriptions, most of which are located in Italy, διδάσκαλος is found among those in Venosa[112] and those in or near Rome, the former inscriptions being basically from the 5th or 6th centuries A.D., while those from Rome are from the earliest centuries of the Christian era. Venosa yields an Aramaic inscription[113] with a questionable reading which may be translated, "Severa, daughter of Jacob. Peace." The expanded Greek on the same remains reads, "Here lies Severa, daughter of Jacob, the teacher (διδάσκαλοσ) may her sleep be in peace."[114] Rome (via Portuensis) also yielded an inscription on a marble plaque which may be from the first or second centuries A.D. It reads: "Here lies Eusebis, διδάσκαλος (the teacher, learned in the law.)"[115] Testimony to the occurrence of both ῥαββί and διδάσκαλος in Jewish inscriptions is consistent from the sixth century A.D. back to the time of Christ, both in the few references in Rome-Venosa inscriptions, and the more numerous ones in Palestine. In two or three instances the conclusion drawn is that ῥαββί and διδάσκαλος are equivalent, not only in the latter part of the third century A.D. at Beth Shearim,[116] but also at the time of Christ in Jerusalem,[117] the usage being as described in the NT where ῥαββί, can be interchanged with teacher.

Based on the findings of the ossuary Shanks concludes that "if the title διδάσκαλος was used, "Rabbi" was used also."[118] Brown refers to Shanks and states "If διδασκαλοσ represents Rabbi, the ossuary may indicate that the NT usage of Rabbi is not anachronistic after all."[119] This conclusion may look over- simplistic but it could be that these two titles are interconnected, which would indicate that the title ῥαββί could have been in use at the time of Jesus. It certainly seem evident that the title ῥαββί was used as a honorific title even if someone did not have teaching or adjudicating authority. Furthermore, this title was originally used in the land of Israel to address sages, but in the later days gradually developed into a title for a person qualified to pass decisions or judgements on Jewish Law, or a person who was qualified to interpret Jewish Scriptures and to teach them to his disciples and audience.

Cohen, in his article on Epigraphical Rabbis, has compiled a list of 57 Rabbis who lived at various times in the period of the history being discussed. Of those Rabbis, belonging to different categories and different times, he confidently says, "three apparently lived before 100-400 C.E."[120] Cohen's compilation and conclusion cannot easily be dismissed. Gerd Theissen and Annette Merz propose that earlier Christian sources, which speak about various events before the destruction of the second temple, attest that the title ῥαββί, was the Aramaic equivalent of διδάσκαλέ, and further, that the Scribes and Pharisees who were responsible for interpretation of the Mosaic Law were themselves called ῥαββί (Mt:23:2.7). Like them, the early Christian leaders also claimed this title (Mt 23:8; 13:52).[121] In sum, it would seem unwise to assume that the earlier usage of the term 'Ραββί, is anachronistic.

'Ραββί in the NT: A Conflict between Context and Content

In the context of the broader usage of the title *rab* in the OT, Shanks notes the possessive term ῥαββί in NT texts as a title for an itinerant preacher. Thus he concludes, "It is understandable that the Gospel use of the title might well be authentic."[122] But at the same time, this study is not content with the simple data of the OT texts and with some of the etymological roots of *rab*. From these it cannot be concluded that the Gospel use of ῥαββί is authentic. Consider that it is accepted by most scholars that use of the title Rabbi for ordained scholars does not appear in any Jewish sources before 70 A.D. Shanks himself warns the reader very strongly to avoid any claim that the OT uses of *Rab* is authentic evidence for the use of *Rabbi* in the Gospels. "I do not suggest that these earlier uses of Rab prove that the Gospel use of the title Rabbi is authentic."[123] He once again affirms that the currently available materials do not show a use of the term ῥαββί, as a title for ordained scholars prior to the Roman destruction of the Temple. But a careful observation denotes that he does not say that the title ῥαβ, ῥαββί, or ῥαββουί never existed before the time of the destruction of the Temple.

There is a certain difficulty with the position of Zeitlin in his review of the frequent occurrence of the title Rabbi in the Gospels. If this title does not exist, how is it that the term Rabbi occurs at least fourteen times in three of the four Gospels? Ferdinand Hahn notes that "the fact that ῥαββί in Greek has in part been left untranslated is an indication of the ancient character and currency of this mode of address."[124] For Hahn, the term belongs to a tradition even earlier than the gospel traditions. Hahn also further observes that ῥαββί, and its intensified form ῥαββουί are to be found in an old stratum of the traditions behind the gospels of Mark and John. In this context, one may quote the Gospel of Luke and say that he has not used it at all. But at the same time, it appears in the other three Gospels, notably three times in the earliest Gospel of Mark, and seven times in the Fourth Gospel. In addition, the more respectful term ῥαββουί also occurs once both in Mark and John. Hahn writes that "there is no evidence of the word in the logia source."[125]

Gerhard Schneider opines that "the tradition's inclination to suppress this title (Matthew) or to avoid it completely (Luke) suggests that ῥαββί really was applied to Jesus during his earthly ministry."[126] Hahn, in analysing the title ῥαββί as used for Jesus, suggests that "the address "Rabbi" was in general use at the time, and was especially preferred in respect of the scholars and teachers of the Law." But at the same time, Hahn adds that at the time of Jesus "it was not yet limited to the highly accomplished and ordained scholars."[127] Rainer Riesner agrees that, "In the first century AD Rabbi was not a fixed title for an academically trained and ordained scribe as it became later."[128] But at the same time, Riesner points out that the actual address, 'Rabbi' was used mainly, though not exclusively, for a teacher, and the Gospels accurately reflect this usage. Also consider the position of

Ephraim Kanarfogel, who says that, "The references in the Gospels to Jesus as Rabbi (which occur for the most part in John, and not at all in Luke) have been explained in different ways. Some have suggested that this is an anachronism that was applied after the destruction of the Second Temple. Others have argued that it was an unofficial title for a personal teacher or spiritual leader, a usage that was to be found in the pre- destruction period."[129] Again, this supports the view that the title Rabbi in the Gospels had the sense of teacher and was given to Jesus to designate him a teacher.

It is not fully convincing that the occurrences of the title ῥαββί in the Gospels explain that it was in use at the time of the historical Jesus. Shanks says that the use of the title ῥαββί was evident due to the occurrences in the Gospels. But for Zeitlin this argument is not acceptable. He maintains that in the Fourth Gospel the title Rabbi has been used in various places but that does not necessarily imply that it was in use at the time of Jesus of Nazareth. It merely means that the title Rabbi was in use when the Fourth Gospel was written. For Zeitlin, it is a historical fact that the Fourth Gospel was written or composed not earlier than the middle of the second century A. D. It is also historical that the Gospel was written for the Gentile Christians. Now the title Rabbi should have been a familiar title among the Jews, but for the gentiles, he translates it as teacher. Thus, Zeitlin tries to differentiate the time of the historical Jesus and the time of the Gospels. He maintains the occurrence of the title in the Gospels does not prove that it was used in the time of Jesus. But here the question is, if John writes to the Gentiles, what is the purpose of introducing a term which is unfamiliar to his readers or community and then translates it at the beginning as well as at the end of the Gospel? Even if Zeitlin can ably defend his analysis of the Fourth Gospel, the latest one, what is his answer for the earliest Gospel of Mark, where there are four occurrences of the title Rabbi? From the occurrences of the title Rabbi, in both the Gospels of Mark and John (earliest and latest gospels) as evidence, it can be concluded that the title Rabbi was in use even at the time of the historical Jesus.

In his early work on "Beginnings of Christianity in Judaism," Zeitlin is aware of this problem when he says that, "we must admit that the name ῥαββί "Rabbi" in the Gospels presents a problem." But it seems to be rash to continue, as he does, "in each instance the term was inserted later."[130] He gives no evidence for this, nor does he explain how the terms were inserted later into the texts. As Shanks has rightly pointed out, "Surely this frequent appearance of the term in the Gospels is more persuasive evidence that the title was in fact used at the time of

Jesus than the absence of the term in pre-destruction tannaitic literature is evidence that it was not used."[131] In agreement with Shanks, there is evidence for the use of the title ῥαββί even before the Destruction of the Temple, and so the use of the title Rabbi in the Gospels cannot be entirely rejected as anachronistic.

Summary and Conclusions

Jewish history was reviewed to see how the term ῥαββί was used in the society in which Jesus lived. This was done with a view to see whether the occurrence of the title ῥαββί in the Gospels is anachronistic. In addressing the possibility of the title ῥαββί being a simple anachronism in the turbulent times in which Jesus lived, this study looked in depth at the opposing views of Hershel Shanks and Solomon Zeitlin. Shanks maintains that the use of the title ῥαββί in the Gospels is not anachronistic whereas Zeitlin asserts that the title ῥαββί in the Gospels is purely anachronistic. *With respect to the question of anachronism, it was noted that the term* ῥαββί has been found written on two ossuaries which were dated as being from the Jerusalem area before A.D. 70. It seems probable that the term 'Rabbi' (or an earlier form *rab*) originated shortly before the time of Jesus as a general term of respect for various leading figures, including teachers. A broad overall study of Jewish history clearly indicated that the title ῥαββί in different stages of its development was not necessarily used to denote master-disciple relationship.

It was noted that the title ῥαββί predates the earliest Gospel of Mark and is not used at all in the Gospel of Luke. Furthermore, John appears to use the term interchangeably with the title διδάσκαλος. Finally the significance of the title ῥαββί in the post-resurrection period was also analysed, specifically from the time of the destruction of the Temple in A.D. 70. If it was only after A.D. 70 that ῥαββί became a formal title for a teacher, then it cannot correctly be applied to Jesus. Sherira's letter could be said to confirm the view that, at the time of Jesus, there were no titles and therefore one should regard the title ῥαββί, as given in the Gospels to John the Baptist and Jesus, as anachronisms. Regardless, the designation "Rabbi" may still be more helpful than any other in conveying a true image of Jesus to the average Christian reader of the first century A.D. even today. If it suggests that Jesus was recognized as a teacher in his day and that he was famous enough to draw students to himself, then "Rabbi," although possibly anachronistic, serves a useful purpose.

After much discussion and analysis, we can adopt the position of Hershel Shanks, namely that the many occurrences of ῥαββί in the Gospels cannot simply be rejected as anachronistic, basing the arguments on the broad use of this title in three of the four Gospels, and particularly in Mark and John. The warnings given by many scholars on the question of the use of this title only after the destruction of the second Temple in 70 A.D. have not been ignored. Regarding this we referred to different scholars and finally again agreed with Shanks who says, if the title ῥαββί was in use officially after 70 A.D., it is possible that it was unofficially used in the time of Jesus. We can therefore opt for this view as being the most probable. It seems certain that, in the second century, ῥαββί came to be used as a formal title for an ordained Scribe. In sum, the title ῥαββί in the NT is not anachronistic, but a deeper understanding of its use and meaning is necessary.

It appears that the title ῥαββί, in the first century AD, was attributed to any charismatic religious leader, like Jesus or John the Baptist. Was it used in the sense of a leader being seen as a 'teacher' or dispenser of wisdom? However, even in the time of Jesus, ῥαββί was mainly not used, if it was used at all, exclusively for a teacher. Whether this should be understood in a technical or formal sense of a Rabbi being an 'ordained' official, or in an honorific sense in which the high esteem of their disciples or followers is expressed, is a matter which will be looked at in greater depth in part II. The detailed explanation of the title ῥαββί and its replacement in the Synoptic Gospels with equivalent titles and their significance will be dealt with in detail. The same questions that are raised by David B. Ruderman[132] in his study "Rabbi and Teacher" will be discussed: how to explain the power or authority of a ῥαββί over his community in and before the time of the historical Jesus? Did the ῥαββί hold power over the Jewish community by virtue of his sanctified status as scholar or did he derive his authority from the community itself? Was the Rabbinic function a concept of leadership emerging primarily within the context of Jewish communal institutions or a concept of learning and scholarship unrelated to public service? This approach will help clarify the proper definition as well as the different interpretations of the term ῥαββί in history, but more specifically at the time prior to Jesus and in the first century Judaism. This approach will also provide a strong base to further study the question of whether or not Jesus was called ῥαββί by his contemporaries and whether Jesus was primarily perceived as a Jewish teacher in the early Christian community.

Endnotes

[1] The gospel narratives show Jesus travelling from place to place, depending upon the hospitality of the people; he taught outdoors, in homes, in villages, in synagogues and in the Temple; he had disciples who followed him as he travelled. This is the very image of a Jewish teacher in the land of Israel at that time. Perhaps the most convincing proof that Jesus was a sage was his style of teaching, for he used the same methods of scripture interpretation and instruction as other Jewish teachers of his day. A simple example of this is Jesus' use of parables to convey his teachings. Parables such as Jesus used were extremely prevalent among ancient Jewish sages and over 4,000 of them have survived in Rabbinic literature. The Gospels depict Jesus likewise moving from place to place a great deal, often accompanied by crowds. Mk 6:6, for example, records that Jesus "went around from village to village teaching." He travelled considerably in Galilee, especially in the vicinity of the Sea of Galilee, and there may be evidence in the synoptic gospels of at least one teaching tour in Judea. Much of Jesus' teaching was done indoors: in homes (Lk 10:38-42), synagogues (Mt 4:23), even in the Temple (Mt 21:23; Lk 21:37). But Jesus is also found like a typical first-century Rabbi, teaching outside in impromptu situations. There is a picturesque account in Luke 5:3 of Jesus teaching from a boat. The feeding of the five thousand occurred in a lonely place (Mt. 14:13; Mk. 6:32; Lk. 9:12), and the Sermon on the Mount was so named because it was delivered in a rural location. See, Dennis INGOLFSLAND, "Kloppenborg's Stratification of Q and Its Significance for Historical Jesus Studies", *Journal of the Evangelical Theological Society* 46.2 (2003) 217-232

[2] See, Reginald FULLER, "Jesus Christ", in *The Oxford Companion to the Bible* (1993) 361. Other sources include Richard A. NORRIS, *Understanding the Faith of the Church*, 1979, pp. 159f; Owen C. THOMAS, *Introduction to Theology*, 1983, pp. 155 -171; *The Cambridge Companion to the Bible*, 1997, pp. 460-539; "Son of God" in *The Harper Collins Bible Dictionary*, rev. ed., 1996, pp. 1051ff. The New Testament usage of the Greek noun μαθητής commonly translated "disciple," is a key to understanding what it means to call Jesus a Rabbi. The New Testament uses this word in contexts that give it new significance because of its association with Jesus. The word occurs frequently in the New Testament. Historically, in the Greek language, μαθητής referred to a "student" who would attach himself to a teacher, διδάσκαλος) to acquire theoretical and practical knowledge in a certain discipline. Likewise in the Rabbinic tradition a *talmid* was a student of Torah who would attach himself to a teacher to learn the Scriptures and the traditions of the fathers. In both instances, the pupil would eventually qualify to become a teacher in his own right with the authority to establish his own school, often carrying on and developing further the traditions of his master. In the New Testament the word is used in similar fashion with regard to John the Baptist's disciples (e.g., Mt 11:2; Mk 2:18; Lk 5:33) and the Pharisees (e.g., Mt 22:16; Mk 2:18). However, the primary interest here is

the use of the word to identify followers of Christ. This particular usage is not restricted to the Twelve; in fact, only a small percentage of the occurrences refer exclusively to the Twelve. By far the most common usage generally refers to followers of Christ, and in these contexts there are similarities as well as some striking differences with the common usage of the word disciple. "Disciple" cannot be defined apart from the teacher to whom the disciples in question are attached. Jesus presented himself publicly as a teacher and was well versed in the Rabbinical traditions, even from an early age (Mk 12:18; Lk 2:41–50; 12:13). Although some in the religious hierarchy refused to acknowledge his authority (e.g., Mk 2:1–11; 6:2; Jn 7:15; 8:13–59), he was nevertheless regarded or recognized as a Rabbi by His own disciples as well as the broader public (Jn 1:38; 3:2; Mk 9:5; 11:21). But His teaching and ministry were clearly unique, a fact that is demonstrated in the responses of the crowds who heard and saw Jesus, and recognized in him an authority that was absent from the traditional Rabbis (Mt 7:28,29; Mk 1:27; Lk 4:32,36). Also noted is Jesus' disapprobation of the ambition of the Jewish doctors who preferred to be called by this title, and his admonition to his disciples not to suffer themselves to be so styled (Mt. 23: 7. 8). For a detailed description of this background see, *New International Dictionary of New Testament Theology*, vol. 1, 485–486; *Theological Dictionary of New Testament*, vol. 4, 417-428.

[3] J. C. TURRO, *Rabbi*, p. 882. To find out the exact places and number of occurrences of the title Rabbi in the Gospels, see, ῥαββί in Kurt ALAND, *Vollständige Konkordanz zum griechischen Neuen Testament*, Vol. I, Part 2, Berlin, New York, Walter De Gruyter, 1983, p. 1192.

[4] Cf. esp. P. S. ALEXANDER, *"Rabbinic Judaism and the New Testament"*, *ZNW* 74 (1983) 237–246; J. NEUSNER, *Rabbinic Literature and* the New Testament: What We Cannot Show, We Do Not Know, Valley Forge, Pa., Trinity Press International, 1994; *Idem, The Rabbinic Traditions about the Pharisees before 70,* 3 vols., Leiden, E. J. Brill, 1971. On criteria for the use of Rabbinic materials, see esp. C. EVANS, *Word and Glory*, pp. 20–28. Cf. L. H. SILBERMAN, *"Anent the Use of Rabbinic Material,"* *NTS* 24 (1978) 415–417 and "Once Again: The Use of Rabbinic Material," *NTS* 42 (1996) 153–55; B. GERHARDSSON, *Memory and Manuscript: Oral Tradition and Written Transmission in Rabbinic Judaism and Early Christianity*, Uppsala, C. W. K. Gleerup, 1961, pp. 15. 77–78; G. F. MOORE, *Judaism in the First Centuries of the Christian Era*, Cambridge, MA, Harvard University Press, 1962, 3:17–22.

[5] Joseph KLAUSNER, *Jesus of Nazareth*, translated by H. DANBY, New York, Macmillan, 1945, p. 43, footnote 93, and p. 256, footnote 16.

[6] G. GRAETZ, *Geschichte der Juden*, Ill, 2

[5] J. KLAUSNER, *op. cit.*, pp. 29, 43. 759; IV[3], n. 9, pp. 399- 400;

[7] Erwin R. GOODENOUGH, *Jewish Symbols in the Greco-Roman Period*, Vol. 1, New York, Pantheon Books, Bollingen Series, XXXVII, 1953, p. 90, footnote 200.

[8] Solomon ZEITLIN, *The Title Rabbi in the Gospels is Anachronistic*, in *JQR* 51 (1961) p. 122. To learn more about the problem of anachronism with regard to the title "Rabbi" given to Jesus, read, S. ZEITLIN, *JQR* 53 (1962-63) 345-349; H. SHANKS, *JQR* 53 (1962-63) 337-345; H. SHANKS, *JQR* 59 (1968-69) 152-157; S. ZEITLIN, *JQR* (1968-69) 158-160; G. VERMES, *Jesus the Jew*, pp. 115-122, ELLISON, *NIDNTT* III, 115f; VIVIANO, *RB* 97 (1990) 207-218; R. RIESNER, *Jesus als Lehrer,* WUNT 2/7, 3d ed., Tübingen, J. C. B. Mohr, Paul Siebeck, 1988, p. 186; H. LAPIN, *ABD* 5 (1992) 600-602.

[9] H. SHANKS, *Is the Title "Rabbi" Anachronistic in the Gospels?*, p. 337.

[10] *Ibid.*, p. 338.

[11] When discussing the letter of Sherira Gaon, written to the community of Kairwan in the 10th century AD, it seems reasonable to doubt the validity of using a document written in the 10th century to substantiate an argument about a matter concerning first century Judaism. Zeitlin rightly questions to what extent it can be given serious attention and to what extent it can be considered as a historical proof. Zeitlin also holds this idea when he says that "no medieval document written in the tenth century can be employed and used as the source for the history of the second Jewish Commonwealth." For more details, refer to the Reply by Solomon ZEITLIN to Hershel SHANKS, *"Is the Title "Rabbi" Anachronistic in the Gospels?"*, p. 345. But at the same time, this study thinks that one may not simply reject this document as outdated. One must remember that it has been quoted by many authors and has been widely referred to on this question of the usage of the title ῥαββί before the destruction of the Second Temple. It is from the letter of Sherira that Zeitlin comes to a conclusion that ῥαββί is anachronistic in the Gospels. On the other hand, Hershel Shanks who maintains that the use of the title ῥαββί in the Gospels is not an anachronism, also quotes from the first part of the letter where it speaks about the use of ῥαββί and ῥαβ respectively in Palestine and Babylon. Thus for this study, the letter of Sherira has led not to conclusions but to complications.

[12] Cf. Jonathan Z. SMITH, ed., *Judaism 101*, in *The Harper Collins Dictionary of Religion,* Harper Collins Publishers Inc., 1995.

[13] S. BYRSKOG, *Jesus the Only Teacher*, p. 95. Though the letter of R. Sherira describes the history of the title, for Byrskog it is too late to serve as primary evidence for the tannaitic and amoraic periods.

[14] S. ZEITLIN, *Beginnings of Christianity and Judaism*, p.392.

[15] *Ibid.*

[16] H. SHANKS, *Is the Title "Rabbi" Anachronistic in the Gospels?*, p. 338. It is advisable to be careful about this question: is the Hillel I mentioned in this letter the contemporary of Jesus or the father of the Hillel who is said to be the contemporary of Jesus of Nazareth? According to tradition, Gamaliel the Elder who first bore the title ῥαββαν is said to be the son or grandson of Hillel.

According to Shanks, it is impossible to date lives such as Hillel's with accuracy. A reasonable estimate is that his important activity occurred during the period 30 B. C. -10 A.D.

[17] L. I. RABBINOUITZ, *Rabbi & Rabbinate*, p. 1447.

[18] C. COULOT, *Jésus et le Disciple*, p. 259.

[19] *Ibid.*

[20] S. ZEITLIN, "*The Title Rabbi in the Gospels is Anachronistic*", p. 160.

[21] H. LAPIN, *Rabbi*, p. 601.

[22] *Ibid.* In the Period before 135 A. D., *Rabbî* is used as an address for a judge. In legal disputes, presumably, the senior member of the dispute was called *Rabbî*.

[23] According to J. L. McKenzie, the Rabbis whose opinions are collected in the Mishna are called *Tannaim*, which means 'teachers.' See, J. L. MCKENZIE, "*Talmud*" in *Dictionary of the Bible*, p. 866.

[24] J. L. McKenzie says that the Rabbis whose opinions are collected in the Talmud are called *Amoraim* which means 'speakers' or 'interpreters.' See, J. L. MCKENZIE, "*Talmud*" in *Dictionary of the Bible*, p. 866.

[25] Bruce CHILTON, *A Galilean Rabbi And His Bible, Jesus' Own Interpretation of Isaiah*, London, SPCK, 1984, p. 20.

[26] *Lev. Rab.* 34, 130d.

[27] Cf. Str-B 1:917, 971; E. LOHSE, "Rabbi", p. 962, n. 19; and R. RIESNER, *Jesus als Lehrer*, p. 268.

[28] '*Abot R. Nat.* 14.

[29] E. KANARFOGEL, "*Rabbinate*", p. 7578. Kanarfogel affirms his position by saying that, prior to the destruction, even the greatest sages such as Hillel and Shammai were referred to without any honorific title.

[30] H. LAPIN, *Rabbi*, p. 601. W. Dennis Tucker agrees with this proposition. See, W. Dennis TUCKER, Jr., "*Rabbi, Rabboni*" in David Noel FREEDMAN, ed., *Dictionary of the Bible*, Grand Rapids, M. I., Cambridge, U. K., William B. Eerdmans Publishing Company, (2000) 1105-1106, p. 1106. Tucker affirms that the use of Rabbi as an official term for an ordained scholar belongs to the period after the destruction of the temple in 70 A.D.

[31] W. D. TUCKER, Jr., *Rabbi, Rabboni*, p. 1106.

[32] S. HIMELSTEIN, *Rabban*, p. 567. Himelstein asserts that the first person in Jewish history to receive the title *rabban* was Rabban Gamaliel the Elder. "*Rabban*" becomes a title given only to patriarchs, the presidents of the Sanhedrin. The first person to be called by this title was the patriarch Gamaliel I. The title was handed down from him to all succeeding patriarchs. Gamaliel I received this title because he presided over the Sanhedrin alone without an *ab bet din* beside him, thus becoming the sole master. This derivation, however, is disproved by the fact that Gamaliel' father, Simon b. Hillel, was not called by that title,

although he was the sole president of the Sanhedrin and had no *ab bet din* beside him. It is more likely that there was no special reason for the title, beyond the fact that the people loved and honoured R. Gamaliel, and endeavoured in this way to express their feeling.

[33] H. SHANKS, *Is the Title "Rabbi" Anachronistic in the Gospels?*, p. 338.

[34] S. ZEITLIN, *The Title Rabbi in the Gospels is Anachronistic*, p. 159.

[35] H. SHANKS, *Is the Title "Rabbi" Anachronistic in the Gospels?*, p.392. According to Jewish history, it is from the time of Gamaliel that the Sanhedrin was led by a single leadership who was named as *Nasi* also called ραββαν meaning 'our Master'. The great body of the Jews was entrusted under the leadership of *Nasi*, abolishing the previous structure of the leadership of two men. The first *Nasi* was Gamaliel the First. Thus according to Zeitlin, it is clear that this title ραββί which evolved from the position of *Nasi* is concerned with authority over the law and the Scriptures which are very important in the Jewish Religion and history. ραββί is not the title for any scholar and it is not for the whole body of the Sanhedrin. Only those who were the authorities over the law were called Rabbis. So a ραββί in this period is the one who decides, teaches and interprets the law.

[36] S. HIMELSTEIN, *Rabbi and Rabbinate*, p. 567.

[37] R. HERTZ, *Rabbi, Rabbinate*, p. 788.

[38] J. E. SAFRA, (ed.), *Rabbi*, p. 871.

[39] To learn more on this subject, read, Emil SCHÜRER & Geza VERMES et al., *The History of the Jewish People in the Age of Jesus Christ*, Vol. II, Edinburgh, Clark, 1973, pp. 325-326. To read more about the Jewishness of Jesus read, S. SAFRAI & M. STERN, ed., *The Jewish People in the First Century: Compendia Rerum Iudaicarum ad Novum Testamentum*, Philadelphia, Fortress, 1974, 1976; Jacob NEUSNER, ed., *Christianity, Judaism, and Other Greco-Roman Cults*, Leiden, Brill, 1975; James ROBINSON, *The Nag Hammadi Library in English*, San Francisco, Harper and Row, 1977; James H. CHARLESWORTH, *The Old Testament Pseudepigrapha*, Garden City, Doubleday, 1983, 1985; James H. CHARLESWORTH, *"From Barren Mazes to Gentle Rappings: The Emergence of' Jesus Research"*, *Princeton Seminary Bulletin* 7 (1986); E. P. SANDERS, *Jesus and Judaism*, Philadelphia, Fortress, 1985; Donald GOERGEN *The Mission and Ministry of Jesus*, Wilmington, Michael Glazier, 1986; Richard HORSLEY, *Jesus and the Spiral of Violence*, San Francisco, Harper and Row, 1987; Burton MACK, *A Myth of Innocence: Mark and Christian Origins*, Philadelphia, Fortress, 1988; Marcus BORG, *Jesus: A New Vision*, San Francisco, Harper and Row, 1987.

[40] A. J. KÖSTENBERGER, *Studies on John and Gender*, p. 71. Theissen and Merz comment that there is a widespread view that in the case of Jesus, 'Rabbi' was merely "a respectful form of address for people in higher positions." See, G. THEISSEN & A. MERZ, *The Historical Jesus*, p. 358. The above opinion is based on the use of ραββί in Rabbinic writings, which refer to the conferring of

the 'title' Rabbi only to scholars living after 70 AD. In the opinion of Theissen and Merz, there is little connection between Jesus and these Scribes.

[41] Gustaf Hermann DALMAN, *The Words of Jesus: Considered in the Light of Post-Biblical Jewish Writings and Aramaic Language*, Edinburgh, Clark, 1902, p. 331.

[42] *Ibid.* Indeed, the fact that the same designation was attributed to Jesus implies that he was seen as a Rabbi in that society.

[43] H. SHANKS, *Origins of the Title "Rabbi"*, p. 155. On the existence of the title 'Rabbi' in ancient history, see, S. J. D. COHEN, *Epigraphical Rabbis*, pp. 1-17.

[44] Idem., *Is the Title "Rabbi" Anachronistic in the Gospels?*, p. 340.

[45] S. ZEITLIN, *The Title Rabbi in the Gospels is anachronistic*, p. 158. According to Zeitlin, in no literature is the title mentioned. He also mentions some historical literature where one might expect the title to appear but does not. In the writings of Josephus, the Apocryphal literature and Philo, the early tannaitic literature, before the destruction of the Temple the title 'Rabbi' is not mentioned.

[46] Cf. Rainer RIESNER, *Jesus as Preacher and Teacher in Jesus and the Oral Gospel Tradition*, Sheffield, UK, JSOT, 1991, p. 188; S. J. D. COHEN, "Epigraphical Rabbis", *JQR* 72 (1982) 1–17. Cf. further M. HENGEL, *Charismatic Leader and His Followers*, p. 43, n. 20.

[47] H. SHANKS, *Is the Title "Rabbi" Anachronistic in the Gospels?*, pp. 339-340.

[48] The details on "The *Tosefta*" that are mentioned in the article of H. SHANKS, *Origins of the Title "Rabbi"*, p. 155 were originally taken from Rabbi A. N. Orenstein who refers to the use of Rabbi before the destruction. The Tosefta reads as follows: "He who has disciples and whose disciples again have disciples is called *Rabbi*. When his disciples are forgotten i.e. because they taught so long ago or perhaps "are ordained", he is called *Rabban*..."

[49] According to McKenzie, there are quite number of bodies of Rabbinical literature which are similar in form and content. The *Tosefta* is one of them and means 'additions.' The Tosefta is a collection of opinions of the *Tannaim* (teachers) found outside the Mishna. But the source and origin of this collection (The *Tosefta*) is obscure. See, J. L. MCKENZIE, *"Talmud"* in *Dictionary of the Bible*, p. 866.

[50] H. SHANKS, *Origins of the Title "Rabbi"*, p. 155. Here Shanks refers to Professor Saul Lieberman of the Jewish Theological seminary who is considered to be an authority on Tosefta.

[51] S. ZEITLIN, *The Title Rabbi in the Gospels is Anachronistic*, p. 160.

[52] *Idem., Beginnings of Christianity and Judaism*, p. 293.

[53] W. BACHER, *"Gamaliel I"*, in *JE* 5 (1903) 558-559, p. 559.

[54] H. SHANKS, *Is the Title "Rabbi" Anachronistic in the Gospels?*, p. 339. According to Hershel Shanks, it is difficult to establish with precision the time when Gamaliel lived. In the NT, the name Gamaliel is mentioned twice, once in Ac 5:34 as a doctor of the law and in Ac 22:3 as Paul's teacher. But it is not certain whether this Gamaliel in Acts is the same as Rabban Gamaliel. If Gamaliel, as many claim, was a contemporary of Jesus then one can definitely say that the title Rabbi in the Gospels is not anachronistic.

[55] S. ZEITLIN, *The Title Rabbi in the Gospels is Anachronistic*, p. 159.

[56] H. SHANKS, *Origins of the Title "Rabbi"*, p. 154.

[57] *Idem, Is the Title "Rabbi" Anachronistic in the Gospels?*, p. 340.

[58] W. Harold MARE, *Teacher and Rabbi in the New Testament*, Grace *Theological Journal* 11.3 (1970)11-21.

[59] P. J. B. FREY, *Corpus Inscriptionum Judaicarum*, vol. I, Europe; vol. II, Asia, Africa, Rome, Pontificio Instituto di Archeologia Cristiana, 1936 (vol. I), 1952 (vol. II).

[60] E. R. Goodenough states that, outside Palestine, the names and little inscriptions are predominantly in Greek till the third or fourth centuries, then in Latin. See, E. R. GOODENOUGH, *Jewish Symbols in the Greco-Roman Period*, vol. 12, New York, Pantheon Books, Bollingen Series XXXVII, 1965, p. 51.

[61] According to Frey's second volume on Asia-Africa, occurrences of Rabbi-didaskalos in that volume are to be found only on Palestinian inscriptions. See, P. J. B. FREY, *Corpus Inscriptionum Judaicarum*, vol. I, Europe, vol. II, Asia, Africa, Rome, Pontificio Instituto di Archeologia Cristiana, 1936 (vol. I), 1952 (vol. II).

[62] According to R. H. Gundry, from archaeological data, proof now exists that all three languages in question such as Hebrew, Aramaic, and Greek were commonly used by Jews in first century Palestine. R. H. GUNDRY, *The Use of the Old Testament in St. Matthew's Gospel*, Leiden, E. J. Grill, 1967, p. 175.

[63] Cf. R. H. GUNDRY, *The Use of the Old Testament in St. Matthew's Gospel*, Leiden, E. J. Grill, 1967, p. 176.

[64] P. J. B. FREY, *Corpus Inscriptionum Judaicarum*, n. 1165.

[65] *Ibid.*, n. 857. See also, E. R. GOODENOUGH, *Jewish Symbols in the Greco-Roman Period*, Vol. 1, p. 24.

[66] See M. AVI YONAH, "*Mosaic Pavements in Palestine*," Quarterly of the *Department of Antiquities in Palestine, London*, II (1932) 178; III (1933) 40.

[67] P. J. B. FREY, *Corpus Inscriptionum Judaicarum*, n. 989.

[68] *Ibid.*, n. 990.

[69] *Ibid.*, n. 979.

[70] Compare, E. R. GOODENOUGH, *Jewish Symbols in the Greco- Roman Period*, Vol. 1, p. 213; and AVI YONAH, *Q. D. A. P. X* (1942), plate XXVI, 8, and p. 131.

[71] M. Schwabe in his work on Greek inscriptions found at Beth-Shearim in the fifth excavation season of 1953 suggests a date of the third or the first half of the fourth century A. D. for these inscriptions. See, M. SCHWABE, *Israel Exploration Journal*, IV (1954) 260.

[72] P. J. B. FREY, *Corpus Inscriptionum Judaicarum*, nn. 1039, 1041, 1052, 1055, 1158.

[73] *Ibid.*, n. 994.

[74] *Ibid.*, n. 1055.

[75] *Ibid.*, nn. 995, 1033.

[76] *Ibid.*, nn. 1006, 1041.

[77] *Ibid.*, n. 1052.

[78] *Ibid.*, n. 1158.

[79] Compare, E. R. GOODENOUGH, *Jewish Symbols in the Greco- Roman Period*, Vol. 1, p. 90.

[80] Compare the remarks of G. Dalman: "In the time of Jesus rabben had not yet became ribbon." See, G. DALMAN, *op. cit.*, p. 324 footnote 3. See, P. J. B. FREY, *Corpus Inscriptionum Judaicarum*, nn. 1006 and 1052.

[81] P. J. B. FREY, *Corpus Inscriptionum Judaicarum*, vol. 1, p. 118.

[82] *Ibid.*, p. 119.

[83] *Ibid.*, n. 892.

[84] *Ibid.*, n. 893. Frey says in a note that "biribi is a contraction for *birribi* (Jerusalem dialect), son of Rabbi with which they would honor the doctors of the law." P. J. B. FREY, *Corpus Inscriptionum Judaicarum*, vol. 2, p. 121.

[85] *Ibid.*, n. 895.

[86] *Ibid.*, n. 900. "The title *Rab* is Babylonian and that of *Rabbi* is Palestinian." Cf. I. BROYDE, "*Rabbi*" in *The Jewish Encyclopedia*, I. SINGER, ed., vol. X, New York, Funk and Wagnalls, 1912, p. 294.

[87] While granting some problems regarding the paleography of the inscription, Vincent argues epigraphically and archaeologically for a date not later than the time of Herod, the Great, seeing in the Jordan Valley a blend of Jewish settlers, possibly the Idumeans, and free artistic energy in which animals and even the human figure are portrayed in architecture which fits in with this time. See, L. H. VINCENT, *Revue Biblique*, XXVIII (1919), p. 558; S.A. COOK, "*The 'Holy Place' of Ain Duk*", *Palestine Exploration Fund Quarterly Statement* (1920) 86-87. See also, P. J. B. FREY, *Corpus Inscriptionum Judaicarum*, vol. 2, p. 245.

[88] P. J. B. FREY, *Corpus Inscriptionum Judaicarum*, n. 1199.

[89] Compare Dalman's remarks, "The Targumic mode of using rabban is recalled in Mk 10:51, Jn 20:16, by the term addressed to Jesus, rabbounei (another reading, rabboni; D Mark, rabbei; John rabbonei...)" G. DALMAN, *Op. cit.,* R. H. Charles in a note on *Pirke Aboth* 1:16 says that Rabban was a title first used for Gamaliel to indicate his being the head of the house of Hillel. R. H. CHARLES, *Apocrypha and Pseudepigrapha of the Old Testament,* vol. 2, Oxford, At the Clarendon Press, 1913, p. 686.

[90] *Ibid.,* n. 1353.

[91] See, P. J. B. FREY, *Corpus Inscriptionum Judaicarum,* vol. 2, p. 305, who refers this inscription to Sukenik, *Juidische Graber Jerusalems um Christi Geburt,* 1931.

[92] It is interesting that in Ac 5:34 Gamaliel is called *nomodidaskalos timos panti toi laoi*

[93] P. J. B. FREY, *Corpus Inscriptionum Judaicarum,* nn. 1264-1272.

[94] *Ibid.,* n. 1269.

[95] *Ibid.,* n. 1268. The word there is somewhat deformed as *Decdekallou* which Frey readily recognized as *didaskalou.* Cf. *Idem., Corpus Inscriptionum Judaicarum,* vol. 2, pp. 267-268.

[96] P. J. B. FREY, *Corpus Inscriptionum Judaicarum,* n. 1218.

[97] *Ibid.,* n. 1285.

[98] P. J. B. FREY, *Corpus Inscriptionum Judaicarum,* Vol. 1, n, 1266.

[99] R. SUKENIK, *Judische Graber Jerusalems urn Christi Geburt,* 1931, pp. 17f., through P. J. B. FREY, *Op. cit ,* vol. 2, p. 266.

[100] Frey takes, Διδάσκαλος in nn. 1266 and 1269 as equivalent to ραββί. P. J. B. FREY, vol. 2, pp. 267-268. See also A. ALBRIGHT, *op. cit,* p. 158.

[101] P. J. B. FREY, *Corpus Inscriptionum Judaicarum,* n. 1403, El-Aqsa. Yet, the text here is uncertain.

[102] *Ibid.,* n. 1410.

[103] *Ibid.,* n. 1414.

[104] *Ibid.,* n. 853.

[105] *Ibid.,*n. 971. See J. W. JOSEPHUS, III, 3, 1 for the location of this place.

[106] R. E. BROWN, *The Gospel According to John* (AB 29 & 29A), 2 vols., Garden City, NY, Double Day, 1966-1970, p. 74.

[107] W. F. ALBRIGHT, *"Discoveries in Palestine and the Gospel of John",* in *The background of the New Testament and Its Eschatology, Studies in Honor of C. H. Dodd,* ed., by W. D. DAVIES and D. DAUDE, Cambridge, The University Press, 1964, pp. 157-158.

[108] Cf. G. KITTEL, *Theologisches Worterbuch Zum Neuen Testament,* Vol. II (1935) 150-162, p. 154. For Albright, it should have been emphasized that

rabbounei (Jn 20:16) like the corresponding Rabbinic expression is a caritative of Rabbi standing for rabboni, 'my dear or little master.' See, ALBRIGHT, *"Discoveries in Palestine and the Gospel of John"*, in *The background of the New Testament and Its Eschatology*, p. 158.

[109] G. H. JOHNSTON, p. 1032. The oldest example that can be dated with certainty is a Jerusalem ossuary from before 70 AD that has διδάσκαλος. See also, H. LAPIN, *"Rabbi"*, p. 601.

[110] H. LAPIN, *Rabbi*, p. 601. When the term 'office' is used, it always implies that there are a set of rights and duties connected to the position one holds. The person who has acquired or is entrusted with such a position has functional responsibilities. By the term "title" is meant that it is an honorary designation/ name given to a person with no connection to any specific office.

[111] W. Harold MARE, *Teacher and Rabbi in the New Testament, Grace Theological Journal* 11. 3 (1970) 11-21.

[112] The inscriptions of Venosa, dating from the sixth century after Christ, still present us with substantially the same picture as those of Rome, the oldest of which probably belong to one of the earliest centuries A. D. Cf. Emil SCHLIRER, *A History of wish People in the Time of Jesus Christ*, Second Division, tr. S. TAYLOR and P. CHRISTIE, vol, II, New York, Chas Scribner's Sons, 1891, p. 247.

[113] P. J. B. FREY, *Corpus Inscriptionum Judaicarum*, n. 594.

[114] *Thegater Iakob didaskalou.*

[115] P. J. B. FREY, *Corpus Inscriptionum Judaicarum*, n. 333. Frey says that "the catacomb was certainly not in use in the first century; but the second and third centuries was the period of greatest activity." See, P. J. B. FREY, *op.cit.*, vol. 1, p. 211.

[116] *Ibid.*, nn. 994, 1055, 1006, 1041, and 1052.

[117] *Ibid.,* n. 1266.

[118] H. SHANKS, *Is the Title "Rabbi" Anachronistic in the Gospels?*, p. 345. See also, Graham N. STANTON, *The Gospels and Jesus*, The Oxford Bible Series (1989), pp. 184-5.

[119] R. E. BROWN, *John*, p. 74.

[120] S. J. D. COHEN, *Epigraphical Rabbis*, p. 10.

[121] G. THEISSEN & A. MERZ, *The Historical Jesus*, p. 355.

[122] H. SHANKS, *Origins of the Title "Rabbi"*, p. 154.

[123] *Ibid.*, p. 155.

[124] F. HAHN, *The Titles of Jesus in Christology*, p. 74.

[125] *Ibid.* For Hahn, conversations and narratives scarcely occur in Q. Though Rabbi does not appear in the saying source, its equivalent διδασκαλε

is found in Mt 8:19 & 12:38 and can possibly go back to Q. Hahn also agrees that a sure conclusion cannot be drawn.

[126] G. SCHNEIDER, *Rabbi,* and *rabbouni,* p. 206. Schneider maintains that the title Rabbi belongs to the pre-Markan tradition but he also agrees that there is no single utterance in the logia source, the Q.

[127] F. HAHN, *The Titles of Jesus in Christology,* p. 74. Thus Hahn makes two things clear, or he puts forward two opinions 1. The title Rabbi was in general use and the ordination or high scholarly studies were not pre- requisites. 2. Rabbi was in general use but specially preferred for the teachers of the law who are specifically mentioned as Scribes.

[128] Rainer RIESNER, *Jesus as Preacher and Teacher in Jesus and the Oral Gospel Tradition,* Sheffield, UK, JSOT, 1991, p. 186.

[129] E. KANARFOGEL, *"Rabbinate",* p. 7578.

[130] S. ZEITLIN, *Beginnings of Christianity and Judaism,* p. 393.

[131] H. SHANKS, *Is the Title "Rabbi" Anachronistic in the Gospels?,* p. 342.

[132] D. B. RUDERMAN, *"Rabbi and Teacher",* p. 741-742.

Part - II

The Relevance of the Title 'Ραββί, A Synoptic Perspective for Jesus

This book's quest to understand fully the meaning of the title ῥαββί in the Gospel of John began in part I, by looking at the historical genesis of the term ῥαββί. Now with some understanding of why Jesus was addressed as Rabbi, this study will move into the area of the Synoptic Gospels. In the gospels, besides ῥαββί, Jesus is given many titles such as Messiah, Prophet, Lord, Son of man, and Son of God. It is mostly understood that these titles attest to Jesus' divinity and very rarely to his humanity. Some historians argue that when used in other Hebrew and Aramaic texts of the time, these titles also have other meanings, and therefore may have other meanings when used in the gospels as well. In the gospels, it is understood that titles or names have a significance which shed light on the characters and are not just a means of identification. That is, any occurrence of a title has a significance intended to help identify their characteristics.

In an exegetic method, understanding the names or titles given to Jesus help to understand the account in which he appears. In other words, the analysis of denotations and connotations by names and titles makes it possible to say, from the viewpoint of the author, that in each account it allots a character to Jesus. It helps reveal whether the person who speaks gives the titles or names is in the group of Jesus' disciples or, on the contrary, in the group of opponents or non-believers. In the Synoptic Gospels, it is a fact that the same terms or titles for Jesus can be understood differently from one gospel to the other. The meaning of the names or titles with which Jesus is usually addressed is also connected to the Christological understanding or revelation of each author. If these questions about the use of such titles are looked at in more detail, it becomes clear that there are systematic comparisons among titles in the three gospels. It will be noted that certain episodes contain several occurrences of the same address or different addresses. The question is whether the connotations which are used are the same for each evangelist. When the titles attributed to Jesus are analysed, the historical question of whether he himself used titles or whether he acted in such a way that they were naturally assigned to him after his Resurrection, must remain an open one. In a nutshell, the above questions form the scope for Part II, chapter one in this book.

Chapter two takes a different stand on the discussion of how and why Jesus could be considered a Rabbi. It will embrace the synoptic perspective but still incorporate certain comparisons with the Fourth Gospel, which is the core of this present study. Part I of the book clearly showed that the title 'Rabbi', in the first century AD, was attributed to any charismatic religious leader. John P Meier,[1] in his study on the historical Jesus, very specifically embraces the category of ραββί as a most suitable title or designation for him. In addressing Jesus as Rabbi, the question is whether this should be understood in a technical or formal sense of being an 'ordained' official, or whether it should be understood in an honorific sense, in which his disciples or followers express their high esteem for him. This is discussed in greater depth in chapter two.

Endnotes

[1] J. P. MEIER, A Marginal Jew: Rethinking the Historical Jesus, Vol. 3., p. 276. There are many indications in the New Testament that Jesus was regarded as Rabbi and a teacher. In Mark, his main activity is shown as teaching the disciples and other people (Mk 4:38). Therefore his disciples and others naturally addressed him 'teacher' (Mt 8:19). He followed the Jewish customary practise of a Rabbi in going to the synagogues (Mk 4: 23, Lk 4: 15-16) and teaching others. Read also, James M. ROBINSON, A New Quest for the Historical Jesus, Studies in Biblical Theology 25, London, SCM Press Ltd., 1959; David FLUSSER, Jesus: Biography of the Life of Jesus, Jerusalem, Magnes Press, 1998; William R. FARMER, Jesus and the Gospel, Philadelphia, Fortress Press, 1982; Paula FREDRIKSEN, Jesus of Nazareth, King of the Jews: A Jewish Life and the Emergence of Christianity, Vintage Books, USA, 2000; Sean FREYNE, Jesus, a Jewish Galilean: A New Reading of the Jesus Story, Edinburgh, Continuum International Publishing Group, T & T Clark, 2004.

Chapter - 1

Terms Equivalent to ʽΡαββί
in the Synoptics

Introduction

Part I of this book briefly noted that in the New Testament the title ῥαββί was one sought by religious leaders, evidently for its flattering effect (Mt 23:2,7). It is used: by disciples of their teacher (Jn 9:2); in a general sense by the public as a whole (Jn 6:25); as a term of respected authority (Mk 9:5), of one coming from God himself (Jn 3:2); and perhaps even as a term of endearment (ῥαββουνί Jn 20:16). The terms ῥαββί and διδάσκαλος appear to be understood in the Gospels as equivalents (cf. Jn 1:38 and Jn 20:16). The complex of ῥαββί διδάσκαλος and μαθητὴς (disciple, learner), that is, the master- teacher and his group of followers is presented regarding Jesus and his disciples in Jn 1:37-38; 4:31; 9:2; 11:8, and also for John the Baptist and his group (Jn 3:26). It is an established fact that the terms ῥαββί and διδάσκαλος are to be found in, and belong to, the first century A.D.

W. Harold Mare observes that there exists "in the New Testament one of the clearest illustrations that the two terms are to be taken as equivalents in meaning."[1] This is very clear in Mt 23:8 where Jesus warns his disciples against taking the title "Rabbi" because he alone is their διδάσκαλος and again in Jn 1:38 and 20:16 where Rabbi (Jn 20:16, ῥαββουνί) is interpreted as διδάσκαλος. In the contemporary New Testament literature the "doctors" or teachers were considered to be experts in the law[2] and they were to be respected and obeyed.[3] In the writings of the

Apostolic Fathers,[4] a special attention is given to Jesus, as "our only teacher" (διδάσκαλος). That an equivalence is meant to be taken at face value in Jn 1:38 is seen in a similar equivalence between Μεσσίας and Χριστός in Jn 1:41. Sometimes, however, κύριος and ἐπιστά# are given as equivalents of rabbi (Mk 9:5, rabbi compared with Mt 17:4, κύριε and Lk 9:33[5] ἐπιστάτης and Mk 10:51, ῥαββουνί with Lk 18:41, κύριε) and διδάσκαλος (Mk 4:38, διδάσκαλέ compared with Mt 8:25 and Lk 8:24, ἐπιστάτα and Mk 9:17, and Lk 9:38 διδάσκαλος compared with Mt 17:15, κύριε).[6] It is necessary, therefore, to explore the various terms used by the synoptic authors in order to determine the equivalent of the term 'Rabbi' in various contexts. In the Synoptic Gospels, there are various occurrences: the most frequent address for Jesus is, κύριε. 35 times versus 27 for διδάσκαλέ 6 for ἐπιστάτα 5 for ῥαββί; 1 for ῥαββουνί plus 25 occurrences of other addresses. The principal addresses for Jesus in the synoptic Gospels are distributed as follows:

Titles	Mark	Matthew	Luke	Total
διδάσκαλε	10	6	11	27
ῥαββί	3	2	-	5
ῥαββουνί	1	-	-	1
κύριε	1	18	16	35
ἐπιστάτα	-	-	6	6

A number of persons in the gospels address Jesus by a title - e.g. teacher, sir, master - when they speak to him. In parallel episodes in the synoptic Gospels these titles undergo changes. In the New Testament there are five Greek words[7] and one Aramaic word that are translated into the English word 'master' with reference to Jesus as a "master" or a "teacher." Byrskog[8] opines that the primary terms describing the basic trait of Jesus as teacher are different forms of διδάσκαλος and of the related verb διδάσκειν and noun διδαξῆ; yet the depiction of Jesus as teacher is of course not restricted to uses of this term only. Byrskog states that there are other relevant terms and concepts as well. This chapter begins with a comparative study of the titles addressed to Jesus in Matthew, Mark and Luke and ends with a description of the titles proper to each Gospel. The first observation is that the addresses and titles for Jesus in the Synoptic Gospels are not uniform. One finds a variety of expressions in each evangelist. Part II chapter one presents some charts[9] covering the occurrence of different terms or titles that are used in addressing Jesus. The chart given below demonstrates that Jesus is called ῥαββί in the gospels.

1. Occurrence of the Title ῥαββί in the Gospels

Events	Mt	Mk	Lk	John
Call of the First Disciples	-	-	Cf. 5:8 κύριε	1:38 ῥαββί διδά σκαλε 1:49 ῥαββί,
Stilling the Storm	8:2 5 κύριε	4:38 διδάσκαλε	8:24 ἐπιστάτα ἐπιστάτα	-
Discourse With Nicodemus	Cf. 22:16 διδάσκαλε	Cf. 12:14 διδάσκαλε	Cf. 20:21 διδάσκαλε	3:2ῥαββί διδάσκαλος
John's Testimony	-	-	-	3:26 ῥαββί,
Discourse with the Samaritan woman	-	-	-	4 : 3 1 ῥαββί
Jesus at Gennesaret	-	-		6:25 ῥαββί,
Transfiguration	17:4 κύριε	9:5 ῥαββί	9:33 ἐπιστάτα	-
Healing of the Man born Blind	-	-	-	9:2 ῥαββί,
Healing of the Blind Men	20:33 κύριε	10:51 ῥαββουνί	18:41 κύριε	Cf.9:36 κύριε (Sir) Cf.9:38 κύριε (Lord)
Raising of Lazarus	-	-	-	11:8 ῥαββί, 11:27 κύριε 11:28 διδα/σκαλος
Withered Fig Tree	21:20	11:21 ῥαββί,	-	-

Woe to the Scribes and	23:7 ῥαββί, 23:8 ῥαββί,			Cf. 13:13 διδάσκαλος
Jesus Foretells His Betrayal	26:22 κύριε 26:25 ῥαββί	-	-	13:25 κύριε
Jesus Arrested	26:49 ῥαββί,	14:45 ῥαββί	-	-
Resurrection appearance	-	-	24:34 κύριος	20:2.13 κύριον 20:16 ῥαββουνί, 20:18.20.25 κύριον 20:28 κύριος 21:7 κύριος

The above chart is useful in reviewing, by event, Jesus' various titles, including ῥαββί in the Gospels. With this chart one can quickly note that the title ῥαββί occurs more in the Fourth Gospel than in the Synoptic Gospels and are ascribed mostly to Jesus. Hershel Shanks also observes that "The title Rabbi is used frequently in the Gospels, especially as a form of address for Jesus."[10] In these passages Jesus is either referring to himself as a teacher, or the adherents confer the title ῥαββί or teacher to Jesus. The New Testament uses ῥαββί to mean 'teacher' or 'master.' In the New Testament the title ῥαββί is used in only three of the gospels. John was writing in Greek, but ῥαββί is an Aramaic or Hebrew word, so he explains to the reader what ῥαββί means. John uses 'teacher' as a translation of the title ῥαββί The New Testament calls Jesus 'teacher' about 47 times. When Dalman observes the synoptic use of the term ῥαββί in the Gospels, he says that the Aramaic term *Rab*, transliterated into Greek ῥαββί "is explicitly recognised as the common form of address to Jesus."[11] But it is evident that the synoptic writers have not only used the title ῥαββί for Jesus. The following section will focus on the terms equivalent to ῥαββί that occur in the synoptic Gospels.

2. ῥαββί and ῥαββουνί in Mark

Events	Mk	Mt	Lk
Transfiguration (Peter)	9:5 ῥαββί	17:4 κύριε	9:33 ἐπιστάτα
Announcing the betrayal by Judas (Judas)		26:25 ῥαββί	
Arrest of Jesus (Judas)	14:45 ῥαββί	26:49 ῥαββί	[22:47-48]
The fig tree (MK: Peter; Mt: The disciples)	11:21 ῥαββί	21:20	

Looking at ῥαββί first, it is noted that the address ῥαββί appears only in Mark and Matthew. In the previous section, the occurrences of ῥαββί in the gospels were noted to demonstrate that the title was in use at the time of Jesus of Nazareth. Mark uses ῥαββί three times (9:5; 11:21; 14:45) and in one place he uses the term ῥαββουνί (10:51). But, the meaning or interpretation of the title ῥαββί is not equal in every case. Mark allows only disciples[12] to address Jesus as ῥαββί (9:5; 11:21; 14:45); both disciples and "outsiders" call him "teacher." Among the synoptic writers, when Mark uses the term ῥαββί in three instances, it is always used for the sole purpose of the disciples' response to Jesus' miraculous actions. The term ῥαββί is used by Peter at the Transfiguration (Mk 9:5) and again in the episode of the withered fig tree in 11:21.

Riesner, speaking of Mark's use of ῥαββί for Jesus, states that "on theological grounds the first evangelist preferred for Jesus the more distinguished κύριε as the address by the followers." For Riesner, there is no clear tendency in Mark to use these titles for Jesus. There is a very different pattern in Matthew and in Luke, where disciples are not allowed to call Jesus διδάσκαλε 'teacher', although other people do so (six times in Matthew, twelve in Luke). Matthew reserves ῥαββί for Judas (Mt 26;25. 49) and in several passages has disciples call Jesus 'Lord' (e.g. Mt 8:25; 17:4. 15). Luke avoids the Aramaic word ῥαββί in six places .

Jesus is addressed ἐπιστάτα as 'master', a word found only in Luke. These variations seem to reflect concern about the special relationship between Jesus and the disciples.

Events	Mk	Mt	Lk
Curing the Blind Men	10:51 ῥαββουνί,	20:33 κύριε	18:41 κύριε

Looking next at ῥαββουνί, it is noted that in Mark, "Jesus is addressed by both followers and outsiders as ῥαββί or with the more dignified parallel form ῥαββουνί and διδάσκαλε."[13] This shows that, in the Synoptic Gospels, Mark is the only one to use the title ῥαββουνί and that appears only once in his Gospel. It is the title by which Bartimaeus, the blind man, addresses Jesus immediately before being cured (10:51). The account belongs to the triple tradition. Matthew (20:33) and Luke (18:41), both replace it by κύριος. Luke avoids it here perhaps because it would be an incomprehensible term for his readers of Greek origin. The two evangelists in any case choose an address which is frequently used in their accounts, thus avoiding the problems of interpretation. James Donaldson notes the title ῥαββί in the Markan Gospel and opines that "on each occasion the use of ῥαββί as a form of address is made by a disciple of Jesus, while ῥαββουνί is used by one who becomes a disciple."[14] Solomon Zeitlin observes this occurrence in Mark and opines that it is a "real translation from the Hebrew *adonai*, my Lord."[15]

ʽΡαββί in Matthew

In the Gospel of Mark, the term ῥαββί occurs only in three episodes. The same is true in the Gospel of Matthew but with different connotations. Of his four uses of the term, two caution Jesus' disciples against allowing themselves to be addressed as Rabbi and two are by the traitor Judas (26:25.49). According to Riesner,[16] in the Gospel of Matthew, Jesus discouraged his disciples from appropriating the title Rabbi (23:8.48), which stood in contrast with contemporary Jewish practice[17] where a student, after several years of association with his teacher, earned the right to be addressed as Rabbi. The one similarity is that whether it is of Peter in Mark or Judas in Matthew, this address is used only by one of the Twelve. The three Markan episodes have parallels in Matthew. However, Matthew avoids the address ῥαββί by Peter and uses it only in the mouth of Judas, during the arrest of Jesus (Mt 26:49). The only other occurrence of ῥαββί in Matthew is in a specific addition. In the triple tradition, during the last meal of Jesus with his disciples, the disciples start to question Jesus as to who will betray him. Each one asks him while saying, "Would this be me, κύριος "(Mt 26:22). Matthew then repeats the same question by Judas, but the address is then ῥαββί (26:25). The traitor is distinguished by using an address different from the other disciples. The address ῥαββί is thus used negatively by Matthew; it comes from the mouth of him who will betray Jesus, and always in a context where treason is spoken of; whereas Mark places this address in the mouth of Peter, and Matthew replaces it by κύριος. In the account of the Transfiguration (Mt17:4) and in the account of the fig tree (Mt 21:20) it is replaced with κύριος.

F. Hahn observes that in comparison with Mark, "Matthew ...has quite deliberately restricted the use of the term; Rabbi is the mode of address which is accepted by the scribes, but of which there is no question as far as the disciples of Jesus are concerned."[18] In Matthew, in regard to Jesus, the term ῥαββί is used only by the traitor Judas, but Matthew consistently avoided its use by the other disciples of Jesus. Hayim Lapin observes that the occurrences of ῥαββί in Matthew are purely polemical.[19] In Matthew, Jesus is more often presented as διδάσκαλος than ῥαββί. Could it be to safeguard Matthew's presentation of Jesus *as the Jewish Messiah* that Matthew avoids presenting Jesus as a Jewish Rabbi? Samuel Byrskog[20] opines that Matthew maintains or adds such terms as ῥαββί and διδάσκαλος only when persons who are not positively related to Jesus use them. When it is a didactic designation to Jesus, Matthew replaces it either with κύριε or omits it altogether. With Mark, whether this address r'abbi, comes from Peter or Judas, it still comes from one of the Twelve. Three Markan episodes have parallels with Matthew but the latter avoided the address ῥαββί.

There are two more references in Matthew which do not directly refer to Jesus but the term ῥαββί is mentioned. In these particular occurrences, Dalman observes, "Jesus forbade his disciples to allow themselves to be called ῥαββί on the ground that he alone was their 'Master.'"[21] In Mt 23:7-8, one may note both the use of the terms ῥαββί and διδάσκαλος. Jesus is warning his disciples not to seek to be called ῥαββί and he continues to tell them that they have only one διδάσκαλος. Zeitlin notes here that διδάσκαλος is found in some of the manuscripts with κύριος which means 'guide or master' instead of teacher. Zeitlin holds that the correct reading should be κύριος. Moreover, for Zeitlin, the whole passage of Mt 23:7-8 where the terms ῥαββί and διδάσκαλος appear, are to be seen as a "later interpolation or that the Greek translator did not fully comprehend the original text."[22] Thus, the use of the title ῥαββί in Matthew is disputed by some and, indeed, seems to have a negative connotation when it is used.

'Ραββί in Luke

Although Luke does not completely avoid the term "master" in addressing Jesus, "he does not incorporate the Aramaic word ῥαββί."[23] However, Luke often used διδάσκαλος even though he "preferred ἐπιστάτα which at times he has editorially inserted."[24] Luke probably has several reasons for avoiding the title ῥαββί. First, some hold that he wanted to avoid Aramaic terms, considered incomprehensible for most of the Greek converts. Donaldson opines that "this is thoroughly consistent with Luke's policy of omitting all Hebrew or Aramaic words from his Gospel."[25] Ed Tenhor, while quoting Pelikan over this issue, observes the following: "Luke takes Mark's use of the word rabbi and substitutes it with the word "Master" or "Lord", doing a little reducing of the Jewishness or "de-judaizing."[26] The second reason might be to contrast with Matthew. He could have wanted to avoid the title ῥαββί which is used by Matthew in a negative way.

Thus, the two occurrences of ῥαββί in Mark, belonging to passages which have parallels in Luke, were modified by Luke. He replaced this address by another term ἐπιστάτα in the mouth of Peter during the Transfiguration (Lk9:33). And Judas does not say anything during the arrest of Jesus (Lk22:47-48). This explains why the connotation attached to ῥαββί in Mark is not absolutely obvious. What is clear is that neither Matthew nor Luke perceive the real meaning of Markan use of the title ῥαββί and they both fail to develop the term ῥαββί in a particularly positive way when it is pronounced in their gospels. From this, one may conclude that the term ῥαββί is distinctive to Mark but as to why is not absolutely clear. What is clear is that the title ῥαββί is not often used by Matthew or Luke. Even when Matthew does use the term, he does so with a negative connotation. By neglecting the title ῥαββί in the case of Judas, one may infer that Luke deliberately wished to downgrade the place of Judas in his gospel. In other words, the absence of any address by Judas to Jesus could indicate that Luke is reluctant to give Judas the same status as the other disciples of Jesus. At the same time, when the title ῥαββί is used by the disciples Peter and Judas, it may be inferred that this title was used to address the historical Jesus, although this cannot be said with any certainty. Another possibility is that both Matthew and Luke chose a form of address that was in common use. And it avoids any confusion with the Aramaic term ῥαββουνί.

3. Jesus as Διδάσκαλος in the Synoptic Gospels

In the New Testament the term διδάσκαλος is used 58 times, 48 of which are in the gospels, mostly applied to Jesus.[27] There are also various instances where the evangelists portray Jesus as διδάσκαλος[28] The following chart shows the various occurrences of the vocative διδάσκαλε in the Synoptic Gospels.

Events	Mk	Mt	Lk
Stilling the Storm	4 :38 διδάσκαλε	8:25 κύριε	8:24 ἐπιστάτα 2x
Healing of the demoniac child	9:17 διδάσκαλε	17:15 κύριε	9:38 διδάσκαλε
The rich young man	10:17.20 διδάσκαλε ἀγαθέ διδάσκαλε	19:16.20 διδάσκαλε	18:18.21 διδάσκαλε ἀγαθε
The entry into Jerusalem		(21:16)	19:39 διδάσκαλε
The tax to Caesar	12:14 διδάσκαλε	22:16 διδάσκαλε	20:21 διδάσκαλε
On Resurrection	12:19.(28) διδάσκαλε	22:24.(33) διδάσκαλε	20:28.39 διδάσκαλε διδάσκαλε
First Commandment	12:28.32 διδάσκαλε	22:36 διδάσκαλε	10:25 διδάσκαλε
On the Destruction of the Temple	13:1.4 διδάσκαλε	24:1.3.	21:5.7 διδάσκαλε

The demand of the Sons of Zebedee	10:35 διδάσκαλε	20:21	
Who is not against us ...	9:38 διδάσκαλε		9:49 ἐπιστάτα
To follow Jesus		8:19 διδάσκαλε	9:57
The sign of Jonas		12:38 διδάσκαλε	
Against the Pharisees			11:45 διδά σκαλε
At the house of Simon the Pharisee			7:40 διδάσκαλε
As an Arbiter of inheritance			12:13 διδάσκαλε

Vincent Taylor asserts that "Teacher is a much more common term in the synoptics."[29] Taylor adds that, of twenty-four examples of διδάσκαλός nineteen are in the vocative. These, with the remaining five, "show that during his ministry Jesus was spoken of as the Teacher."[30] It is clear that the title διδάσκαλος is used by the evangelists to intimate that Jesus was perceived as a teacher in that community. But to what extent is this true in the Synoptic Gospels? Seven of the nine episodes in which the address διδάσκαλε appears in Mark belong to the triple tradition. Among these episodes, one can distinguish the cases where the address is the same in the three evangelists and the cases where it varies. The address διδάσκαλε is common to the three evangelists in four episodes. One finds it in the mouth of the rich man who meets Jesus, and in the three questions which are posed to Jesus in the Temple of Jerusalem concerning the tax due to Ceasar, the resurrection of the dead and the first commandment. In the three other episodes belonging to the triple tradition where Mark uses διδάσκαλέ Matthew prefers the title κύριος. These are the episodes of the storm and of the demoniac child. Again, Matthew avoids any address at the episode of the destruction of the Temple. On the other hand, Luke preserves the address διδάσκαλε in the demoniac child and the destruction of the Temple, but replaces it by ἐπιστάτα in the account of the stilling of the storms. The following references are given to substantiate how the applications of the titles to Jesus differ among the evangelists. Mt 8:25: "And his disciples came to him, and awoke him, saying, Lord, save us, we perish." Mk 4:38: "And he was in the hinder part of the ship, asleep on a pillow, and they awake him, and say unto him, Master, do you not care that we perish?" Did the disciples address Jesus as "Lord" κύριος or as "master" διδάσκαλος In Aramaic, there may have been no difference, nor in Greek. Both Greek words can carry the sense of the master. The use of κύριος as a divine title in the early church may have led Matthew to select it here, though he does have others (mostly non-believers) call Jesus διδάσκαλος and Mark does have people call Jesus κύριος (Mk 9:24).

Among the episodes belonging to the triple tradition, the address διδάσκαλε is used in Lk 19:39, in the entry into Jerusalem. It is at the end of the account and appears to be an addition specific to Luke. Two last occurrence of διδάσκαλε in Mark belong to the episodes, which have parallels only in one of the two other evangelists. In "The request of sons of Zebedee" which occurs in the double tradition Mk/Mt, James and John ask Jesus that they sit on his right-hand side and his left when he comes in glory (Mk 10:35; in Mt 20:21. It is the mother of the disciples who formulates the request, but without giving any address to Jesus). In "Who is not against us is with us", double tradition of Mk/Lk, the disciples of John ask Jesus to prevent a foreign exorcist from driving out demons in his name (Mk 9:38), Lk 9:49 replaces διδάσκαλε by ἐπιστάτα. Three episodes of the double tradition Mt/Lk comprise the address διδάσκαλε but always in only one of the two evangelists, and there is no mention of a different address in the other evangelists. This may indicate an editorial intervention. In Mt 8:19 in the episode, which shows a scribe maintaining that he wishes to follow Jesus, it is the scribe who says to Jesus that he wants to follow him everywhere; in the parallel of Luke (9:57), it is about an anonymous character. In Mt 12:38 in the episode of the sign of Jonas, they are scribes and Pharisees who address Jesus to ask him for a sign by calling him διδάσκαλε. There is no occurrence of the address διδάσκαλε in Matthew which explains the Jewish ritual cleansing laws. On the other hand it appears twice in Luke. In Lk 7:40, which speaks about sinners at Simon's place, it is Simon the Pharisee who addresses Jesus and in 12:13, which is the passage asking Jesus to arbitrate between two brothers over the question of a heritage, it is an anonymous character who asks Jesus, as διδάσκαλε, to arbitrate a division.

Διδάσκαλος in Mark

Mark, while depicting Jesus as ῥαββί, frequently also uses the Greek term διδάσκαλος.[31] Seven of the nine episodes in which διδάσκαλος appears in Mark belong to the triple tradition. In the three other episodes belonging to the triple tradition when Mark uses διδάσκαλος, Matthew prefers the title κύριε both in the stilling of the storm, and the cure of the demoniac. But Matthew uses neither διδάσκαλος nor κύριε when it comes to the passage on the destruction of the Temple.

The last two occurrences of διδάσκαλε in Mark belong to the episodes that have no parallels with either of the other evangelists. As has already been noted, in the request of the sons of Zebedee in the double tradition of Mark and Matthew, James and John request Jesus to give them the right to sit one at his right and one at his left when he comes in his glory (Mk 10:35). In Mt 20:21 it is the mother of the disciples who formulates the request, but without any title addressed to Jesus. In the verse with "one who is not against us is with us" in the double tradition of Mark and Luke, Mark's διδάσκαλε (Mk 9:38) is changed to Luke's ἐπιστάτα (Lk 9:49). Thus, the variety of usage shows that this form of address was not only used and recognised by his disciples, but also by others. Hence, in the opinion of Donaldson, "there is no distinction made in Mark's gospel as to who uses διδάσκαλε"[32] The wide usage of διδάσκαλος in Mark shows that Jesus is not receiving any attribute of special dignity.

Jesus was accorded this form of address "because he outwardly conformed to the picture of a teacher of his day."[33] Rudolf Schnackenburg in his *Jesus in the Gospels* observes that in Mark, the image of the teacher Jesus is strengthened by his frequently being addressed as διδάσκαλος, both by his disciples (Mk 4:38; 9:38; 10:35; 13:1) and by other people. Thus for Schnackenburg, the address 'teacher' for Jesus is certainly used in the gospels. Schnackenburg adds that in the Gospel of Mark, "we have the usual respectful addressing of a Jewish teacher, not yet limited to educated scribes; it is the translation of the Aramaic *Rabbi* or *rabboni*."[34] James Donaldson notes that διδάσκαλε being the Greek equivalent of *teacher* is the most common form of address in the Gospel of Mark, and it is used there "instead of the transliteration of the Hebrew *Rabbi*."[35] Lapin[36] notices that the term διδάσκαλος in Mark is used to refer to Jesus both by his disciples and non-disciples alike. Dalman opines with regard to Mark's use of διδάσκαλος that "the Greek διδάσκαλε is attested with special frequency"[37] as an address given to Jesus.

Διδάσκαλος **in Matthew**

Jesus is referred to as διδάσκαλος (*Didaskalos* as transliteration) in Mt 8:19; 9:11; 12:38; 17:24; 19:16; 22:16; 22:24.36; 26:18. Samuel Byrskog states that, "within an intersynoptic perspective, the material occurs in the triple tradition, the double tradition and Matthew's special material."[38] Matthew uses the term διδάσκαλος twelve times,[39] altogether more often than ῥαββί. Samuel Byrskog states that "all instances refer explicitly or implicitly to Jesus."[40] From this he concludes (p. 208) that "Jesus should be referred to merely as "the teacher." For Byrskog, "Ὁ διδάσκαλος is at this point a clear reference to the only teacher of the disciples." On p. 212 he asserts that, "nowhere is there an indication that Jesus would reject the terms. On the contrary, Jesus – the main character whose point of view is normative in the story - acknowledges the terms providing the didactic characterization." On p. 214, Byrskog adds that, "In the Matthean story, the foundational and normative connotations of the didactic terms find their concretisation in texts showing that Jesus interacts as διδάσκαλος with various characters." On p. 215, Byrskog explains that "Jesus often interacts with persons outside of the group of the disciples. In three out of the twelve cases of διδάσκαλός the person using the term, though not antagonistic to Jesus, reveals no attitude of confessional belief (8:19; 17:24; 19:16)." The term expresses merely that they interact with Jesus as teacher. Byrskog also holds the view (p. 207) that the narratives frequently depict Jesus as a teacher, presumably active close to the temple (21:23; 26:55).

Byrskog states (pp. 215-216) that in the Gospel of Matthew, the Pharisees use διδάσκαλος on four occasions. They use διδάσκαλος either directly (9:11; 12:38) or indirectly through others (22:15f. 34-36). "When they speak about Jesus as διδάσκαλος, they are alone (9:11); when they address Jesus, they appear together with other characters. Their use of the term indicates an interaction of conflict." In Mt 9:11; 12:38; 22:15f. 23f. 34-36, the characters with evident negative traits use διδάσκαλος in reference to Jesus. They represent the religious leaders of the Jewish people. Byrskog concludes the whole discussion with the following statement (p. 218). What we see in the gospel of Matthew is that "out of the twelve occurrences of διδάσκαλος, eight occur on the lips of characters expressing a lack of faith or a thoroughly negative estimate of Jesus' person and teaching. But this does not give the term a derogatory connotation." Hence, the term διδάσκαλος is not derogatory in itself but is when the persons who apply that title to Jesus appear to be opposed to him or indifferent. The foundational and normative connotations that the Matthean story attaches to the didactic terms oppose such a negative understanding. The terms express a confessional or a faith attitude of the person towards Jesus. Διδάσκαλος as a title for Jesus emerges to express that Jesus is a teacher by virtue of his teaching and dialogue. Again, Jesus as διδάσκαλος in the sense of 'teacher' enters into open debate with his detractors, and shows himself as ready to defend his arguments, the proof of a genuine teacher.

In the opinion of Donaldson, "the only use of διδάσκαλος by a disciple of Jesus, is found in Matthew 26:49, when Judas betrays Jesus, and so denies his discipleship."[41] So for Donaldson it is only those who are opponents of Jesus, or who are neutral with regard to his identity, who address Jesus as διδάσκαλος in Matthew. Bornkamm[42] observes that Matthew maintains or adds such terms as διδάσκαλος and ῥαββί only when persons who are not positively related to Jesus use them. Kittel opines that "Mt. in his reshaping of the Markan material reserves διδάσκαλε for the Pharisees, Judas Iscariot and the uncommitted."[43] Thus, for Matthew, reservations about Judas addressing Jesus as διδάσκαλε are clearly implied. Donaldson also states that "In Matthew's Gospel διδάσκαλε is not used as a form of address by the disciples of Jesus, but is restricted to those who do not recognise Jesus as κύριος."[44] A separate study of the use of the title κύριος in reference to Jesus would be needed to address this point.

Διδάσκαλος in Luke

Jesus is addressed as διδάσκαλος in Lk 7:40 (Peter), 9:38 (man from the multitude), 10:25 (a certain lawyer), 11:45 (one of the lawyers), 12:13 (someone in the crowd), 18:18 (a certain ruler), 19:39 (some of the Pharisees), 20:21 (scribes and chief priests), 20:28 (Sadducees), 20:39 (some of the scribes), 21:7 (disciples). To this should be added the references in 8:49 and 22:11. Luke retains the address διδάσκαλε in the episodes of the demoniac and the destruction of the Temple, while it is replaced by ἐπιστάτα in the narrative of the stilling of the storm. Among the episodes belonging to the triple tradition, it is necessary to mention the address διδάσκαλε in Lk 19:39, in the narration of the entry into Jerusalem. Thus, Kittel observes here that "Lk. in his Markan material either keeps διδάσκαλε or substitutes ἐπιστάτα."[45] Riesner observes that, "Luke, writing mainly for non-Jews, did not use the term ῥαββί at all. Apparently he was also careful to avoid the address διδάσκαλε in the mouth of the disciples although he preserved this form of address on the lips of non-followers."[46] Here Riesner asserts that, based on the historical information of his sources, the evangelist Luke accepted that Jesus was addressed as a Jewish teacher, but "with the suppression or alteration of the address διδάσκαλε in the mouths of believers, Luke underlined that for him Jesus was far superior to any teacher."[47] Riesner also applies the same principle to Matthew. "There is no use of διδάσκαλε on the lips of the disciples, and when Judas addresses Jesus twice as ῥαββί (Mt 26:25.29), it is only an exception which confirms the rule: the traitor is no longer a disciple."[48] All these observations indicate that in contrast to Mark, the evangelists Matthew and Luke carefully avoid placing the address διδάσκαλε in the mouth of the disciples. When such an occasion does arise, Matthew replaces the address διδάσκαλε by κύριε (Mt 8:25) or avoids it (Mt 20:21; 24:1). Luke chooses to place ἐπιστάτα in the mouth of the disciples (8:24; 9:49) to distinguish them from those who address Jesus as διδάσκαλε (Lk 21:7). Here the question arises; why do Matthew and Luke carefully avoid putting διδάσκαλε into the mouths of the disciples? Is it because διδάσκαλε implies a negative attribution towards Jesus?

It may be noted that, contrary to what one might conclude at first reading, the title διδάσκαλε in the gospel of Matthew and Luke is not reserved to requests for teaching. Therefore it is possible that Matthew and Luke modify this address διδάσκαλε to other terms, when they place it in the mouth of the disciples, since in their view it implies a kind of negative connotation, something they do not wish to attribute to Jesus. If Matthew and Luke do not replace the term διδάσκαλε with another term, it could mean that it has a neutral connotation or sometimes a negative understanding of Jesus on the part of the disciples rather like the opponents of Jesus. However, when διδάσκαλε comes from the mouth of the disciples, Luke and Matthew distinguish them from the general public who see Jesus merely as a teacher. The fact that the disciples – particularly those who had a direct and close association with Jesus – use the term ἐπιστάτα or κύριος implies that they have reached a deeper understanding of who Jesus is. For Luke and Matthew, this is an important factor in the portrayal of the disciples, and of course of Jesus himself, to their respective communities.

Parallels between ῥαββί and διδάσκαλος

In the Gospel, there are different titles for Jesus but each one reflects a particular "colour", namely, an aspect of his profound reality. The prevalent title of teacher has already been discussed. It is known that, according to the New Testament Gospels: the scribes and Pharisees desired the title (Mt 23:2, 7); that it was used of formally unschooled teachers such as John the Baptist and Jesus by their inner circle of μαθηταί and by the crowds; and that it carried with it a sense of respect and authority. Apart from the title ραββί meaning the equivalent of the term διδᾶσκαλος[49] (with the connotation of 'teacher') the title is used extensively in all the four gospels. In looking at Jesus as a 'teacher' and making a comparison between the Synoptic Gospels and the Fourth Gospel, it is noted that while John frequently provides the Hebrew/Aramaic term ραββί the Synoptists generally use the Greek equivalent διδᾶσκαλος. In the first instance where ραββί is used, John translates ραββί as διδᾶσκαλος (1:38). He does the same at the end of the Gospel where the variant ραββουνί is used (20:16). Dalman[50] also notes the frequent occurrence of the term διδᾶσκαλος in the gospels. He opines that the fact that the Gospels often employ διδᾶσκαλε as a form of address presupposes that ραββί was the original title used.[51] Consequently, it can be inferred that ραββί was already a designation for a teacher. R. Riesner[52] observes that in all the four gospels Jesus is addressed as διδάσκαλε, the vocative of διδάσκαλος, which translates in Hebrew/Aramaic as Rabbi. From a historical review it was found that the term ραββί at the time of Jesus was not a new term. For Riesner, if Jesus was seen and addressed as a Rabbi, then it can further be assumed that he also acted in some ways like a Jewish teacher. Hans Schwarz in his *Christology* opines that "the first impression Jesus gave to his contemporaries was that he acted like a scribe. Accordingly he was addressed as "Rabbi" (Mk 9:5) or synonymously as "teacher" (*didaskalos;* Mk 9:17)." He cites Jesus' entry into the synagogue and teaching (Mk 1:21), his immediate followers (or disciples) (Mk 3:7); the way he taught them (Mk 8:31) and how they, in turn, instructed others (Mt 10:7). Thus he observes, "Jesus may indeed be seen in close connection with the Rabbinic tradition."[53] H. F. Weiss also observes that Jesus' teacher role and his connection with the Jewish tradition is unmistakable. Jesus' teaching in the synagogue and his Sermon on the Mount correlate to his being seen as a διδάσκαλος in the eyes of the Jewish community. He also agrees that "The term διδάσκαλος corresponds to the term ραββί."[54] For Weiss, all these instances are evidence to support his view that Jesus is a teacher in the line of ordinary Jewish tradition.

Although inscriptions could not be expected to yield much in the way of enlightenment regarding the full meaning of ραββί and διδᾶσκαλος, they now and again reveal additional information as to the import of the concepts, and to the type of person who was given these titles.[55] In the third and fourth centuries A.D., according to the Jewish history, rabbis were honoured as having helped monetarily with a building at Sepphoris[56] and an inn at Er Rama in Galilee.[57] In an inscription of questionable date, Rabbi Mathiah is commemorated for having given money for the construction of a pillar before the synagogue at Thella.[58] It cannot be proved, however, that the persons were addressed as ῥαββί due to having contributed funds. One Rabbi Tanhum[59] is identified as being a Levite and one Rabbi Samuel,[60] on a Jerusalem inscription, is called chief of the synagogue. On one of the early Roman inscriptions[61] the title διδάσκαλος is supplemented with the adjective *nomomathes*, learned in the law.

To summarize, it is observed that the title ῥαββί together with διδάσκαλος, began to be used in the sense of teacher-master about the time of Jesus, as is evidenced by the New Testament Gospels. Some evidence from early archaeological inscriptions and the corroborative evidence from Josephus and Philo also bear testimony to the use of equivalent terms like ῥαββί and διδάσκαλος. Then, as the transition between the Jewish tradition and Christian Church continued, the term ῥαββί no longer had a place in the latter as is evidenced by the lack of the use of the term ῥαββί in the New Testament outside of the Gospels.[62] Even διδάσκαλος outside the Gospels is sparingly used in the Acts and the Epistles. This latter term seems to be reserved basically for Jesus.[63] This is corroborated in the Apostolic Fathers where ῥαββί does not occur at all and where διδάσκαλος is used but relatively infrequently. On the other hand, as Judaism continued and developed in its own way, the title ῥαββί became increasingly important in Jewish practice and tradition as is evidenced by Talmudic tradition. How much official technical significance the title ῥαββί– διδάσκαλος carried in the New Testament period would be very difficult to determine on the basis of literary and archaeological records.[64] The available early evidence simply does not allow going beyond that.

4. Lukan Jesus as ἐπιστάτης

In the New Testament, this word ἐπιστάτης occurs only in the Gospel of Luke where it is used seven times, always in the vocative, to address Jesus. ἐπιστάτα is given as a noun used in the vocative singular masculine, which means, an appointee over, i.e. commander, (teacher), master. It occurs five times as an address to Jesus (Lk 5:5; 8:24, 24.45; 9:33.49; 17:13). In two cases, ἐπιστάτα modifies the pre-existing addresses: in the episode of the stilling of the storm, ἐπιστάτα replaces the διδάσκαλε of Mark. In the episode of the Transfiguration, ἐπιστάτα (Lk 9:33) replaces ῥαββί, which was placed by Mark in the mouth of Peter (Mk9: 5). Finally in Lk 8:45, Luke introduces ἐπιστάτα in the remarks of Peter which Mark allotted without any address to the group of the disciples (5:31). In 9:49, "Who is not against us is for us..." in the double tradition Mk/Lk, Luke reproduces almost word for word the text which one finds in Mk 9:38, but replaces διδάσκαλε by ἐπιστάτα For greater clarity, the occurrence of ἐπιστάτα in the Synoptic Gospels is shown in the chart.

Events	Mk	Mt	Lk
Stilling of storms	4:38 διδάσκαλε	8:25 κύριε	8:24 ἐπιστάτα 2x
Woman with hemorrhage	5:31		8:45 ἐπιστάτα
The Transfiguration	9:5 ῥαββί	17:4 κύριε	9:33 ἐπιστάτα
Who is not against us...	9:38 διδάσκαλε		9:49 ἐπιστάτα
Miraculous catch of fish			5:5 ἐπιστάτα
Ten lepers			17:13 ἐπιστάτα

The first and the last occurrence of ἐπιστάτα in the Gospel of Luke belong to the simple tradition of Luke: (Lk 5:5 and 17:13). In 5:5, Simon responds to Jesus who invites him to throw the nets into the sea for a catch. He points out to Jesus, calling him ἐπιστάτά that they have spent the night without success. Nevertheless, he responds to Jesus and throws out the nets. After the miraculous catch, he falls at the knees of Jesus and addresses him as κύριε. This change of title should be noted carefully: this variation in address occurs in the same episode, and from the same person. In 17:13, ten lepers plead with Jesus: "Jesus, ἐπιστάτα have pity on us." The ten are cured, but only one returns to thank God. He is a Samaritan, and it appears that the episode takes place on the border between Galilee and Samaria. This address was previously reserved to the disciples in the first part of the Gospel of Luke (1:1 - 9:50) and appears only once more, from the ten lepers.

It may be useful to note here the interchange of address: when Mark gives Jesus the title ῥαββί, Luke uses an alternative for the same episode. As was already noted, Luke has completely avoided using the Hebrew/Aramaic term ῥαββί with reference to Jesus. However, Luke does use the

Greek term διδάσκαλος and he introduces another Greek term ἐπιστάτα which also has the equivalent meaning of *teacher*. Luke uses the term διδάσκαλος in Lk 7:40; (8:49); 9:38; 10:25; 11:45; 12:13; 18:18; 19:39; 20:21; 21:7; (22:11) 28:39. The two references within brackets are of the term being used when not directly addressed to Jesus but when spoken of Jesus.

Ἐπιστάτης: **Replacing the Inadequacy in** ῥαββί **and** διδάσκαλος
Kittel observes that ἐπιστάτα in Luke has its "independent rendering."[65] In two cases, Luke modifies the synoptic address that already exists. In the case of the 'Stilling of the Storm' Markan διδάσκαλε is replaced by ἐπιστάτα. Again, in the episode of the Transfiguration, ἐπιστάτα (Lk 9:33) replaces Markan ῥαββί (Mk 9:5) coming from Peter. And finally, in the case of the woman with a haemorrhage, Luke introduces ἐπιστάτα (Lk 8:45) spoken by Peter, whereas in Mark (Mk 5:31) it is attributed to the group of the disciples in general. In Lk 9:49, in the case of "Who *is not against us is with us...*", in the double tradition of Mark and Luke, Luke replaces the Markan διδάσκαλε (Mk 9:38) by ἐπιστάτα (Lk 9:49). The last two occurrences of ἐπιστάτα (Lk 5:5; 17:13), shown in the above chart, belong to the simple tradition of Luke. In Lk 5:5, Simon responds to Jesus before the event of the astounded catch of fishes. After the miracle, Simon falls to the knees of Jesus and addresses him by the title κύριε (Lk5: 8). In Lk 17:13, the ten lepers address Jesus with the title ἐπιστάτα.

When Taylor observes the equivalent titles that present Jesus as a teacher in the gospel of Luke, he adds that "Luke appears to have felt the inadequacy of διδάσκαλος, for when the disciples are the speakers he prefers to use ἐπιστάτα (Master), a word which he has used six times."[66] L. Sabourin observes that in the Synoptic Gospels the occurrence of διδάσκαλος, in the proper sense of teacher, is frequent. Sabourin agrees that the Synoptists have also used διδάσκαλος in place of ῥαββί or ῥαββουνί. But coming to Luke, Sabourin notes that, "finding the term inadequate for the Saviour, Luke often preferred the expression ἐπιστάτα."[67] In Dalman's observation, "the form ἐπιστάτα occurring six times in Luke alongside the commoner διδάσκαλε is a Greek synonym for the latter."[68] Dalman adds that both ἐπιστάτα and διδάσκαλος in Luke can be traced back to the Aramaic term ῥαββί. For Lapin, ἐπιστάτα in Luke "corresponds once to the Markan Rabbi (Lk 9:33; Mk 9:5) and twice to διδάσκαλος (Lk 8:24; Mk 4:38; Lk 9:49; Mk 9:38)."[69] But Donaldson disagrees with this position of Dalman and Lapin and says that in the original Hebrew roots ἐπιστάτα reveal the meaning related to "authority" "superintendent" or "overseer." So for Donaldson, Luke's use of ἐπιστάτα "as a synonym for διδάσκαλε cannot be accepted."[70] The word ἐπιστάτα in the NT occurs only in Luke and one finds six occurrences, always in the vocative form, to address Jesus. All these occurrences are found when Jesus is challenged to reveal his full authority. Thus in the opinion of Donaldson "ἐπιστάτα is not a neutral word for Luke, but is used to express the idea that for him Jesus is a man with full authority."[71] As already noted, in the Gospel of Luke, the title ἐπιστάτα has been reserved only for the disciples in the first part of the gospel (1:1–9:50) and later only for the ten lepers in Lk 17: 13. A second observation is that Luke uses ἐπιστάτα to replace the Markan ῥαββί or διδάσκαλε. This replacement seems to be an alternative that Luke uses in addition to κύριε.

5. Synoptic Jesus as κύριος

The word κύριος is difficult to translate because it has a very wide range of meanings. It can mean "sir," a term of polite address or it can mean "master." For example, when a servant (slave) addressed his master, he would most likely call him κύριος meaning "master" or "owner", because κύριος also describes one having "power" or "authority." But there is another use of κύριος that is more significant here. In the Greek translation of the Old Testament, the Greek word κύριος was used to translate the most holy name of God in the entire Old Testament; the name of YHWH[72] or the name of God; two different ways of pronouncing the same thing. In the New Testament, κύριος is very often employed in reference to Jesus; in other cases, it keeps its significance of "Master" in a general sense. κύριος means "owner" and is so translated in Lk 19:33. It expresses the authority and lordship arising from, and pertaining to, ownership.

Joseph A. Fitzmyer observes the development of the terms ῥαββί and κύριος[73] in New Testament usage and is of the opinion that the word ῥαββί lies behind διδάσκαλος which means "teacher." The Aramaic *Rab* originally meant "master" or "teacher" but in the course of time it came to be simply a title, ῥαββί. So for Fitzmyer, "one could assume a similar development in the case of κύριος."[74] Fitzmyer also notes that, as a title for Jesus, κύριος is used by various New Testament writers and that "it is but one of the several titles given to him."[75] Fitzmyer has mentioned the same point in his earlier work, saying that "the gospels attest that various persons, disciples or pagans, addressed the earthly Jesus as κύριε."[76] Bruce Vawter asserts, "Jesus was undoubtedly in his own lifetime called *mara* or

mare (master), *mari* (my master), *maran* or *marana* (our master), etc."[77]
For Vawter, all the above terms correspond with the more familiar Hebrew
word equivalent to the Greek word meaning master or teacher.

Morio – Moran - Mar

The Gospels frequently use "Lord" as a title for Jesus. Jesus himself never
seems to have claimed the title, it is only ascribed to him by others. This
has led to various interpretations. The Gospels frequently use "Lord" as a
title for Jesus. Many interpret the term as a reference to divinity. In John,
Jesus is addressed as "My Lord and my God." Scholars explain the use
of this title in various ways: some believe that Jesus' disciples called him
"Lord", not because he was divine, but because this was merely a title used
when students addressed their teachers. According to Geza Vermez, a close
reading of the Gospels suggests that most people addressed Jesus as Lord
as a sign of respect for a miracle-worker, especially in Mark and Matthew,
or as a teacher, especially in Luke. In many cases one can substitute the
words "teacher" for "lord", though in some instances the substitution would
make little sense. Others believe that the New Testament uses the term
Lord to indicate Jesus' divinity,[78] but only after his death. Others argue
that neither Jesus nor his disciples used the Aramaic term for Lord, *Mara*,
and that the Greek term κῦριος was borrowed from Hellenistic usage. Still
others maintain that it identifies Jesus as the YHWH of the Old Testament.

Some believe that the New Testament uses the term Lord to mean
divine. But it was only after Jesus' death and resurrection that his followers
ascribed divinity to him. The Greek word κῦριος in the New Testament
carries the same meaning as *Adonai* in the Old Testament. *Adonai* is a
special plural form of *adon*, which means lord, master or owner; "one
possessed of complete control." When *adon* appears in the special plural
form, with a first common singular pronominal suffix, it always refers to
God. It appears in this form more than three hundred times, mostly in
Psalms, Lamentations, and the latter prophets. It is usually translated in
English Bibles as "Lord." The Hebrew Bible distinguishes between "Lord"
(*adon*) and "God"; the word "Lord" does not necessarily imply divinity,
although God is often described as "the Lord". Surviving inter-testamental
Aramaic texts frequently use the Aramaic *mara* to mean "the Lord", that
is God, but they also provide evidence of people using *mara* and κῦριε
as personal titles used to address a husband, father, or king. There is little
evidence that either term was used specifically to mean "teacher", but there

is much evidence of students using the term "*mar*" to refer to their teachers respectfully, or to refer to an especially respected and authoritative teacher.

In the Syriac version of the New Testament, it is *moran*[79] which is employed to designate Jesus as the Christ. In the New Testament, *morio* is employed each time in a reference to the Old Testament, and it distinguishes between morio and *Mor*, as between God and Jesus the Christ. It should be noted that in the Gospel of Luke, Jesus is referred to as *morio*. One finds *morio* in the first five chapters of Luke, except in 1:28 where *moran* is used as if the angel announced that Mary was already pregnant of Jesus: the Lord is with you. So the term *moran* is used infrequently: on the other hand, when it is used, *Mor* or moran replaces the vocative κύριε. It is worth noting that the form κύριος is applied to Jesus, as if it were necessary to show the difference between the God of Israel and Jesus the Christ. Matthew, like Luke, reserves *morio* for the quotations from, or allusions to, the Old Testament. It is particularly employed by Luke, in the Infancy Narratives. Luke employs the word κύριος in the same way as Mark. In Mk 5:19 one may note Jesus telling the demoniac after the cure, "Go and tell what the Lord (*morio*) did for you". This means that he who cures is the Lord of Israel. Paul employs *morio* without reference to the Old Testament in I Cor 10:12 to affirm that the Christians and the Jews have the same Lord. Finally a particular case may be noted; in Jn 12:20 in the Sinaitic codex texts, κύριος designates a man (Philip) and not God. How can Philip be named *morio*? One can suggest that it was the redaction of a Scribe. *Morio* could testify here to an old use before it becomes used exclusively to indicate YHWH. It is the philological explanation. In another way it may be said that the request made by the Greeks to see Jesus is not addressed to Philip but is a request to God.

To summarize: *morio*, which is translated as κύριος in the New Testament, where the Old Testament is quoted, can also designate God in a more general way as one who directs men and the Church. But Jesus can also be called *morio* to underline his divinity and the continuity of his action as God of Israel. In general, the Syriac translation of κύριος makes the distinction between God of the Old Testament as *morio* and Jesus the Christ as *moran*, a distinction between the divine lord and the human Master. On the other hand, there are instances of *morio* being used for Jesus. It seems that this is the desired theological intention, to identify Jesus with the God of the Old Testament, and thus to affirm the divinity of Jesus Christ as seen in Ac11:21, I Cor 8:6; Phil 12:3, Ac 2:11; 4:29 where one would see *Mor* applied to Jesus. In the same way, one finds examples of *moran* employed for *Mor* in Lk 16:8. This may be the choice of the translator and his theological intentions, or it could even be a human error. One can even speculate that the employment of this term is the result of several translators working on the same text, each of whom had his own preference for a particular word.

Morio is[80] a word especially used to indicate YHWH in the Old Testament, whereas *Moran* (our Lord) is used as an honorific title like *mor* in the Old Testament (2 Kings 2:19; Ps 8:1 where both *morio* and *moran* are used interchangeably. In the New Testament, the word is employed to designate Jesus as Christ, mainly in the letters of Paul but also in John. In Paul, it is the equivalent of κύριος. One finds *moran* associated with both the name Jesus and the title Christ. Moran in Romans 16 (verses 2, 8, 11, 12, 13, 18, 20, and 22) is used to underline the One Lord in whom they all believe. In I Corinthians, one also finds *moran* employed with determinative: e.g. brothers of the Lord (9:5). In some expressions such as "fear of the Lord" (II Corinthians) or "I say according to the Lord" (II 11:17 Corinthians), the translator could have hesitated between *moran* and *morio*. In certain passages it is *morio* which is preferred. They are notable exceptions because the general rule is for Paul to use *moran*. In the case of the letter of James, it is obvious that there was a plurality of translators, whereas in the case of Paul, the choice is made for a particular theological reason. In his letter to the Galatians, *Moran* applied to Jesus occurs six times.

One can frequently find *morio* in the Acts and again in the Gospel of Luke. Morio derives from the root *MR* but the form is difficult to explain. It seems to keep the primitive form *MR* or *MRY* in the quotations of the Old Testament. In expressions drawn from the Old Testament it refers to something like "angel of the lord." However, had long been used by the Septuagint to translate יבר (*adon*). The Hebrew Bible distinguishes between "lord" (*adon*) and "God"; the word "lord" does not necessarily imply divinity, although God is often described as "the Lord". Inter-testamental Aramaic texts frequently use the Aramaic *mara* to mean "the Lord", that is, God; but they also provide evidence of people using *mara* and κύριος as personal titles to address for example a husband, father, or king. There is little evidence that term was used specifically to mean "teacher", but there is much evidence of students using the term *mar* to refer to their teachers respectfully, or to refer to an especially respected and authoritative teacher. In one passage in the New Testament "Lord" and "teacher" are distinguished by two different Greek words. In most cases one can substitute the words "sir" or "teacher" for "Lord" and the meaning of the passage in question does not change.

Morio is the simplest form as both absolute and emphatic. It is employed to designate an unspecified man who is a Master or owner. *Morio* is used in Luke 10:2 where it refers to the Master of the harvest, or in Luke 12:36 and following where it is a question of the master returning from the wedding feast. When the subject is Jesus or God, the term *moro* is used. But in the expression "Lord of the Sabbath" of Lk 6:5 the term *moro* is replaced by *morio*. One can also translate this as *mor*. *Mor* is found in the Old Testament for "Master" in Gen18:2; 24:14; 24:18; 42:10; II Samuel 19:19-20 for a king; I Kings 2:19 for a prophet; Ps 16:2 for God. Very often in the Gospels, *mor* is replaced by the vocative κύριε when they address Jesus. When the interlocutors are in the plural, it is logical to use *moran* as "our Lord." *Mor* which literally means "my lord" in its ecclesiastical usage, is used to address a superior. Its vocative value appears where *morio* is applied as is the case for a quotation from the Old Testament: in Rom10:16 which quotes Isaiah 53:1, and in Rom 11:3, which quotes I Kgs 19:10. There is a tendency to use the term *morio* rather than *moran*, which is employed only when it explicitly speaks about Jesus the Christ. In the Syriac translation of the Acts, one has the impression that it is God YHWH who directs the Church and not Jesus. This can be substantiated with examples such as the reaction of Ananias to the instruction to visit Paul (Ac 9:10), and in the account of Peter's liberation from prison (Ac 12:17). The prayer is addressed to God, YHWH, as *morio* (Ac 1:24; 4:29; 8:22). The Spirit of the Lord who is YHWH, is named as *morio* (Ac 5: 9; 8:39) and in the Gospel of Luke (Lk 4:18). Putting aside the assumption that several translators or redactors used their own preferential choices, it would appear that the original writers (notably Luke and Paul) preferred certain options based on their theological intentions. Finally, translations of κύριος as "God" or "Jesus" (which one finds in the work of Luke and the letters of Paul), are related to alternatives one finds in the Greek text. If the Syriacs, in their biblical reading made the distinction between Jesus and the God of Israel, how do they begin to identify Jesus with the OT God? One could deduce from this that these readings of "God" or "Jesus" are the oldest, and that the use of κύριος is a later theological interpretation. But this may be an over-simplification. It is also possible that what may have dictated the choice was the audience the writer had in mind rather than theological connotations.

Κύριος as a Title given to Jesus in the Synoptics

The following chart[81] and subsequent discussion will primarily deal with the specific question of whether the synoptic Jesus was addressed as κύριε and, if so, what the term κύριος means to the synoptists. This discussion will shed further light on the Johannine perspective of addressing Jesus as ῥαββί and κύριος

Events	Mk	Mt	Lk
Purification of the leper	1:40 d.i.	8:2 κύριε	5:12 κύριε
Stilling of storms	4:38 διδάσκαλε	8 :25 κύριε	8 :24 ἐπιστάτα
First announcement of the Passion	8 :32 d.i.	16 :22 κύριε	
The Transfiguration	9:5 ῥαββί	17:4 κύριε	9:33 ἐπιστάτα
The demoniac child	9:17 διδάσκαλε	17 :15 κύριε	9: 38 διδάσκαλε
The curing of the blind	10:48.51 ῥαββουνί	20:31.33 κύριε κύριε 9:28 κύριε	18: 39.41 κύριε
Announcing the betrayal by Judas	14: 19	26: 22 κύριε	[22: 23]
Prediction of the denial of Peter	14: 29	26: 33	22: 33 κύριε
Arrest of Jesus			22: 49 κύριε
Jesus walking on the waters		14 :28.30 κύριε κύριε	

The Canaanite or Syro-Phoenician woman	7:[25].26.28 d.i. κύριε	15 :22.25.27 κύριε κύριε κύριε	
Our Father			11:1 κύριε
The two ways			13: 23 κύριε
The Centurion at Capernaum		8 :6.8 κύριε κύριε	7: [2]. 6 κύριε
To follow Jesus...		8 :21 κύριε	9 :59.61 [κύριε] κύριε
How many times to forgive...		18 :21 κύριε	
The vultures			17: 37 κύριε
The Faithful			12: 41 κύριε
The miraculous catch of fish			5: 8 κύριε
Bad reception at Samaria			9: 54 κύριε
The Return of the Seventy-Two			10: 17 κύριε
Martha and Mary			10 :40 κύριε
Zacchaeus			19: 8 κύριε
Two swords			22: 38 κύριε

Obviously Jesus was often addressed as κύριε in the synoptic gospels. However, according to Kittel "Jesus was neither addressed as Lord during His days on earth, nor was He referred to as the Lord."[83] In short, the address κύριος has, in the three evangelists, a positive connotation. Whereas in Mark, κύριος is employed only once (7: 28) by the Syro-Phoenician woman, in Matthew it is found 18 times in 13 episodes, and in Luke 16 times in 16 episodes. κύριος appears only once in Mark, in the meeting between Jesus and the Syro-Phoenician woman. It is probably necessary to read here the equivalent story of a confession of faith in the Gospel of Matthew: it is only a foreigner, not a Jew, who addresses Jesus as "Lord." Matthew restricts this form of address to those who believe, particularly to the disciples, apart from Judas. When he adds κύριος at his own initiative, it often comes from Peter. In other words, by this means, Matthew underlines the exceptional status of Judas among the close group of Jesus' followers. But it can be noted that Matthew reiterates this address in some episodes; the centurion, Jesus walking on the water, the Canaanite woman (who is a Syro-Phoenician in Mark) and the cure of the blind men (who is Bartimaeus in Mark). This underlining of the particular role of Jesus in these episodes is probably intended to indicate those who showed strong faith.

Jesus as κύριος in Mark

In studying the term κύριος in the synoptic passages, it is found that Mark has used this term just once (Mk 7: 28), in reference to the Syro-Phoenician woman for which Matthew has a parallel. Apart from that, there is no case where all the three evangelists maintain the use of κύριος. There are, however, two instances in the triple tradition where Matthew and Luke use κύριος at the same place. In the purification of the leper, Matthew and Luke put into the mouth of the leper the address κύριος whereas Mark uses indirect speech. In the cure of the blind men in Mark, it is ῥαββουνί, replaced in Mt and Lk with κύριος. As Gerhard Kittel notes, "In Mark only the Syro-Phoenician woman uses the vocative κύριε (7: 28). The disciples, Pharisees and people all use διδάσκαλε."[84] Vincent Taylor notes, "It is important to observe that St. Mark does not apply the title 'the Lord' to Jesus, unless he does so in 11:3. He contents himself with the names 'Teacher', 'Jesus', and 'Son of Man.'"[85] Christopher M. Tuckett observes that "the term Lord (*Kyrios*) seems to play a rather insignificant role in Mark".[86] Tuckett adds "*Kyrios* does not seem to have been a very important term christologically for Mark."[87] Geza Vermes observes, "If scholarly opinion is to be believed, this oldest Gospel gives no hint whatever that Jesus was addressed as

'Lord' in Palestine."[88] And Vermes concludes "If all the Marcan witnesses are allowed to testify, the old axiom that 'lord' appears only in the mouth of Gentiles in the earliest Gospel tradition will have to be discarded." But Vermes agrees that in the Markan occurrences of κύριος "the appellation was the regular mode of address to a miracle-worker."[89] Hence it is found that Mark has a very limited use of the address κύριος given to Jesus, and that only in the context of presenting Jesus as a miracle-worker.

Jesus as κύριος in Matthew

With regard to the tradition of Mark and Matthew, six occurrences (one in Mk, five in Mt) of κύριος are distributed throughout two episodes. When Jesus walks on water, the address κύριος appears twice in the mouth of Peter. It is the occasion for Matthew to express the faith of Peter. In Matthew, Peter is a disciple when he uses the term κύριός even though his faith is limited (Mt 14:31). In the meeting of Jesus with the Canaanite woman, Matthew maintains and repeats three times the address κύριός whereas it is only used once in Mark during the conversation with the Syro-Phoenician woman. In Matthew and Luke there are ten occurrences in seven episodes, four in Mt and six in Lk where the title κύριος is used as parallel address by both evangelists. In the episode of the centurion, there is no explicit address. In the narration on forgiveness, there is an address in Mt whereas it is missing in Luke. Matthew introduces this teaching by a question from Peter, which may be an editorial addition. On the other hand, one finds the address four times in a short editorial addition in Luke whereas it is missing in Mt in the teachings on Our Father, two ways, the body and vultures, and the faithful servant. There is a request for teaching in each episode.

In the triple tradition, Matthew puts κύριος in the mouth of the disciples, taken collectively or singly, while Mark has διδάσκαλε in certain cases, such as the calming of the storm and Peter calling Jesus at the first announcement of the Passion. Again ῥαββί is used by Peter at the Transfiguration, but there is no address given in the announcement of the treason of Judas. The only exception is Judas who does use, in Matthew, the address ῥαββί to Jesus (26:25. 49) at the Last Supper (Mt 26). This makes one wonder whether Matthew still regards him as a disciple. This enables Matthew to underline the contrast between Judas, who addresses Jesus by calling him ῥαββί, and the disciples who had called Jesus κύριος. In the account of those who express their desire to follow Jesus (Mt 8:19-21), this contrast is evident; the scribe (Mt 8:19) calls him διδάσκαλε, whereas another man, one of his disciples, addresses him as κύριος (Mt 8:21). The use of κύριος by Matthew, in place of διδάσκαλε in the exorcism of the demoniac child, might mean that Matthew compares the father of the child to a disciple of Jesus.

Matthew applies κύριε systematically in the mouths of the disciples, either collectively or individually,[90] whereas Mark uses διδάσκαλε collectively only. With regard to the double tradition[91] of Mark and Matthew, there are six instances of the term κύριε being used. With Matthew[92] one finds a total of eighteen times in thirteen episodes and with Luke sixteen times in sixteen episodes. Vermes suggests that "examination of Matthean passages containing the term 'lord' reveals the same predominant usage as in Mark."[93] So in Vermes' observation, like Mark, Matthew also has principally employed the vocative κύριε in miracle stories. But the novelty in Matthew's employment of κύριε is that the miraculous setting "is found not only in the mouths of strangers, but also four times in those of his regular companions."[94] However, Matthew "testifies to an extension of the meaning to include other aspects of Jesus' personality - those of teacher and religious leader."[95] we can agree with Vermes that the title κύριος given to Jesus has also the connotation of teacher and religious leader. But it does not stop with that, as the following will show.

According to Tuckett, regarding Matthew's use of the title κύριος to Jesus, "Matthew appears to restrict the use of the term either to those who are recipients of Jesus' miraculous powers (e.g. the leper in 8:2, the centurion in 8:6), or the disciples and other followers of Jesus (e.g. Peter in 14:28. 30)."[96] Hence for Tuckett, the usage of the title κύριος is characteristic and revealing. In Mt 26: 21-25, during the Last Supper, the disciples are anxious to know who would betray Jesus. Unlike Mark, Matthew alone adds the question of Judas here (v.25.) When all other disciples ask 'Is it I Lord'? (v. 22) Judas the betrayer asks Jesus, 'Is it I, ῥαββί?' Thus Tuckett concludes "only the true followers of Jesus are apparently allowed by Matthew to address Jesus as *Kyrios*."[97]

Jesus as κύριος *in Luke*

In Luke, Jesus is called κύριε 18 times. Among the occurrences, 13 are of the instances in which the term κύριε "always implies teacher, with the occasional suggestion that he is the head of a group, the master of a circle of disciples."[98] In Luke, the term κύριε usually comes from the mouths of various persons showing a faith attitude. Kittel notes that, when there is no

Marcan original, Luke often "uses κύριε especially on the lips of disciples."[99]
Vermes states that "By comparison with Mark and Matthew, the title 'lord'
in a miraculous context is much less evident in the third Gospel."[100] In
the observation of Tuckett on the use of the title κύριος in Luke, the word
is "capable of a wide range of meanings. Thus kyrios can be (just) a term
of polite respect, or a reference to a human master."[101] Tuckett agrees that
the title κύριος can also be used by Jews to refer to God himself, but he
insists that "it is unlikely that Luke intends any great claims to divinity
by his use of the term kyrios for Jesus."[102] Tuckett also suggests that
occasionally the term κύριος is used of Jesus in Q. The centurion in Q
7:6 addresses Jesus as 'Lord.' And the word κύριε here "means no more
than a polite form of address."[103] Luke, by maintaining διδάσκαλε, makes a
distinction between the father and the disciples (Mt17:17). While it would
include the father, or even address the father exclusively, it is certainly not
addressed to the disciples in Luke (9:41). In the prediction of the betrayal
by Peter, Matthew has, like Mark, a text without address; but Luke puts
κύριος into the mouth of Peter. In the arrest of Jesus, Luke inserts an addition
in which the disciples use the same term κύριος to Jesus. The address
κύριος does not appear in the episodes belonging to the simple tradition of
Matthew. On the other hand, it appears six times in the simple tradition of
Luke. One always finds it in the mouth of disciples or people close to Jesus.
Four episodes illustrate it in an obvious way: the bad reception in Samaria
(Lk 9:54) the return of the seventy two (10:17) Martha and Mary (10:40)
and two swords (22:38). Moreover, in the episode of the miraculous
catch of fish, it is only after the experience of the miracle that Simon
throws himself at the feet of Jesus and calls him κύριος. Previously, he
had addressed Jesus as ἐπιστάτα In the same way, Zachaeus does not use
κύριος for Jesus at first but only after he has been re-instated by Jesus.
Thus, in his Gospel, Luke makes a broad use of κύριος.

Κύριος: Presentation of Synoptic Jesus as more than a Teacher

From the synoptic passages where the title κύριε is given to Jesus, it is
observed that the address κύριε has, among all three evangelists, a positive[104]
connotation. In Mark, it appears only once (in the encounter between
Jesus and the Syro-Phoenician woman), but Matthew reserves the term
exclusively for those who believe, in particular the disciples (except Judas).
Donaldson observes that "the disciples of Jesus, who are in Matthew's
Gospel in a state of faith and understanding, address Jesus as κύριε which
for Matthew has a Christological significance, and means more than κύριε
when this is understood in a sense of 'my master.'" It would appear then

that, in Matthew, occurrences of the term κύριε are to be seen as more than simply an expression of human respect. Moreover, as Donaldson states, "Matthew has expanded his Marcan source to express the recognition of Jesus as more than a teacher, by those who encounter him."[105] Hence for Matthew the title κύριος given to Jesus means that he was seen both as a teacher and as *more* than a teacher. According to Donaldson, the use of κύριε and ἐπιστάτα in the parallel texts of Matthew and Luke show that these writers wish to distinguish Jesus from being a mere teacher. "Their usage in fact is in harmony with their theological intention and with the Christian Church's confession that Jesus is more than a teacher."[106] Thus in the synoptic perspective, the use of the title κύριος, when attributed to Jesus, denotes that he was perceived or understood to be someone who is more than teacher. By being given the title κύριος, Jesus is acknowledged as of a higher status that distinguishes him from all other teachers or masters in his contemporary society.

6. Application of a Title and Expression of Faith: A Continuity

The chart below shows how each evangelist had his own choice of name or title given to Jesus for the same event. This chart is a clear portrayal of the application of various titles to Jesus as well as showing that each evangelist felt free to choose the titles or names given to Jesus in his own Gospel. This study discusses how the evangelists chose a title or name of their own choice for the same episode:

Events	Mk	Mt	Lk
The rich young man	10:17.20 διδάσκαλε ˙ γαθὲ διδάσκαλε	19:16.20 διδάσκαλε	18:18.21 διδάσκαλε ˙ γαθὲ
The curing of the blind	10:47.48.51 υἱὲ Δαυιˑδ Ἰησοῦ υἱὲ Δαυῖδ ῥαββουνί	20:30.31.33 [κύριὲ υἱὸς Δαυῖδ κύριε υἱὸς Δαυῖδ κύριε 9:27.28 υἱὸς Δαυῖδ κύριε	18:38.39.41 Ἰησοῦ υἱὲ Δαυῖδ υἱὲ Δαυῖδ κύριε

Announcing about the betrayal of Judas	14:19	26:22.25 κύριε ῥαββί	[22:23]
The Syro-Phoenician woman	7:26.28 d.i κύριε	15:22.25.27 κύριε υἱὸς Δαυὶδ κύριε κύριε	9:57.59.61 [κύριε] κύριε
To follow Jesus		8:19.21 διδάσκαλε κύριε	
The miraculous catch of fish			5:5.8 ἐπιστάτα κύριε

The title διδάσκαλε is given to Jesus in the passage about the rich young man. This is probably intended to show that he fails to understand who Jesus really is. The passage portrays a negative evolution in the understanding of discipleship and stands in contrast to that concerning the cure of Bartimaeus who calls Jesus ῥαββουνί. This is a kind of transformation in a man who passes from blindness to the enlightenment of faith. Thus, this passage marks a positive evolution. Matthew uses κύριος for the same episode in his Gospel (9:27.28).

Thus the evolution proceeds from one address to another in two stages. Luke inserts another evolution in the episode of the miraculous catch of fish. He begins by calling Jesus ἐπιστάτα but after the miracle he calls him κύριος. Then, in the episode of the call of the first disciples, Luke presents another evolution. A question then arises: what determines the evangelist's choice of the title or name in any given passage in his Gospel? To answer this question, it is necessary to find evidence which may indicate why the choice was made. Is it to convey a particular message to a particular audience? This "system of the address" adopted by each evangelist must be based initially on an examination of the speaker who pronounces the address. It can be supplemented by observations based on the narrative features of certain episodes and by the conclusions reached, starting from the literary units containing several addresses. If the characters of the gospels are divided into several groups, three separate groups can be discerned. The first group consists of "the sympathizers" who follow him and who are designated his disciples. The second group consists of "the declared opponents" such as lawyers, scribes, the High priest, and those who are sent by the priests such as Herodians, Sadducees or Pharisees. The third group consists of characters who have met occasionally, and one cannot know for sure on which side they should be placed. This group is comprised of lepers, blind men, tax collectors, foreigners, and so on. When they come on the scene, they have a neutral connotation. The way they react will modify this connotation, that is to say, either they will be presented as belonging to those who believe in Jesus or those who become opposed to him. When they believe in Jesus, they will be connoted positively and when they are characterized by their unfaithfulness, they will be connoted negatively.

7. Reasons for Adaptation or Avoidance of the Term Ῥαββί

In summary, some of the very specific observations that have been made can now be identified. In Mark, the title ῥαββί is used by both Peter and Judas. When Mark applies the same title ῥαββί for both Peter and Judas, it may not mean that Peter is no better than Judas in regard to his relationship (discipleship) with Jesus. However, a question arises: why was Mark so keen on keeping the term in Aramaic? It may be that he wanted to preserve the Aramean term specifically for the sake of the faith community. Like Mark, John in his Gospel retains the original Aramaic appellation ῥαββί. Thus John, who is often considered to be less interested in preserving original parlance or historical accuracy, is in this instance found to be closer to the actual address of the earthly Jesus than the Synoptic writers. Interestingly, Mark thus comes closest to John in reflecting the probable historical address of Jesus as Rabbi by his contemporaries. And yet another question: why did Mark not feel obliged to translate the term "Rabbi" in his gospel as διδάσκαλος when John apparently felt free to translate it in that way?

Matthew, the author, uses equivalent titles to distinguish three groups of people by the way they address Jesus. Those who use κύριε are portrayed by Matthew as the group of 'believers', including those disciples who accompanied Jesus during his earthly ministry. Secondly, there are those who are portrayed as being *opposed* to Jesus' teaching or, at least, not adhering to his teaching. For these Matthew uses the term διδάσκαλε. And thirdly, there is the single case of Judas. Matthew uses the term ῥαββί when Judas addresses Jesus in an act of betrayal. This could imply that for Matthew,

Judas is no longer a disciple but rather a member of the opposition camp. Two problems arise (which could be an area for further research): why does Matthew, who sees Moses as an important figure of the OT and as a great ῥαββί (*Rabbenu*), not use the same term for Jesus, whom he portrays as a "New Moses"? Secondly, why does he use the honorific title 'Rabbi' as coming from Judas, the betrayer?

In Luke's Gospel, there are three distinct groups. Firstly, there are those who do not understand who Jesus really is. These are portrayed as using the title διδάσκαλè Secondly, there are those who do recognise him (in a proper sense) and address him using the title κῦριε. Thirdly, the title ἐπιστάτα addressed to Jesus has been reserved to the disciples. When Donaldson observes the use of ῥαββί and other equivalents in the synoptic writings, he states that either the adaptation or avoidance of the term ῥαββί occurs in the gospels "precisely for Christological reasons and not because of any reluctance to use ῥαββί as a title."[107] This position of Donaldson appears convincing. But at the same time when they wrote the gospels for their faith communities, the evangelists presented Jesus as someone who is more than a teacher. According to Andreas Kostenberger, Luke does not use the Hebrew/Aramaic term Rabbi at all and generally substitutes the Greek expressions διδάσκαλος or ἐπιστάτα in deference to his Gentile audience. He does this, however, without downplaying the significance of Jesus' role as a teacher.[108] The term ῥαββί, in the sense of a teacher, occurs in all the gospels except Luke. This indicates that Luke might have had a special reason to replace ῥαββί by the term ἐπιστάτα which was very common among his particular believers or readers. But at the same time, as Dalman and Lapin have observed, Luke's ἐπιστάτα and διδάσκαλος to Jesus can be traced back to the Aramaic term ῥαββί .

Robert H. Stein makes a valid point when he notes that, "Within certain circles some titles tend to be more emphasised than others, and frequently the choice of titles given to Jesus reveals a great deal about the views of that particular circle."[109] All of this raises the familiar question of whether the titles ῥαββί and ῥαββουνί were actually used to address Jesus in his lifetime, or whether they were used by the writers of the Gospels some decades after the life and mission of Jesus of Nazareth. That leads immediately to ask another question. Was the title ῥαββί given to Jesus in the sense of his holding a position of teacher? From the previous study in part I of this book and the results that were inferred, we try to prove that the title Rabbi was a title used mostly at the time of Jesus. There is a substantial amount of recorded evidence that this title was in use both before and during the lifetime of Jesus of Nazareth. The term ῥαββί in the time of Jesus did not necessarily refer to a specific office or occupation. That would be true only after the Temple in Jerusalem was destroyed (70 A.D.). Rather, it was a word meaning 'great one' or 'my master', which was applied to different kinds of people. It was clearly used as a term of respect for one's teacher as well, even though the formal position of ῥαββί would come later. In one sense then, as has been discussed in part I of this book, calling Jesus Rabbi would be an anachronism. In another sense the use of this term for him by the people of his day is a measure of their great respect for him as a person and as a teacher, and not just a reference to the activity of teaching he was engaged in. One thing is clear: every author of the Synoptic Gospels agrees in presenting Jesus as a master or a teacher.

Summary and Conclusions

The titles that are applied by the different authors and by redactors play an important role in revealing the characteristics of the person of Jesus. Certain episodes in the gospels have a significant function: these occur when people address Jesus with varying names and titles. These episodes not only reveal more about Jesus himself, but function as a model which the reader can imitate. By their revealing function, it should be understood that, for each addressing or naming of Jesus, the believer is somehow highlighted and the relation of the believer to Jesus is revealed or, for that matter, the relation of the non- believer. One of the tasks of the gospel writer is to provide indications to his readers which will enable them to determine correctly the value of certain titles or names that are given to Jesus by different people. In this greeting or naming, the address is a precise indicator of the mode of relation existing between the one who speaks and the one to whom it is addressed.

A synthesis can be made of what has been observed in the gospel of each evangelist, because each evangelist is putting forward his own theological interpretation, appropriate to his audience. But the expression of a particular thought by means of language does not stop with lexicon, because it also reveals its characters. So it is necessary to make a systematic study of how Jesus is addressed by considering the various speakers in the accounts. This provides the means to understand the particular representation of the relation between believer and Jesus that each evangelist wants to present to his readers.

The inventory of the occurrences was restricted to the names or titles applied to Jesus in the Synoptic Gospels. To begin with, all the addresses applied to Jesus were catalogued. It is noted that when two evangelists recount the same episode comprising an address to Jesus, they do not necessarily use the same address. For example, in the account of the storm, the frightened disciples call on Jesus as διδάσκαλε in Mk 4:38, whereas it is κύριος in Mt 8:25 and e,pista,ta in Lk 8:24. In other cases an episode in which Jesus is addressed in a particular way in one gospel is not replicated in the account of the same episode in another gospel. For example, in the account of the prediction of the denial of Peter, Jesus is not addressed directly in Mk 14:29 and Mt 26:33, whereas Luke uses κύριος (Lk 22:33). Thus there are various gospel titles for Jesus, but each writer of the New Testament approaches the faith story of Jesus in a different way with different titles and names.

Chapter one, on the equivalent terms to ῥαββί that are used to address Jesus in the synoptic Gospels, presents him as being perceived not merely as a teacher but much more than a teacher. A detailed study was made of the various equivalent terms used by the synoptic authors to address Jesus as 'Rabbi' in different circumstances. This study has not excluded the possibility that many of these terms may have been inserted when the gospels were eventually written some decades after the event. This was done, no doubt, in the light of the faith experience of the first generation Christians.

Gospel readers will often have heard many titles ascribed to Jesus without really understanding their background, meaning and significance. Furthermore, it is noted that the full significance of some of Jesus' titles were not immediately realised by his contemporaries, even those who were close to him. The gospels involve a gradual unfolding of the message of Jesus, and the meaning of the titles given to him also gradually unfolds. In the gospels, Jesus refers to himself, and is referred to, by certain Christological titles. There has been much debate over the historicity of Jesus' use and acceptance of these titles as portrayed in the gospels. It is safe to say that the majority of scholars view many, if not most, of the traditions about Jesus in which he uses one of these titles of himself, or is so addressed, as being "community creations," that is, the reading back of later Christological beliefs into the time of Jesus.

If the synoptists agree that Jesus was a teacher, in what way is he a teacher or a master? Is he just one among the many teachers of his time? Again, in what ways is he different from his contemporaries? The following chapter is an attempt to answer the question whether Jesus could be considered as a Jewish teacher, and if so, in what regard.

Endnotes

[1] W. HAROLD MARE, Teacher and Rabbi in the New Testament, Grace Theological Journal 11.3 (1970) 11-21.

[2] JOSEPHUS, J W I, p. 648.

[3] PHILO, On Dreams II, p. 68.

[4] IGNATIUS, Mag. IX and Polycarp calls Jesus, a famous teacher. See, Martyrdom of Polycarp XIX, p. 1.

[5] For Lk 9:33, P 45 has διδάσκαλε

[6] See G. DALMAN, The Words of Jesus, pp. 327- 328.

[7] In Hebrew literature, there are instances of the use of the titles "rabbi" and "talmid" occurring together. Talmidim is used throughout the Hebrew version of the New Testament to describe the Twelve Disciples. Rabbi is the Hebrew equivalent of διδάσκαλος (Teacher). In NT, Jesus used these words in parallel when he said "But be not you called Rabbi: for one is your Master ,διδάσκαλος., even Christ; and all you are brethren" (Mt 23:8). The same parallelism is found in Jn 1:38, where the equivalence of the Hebrew and Greek words is made explicit: "And the two disciples heard him speak, and they followed Jesus. Then Jesus turned, and saw them following, and said unto them, what do you seek? They said unto him, Rabbi, (which is to say, Teacher - διδάσκαλος. where do you stay?" First, the Greek word διδάσκαλος means a teacher or one who teaches. It is indicative of a teacher/disciple relationship. Second, the Greek word κύριος indicates a lord or one who exercises authority. It is translated as Lord 663 times in total. It indicates a master/servant relationship. It is in this relationship that the people of God most frequently view their relationship with God. They see God as the Master/Lord and themselves as his servants. Eph 6:5-9 instructs that our relationships as natural servants/masters should be mirrored in our relationship with Christ as our master. Third, the Greek word despotes, indicates one who has absolute ownership and full authority. This principle is elaborated in 2Tim 2:21. Fourth, the Aramaic word, ῥαββί signifies "my master" a title of respectful address to Jewish teachers. This word can be distinguished from διδάσκαλος in the following manner: there are many διδάσκαλος (teachers) but Jesus is "the teacher." ῥαββί is also used to indicate a great teacher. Fifth, the Greek word, ἐπιστάτηὸ denotes a chief, a commander, an overseer or master. It appears to have been used by the disciples in addressing the Lord, in recognition of his authority. This word only appears in the book of Luke: Lk 5:5; 8:24; 8:45; 9:33; 9:49; 17:13. Sixth, the Greek word, kathegetes indicates a guide or leader. It appears only in Mt 23:10.

[8] S. BYRSKOG, Jesus the Only Teacher, Didactic Authority and Transmission in Ancient Israel, Ancient Judaism and the Matthean Community, p. 201. Also

cf. James DONALDSON, "The Title Rabbi in the Gospels—Some Reflections on the Evidence of the Synoptics", JQR 63 (1972–73) 287–291; Hershel SHANKS, "Is the Title 'Rabbi' Anachronistic in the Gospels?", JQR 53 (1963) 337–345; S. ZEITLIN, "Is the Title 'Rabbi' Anachronistic in the Gospels?", JQR 53 (1963) 345–349; R. RIESNER, "Jesus as Preacher and Teacher", p. 188.

[9] The charts of various titles for Jesus in the synoptic passages have been prepared with the help of the following sources. A detailed chart on the occurrence of the titles of ῥαββί and ῥαββουνί in the Four Gospels, was prepared by Prof. Dr. Reimund Bieringer. See, Reimund BIERINGER, *Leadership in the New Testament* (Course material for the summer course of Leuven summer school), Leuven, 2002, p. 71. Some of the very important sources include M. E. BOISMARD & A. LAMOUILLE, *Synopsis Graeca Quattuor Evangeliorum*, Leuven & Paris, Peeters, 1986; Kurt ALAND, *Concordance to the Novum Testamentum Graece*, Berlin & New York, Walter de Gruyter, 1987; Robert B. STRIMPLE, *The Modern Search for the Real Jesus: An Introductory Survey of the Historical Roots of Gospels Criticism*, P & R Publishing, 1995; John J. KOHLENBERGER III, Edward W. GOODRICK & James A. SWANSON, *The Exhaustive Concordance to the Greek New Testament*, Grand Rapids, MI, Zondervan, 1995; Paul HOFFMANN, Thomas HIEKE & Ulrich BAUER, *Synoptic Concordance*, Vols. 1&2, Berlin & New York, Walter de Gruyter, 2000; Alexander SOUTER, *The Text and Canon of the New Testament*, rev. C. S. C. WILLIAMS, 2nd ed, London, Gerald Duckworth & Co. Ltd., 1954, p. 144; R. P. C. HANSON, *Tradition in the Early Church*, Philadelphia, Westminster Press, 1962, p. 249; Cf. Harry Emerson FOSDICK, *The Man from Nazareth: As His Contemporaries Saw Him*, London, SCM Press Ltd., 1950; Etienne TROCME, *Jesus: As Seen by His Contemporaries,* trans. R. A. WILSON, Philadelphia, Westminster Press, 1973; C. H. DODD, *The Founder of Christianity*, London, Collins, 1971, p. 36; M. S. ENSLIN, "*Apocrypha, NT*", in The *Interpreter's Dictionary of The Bible*, New York, Abingdon Press, 1992, pp. 166-169; IRENAEUS, *Against Heresies*, ed. Cyril C. RICHARDSON, in *Early Christian Fathers, Vol.* I, *Library of Christian Classics,* Philadelphia, Westminster Press, 1953, iii. 11. 8; J. DONALDSON, *The Title Rabbi in the Gospels: Some Reflections on the Evidence of the Synoptics, JQR*, pp. 287-291.

[10] H. SHANKS, *Is The Title 'Rabbi' Anachronistic in the Gospels?*, p. 337.

[11] G. H. DALMAN, *The Words of Jesus,* p. 336. Geza Vermes in his work on *Jesus and the World of Judaism* notes that in addition to his ministry as healer and exorcist, Jesus also taught as a teacher. For Vermes, it is not only the disciples, but also "sympathizers and even passers-by regularly address him as teacher or master, *Rabbi* or *rabbuni* in Aramaic, rendered as *didaskale* or *epistata* in Greek." See, G. VERMES, *Jesus and the World of Judaism*, p. 30.

[12] F. Hahn observes that ῥαββί and ῥαββουνί are found as mode of address in the traditions behind the gospels of Mark and John.

[13] R. RIESNER, *Jesus as Preacher and Teacher*, p. 187. On the contrary Matthew preserved διδάσκαλε in the mouth of non-followers.

[14] J. DONALDSON, *The Title Rabbi in the Gospels,* p. 287. Donaldson notes that this Markan ῥαββουνί is rendered κύριε in some of the manuscripts. Codex Bezae has κύριε ῥαββί which is a conflation based on the parallel texts.

[15] S. ZEITLIN, *A Reply- Is the Title Rabbi Anachronistic in the Gospels*, p. 346. Zeitlin, in his observation of ῥαββί in Mk 9:5 which in Mt 17:4 has been rendered with κύριε makes the same observation that in Mt, κύριε is given instead of ῥαββί. For Zeitlin apparently the original Hebrew is *adonai* which Mt gives κύριε whereas Mk renders as ῥαββί in the Aramaic form.

[16] Cf. R. RIESNER, *Jesus als Lehrer*, pp. 259–264; 269–272.

[17] Cf. LOHSE, *Rabbi*, pp. 962-965.

[18] F. HAHN, *The Titles of Jesus in Christology*, p. 74. Matthew at many points has effaced the mode of address ῥαββί and has retained it only in the mouth of the adversaries of Jesus or those who stood aloof.

[19] H. LAPIN, *Rabbi*, p. 601. When Lapin says that the use of ῥαββί in Matthew is polemical, we need to pay special attention to that point, since the only person to address Jesus as Rabbi is Judas (Mt 26:25. 49). One can note that in both occurrences, where Jesus has been addressed as ῥαββί, it is coming from the lips of a traitor and at no time from his other disciples.

[20] S. BYRSKOG, *Jesus the Only Teacher,* p. 200. In p. 201, footnote 1, Byrskog observes that the term ῥαββί in Matthew is either negative or goes beyond the purely didactic one.

[21] G. DALMAN, *Words of Jesus*, p. 336. Here in Mt 23: 7-8 according to the understanding of Dalman, Jesus recognised that, in reference to himself, the term ῥαββί was the designation of the real relation between his disciples and himself.

[22] Solomon ZEITLIN, *A Reply - Is the Title Rabbi Anachronistic in the Gospels*, in *JQR* 53 (1963) 345-349, p. 346.

[23] F. HAHN, *The Titles of Jesus in Christology*, p. 74.

[24] *Ibid.*, p. 75.

[25] J. DONALDSON, *The Title Rabbi in the Gospels- Some Reflections on the Evidence of the Synoptics, JQR* 63, p. 289. In Luke's avoidance of the Hebrew-Aramaic terms, Donaldson notes the single exception of αμην, the only non-Greek word that occurs in Luke's Gospel.

[26] Ed TENHOR, *That Rabbi from Nazareth: A Quest for Historical Jesus*, Bloomington, IN, 2004, p. 43.

[27] Cf. *TDNT* 2:148-161. Διδάσκαλος is a noun and its use is masculine. The terms are used variously as διδάσκαλε 31, διδάσκαλω 15, διδάσκαλον 5, διδάσκαλοι 4, διδάσκαλοω 3 times. The verb διδάσκειν which means "to teach" occurs 95 times and two thirds of these are used in the gospels. In this case,

the teaching action is prevalently applied to Jesus. As διδάσκαλος it stands for someone who is a teacher. In the NT, a teacher is the one who teaches concerning the things of God, and the duties of man. Vernon K. Robbins in his "*Jesus the Teacher: A Socio-Rhetorical Interpretation of Mark*" quoting from E. Schweizer and A. H. Howe, affirms that by the end of the first century C.E., the terminology and pattern of a teacher and his disciple- companions are well established in the writings of Flavius Josephus, tannaitic rabbinic traditions, and the gospels. The Gospel of Mark is representative of this shift in pattern and terminology, containing seventeen occurrences of the verb διδάσκειν (to teach), twelve occurrences of the noun διδάσκαλος (teacher), and forty-five occurrences of the noun μαθητής (disciple-companion). See, Vernon K. ROBBINS, *Jesus the Teacher: A Socio-Rhetorical Interpretation of Mark*, Philadelphia, Fortress Press, 1984, p. 88. In the Jewish tradition διδάσκαλος meant also teachers of the Jewish religion διδάσκαλος refers to those who by their great power as teachers draw crowds around them (such as John the Baptist and Jesus). Jesus acted as one who showed men the way of salvation. διδάσκαλος is also for the apostles, and for Paul who in the religious assemblies of the Christians, undertook the work of teaching, with the special assistance of the Holy Spirit. In the sense of Teacher, or "Doctor", it occurs fifty-eight times, and is twice explained as meaning "Rabbi." Jesus was addressed as διδάσκαλος (Teacher), rendered "Master" thirty-one times; six times in Matthew (8:19; 12:38; 19:16; 22:16.24.36); ten times in Mk 4:38; 9:17.38; 10:17.20.35; 12:14.19.32; 13:1; twelve times in Lk 3:12; 7:40; 9:38; 10:25; 11:45; 12:13; 18:18; 19:39; 20:21.28.39; 21:7; three times in Jn 1:39; 8:4; 20:16. Jesus is spoken of διδάσκαλος as "Master" by himself eight times: three times in Mt 10:24,25; 26:18; once in Mk 14:14; thrice in Lk 6:40.40; 22:11; once in Jn 13:14. Jesus is spoken of διδάσκαλος as Ὁ διδάσκαλος "Master" by others than himself six times: twice in Mt 9:11; 17:24; once in Mk 5:35; once in Lk 8:49; twice in Jn 11:28; 13:13. Again Jesus as διδάσκαλος is spoken of others than himself twice, and rendered "master" in Jn 3:10; Jam 3:1. In other renderings, once "doctor" (Lk 2:46), and ten times "teacher", once of Jesus (Jn 3:2), and nine times of human teachers (Ac 13:1; Rom 2:20; 1Cor 12:28.29; Eph 4:11; 1Tim 2:7; 2Tim 1:11; 4:3; Heb 5:12).

[28] Justin Martyr (+ 165), who himself acted as a teacher, uses the title διδάσκαλος for Jesus to portray him as a teacher. Cf. *Apol.* I 4:7; I 15:5; I 19:6; I 21:1; I 46:1; *Dial*, 108:2. To read more about Jesus as Teacher in the Gospels, please read, L. GASTON, *The Messiah of Israel As Teacher of the Gentiles, The Setting of Matthew's Christology*, INT 29 (1975) 24-40; F. W. BEARE, *Jesus as Teacher and Thaumaturge: The Matthean Portrait*, SE 7 (TU 126) (1982) 31-39; F. BRANDLE, *Jesucristo, unico maestro y sabiduria de Dios en Mateo*, RevistEspir 43 (1984) 187-209; J. J. PILCH, *Teacher for a Troubled Church: Matthew's Jesus*, BibTod 25 (1987) 23-28; D. ZELLER, *Jesus als vollmächtiger Lehrer (Mt 5-7) und der hellenistische Gesetzgeber*, in L. SCHENKE (ed.), *Studien zum Matthäusevangelium*. FS W. Pesch, SBS, Stuttgart, 1988, pp. 299-317; F. NORMANN, *Christos Didaskalos, Die Vorstellung von Christus*

als Lehrer in der christlichen Literatur des ersten und zweiten Jahrhunderts, *MBT* 32, Munster, 1967, pp. 23-44; J. DONALDSON, *The Title Rabbi in the Gospels-Some Reflections on the Evidence of the Synoptics, JQR* 63, p. 288; J. BLANK, *Lernprozesse im Jüngerkreis Jesu, TQ* 158 (1978) 163-173, p. 163; R. T. FRANCE, *Mark and the Teaching of Jesus*, in R. T FRANCE et al, (eds.), *Gospel Perspectives*, Vol 3, Sheffield, 1983, 101-136, pp. 106-109; H. F. WEISS, διδάσκω κτλ., *EWNT* 1 (1980) 764-769, p. 767; F. G. DOWNING, *The Social Contexts of Jesus the Teacher: Construction or Reconstruction, NTS* 33 (1987) 439-451, p. 447; R. RIESNER, *Jesus als Lehrer, Eine Untersuchung zum Ursprung der Evangelien-Überlieferung, WUNT* 2:7, Tubingen, 1988, pp. 249-251. 367; idem, *Jesus as Teacher and Preacher*, in H. WANSBROUGH (ed.), *Jesus and the Oral Gospel Tradition, JSNTSup* 64, Sheffiled 1991, pp. 185-210; A. F. ZIMMERMANN, *Die urchristlichen Lehrer, Studien zum Tradentenkreis der* διδά σκαλοι *im frühen Urchristentum, WUNT* 2:12, Tubingen, 1988, pp. 144-193; P. PERKINS, *Jesus as Teacher*, Cambridge, 1990, pp. 72-84; B. T. VIVIANO, *Rabbouni and Mark 9:5, RB* 97 (1990) 207-218, pp. 209f; M. KARRER, *Der lehrende Jesus, Neutestamentliche Erwägungen, ZNW* 83 (1992) 1-20, pp. 3f. 16-18. Authors like Gaston consider that the didactic designation of διδάσκαλος to Jesus as a teacher is the "most appropriate title." Cf. L. GASTON, *The Messiah of Israel As Teacher of the Gentiles, The Setting of Matthew's Christology, Int* 29 (1975) 24-40, p. 38. There are some other authors who remain sceptical and even negative about didactic portrayal of Jesus. Cf. G. D. KILPATRICK, *The Origins of the Gospel According to St. Matthew,* Oxford, 1946, p. 80; D. R. BAUER, *The Structure of Matthew's Gospel, A Study in Literary Design, JSNTSup* 31, Sheffield, 1988, p. 35. R. T. France in his *"Mark and the Teaching of Jesus"*, in p. 109, describes the teacher language in Matthew as "almost derogatory." Cf. R. T. FRANCE, *Mark and the Teachings of Jesus*, in R. T. FRANCE et al. (eds.), *Gospel Perspectives*, Vol. 1, Sheffield, 1980; C. K. BARRETT, *The Journal of Theological Studies* XX (1), Oxford University Press, 1969, pp. 271-273; G. H. R. HORSELY, *The Journal of Theological Studies* 49(1), Oxford university press, 1998, pp. 265-273.

[29] V. TAYLOR, *The Names of Jesus*, p. 12.

[30] *Ibid.* G. Kittel notes that "διδάσκαλος is also a word which is used both by Jesus Himself and by others to describe the position of Jesus in relation to His disciples." See, G. KITTEL, κύριος in *TDNT* 3, p. 1093. Hence the term διδάσκαλος which is attributed to Jesus in the synoptics portray him both as a teacher as well as the master of his disciples.

[31] Mark uses the term ῥαββί three times and on one occasion ῥαββουνί in his Gospel. But his use of διδάσκαλος and the action of teaching occurs numerically more than the use of ῥαββί in the gospel. Cf. Mk 4:38; 5:35; 9:17, 38; 10:17, 20, 35; 12:14, 19, 32; 13:1; 14:14. Among these episodes, one can distinguish the cases where the addresses given to Jesus are the same and where they are different from the other two evangelists. The address διδάσκαλος is common

to the three evangelists in four episodes. One finds it in the mouth of the rich man who meets Jesus and in the three questions that are put to Jesus in the Temple of Jerusalem concerning the tax to Caesar, the Resurrection of the dead and the greatest commandment. For Jesus as διδάσκαλος in Mark, See R. P. MEYE, *Messianic Secret and Messianic Didache in Mark's Gospel*, in F. CHRIST (ed.), *Oikonomia, Heilsgeschichte als Thema der Theologie*, FS O. Cullmann, Hamburg, 1967, pp. 57-68; F. NORMANN, *Christos Didaskalos, Die Vorstellung von Christus als Lehrer in der christlichen Literatur des ersten und zweiten Jahrhunderts*, MBT 32, Münster, 1967, pp. 1-23; R. P. MEYE, *Jesus and the Twelve, Discipleship and Revelation in Mark's Gospel*, Grand R a p i ds, 1 9 6 8 , p p . 3 0 - 8 7 ; R . H . S T E I N, *T h e "Redaktionsgeschichtilich" Investigation of a Markan Seam* (Mc 1:21f), ZNW 61 (1970) 70-94, pp. 91-94; J. DONALDSON, *JQR* 63 (1972-73) 287f; R. T. FRANCE, *Mark and the Teaching of Jesus*, pp. 101-136; H. F. WEISS, *EWNT* I, pp. 766f; R. RIESNER, *Lehrer*, pp. 251-252; B. T. VIVIANO, *RB* 97 (1990) 207-218; R. K. ROBBINS, *Jesus the Teacher*, pp. 75-196; K. SCHOLTISSEK, *Die Vollmacht Jesu, Traditions-und redaktionsgeschichtliche Analysen zu einem Leitmotiv markinischer Christologie*, NTAbh Neue Folge 25, Münster, 1992, pp. 119-125. 213ff.

[32] J. DONALDSON, *The Title Rabbi in the Gospels*, p. 288.

[33] *Ibid*.

[34] R. SCHNACKENBURG, *Jesus in the Gospels*, p. 20. Schnackenburg observes that in Mark, Jesus is addressed as a teacher. Mark speaks 15 times of Jesus' teaching and in 6: 30, he speaks of the teaching of the disciples, which is commissioned by Jesus. But Schnackenburg agrees that in Mark whenever Jesus is addressed as either ραββί or ραββουνί, it is used in place of teacher in four places (Mk 9:5; 10:51; 11:21; 14:45), and in these places, one cannot generally see any particular reference to Jesus' teaching. For Schnackenburg, on the whole, in any case, one cannot infer a prominent teaching function from the addressing of Jesus as "teacher" or, ραββί,

[35] J. DONALDSON, *The Title Rabbi in the Gospels*, p. 287.

[36] H. LAPIN, ραββί, p. 601. Lapin observes that after being healed of his blindness, Bartimaeus addresses Jesus with the term ραββυνί not in the sense of διδάσκαλος but with the meaning of "sir" or perhaps "lord." However, in another instance (of the healing of a boy possessed with a mute spirit in 9:17), the term διδάσκαλος is used. In general, Jesus is addressed with διδάσκαλος by his disciples in 4:38; 9:38; 10:35; 13:1) and the non-disciples use the same address to Jesus in 9:17; 10:17, 20; 12:14, 19, 32.

[37] G. DALMAN, *The Words of Jesus*, p. 336.

[38] S. BYRSKOG, *Jesus the Only Teacher*, p. 202. Byrskog observes that the use of διδάσκαλος in Matthew harmonizes with Mark and/or Luke in seven cases. Mt 10:24.25/Lk 6:40; Mt 19:16/Mk 10:17/Lk:18:18; Mt 22:16/Mk 12:14/Lk 20:21;

Mt 22:24/Mk 12:19/Lk 20:28; Mt 22:36/Lk 10:25; Mt 26:18/ Mk 14:14/ Lk 22:11. The presence of the term διδάσκαλος constitutes in Mt 22:36/Lk 10:25 a minor disagreement with Mk 12:28. On certain occasions, Matthew is alone in using διδάσκαλος in reference to Jesus. Apart from seven instances where Matthew harmonizes with Mark and Luke in using διδάσκαλος to Jesus, in the rest of the five instances, three are very specific to Matthew (Mt 8:19; 9:11; 12:38) in spite of the presence of the traditions in one or both of the other synoptics. The whole picture of διδάσκαλος as reference to Jesus as a teacher in Matthew makes us seriously refute the idea of Hahn who thinks that Matthew never adds διδάσκαλος to his sources. See, F. HAHN, *Christologische Hoheistitel*, p. 84.

[39] In Matthew Jesus is more often presented as διδάσκαλος than ραββί. To read more about the portrayal of Jesus as a teacher in the gospel of Matthew, read, K. H. RENGSTORF, διδάσκω κτλ., *TDNT* 2 (1964) 1 3 5 - 1 6 5 , p . 1 3 9; F L E N D E R , *E v T* 2 5 (1 9 6 5) 7 0 4 ; DAVIES/ALLISON, *Matthew* I, p. 413; WILKINS, *Concept of Disciple*, pp. 116-124; D. PATTE, *Prolegomena to a Study of the Disciples in Matthew*, Paper Presented at the SNTS Conference at Cambridge, 1988, pp. 1-54; A. T. LINCOLN, *Matthew-A Story for Teachers?*, in, D. J. A. CLINES *et al*, (eds.), *The Bible in three dimensions*, Essays in celebration of forty years of Biblical Studies in the University of Sheffield, *JSOTSup* 87, Sheffield, 1990, pp. 103-125; R. A. EDWARDS, *Characterization of the Disciples as a Feature of Matthew's Narrative*, in, F. VAN SEGBROECK et al. (eds.), *The Four Gospels*, 1992, FS F. NEIRYNCK, *BETL* 100, Leuven, 1992, pp. 1305-1323; *Idem, Uncertain Faith: Matthew's Portrait of the Disciples*, in F. F. SEGOVIA (ed.), *Discipleship in the New Testament*, Philadelphia, 1985, pp. 47-61.

[40] S. BYRSKOG, *Jesus the Only Teacher*, p. 202. In the opinion of Byrskog, the reference to Jesus as διδάσκαλος is implicit in 10:24. 25 and it is probable in 23:8. We note that in Mt 8:19; 9:11; 12:38; 17:24; 19:16; 22:16; 22:24, 36; 26:18 that Jesus is presented as διδάσκαλος. Jesus' teaching activity in Matthew is explained in Mt 9:35; 11:1; 13:54. In 23:8 and 26:18, the term διδάσκαλος is apparently used in reference to Jesus. From a total of twelve occurrences of διδάσκαλος, Jesus uses the term four times referring to himself in Mt 10:24. 25; 23:8; 26:18). In addition, four of the twelve relevant instances of διδά σκειν appear on the lips of Jesus in Mt. 5:19 (bis); 26:55; 28:20 and the opponents use of the verb διδάσκειν which is seen just once in Mt 22:16. The final instance of διδάσκαλος occurs in Mt 26:18 where Jesus tells his disciples to refer to him merely as Ὁ διδάσκαλος which is a definite form, when they meet the man in whose house they are to celebrate the Passover meal.

[41] J. DONALDSON, *The Title Rabbi in the Gospels*, p. 288.

[42] G. BORNKAMM, *End-Expectation and Church in Matthew*, in, G. BORNKAMM et al., *Tradition and Interpretation in Matthew*, London, 1982, 15-57, p.41. According to scholars like Bornkamm, when a didactic designation

occurs on the lips of characters revealing a confessing attitude towards Jesus in the alleged source(s), Matthew either replaces it with κύριε *or omits it altogether.*

⁴³ G. KITTEL, κύριος, p. 1093.

⁴⁴ J. DONALDSON, *The Title Rabbi in the Gospels*, p. 289.

⁴⁵ G. KITTEL, κύριος, p. 1093. To read more about Jesus as a teacher in the gospel of Luke, see, L. SAGGIN, *Magister vester unus est, Christus* (Mt 23:10), *VD* 30 (1952) 205-213, pp. 208f; O. GLOMBITZA, *Die Titel* διδάσκαλος *und* ἐπιστάτçò *für Jesus bei Lukas, ZNW* 49 (1958) 275-278; A. OEPKE, ἐπιστάτçò *TDNT* II (1964) 622-623, 622f; F. NORMANN, *Christos Didaskalos, Die Vorstellung von Christus als Lehrer in der christlichen Literatur des ersten und zweiten Jahrhunderts, MBT* 32, Münster, 1967, pp. 45-54; J. DONALDSON, *JQR* 63 (1972-73) 288f; M. BACHMANN, *Jerusalem und der Tempel, Die geographisch-theologischen Elemente in der lukanischen Sicht des jüdischen Kultzentrums, BWANT* 109, Stuttgart, 1980, pp. 261-289; H. F. WEISS, *EWNT* I, 767f; W. GRIMM, ἐπιστάτçò *EWNT* II (1981) 93-94, pp. 93f; R. RIESNER, *Lehrer*, pp. 247-249.

⁴⁶ R. RIESNER, *Jesus as Preacher and Teacher*, p. 187.

⁴⁷ *Ibid.* Riesner here claims that Luke was also careful to avoid the address διδάσκαλε from disciples although he preserved this form of address from non-followers for the purpose of underlining "that for him Jesus was far superior to any teacher."

⁴⁸ *Ibid.*

⁴⁹ The NT frequently also uses the equivalent *Greek* word διδάσκαλος (meaning 'teacher' – 12 in Mk, 12 in Mt, 17 in Lk and 8 in Jn), usually when Jesus is addressed by various people (disciples and others), but sometimes in Jesus' own sayings about "teachers" (see esp. Mt 10:24-25 & 23:6-12). In John, both in the beginning (Jn 1:38) and at the end (Jn 20:16) where we see these titles ῥαββί and ῥαββουνί occurring, they are explicitly translated as διδάσκαλος meaning "teacher." In NT other than the gospels, some early Christian leaders are also called "teachers" (Ac 13:1; Rom 2:20; 1Cor 12:28-29; Eph 4:11; etc.) But when the title 'teacher' is conferred upon Jesus, "Jesus' activity as Rabbi is well attested." See. G. L. MÜLLER, *Christological Titles*, p. 84.

⁵⁰ G. DALMAN, *The Words of Jesus*, p. 333.

⁵¹ This may also be an interesting point for a historical study of the 'faithfulness of the evangelists'. It is interesting to note that John seems to preserve the original form of addressing the 'historical Jesus' as ῥαββί. This will be dealt with in the next part of this book.

⁵² See, R. RIESNER, *Jesus as Preacher and Teacher*, p. 189. The equivalence of the terms Rabbi and διδάσκαλος is also confirmed by the synonymous parallelism in Matt 23:8. Cf. RIESNER, *Jesus as Preacher and*

Teacher, p. 186, who refers to epigraphical evidence from pre-70 A.D. Jerusalem (*CCII*, II, 1266, 1268/69).

[53] Hans SCHWARZ, *Christology*, Grand Rapids, MI, Cambridge, UK, Eerdmans, 1998, p. 99.

[54] H. F. WEISS, διδάσκαλος and διδάσκω, in *EDNT* 1 (1990) 317-319, p. 318.

[55] Cf. E. R. GOODENOUGH, *Jewish Symbols in the Greco-Roman Period*, Vol. 1, p. 53.

[56] P. J. B. FREY, *Corpus Inscriptionum Judaicarum*, n. 989.

[57] *Ibid.*, n. 979.

[58] *Ibid.*, n. 971.

[59] *Ibid.*, n. 857.

[60] *Ibid.*, n. 1414. 189

[61] *Ibid.*, n. 333, Rome, via Portuensis.

[62] Compare the fading use in the New Testament of another Jewish religious term, *synagogue*, as the New Testament *ekklesia* becomes dominant.

[63] Compare also, IGNATIUS, *Mag.* IX, Here Ignatius writes that "Jesus Christ, our only διδάσκαλος."

[64] E. R. GOODENOUGH, *Jewish Symbols in the Greco-Roman Period*, Vol. 1, p. 90 says that "The word was very casually used in early Christian circles with no reference to 'scholarship' of any kind. ..."

[65] G. KITTEL, κύριος, p. 1093.

[66] V. TAYLOR, *The Names of Jesus*, p. 13.

[67] L. SABOURIN, *The Names and Titles of Jesus*, p. 15.

[68] G. DALMAN, *The Words of Jesus*, p. 336.

[69] H. LAPIN, *Rabbi*, pp. 601-602. Apart from Lk 17:13, the address ἐπιστάτα is always found in the mouths of the disciples.

[70] J. DONALDSON, *The Title Rabbi in the Gospels*, p. 289.

[71] *Ibid.*

[72] This is the name, revealed to Moses in the episode of the burning bush (Ex. 3). God calls Himself, "I AM who I AM", a name translated into English as YHWH, but in the Greek Old Testament as κύριος. What Peter is preaching in Ac. 2 is that Jesus is God.

[73] The Greek word κύριος is very frequent in NT, as many as 717 times with varied meanings. (80 Mt; 18 Mk; 104 Lk; 107 Ac; 274 Paul). In John, there are a total number of 52 occurrences. Some people (sometimes the foreigners) call Jesus Κύριε simply as a sign of respect. This title can be the equivalent of "Sir." It occurs in Mk 7:28; Jn 4:11; etc. and in all these places the disciples usually refer to Jesus as their "master." In later texts, calling Jesus "Lord" is an indication of his messianic or divine status (Ac 2:34-36). In Paul, "the Lord" is

often a substitute for the name of Jesus. It is to be noted that the use of 'Lord' in other contexts occurs like "the Lord's Day" (Rev 1:10), "the Lord's Supper" (1 Cor 11:20).

[74] Joseph A. FITZMYER, *A Wandering Aramean, Collected Aramaic Essays*, MI, USA, Scholars Press, 1979, p. 117. Fitzmyer agrees that there is no clear historical evidence to prove the evolution of the title κύριος meaning "Lord." In McKenzie's observation, the term ραββί "is often translated by κύριος ('Lord') or διδάσκαλος 'teacher.'" See, J. L. MCKENZIE, *Rabbi*, p. 718.

[75] *Idem.*, *To Advance the Gospel*, The Biblical Resource Series, Grand Rapids, MI, Cambridge, UK, Eerdmans, 1981, p. 218.

[76] J.A. FITZMYER, *A Wandering Aramean, Collected Aramaic Essays*, p. 127.

[77] Bruce VAWTER, *This Man Jesus, An Essay Toward a New Testament Christology*, London, Geoffrey Chapman, 1975, p. 100.

[78] The divine name was increasingly regarded as too sacred to be uttered; it was thus replaced vocally in the synagogue ritual by the Hebrew word Adonai (My Lord), which was translated as κύριος (Lord) in the Septuagint, the Greek version of the Old Testament. Cf. *The New Encyclopaedia Britannica*, 15th edition, vol. 10, p. 786. The Greek translators of the Bible took great care to render the name κύριος Lord, as if they knew of no other reading but Adonai. Translations dependent upon the Septuagint have the same reading of the Name. Cf. *Jewish Encyclopedia*, 1901, vol. 1, pp. 201-203.

[79] For a detailed study, See, Harris, R. LAIRD, (ed.), *Theological Wordbook of the Old Testament* (TWOT), Chicago, Moody Press, 1980. See also, Gerhard KITTEL and Gerhard FRIEDRICH (eds.), *Theological Dictionary of the New Testament* (TDNT), Abridged in One Volume by Geoffrey W. BROMILEY, Grand Rapids, Eerdmans, 1985, Reprinted 1992. Read, Kenneth S WUEST, *Wuest's Word Studies from the Greek New Testament*, Volume One, Grand Rapids, Eerdmans, 1955, Reprinted 1989. See also, *Easton's Illustrated Bible Dictionary*, Electronic text and markup, Epiphany Software, 1995.

[80] Alain-Georges MARTIN, *La traduction de KURIOS en syriaque, Filología Neotestamentaria* **12 (1999) 25-54, p. 25.**

[81] As before, this chart has been prepared with the help of the following sources: M. E. BOISMARD & A. LAMOUILLE, *Synopsis Greaca Quattuor Evangeliorum*; K. ALAND, *Concordance to the Novum Testamentum Graece*; J. J. KOHLENBERGER III, E. W. GOODRICK & J. A. SWANSON, *The Exhaustive Concordance to the Greek New Testament*; P. HOFFMANN, T. HIEKE & U. BAUER, *Synoptic Concordance*. The sequence in the chart is as follows: The occurrence of the title κύριος appears first in the triple tradition, then the double tradition, and finally the single tradition. Hence, the occurrences are not in chronological order. The next point to be mentioned here is why some of the entries do not have any title but only the biblical reference. This means that

the author has presented that episode in his gospel but there is no title given to Jesus in that particular context.

[82] G. KITTEL, κύριος in *TDNT* 3, p. 1093. Matthew and Luke do reduce a couple of Markan addresses, in their accounts, to κύριε. For example, the two blind persons of Matthew and the blind person of Luke say κύριε whereas Markan blind Bartimaeus calls Jesus ραββουνί. In the Gospel of Mark, this narrative is situated just before the entry of Jesus into Jerusalem as in both Matthew and Luke. Having studied closely the synoptic narratives, the blind person can be seen as symbolic of a disciple whose 'eyes' (of the mind, heart and soul) have been opened. Like the disciple, the healed blind person follows Jesus when Jesus enters into the city of Jerusalem to suffer on the cross.

[83] G. KITTEL, κύριος, p.1093.

[84] Vincent TAYLOR, *The Person of Christ in New Testament Teaching*, London, Macmillan, 1958, p. 6. Taylor opines that Mark's restraint from using κύριε is remarkable, since the confession 'Jesus is Lord' was widespread in the primitive Christian communities long before he wrote his Gospel.

[85] Christopher M. TUCKETT, *Christology and the New Testament, Jesus and His Earliest Followers*, Edinburgh, University Press, 2001, p. 110. For Tuckett, it is surprising that Mark has not given a significant place to Jesus κύριος despite its very probable Hellenistic Christian milieu.

[86] *Ibid.*, Even when the term κύριος occurs in Mk 5:19 (The Lord has done for you...), it is not clear whether the title 'lord' refers to Jesus or God. In Mk 11:3 (The Lord needs it...), it is uncertain how significant is this form a Christological point of view.

[87] G. VERMES, *Jesus the Jew*, p. 122.

[88] *Ibid.*, Vermes also observes that the peculiar style κύριε is employed by the disciples when mentioning, or speaking to, their master.

[89] Matthew uses κύριος first in the event of the stilling of the storm and secondly, when using indirect speech (by Peter) in the event of the first announcement of the passion. During the Transfiguration, Mark uses the address Rabbi and no address in the event of the betrayal of Jesus in Gethsemene by the traitor Judas. However, Matthew has Judas use the address 'Rabbi' in the betrayal event (Mt 26: 25&49). This leads one to wonder whether Matthew considers Judas no longer a disciple. On the other hand, the way Matthew uses κύριε in place of διδάσκαλε in the episode of the exorcism of the demonic child could imply that Matthew considers the father of the child to be a disciple of Jesus.

[90] In the event of Jesus walking on the waters the address κύριε comes twice from Peter. Adopting this Markan narrative, Matthew mentions the faith of Peter and says that Peter is a disciple. In Matthew, when it concerns *faith in Jesus*, the term κύριε is used, and even when the faith is limited the term κύριε (Mt 14:31-32) is still used in a proportionately limited way. Again at the encounter

of Jesus with the Canaanite woman, Matthew maintains (and even repeats three times) the same address κύριε.

[91] With regard to Mark's single occurrence of the address κύριε of the Syro-Phoenician woman, a parallel use is noted in Matthew. It seems that the synoptic writers have no unanimous application of the term κύριε in any Gospel event. Nevertheless, it is noted that in two cases of the triple tradition, Matthew and Luke use the term κύριε in the same context. In the episode of the leper, Matthew and Luke have the leper use the address κύριε while Mark relates the event in indirect speech. In the healing of the blind person, Mark's Bartimaeus calls Jesus ῥαββουνί, which is rendered by Matthew and Luke as κύριε.

[92] G. VERMES, *Jesus the Jew*, p. 123.

[93] *Ibid.*, p. 124.

[94] *Ibid.*, p. 126.

[95] C. M. TUCKETT, *Christology and the New Testament*, p. 123.

[96] *Ibid.*

[97] G. VERMES, *Jesus the Jew*, p. 125.

[98] G. KITTEL, κύριος, p. 1093. In the 'prediction of denial by Peter', Mark and Matthew have not used any address while Luke puts κύριε in the mouth of Peter. In the event of the arrest of Jesus, Luke does place κύριε in the mouth of the disciples.

[99] G. VERMES, *Jesus the Jew*, p. 125. In the double tradition of Matthew and Luke, there are ten occurrences of the term κύριε of which four are from Matthew and six from Luke. Matthew uses the title κύριε in the context of Jesus giving instruction to his followers or engaging in some kind of teaching activity. It is mostly used when placing a request to Jesus, following his teaching. There is not even a single address of κύριε in the simple tradition of Matthew. On the other hand, κύριε appears six times in the simple tradition of Luke, especially when spoken by those close to Jesus. Four episodes illustrate this point clearly; i) The case of the event in the Samaritan Village (Lk 9:54); ii) The return of the seventy-two (Lk 10:17); iii) The episode of Martha and Mary (Lk 10:40); iv) and the case of the dialogue of Jesus just before he makes his way to the Mount of Olives (Lk 22:38). In addition, it is noted that in Luke the term κύριε is used in the context of the miraculous catch of fish (Lk 5:8). However, note that this term is used only *after* the catch, when Simon throws himself at the feet of Jesus saying κύριε (prior to that event he addressed Jesus with ἐπιστάτα). Similarly, Luke puts this term κύριε addressed to Jesus, by Zachaeus, but only *after* he welcomed Jesus to his place.

[100] C. M. TUCKETT, *Christology and the New Testament*, p. 141.

[101] *Ibid.*

[102] *Ibid.*, p. 193.

[103] Apart from this, Fitzmyer notes that the title κύριος at least once in the synoptic tradition, has also a "regal connotation" when Jesus is presented in debate with a temple audience (Mk 12:36), or Pharisees (Mt 22:41), or scribes (Lk 20:39). See, J. A. FITZMYER, *A Wandering Aramean,* p. 127.

[104] J. DONALDSON, *The Title Rabbi in the Gospels,* p. 288. When Matthew adds κύριε *in his own simple tradition* this is often placed in the mouth of Peter. It underlines the exceptional status of this disciple among those closest to Jesus.

[105] *Ibid.*

[106] *Ibid.*

[107] J. DONALDSON, *The Title Rabbi in the Gospels,* p. 288.

[108] A. KOSTENBERGER, *Studies in John and Gender,* p. 74.

[109] Robert H. STEIN, *The Method and Message of Jesus' Teachings,* Philadelphia, The Westminster Press, 1948, p. 1. Stein explains that when one group places an emphasis on "Prophet" as a title to Jesus, another group or circle understands Jesus either as "savior" or "Lord." This is the same when Jesus is understood as "Messiah" whereas another group merely calls him a "teacher."

Chapter - 2

Jesus:
A Jewish Rabbi and Teacher?

Introduction

In part I of this book, the study of the historical development of the title "Rabbi", it was shown that the term ῥαββί in the time of Jesus did not necessarily refer to a specific office or occupation. That would be true only after the Temple in Jerusalem was destroyed in 70 A.D. Rather, it was a word meaning "great one" or "my master" which was applied to many kinds of people in everyday speech. The present study uses the term "rabbi" in the former sense without implying in any way that Jesus conforms to the formalized picture of the institutionalized rabbinate that emerged after the destruction of the Jewish Temple in 70 A.D. and the bar Kochba revolt in 135 A.D. It was clearly used as a term of respect for one's teacher as well, even though the formal position of rabbi would come later. In one sense then, calling Jesus "Rabbi" is an anachronism. In another sense the use of this term by the people of his day is a measure of their great respect for him as a person and as a teacher and not just a reference to the teaching in which he was engaged. This chapter will look at the term 'Rabbi' as it was applied to Jesus in a Jewish context through the eyes of the authors of the Synoptic Gospels.

To begin with, it is clear that all three synoptic authors portray Jesus as a 'teacher' with his own followers or disciples. They all portray him as being addressed as 'Rabbi' both by his disciples and others. The obvious questions are 'How was this term used?' and 'Was Jesus seen as being of the same order as any other Rabbi of his time?' This chapter will attempt to answer these crucial questions. Thus, the relationship that existed between Jesus and other Rabbis of his time will be explored. Comparisons will be drawn of master/disciple relationship between Jesus and his followers, and that which existed between other Rabbis and their followers. Also, the content of his teaching and the authority by which he proclaimed his message will be looked into. In all these areas the similarities with the Rabbinical method of operation will be noted and perhaps more important, the significant differences too.

1. Calling Jesus a Jewish Rabbi: A Valid Title?

Rudolf Bultmann suggests, "If the gospel record is worthy of credence, it is at least clear that Jesus actually lived as a Jewish Rabbi."[1] To justify his point he draws attention to the way Jesus taught in the synagogue, and the way Jesus is portrayed in the gospels as disputing "questions of law with pupils and opponents or with people seeking knowledge who turn to him as the celebrated Rabbi."[2] Jesus' contemporaries viewed him first of all as a ῥαββί because they observed him keeping the established Jewish customs.

However, Martin Hengel, in his significant work "The Charismatic Leader and His Followers", flatly states that "Jesus was not a 'rabbi.'" Martin Hengel concludes, "He [Jesus] is for them [his disciples], not the ῥαββί / διδάσκαλος but their Lord." While acknowledging that "Jesus was doubtless addressed as 'Rabbi,'"[3] Hengel suggests that, "we should desist altogether from the description of Jesus as a 'Rabbi.'" However, Hengel himself considers Jesus primarily as an "eschatological charismatic," the focus of whose message was no longer the Old Testament. For Hengel, Jesus "stood outside any discoverable uniform teaching tradition of Judaism," so that he concludes that, "There was between him [Jesus] and the rabbis not a difference in degree as between two different teachers, but a difference in principle. He taught as someone specially authorized by God, so that his Word was God's Word, which men could not evade." Hengel contends that this expression did not necessarily carry the connotation of teacher but may merely have functioned as a term of respect. However, Hengel's treatment has been eclipsed by the magisterial work of R. Riesner[4] on Jesus as a teacher. While Riesner focuses primarily on the Synoptic Gospels, he argues that Jesus operated within the Palestinian framework of a Jewish religious teacher. Riesner's work remains to be supplemented by an equivalent study on Jesus as a rabbi in the Gospels.

Jesus, according to the Jewish writer Josephus Flavius, appeared on the scene as a respected ῥαββί[5] It is important to remember that Jesus operated in the context of the theology of his time because there has been a tendency in recent literature on Jesus to view him simply as Jewish by background. Historical and archaeological researches have revealed the Judaism of his time in its wide variety. Thus, this study places Jesus back into his own Jewish environment. Rather than reading the gospels superficially, as texts either to be embraced as infallible or relativized as symbolic, they are placed in the context of what was happening when they were written. This includes comparing them to early Jewish literature such as the Torah and the Prophets in Hebrew, the Talmud, the Mishnah, and the Jewish historian Josephus, of the Targums. This last item represents the oral Aramaic folk renderings of Scripture which depart from the Hebrew texts in significant ways. Geza Vermes opines that, "In fact, with the discovery and study of the Dead Sea Scrolls and other archaeological treasures and other corresponding improvement in our understanding of the ideas, doctrines, methods of teaching, languages, and culture of the Jews of the New Testament times, it is now possible not simply to place Jesus in relief against this setting (as students of the Jewish background of Christianity pride themselves on doing) but to insert him foursquare within first-century Jewish life itself. The questions then to be asked are where he fits into it, and whether the added substance and clarity gained from immersing him in historical reality confer credibility on the patchy gospel picture."[6] This leads to more questions. What kind of cultural environment formed his personality? Why does history first encounter him in public among the disciples of John the Baptist? When and where did Jesus begin to develop his own following, so that he was recognized as a teacher, a ῥαββί, in his own right? The starting point in this section will be basically and primarily the identification of Jesus as a Jew. The following section will look at the academic (Rabbinical?) formation of Jesus in Nazareth to see whether Jesus was qualified as a Rabbi to teach and interpret both the scripture and the law to his audience. The position of certain scholars such as Rudolf Bultmann, Geza Vermes and E. P. Sanders will also be reviewed. In his *Jesus the Jew*, Geza Vermes[7] seeks to set the scene for Jesus' activity and determine what kind of Jew he was. E. P. Sanders[8] in his *Jesus and Judaism*, criticises scholars who refuse to take seriously the Jewishness of Jesus. These scholars in their research of the historical Jesus attempt to illustrate the historical settings of Jesus' life and ministry in the context of first-century Judaism.

Jesus was raised a Jew

To begin with, no one disputes that Jesus was a Jew by birth, and the identification of Jesus as a Rabbi basically emerges from the general acceptance of his Jewish identity. This is confirmed by his very Jewish genealogy. As noted in the gospels, Jesus was circumcised[9] on the eighth day (Lk 2.21) and bore a common Jewish name, *Yeshua*, 'God saves'[10] (Mt 1.21). After his birth, Jesus was presented to the Lord in the Jerusalem temple.[11] In the Synoptic Gospels the matter of Jesus' whereabouts after he was found in the temple of Jerusalem at the age of twelve is missing. Though little is stated about the childhood of Jesus,[12] it is understood that he grew in wisdom as a boy and that he reached the fulfilling of the commandments of the Passover at the age of twelve. When Jesus was a young adolescent he did stay behind in Jerusalem as Luke 2:41-52 describes. Perhaps his family was prospering or was particularly dutiful, for most of them only went up to Jerusalem occasionally. Jesus' parents went up to Jerusalem to celebrate Passover (Lk 2:41-43), a tradition which Jesus continued (Jn 12:12; Mk 14:12-26). By the age of 12 Jesus was growing in understanding as he was found in the temple[13] precincts "both listening and asking questions" (Lk 2:46). The method of teaching in Jesus' time included questioning to elicit intelligent responses. So Jesus' asking questions may not have been just to obtain knowledge but also to teach it, indeed "they

were astonished at his understanding and answers." Bruce Chilton raises the question, "What exactly became of Jesus after he disappeared into the milling crowds at the Temple? The gospels are nearly silent. There is just one lone reference in Lk 2:41-52. Jesus evades his family and remains in Jerusalem…"[14] If all that happened according to the Jewish laws and customs, Jesus would also surely have pursued a Jewish education as any boy of his age was expected to do.

Rudolf Bultmann in the beginning of his work on *Jesus and the Word makes a critical comment emphasizing,* "We can know almost nothing concerning the life and personality of Jesus."[15] Even though Bultmann seems to be sceptical, in this same work he recognises that Jesus is called a Rabbi in the gospels.[16] It is at least clear, said Bultmann, "that Jesus actually lived as a Jewish Rabbi. As such, he takes his place as a teacher in the synagogue. As such he gathers around him a circle of pupils. As such, he disputes over questions of the Law with pupils and opponents or with people seeking knowledge who turn to him as the celebrated Rabbi. He disputes along the same lines as Jewish Rabbis, uses the same methods of argument, the same turns of speech; like them he coins proverbs and teaches in parables. Jesus' teaching shows in content also a close relationship with that of the rabbis."[17] The term ῥαββί, in his case, can be taken to mean "belonging to the class of scribes."[18] If this point is taken seriously, according to Bultmann, it implies that Jesus, being a scribe, had received the necessary scribal training and also passed the scribal tests. Even when Bultmann says that Jesus must have undergone scribal training, he further agrees that it is uncertain how strictly and comprehensively the course would have been at that time. It was only a century later that it was formalised and 'well regulated.' From this proposition it seems that by the time Jesus began his public ministry, he had not only received the thorough religious training typical of the average Jewish man of his day, he had probably spent years studying with one of the outstanding Rabbis in Galilee. Was Jesus' education the same, as any other Jewish boy of his time? This will be the main concern for the discussion in the following section.

Education for Jesus as a Jewish Boy

Besides many designations attributed to Jesus, Rabbi appears, in the gospels, to present him as a teacher or scribe. The implication being that Jesus had received the necessary scribal training and had passed the requisite scribal tests. Although it is uncertain how strictly the course of study, which is known from Rabbinic literature, was regulated at the time of Jesus, it can probably be assumed that it was less defined than it was a century later.

Jacques Baldet while speaking on the Judaism of Jesus in his recent book on "*Jesus the Rabbi Prophet*" notes that "to understand Jesus' message, we must first understand the religion in which he was educated."[19] It certainly demands a closer look at the education process in Galilee. The Mishnah[20] describes the educational process for a young Jewish boy at the time when the oral Torah was transformed into Mishnah after the time of the historical Jesus. According to Samuel Byrskog, "The rabbinic literature contains numerous traces of a developed educational system, on the elementary as well as on the advanced level."[21] At five years old, a boy began to study Scripture, at ten years the Mishnah, the oral Torah and the interpretations at thirteen for the fulfilling of the commandments. Byrskog states that "The Scripture school provided the basic education in reading the Torah."[22] At the age of fifteen, a Jewish boy learnt the Talmud which is of the making of Rabbinic interpretations, at eighteen he went to the bride-chamber, at twenty he began pursuing a vocation, and eventually at thirty he exercised his authority to teach others.[23] This clearly describes the centrality of Scripture in the education of a Jewish boy in Galilee. However, Ed Tenhor is of the opinion that in Jesus' hometown, "There was little opportunity for a formal education."[24] Most of the scholars who deal with the study or research on "The Historical Jesus" agree that Jesus would have learnt the Scripture and Torah as was expected of any Jewish boy. The following section sets forth the ideas of some scholars regarding the languages that Jesus might have spoken.

Did Jesus Learn and Speak Hebrew?

Irving M. Zeitlin, in his work on *Jesus and the Judaism of his time* speaks about the Jewish identity of Jesus in his Judeo- Palestinian context. "He was circumcised as a Jew, lived as a Jew and prayed as a Jew; he performed the Jewish rites and he preached in Aramaic to his fellow Jews in the synagogues of Palestine."[25] John P. Meier believes that Jesus, almost certainly, would have been literate in Hebrew. Meier deals with the subject of the various languages Jesus spoke in the course of his public ministry. He notes that "since the adult Jesus became an itinerant teacher traversing both Galilee and Judea and since as a teacher he obviously wished to be understood by his audience, which was largely made up of ordinary Palestinian Jews, Jesus would have spoken whatever was the language commonly used by the ordinary Jews in their daily lives in Palestine."[26] Of course, the question of the language that Jesus spoke is greatly discussed today and the above would in no way simplify that argument. For Irwin M. Zeitlin, there are good reasons to suppose that "Jesus knew and employed the language of the Scribes and Pharisees. To the unlearned people, however, Jesus spoke Aramaic, the only language in which many of them could converse."[27] When Jesus had thus progressed from a learner to a Rabbi, according to Zeitlin, it was possible that he might have learnt Hebrew and Aramaic as any other boy usually did in his time and at his age.

Ed Tenhor thinks that Aramaic is the language that was spoken by Jesus. He states that, "He probably did know some Hebrew, having read the Hebrew Bible in the synagogue, certainly knew quite a lot of Greek, a large Greek-speaking city, Sephorris, being just a little over an hour's walk from his childhood home, but his actual language was a Galilean form of Aramaic."[28]

R. H. Stein is of the same opinion; he says that "to be more exact, we can say that he spoke "a Galilean version of western Aramaic" which differed somewhat from the Aramaic of Judea."[29] Scholars like Joachim

Jeremias and Vincent Taylor agree that certain expressions of Jesus in the gospels are "Aramaisms",[30] or Greek translations of sayings that were originally Aramaic. According to Stein, it is evident that Jesus also spoke Hebrew. He concludes, "Furthermore, it is doubtful that Jesus would have been addressed as "Rabbi" unless he was capable of discussing the Hebrew texts."[31] Yet, Stein does not deny that Jesus could also have spoken Greek, which was undoubtedly spoken at his time in Palestine.

When Riesner speaks about *Jesus as Preacher and Teacher*, he agrees that Jesus could have learned some of his rhetoric through the education of the Synagogue. "The synagogues provided even in small Galilean villages such as Nazareth a kind of popular education system."[32] In the synagogues, like many other Jewish men, Jesus also could have read the Scriptures and expounded them.[33] Riesner himself goes further to say that Jesus, apparently, had also a natural, God-given talent for speaking. This will be dealt with in more details later in this chapter.

From the gospels, it is known that it was mostly the ordinary people who were Jesus' audience. In that context, this study suggests that Jesus would have spoken the language of these ordinary people. Yet there is not any concrete evidence as to which languages Jesus did speak at his time. This study is not fully convinced that Jesus as a Jew had the formal training to ultimately become a Jewish teacher, a Rabbi. But it is wholeheartedly agreed that Jesus was born and brought up a Jew. The fact must be accepted that in the Gospels there are no elaborate arguments about Jesus' academic formation before the public ministry. It is clear that, arrive at any definite conclusion, further research is needed in the area of the historical Jesus.

Did Jesus observe Jewish Religious Customs?

According to many writers and historians, based on his life and mission in a Jewish environment, Jesus behaved and looked like a Jew. Certainly, being faithful to the Law, he wore the *tsîtsit* 'tassel.' Ed Tenhor writes, "Since Jesus was a teacher, it would be appropriate that he dress as a religious Jew, and thus, had tassels, smaller ones, at the hem of his cloak."[34] Jesus also kept Tabernacles (Jn 7:1-39). Jn 10:22-23 may also indicate that Jesus celebrated the *Hanukkah* festival, which commemorated the 2nd century B.C. rededication of the Temple under the Maccabees. "As was his custom" he also attended synagogue every Sabbath (Lk 4:16) even during his travelling ministry (Mk 1:39; Mt 4:23; 9:35; Lk 4:15.16-27.44). In tithing, fasting and alms giving he was totally Jewish. In every respect, therefore, Jesus was a Jew, and was not ashamed to call himself one: "*We* know what *we* worship, for salvation is from *the Jews*" (Jn 4:22).

Another question here is; to what extent did Jesus observe the practices of the Oral Torah? Zeitlin's research informs us that Jesus was a teacher who even questioned the Scribes and Pharisees on law and authority.[35] The important point is, Jesus taught *as a Rabbi* quoting from the Scriptures. This attracted many to listen to him, in particular a wide group of ordinary people. In Zeitlin's view, Jesus was their Rabbi, a teacher who had authority and he manifested his authority over and above the Scripture and Law. Jesus was not often charged with breaking any part of it, although his disciples occasionally were accused of disobeying aspects of the Oral Torah (Lk 6:1-2). Only one such accusation was made against Jesus that he broke the Sabbath by healing the sick (Lk 14:1-4).[36] It may seem that there is a shortage of hard evidence in the New Testament concerning Jesus' religious observance. Nonetheless, one is able to gather enough evidence from the Gospels to conclude that Jesus observed[37] the biblical commandments as they were interpreted in the Oral Torah. To limit the scope of whether Jesus functioned as a Jewish Rabbi, this study will not further discuss this area of Jesus' academic formation. Rather that is suggested as an area for later research. The following section will analyse the concept of considering Jesus as a disciple of John the Baptist. Is it valid and authentic that Jesus should be considered a disciple of the Baptist? Was Jesus a member of the group gathered round the Baptist, and did John the Baptist affect Jesus in any way in his religious and ethical formation?

Is Jesus a Disciple of John the Baptist?

Jacques Baldet raises a question as follows: "Like so many other religious people of his time, did not Jesus also have a teacher, one who opened the way for him? Might this teacher have been John the Baptist?"[38] There are some scholars who support the view that Jesus stayed with the Baptist for a while as a disciple. A. N. Wilson, for example writes that Jesus "was also brought up with religious training, perhaps as a disciple of his cousin John the Baptist."[39] According to Bruce Chilton, "Jesus moves straight from early adolescence into a close relationship with John, and is only referred to again in Galilee much later, as a mature adult. That suggests he did not return with his family to Nazareth, but remained near Jerusalem and sought out the company of John." Thus Jesus might have became a student or disciple of John.[40] Bruce Chilton opines that "Jesus joined the other disciples in John's practice only after he had watched, listened, absorbed, then mastered John's *mishnah*."[41] This is a clear description of how Jesus might have become a disciple of the Baptist and also a rather bold presumption that, both in the intellectual and charismatic formation of Jesus, John the Baptist had a very important role to play.

However, P. Johnson holds the view in *History of Christianity*, that "Our ignorance about the personality of the Baptist obscures our appreciation of the uniqueness of that of Jesus. The problem is that we do not know much about what John taught, very little about his life, and nothing about his education. We do not even know if he taught his own version of theology or cosmology, nor if his eschatology was limited to the simple Messianic message given in the gospels; nor do we know whether on the contrary (which seems more plausible), his teachings were quite elaborate and sophisticated."[42] In any case as Baldet opines, "one point on which little doubt remains is that Jesus was baptised by John."[43] Jesus probably grew up in an environment where some people nurtured his hopes for divine intervention into human history. Jesus may have shared these hopes at some point in his life since he was baptised by and may have been a disciple of John the Baptist. If John the Baptist was such an apocalyptic preacher, it is entirely reasonable to presume that Jesus had some connection with eschatological hopes.[44] Ed Tenhor says that Jesus was "perhaps exposed to many groups during his young adult years, deliberately searching them out, picking up ideas, and exploring practices, learning all the time."[45] Ed Tenhor is convinced that Jesus was strongly influenced by John the Baptist and his apocalyptic movement. It is to be noted that Jesus, after his baptism by John, begins to choose disciples for his own movement, but a movement that shared something of the influence of John the Baptist. Yet there is always a difference, both in the method and content of the preaching, between that of John the Baptist and Jesus. John P. Meier rightly observes: "Although Jesus followed in the Baptist's footsteps, perhaps even baptizing for a while (see Jn 3:22, 26; 4:1), there was a major shift in his message."[46] So the possibility exists that Jesus was a disciple of the Baptist. However any attempt to depict Jesus merely as a disciple in the group gathered around the Baptist would not be credible.

John the Baptist: Jesus' Rabbi?
In the first century AD, Jesus was not the only one who had disciples. The gospels state that there were other groups, each with their own leader and teachings. However, J. P. Meier observes, "apart from a relatively small number of references to the disciples of the Pharisees, of the Baptist, and

of Moses, the word "disciples" in the gospels refers solely to the disciples of Jesus."[47] The Pharisees had their own disciples (Mt 22:16; Mk 2:18; Lk 5:33). Similarly, the New Testament speaks about the 'disciples of John the Baptist' (Mt 9:14; 11:2; Jn 1:35.37). Interestingly, the term Rabbi, in the sole instance in John where it does not refer to Jesus, is applied to the Baptist (3:26). According to Andreas Kostenberger, "This indicates that the Baptist was awarded the respect commensurate to a religious teacher by his disciples."[48] Even the Synoptic Narratives (cf., Mk 2:18; Mt 11:2ff; Lk 7:18ff; 11:1) testify that the Baptist had his own circle of disciples. But was John the Baptist Jesus' Rabbi?

J. P. Meier in an attempt to gain greater clarity observes, "By definition, the very fact that Jesus left Nazareth, came to the region of the Jordan to hear John, and accepted his message to the point of receiving his baptism means that, in the broad sense of the word, Jesus became John's disciple."[49] Meier agrees that John the Baptist was both an eschatological prophet and spiritual master who taught his disciples. "To that extent, by submitting to his message and baptism, Jesus became the disciple, the pupil, the student of this rabbi called John."[50] Meier also wonders whether after his baptism Jesus stayed with the Baptist and joined the inner circle of the baptised "who followed John on his baptising tours up and down the Jordan valley (cf. Jn 1:28. 35-37; 3:23), assisted John in his preaching and baptising (Jn 3:25) and received more detailed teaching from him about his message (Jn 3:26-30)."[51] Geza Vermes asserts that Jesus imitated John the Baptist in his preaching. He also asserts that the content and mode of Jesus' preaching cannot be equated with the Essenes. "Contrary to the Essene practice reserving instruction to initiates only, but imitating John the Baptist, Jesus addressed his preaching in Galilee and all throughout Judea."[52] In sum, one can only speculate whether or not Jesus was a disciple of the Baptist.

The School of the Baptist and His Disciples

The important element seen in all the gospels is that Jesus and John the Baptist were contemporaries, and that John the Baptist is portrayed as the forerunner of Jesus and his ministry. J. P. Meier notes that "there is no indication, however, of any structured community during John's life time, or indeed after his death."[53] Martin Hengel's position is that John the Baptist is never shown expounding Scriptures to his disciples. When Hengel speaks about John the Baptist he opines that "We hardly know anything about how he gathered his disciples around him, but it may nevertheless be indicative that we hear nothing about his expounding Scripture but only of his teaching his disciples special prayers and of their having their own fasting practices."[54] But the fact that John the Baptist knew the coming of the Messiah was imminent implies he knew the scriptures very well. From what is known of the Rabbi/disciple mode of operation, he must have taught this to his disciples.

Hahn notes, "The address 'Rabbi' is quite normally used to the Baptist."[55] The Lukan presentation of John the Baptist with the title διδάσκαλος (Lk 3:12) must also be noted. According to Schnackenburg, the disciples of the Baptist were found as "a group with religious practices of their own, distinct from the disciples of Jesus."[56] Raymond Brown, too, maintains that the Baptist had his own circle of disciples who formed a religious school. "All the Gospels agree that John the Baptist had disciples."[57] Brown's commentary cites the gospels stating that John the Baptist had his own group of disciples chosen by baptism and that this group had their own rules of fasting (Mk 11:18; Lk 7:29-33) and their own prayers (Lk 5:33; 11:1).[58] These disciples had their own ascetic practices (Mk 2:18). Presumably the disciples of the Baptist had to fulfil the demands of their master. According to Nepper-Christensen "Those who followed John were baptized for repentance and subjected themselves to new ascetic ethical demands."[59] Andreas J. Köstenberger agrees that, in the Gospels, the term ῥαββί is also applied to John the Baptist which means that "the Baptist was awarded the respect commensurate to a religious teacher by his disciples."[60] So it can be seen that John the Baptist is presented as a ῥαββί in the sense of a teacher and master of a particular group with its own disciples, and it can be assumed that John he Baptist functioned as a Rabbi and taught his disciples.

It seems reasonable to agree with John P. Meier who concludes that Jesus' exact relation to the various Jewish parties of the day is extremely difficult to fix, all the more so because most of the rabbinic material comes from a later date."[61] The relation of Jesus to the various Jewish groups of the first century A.D, is thus vastly more complicated. Different scholars have identified Jesus with almost every Jewish party known to exist. Among them, the favourite designation is "Jesus the Pharisee." Here in the following section we shall attempt to study the concept of calling Jesus a Pharisee and its relevance to our theme of considering Jesus a Jewish teacher.

Is Jesus A Pharisee?

A number of scholars hold that Jesus could have been a Pharisee.[62] In his *Jesus the Pharisee*, Harvey Falk[63] situates Jesus in the struggle between two different Pharisaic schools such as the school of Shammai and the school of Hillel. Falk claims that about 20 B.C. the school of Shammai gained control of the Jewish community in Palestine and the Hillelites joined the Essenes. For Falk, Jesus' background was in the Essene branch of the Pharisaic movement gathered around Hillel and he remained an Orthodox Jew all his life and never wished his fellow Jews to change any aspect of their traditional faith. John P. Meier takes a contrary view: he observes that "Jesus has been painted as a nonconforming Pharisee because of his freedom *vis-à-vis* the Law and tradition, a Pharisee of the Shammai school because of his strict views on divorce, and a Pharisee of the Hillel school because of his humane emphasis on love of neighbor as central to the Law."[64] As the NT shows, there were certainly points of contact between the Pharisees and Jesus.[65] Yet, it is neither easy to include Jesus as a member in a group of the Pharisees, nor is it possible to label him as someone against the Pharisees. E. P. Sanders in his *Jesus and Judaism* argued that, in spite of denunciations of Pharisees attributed to Jesus in the gospels, Jesus himself was a Pharisee. Phipps concludes that Jesus belonged to the Pharisaic movement. According to Phipps, "it seems clear that Jesus' message and mission cannot properly be understood without seeing him as a Pharisaic Jew."[66] Their claims are based on the similarity[67] of his teaching methods as they are shown in the gospels and those offered by the rabbis and the sages in the Rabbinic texts.

Asher Finkel[68] in his study on *"The Jewishness of Jesus"* cites many examples to prove how Jesus acted, and preached,[69] in his Galilean countryside as a Jew himself. He points out, "The Pharisaic masters recognised Jesus at first as a colleague and the people addressed him with the title 'Rabbi'.[70] Thus, Jesus was identified as a Jewish Rabbi and was addressed a teacher in almost all circles.

2. Jesus' Public Ministry: Mission of a Rabbi

According to Robert H. Stein, "It is unanimous witness of the Gospel tradition and redaction that one of the prominent functions of Jesus during his public ministry was teaching."[71] Stein affirms that, "the teachings of Jesus possess qualities in common with the teachings of both the wise men and the prophets of the Old Testament."[72] Many scholars argue that the world seemed to forget that Jesus was a Jew, and that they seem to forget or ignore the fact that Jesus functioned as a Rabbi. Until these facts about Jesus are understood, some of the things he said cannot be fully understood: the implications of what he said can only be understood through the framework of who he was as a human, a Jew and a ῥαββί.

Ed Tenhor in the introduction to his work, *"That Rabbi from Nazareth: A Quest for Historical Jesus"*, summarises the life of Jesus as follows; "I would like to introduce you to the ῥαββί named Jesus, the one from Nazareth. He was a Jewish teacher, identified as a prophet, a unique wandering sage involved in healing and exorcisms, a popular Galilean who often provoked religious people and authorities, who was also an unpopular seemingly homeless person who agitated until arrested, and who was found guilty enough to have been executed."[73] Focusing on whether Jesus was a Rabbi, this section will present a number of elements to prove that Jesus was indeed considered a Rabbi of his time. Evidence will be used based on the research of scholars who have looked at Jesus and his teachings with the view of identifying him as a Jewish teacher.

Jesus: Teacher of Jewish Tradition and Morals

To establish that Jesus acted like any other Jewish teacher, a number of instances can be cited of his ways of teaching: for example, Jesus disputes questions of the Law with pupils and/or opponents and also with people who are seeking knowledge and turn to him as a celebrated Rabbi. He disputes along the same lines as Jewish Rabbis, uses the same methods of argument, the same turns of phrase and, like them, he coins proverbs and teaches in parables. Jesus' teaching also shows that, in content, he bears a close relationship with the Rabbis.[74] Hence in the following section it will be seen how, in the method and the content of his preaching, Jesus showed himself to be a Jewish teacher like others of his time.

The Jewishness of Jesus' teaching is well summarized by Franz Mussner: "Jesus of Nazareth stood for the great religious ideas of Israel as they are found in the Hebrew Bible and the Jewish Tradition. His teachings on God, obedience to God's will, creation, expiation for sin, Covenant, the piety of the poor, the better righteousness, eschatology, and fidelity are consistent with his Jewish heritage."[75] Franz Mussner states that through Jesus the great heritage of Israel has been mediated to all nations. According to C. H. Dodd starting from the point where Jesus occupied common ground with his Jewish contemporaries, it may help to appreciate both the organic relationship of his teaching to its matrix in Judaism, and the new departure it marks. According to C. H. Dodd, Jesus "was addressed as "Rabbi" (Master), and not only by his immediate followers, but also by strangers, including some who would themselves have claimed the same title."[76] It is clear that on many issues (both religious and ethical), Jesus operated from a common ground, which he shared with other Rabbis of his time.

Uniformity in Teaching by Jesus and Jewish Teachers

Geza Vermes in his work on *Jesus the Jew* observes that "from the outset the Gospels portray Jesus as a popular preacher and preserve various types of sayings ascribed to him."[77] With the help of the evangelists' presentation, Vermes tries to determine what kind of a teacher Jesus was in that society. He notes that Jesus only preached to the Jews, for he never envisaged a systematic mission to Gentiles. Then coming to the ethical message of Jesus, he observes the parables Jesus used in his preaching. He explains that the parables of Jesus are "a form of homiletic teaching commonly used by Rabbinical preachers."[78] For Vermes, it is clear that there are many similarities to the rabbinical preachers in the sayings of Jesus. Vermes wonders, "if Jesus was primarily a teacher of morals, he might be expected to have shown a liking for short, pithy, colourful utterances, the kind of Rabbinic logia with which the pages of the sayings of the fathers in the Mishnah are filled."[79] When Vermes analyses the ethical teaching of Jesus, he opines that Jesus was familiar with the Rabbinic logia.

In his discourses, Jesus followed the same pattern of debate as other Jewish Rabbis. He had the same methods of speech and argument and he also used proverbs and parables. "Thus Jesus' teaching shows in content also a close relationship with that of the Rabbis."[80] Thus Bultmann agrees with other scholars that Jesus actually lived and taught as a Jewish Rabbi. One of the most familiar methods is the question and answer, with the question often phrased as a teaser. A woman had seven husbands; whose wife will she be in the life to come (Mt. 22:23-33)? Is it lawful for a devout Jew to pay taxes to the Roman authorities (Mt. 22:15-22)? What must I do to inherit eternal life (Mk 10:17-22)? Who is the greatest in the Kingdom of Heaven (Matt. 18:1-6)? The one who puts the question acts as a straight man, setting up the opportunity for Rabbi Jesus to drive home the point, often by standing the question on its head. To the writers of the New Testament, however, the most typical form of the teachings of Jesus was the parable: "He said nothing to them without a parable" (Mt. 13:34). But the Greek word *parabole* was taken from the Septuagint, the Jewish translation of their Bible into Greek. Thus here too the evangelists' accounts of Jesus as a teller of parables[81] make sense only in the setting of his Jewish background. John P. Meier also expresses the same view when he says, "Prophet and wisdom teacher that he was, Jesus used the rich rhetorical traditions of Israel to hammer home his message. Oracles, woes, aphorisms, proverbs, but above all parables served to tease the minds of his audience, throw them off balance, and challenge them to decide for and against his claim on their lives."[82] So, various scholars make convincing arguments to prove that Jesus acted like any other Jewish teacher of his time both in the method and the content of his teaching. However, there are also opposing views against this stand.

Martin Hengel in his *Charismatic Leader and His Followers* contends that the Old Testament is no longer the central focus of Jesus' message. He comments, "As a rule Jesus argues exegetically only when he is questioned or attacked by third parties about the Torah, and, in addition, also at times when his claims and authority are at stake, and here it is often methodologically difficult to distinguish between Jesus' use of scripture and that of the Christian community, as the latter again was for apologetic reasons very much more interested in proofs from scripture."[83] Andreas Köstenberger has only a few critical remarks on Martin Hengel's position. Apart from Hengel's methodological skepticism, it seems precarious to brush aside instances where Jesus uses the Hebrew Scriptures, "when he is questioned or attacked by third parties about the Torah, and, in addition, also at times when his claims and authority are at stake" as merely exceptional. Köstenberger concludes, "It seems extreme to deny completely that Rabbi carried the connotation of teacher in the instances narrated in the gospels when applied to Jesus."[84] Moreover, when Hengel claims that the new content of Jesus' teaching "was not 'scribal' and 'rabbinic' but 'charismatic' and 'eschatological,'" he seems to use the term 'rabbinic' in its later, post-70 A.D. sense.

Jesus the Rabbi: A Master

According to Alan Culpepper,[85] in the Mediterranean world, the Pythagoreans, Platonists, Aristotelians, Epicureans, Stoics, the disciples of Hillel, and Philo all formed schools which consisted of a circle of disciples. Jacques Baldet brings out the difference between them and Jesus' followers; "In the Mediterranean world, philosophers, prophets, and rabbis were commonly accompanied by disciples. What made Jesus' disciples unusual is that they were chosen by him and in order to follow him, they had to abandon home, family, friends, and possessions, with no hope of return."[86] Samuel Byrskog states, "Although it is possible for a teacher to exhibit his functions in interaction with various discussion partners only, the Matthean Jesus appears together with a defined group of disciples."[87] Jesus had an inner circle of twelve disciples who received special training, but these were not his only disciples. He called them to follow him[88] and to be with him. They were invited to imitate[89] his actions and were to make everything else secondary to their learning from the Rabbi.

Jesus as Διδάσκαλος *and His Disciples as* Μάθηταί

As presented in the gospels, Jesus takes his place as a teacher in the synagogue. As such he gathers around him a circle of pupils[90] and teaches them, as any other master would do to his disciples (pupils). Μαθητής as a learner, pupil, student is in contrast to διδάσκαλος, a teacher; hence it denotes one who follows one's teaching, as the disciples of John, Mt 9:14; of the Pharisees, Mt 22: 16; and of Moses, Jn 9:28. Μαθητής is used of the disciples of Jesus (*a*) in a wide sense, of Jews who became his adherents (Jn 6:66; Lk 6:17), some being secretly so (Jn 19:38); (*b*) especially of the twelve Apostles (Mt. 10:1; Lk 22:11); (*c*) of all who manifest that they are his disciples by abiding in his word (Jn 8: 31; cf. 13:35; 15:8); (*d*) in the Acts, of those who believed upon him and confessed him (6:1. 2. 7; 14:20. 22. 28; 15:10; 19:1). A disciple was not only a pupil, but an adherent; hence they are spoken of as imitators of their teacher (cf. Jn 8:31; 15:8). When a general survey is taken of the study of "disciples in NT"[91] it is found that Jesus is not the only "teacher" to have "disciples", for there are also other disciples such as "disciples of John the Baptist" and "disciples of the Pharisees" (Cf. Mk 2:18; 6:29; Mt 9:14; Lk 5:33). By definition, a teacher requires a disciple just as a disciple requires a teacher. They always come in pairs. In Greek, the paired words are διδάσκαλος (Master) and Μάθηταί(Disciple), the latter being consistently used throughout the Gospels to describe the Twelve Disciples. In that light, we need to consider whether the disciples of Jesus were disciples[92] as understood by the people of his time.

The disciple of Jesus is anyone who is deeply and personally committed to Jesus, who manifests the power and authority of his master, and who continues and extends his work. Quoting W. D. Davies, Robbins states that "it is customary to presuppose that the teacher/disciple relation in Mark derives from the rabbi/disciple relation in first-century C.E. Judaism."[93] In the first century, the decision to follow a ῥαββί as a disciple meant total commitment, and the *talmidim* were expected to obey the ῥαββί as they would obey their fathers.[94] Since a *talmid* was totally devoted to becoming like the ῥαββί, he would have spent his entire time listening and observing the teacher to know how to understand the Scripture and how to put it into practice.[95] Phrases like "to follow after" or "to come after" are not simply biblical phrases but connected with rabbinic accounts where disciples are featured in a position of following behind. Referring to D. Daubbe, Robbins proposes that "the titles *rabbi* or *rabbouni* and in many other stories Jesus' dialogue with his disciples follows patterns akin to patterns in rabbinic accounts."[96] M. J. Wilkins points out that "a major device in the inclusion of the term Μαθητής was to create units where Jesus delivers some kind of teaching to the disciples."[97] The teaching of Jesus usually consists of certain information or instruction that Jesus conveys to his disciples; often in response to something they say or ask for. Byrskog also observes that the term Μαθητής is often associated with the appearance of Jesus as teacher. "Through the association between Μαθητής and διδάσκαλος /διδάσκειν, the disciples appear as followers of Jesus the teacher."[98] Gerhard Kittel in his article on Jesus as διδάσκαλος in *TDNT* opines "That Jesus is addressed as διδάσκαλε presupposes the fact that he outwardly conforms to the Jewish picture of διδάσκαλος."[99] According to Kittel, if the gospel record is accurate, it is at least certain that Jesus actually lived as a Jewish Rabbi. In the observation of Kittel, Jesus conforms to the Jewish expectation of a ῥαββί in the sense of a teacher. Kittel sets out all the elements that associate Jesus with the scribes of his time. He also notes that Jesus was indeed a διδάσκαλος for he had gathered a group of disciples around him. The very fact that his disciples addressed him as διδάσκαλος implies that he was regarded as a teacher among the people. Thus "the Gospels make it clear point by point that the relation between Jesus and the disciples corresponds to the Rabbinic pupils to their masters and that the crowd treated him with the respect accorded to teachers."[100] When Kittel agrees that Jesus outwardly conformed to the Jewish picture of a teacher, he concludes that Jesus may be associated with the Scribes both from the form and the content of his teaching. Because of all these factors, according to Kittel, Jesus proves to be both a powerful and effective teacher and is in line with his contemporary Jewish teachers. However, categories such as "teacher of wisdom" or "teacher after the manner of rabbinic authorities"[101] fail to do justice to the uniqueness of Jesus as teacher.

The opinions of the various authors over Jesus' conformity with the Jewish picture of a Rabbi result in two important points. They are basically: 1. The method and content of his teaching which also includes Jesus' presence and teaching in the synagogues 2. The formation of the pupils who formed a group of disciples of Rabbi, their master. All the authors discussed in this study (and indeed many more) make the scholarly observation that Jesus, in his public ministry, acted in the same way as other Rabbis of that time in Galilee and as such they called Jesus a Rabbi. In the case of Jesus, it was certainly used in the sense of a leader who was seen as a 'teacher' or a dispenser of wisdom. But it must also be acknowledged that if one tries to see Jesus as a Rabbi, understood as meaning 'an ordained scholar,' then clearly Jesus would have been unlikely to have qualified for the title, and the gospels do not express such an idea anywhere.

However, at the same time, there are also opposing views and arguments about considering Jesus a Jewish Rabbi. Some of the scholars themselves who identify Jesus as a Jewish teacher have expressed their opinion that Jesus cannot be called a Rabbi in any formal sense of the term. Apart from a few authors, who totally reject the idea of calling Jesus a Rabbi, the majority of scripture scholars do consider Jesus a Rabbi, even if some add that Jesus differed in some significant respects from his Jewish contemporaries. In the following section, those arguments will be explored and also attempt to identify the 'differences' they reveal that makes Jesus stand out from other Rabbis of his time.

3. The Uniqueness of Jesus: Jesus was more than a Rabbi

Geza Vermes opposes Bultmann's view of portraying Jesus as a 'Jewish Rabbi'. He believes this view is, in fact, somewhat misleading. For Vermes, "the title of Rabbi does not seem to have acquired by Jesus' life time the meaning attached to it in later ages of a fully trained exponent of Scripture and tradition."[102] From this Vermes asserts that the term Rabbi when applied to Jesus "must be taken here in its broader sense, without prejudging the type and style of either the teacher or his teaching."[103] For Vermes, it is clear that there is no NT evidence to speak of Jesus having received any specialised training. It was the pharisaic scribes who normally expounded and interpreted the Hebrew Scriptures, but in the NT there is no mention of Jesus belonging to this group of Scribes. The doctrinal discussions Jesus had with others, and in particular the literary forms that Jesus used to express his ideas, do not necessarily prove that he had received any specialised training. For example, his words of wisdom, his prophetic warnings and his use of parables, Vermes observes "demand no skill in Bible interpretation proper, or particular familiarity with the intricacies of Jewish law."[104] Martin Hengel, in his work on *The Charismatic Leader and His Followers* categorically says, "Jesus was not a Rabbi."[105] At the same time Hengel does not fail to recognise that the expression 'Rabbi' was used by some when addressing Jesus. Hengel acknowledges that Jesus was undoubtedly addressed as Rabbi, but cautions that the title ῥαββί did not mean the same as it did one or two hundred years later. At this point it is worth noting that Hengel himself has spoken of Jesus as a teacher who taught his disciples (and others) in the course of his public ministry. Hengel, in fact, notes that Jesus was first and foremost a teacher who, like the Rabbis, taught in parables and ingeniously contrived sayings. Hengel also notes that Jesus spoke in the synagogue, gathered pupils around him, debated with his opponents, and in so doing was able to use the Torah with amazing skill. However, Hengel asks a counter question "By what right do we consider these features in Jesus' day as the exclusive preserve of Rabbinic legal scholars."?[106] Thus, Hengel very strongly affirms that Jesus of Nazareth was not a Rabbi in the ordinary sense of a 'Rabbinical teacher'.

I. M. Zeitlin says "The Gospels regard Jesus as a teacher or Rabbi, among other things. He was addressed as 'teacher' by his disciples, by his learned adversaries and by the crowds."[107] Zeitlin also observes, "In Hebrew the major school or academies in Jesus' time were in fact called 'houses'- Bet Hillel (the House of Hillel), Bet Shammai (the House of Shammai). He raises a question 'was there a Bet yeshu or House of Jesus as well? Ben Witherington III in his *The Christology of Jesus* states that there is no doubt that "Jesus was perceived to be a great teacher by his intimates and others"[108] and thus he was honoured with terms of respect like Rabbi and Rabbuni or just Teacher. But Witherington does not agree that Jesus falls into the same category as the other Jewish Rabbis of his time. He notes that, contrary to his contemporaries, Jesus *as* a Rabbi did not have some sort of a formal school to 'instruct and train' his disciples. Again, when it comes to the content of his preaching, "apparently Jesus was not and did not set out to be like a "teacher of the Torah" per se, passing along legal judgements or exegesis of various texts."[109] He further notes that Jesus does not involve himself in disputations about the Scripture and in particular the Law, but rather directly announces the will of God for the present time. What Jesus taught and preached "was not something he had learned from Jewish teachers"[110] but an eschatological revelation given by God. Thus, for Witherington, Jesus does not fall into the normal category of contemporary Jewish Rabbis. The following pages will show how distinctly Jesus, as a teacher, acted in that society, and how relevant it would be to call Jesus a Rabbi.

Rabbi Jesus: A Distinction from Rabbinic and Hellenistic Groups
R. H. Stein, speaking about Jesus as a teacher, says that the actions of
Jesus look "unrabbinic."[111] Samuel Byrskog observes that the means of
transmission of the message in Jesus' teaching to his disciples is distinct
and very different from others. "It conveys an emphasis on appropriating
Jesus' teaching in word and deed through active hearing and practise."[112]
Though there could be seen a kind of master and disciple relationship
(Jn 15:20a), the practice of Jesus and his relationship was based on love and
trust. "But Jesus informed his disciples about what his father told him, so
that their relationship might be based on trust (15:15)."[113] Hengel observes
that the changing of the masters from one to the other was sometimes
recommended in the Rabbinical way of thinking and learning, whereas,
"it was unthinkable in following Jesus. In what he did, Jesus' aim was not
to form tradition or to nurture exegetical or apocalyptic scholarship but
to proclaim the nearness of God in word and deed."[114] Quite clearly, the
master/disciple relationship in Jesus' circle is both distinct and different.
In this present section we will move to the next stage, which we consider a
significant one. The next section will look at the distinctive features which
identify the differences that make Jesus stand out from other Rabbis of his
time with regard to the master/disciple relations in his circle.

The Concept of Master/Disciple Relationships
In the Jewish world of his day, Jesus was called ῥαββί and διδάσκαλος,
the terms used to address any Rabbi of that time. Like any other Jewish
scribe, he was also teaching his disciples and the people who listened or
questioned him from the Scriptures. (see. Mt 26:25; 8: 19; 12:38; 26:55).
But it is evident that there is a difference[115] between Jesus' concept of
Master- disciple relationship and that of his contemporaries. As has already
been noted above, it was common at the time of Jesus for scribes to take
on the role of teaching the Torah, and for this purpose, they had their own
disciples. The Pharisees, too, had their own disciples and, at least once,
they even claimed to be disciples of Moses (Jn 9:28-29.) In a similar way,
Jesus also gathered his disciples around him, and together they formed a
group. It is clear, from a variety of statements, that the relationship between
Jesus and his disciples rested upon this notion of a Rabbi and master.[116]
Bultmann, in his observation of Jesus' circle of disciples, notes that Jesus
was addressed as 'a Rabbi'. He further notes that it is significant that his
adherents were also called 'his disciples'. The term 'adherent' or 'disciple'
in this context refers to the pupils of a Rabbi. Bultmann notes that "Jesus
was less bound by the forms than other Rabbis."[117] Bultmann also agrees

that, at the time of Jesus, the practices of a scribe were less fixed than there were two generations later. When Bultmann says that, he specifically notes that Jesus included women in his circle of followers "who are elsewhere never included among the followers of a Rabbi.[118] Furthermore, no Rabbi would converse with certain categories of people in their society, such as sinners, prostitutes and publicans. Another observation is that Jesus calls his followers to 'follow him'. That Jesus did this is surely historical but it is alien to the known practices of a Rabbi in his day. After all this Bultmann concludes, "However we cannot doubt that the characteristics of a Rabbi appeared plainly in Jesus' ministry and way of teaching."[119] In the observation of Metzger, Jesus was addressed by the title 'Rabbi' by different persons and, of course, with great respect and esteem in that society "It will be obvious that in many respects Jesus of Nazareth was like a typical Jewish scribe."[120] Metzger adds that Jesus "gathered about himself a group of disciples who had responded to his call, "Follow me.""[121] The disciples of Jesus as presented in the gospels gave him the respect due to him by calling him Rabbi (Jn 1:38; 4:31; 9:2; Mk 9:5; 11:21; 14:45). Could this be taken as indicative of a 'master/student' relationship typical of that society at the time of Jesus?

For Irwin M. Zeitlin,[122] it is important that Jesus is addressed as Rabbi, so it is also significant that his adherents (including the twelve apostles) are all called 'disciples'. That, too, is a technical term, and denotes the pupils or followers of a Rabbi. However, Zeitlin does note a difference. He agrees with Bultmann that at the time of Jesus, the practices of the scribal profession were less fixed than two generations later, and it may also be indicative that Jesus felt less bound[123] by conventional norms, than did other Rabbis of his time. Thus, there is a fundamental difference between the relation of Jesus to his own disciples and that of the scribes to their pupils.[124] What is it about Jesus that makes him appear different from other Rabbis to his disciples? This will be discussed below.

Choosing Disciples: 'Follow Me' and 'Following After'

W. D. Davies in his *The Setting of the Sermon on the Mount* considers that it is customary to presuppose that the 'teacher/disciple' relation, in the case of Jesus and his disciples, derives from the 'Rabbi/disciple' relationship of first century AD Judaism. Davies agrees that "Evidence of a Rabbinic colouring in the activity of Jesus emerges also in the terminology employed of the disciples."[125] However, Davies also observes that the nature of the discipleship to Jesus differs from the Rabbinic traditions. Jesus discipleship "involved certain elements which differentiated it from the life of the Rabbinic students."[126] Davies notes that "discipleship arose in response to a call from Jesus to follow him, a call directed to the individual in isolation or to the hearers at large."[127] John P. Meier looks at the relationship that existed between Jesus and his disciples and observes, "Jesus' relation to his disciples differed from that of the later Rabbis in a number of ways. Jesus often took the initiative in calling people - including some not very promising candidates - to discipleship, even ordering them to forsake sacred duties to follow him: 'Let the dead bury their dead.'"[128] Following Jesus as a disciple[129] meant that one was bound to live according to his teachings as well as to pass on his teachings to others. The link between discipleship and teaching is clear in the Great Commission[130] of Matthew 28:18–20. Moreover, in this text Jesus' fundamental expectation of his disciples is evident, specifically that his disciples will "observe all things...I have commanded you" (verse 20). Thus obedience to his commandments is definitive of living as his disciple.

Martin Hengel[131] states that it is *extremely* improbable that the very specific aspects of 'following after' and 'discipleship' are derived from the model of the Rabbinical scribes and the Rabbinical school. He further states that there are no Rabbinical stories of 'calling' and 'following after' and there is no 'follow me' in any of the known Rabbinical 'teacher-pupil' relationships. When it comes to the 'master-disciple relationship' in the case of Jesus and his disciples, it is well known that in Jesus' day the normal practice was for potential followers to choose their own master. The entry into the Rabbinical school was mostly on the basis of an initiative taken by the student, whereas in the gospels, the reverse is true. The decisive call comes from Jesus, 'the master'. In Judaism, when a pupil joined himself to a particular teacher, he was bound to him for the rest of his life in the belief that he might acquire knowledge and wisdom from him. Familiarity with the oral tradition of Judaism and the knowledge that he acquired of Sacred Scripture from his 'master' allowed him to be addressed as a Rabbi by others. Irwin Zeitlin observes that "the usual pattern was that after one started as a pupil, as did Paul, and mastering the Scriptures and the traditional oral commentaries, one became a teacher with pupils of one's own."[132] So, in the actual context of the ancient Jewish or Hellenistic world, disciples usually sought out a teacher (cf. Lk 9:57-62) whereas Jesus often reverses this in calling people to become his disciples (Mk 1:16-20; 2:14-17; 3:13).

Observing the 'Rabbi/disciple' relationship in the gospel of Mark, Vernon K. Robbins states that "analysis of the initiation of the teacher/ disciple relation, however, suggests that the portrayal of the teacher/ disciple relation in Mark is a distinctive adaptation of aspects from both Jewish and Greco-Roman traditions."[133] Robbins further observes, that in the "Rabbinic literature, Rabbis are not depicted travelling around as Jesus does to find people who will respond to his summons to become disciple-companions."[134] In sum, the singular common phenomenon in all the gospel narratives is the choice of the apostles by the master, which is found in both the synoptic tradition and John. It is clear that they did not choose him, he chose them and commissioned them to be his disciples. This is another example of a practice, different from the Jewish and Hellenistic perspective.

Call to Discipleship, Not to Leadership

On the question of 'choice of disciples' Riesner, like other scholars, insists on a specific difference in the way Jesus called his followers to discipleship. Whereas "the disciples of the proto-Rabbis selected the appropriate teacher themselves, Jesus called his disciples with complete sovereignty"[135] (cf. Lk. 9: 57- 62). For Jesus' disciples, there was no end to learning and they were bound to his personality (cf. Mk 10:34-38.). The specific element to be noted in Jesus' discipleship is that Jesus called individuals and not crowds. As an itinerant preacher, the immediate disciples of Jesus literally had to follow him around (cf. Mk 8:34; 10:21; Lk 9:57-62; Jn 1:43). Perhaps this is the main reason why it was Jesus who chose his disciples (cf. Jn 15:16). Note that in each case the 'call' was extended from the master to the disciple. This is in not in line with the tradition that "emphasises the initiative by individual people to receive permission from a Rabbi to become one of his student-disciples."[136] As Collins notes, "a disciple is one who follows, one who answers Jesus' call "follow me."[137] As Hans Weder states, "The initiative lay with Jesus alone; apart from his call, there is no recognisable motive for one to become a disciple and follow Jesus."[138] In Mark, all the early disciples receive their call from Jesus with this same call formula, 'Follow me.' The Synoptic call formula of "follow me" by Jesus is extended to Philip in the Fourth Gospel (Jn 1:43). This word "characterises the central quality of existence as a disciple."[139] Furthermore, the call 'follow me' explains the characteristic description of discipleship in all the gospels.

John P. Meier, when he speaks about the discipleship of Jesus and the relationship between Jesus and his disciples, insists that at least in his inner group, Jesus expected from his disciples the strong commitment to himself to be a permanent affair. "His disciples were not studying to be rabbis who would then leave him and set up schools of their own."[140] Hence it seems that Jesus called his disciples to be faithful followers rather than becoming Rabbis or leaders.[141] H. F. Weiss points out that the unique character of the 'teacher/pupil' relationship with Jesus where "one does not attach himself to Jesus the teacher; rather, one is called to discipleship."[142] In the words of Collins, "that is the call to discipleship."[143] Jesus often had to correct his disciples because they fell into two temptations that hindered their service for him. On several occasions they argued among themselves as to who was the greatest. A Rabbi's disciple might have given up most material benefits in order to study the Torah, but he would have known that the sacrifice was for a limited time. At a later stage he would be rewarded financially for his diligence when he became a Rabbi himself. In contrast, Jesus called his disciples to a life of humility and poverty. They were to sell their possessions, and give alms. They were to take with them "no gold, nor silver, nor copper in your belts, no bag for your journey, nor two tunics, nor sandals, nor a staff." Jesus called his disciples to suffer. When Jesus called his disciples to follow him, they had to be willing to walk his way, which was the way of the cross. If they were to share their lives together, they would share not only their joys but also their sorrows. Jesus had constantly warned his disciples about the physical dangers that lay ahead.

Robbins states, "the teacher/disciple tradition in Mark represents an adaptation of biblical and Greek traditions that is not entirely paralleled either in Rabbinical literature or in Philostratus's *Appollonius* in which a potential disciple seeks out a teacher and attempts to convince the teacher to accept him as a student/disciple."[144] At the same time the writers of the Gospels also make mention of some who came forward to offer their services and were put off by the Master (cf. Lk 9:57.58.61.62). Jesus was also able to command his followers and caution them wherever and whenever it was necessary. In the gospels, Jesus stakes out a claim for his status as "Rabbi" in the face of potential competing claims among his own followers. For example, in the context of Rabbinical pride and intellectualism, Jesus finds fault with the pride which demands exaggerated respect (cf. Mt 23:7-8) and forbids his disciples to accept the titles of Rabbi or Father, another title given to scribal teachers. Here, Jesus' rejection of the use of the title 'Rabbi' in Mt 23:7-8 marks a great contrast between the teaching ministry of Jesus and that of other Rabbinical teachers. In the circumstance of Mt 23:7-8, Jesus objects to any seeking 'respect and honour' with titles such as 'Rabbi' and he censures the desire of the scribes who seek to be greeted as Rabbi in that society.

In Rabbinical circles, a disciple chose his own master and voluntarily joined his school. With Jesus, the initiative lay entirely with him. Simon and Andrew, James and John, Levi, Philip and others - all were personally called by Jesus to follow him. He laid down for them the conditions that he required (Jn 15:15). The Rabbis accepted disciples who were ceremonially 'clean', who were righteous according to the law, and who had sufficient intelligence to study the Torah with a view to becoming Rabbis themselves. Jesus called to himself a curious cross-section of contemporary society. James and John the sons of Zebedee were fishermen; there was a despised Levi; and among the twelve we find Greek and Semitic names, and probably a Judean as well as Galileans. Jesus' group of disciples reflected a microcosm of society at that time. Jesus' disciples saw themselves as personally chosen by Jesus, and this altered their whole attitude towards him and motivated them for the work he had given them. A Jewish Rabbi expected disciples to commit themselves to a specific teaching or to a definite cause. But the call of Jesus was personal: his disciples were to follow him, to be with him, and to commit themselves totally to him. When Jesus called individuals to be his disciples, he shared his life with them. Although Jesus' relationship with the twelve showed a depth of sharing that was not experienced by everyone, he still gave himself to everyone who responded to his call. However, with Jesus, discipleship means knowing him, loving him, believing in him and being committed to him. Jesus called his disciples to life-long obedience. The disciples of a Jewish Rabbi would submit themselves as slaves to their master until the time came when they left their schooling and became Rabbis themselves. Jesus called his disciples to unconditional obedience for the whole of their lives. To be a disciple of Jesus meant to follow him, to go the way that he went, to accept his plan and will for their lives. The disciples were also commissioned to go and preach and to 'heal the sick, raise the dead, cleanse lepers, cast out demons'. When Jesus called Simon and Andrew to follow him, he told them that he would make them fishers of men.

Rabbinic discipleship was based on the belief that the Rabbi's special knowledge gave him a direct access to God and the Torah that was denied to others. Unlike the traditional communities of learning, in Jesus' style of discipleship the master served and the disciples received. They allowed

Jesus to wash their feet, a task usually done by the lowest household slave. He prepared the fire and cooked the fish (Jn 21:12). The relationship between the master and the disciples was a reciprocal one. Jesus called his disciples to share their lives with him and with one another in love. His statement "You did not choose me, but I chose you" is a command to love one another. He said that it would be by this love that people would identify them as his disciples. Jesus called his disciples to become like him. The call to discipleship involves Jesus' unique invitation to become like him (Lk 6:40) and to be a full participant in his mission. "Come, follow me, and I will make you fishers of men" links discipleship with carrying the good news to all (Mk 1:15,17; Lk 5:10), while the occasions on which Jesus sent the twelve or the seventy out in twos (Mk 6:7-13; Lk 10:1-20) show that he expects disciples to be fully involved in service to others. Thus, there are many examples of Jesus' choice of disciples and the purpose of his group as being different from the customary role on learning and being a disciple of a typical Rabbi of that time. What then is unique in Jesus' teaching method that makes him a different sort of teacher? This needs to be analysed further. A further question is, 'what made Jesus' teaching superior to those of his contemporary teachers of Scripture and law'?

Teaching Methods of Rabbi Jesus: Distinct from His Contemporaries

Bruce Chilton in his work "A Galilean Rabbi and His Bible"[145] presents Jesus of Nazareth as a Galilean Rabbi. The way Jesus interpreted Scripture and the authoritative way he taught are sufficient grounds for Chilton to see Jesus as a Rabbi who spent most of his life in Galilee. Luke tells us (Lk 4:16-30) that Jesus came to Nazareth, where he had been brought up; and he went to the synagogue, as was his custom,[146] on the Sabbath day. For Riesner, the style of Jesus' preaching could be described in three ways. Firstly, Jesus' preaching was impressive; secondly, Jesus made his teaching understandable; and thirdly, Jesus made his teaching memorizable.[147] In order to make his style of preaching effective, Jesus taught by using parables "the use of the parables, which in the opinion of almost all exegetes is so typical for him, could catch the attention of all kinds of hearers."[148] Jesus made his teaching understandable to his audience with the help of parables and examples from the daily life experience of the people "Like other Jewish teachers, he liked word play, but he outdid all of them in creating parables."[149] Riesner calls this style of preaching of Jesus a vivid style.

With regard to the Synoptic Gospels, Riesner holds the view that "many synoptic summaries mention that Jesus taught in the synagogues."[150]

However, when Riesner begins to observe the distinctive elements in the teachings of Jesus, he refers to 'outdoor preaching' (cf. Lk 13: 26-27) as something typical of Jesus. He also notes that the practice of preaching and teaching outside synagogues was also known to have taken place for other Jewish Rabbis, "but to do so in front of crowds was rather the exception to the rule."[151] Ed Tenhor agrees on this point with Riesner in saying, "Jesus did not teach in one place and in one school, but taught in many locations, and was a peripatetic, itinerant teacher."[152] Indeed, this study agrees that both outdoor preaching and an audience of large crowds were typical for Jesus.

Jesus the Rabbi: A Teacher Par Excellence

R. H. Stein asks, "Why was Jesus such a fascinating teacher? What caused these large crowds to follow him? In reply one might say that it was *what* Jesus said that drew the crowds."[153] It is clear that there was some difference in the teachings of Jesus which caused the people to listen to him and to follow him wherever he went. The Jewish historian Josephus of the first century A.D. mentions that "there lived Jesus, a wise man…a teacher of such people as accept truth gladly. He won over many Jews and many of the Greeks…"[154]

Ed Tenhor presents Jesus as a pedagogue: "Jesus was a teacher, a Rabbi of his day."[155] Ed Tenhor does not stop at calling Jesus a teacher, he has more to say; "Rabbi Jesus was a teacher who put various pedagogical principles into words and action."[156] In the observation of Asher Finkel, Jesus is identified with different Jewish groups but it was his teachings and actions that differentiate him as a teacher *par excellence*. Jesus was known as a teacher by the people; he set time aside specifically to teach the people in the Temple, in synagogues in Galilee and Judea, out of doors and even in a boat (Mk 4:1; Lk 5:3). In addition, he taught his disciples privately. It is implied in *m. Abot* 1.4; 3.2, 6 that for the early Rabbis sitting was the common position for teaching. Jesus likewise is said to be sitting when teaching (Mt 5:1; Mk 4:1; Lk 5:3). But Jesus is also said to stand when teaching (Lk 6:17). He was well received by the people as a teacher, and was perceived as having an authority that the scribes did not have. The very essence of his mission and preaching differentiates him from his contemporaries and the vision he had for that society makes him a different Rabbi or teacher. Finkel concludes, "Although Jesus showed tendencies both as a Pharisaic and Essene teacher, a deviation from their ways emerged to clear the obstacles on the road of his proposed mission."[157]

He brings out the uniqueness of Jesus and points out how Jesus differs from the Pharisees and Essenes both in his actions and in his teachings. Though Jesus is shown dissatisfied with Roman rule, he differed from the Zealots in the approach to that problem. While the Zealots insisted on an immediate solution by force to purify the religious authority from the Romans, Jesus focussed on the repentance of the people (Mt 3:2; 4:17; Mk 1:15). He preached on the golden rule as the cornerstone of the Mosaic Law and of the prophetic teachings, which echoes the teachings of Hillel (See. Abot 1:12). Likewise, when Jesus observed the teachings of Torah with regard to Sabbath, he was not simply acting like the Pharisaic teachers but exceeded them in his teachings. Again, at a meal, Jesus is seen following the Jewish religious procedures (Mt 14:19; Mk 6:41; Lk 9:16). It also appears that Jesus adhered to the pharisaic code of purity, but Jesus' teaching on purity differs greatly from the interpretation of the Pharisees and Scribes. Some sources suggest that Jesus, in the context of his time, could not escape the teachings and the mode of life of the Rabbinical masters. But there is ample evidence, not least from the Gospels, to prove that Jesus deviated from the path of his contemporaries and, in doing so, proved to be a different teacher and master altogether. Byrskog confirms that "Jesus is a διδάσκαλος, but not one among the many Jewish teachers. He is the teacher - the only teacher of the disciples."[158] Consequently, any understanding of Jesus *as a Rabbi* cannot be the same as understanding any other Rabbi of his time.

Rabbi Jesus: Speaking with a New Authority

The evangelists all portray Jesus as a teacher. In his first comment on the teaching of Jesus, Mark notes that Jesus taught in the synagogue at Capernaum 'as one who had authority, and not as the Scribes' (Mk 1:22). Mark soon shows that, unlike the scribes, the teaching of Jesus did not centre on learned interpretation of the law, although he could and did dispute with scribes, cf. Mk 7:1. 5; 9: 11. Jesus seemed to be a type of Rabbi believed to have authority (in Hebrew *semikhah*, in Greek *exousia*) to make new interpretations. Most teachers were Torah teachers (teachers of the law) who could only teach accepted interpretations. Those with authority could pass legal judgments. Crowds were amazed because Jesus taught with authority, unlike their Torah teachers. While this makes Jesus one of a small group of teachers, he was not the only one with authority. Rabbis invited people to learn in order to keep the Torah. Fulfilling the Torah was the task of a first century Rabbi. The technical term for interpreting the Scripture so that it would be obeyed correctly was 'fulfilled'. To interpret

Scripture incorrectly so it would not be obeyed as God intended, was to destroy the Torah. Jesus uses these terms to describe his task as well. Contrary to what some think, Jesus did not come to do away with God's Torah or Old Testament. He came to complete it and to show how to keep it correctly. One of the ways Jesus interpreted the Torah was to stress the importance of the right attitude of heart as well as the right action.

Robert H. Stein, describing the method and message of Jesus' teaching, states that "Jesus' message, unlike that of the scribes and the rabbis, did not possess a derivative authority from the rabbis of the past but possessed an immediate authority."[159] The teaching of Jesus was 'a new teaching, with authority' (Mk 1:27). Bruce Chilton notes that "the close of his successful although chaotic period in and around Capernaum brought Jesus to a clear articulation of what made his practice of Judaism distinct from others."[160] The Greek word translated as 'authority' includes the notion of power, which comes from God. So in these two verses we may translate: 'Jesus *taught with prophetic* authority.' The other passages in Mark in which reference is made to the 'authority' of Jesus confirm this interpretation. (See, Mark 11:27-33; also 2:10; 3:15 and 6:7). The conclusion of the Sermon on the Mount confirms the special status of Jesus' new authority. "And when Jesus finished these sayings, the crowds were astonished at his teaching, for he taught them as one who had authority, and not as their Scribes."(Mt. 7:28-29). In sum, Jesus did not speak like a prophet. A prophet spoke a message he received from God. He began his message with the words, "Thus says the Lord." Jesus never said, "Thus says the Lord." His teaching and words were his own; therefore, Jesus taught and spoke on his own authority. He did not need the support of human opinions or any other Rabbi.

Rabbi Jesus: Proponent of New Ethics

When the salient features of Jesus' teaching are analysed, the significant factor that differentiates Jesus from his contemporaries may be called the 'New Ethics of Jesus.' The following, will show the views of some of the authors who present Jesus as the proponent of 'New Ethics.' Joseph Klausner, at the end of his book, "*Jesus of Nazareth*", says "If ever the day should come and this ethical code be stripped of its wrappings of miracles and mysticism, the Book of Ethics of Jesus will be one of the choicest treasures in the literature of Israel for all time."[161] Gerd Theissen and Annette Merz also note the difference between Jesus and his contemporaries. They write, "Unlike the Essenes and Rabbis, Jesus did not see his task as being the exegesis of scripture for its own sake."[162] Jesus applied the Scriptures to promote a new form of conduct and a new ethics not only for those who heard him but for the whole of humankind. Jesus uses the techniques of teachers, that is, he also is equipped with pedagogical tools. Jesus is also an *authoritative teacher.* Mark's statement is to the point (1:22): "He taught them with authority, not like the scribes." Another passage from Mark (12:14) is very significant: "Teacher, we know that you are a truthful man and that you are not concerned with anyone's opinion. You do not regard a person's status but teach the way of God in accordance with the truth." This is a wonderful portrait of the true teacher, who does not bend when he meets with opposition. Two passages are emblematic in this sense: Jn 8:28: "I say only what the Father has taught me (διδάσκειν)." Mt 11:27: "No one knows the Son except the Father, and no one knows the Father except the Son and anyone to whom the Son wishes to reveal him." In summary: Jesus is a historical Teacher who uses the techniques of the world, of which he is a part (the parables, for example); but he does something different and original, like the choice of disciples. Furthermore, he is an authoritative and free teacher. But he is much more: he is a transcendent teacher who teaches the truth that goes beyond the boundaries of human knowledge and originates from revelation.

According to Ed Tenhor, "Jesus' ethics calls for a new attitude, but not only in the heart, but in actions themselves. Doing is important. One must do them."[163] Ed Tenhor quotes from Stein[164] who lists six outstanding characteristics of Jesus' ethics as follows. There is a wise selection of key moral commands as opposed to the hundreds of less important ones of his contemporaries. There is a removal of the more unhealthy traditions that undermined the real spirit of the teachings of the Old Testament. There is an intensification of the emphasis of the law but with a need for a new heart to love one's neighbour, including Samaritans, publicans, sinners and enemies, excluding legalism and elitism. There is a new attitude of acceptance toward outcasts, acceptance of women, children, enemies, tax collectors, Samaritans, publicans and sinners. There is a new motive for religion, not legalism, but gratitude for God's grace, as opposed to an ethic of merit or achievement. There is a positive emphasis, not simply refraining from sin, but the doing of good. Thus to Stein, "There was the perfect example in Jesus' own life, a fulfilment of his own moral teachings."[165]

John P. Meier expresses that very categorically when he says, "trying to formulate Jesus' moral teaching into some codified, rational system is futile, especially since it is in his attitude to morality and law that Jesus proves himself the true charismatic in the classical sense."[166] Thus in the approach of Jesus with regard to morals and ethics, there is a distinction which faces a crisis with the traditional authority. According to Dodd, Jesus accepted the Old Testament as containing divine revelation like any other Rabbi of his time. He offered interpretations of the Law of Moses, as other Rabbis did, as well as some criticisms,[167] an area where other Rabbis would not have dared to venture. Jacques Baldet opines that "some scholars, especially authors of Jewish origin, have pointed out a number of inconsistencies in Jesus' relation to Mosaic Law as described in gospel and other accounts, raising questions about the meaning of certain sayings that refer to the Law."[168] Jewish scholars have shown that there is a considerable amount of Rabbinical teaching which is markedly similar to that of Jesus in the Gospels, which is, after all, not surprising. Indeed, we can suppose that a good deal of the current ethics of Judaism are, in an unspoken way, taken for granted. However Baldet did not fail to note that "contemporary literature brings out the nonconformist and the non-normative character of Jesus' teaching...Far from being a Puritan, he was a provocateur."[169] Thus there is certainly a difference in Jesus' teaching and in the content of his teachings. To Baldet, Jesus appears a nonconformist teacher, who teaches with new authority.

Rabbi Jesus: A Revolt against Authorities and Traditions

John P. Meier, while agreeing that Jesus acted like any other Jewish teacher in his way of teaching, observes certain elements which differentiate him from them. "Jesus' impact did not come simply from powerful rhetoric. As with the Old Testament prophets, word was also deed. Jesus consciously willed his public activity to be a dramatic acting out of his message of God's welcome and forgiveness extended to the prodigal son. He insisted on associating and eating with the religious low-life of his day, "the tax collectors and sinners," Jews who in the eyes of the pious had apostatised and were no better than gentiles. His practise of sharing meals (for Orientals, a most serious and intimate form of social intercourse) with the religiously "lost", put Jesus in a continual state of ritual impurity, as far as the stringently law-observant were concerned."[170] In other words, Jesus rebelled against the practice of the Jews and the contemporary Jewish teachers.

When Sherbok looks at the *content* of Jesus' teaching, he states that throughout his ministry the kingdom of God was the subject of Jesus' teaching. However, the kingdom aspect never excluded one's duties and obligations towards one's neighbour. This is not something restricted to an individual's relationship with God. "Much of his teaching concerns a person's responsibilities to others."[171] When Sherbok comes to the 'series of objections' disputes, he notices the difference between Jesus' teaching and the Rabbis of his time. "The Rabbis sought to provide adequate social legislation, but Jesus had a view different from others."[172] For example, in Jewish eyes, poverty is seen as an evil, and the Rabbis sought to alleviate it by enacting laws to tax the wealthy for the benefit of the poor, whereas for Jesus poverty was not a deprivation but meritorious. For him, to be perfect or to have treasure in heaven, one has to sell everything that he possesses and give the proceeds to the poor. Thus the teaching and demands Jesus placed on his followers greatly differed from the teachings and instructions of the Rabbis. Sherbok, further notes, "finally Jesus' teaching is rejected by the Jews because his interpretation of Jewish law is at variance with Rabbinic tradition."[173] John P. Meier argues: "By assuming unlimited power over Torah and by rescinding a key boundary marker between Jews and gentiles, Jesus inevitably put himself on a collision course not only with the temple priests but also with sincere Jews in general."[174] Thus the message of Jesus' teaching and the contextualisation of his teachings not only differentiated him from other Rabbis but also provoked opposition to his teachings.

Rabbi Jesus: A New Moses

Moses, as the teacher of the Torah, is considered in general as the great Rabbi and his teachings are considered as the basis for learning. Jacob Neusner writes, "The rabbis taught that the "whole Torah" - oral and written - was studied by David, augmented by Ezekiel, legislated by Ezra, and embodied in the schools and by the sages of every period in Israelite history from Moses to the present... The Torah myth further regards Moses as "our rabbi", the first and prototypical figure.[175] It holds that whoever embodies the teachings of Moses, "our rabbi", thereby is himself a rabbi and conforms to the will of God - and not to God's will alone, but also to his way."[176] Moses was, in the final analysis, only a servant of God, one *through whom God revealed himself.* Thus Moses has an important place in the history of Rabbis and teachings of Torah. All those who wanted to become Rabbis would have been expected to be, and were assumed to be, steeped in the wisdom of the Torah[177] and the Scripture. This would have made them Rabbis.

Geza Vermes in his work on *Jesus the Jew* observes quite a number of similarities indicating that Jesus was acting like a teacher in his community.

At the same time Vermes has pointed out a number of variations too. He observes that Jesus preached like a Jewish teacher but the authority with which he taught his disciples made him different from other Rabbis of his time. "New Testament commentators usually see in this a contrast between Jesus' method of teaching and the Rabbis' habit of handing down a legally binding doctrine in the name of the master from whom they learned it, which was held to derive from a chain of tradition traceable (ideally) back to Moses."[178] He makes a distinction between the scribal authority of the Rabbis and the prophetic authority of Jesus. He concludes that Jesus was not an expert in Jewish law and therefore it is misleading to attempt to compare his style of instruction with that of later Rabbinic academies. The identification of Jesus as a 'prophet' was a means both of affirming his continuity with the prophets of Israel and of asserting his superiority to them. By this, this study implies that Jesus was the Prophet whose coming they had predicted and to whose authority they had been prepared to yield. In Dt 18:15-22, God tells Moses, and through him the people, that he "will raise up for them a prophet like me from among you," to whom the people are to pay heed. In its biblical context, this is the authorisation of Joshua as the legitimate successor of Moses, but in the New Testament and in later Christian writers, the prophet to come is taken to be Jesus. He is portrayed as the one Prophet in whom the teaching of Moses was fulfilled and yet superseded, the one Rabbi who both satisfied the law of Moses and transcended it: "the law was given through Moses; grace and truth came through Jesus Christ" (Jn 1:17). Behind the confrontations between Jesus as Rabbi and the representatives of the Rabbinical tradition, the affinities are nevertheless clearly discernible in the forms in which his teachings appear in the Gospels. Byrskog affirms that the story of Jesus as a teacher in the gospels does not concern merely one teacher among many others. "Jesus carries as teacher a specific authority based on his extraordinary origin and identity."[179] Thus Jesus had his own approach and his own authority as a teacher. John P. Meier asserts that there was a clear distinction in the approach of Jesus, "and it led to a basic tension in his treatment of the Mosaic Law."[180] Meier explains that Jesus the Jew fundamentally affirmed the Law as God's will, though with a radicalising thrust seen also at Qumran. At times, Jesus would engage in rabbinic-style debate to solve concrete problems. Yet on certain specific issues (divorce, oaths, unclean foods), he claimed to know intuitively and directly that Jewish Law or custom was contrary to God's will. In such cases, the Law had to give way to, or be reinterpreted by, the command of Jesus, simply because Jesus said so: "I say to you." Jesus made no attempt to authenticate such teachings in the manner of the Old Testament prophets or the later rabbis, but emphasised that he knew and taught God's will with absolute certitude. R. H. Stein states that "the words of Jesus reveal that he thought he possessed an authority such as no other man had,"[181] for whereas the prophets and Moses spoke what God had revealed to them, Jesus spoke his own words which were nevertheless the Word of God.

In the opinion of Donald Senior, the title 'Teacher' is one of the most characteristic titles of Jesus in the Gospels and "in fact, he is called "teacher" more than anything else."[182] At the same time, Senior observes that "the Gospels also insist that Jesus was not a teacher in the sense commonly accepted in his day."[183] To substantiate that point, Senior puts forward the following considerations. First of all, Jesus preached with his own authority and consequently, his statements are decidedly different in that respect. Secondly, he never cites the authority of the other Rabbis to support what he says. "Even his citations of Scripture appear as mere confirmation or illustration of what he declares rather than as clinching proof."[184] Thirdly, to emphasise that awesome authority, most of his solemn statements begin with 'Amen, amen I say to you.' This 'Amen' for Jesus is a kind of confirmation of what he says and this usage has no parallel in Jewish literature. When Senior writes of the 'teaching authority' of Jesus, he asserts that Jesus "contrasts his own teaching with traditional interpretations"[185] and 'he taught them as one who had authority, and not as their scribes' (Mt 7.29). Thus, in the observation of Senior, Jesus was indeed addressed as a teacher in the gospels, but this should not be understood in the same way as any of his contemporaries.

Rabbi Jesus: A Personal Authority (I Say to You)
According to W. D. Davies, it is certain that Jesus was called a Rabbi. "For the Rabbinic traits in Jesus are unmistakable."[186] Davies basically agrees that in the days of Jesus the title Rabbi did not have the exact connotation of 'one officially ordained to teach', which would have been the case in a later period. When Davies opines that Rabbinic traits are found in Jesus, he refers to the gospels where the functions of the disciples of Jesus are of 'servant/disciple.' But in Jn 13, Jesus repudiates the need for a servant/disciple for himself and then demands the same spirit from his disciples. Only then did Jesus accept the honour given to him.

The next point to note is that when Jesus taught, he sat down to do so, as did Moses and other Jewish teachers. Davies goes on to the extent of identifying Jesus, and his disciples, as having a Rabbinic style of school. But, Davies does not go so far as to interpret that as being in the strict sense of a Rabbinic school. However, he does hold that there is a distinction to be made between the teaching of Jesus and other Rabbis. "There were certainly many things that set him apart from the Rabbis."[187] Davies agrees that Jesus spoke with the authority of a Rabbi, though he had not been taught in the formal sense, or ordained. The authority of his teaching differed from that of the scribes. Davies notes that the authority with which Jesus spoke "was therefore not derivative but autonomous."[188] Jesus expressed his teaching in the imperative and not in a participial form, customary among Rabbis. "The content of Jesus' teaching perhaps most radically differs from that of the Rabbis."[189] Again, in the observation of Davies, it is clear that Jesus made use of Scripture when he claimed it gave witness to himself, which a normal Rabbi would never do.

When ascribing the title 'teacher' to Jesus, I. M. Zeitlin sees many similarities between the teachings of Jesus and the other Rabbis. At the same time, Zeitlin points out those elements that present Jesus as significantly differing from other Jewish teachers: "But if Jesus was a Rabbi, it is also evident from everything we have learned about him so far that he differed significantly from the other Jewish teachers and learned Pharisees of his era."[190] Jesus did teach like other Rabbis, but with distinctive features. When a Rabbi gave his opinion on a religious question, he supported his position by quoting the great Rabbis of the past. His authority rested on the authority of other Rabbis. Jesus never quoted another Rabbi to support any of his teachings and his authority rested on nobody but himself. As Zeitlin opines, "the source of his authority, as he understood it, differed from that of the Rabbis." He always taught in a challenging way; for example he would prefix some statements with "I say to you" and directly justify his stance by quoting Scripture. In the words of Zeitlin, this is something

"a pharisaic teacher would not normally do without basing himself on previous Rabbinical authorities."[191] Indeed, Jesus displayed an intimate relationship with God and that could explain his authoritative involvement with the Scriptures.

When Riesner speaks about Jesus' authority as a teacher he asserts that "There is no word extant where the authority of another teacher is invoked."[192] For most Rabbis, the Hebrew Scripture was the sole authority for their teaching. He notes the OT was not the sole source of authority for Jesus. "Jesus could base a statement solely on the argument that he himself made"[193] and adds that "not only after but even before Easter it was felt that Jesus claimed more authority than that of a scribe or proto- Rabbi."[194] To show that his authority came from himself, he sometimes began a sentence with the words, "I say to you." Thus, Jesus expressed himself in the style of a prophet. "A great fear swept the crowd, and they exclaimed with praises to God, A mighty prophet has risen among us," and, "We have seen the hand of God at work today." Lk 7:16. "When the people realized what a great miracle had happened", they exclaimed, "Surely, he is the Prophet we have been expecting!" Jn 6:14. "Jesus travelled all through Galilee teaching in the Jewish synagogues, everywhere preaching the Good News about the Kingdom of Heaven. And he healed every kind of sickness and disease. The report of his miracles spread far beyond the borders of Galilee so that sick folk were soon coming to be healed from as far away as Syria. And whatever their illness and pain, or if they were possessed by demons, or were insane, or paralysed, he healed them all" (Mt 4:23-24). They said to Jesus, "Sir, we know what an honest teacher you are. You always tell the truth and don't budge an inch in the face of what others think, but teach the ways of God." Lk 20:21. However, by his actions and his authority, he shows that he is indeed much *more* than a prophet.

Riesner says, "All those who believed in a prophetic mission of Jesus had a deep interest in his words." At the same time, "revelatory statements especially, such as the Amen-sayings, required that they be regarded and remembered as divinely inspired speech."[195] Martin Hengel holds that Jesus was not a ῥαββί and consequently may be called neither a scribe nor a prophet. He maintains that Jesus only occasionally used exegetical arguments and then only when he was questioned (or attacked) by third parties about the Torah. Occasionally he would do so when his authority, or his claims, were at stake. Hence calling Jesus a scribe is going too far. For Hengel, Jesus proved that "the Old Testament is no longer the central focus of his message; and this distinguishes him both from the 'prophets' of his day and from the scribes."[196] Jesus is not shown in the Gospels as presenting his message using the formulas of the O.T prophets such as 'thus says the Lord.'[197] Hengel appears to not understand the prophetic actions of Jesus in their distinctive form. He contends that the two terms 'prophet' and 'teacher' should in no way be regarded as opposites, "Nor should the prophet and teacher be regarded in any sense as opposites."[198] While not claiming that Jesus was solely a prophet, the prophetic elements can be discerned in his public ministry. More specifically, this can be inferred from the teachings of Jesus. He was seen, by many, as a prophet who spoke and acted with a new authority.

In the above study of the various scholarly agreements and disagreements regarding Jesus as a Rabbi within his world of contemporary Judaism, a number of distinct variations have been highlighted that makes Jesus different from the other Rabbis, teachers or scribes of his time. Among them, one of the most important is the 'new authority' that Jesus expressed in his teachings. He shows himself, time and again, to be a teacher but one who teaches with an authority that seems to place him as being even greater than a prophet. Thus Jesus is portrayed both as a teacher with a new authority and at the same time a prophet who spoke with a divine inspiration. The following section will explore this important aspect further.

Rabbi Jesus: Teacher and Prophet

The conclusion of the Sermon on the Mount confirms the special status of Jesus as not only Rabbi but Prophet (Matt. 7:28-8:1): "And when Jesus finished these sayings, the crowds were astonished at his teaching, for he taught them as one who had authority, and not as their scribes. When he came down from the mountain, great crowds followed him." Then there emerges several miracle stories. The New Testament does not attribute the power of performing miracles only to Jesus and his followers (Mt 12:27), but it does cite the miracles as substantiation of his standing as Rabbi-Prophet.[199] This identification of Jesus was a means both of affirming his continuity with the prophets of Israel and of asserting his superiority to them as the prophet whose coming they had predicted and to whose authority they had been prepared to yield. R. H. Stein observes from the New Testament that "during his ministry Jesus was also considered by many to be a prophet."[200] According to the New Testament, many Jews of the time thought of Jesus as a prophet (Mk 6:15; 8:28; 14:65; Lk 7:16; Mt 21:11.46). The New Testament also indicates that Jesus considered himself to be a prophet (Mt 6:4). "People were astonished at his doctrine: for he taught them as *one* having authority" (Mt 7:28-29). Officers sent to arrest him did not, declaring, "No man ever spoke like this man!" (Jn. 7:46). In some instances, when Jesus is presented in the Gospels as 'teacher', he is also viewed as a prophet. Many argue that Jesus, as so presented, has indeed acted and witnessed as a 'prophet of old.' He revealed truths that were unknown before: "I will open my mouth in parables; I will utter things which have been kept secret from the foundation of the world" (Mt 13:35). Several questions arise. When the evangelists perceive Jesus' as a prophet, in what sense do they distinguish the two roles of 'teacher' and 'prophet'? Are the two roles incompatible? Are they complementary, or are they two aspects of the same thing?

The words prophet and prophecy are used in two distinct ways in the scriptures. Prophet means "an inspired speaker", who speaks by divine inspiration. They also imply 'a fore teller' who foretells or predicts future events. The two-fold role of God's prophet is seen in scripture to "speak or teach by Divine inspiration" and to "foretell future events" as God revealed them. On occasion the prophet may speak inspired words as powerful truths that do not include the foretelling of the future. There have been numerous men throughout history who were chosen of God as prophets and who spoke powerful truths as God inspired them to do so. In the Hebrew Bible, prophets were men who spoke for God, proclaiming God's words to the people, and often predicting future events (Mt 21:11; Lk 7:16). The two-fold role of a prophet as inspired teacher and foreteller of future events was extraordinarily expressed in the life of Jesus.[201] According to Vincent Taylor, "the Synoptic Gospels show that in popular estimation Jesus was looked upon as a prophet."[202] But Taylor observes the important distinction between Jesus and the OT prophets. "Like the prophets of old, Jesus was seen to be filled with the Spirit and to speak the words of God, but unlike them, He left the abiding impression of possessing far more than the prophetic commission."[203] Rudolf Bultmann, in his work, *Theology of the New Testament,* discusses Jesus' adherence to the Jewish faith and also the elements that make him distinct from other adherents. In the Jewish society of his time, Jesus was regarded as a prophet and a teacher of 'religion and morals.'[204] Bultmann acknowledges that, "however much his preaching in its radicality is directed against Jewish legalism, still its content is nothing else than true Old Testament Jewish faith in God radicalised in the direction of the great prophets' preaching."[205] As Bruce Chilton rightly observes, "Jesus knew that his reputation as a prophet brought the threat of death. Galilee was no longer the safe haven for him it had once been. Jerusalem, too, offered no security. That had been a place of resistance to the great prophets of Judah."[206] Kittel in his article on Jesus as διδάσκαλος observes that Jesus faced much opposition and non-acceptance of his teaching "This took place at the point where Jesus as διδάσκαλος took up again the line of the OT prophet who goes beyond traditional formulations and proclaims the will of God afresh and directly."[207]

In two of the gospels, Pharisees ask for a sign from heaven to be given by Jesus "to test him." It is hard to imagine any other reason for this than the claims that Jesus was a prophet. The gospels tell of a number of occasions where his claim to be a prophet is unambiguous. With this possibility as a starting point, how would one expect the Pharisees to react to the claim that Jesus was making? First of all, they would need to test that claim. If he were truly a prophet, he would be speaking the message of the Lord, and it would be their duty to support him in every way, and to allow the Lord's message to be proclaimed. On the other hand, if he were a false prophet, it would be their solemn duty to denounce him and to find some way of removing him from the situation. A false prophet would be guilty of blasphemy. To allow such a false prophet to continue to speak would have very dangerous consequences. This would be especially true in the fragile political climate that existed. In this way of reasoning, the Pharisees were acting correctly and properly in their questioning of Jesus. One can see from the gospels that they needed to be assured of his orthodoxy. And the questions that the Pharisees asked, and the answers that Jesus gave to them were always supported by the Torah, both written and oral. The gospels show the prophetic claim of Jesus as being confirmed by the works he performed. In the Hebrew Bible, miracles,[208] healing and other works are associated with the task of the prophet. In some cases these works are proof that the person concerned was indeed a prophet of the most high.

Is Rabbi Jesus an Eschatological Prophet?

Ed Tenhor states that "Rabbi Jesus was a first century Palestinian Prophet."[209] He adds that Jesus' mission, as a prophet was to bring in the God movement, to restore Israel to where it once again would be a nation where God rules, thus a kind of "restoration movement prophet."[210] Jesus seems to have had a concern for the reign of God as something that affects the people as a whole. For example, he called people together in some sort of fellowship and probably used symbols that in some way related to the tradition of the people of Israel. He was, in effect, constituting a call for the reform of the people in Israel. So those elements in his teaching and his proclamation that have to do with the reign of God bring him closer to what we might describe as an apocalyptic preacher or someone who was concerned for God's intervention into human history to set Israel right. In the Gospel of Mark, Chapter 13, there are series of predictions of the end of the world; the skies will be darkened, the stars will fall from heaven, there will be earthquakes, trials and tribulations, war, and rumours of war. And then at the end of that period, a divine figure, the Son of Man, will come, will enter into human history and will inaugurate God's kingdom. These predictions are examples of apocalyptic prophecy. That is, a prophecy of God's intervention into human history at the end of time to bring to realization all the things that God has promised to his people. This is what is meant by the term 'Apocalyptic Eschatology.'

If the attribution of that series of prophecies to Jesus is taken seriously, then Jesus would have to be classified as an eschatological prophet. There is, however, reason to believe that some of those prophetic statements attributed to Jesus were probably the creation of the early church. These statements were put into the mouth of Jesus, in order to help his followers to understand their relationship to their own history and to make sense of the catastrophes that were developing during the course of the first century. If some of the other elements in the teaching of Jesus are reviewed, there seems to be on his part a somewhat critical attitude towards some of these prophetic elements. For instance, there are sayings where Jesus says that he does not know when the end will come.

Albert Schweitzer, in his *Quest of the Historical Jesus*, saw Jesus as a Jewish "apocalyptic prophet",[211] overthrowing evil and bringing in a new dominion. Willem S. Vorster in his work *Speaking of Jesus* discusses the question of who Jesus was in the Palestinian context of his time. He suggests three possible answers: (1) an eschatological prophet, (2) a wisdom teacher, (3) perhaps both. Vorster thinks that, "it is undoubtedly possible that Jesus was an eschatological prophet, in the first-century Galilee."[212] It is interesting to note that Vorster has not failed to see and evaluate the aspect of seeing Jesus as the 'eschatological prophet'. This had been called into question in the recent past on several grounds. Is Jesus *merely* an eschatological prophet? Is it *relevant* to present Jesus 'the Rabbi' as an eschatological prophet? In what *sense* can he be seen as an 'eschatological prophet'? Vorster says that the images of prophet and teacher "are forced upon us by the New Testament as well as by the results of New Testament scholarship."[213] He insists that "both the state of scholarship and the images of Jesus in the ancient sources at our disposal make it necessary for us to take seriously the images of prophet and teacher."[214] Vorster also notes that there is a prevailing opinion that these two images are viewed by some as two opposing images. He argues further that, "it is possible to conceive of Jesus as a wisdom teacher in non- eschatological terms."[215] Even in his reading of the Beatitudes, Vorster continues "it is possible to interpret the sayings tradition of Jesus within a wisdom framework and not an apocalyptic, eschatological one."[216] Vorster also agrees that for almost a century Jesus was interpreted within the framework of Jewish eschatology and apocalyptic writings. For many commentators, if not most, the eschatological interpretation of Jesus' teaching and his role as an eschatological prophet,[217] became the dominant way of seeing him. But Vorster draws attention to recent studies, where it is argued that the idea of 'apocalyptic eschatology' in the teachings of Jesus was a later development in the Jesus tradition, and that Jesus himself was probably more of a sage than an eschatological prophet.

To conclude, it can be agreed that the oscillation between describing the role of Jesus as Rabbi and attributing to him a new and unique authority made additional titles necessary. One such was Prophet, as in the acclamation in Mt 21:11, "This is the prophet Jesus from Nazareth of Galilee." Probably the most intriguing version of it is once again in Aramaic (Rev 3:14): "The words of the Amen, the faithful and true witness." The word Amen was the formula of affirmation to end a prayer, as in the farewell charge of Moses to the people of Israel, where each verse concludes (Dt 27:14-26): "And all the people shall say, Amen." In the New Testament an extension of the meaning of Amen becomes evident in the Sermon on the Mount. "Amen, Truly, I say to you." Some seventy-five times throughout the four Gospels, Amen introduces an authoritative pronouncement by Jesus. As one who had the authority to make such pronouncements, Jesus was the Prophet. From the above, this study concludes that Jesus had a prophetic ministry which far exceeded that of other prophets and who emerges as a new Moses who speaks for God with new authority both in his words and deeds.

Summary and Conclusions

Part II chapter two of this book began by looking at the context in which Jesus started and continued his public ministry in Palestine. As I. M. Zeitlin (and others) have noted, Jesus was steeped in the Jewish faith and tradition from the outset. His knowledge of the Hebrew Scriptures and of his Jewish heritage was such that, as Kittel notes, Jesus acted like a Jewish Rabbi of his time. Therefore those who followed him naturally accepted him as such. Nevertheless, as Davies and Hengel note, Jesus did not fit completely in the mould of a typical Rabbi. The Gospel accounts of Jesus quite clearly demonstrate that it is the content of his teaching that distinguished him from all other Rabbis of his day. In fact it was the uniqueness of his message, the way he claimed to justify his teaching by his own authority and not by citing either Scripture or past Rabbinical sources, that ultimately brought him into conflict with the whole Sanhedrin.

This was not the only difference noted between Jesus and other Rabbis. The relationship that Jesus had with his most intimate followers, his disciples, was also different. First of all, he 'called' (or chose) them rather than the other way round. They remained close to him throughout his ministry, which was not confined to the synagogue or temple but included travelling in the countryside and towns and speaking to large crowds. Jesus called them to discipleship, rather than that they would increase their knowledge of the Law and the Prophets. This has led to the conclusion that Jesus was not a formally 'ordained' Rabbi in the ordinary accepted sense of the term. He was, rather, perceived as 'one who teaches' and as such his disciples (and others) gave him all the respect and honour due to a Rabbi of his time.

Two different positions in two different stages were presented to see whether Jesus was perceived as a Rabbi in the same way as any other Rabbi of his time. The preceding chapter, chapter one dealt with quite a number of ideas and arguments to prove that Jesus was in fact called and considered a Rabbi. Even while chapter one very strongly affirmed that Jesus acted like a Rabbi, we have never agreed that Jesus of Nazareth was a Rabbi in the ordinary sense of a 'Rabbinical teacher'. This current chapter, chapter two, presented the arguments of some scholars like Martin Hengel who objected to the proposition that Jesus was a formal Rabbi. He, along with other authors, offers several objections to explain why in their view Jesus cannot be called a Rabbi. First of all, for Hengel, Jesus does not come from the line of Scribes or Rabbis as his message was not a Rabbinical instruction, but charismatic. He claims that the new content of Jesus' teaching was neither scribal nor Rabbinic, but charismatic and eschatological. For Hengel, Jesus "stood outside any discoverable uniform teaching of Judaism"[218] and hence Jesus cannot be called Rabbi in the normal sense of the term. In Hengel's words, Jesus "taught as someone specially authorised by God, so that his Word was God's Word, which men could not evade."[219] But he maintains that, for reasons of clarity, the description of Jesus 'as a Rabbi' should never be used. Thus his objections could be summed up as follows: "to his contemporaries Jesus was not at all like a scribe of the Rabbinical stamp;"[220] and there is no trace of the typical method of the Rabbinical way of debating. "Even the controversies between Jesus and the Scribes who opposed him can hardly be used to show that Jesus was a teacher taught in accordance with the Rabbinic method."[221] Again, in the use of scripture, Jesus presented a new angle or interpretation and this new content "was not scribal and Rabbinic but charismatic and eschatological in type." Hengel also maintains that in his preaching Jesus was in fact not an exegete: "In addition he is innocent of the spirit of Rabbinic learning."[222] Thus, for Hengel, Jesus stood outside any teaching tradition of Judaism of his time.

Endnotes

[1] R. BULTMANN, *Jesus and the Word*, p. 49. F. Hahn also notes that "It is certain that in His own lifetime Jesus was addressed as "Rabbi", and in His outward appearance He was not essentially distinguished from the scribes of the day." See, F. HAHN, *The Titles of Jesus in Christology*, p. 74. Theissen and Merz observe that the historical Jesus, in his lifetime, behaved like a Rabbi in his public ministry. His discussions with other scribes, his gathering of μαθηταί around him, his teachings in the synagogues and his method of answering theological and scriptural enquiries by different sorts of people "corresponded to the contemporary notions of a Rabbi." See, G. THEISSEN & A. MERZ, *The Historical Jesus*, p. 355. They contend that Jesus displayed a strong adherence to Sacred Scripture that was expressed in both his teachings and interpretation of Scripture, especially of the Mosaic Law. They further note he had a group of disciples around him. Moreover, the specific way he taught his disciples strongly suggests he was acting as a scribe or a Rabbi of that time.

[2] *Ibid.* There are occurrences of Jesus' teaching in the synagogue (Mk 1:21; 6:2; Mt 4:23; 9:35; 21:23; Lk 4:15; 6:6; 13:10; Jn 6:59; 18:20). Jesus has also been presented as teaching in the Temple (Mk 11: 17; 12: 14; 12:35; 14:49; Mt 21:23; Lk 19:47; 21:37; Jn 7:14; 8: 2; 8:20; 18:20). These instances may demonstrate that the manner of Jesus' teaching is in accordance with that of a Jewish teacher or scribe. In addition, Jesus has been viewed as a teacher (Mk 10:1; Mt 4:23; 9:35; Lk 4:15) in the line of contemporary Jewish teachers.

[3] Martin HENGEL, *The Charismatic Teacher and his Followers*, Edinburgh, T. & T. Clark, 1981, pp. 42–50. The quotation is from the heading on p. 42. Cf. also K.H. RENGSTORF, "μαθητης" *TDNT* 4:455. See also, Martin HENGEL, *The Johannine Question*, SCM Press, London, 1989; Mark Allan POWELL, *Jesus as a Figure of History: How Modern Historians View the Man from Galilee*, Louisville, John Knox, 1998.

[4] R. RIESNER, *Jesus als Lehrer,* WUNT 2/7, 3d ed., Tübingen, J. C. B. Mohr, Paul Siebeck, 1988.

[5] Josephus writes, "Now there was about this time Jesus, a wise man, if it be lawful to call him a man; for he was a doer of wonderful works, a teacher of such men as receive the truth with pleasure. He drew over to him both many of the Jews and many of the Gentiles. He was [the] Christ." Cf. JOSEPHUS, *Ant.* 18 - 3:3. See also, Henry WANSBOROUGH, ed., *Jesus and the Oral Gospel Tradition, Journal for the Study of the New Testament Supplement*, Sheffield, Continuum International Publishing Group, Sheffield Academic, 1991; Robert E. VAN VOORST, *Jesus Outside the New Testament: An Introduction to the Ancient Evidence*, Studying the Historical Jesus, Grand Rapids, Eerdmans, 2000. Jesus was recognized as Rabbi by his contemporaries as passages in the New Testament illustrate: And Jesus answered and said to him, "Simon, I have something to say to you." And he said, "What is it?" (Lk 7:40). A lawyer asked him a question to test him: "What is the greatest commandment in the

Torah?" (Mt 22:35-36). And behold, a rich man came up to him and said, "ῥαββί What good thing must I do to have eternal life?" (Mt 19:16). And someone in the crowd said to him, "ῥαββί order my brother to divide the inheritance with me." (Lk 12:13). And some of the Pharisees in the crowd said to him, "ῥαββί rebuke your disciples." (Lk 19:39). Some of the Sadducees came up to him...and they asked him, saying, "ῥαββί " (Lk 20:27-28).

[6] Geza VERMES, *Jesus the Jew*, in James H. CHARLESWORTH (ed.), *Jesus' Jewishness, Exploring the Place of Jesus Within Early Judaism*, NY, Crossroad, The American Interfaith Institute, 1991, p. 110.

[7] Cf. Geza VERMES, *Jesus the Jew: A Historian's Reading of the Gospels*, rev.ed, Philadelphia, 1981; Idem, The Gospel of Jesus the Jew, Newcastle upon Tyne, 1981; *Idem, Jesus and World of Judaism*, Philadelphia, 1984; Gerd THEISSEN & Annette MERZ, *The Historical Jesus: a Comprehensive Guide*, Augsburg, Fortress Publishers, 2003.

[8] Cf. E. P. SANDERS, *Jesus and Judaism*, Philadelphia, 1985.

[9] Jacques Baldet agrees on the point of circumcision and he adds that "there is no doubt that Jesus was Jewish, circumcised in his body and in his heart." Jacques BALDET, Trans. Joseph ROWE, *Jesus the Rabbi Prophet, A New Light on the Gospel Message*, Rochester, Vermont, Inner Traditions, 2005, p. 74; Bruce Chilton holds the view that Jesus' life in Judaism opened with his *berith*, the ritual circumcision mandated by the Torah for every male child of Israel. (Cf. Gen 17:9-14). See, See, B. CHILTON, *Rabbi Jesus, An Intimate Biography: The Jewish Life and Teachings that Inspired Christianity*, p. 3.

[10] In fact, *Yeshua* was the fifth most common Jewish name, 4 out of the 28 Jewish High-Priests in Jesus' time were called *Yeshua*. Joseph was the second most common male name and Mary the most common amongst women, this in itself is sufficient evidence to throw doubt on the recently found tomb of 'Jesus, Mary and Joseph.' Ed Tenhor opines that "the name Jesus has been found on a few burial ossuary chests and this is so because it is one of the common names of the day." See, Ed TENHOR, *That Rabbi from Nazareth: A Quest for Historical Jesus*, Bloomington, IN, 2004, p. xxix.

[11] Cf. Lk 2: 22; Dt 18:4; Ex 13:2.12.15. At the conclusion of Mary's period of uncleanness (cf. Lev 12: 2-8) a sacrifice was offered for the child Jesus, a pair of doves and 2 young pigeons, which indicates that his family was not wealthy (Lev 12: 2. 6. 8; Lk 2: 22-24). It is clear from these small details that Jesus was raised according to the law (Lk 2:39).

[12] The primary sources for Jesus' life and teaching are the Gospels of Matthew, Mark, Luke, and John (see articles on the individual books, e.g., Matthew, Gospel according to), though these are not biographies but theologically framed accounts of the ministry, death, and resurrection of Jesus, i.e., of the basic subject matter of Christian preaching and teaching. Other books of the New Testament add few further details. Among non-Christian writers of antiquity,

Tacitus (A.D. 54-119), Suetonius (A.D. 75-160) and Pliny the Younger (about A.D. 61-115), refer to Jesus, as does Josephus (A.D. 37-94) in at least one passage. The second century Gospel of Thomas sheds light on the development of the tradition of Jesus' sayings. The Gospels of Matthew and Luke contain narratives of Jesus' birth and infancy, which disagree in many points but concur in asserting that he was the miraculously conceived son of Mary the wife of Joseph, and that he was born at Bethlehem in Judea. All four Gospels agree in dating his call to public ministry from the time of his baptism at the hands of John "the baptizer," after which he took up the life of an itinerant preacher, teacher, and healer, accompanied by a small band of disciples. However the activities of Jesus after he was found at the Jerusalem temple are not given in the gospels and that raises many presumptions about his formation as a student. Read, David CAIRNS, "The Motives and Scope of Historical Inquiry About Jesus", *Scottish Journal of Theology* 29 (1976) 335ff; Robert H. STEIN, "The 'Criteria' for Authenticity", R. T. FRANCE & David WENHAM, eds., *Gospel Perspectives*, Vol. 1, *Studies of History and Tradition in the Four Gospels*, Sheffield, JSOT Press, 1980, pp.225-263.

[13] See, B. CHILTON, *Rabbi Jesus, An Intimate Biography: The Jewish Life and Teachings that Inspired Christianity*, pp. 23-32.

[14] *Ibid.*, p. 32.

[15] Rudolf BULTMANN, *Jesus and the Word*, NY, Charles Scribner Sons, London & Glasgow, Fontana Books, 1958, p.8.

[16] In two passages among many occurrences of the title "Rabbi" in the gospels, certain passages (for example Mk 9:5 and 10:51) bear witness to Jesus being addressed a ῥαββί He is a ῥαββί who speaks in public, like the teachers were doing in Israel: in synagogues, in squares, in the temple. Jesus is a teacher surrounded by *mathetai,* that is, by the disciples; he seems to have a school. In the New Testament the word ῥαββί is used in similar fashion with regard to John the Baptist's disciples (e.g., Mt 11:2; Mk 2:18; Lk 5:33) and the Pharisees (e.g., Mt 22:16; Mk 2:18). However, the primary interest here is the use of the word to identify Jesus as a teacher and his followers or disciples. This particular usage is not restricted to the Twelve; in fact, only a small percentage of the occurrences refer exclusively to the Twelve. By far the most common usage generally refers to the disciples of the later time, and in these contexts there are similarities as well as some striking differences with the common usage of *Mathethes* in NT. "Disciple" cannot be defined apart from the teacher to whom the disciples in question are attached. Jesus presented himself publicly as a teacher and was well versed in the rabbinical traditions, even from an early age (Mk 12:18; Lk 2:41–50; 12:13). Some of the religious hierarchy refused to acknowledge his authority (e.g., Mk 2:1–11; 6:2; Jn 7:15; 8:13–59). He was nevertheless recognized as a ῥαββί by his own disciples as well as the broader public (Jn 1:38; 3:2; Mk 9:5; 11:21). But his teaching and ministry were clearly unique, a fact that is demonstrated in the responses of the crowds who heard and

saw Jesus, and recognized in him an authority that was absent from the traditional Rabbis (Mt 7:28,29; Mk 1:27; Lk 4:32.36). When people called Jesus ῥαββί Jesus never seemed to object. Very often the adherents of Jesus say ῥαββί either by contacting Jesus or by speaking about him. Matthew informs us in Mt 23:8 and Mt 26:17-19 that when he uses 'teacher' as a title for Jesus, he is translating the word ῥαββί Does that mean that Jesus considered himself a rabbi? Recall that the Aramean word 'rabbi', used at the time of Jesus, is reproduced or translated by words to denote either master or doctor of law and in this context Jesus as a ῥαββί is considered to be a great teacher of Torah. See also, John Dominic CROSSAN, *The Historical Jesus: The Life of a Mediterranean Jewish Peasant*, San Francisco, Harper Collins, 1993; *Idem, Jesus: a Revolutionary Biography*, San Francisco, Harper San Francisco, 1995; *Idem, Who Is Jesus? Answers to Your Questions About the Historical Jesus*, Westminster John Knox Press, 1999.

[17] R. BULTMANN, *Jesus and the Word*, p. 58.

[18] *Ibid*, p. 48.

[19] J. BALDET, p. 63. See also, George WESLEY BUCHANAN, "The Age of Jesus," *New Testament Studies* 41.2 (1995) 297; Henry WANSBOROUGH, ed., "Jesus and the Oral Gospel Tradition"*, Journal for the Study of the New Testament*, Supplement 64, Sheffield, Continuum International Publishing Group, Sheffield, Academic Press, 1991; Ken M. CAMPBELL, "What was Jesus' occupation?", *Journal of Evangelical Theological Society* 48.3 (Sept. 2005) 501- 519.

[20] Mishnaic or Talmudic references, even if dated post-CE 70, may still reflect traditions current in Jesus' day. Cf. H. L. STRACK and G. STEMBERGER, *Introduction to the Talmud and Midrash,* (trans. M. Bockmuehl), Minneapolis, Fortress, 1992. In using rabbinic materials for the purpose of establishing a framework for understanding John's portrait of Jesus as a Rabbi, see, e.g., C. K. BARRETT, *The Gospel According to St. John* (2d ed.), Philadelphia, Westminster, 1978, p. 33. "Great caution is necessary. No part of the rabbinic literature was written down until a date later than the composition of John. Direct literary relationship is out of the question, and some apparent parallels may be merely fortuitous. But when all such allowances have been made it remains very probable that John himself (or perhaps the authors of some of his sources) was familiar with the oral teaching which at a later date was crystallized in the Mishnah, the Talmud, and the Midrashim." According to Riesner, the portrayal of Jesus as a teacher cannot be explained merely by a later Jewish-Christian "rabbinization" Cf. R. RIESNER, *Jesus als Lehrer*, p. 252. The Mishnah contains rabbinic interpretations of Scripture written down during the second century AD. Jewish scholars believe it contains the oral traditions present during the 1st century BC to 1st century AD and therefore would reflect what was true during Jesus' lifetime. Cf. Aboth 5:21. See also, Herbert DANBY, ed., *The Mishnah*, Oxford University Press, Oxford, 1985. The Jewish people call the Hebrew Bible (Old Testament) *Tanakh* an acronym taken from *Torah* (Pentateuch), *Neviim* (Prophets including the history books since history is prophetic), *Ketubim*

(writings). Boys studied Torah since it was the foundation of the Jewish faith and the others (writings and prophets) were believed to comment on and apply the Torah. The Oral Torah was interpretation and application of the Torah believed to originate with Moses and to have been handed down orally for centuries. Many of Jesus' debates with the scribes were over issues of the Oral Torah. God had commanded the wearing of tassels but the oral Torah specified the length. Torah is not a matter of laws and commandments, but rather instructions from God to man for living a life of blessing and joy. Torah consists of two elements-one written and one oral. Jesus apparently attached great importance to the oral Torah (unwritten in his day), and it seems he considered it to be authoritative. When he admonished his disciples to "do and observe everything they (the scribes and Pharisees) command you" (Mt 23:3), he was referring to the Pharisees' oral traditions and interpretations of the Written Torah. The Written Torah itself could not have been in question, for it was accepted by all sects of Judaism, and Jesus himself said, Heaven and earth would sooner disappear than one *yod* or even one *kotz* from the Torah. (Mt 5:18) Many rabbinic statements express similar ideas, such as: Should all the nations of the world unite to uproot one word of the Torah, they would be unable to do it. An excellent treatment of this education can be found in, Shmuel SAFRAI, *Jewish People in the First Century*, Vol. ll, Amsterdam, Van Gorcum, 1974; Paul FOSTER, "Educating Jesus: The Search for a Plausible Context", *Journal for the Study of the Historical Jesus* 4.1 (January 2006) 7-33. The study of Greek in Palestine in Jesus' day was not encouraged, although it was a necessity of daily life in the *Diaspora* lands outside of Palestine. Greek philosophy was equally deprecated in Palestine. Jewish writings such as the Talmud and Mishnah as two rabbinic stories gave a flavour of the Palestinian attitude towards Greek. Access to copies of the Hebrew Scriptures was virtually universal via the synagogues and schools. In addition, every household might purchase one scroll or another according to their wealth. However, it was unlawful to make copies of small portions out of context through fear of transmission of error. Since Scripture was memorised from youth these manuscripts were luxuries rather than essential. Given all of this we can assume that Jesus did not have supernatural help in learning his Scripture but being a Jew he might have learnt it as any other Jewish boy. For example, we read that Timothy had known the Scriptures from his childhood and those were able to make him wise for salvation (Cf. 2Tim 3:15). The Jews of Jesus' era were world innovators in comprehensive education. The majority, if not all, were taught to read and write. The philosopher Seneca remarked that the Jews were the only people who knew the reasons for their religious faith. Jewish education began at the age of five or six and from then on the boy was crammed with Scriptural teaching. Lessons began with the book of Leviticus at age five or six and progressed onward. Higher education began at 15 when he would embark on theological discussion with learned teachers or Rabbis. Read, Craig A. EVANS, *"The Need for the 'Historical Jesus' A Response to Jacob Neusner's Review of Crossan and Meier"*, *Bulletin for Biblical Research*

4 (1994) 127-134; Craig A. EVANS, "Assessing Progress in the Third Quest of the Historical Jesus",

[21] S. BYRSKOG, *Jesus the Only Teacher*, p. 75. Byrskog states that the rabbis in principal maintained the biblical ideal (Dt 4:9f; 6:7. 20f; 11:18f; 32:7. 46) about the responsibility of the father to teach his son. The following rabbinic literatures will help us in this regard. Cf. m. *Pesah.* 10:4; t. *Hag.* 1:2; t. *Qidd.* 1:11; b. *Sukk.* 42a; b. *Nazir* 29a; b. *Qidd.* 29b, 30a; b. B. *Bat.* 21a; *Mek.* on 13:13. Rainer Riesner in his work "Jesus as Teacher" affirms that this practice of education for the Jewish boys was deeply rooted in antiquity. Cf. R. RIESNER, *Lehrer*, pp. 102-110. Samuel Byrskog concludes that "the rabbinic literature shows that the accounts about the teacher-pupil relationship corresponded to the actual existence of schools. The colleges, in particular, were often schools in which the teacher himself provided the circle of disciples with its basic identity and coherence." S. BYRSKOG, *Jesus the Only Teacher, Didactic Authority and Transmission in Ancient Israel*, p. 77.

[22] *Ibid.*, p. 75. According to a Rabbinic literature *y. Ketub.* 32c, *Simeon B. Shetah* (c. 90 B. C. E.) was the first to decree that children should go to the Scripture school. Riesner adds that scripture teachers were appointed in each district and each town. See, R. RIESNER, *Lehrer*, pp. 200-206. Thus, the scripture schools existed in practically every inhabited place of some size in Israel. Cf. *b. Git.* 58a ; *b. Sanh.* 17b ; *y. Meg.* 73d ; *y. Hag.* 76c. *y. Ketub* 35c. *Journal for the Study of the Historical Jesus* 4.1 (January 2006) 35-54.

[23] A basic teaching is that no one should forget even one word of Mishnah or Scripture. (cf. *Avoth* 3:8). To read more about the process of learning in the Jewish system, read, S. BYRSKOG, *Jesus the Only Teacher*, p. 76; S. SAFARI, *Elementary Education, its Religious and Social Significance in the Talmudic Period*, in H. H. BEN-SASSON et al. (eds.), *Jewish Society Through the Ages*, London, 1971, pp. 148-169; idem, *Education and the Study of the Torah*, in S. SAFARI et al. (eds.), *The Jewish People in the First Century, Historical Geography, Political History, Social, Cultural and Religious Life and Institutions*, CRINT I 2, Assen, 1976, pp. 945-970. Cf. Z. H. CHAJES, *The Student's Guide Through the Talmud*, New York, 1960, pp. 35-117. D. PATTE, *Early Jewish Hermeneutic in Palestine*, SBLDS 22, Missoula, 1975, pp. 100-104. C. ROTH, *Minhagim Books*, EncJud XII (1971) 23-31, pp. 26-31. M. ELON, *Takkanot*, EncJud 15 (1971) 712-728, p. 714.

[24] Ed TENHOR, *That Rabbi from Nazareth: A Quest for Historical Jesus*, Bloomington, IN, 2004, p. 10. However, Byrskog states that the field of cultural continuity in ancient Israel and ancient Judaism shows a development towards more organised schools. The development is probably due both to internal needs and external influences from the Greek-Hellenistic world. Read, Willem S. VORSTER & J. Eugene BOTHA, eds., *Speaking of Jesus: Essays on Biblical Language, Gospel Narrative and the Historical Jesus, Biblical Studies*, Leiden, Brill, 1998.

[25] Irving M. ZEITLIN, *Jesus and the Judaism of His Time*, Cambridge, UK, Polity Press, 1988, p. 48. It is obvious and yet, to judge by the tragedies of later history, not at all obvious that Jesus was a Jew, so that the first attempts to understand his message took place within the context of Judaism. Luke tells us (4:16-30) that after his baptism and temptation by the devil, he "came to Nazareth, where he had been brought up; and he went to the synagogue, as his custom was, on the Sabbath day. And he stood up to read." Following the customary rabbinical pattern, he took up a scroll of the Hebrew Bible, read it, presumably provided an Aramaic translation-paraphrase of the text, and then commented on it. The words he read were from Isaiah 61:1-2: "The Spirit of the Lord is upon me, because he has anointed me to preach good news to the poor. He has sent me to proclaim release to the captives and recovering of sight to the blind, to set at liberty those who are oppressed, to proclaim the acceptable year of the Lord." But instead of doing what a rabbi would normally do, apply the text to the hearers by comparing and contrasting earlier interpretations, he declared: "Today this scripture has been fulfilled in your hearing." Although the initial reaction to this audacious declaration was said to be wonderment "at the gracious words which proceeded out of his mouth," his further explanation produced the opposite reaction, and everyone was "filled with wrath." Behind the confrontations between Jesus as ῥαββί and the representatives of the rabbinical tradition, the affinities are nevertheless clearly discernible in the forms in which his teachings appear in the Gospels. Read, R. T. FRANCE, "The Authenticity of the Sayings of Jesus," Colin BROWN, ed., *History, Criticism, and Faith,* Downers Grove, Illinois, IVP, 1976, pp. 101-141; Paul COPAN, ed., *Will the Real Jesus Please Stand Up?*, A Debate Between William Lane Craig and John Dominic Crossan, Grand Rapids, Baker Book House, 1999; N. T. WRIGHT, *The Contemporary Quest for Jesus*, Augsburg, Fortress Publishers, 2002.

[26] J. P. MEIER, *A Marginal Jew: Rethinking the Historical Jesus*, Vol.1. p. 255. To the question of what language Jesus spoke, Meier agrees to a certain extent with Joachim Jeremias that the language that Jesus spoke is a complex one. Latin is ruled out whereas Greek is likely. But, in the context of Jesus' public life, fluency in Greek was not called for. As for Hebrew, Meier opines that Jesus would have learned that either in the synagogue at Nazareth or a nearby school. Jesus probably used Hebrew when he was debating with Pharisees and scribes on Law and scripture. But as for his preaching to the ordinary folk, Jesus as a teacher almost certainly spoke in Aramaic. From Meier's observation we can infer three salient features: 1. Jesus was a teacher in the Jewish land of Galilee and Judea 2. His audiences mostly comprised ordinary Palestinian Jews. 3. Jesus wished to be understood by them and so spoke the language of those ordinary people. Here with the following arguments, one needs to raise a concrete question, which certainly brings an objection to Meier's views, which was seen above. Did Jesus use both the Aramaic and the Greek expressions for "Father" as Mark recorded in Mk. 14:36?. "Abba, Father" (Mk.14:36; Rom. 8:15; Gal. 4:6). The term abba

is the Aramaic word for father. The Greek term is added not to tell the reader what the Aramaic means, but to express Jesus' dependence on his Father as he faced the sufferings of the crucifixion (Mk 14:36). No doubt Jesus loved to utter his Father's name in both forms, first in his cherished mother tongue and then in the common language of his day. In this view the use of both words has a charming simplicity and warmth. Paul uses the phrase 'Abba, Father' in Rom. 8:15 and Gal. 4:6 to express the intimate relationship the believer has with God. Cf., *Nelson Study Bible, Word focus*, p. 1675; Stephen WESTERHOLM, *Jesus and Scribal Authority,* Lund, Gleerup, 1978, pp. 178ff.

[27] I. M. ZEITLIN, *Jesus and the Judaism of His Time*, p. 48.

[28] E. TENHOR, *That Rabbi from Nazareth: A Quest for Historical Jesus*, p. 67. For an excellent discussion on the entire question of the languages of Jesus, see Joseph A. FITZMYER, "*The Languages of Palestine in the First Century A.D.*," *CBQ*, Vol. 32 (1970), pp. 501-531; Pinchas LAPIDE, "*Insights from Qumran Into the Languages of Jesus*," *RQ*, Vol. 8 (1975), pp. 483-501. It is known from early church records that Matthew's gospel was written in Hebrew. Some scholars assume that Jesus himself must have taught in Hebrew as all rabbis did. Jesus says that "not one *yodh* or little horn shall pass away from the law" (Mt 5:18) referring to the smallest Hebrew letter *yodh* and the small hook or serif on others. The Greek gospels are translations themselves of Jesus' Hebrew teachings and possibly too of an original Hebrew gospel. Cf. P. M. CASEY, "In Which Language Did Jesus Teach?", *Expository Times* 108.11 (1997) 326-328.

[29] Robert H. STEIN, *The Method and Message of Jesus' Teachings*, Philadelphia, The Westminster Press, 1948, p. 4. Stein states categorically that Greek was not the mother tongue of Jesus. Rather Stein sets out with Gustaf Dalman to demonstrate that the native tongue of Jesus was Aramaic. Stein observes that although the sayings of Jesus recorded in the NT appear in the Greek language, it is apparent from the gospels that Greek was not his mother tongue, but that it was Aramaic. That Jesus spoke Aramaic is evident from the fact that even in the Greek NT, a number of Aramaic terms and phrases come from the lips of Jesus. Stein observes that Aramaic was the native tongue of Palestine in the first century. However, it cannot be denied that Hebrew also was spoken at that time. Hence it is not baseless to say that along, with Aramaic, Jesus could have also spoken and read Hebrew. The discovery of the Dead Sea Scrolls, which are primarily in Hebrew, and of the Bar Cochba correspondence (Bar Cochba was the messianic pretender who led the Jewish revolt against Rome in A.D. 132-135), which is also in Hebrew, has demonstrated that Hebrew was still used extensively at least in certain circles. Cf. Lk 4:16-20, where Jesus reads the Hebrew Scriptures in the synagogue of Nazareth. Moreover, Stein does observe that it is not surprising to discover that Jesus, raised in Galilee of the Gentiles and living only three or four miles from the Greek city of Sepphoris, could probably speak some Greek. Read also, F. F. BRUCE, "Did Jesus Speak Aramaic?", *Expository Times* 56 (1944-45) 328; Stanley E. PORTER, "Did Jesus

Ever Teach in Greek", *Tyndale Bulletin* 44.2 (1993) 199-235; M. WINGER, "Why Didn't Jesus Write?", *Expository Times* 111.8 (2000) 259-261; Stanley E. PORTER, "Jesus and the Use of Greek: A Response to Maurice Casey", *Bulletin for Biblical Research* 10.1 (2000) 71-88.

[30] See, Joachim JEREMIAS, *New Testament Theology*, trans. John BOWDEN, Charles Scribner's Sons, 1971, pp. 6-7; Vincent TAYLOR, *The Gospel According to St. Mark*, London, Macmillan and Co., Ltd.,1959, pp. 55-66.

[31] R. H. STEIN, *The Method and Message of Jesus' Teachings*, p. 5. See also J. A. EMERTON, "*The Problem of Vernacular Hebrew in the First Century a.d. and the Language of Jesus*", *JTS*, Vol. 24 (1973), pp. 1-23; Matthew BLACK, *An Aramaic Approach to the Gospels and Acts*, 3rd ed., Oxford, Clarendon Press, 1967, pp. 41-49. Jesus' inaugural sermon in Nazareth is prefaced only in Lk 4:16-21 which is a direct quote from the LXX, and the claim that the prophecy is now being fulfilled. In these stories (Lk 1-4), not only the content of the LXX is reflected, but also the narrative and semantic style of the LXX translators. Note that Jesus began his public ministry not in Jerusalem, or Judea, but in the region called Galilee, that is, Galilee of the Gentiles. "Traditionally Galilee has been regarded as a relatively isolated region within Palestine, particularly subject to Hellenization and a hotbed of revolution." See, Allen C. MYERS, (ed.), *Eerdmans Bible Dictionary*, 1989, p. 399. Lower Galilee remained outside the main stream of Israelite life until NT times, when Roman rule first brought security. Even then Sepphoris was the chief town of the area, a little to the north of Nazareth. But Nazareth lay close enough to several main trade routes for easy contact with the outside world, while at the same time her position as a frontier town on the S border of Zebulon overlooking the Esdraelon plain produced certain aloofness. It was this independence of outlook in Lower Galilee which led to the scorn in which Nazareth was held by strict Jews (Jn 1:46) Cf. DOUGLAS, *New Bible Dictionary*, 'Nazareth,' p. 819. According to the Catholic Encyclopaedia, it was called the district of various peoples. It was here in the centrally located town of Nazareth, 20 kilometres from the Mediterranean, that Jesus spent his early years; as a province it was ruled at that time by Herod Antipas (4 B. C. to A. D. 39). Here also Jesus began and continued the early years of his ministry. In NT times the languages spoken there were Aramaic, Greek, and Hebrew. See, Robert C. BRODERICK, p. 235. It is probably safe to assert that Jesus habitually spoke Aramaic and occasionally Greek, and read and spoke Hebrew. It is known that Jesus did use, at least at times, the Septuagint, rather than the Hebrew text. For example, when teaching in the synagogue in Nazareth, Jesus was handed the scroll of Isaiah. It is recorded for us in Lk 4:18 that he read from Isaiah (Is 61:1-3). The Luke passage states: "The Spirit of the Lord is upon me, because he has anointed me to preach the gospel to the poor; he hath sent me to heal the broken-hearted, and recovering of sight to the blind, to set at liberty them that are bruised." The phrase "and recovering of sight to the blind", is not in the Hebrew text. It only appears in the Septuagint. It seems reasonable to

assume, since Jesus was reading from the Greek text, he most likely continued his teaching in Greek. See, Dr. Charles GOODWIN & David MCBRAYER, *The Original Word Teaching Series II, New Testament Greek*, Bible Study, 1997, p. 101, footnote 21. In addition, there are several incidents in Jesus' ministry when he spoke to people who knew neither Aramaic nor Hebrew. Probably Jesus spoke Greek during the following occasions: the visit to Tyre, Sidon and the Decapolis (Mk 7:31ff.), the conversation with the Syro- Phoenician woman (Mk 7:24-30; compare especially 7:26) and the trial before Pontius Pilate (Mk 15:2-15; compare also Jesus' conversation with the "Greeks" in Jn.12:20-36.) Cf. Robert H. STEIN, *Jesus The Messiah, A Survey of the Life of Christ*, 1996, p.87. The extent to which Jesus may have used Greek is subject to debate. The fact that he read in the synagogue proves that he was an educated man. His speaking to the Samaritan woman (Jn 4) and the calling of the Gentiles proves that Jesus was not an exclusivist. To say that he was not more than just acquainted with the Greek language is to ignore the evidence of the pervasiveness of the Hellenistic culture, even in Palestine, at that time in history. To argue that he could not speak Greek at all is, to say the least, simply illogical. Indisputable evidence of the forceful impact of Hellenism is furnished by numerous Greek inscriptions written in Palestine and second-century A.D Greek translations of the Bible. Greek fragments of the Dead Sea Scrolls, and the Graecisms found throughout rabbinic literature. Studies on a wide range of Greek influence have made absolutely clear the importance and pervasiveness of the Hellenistic language and culture in Palestine. Cf. Angel SAENZ-BADILLOS, Translated by John ELWODE, *The History of the Hebrew Language*, 1993, p. 168. The entire point of this passage is to show that the ancient Greek language was rather the dominant language of the early Christian era, and it was the language by which the Gospel was spread so rapidly throughout the ancient Roman Empire and beyond. The strongest evidence that the original New Testament was written in Greek is the use of a Greek translation, the Septuagint, as the primary source for quotations from the Old Testament. Notice that in Jn 1:42, John uses the name Jesus, which in the Greek is Iesous (transliterated into English). John, writing in Greek, uses the Greek equivalent of the Hebrew Yeshua in his writings. If anyone doubts that Iesous is indeed the equivalent of the Hebrew expression, then recall the trilingual sign that Pilate placed above Christ at His crucifixion. The sign read, "Jesus of Nazareth, King of the Jews"; and it said this in three languages (Jn 19:19-20). What did the people see? They saw the name of Jesus written in each of these languages: In the Hebrew, Yeshua; in Latin, Iesous; and, in the Greek, Ἰησοῦς. "The languages of Palestine in the 1st century AD are a complex problem. It seems clear that Aramaic, Hebrew and Greek were all spoken. Aramaic was most probably Jesus' vernacular, but a Galilean would almost certainly also have a working knowledge of Greek and Hebrew in a form akin to the later Mishnaic Hebrew, may well have been the medium for his debates with the religious authorities in Jerusalem." To read more on this subject, consult, F. F. BRUCE, *New Testament History*, 1969, chs. 1-9; P.E. HUGHES, *The Languages spoken by Jesus*, in R. N. LONGENECKER and M. C. TENNEY, (eds.), *New Dimensions in New Testament Study*, 1974, pp.127-143; G. VERMES, *Jesus the Jew*, 1973, ch. 2 (on Galilee). See also, *Jesus Christ*, in *The Illustrated Bible Dictionary*, Vol. 2, pp. 761-771; Gary R. HABERMAS, *The Historical Jesus: Ancient Evidence for the Life of Christ*, College Press Publishing Co., 1996.

[32] R. RIESNER, *Jesus as Preacher and Teacher*, p. 191. Dan Cohn- Sherbok, in his work on *The Jewish Messiah*, states that "although little is known of Jesus' earthly life, it appears that he received a traditional Jewish education." See, Dan Cohn- SHERBOK, *The Jewish Messiah*, Edinburgh, T & T Clark, 1997, p. 61. Sherbok refers to the event of Lk 4:16-20, the presence of Jesus in the synagogue and opines that Jesus "was deemed worthy to read the Torah in the synagogue in Nazareth. As a Jewish boy and according to the custom he took part in the pilgrimage to Jerusalem and he is seen there debating with others. Thus, in the understanding of Sherbok, Jesus was brought up in a Jewish environment and he in fact observed the Jewish customs and their obligations. Thus, he concludes that in the Jewish environment Jesus should have also received the Jewish traditional education. Jesus would have been influenced by Scriptural writings. See, Gary M. BURGE, "A Jesus Quest without a Compass? Article- Review", *Evangelical Quarterly* 74.1 (2002) 59-66.

[33] By the time Jesus began his public ministry, it seems that he had not only received the thorough religious training typical of the average Jewish man of his day, he had probably spent years studying with one of the outstanding rabbis in the Galilee. Jesus thus appeared on the scene as a respected rabbi himself. He was recognized as such by his contemporaries. Clearly, there was a wide range of Jesus' contemporaries who saw him as a ῥαββί. Read, Bruce CHILTON, Craig A. EVANS & Jacob NEUSNER, *The Missing Jesus: Rabbinic Judaism and the New Testament*, Leiden, Brill, 2003.

[34] E. TENHOR, *That Rabbi from Nazareth: A Quest for Historical Jesus*, p. 3. Ed Tenhor also refers to the Jewish scholar Geza Vermes who suggests that the garment of Jesus was the kind the Pharisees wore (Mt 23: 5) with the traditional tassels hanging from the edges. Cf. Nu 15.37-41; Mt 9:20; 14:36; Lk 8:44; in English these are obvious by the translations 'hem' or 'fringe of his garment' which the crowds were keen to touch in order to be healed. He may also have worn the *tephillin* 'phylacteries', Dt 6:8, small boxes bound to arm and head containing the Scriptural verses: Ex 13:1-16, Dt 6:4-9 and 11:13-21. Jesus only criticised the exaggerated form of these for ostentatious exhibitionism (Mt 23.5), a practice also condemned by later rabbis. Conventionally, these were meant to be discreet, and the arm one was invisible under clothing. A rabbinic source suggests that the head one should only be worn in winter under a headband, and not in summer when it would have been conspicuous. Actually, it is unlikely that Jesus wore them as the practice was not universal in his time and, apparently not strictly required (cf. Dt 6:8).

[35] I. M. ZEITLIN, *Jesus and the Judaism of His Time*, p. 48.

[36] However, as Hebrew University professor and Jerusalem School scholar Shmuel Safrai notes even the Sabbath healings which were performed by Jesus were permitted by rabbinic ruling. See, Shmuel SAFRAI, *"Religion in Everyday Life" The Jewish People in the First Century*, volume II, p. 805.

[37] Cf. B. CHILTON, *Galilean Rabbi*, p. 31: "The early Judaism of Jesus' time seems to have been so heterogeneous that to claim his continuity or discontinuity with the religion of his day in general terms is problematic in the extreme: in almost anything he did or said, he would have been accepted by some Jews and rejected by others." The normal Jewish religious practices were so well known and followed by the Jews. One of the most basic examples of a rabbinic command, which Jesus obeyed, is in the realm of blessings. The sole scriptural basis for the many blessings that an observant Jew still says daily is Deuteronomy 8:10: *Ve'akalta vesavata uverakta et Adonai eloheka*, "When you have eaten your fill, thank the Lord your God..." which is literally, "And you will eat and you will be full and you will bless the Lord your God"). The rabbis found justification in this verse for saying a blessing before the meal as well as after, and on many other occasions—indeed, on almost every occasion. The general rule, as delineated in the Babylonian Talmud, Berachot 35[a], was *Kol davar sheneheneh ta'un berakah*, "Anything that is enjoyed requires a blessing." Jesus said grace, or rather a blessing, before and/or after meals (Dt 10; Mt 6:41; 26:26 and Lk 24:30 which is post resurrection; cf. *Didache* 10:1). The object of the blessing was not the food but God. When the New Testament inserts 'it' or 'the bread' in such verses it is not found in the Greek. It was inconceivable that a Jew would bless the object and not the originator/creator. The traditional blessing is: "*Barukh attah 'Adonai 'elohenu Melekh ha-olam ha-motsi lechem meen ha-arets*" "Blessed are You, our Lord God, King of the Ages/Universe, who brings forth bread from the earth." There is evidence that Jesus adhered to the rulings of the Oral Torah in his use of various blessings. In conformity with the rabbis' interpretation of Deuteronomy 8:10, Jesus not only recited a blessing after meals, but also said the blessing before meals: *Baruk hamotsi lehem min ha'arets*, Blessed is he who brings bread out of the earth. It is recorded that at the last Passover meal, which Jesus ate with his disciples in Jerusalem, Jesus "took bread and blessed and broke and gave to his disciples" (Mt 26:26). Since in the Greek text there is no direct object following the verbs "blessed," "broke" and "gave," English translators have felt it necessary to supply the word "it" after each of these, or at least after "broke" and "gave." The English reader therefore receives the impression that Jesus not only divided and distributed the bread, but blessed it as well. Before dining with the two disciples from Emmaus, Jesus "blessed, broke and gave," as he did before he fed the five thousand with five loaves and two fish (In Luke's account, but not in Mark's or Matthew's, the text reads "blessed them," but one important Greek manuscript reads "blessed for them" at Lk 9:16). The blessing that was said in Jesus' time before one ate was praise and thanksgiving to God who so wondrously provides food for his children, to

him who "brings bread out of the earth." One does not bless the food, nor does one even ask God to bless the food. One blesses God who provides the food. See also, Bruce D. CHILTON, "An Evangelical and Critical Approach to the Sayings of Jesus", *Themelios* 3.3 (1978) 78-85.

[38] J. BALDET, *Jesus the Rabbi Prophet, A New Light on the Gospel Message*, p. 89. Baldet himself is not sure whether Jesus was a disciple of John the Baptist and he raises this question as a probability. Baldet adds that the various responses offered to these questions by scholars remain incomplete, for the sources available to us offer little information and are often biased. Baldet asks further questions: "Did Jesus himself become a part of the Baptist movement; and/or, did he belong to a group led by John?" Baldet tries to answer this question, saying, "the answer to these questions is still under debate both by historians and theologians. There are lots of questions about which the scholars have a lot of questions. Did John the Baptist live at Qumran? See the Dead Sea Scrolls? Write any of them? These questions have gripped scholars because the Dead Sea Scrolls reveal remarkable similarities between the Essenes and John's teachings and practices. It is seen in the Bible that John the Baptist came from a family of priests. Many of the Essenes were priests who disagreed with the temple authorities. John was called to prepare the way of the Lord and again the Essenes' main purpose for living in the wilderness was to prepare the way for the Lord. John baptized people as a sign of repentance and inner cleansing and the Essenes practiced ritual cleansing in water as a sign of the soul's cleansing. John the Baptist didn't participate in the normal lifestyle of his people and the Essenes lived an isolated, ascetic existence. Despite the remarkable similarities, John was never identified as an Essene, was not a member of any community, and cannot be placed definitively at Qumran. He proclaimed his message publicly rather than seeking the shelter of a monastic setting like that of Qumran. Read also, David R. CATCHPOLE, "John the Baptist, Jesus and the Parable of the Tares", *Scottish Journal of Theology* 31 (1978) 557ff.

[39] A. N. WILSON, *Jesus, a Life*, NY, W. W. Norton and Company, 1992.

[40] B. CHILTON, *Rabbi Jesus, An Intimate Biography*, p. 33. Bruce Chilton affirms that Jesus wanted to become the talmid of John the Baptist. From John he might have learnt that release from sin makes every Israelite pure and thus acceptable in God's eyes. Little by little Jesus began to break from John and surpass him in influence. Sometimes he continued to emphasize the themes of purity that had so characterized the Baptist, but more and more he chose "to celebrate the Kingdom in Israel with wine and food rather than immersion." As he reflected on the Hebrew Scriptures, Zechariah, especially chapter 14, and especially as mediated through its Targumic interpretations, gave him the insight that God's Kingdom would be manifested over all the earth when the sacrifices were offered at the temple by Jews and Gentiles alike.

[41] *Ibid*, p. 49. Chilton explains that a Rabbi's Mishnah was his "repetition," the words and actions that conveyed his teachings. John's insistence on the

dynamic relationship between repentance and release from sin was the source of Jesus' emphasis on the same relationship throughout his own ministry. Chilton concludes that John did more for Jesus than teach his Mishnah. Thus Jesus is portrayed by some of the scholars to be a disciple of the Baptist. The close relationship between John and Jesus, according to Chilton, "was not destined to last. As Jesus grew older and more confident, his success in gathering pilgrims for immersion, his ability to invoke the Spirit, and the power of his vision of God's Throne put him into competition with John." B. CHILTON, *Rabbi Jesus,* p. 58. Having said this, this study takes no position since there is no biblical basis, or any solid proofs, to establish that Jesus was the disciple of John the Baptist.

[42] P. JOHNSON, *A History of Christianity*, New York, Simon and Schuster, 1976, p.21.

[43] J. BALDET, *Jesus the Rabbi Prophet, A New Light on the Gospel Message*, p. 101. To read the event of Baptism of Jesus by John the Baptist, cf. Mk 1:9; Mt 3:13; Lk 3:21.

[44] The way in which Jesus worked out his hopes and the way in which he came to understand the reign of God or the kingdom of God suggest that he did not necessarily express the eschatological vision in the way that his followers, notably (Mk 13) reworks. One of the most interesting and frustrating aspects of the stories about Jesus in the gospel is that they speak about him in so many different ways. There are elements of Jesus' public career, where he seems like a healer. In Mark, Jesus is first of all an exorcist, somebody who drives out demons and drives out sickness. In Matthew he is depicted as a religious teacher. The Beatitudes, which is called the Sermon on the Mount, are part of that teaching. He is constantly having arguments about what the correct way is to live. He is depicted also as somebody who is talking about the coming Kingdom of God. It might be that the attribution of apocalyptic hope to Jesus came after his lifetime, or maybe was the editorial decision of the evangelist, who, after all, is writing sometime between 70 and 100. Jesus dies around the year 30. There is that gap. In other words, these apocalyptic elements may be seen as a kind of literary theme, but not telling us anything about Jesus. And Paul himself also talks about the coming Kingdom of God with a different view on it: that the Son of God, namely Jesus, is going to come back and now the Kingdom is going to arrive. Paul is talking about a coming Kingdom of God, about the transformation of the living and the resurrection of the dead, about a spirit of holiness transfusing Christian communities, about Jesus coming back and about God intervening definitively in history. See, Bruce D. CHILTON & Craig A. EVANS, eds., *Studying the Historical Jesus: Evaluations of Current Research*, New Testament Tools & Studies Series, Leiden, Brill, 1998; Simon J. GATHERCOLE, "The critical and dogmatic agenda of Albert Schweitzer's The quest of the historical Jesus", *Tyndale Bulletin* 51.2 (2000) 261-283.

[45] E. TENHOR, *That Rabbi from Nazareth: A Quest for Historical Jesus*, p. 10. Ed Tenhor speculates about a number of possible influences that could have

affected Jesus during his hidden young adult years. In his early 20's, according to Ed Tenhor, Jesus was exposed to the Pharisee movement and perhaps joined them or was taught by them. Ed Tenhor believes that many of the beliefs of Jesus are very similar to those of the Pharisees. Ed Tenhor in p.12 concludes "Thus there were many possible influences. Jesus had many opportunities to be a pupil and study. His keen mind absorbed so much, all the while struggling with the specific form that mission ahead of him would take, in the context of a growing self-consciousness of messianic stress."

[46] John P. MEIER, *Reflections on Jesus-of-History Research Today*, in James H. CHARLESWORTH (ed.), *Jesus' Jewishness, Exploring the Place of Jesus Within Early Judaism*, NY, Crossroad, The American Interfaith Institute, 1991, p. 90. While John emphasized judgement and punishment, Jesus proclaimed the good news that God, like a loving father, was seeking out and gathering in the lost, the poor, the marginalized, even the non-believers.

[47] J. P. MEIER, *A Marginal Jew, Rethinking The Historical Jesus*, Vol. 3, p. 41.

[48] A. J. KÖSTENBERGER, *Studies on John and Gender*, p. 76. Only John notes the fact that some of Jesus' first followers had previously been followers of the Baptist and that the Baptist himself had pointed them to Jesus. The two references in 1:38 and 49 indicate that Jesus' first followers transferred their allegiance from one religious teacher, the Baptist, to another, Jesus, who was more but not less than a Rabbi. Cf. also Lk 3:12 where the Baptist is addressed as διδάσκαλος.

[49] J. P. MEIER, *A Marginal Jew, Rethinking The Historical Jesus*, Vol. 2, p. 116.

[50] *Ibid.*

[51] *Ibid.*, pp. 116-117.

[52] G. VERMES, *Jesus the Jew*, p. 26.

[53] J. P. MEIER, *A Marginal Jew*, Vol. 2, p. 117.

[54] M. HENGEL, *The Charismatic Leader and His Followers*, p. 35.

[55] F. HAHN, *The Titles of Jesus in Christology*, p. 74.

[56] R. SCHNACKENBURG, *John*, p. 307. Also noted is a kind of competition between the two schools, namely that of the Baptist and of Jesus (Jn 3:26; Mt 9:14; 11:2), and this suggests that these two schools were contemporaries.

[57] R. E. BROWN, *John*, p. 74.

[58] *Ibid.* Goulder writes that "the Jerusalem disciples had at least been strongly influenced by the Baptist, and his baptism had become their sacramental initiation." See, Michael D. GOULDER, *John 1,1-2,12 and the Synoptics*, in Adelbert DENAUX (ed.), *John and the Synoptics*, BETL 101, Leuven, Leuven University Press & Peeters (1992) 201-237, p. 215.

[59] NEPPER- CHRISTENSEN, Μαθητής, in *EDNT 2* (1991) 372-374, p. 372.

[60] A. J. KÖSTENBERGER, *Studies on John and Gender*, p. 77.

[61] J. P. MEIER, *Reflections on Jesus-of-History Research Today*, p. 96. Among the scholars, when there is an attempt to label Jesus as a Pharisee, there are others, who have seen his critique of the Pharisees' oral tradition, advocate that Jesus had a preference for the Sadducees. Meier notes that there are still others who suggest that, since Jesus radicalised the obligations of the Law and proclaimed the imminent end of the present age, he had ties with the sectarians at Qumran. From the discovery of the Dead Sea Scrolls, and from the approach of Jesus to the written Law and his critique of purity laws, and his distance from priestly concerns, and his openness to Jewish sinners, the identification of Jesus as a member of any Jewish group is improbable. Read, Jacob NEUSNER, "Who Needs 'The Historical Jesus'? An Essay-Review", *Bulletin for Biblical Research* 4 (1994) 113-126; John P. MEIER, "The Present State of the 'Third Quest' for the Historical Jesus: Loss and Gain," *Biblica* 80 (1999) 459-487.

[62] Cf. E. TENHOR, *That Rabbi from Nazareth: A Quest for Historical Jesus*, p. 61. Tenhor states that it is not easy for Christians to think of Jesus as a Pharisee. The battles in the Gospels always seem to have Jesus, not as a part of this religious group, but in conflict with them. For Tenhor, if we can speak of "Jesus as Pharisee," it will have to be understood as "Jesus' teaching having some of its roots in the Pharisaic movement." E. TENHOR, *That Rabbi from Nazareth: A Quest for Historical Jesus*, p. 63. If Jesus were a Pharisee, there seems to be a problem when "the Pharisees" are presented in an apparently negative light in the gospels, and in particular when Jesus' own words about them are read. The NT does not present a simple picture of the relationship between the Pharisees and Jesus. Pharisees warn Jesus of a plot against his life (Lk 13:31); in spite of their dietary scruples they invite him for meals (Luke 7:36-50; 14:1); some of them even believe in Jesus (Jn 3:1; 7:45-53; 9:13-38); later, Pharisees are instrumental in ensuring the survival of Jesus' followers (Ac 5:34; 23:6-9). Nevertheless, Pharisaic opposition to Jesus is a persistent theme in all four gospels. This opposition has been explained differently by those who hold differing views on the nature and influence of the Pharisees. Those who see the Pharisees as a class of political leaders posit that Jesus came to be understood as a political liability or threat. Those who understand the Pharisees as a society of legal and religious experts suggest that Jesus became viewed as a dangerous rival, a false teacher with antinomian tendencies. To the extent that there were Pharisaic leaders and scribes, both these factors probably played a part. Yet other scholars point out that according to the gospels the disputes between Jesus and the Pharisees centred primarily on the validity and application of purity, tithing, and Sabbath laws (e.g., Mt 12:2, 12-14;15:1-12; Mk 2:16; Lk 11:39-42). In the light of this evidence it would seem that at least part of the Pharisaic opposition to Jesus was occasioned by the obvious disparity between Jesus' claims about himself and his disregard for observances regarded by the Pharisees as necessary marks of piety. In the end, the Pharisees could not reconcile Jesus, his actions and his claims, with their own understanding of piety and godliness. Cf. J. BOWKER, *Jesus and the Pharisees*; E. RIVKIN, *"Defining the Pharisees;*

The Tannaitic Sources", *HUCA* 40-41:205-49, and *A Hidden Revolution*; L. FINKELSTEIN, *The Pharisees: The Sociological Background of Their Faith*, 2 vols.; R. T. HERFORD, *The Pharisees*; E. SCHURER, *The History of the Jewish People in the Age of Jesus Christ*; H. D. MANTEL, "*The Sadducees and the Pharisees*", in *The World History of the Jewish People*, VIII; M. AVI- YONAH and Z. BARAS, eds., *Society and Religion in the Second Temple Period*; J. NEUSNER, *From Politics to Piety: The Emergence of Pharisaic Judaism*. Also, Cf. J. D. KINGSBURY, *The Developing Conflict Between Jesus and the Jewish Leaders in Matthew's Gospel: A Literary-Critical Study*, CBQ 49 (1987) 57-73, suggests that evil is the root trait of all religious leaders in Matthew.

[63] Harvey FALK, *Jesus the Pharisee: A New Look at the Jewishness of Jesus*, NY/ Mahwah, NJ, 1985.

[64] J. P. MEIER, *Reflections on Jesus-of-History Research Today*, p. 96. One of the similarities noted between Jesus and the Pharisees is that both were religiously committed and both were disgusted with the corrupt rulers and high priests of Israel and sought personal and national reform through a fierce commitment to doing God's will in ordinary daily life. Yet, while Jesus and the Pharisees could agree on the basic goal of personal reform and national restoration along spiritual lines, they were diametrically opposed on the way to achieve such renewal. Hence, there is always a difference and distinction which sets Jesus aside to be a different Jew and a different teacher. Bruce D. CHILTON & Craig A. EVANS, eds., *Authenticating the Words of Jesus*, New Testament Tools & Studies Series, Vol. 28, Part 1, Leiden, Brill, 1998; Bruce D. CHILTON & Craig A. EVANS, eds., *Authenticating the Activities of Jesus*, New Testament Tools & Studies Series, Vol. 28, Part 2, Leiden, Brill, 1998.

[65] See, David SMITH, "Jesus and The Pharisees In Socio- Anthropological Perspective", *Trinity Journal* 6.2 (1985) 151-156. The Pharisees are portrayed in the Gospels as rejecting Jesus' person and ministry and appear as his main opponents. Cf. G. D. KILPATRICK, *The Origins of the Gospel According to St. Matthew*, Oxford, 1946, p. 121; R. HUMMEL, *Die Auseinandersetzung zwischen Kirche und Judentum im Matthäus-evangelium*, BevT 33, München 1966, pp. 12-14; S. LÉGASSE, *Scribes et disciples de Jésus*, RB 68 (1961) 321-345, 481-506; S. LÉGASSE, *L'antijudaïsme dans l'Evangile selon Matthieu*, in M. DIDIER (ed.), *L'Evangile selon Matthieu: Rédaction et théologie*, BETL 29, Gembloux, 1972, 417-428, p. 418. There is a considerable tension between this view, and the traditional view based on the many speeches of Jesus in the gospels, which criticise the Pharisees. The Pharisees had devised a system in which they had codified the Mosaic Law into some 365 prohibitions and 250 commandments. They required those who followed them to submit to their interpretations of this Law. Because the Pharisees considered themselves the official interpreters of the Law, they promoted themselves to a position of authority in Israel. In Mt 23:2, Jesus referred to the Scribes and the Pharisees as men who "sit in Moses' seat." Claiming the authority of Moses as interpreters and teachers of the Law, they demanded that all in Israel who submitted to Moses also submit themselves

to them. They demanded that men become disciples of the Pharisees, and that individuals in Israel recognize themselves not only as disciples of Moses but also as disciples of the Pharisees. This is seen in a passage such as Mk 2:18 where Jesus is asked the question, "The disciples of John and of the Pharisees used to fast: and they come and say unto him, why do the disciples of John and of the Pharisees fast, but your disciples fast not?" This shows us that those who submitted themselves to the Pharisees were disciples of the Pharisees. They became disciples by voluntarily submitting themselves to the rule of the Pharisees over them." J. Dwight PENTECOST, *Design for Discipleship*, Grand Rapids, Zondervan, 1971, p. 24. In addition, some modern scholarship after the school of Bultmann discounts the accuracy with which the sayings of Jesus are reported, and claims that what exists in the gospels is later construction written at a time after the destruction of the temple, and written against the emerging pharisaic leadership among the Jews. Firstly, the high view of Jesus that is held by all four evangelists makes it very unlikely that they would wish to distort what was known of the actual sayings of Jesus as they were handed down. Secondly, the events of the gospels all took place in a society that was for the most part non-literate, and there is modern anthropological evidence to the effect that transmission of information in such a culture has a very high degree of accuracy. From this, it may be concluded that the words that Jesus spoke to, and about, the Pharisees are very probably accurately reported. Bruce Chilton observes that "not all Pharisees were Jesus' enemies." B. CHILTON, *Rabbi Jesus*, p. 133. Chilton adds that many of the Pharisees had at least a modicum of respect for him and were curious about his teaching. By inviting Jesus into his home, the Pharisee (Lk7: 36-50) opened it to Jesus' disciples, followers, and others who came to listen to the rabbi and sit with him out of simple curiosity. Ed Tenhor in p.63 concludes that "the gospel writers, years later, remembering Jesus' angry words with the Pharisees, projected into their writing of the Gospels their own bias reflecting where they were in their late first century controversies between early Christian communities and members of the Pharisaic party." E. TENHOR, *That Rabbi from Nazareth: A Quest for Historical Jesus*, p. 63. On the question of whether or not the Gospel portrait of the Pharisees is accurate, see M. SILVA, *"Historical Reconstruction in New Testament Criticism"*, in *Hermeneutics, Authority, and Canon*, (ed.), D. A. CARSON and J. D. WOODBRIDGE, Grand Rapids, Zondervan, 1986, pp. 112–121. Cf. also J. NEUSNER, *Rabbinic Traditions about the Pharisees*, pp. 244–248; Stephen E. WITNER, "The Lost Message of the Lost Message of Jesus", *Themelios* 31.1 (October 2005) 60-74.

[66] William E. PHIPPS, *The Wisdom and Wit of Rabbi Jesus*, Louisville, Kentucky, Westminster John Knox Press, 1993, p.11.

[67] A number of scholars point to the difference in teaching between the different pharisaic schools, in particular between Bet Shammai and Bet Hillel. Some sayings of Jesus in the gospels are similar to sayings of Hillel and his followers,

while Shammai usually takes a harder line. If it is assumed from this that Jesus is of the school of Hillel, then there is an argument for saying that Jesus is always in confrontation with Shammaites, and simply engaging in the style of debate that the Mishnah presents to us. Varner speaks of the practice of public debate between pairs of Pharisees of differing views. Whilst this view may be part of the reason, we would expect at least one of the gospels to have made reference to these differing views among the Pharisees if it were the whole story. Since this does not occur, it may be concluded that when the gospels speak of "the Pharisees" they are not referring simply to Shammaite Pharisees. The earliest documents about "the Pharisees" of the time of Jesus are the gospels themselves, and some texts from Josephus. Rabbinic sources are not able to be dated with any certainty, but much of the content is probably of much later authorship than the gospels. Most of the information about the Pharisees at the time of Jesus thus comes from Christian biased sources, and there is no certainty that there are any early writings from the Pharisees themselves. It can be argued that the Rabbinical texts offer a good account of what the Pharisees were like, but helpful though they are, these texts carry little which tells of the way in which the Pharisees of his own time viewed Jesus, or what they said about him. Read, Stephen WESTERHOLM, *Jesus and Scribal Authority*, Lund, Gleerup, 1978. If the view is held that Jesus was trained as a Pharisee, and taught as a Pharisee, what was it that his fellow Pharisees were doing and saying to provoke the strong responses from Jesus that the gospels show? To get behind this situation, it is necessary to look at what the Pharisees were doing, and saying. The gospels say that they were trying "to test Jesus" or "to trap him." Why might they want to do this - especially to a fellow Pharisee? This would also serve to explain why there are times when the Pharisees are shown as being supportive of Jesus - again, no distinction is made between "the Pharisees" who offer help, and "the Pharisees" who seem to be in disagreement with him. See Lk 7:36 and 11:37 where Jesus is invited to dine with Pharisees, Lk 13:31-33 where the Pharisees warn Jesus that Herod is wanting to kill him, also Mk 14:1, 12:28-34 and Mt 23:1-2. Read, W. Harold MARE, "The Role of the Note-Taking Historian and his Emphasis on the Person and Work of Christ", *Journal of the Evangelical Theological Society* 15.2 (1972) 107-121; Scott SPENCER, *What Did Jesus Do*, Continuum International Publishing Group, Trinity Press International, 2003.

[68] Asher FINKEL, *The Pharisees and the Teacher of Nazareth, A Study of Their Background, Their Halachic and Midrashic Teachings, The Similarities and Differences*, Leiden, Köln, E. J. Brill, 1964, pp. 129-134. With Klausner, Finkel agrees that "Jesus of Nazareth was true to his Jewish heritage throughout the period of his ministry." See, *Ibid.*, p. 130. For Finkel, in the daily life of the Galileans, the prominent social and religious figures were the Essene teachers, the Pharisaic Shammaites (and their associates) and the Zealots. When Finkel basically identifies Jesus with various groups of Galilean origin, he uses, as evidence, many quotations from the Gospels. Consequently, one may conclude that Jesus did indeed act or preach like them or, at least, had the same ideology

of any one of those groups or, perhaps with all of them. Jesus had much in common with the Pharisees such as; belief in resurrection; summary of the Law which could be summarised under two headings; love of God, love of neighbour. The conflict is so intense in the NT not because Jesus and the Pharisees represented the most different extremes of Judaism, but because they were so similar, and were trying to occupy the same space and to win the hearts and minds of the Jewish people. Jesus condemned the Pharisees for hypocrisy. Yet a little over a century before, they had led the Jewish people in being willing to give their lives for the sake of obedience to God. Yet many of the features of Pharisaic emphasis forged in the crucible of persecution in the time of Antiochus Epiphanes actually led to an unbalanced understanding of Jewish identity later on. Read, Weston W. FIELDS, "Understanding the Difficult Words of Jesus", *Grace Theological Journal* 5.2 (1984) 271-288.

[69] Cf. Shmuel SAFARI, *"Master and Disciple"*, *Jerusalem Perspective* 3 (November-December 1990) 5-13; Jakob VAN BRUGGEN, *Christ on Earth: The Life of Jesus According to His Disciples & Contemporaries*, Grand Rapids, Baker Book House, 1998. Rabbis used similar methods of interpreting Scripture. For example the great teachers used a technique today called *remez* or hint, in which they used part of a Scripture passage in discussion assuming their audiences' knowledge of the Bible would allow them to deduce for themselves fuller meaning. Apparently Jesus used this method often. When the children sang Hosanna to him, the Sadducees demanded Jesus quiet them. He responded with a quotation, "From the lips of children and infants you have ordained praise." Their anger at Jesus is better understood on the next phrase in the Psalm. The reason why children and infants would praise, and the enemies of God would be silenced is explained. In other words the chief priests realized Jesus was implying they were God's enemies. Another example is Jesus' comments to Zacchaeus. The background to this statement is probably Ezekiel 34. God, angry with the leaders of Israel for scattering and harming his flock (the people of Israel) states that he himself will become the shepherd and will seek the lost ones and deliver them. Based on this the people of Jesus' day understood that the Messiah to come would seek and save the lost. By using this phrase, knowing the people knew the Scripture, Jesus said several things. To the people he said 'I am the Messiah and God no less.' To the leaders whose influence kept Zacchaeus out of the crowd, he said 'You have scattered and harmed God's flock.' To Zacchaeus he said 'You are one of God's lost sheep.' This technique indicated a brilliant understanding of Scripture and incredible teaching skills on Jesus part. It also demonstrates the background knowledge of Scripture the common people had. Rabbis used similar teaching techniques like the use of parables. Jesus also used similar themes (e.g., landowner, king, and farmer) as well. See, F. F. BRUCE, *Hard Sayings of Jesus*, Downers Grove, IL, Intervarsity Press, 1983; Bruce D. CHILTON & Craig A. EVANS, eds., Proclamation of Jesus, *Arbeiten Zur Geschichte Des Antiken Judentums & Des Urchristentums*, Leiden, Brill, 1997.

[70] A. FINKEL, *The Pharisees and the Teacher of Nazareth,* p. 132. Finkel tries to identify Jesus with the school of Hillel as opposed to the zealous pharisaic disciples of Shammai's academy. The qualities of "humbleness, restraint, clear argumentative reasoning and liberal stand - was close in spirit to that of the teacher of Nazareth." See, *Ibid.,* p. 134. However, in the present study of Jesus, one cannot conclude that he is someone like Hillel. There is another and contrasting element with regard to the usual places chosen for teaching. Finkel himself observes that Jesus taught not only in the synagogues, but also in the open air, by the Sea of Galilee and on the hills (Mk 4:1; 5:1). Jesus could be seen as a contemporary of Hillel and Shammai but he always produces a new thought, and new way of living. Academic research has not been successful in tracing how Jesus' influence eventually prompted the emergence of his movement as a religion distinct from Judaism. In his years of public ministry, however, Jesus was not setting out to subvert or discredit Judaism. It was his actions such as his authority at the Temple, an attempt to enact the prophecy of Zechariah that led to his death at the urging of the High Priest Caiaphas, whose successful manipulation of Pontius Pilate is described in detail on the basis of Jewish and Roman sources. Crucial within that unfolding of events was Jesus' declaration that the wine and bread served to his disciples during his last meals with them were his own sacrifice. In the Aramaic sense of his words, Jesus designated the wine he shared as the blood of sacrifice, and his bread the flesh which God preferred to what was offered in a corrupt Temple. The blasphemy he was accused of by many in Jerusalem, even some of his own followers, was a natural consequence of what he said.

[71] R. H. STEIN, *The Method and Message of Jesus' Teachings,* p. 1. To prove that Jesus functioned as a Jewish teacher, Stein quotes from Mt 4:23 which has the Markan parallel in Mk 1:39 which uses the word "preaching." Stein goes on to say that despite his lack of formal training (Mk 6:2-3; cf. Jn 7:15) he was correctly recognized as a "Rabbi" (Mk 12:14; cf. Jn 3:2). Although Jesus had not gone through the normal prescribed course of instruction, his wisdom and manner of teaching resembled that of the other Rabbis, so that it was not unnatural to ascribe the title "Rabbi" to him. Stein notes that like other Rabbis, Jesus proclaimed the divine law (Mk 12:28-34), taught in the synagogues (Mk 1:21-28. 39; 3:1-6; 6:1-6), gathered disciples (Mk 1:16-20; 3:13-19; cf. Jn 1:35-51; 1cor 15:5), debated with the scribes (Mk 7:5f; 11: 27-33; 12:13-17. 18-27), was asked to settle legal disputes (Mk 12:13-17; Lk 12:13-15; cf. the post canonical tradition found in Jn 7:53 to 8:11), sat as he taught (Mk 4:1; Mk 9:35; Lk 4:20; Mt 5:1; cf. also Lk 2:46), supported his teaching with Scripture (Mk 2:25-26; 4:12; 10:6-8. 19; 12:26. 29-31. 36; Mt 12:40; 18:16), used poetic-didactic techniques to help his disciples memorize, etc.

[72] *Ibid.,* p. 2. Stein notes that whereas the prophetic aspect of the teachings of Jesus usually receives its due recognition, there is a tendency to overlook and underestimate the role of Jesus as a sage. The evidence in the gospels that Jesus

taught as a wise man, according to Stein, is impressive. His abundant use of proverbs, parables, paradox, metaphor, etc., witnesses to a similarity between the form of his teachings and that of the wise men. Stein compares certain passages of the gospels with the sayings of the prophets and sages to prove that Jesus acted both as a sage and a prophet in that community. See, Mt 5:42 with Sir 4:4-6; Mt 24:28 with Job 39:30; Mk 4:25 with IV Ezra 7:25 (II Esdras); Mt 6:34 with b. Sanhedrin 100b.; Mt 7:1f with Pirke Aboth 1:6; 2:4; Lk 14: 7-11 with Prov 25: 6-7; Mt 11: 28-30 with Sirach 51:23f; 24:19f; Prov 1:20f; 8:1f. To see more comparisons in this regard, read, Rudolf BULTMANN, *The History of the Synoptic Tradition*, trans. By John MARSH, (rev. ed.), Harper & Row Publishers Inc., 1968, pp. 105-108; John L. MCKENZIE, *"Reflections on Wisdom"*, *JBL*, Vol. 86 (1967) p. 2. McKenzie states furthermore that "the debates between Jesus and the scribes and Pharisees are generally couched in wisdom style."

[73] E. TENHOR, *That Rabbi from Nazareth: A Quest for Historical Jesus*, p. xix. In p. 42, Ed Tenhor argues that Jesus was a teacher or rabbi. Though he is much more, he is still nevertheless a teacher. "Rabbi" is a title used by the Jews to address their teacher and a word used to honour their teachers when speaking about them. The Jesus in the Gospels has always been seen as a teacher. He is the master, the rabbi, and the teacher.

[74] Cf. E. TENHOR, *That Rabbi from Nazareth: A Quest for Historical Jesus*, p. 44. Ed Tenhor notes that in his teaching, Jesus used simile, metaphor, proverb, riddle, and paradox. Tenhor adds that there were other teaching techniques identified by scholars, which Jesus used as teacher and public speaker. He used a fortiori, irony, questions, parabolic actions, poetry, synonymous parallelism, synthetic parallelism, step or climatic parallelism, chiasmic parallelism, parables of various kinds, metaphor or figurative sayings, story parable, similitude, example parables, and allegory. Notice that Jesus seldom answered a question directly, but rather would answer with a question of His own. This was a very common way for a Rabbi to teach and often how they debated things. This is proof that he was a Jew and talked and debated like a Jew.

[75] Franz MUSSNER, *"Der Jude Jesus"*, *FrRu* 23 (1971) 3-7; *Idem, Traktat über die Juden*, Munich, 1979, p. 183 ; *Idem, Tractate on the Jews : The Significance of Judaism for Christian Faith*, Philadelphia, 1984, p. 113. T. W. Manson mentions that there are eighty-seven quotations of the Old Testament found on the lips of Jesus. He also affirms that Jesus had an intimate and detailed knowledge of the Hebrew Scriptures. See, T. W. Manson, The Teaching of Jesus, Cambridge, University Press, 1931, pp. 48, n. 1. 82-83.

[76] C. H. DODD, *The Founder of Christianity*, New York, Macmillan Company, 1970, p. 100. Though Dodd notes that Jesus was called a Rabbi, he also points out that, at the time of Jesus, the title 'Rabbi' had not yet become 'formalised' as it did by the end of the first century AD. So the title 'Rabbi' for Jesus is to be understood as something rather like a courtesy title given to a

teacher. It was as such that Jesus was at first regarded and it was as such that he attracted his disciples around him. In the same way when Dodd accepts that Jesus occupied a common ground with his Jewish contemporaries, he also asserts that the teaching of Jesus is oriented in a direction which "differentiates it from Rabbinic Judaism; the angle at which it touches life is different." Dodd speaks about the 'parables of Jesus' as the most characteristic part of the record of the teachings of Jesus. He asserts that Jesus was indeed a Rabbi although different from his contemporaries. For example, his whole *approach* to moral behaviour was different from that of his contemporary Jewish teachers. Jesus would often start from a position, which he largely shared with other Jewish teachers of his time, but in some respects he would go *beyond* their position.

[77] Geza VERMES, *Jesus the Jew, A historian's Reading of the Gospels*, London, Collins, 1973, p. 26.

[78] *Ibid.*, p. 27. To the writers of the New Testament, however, the most typical form of the teachings of Jesus was the parable: "He said nothing to them without a parable" (Mt. 13:34). But the Greek word παραβολή was taken from the Septuagint, the Jewish translation of their Bible into Greek. Thus here, too, the evangelists' accounts of Jesus as a 'teller of parables' make sense only in the context of his Jewish background. Interpreting his parables, on the basis of that context alters conventional explanations of his comparisons between the kingdom of God and incidents from human life. Once again, Vermes says that the teaching of Jesus was difficult to comprehend for non-Jews. This was because they were, by and large, unaccustomed to Palestinian teaching methods. It was the Gentiles and the non- disciples who needed every detail of a similitude to be spelled out and not Jesus' direct disciples, who as Jews themselves were already accustomed to his mode of preaching. Jesus was a very creative and engaging preacher. And contemporary scholars have tried to find analogies between his preaching and the images he uses, the parables he uses, the prophecies that are attributed to him between those materials and contemporary preachers of various sorts.

[79] *Ibid.* To substantiate his view, Vermes notes Jesus' presence in the Temple and his liturgical sermon in the synagogue of Nazareth. Thus, for Vermes, Jesus, as a teacher, has to be seen in his Jewish context. At the same time, Vermes also notes the differences that make Jesus distinct from his contemporaries.

[80] *Ibid.* When Bultmann says that Jesus actually lived as a Jewish Rabbi, he points to the way Jesus gathered disciples to himself, just like any other Jewish Rabbi of his time. Ed Tenhor also observes the same point while saying that many authors have seen Jesus as a great teacher, and some as wise sage, giving instructions to followers. "Jesus used the teaching tools of his day, such as parables and aphorisms, to teach a new style of subject matter, a kind of subversive, alternative wisdom." E. TENHOR, *That Rabbi from Nazareth: A Quest for Historical Jesus*, pp. 42-43.

[81] Interpreting the parables of Jesus on the basis of the settings alters conventional explanations of his comparisons between the kingdom of God and incidents from human life. The point of the parable of the prodigal son (Lk 15:11-32), better called the parable of the elder brother, is in the closing words of the father to the elder brother, who stands for the people of Israel: "Son, you are always with me, and all that is mine is yours. It was fitting to make merry and be glad, for this your brother was dead, and is alive; he was lost, and is found." The historic covenant between God and Israel was permanent, and it was into this covenant that other peoples, too, were now being introduced. The beginnings of this de-Judaization of Christianity are visible already within the New Testament. With Paul's decision to "turn to the Gentiles" (Ac 13:46) after having begun his preaching in the synagogues, and then with the destruction of the temple in A.D. 70, the Christian movement increasingly became Gentile rather than Jewish in its constituency and outlook. In that setting the Jewish elements of the life of Jesus had to be explained to Gentile readers (for example, Jn 2:6). Recently, scholars have not only put the picture of Jesus back into the setting of first century Judaism; they have also rediscovered the Jewishness of the New Testament, and particularly of Paul. His epistle to the Romans (ch. 9-11) is the description of his struggle over the relation between church and synagogue, concluding with the prediction and the promise: "And so all Israel will be saved" not, it should be noted, converted to Christianity, but saved, because, in Paul's words, "as regards election they are beloved for the sake of their forefathers. For the gifts and the call of God are irrevocable" (Rom. 11:26-29). This reading of the mind of Paul in Romans gives special significance to his many references to the name of Jesus Christ there: from "descended from David according to the flesh... Jesus Christ our Lord" in the first chapter, to "the preaching of Jesus Christ," which "is now disclosed and through the prophetic writings is made known to all nations" in the final sentence. Here Jesus Christ is, as Paul says of himself elsewhere, "of the people of Israel, a Hebrew born of Hebrews" (Phil. 3:5). The very issue of universality, supposedly the distinction between Paul and Judaism, was, for Paul, what made it necessary that Jesus be a Jew. For only through the Jewishness of Jesus could the covenant of God with Israel, the gracious gifts of God, and his irrevocable calling become available to all people in the whole world, also to the Gentiles, who "were grafted in their place to share the richness of the olive tree" namely, the people of Israel (Rom. 11:17).

[82] J. P. MEIER, *Reflections on Jesus-of-History Research Today*, p. 92.

[83] M. HENGEL, *Charismatic Leader and His Followers*, p. 46

[84] A. J. KÖSTENBERGER, *Studies on John and Gender*, p. 83. no. 60.

[85] See. Alan CULPEPPER, *The Johannine School*, SBLDS 26, 1975.

[86] J. BALDET, *Jesus the Rabbi Prophet*, p. 109.

[87] S. BYRSKOG, *Jesus the Only Teacher,* p. 221. Byrskog here brings out the difference between the terms disciple and pupil. Being a disciple according to Byrskog is not necessarily the same as being a pupil. A disciple may follow a person or a cause without receiving any particular information from a teaching master. Discipleship is not always a didactic category. In the case of Jesus' company of the disciples, the characterisation of the disciples as persons receiving and understanding Jesus' teaching corresponds directly to the depiction of Jesus as teacher. Cf. Bill HULL, *Jesus Christ Disciple Maker*, Old Tappan, NJ, Fleming H. Revell Company, 1990, Originally Published at Colorado Springs, CO, NavPress, 1984, pp. 9-12; C. Peter WAGNER, *"What is Making Disciples?"*, in *Evangelical Missions Quarterly* 9 (Fall 1973) 285: Donald A. MCGAVRAN, *Understanding Church Growth*, rev. ed., Grand Rapids, Eerdmans Publishing Co., 1980, p. 170; C. Peter WAGNER, *Church Growth and the whole Gospel: A Biblical Mandate*, San Francisco, Harper & Row Publishers, 1981, pp. 130-133; John F. MACARTHUR, Jr., *The Gospel According to Jesus*, Grand Rapids, Zondervan Publishing House, 1988, pp. 29-30. 196-98; James Montgomery BOICE, *Christ's Call to Discipleship*, Chicago, Moody Press, 1986, pp. 13-23.

[88] According to Lk 5:28, Levi, a tax collector is invited to follow Jesus. When Levi was challenged by Jesus to follow him, he immediately "left everything" to respond. Byrskog affirms that the general connection between Jesus as teacher and discipleship is implicit in such pericopes as Mt 8:18-22 and 19:16-22. In Mt 8:19; 19:16, someone approaches Jesus as teacher and Jesus responds by speaking about what it means to follow him (Mt 8:20; 19:21). Cf. S. BYRSKOG, *Jesus the Only Teacher,* p. 222. In Matthew 8:19 another man was warned by Jesus of the price he would have to pay after he perhaps too quickly and easily blurted out, "Teacher, I will follow you wherever you go!" Two would-be disciples were rebuked by Jesus when they asked his permission to tend to important family responsibilities before answering his call (Lk 9:59-62). Jesus also called a rich man, demanding that he gives up his wealth before becoming his disciple (Mk 10:21). The Gospels show that other men and women also listened to Jesus for periods of time. Mary was one such person. As Jesus taught in her home, Mary left her household duties in order to learn at his feet. She had chosen the "best portion," Jesus said, referring to her desire to listen to his teaching (Lk 10:42). Cf. Mark SHERIDAN, *"Disciples and Discipleship in Matthew and Luke"*, *Biblical Theology Bulletin* 3 (October 1973) 240-241.

[89] Being like the Rabbi is the major focus of the life of student or disciple. They listen and question, they respond when questioned, they follow without knowing where the Rabbi is taking them, knowing that the rabbi has good reason for bringing them to the right place for his teaching to make the most sense. This may explain Peter's walking on water. When Jesus (the Rabbi) walked on water, Peter (the disciple) wanted to be like him. Certainly Peter had not walked on water before nor could he have imagined being able to do it. However, because the teacher chose me because he believed I could be like him, I can do. And he

did! It was a miracle but he was just like the Rabbi! And then he doubted. Traditionally this is interpreted as Peter doubting Jesus' power. But Jesus was still standing on the water. It is more likely that Peter doubted himself, or his capacity to be empowered by Jesus. Why did you doubt? (14:31). That is a crucial message for the disciple. In another place, while Jesus walked to Caesarea Philippi, he talked to his disciples in order to teach them a lesson. When they had observed and learned for a time they were sent out to begin to practise being like the teacher. The amazement of the *talmidim* in discovering they could be like their teacher is great. It is most affirming when a student discovers that being like the teacher is possible. When the teacher believed that his *talmidim* were prepared to be like him he would commission them to become disciple-makers. This practice certainly lies behind Jesus great commission. The mission of the disciples was to seek others who would imitate them and therefore become like the master. It also helps to understand the teaching of Paul who sought to make disciples. He invited Herod Agrippa and the Roman governor to become like him. The writer to the Hebrews had the same mission. This is one of the most significant concepts of the New Testament. Jesus, the divine Messiah, chose the rabbi/ *talmid* system. He taught like a rabbi in real life situations, using the most brilliant methods ever devised. He interpreted God's word and completed it. He demonstrated obedience to it. He chose disciples whom he would empower to become like him and led them around until they began to imitate him. Cf. Michael J. WILKINS, *The Concept of Disciple in Matthew's Gospel*, Leiden, F. J. Brill, 1988, pp. 221-222; Wolfgang TRILLING, *Das Wahre Israel: Studien zur Theologie des Matthäus- Evangeliums*, 3d. aulfage, Münehen, Kösel-Verlag, 1964, pp. 21ff.

[90] Cf. R. T. FRANCE, *I Came to Set the Earth on Fire*, Downers Grove, Intervarsity Press, 1976, p. 50. The master's ultimate expectation was that each of his disciples would be proficient in his master's teaching. Cf. Charles C. BING, *"Coming to Terms with Discipleship"*, *Journal of the Grace Evangelical Society*, Spring 1992, Volume 5:1. The word disciple translates the Greek noun Μαθητής, which is found 264 times in the Gospels and Acts. It is not found in the Epistles. The noun has the basic meaning of a pupil, apprentice or adherent. The verb form μάθητεω occurs four times in the Gospels and once in Acts. It means to be or become a pupil or disciple. That the meaning of the word disciple is never explained in the NT indicates that the early readers understood it in relation to contemporary rabbinic or Greek practice. It was used of learners who associated themselves with a teacher, philosopher, or rabbi with the assumption that the pupil would become like his teacher (Mt 10:25; Lk 6:40). In the Gospel of Matthew, the word Μαθητής occurs approximately 73 times. Cf. Mt 8:21.23; 9:27.37; 10:42; 12:49; 13:10; 15:23; 16:5; 17:6.10; 18:1; 19:10; 21:20; 24:3; 26:8.40.45. However, it is not always evident that the disciples of Jesus are given the instructions in the strict sense of teacher/disciple method. The term Μαθητής, (disciple) which is found 46 times in Mark seems to be a deliberate

choice on the part of Jesus. "Disciple" in the contemporary Church is a word
that is applied to all baptized persons but that is not the original understanding
in the gospel accounts and was used rarely in the early Christian communities.
See J. P. MEIER, vol. 3, ch. 25, p. 41. When the word "disciple" is analysed it
is clear that it is a word peculiar to Jesus. No Jewish author uses the precise
word "disciple" and not even *Talmid*, the word for 'learner' in the Hebrew and
this does not appear in the Septuagint translation. A verb cognate of "$Μαθητής$" is
$μάθητεω$ (make a disciple) is used to refer to the making or training of disciples.
This term is used rarely in the New Testament but does appear in one of the
more well-known passages on the topic, Mt 28:18-20. The Greek New Testament
has two other terms that are used to describe the idea of "following after"
Jesus, these are $ἀκολούθεω$ (a verb meaning "come after, accompany, follow
as a disciple") and *opiso* (an adverb meaning "behind, after"). Sometimes only
$ἀκολούθεω$ is used, other times only *opiso* is used. Sometimes these are used
together. However in OT, we have the story of Elisha who is called a disciple
of Elijah. Yet there is not a mention of this word in the Qumran community. *A*
Greek-English Lexicon of the New Testament and other Early Christian Literature,
Compiled by Walter BAUER, (trans. and adapted), by William F. ARNDT and
F. Wilbur GINGRICH, 2nd ed., rev. and augmented by F. Wilbur GINGRICH and
Frederick W. DANKER, Chicago, University of Chicago Press, 1979, pp. 486-487.
$Μάθηταί$ (*Mathethai* as transliteration) the Greek word which denotes a disciple
in Greek is used in the rest of the NT after its use in the Gospels. Disciple is
rarely used by Paul or other writers of the New Testament except for Luke's
Acts which is the second part of Luke's Gospel, and it is not used by the early
Christians. See J. P. MEIER, *A Marginal Jew*, vol. 3, ch. 25, p. 42. Turning
to "the disciples" Meier notes the absence of the Greek term in the LXX and
outside the gospels and Acts in the New Testament and the almost complete
absence in biblical and other literature of the period (including Qumran) of its
Hebrew equivalent *talmid*, which is used from the second century CE onwards
to designate disciples of rabbis (p. 42). $Μάθηταί$ does occur (but only 14 times)
in Philo for people who are taught, including those taught by God, and in
Josephus (15 times), whose use includes it as a description of the relation of Elisha
to Elijah, and reflects the influence of Greco- Roman school traditions. Jesus'
use of the word "may reflect the Hellenistic milieu that had come to influence
Palestine from the days of Alexander the Great onwards. But for Jesus, a
more immediate influence and model would have been supplied by the Baptist
and his group of disciples, to which Jesus may have for a while belonged" (pp.
44-45). The recognition of Greco-Roman school influence prompts Meier to
observe: "As a religious figure within the Greco-Roman period, Jesus not
surprisingly bore some resemblances to other philosophical or religious teachers
of his time, notably in his desire to assemble followers or students around him.
Hence, while Jesus' resemblance to wandering Cynic philosophers has been
greatly overemphasized, one should not deny all similarities to philosophers
in the broad Cynic-Stoic stream, mixed as it sometimes was with Pythagorean

traits" (p. 47). Cf. Richard D. CALENBURG, *The New Testament Doctrine of Discipleship*, Th. D. Dissertation, Grace Theological Seminary, 1981, pp. 20-40.

[91] Cf. K. H. RENGSTORF, "Μάθηταί, in *TDNT* 4, pp. 415-441. Used 261 times in the NT, "disciple" usually refers to the immediate followers of Jesus, but there are also disciples of John the Baptist (Lk 11:1, Jn 1:35), of the Pharisees (Mk 2:18, Mt 22:16), of Moses (Jn 9:28), or of later Christians (Ac 6:1-7). In the New Testament, the picture of a disciple is not as clear or simplistic as one might wish, for the terms Μάθηταί (disciple, learner) and 'ακολούθεω (to follow) are used in a variety of ways. Not only did Jesus have his disciples, but also so did John the Baptist (Mt 9:14; 11:2; Jn 1:35. 37, etc.), the Pharisees (Mt 22:16; Mk 2:18; Lk 5:33), and even Moses (Jn 9:28). There is great diversity among those who are identified as the disciples of Jesus in the Scriptures. John (Jn 6:60.66) uses the term 'disciple' to refer to those who are uncommitted, unbelieving followers of Jesus, motivated mainly by curiosity or impure desires. The masses who have come to faith and trusted in Jesus as their Messiah were also called disciples (Jn 8:30. 31). Then, of course, the term was used particularly and most frequently of the twelve disciples (Mt 10:1, etc.) one of whom was his betrayer (Jn 6:70. 71). Within the circle of the twelve was an inner circle of three: Peter, James and John (Lk 9:28). In the book of Acts, the word 'disciple' seems to be used synonymously with the term 'believer' (cf. Ac 6:1. 2. 7). What is a disciple? Mark summarizes it best in his gospel: "And he went up to the mountain and summoned those whom he himself wanted, and they came to him. And he appointed the twelve, that they might be with him, and that he might send them out to preach, and to have authority to cast out demons" (Mk 3:13-15). It was a remarkable affirmation of the confidence the teacher had in the students.

[92] Cf. John P. MEIER, *"The Circle of the Twelve: Did It Exist during Jesus' Public Ministry?"*, in *Journal of Biblical Literature*, Vol. 116, No. 4 (Winter, 1997) 635-672. The word "disciples" is used 233 times in the Gospels for Jesus' followers, but one should not assume that it refers only to "the twelve" and the phrase "twelve disciples" occurs only three times (Mt 10:1; 11:1; 20:17), and "disciples" often refers to this core group of 12 disciples who are also mentioned as 12 apostles. Other people are also called "disciples" of Jesus (Mt 8:19-22; Lk 6:13, 17, 20; 19:37; Jn 4:1; 6:66; 8:31; 9:28; Ac 6:1-7; etc.). The "twelve" live in close community with Jesus. He chooses them and they remain with him. But there are also the 72 disciples who are sent out on mission. There are others who follow, yet perhaps come and go in relation to other obligations and some among his followers are women, although the term disciple *mathetes* is not used of them. Certainly Mary Magdalene is one of these and there are the friends who appear not to be *mathetes* but whom Jesus loves such as Mary, Martha and Lazarus. In a carefully nuanced discussion Meier takes us through the issues of women among the followers of Jesus. None is called a "disciple" - perhaps the male form *mathetes* included women. Meier concludes: "Did the historical Jesus have women disciples? The sight of a group of women apparently, at least

in some cases, without the benefit of husbands accompanying them travelling around the Galilean countryside with an unmarried male who exorcised, healed, and taught them as he taught male disciples could not help but raise pious eyebrows and provoke impious comments." Cf. J. P. MEIER, *Marginal Jew: Rethinking the historical Jesus; Companions and Competitors*, Vol. 3, p. 100.

[93] Vernon K. ROBBINS, *Jesus the Teacher: A Socio-Rhetorical Interpretation of Mark*, Philadelphia, Fortress Press, 1984, p. 101. Four settings in Mark, where Jesus sits as he teaches (Mk 4:1; 9:35;12:41; 13:3) are the typical characteristic of the rabbinic teacher. However, Robbins did not fail to notice that the teacher/ disciple relation in the case of Jesus and his disciples is a distinctive adaptation of aspects from both Jewish and Greco-Roman traditions. In rabbinic literature, except the case of Rabbi Akiba, Rabbis are not depicted travelling around as Jesus does to find people who will respond to his call to become his disciples. In the case of Rabbi/disciple relation, an individual asks for permission from a Rabbi to become his disciple. The young man is portrayed struggling to receive the acceptance from his master rather than the action and summons of a Rabbi to attain a response from a person whom he wants as a disciple-companion. Persistently in rabbinic tradition, students struggle to initiate and maintain a student-disciple relation with a Rabbi. In turn, Rabbis do not go out to seek and summon people to become disciple-companions to them.

[94] Father is used as a title of honour for a priest (Jud. 17:10; 18:19), and for a prophet (2 Kgs. 6:21; 13:14). In 2 Kgs 2:12, on the lips of the prophet's disciple, it also expresses spiritual relationship. In Rabbinical Judaism, where the title of father was frequently used of respected Scribes (SB I 918 f.), the metaphor of father and child is occasionally applied to the relationship between a teacher of the Torah and his pupil (SB III 340 f.)." See, O. HOFIUS, "*Father*," *New International Dictionary of New Testament Theology*, I, p. 617.

[95] Jesus describes his relationship to his disciples in exactly this way. There were a few exceptional rabbis who were famous for seeking out their own students. If a student wanted to study with a Rabbi he would ask if he might follow the Rabbi. The Rabbi would consider the students potential to become like him and whether he would make the commitment necessary. Choosing someone indicated that the rabbi believed the potential *talmid* had the ability and commitment to become like him.

[96] V. K. ROBBINS, *Jesus the Teacher: A Socio-Rhetorical Interpretation of Mark*, p. 101.

[97] M. J. WILKINS, *Concept of Discipleship*, p. 165, footnote 181. Wilkins claims that Μαθητής is the word in the gospels that denotes 'disciples' and this also refers to the instruction of Jesus to his followers.

[98] S. BYRSKOG, *Jesus the Only Teacher*, p. 222. In Mt 5:1, the narrator uses the word Μαθητής for the whole group of disciples and the activity of Jesus is explained with the word διδάσκειν. In Mt 10:24. 25; 23:8; 26:17f, Jesus uses

the term διδάσκαλος in reference to himself and he speaks to his disciples who are the Μαθητής. In Mt 9:10; 17:24, the outsiders identify Jesus as the teacher of the disciples. Byrskog asserts that Jesus never speaks of himself directly as teacher to anyone but only to his disciples. Jesus is thus constantly characterized as the teacher of his disciples. In the words of Byrskog, Jesus is first of all the teacher of his own group of followers.

[99] Gerhard KITTEL, διδάσκαλος in *TDNT* 2 (1964) 152-159, p. 153. The teacher of the law, or Rabbi, was a common sight during the time of Jesus, and he was generally followed at a respectful distance by his pupils. See, Elmar M. KREDEL, *Disciple*, in *Bauer Encyclopaedia of Biblical Theology* (1978) 209-213, p. 209. The ministry of Jesus throughout Palestine is described as essentially one of teaching, whether to the casual crowds or to his own disciples; whether in the synagogues, public places, or in the audience of the religious leaders (Lk 5:17). The effect upon his gatherings was impressive, and forced the conviction that he taught not as the scribes but as one who possessed authority (Mt 7:28 f.; 13:54; Mk 1:22; 6:5; cf. Lk 4:32). Jesus asserted that God had taught him the words that he spoke (Jn 8:28) and that his teaching was from the Father (Jo 7:16 f.). His teaching was characterized by the frequent use of parables (Mk 4:2). Nicodemus acknowledged Jesus to be a teacher come from God and attested by mighty works (Jo 3:2). The chief priests and scribes interrogated him as to the source of his teaching authority (Mat 21:23; cf. Jn 18:19). Even his opponents frankly admitted that the Lord taught the way of God impartially, regardless of the fear or the favour of man (Mk 12:14; Lk 20:21; Mt 22:16; cf. Jo 18:19). Indeed, all were astonished at his teaching (Mt 7:28; 13:54; 22:33; Mk 1:22; 11:18) and asked whether it was a new teaching (Mk 1:27). In his early circuit of Galilee Christ was glorified by all for his teaching (Lk 4:15). In the last days of His ministry he was daily in the temple teaching (Lk 19:47; 20:1; cf. Mk 14:49; Jo 18:20).

[100] *Ibid.*, pp. 153-154. In the mind of Kittel, it is clear from the Gospel accounts that the people listened to him with respect "nor is it only by the disciples that He is treated as such, for the crowds also honour Him in this way." See, *Ibid.*, p. 154. Wegenast opines that "the use of "Rabbi" as a form of address to Jesus may be historically authentic, for according to the tradition he had all the marks of the Rabbi." See, K. WEGENAST, διδάσκαλος, in *NIDNTT*, Vol. 3 (1975) 766-767, p. 766. Here, Wegenast agrees that the term ῥαββί largely co-incides with διδάσκαλος in the sense of the teacher of the law in Israel. At the same time, he also points out that in history, the semantic meaning (of these two terms) are different. When Wegenast says that Jesus had all the hallmarks of a ῥαββί he justifies his view by pointing to a number of biblical occurrences where the term applies. For example, in the Gospels, Jesus is asked to give rulings on disputed questions of the law (Lk 12: 13f.), and on doctrinal issues (Mk 12:18ff). He also had pupils, which indicates that, indeed, he was a Rabbi. Wegenast also notes that the later conditions for bearing the title Rabbi, namely study and ordination,

were not yet binding at the time of Jesus' public ministry. To summarise, first he agrees that the title ῥαββί is fittingly attributed to Jesus. Secondly, he adds a historical note, that the title ῥαββί had been in common usage at the time of Jesus. Hence for Wegenast, Jesus had all the hallmarks of a Rabbi.

[101] Cf., R. RENGSTORF, "μαθητης, κτλ., p. 454, n. 256.

[102] G. VERMES, *Jesus and the World of Judaism*, p. 30. Vermes goes back into history, where none of the predecessors of Jesus, great scholars like Hillel or Shammai, or the elder Gamaliel, are referred to as Rabbi in the Mishnah or the Talmud. According to Kittel, Jesus always differed in his views from the opinions of Hillel and Shammai. See, G. KITTEL, διδάσκαλος in *TDNT*, p. 155.

[103] G. VERMES, *Jesus and the World of Judaism*, p. 30. On this point of the academic formation of Jesus, Gerhard Kittel notes a number of differences which caused hostility between Rabbi Jesus and the other Scribes and Pharisees. As Kittel observes, if there was any objection to Jesus' activity as a teacher, it arose from the fact that he had not gone through the prescribed course of instruction or received authorisation from any teaching body (Jn 7:15).

[104] *Ibid.*, p. 31. Though Vermes objects to the view that Jesus was a Jewish Rabbi, he accepts that all three synoptic writers assert that, at the outset of the preaching career of Jesus, his style differed from that of the scribes. While the scribes' concern was to invest all religious doctrine with the sanction of tradition by means of exegetical ingenuity in scripture and especially in the Pentateuch, Jesus taught with authority without seeking a formal justification of his words.

[105] Martin HENGEL, *The Charismatic Teacher and His Followers*, Edinburgh, UK, T & T Clark, 1981, p. 42.

[106] *Ibid.*, p. 44.

[107] I. M. ZEITLIN, *Jesus and the Judaism of His Time*, p. 100.

[108] Ben WITHERINGTON III, *The Christology of Jesus*, Minneapolis, Fortress, 1990, p. 179. These forms of address for Jesus are found in various layers of tradition (cf. Mk 5: 35/ Lk 6:40/ Mt 10:24; Jn 20:16). Witherington also notes that with two exceptions (Mt 23:5-7, Jn 3:26) it is only to Jesus these terms Rabbi and Rabbuni are applied. Upon reaching the stage of calling Jesus a Rabbi, in the sense of a teacher, it should not be immediately expected for Jesus to come either in the line of sophisticated philosophers or simply to be like any other Jewish teacher of the Torah.

[109] *Ibid.*, p. 180.

[110] *Ibid.*, p. 181.

[111] R. H. STEIN, *The Method and Message of Jesus' Teachings*, p. 2. When Stein speaks about the differences between Jesus and the rabbis, he observes the following elements: Jesus was different from the rabbis in the way he taught, for Jesus often taught in the open fields and countryside as well as in the synagogues (Mk 4:1; 6:32-44; 8:1-9; Mk 2:13; Mt 5:1) and his association with women, tax

collectors, sinners, and children quite "unrabbinic." The relationship between Jesus and his disciples also differed from that between the rabbis and their disciples. Normally a pupil (*talmid*) was a disciple of the tradition of his teacher, but the disciples of Jesus were exactly that, disciples of Jesus. Their message was not just the words of Jesus, although they did receive them and "delivered" his words; their message consisted of both the message and the person of their teacher as well.

[112] S. BYRSKOG, *Jesus the Only Teacher,* p. 397.

[113] Craig R. KOESTER, *Symbolism in the Fourth Gospel: Meaning Mystery Community*, Minneapolis, Fortress, 1995, p. 246. From Jn 7:3 there is a very strong implication that there are disciples in Jerusalem apart from the disciples of Galilee.

[114] M. HENGEL, *The Charismatic Leader and His Followers*, p. 53.

[115] See, V. K. ROBBINS, *Jesus the Teacher: A Socio-Rhetorical Interpretation of Mark*, p. 103. Robbins observes that the focus of Mark on Jesus' summoning of disciple-companions rather than on people's requests to become disciples creates a different use of language in Mark than in the rabbinic tradition. For example, Jesus goes to Simon and Andrew and tells them he will make them fishers of men. In contrast, the Rabbis say, "You make yourself into another Rabbi and get a fellow disciple. Cf. *Abot* 1: 6. In *Abot* 1:16, "Make for yourself a rabbi" is attributed to Rabbi Gamaliel. In *Abot* 1:12, it is attributed to Hillel. In pp. 103-104 Robbins notes that the language about "being made into" is found in a collection of traditions about Shammai and Hillel in the Babylonian Talmud. Again, the Rabbis do not go to someone with a promise to make them into something different. Instead, different people are portrayed coming to them with a special request. Thus the characteristics of the rabbinic tradition are to place the initiative on the person himself to seek a rabbi and to attempt to become a student-disciple to him. However, there is a difference with regard to biblical concept of discipleship. With regard to the relationship between 'Rabbi' Jesus and his disciples, Jesus called them not for mere knowledge but for *discipleship*. The relationship between Jesus and his disciples was more personal than pedagogical. It is known for certain that in Judaism the relationship between a Rabbi and his disciple was largely a matter of learning the Torah and the Tradition. Though the disciple was expected to depend on his Rabbi, there was never the sense of intimacy. "The attitude of the talmid towards his teacher, the Rabbi, was expressed in the respectful distance at which he followed him." Cf. E. M. KREDEL, *Disciple*, pp. 209- 210. In contrast, the actual relationship between Jesus and his disciples was very different (cf. Jn 15:13-15).

[116] In Lk 6:40 Jesus affirms the traditional Rabbinic notion that "a pupil is not above his teacher, but everyone after he has been fully trained will be like his teacher." The expression 'not above', in view of the contrasting parallel in the second part of the verse, here suggests that the pupil normatively does not deviate from anything the teacher does. In the Gospel of John this pattern of rigidity, in replicating Jesus' life, is repeated in Jn 13:34; 17:18.23; and 20:21, using the

conceptual formula, "As I . . . so you." In Jn 13:15 Jesus states, "For I gave you an example that you also should do as I did." The continuation and replication of Jesus' mission in his disciples is explicit in Jn 20:21, "As the Father has sent me, I also send you." The significance of all this is that, in Palestinian Jewish tradition, at the time of Jesus as well as in the NT itself, no detail of a teacher's life is to be ignored. Although the concept of discipleship was common knowledge in the days of Jesus, his teaching on discipleship differed greatly from contemporary thought. Several of these distinctives will serve to illustrate what is meant here. The main distinctive features can be codified as follows. Jesus called his disciples. In Jesus' day, it was the followers who chose their master. But in Jesus' ministry, it was he who chose them (cf. Jn 15:16). Some of those who 'volunteered' their services were put off by the Master (cf. Lk 9:57.58.61.62). The relationship between Jesus and his followers was more personal than pedagogical. In Judaism, the relationship between a rabbi and his disciple was largely a matter of academics. It was the impartation of knowledge. Granted, on the part of the disciple, there was a very pronounced dependency upon the Rabbi, but there was never the sense of intimacy which existed between Jesus and his disciples (cf. Jn 15:15). Although Jesus taught his disciples, they perceived their commitment as a very personal one. It was only after his death and resurrection that his teaching was fully understood and valued. The path of a disciple of Jesus was far different that than of contemporary Judaism. One who chose to be a disciple of a great rabbi looked forward to the time when he, too, would be a great leader in Israel. The path which a disciple of Jesus chose to walk was the path of service and self-sacrifice. His disciples must take up their cross (Lk 9:23-24). They must suffer rejection and persecution (Jn 15:20.21). They, as their Master, must give up their lives in service (Mk 10:45). Jesus' discipleship was not a burden, but a blessing. It is obvious that the demands of our Lord's discipleship were great. But it is amazing that in the final analysis it is the disciple of the scribes and Pharisees who has the real burden: "And they tie up heavy loads, and lay them on men's shoulders; but they themselves are unwilling to move them with so much as a finger" (Mt 23:4). How different is this from that of Jesus: "Come to me, all who are weary and heavy-laden, and I will give you rest. Take my yoke upon you, and learn from me, for I am gentle and humble in heart; and you shall find rest for your souls. For My yoke is easy, and my load is light" (Mt 11:28-30). Read, Eugene E. LEMCIO & John COURT, eds., *The Past of Jesus in the Gospels*, Society for New Testament Studies Monograph Series, Cambridge, Cambridge University Press, 1991.

[117] R. BULTMANN, *Jesus and the Word*, p. 50.

[118] *Ibid.*

[119] *Ibid.*, p. 51.

[120] B. M. METZGER, *The New Testament: Its Background, Growth, and Content*, p. 51.

[121] *Ibid*. From the life of Jesus the following principles for effective discipleship have been identified. Although Jesus spent some time with the crowds, and at least on one occasion he sent out seventy disciples on a specific mission, he spent most of his ministry on this earth with the twelve disciples. And of those twelve, he concentrated especially on three, James, Peter and John. A number of principles for selecting disciples are seen in Lk 6:12,13: "One of those days Jesus went out to a mountainside to pray, and spent the night praying to God. When morning came, he called his disciples to him and chose twelve of them, whom he also designated apostles": Jesus spent an entire night in prayer before he chose his disciples. There were among the twelve: extroverts and introverts; conservatives and liberals; people who have much to say and those who never say a word. Leaders tend to choose people who are like them which leads to discrimination. Jesus chose people not on the basis of what they were, but on the basis of what they were to become. We also see a kind of close association between Jesus and his disciples. "Jesus went up on a mountainside and called to him those he wanted, and they came to him. He appointed twelve - designating them apostles - that they might be with him and that he might send them out to preach" (Mk 3:13;14). This passage emphasises association before involvement! "Make many disciples" is one of the three earliest sayings recorded in the *Mishnah* (*Avot* 1:1), and a rabbi often would select and train large numbers of disciples. The apostle Paul's teacher Gamaliel, for instance, had large number of disciples who studied with him (Cf. *Sotah* 49b). Jesus, too, had many permanent students, although there must have been others who learned from him for shorter periods of time. Lk 19:37 notes that near the end of Jesus' life, a "multitude" of his disciples accompanied him as he entered Jerusalem. One can gain an idea of the size of that "multitude" from the number of Galilean disciples. 120 persons remained in Jerusalem after Jesus' crucifixion (Ac 1:15). Jesus' twelve disciples were his inner-circle who spent years of intense study and practical training with their master. Later, they themselves were sent out to make disciples and pass on Jesus' teachings.

[122] I. M. ZEITLIN, *Jesus and the Judaism of His Time*, p. 100.

[123] One may at this point note that among the followers of Jesus were women (Lk 8: 2-3), who are elsewhere never included among the followers of a Rabbi. His conversation and company with sinners, prostitutes, and publicans, which is surely historical, is also alien to the practices of a Rabbi. If the tradition in this respect is reliable, it should also be considered that he showed special affection for children, a trait which does not correspond to the typical figure of a Rabbi. All this indicates that the full picture of a Jewish Rabbi's ministry is more complex. Today, due to the fragmentary nature of the sources, one cannot see the whole clearly. However there can be no doubt that the 'characteristics' of a Rabbi appeared plainly in Jesus' ministry and way of teaching. See, Ernst KÄSEMANN, "The Problem of the Historical Jesus", in *Essays on New Testament Themes*, Polebridge Press, Westar Institute, 1982.

[124] Among the differences in Jesus' discipleship, it is certain that disciples do not choose first to follow Jesus either, as do disciples of other rabbis. Jesus calls his disciples and they follow. The commitment is to him and it is not temporary. It is a commitment to take part in Jesus' mission of proclaiming God's coming kingdom. It demands that they leave everything behind, including family and careers.

[125] W. D. DAVIES, *The Setting of the Sermon on the Mount*, p. 133. For Davies, 'coming to Jesus' and 'going after Jesus' have a recognisable distinction. 'Going after Jesus' is to be seen as the equivalent of 'to follow Jesus.' From this, Davies concludes that 'coming to Jesus' and 'to go after' are probably to be understood as the equivalents of Rabbinic technical terms for going to a Rabbi for instruction and following him as Rabbi. In the same way when Jesus addresses the same formula 'come to me' and 'follow me', it is only the disciples who can be said to follow Jesus their master (Rabbi).

[126] *Ibid.* Jesus expected his disciples to learn from him. One of the most important characteristics in a disciple is *teachability,* as people only learn to the extent that they are open to learn. The task is not so much informational as transformational. This transformational aspect is what Jesus demanded of his disciples. He expected that his disciples were to follow him (Mk 2:13-17). A disciple is one who follows or imitates another. John and Jesus having disciples meant showing that disciples follow or imitate the life of the person they follow. Finally Jesus expected that when a disciple is fully trained, he will be like his teacher (Lk 6:40). A disciple has to reproduce the lifestyle of Jesus. Thus, the rabbinical marks of a disciple is also reflected in Jesus' discipleship. In summary, a disciple is a learner who develops through a learning process; a *follower* who provides a significant model for people to follow. In the ancient world, students/ disciples usually sought out a teacher (cf. Lk 9:57-62) whereas Jesus usually reverses the dynamic into another significant way of "calling" people to become his disciples (Cf. Mk 1:16-20; 2:14-17; 3:13; etc.). It is also evident that Jesus did not establish a "school" in a particular location, but was an itinerant or wandering preacher or teacher and his disciples literally had to follow him around (Cf. Mk 8:34; 10:21; Lk 9:57-62; Jn 1:43). The scriptures say that Jesus taught the disciples by speech (Mt 5:2), by example (Jn 13:15), by written word (Mt. 12:3), and by parable (Mt. 13:3). He taught them in the synagogues (Mt. 9:23), in the temple (Mt. 26:55), by the sea side (Mk 4:1), in the villages (Mk 6:6), on the mountain (Mt. 5:1), in the desert (Mt 14:15). Furthermore, "he taught them as one having authority, and not as the scribes" (Mt 7:29). Jesus' call to discipleship does not mean that a disciple is put in a learning relationship from which he can depart as a master (cf. Mt 23:8). Following Jesus as a disciple means the unconditional sacrifice of his whole life (Mt 10:37; Lk 14:26f.; cf. Mk 3:31-35; Lk 9:59-62) for the whole of his life (Mt 10:24f.; Jn. 11:16). To be a disciple of Jesus means to be bound to the master (Jesus) and to do God's will (Mt 12:46-50; cf. Mk 3:31-35). Cf. D. MÜLLER, p. 488.

[127] *Ibid.* In the discipleship of Jesus, the invitation formula "follow me" involved a commitment of a disciple (follower) to Jesus and to his service. This means the forsaking of home, wealth and possessions, comfort and security and to have a readiness to share in the way of Jesus himself.

[128] J. P. MEIER, *Reflections on Jesus-of-History Research Today*, p. 91. Jesus demands that those who follow him do so immediately and unconditionally. To follow Jesus is to accept his message of the Kingdom of God and to repent. As in most cultures, a son had a strong obligation to provide his deceased father with a proper burial (see, Tob 4:3; 6:15); the early rabbis even exempted a man from reciting the Shema, from the Tefillah (Eighteen Benedictions) and from Tefillin (wearing phylacteries) in order to fulfill his duty to bury his dead (m. Ber. 3.1). See M. HENGEL, *The Charismatic Leader and His Followers*, pp. 3-15. Of course, Jesus' directive for the literal dead to bury the literal dead is absurd, which has led many commentators to interpret the first reference to the dead metaphorically as the "spiritual" dead. cf. J. FITZMYER, *The Gospel According to Luke*, pp. 833-37; R. BULTMANN, *TDNT* 4, pp. 893; M. HENGEL, *The Charismatic Leader and His Followers*, p. 8. This is possible, but not as likely as interpreting Jesus as using extreme hyperbole, to the point of absurdity, to make the point that no obligation can take priority over following him and preaching the Kingdom of God. See, PERRIN, *Rediscovering the Teaching of Jesus*, p. 144; MANSON, *The Sayings of Jesus*, pp. 72-73.

[129] To understand the concept of 'disciple' in the NT, one must understand the following terminologies. The New International Dictionary of New Testament Theology discusses several Greek words under discipleship: (1) 'ακολουθέω (follow), which "denotes the action of a man answering the call of Jesus whose whole life is redirected in obedience"; (2) μαθητής (a disciple), "one who has heard the call of Jesus and joins him"; and (3) *mimeomai* (imitate), which "emphasizes the nature of a particular kind of behaviour, modelled on someone else." See also "to be a disciple; to make a disciple"; Mt 13:52, 27:57; 28:19; and Ac 14:21 "female disciple"; Ac 9:36 only. In the NT, a disciple is defined as a follower, from 'ακολουθέω "to follow"; 90 times). Sometimes this verb simply means physically following someone or something else (Mk 10:32; 11:9), but participial forms are also used for "those who follow" in the sense of discipleship (Mt 8:10; John 8:12). Apostle "someone sent out; a messenger, delegate, missionary"; 80 times, "to send out"; 132 times. In the NT this term sometimes refers to "the Twelve" (Mt 10:2; Mk 3:14; 6:30; 6 times in Lk, often in Acts. In Heb 3:1 Jesus himself is called an "apostle" sent by God. See also, "apostleship"; Ac 1:25; Rom 1:5; 1 Cor 9:2; Gal 2:8. The Twelve refers to a core group of Jesus' disciples. The term occurs

23 times in the Gospels, but otherwise only at Ac 6:2 and 1 Cor 15:5. Their names are listed in Mk 3:13-19, Mt 10:1-4, Lk 6:13-16, and Ac 1:13, but not in John. These "twelve" are not the only "disciples" or apostles" in the NT; the number is symbolically derived from the "Twelve Tribes of Israel" (Mt

19:28). The two primary terms relative to discipleship are the verb 'to follow,' and the noun, 'disciple.' For an excellent study of these terms, cf. Collin BROWN, General Editor, *The New International Dictionary of New Testament Theology*, Grand Rapids, Zondervan, 1975, Vol. 1, pp. 480-494. D. MÜLLER, "μαθητής", *The New International Dictionary of New Testament Theology*; K. H. RENGSTORF, "μαθητής", *Theological Dictionary of the New Testament*, Edited by Gerhard KITTEL and Gerhard FRIEDRICH, Grand Rapids, Eerdmans, 1967, Vol. IV, p. 416. See, *Aboth* 1:1,16, as quoted by K. H. RENGSTORF, *TDNT*, Vol. IV, p. 434.

[130] The Great Commission occurs in each of the gospels and in the Acts of the Apostles. These were the last words that Jesus spoke. It is helpful to focus on three details in Mt 28:18-20: Here we see a group of individuals who had, only a few days before, fled at the arrest of Jesus. He said to this group, "I am going to give you all authority and this is what I want you to do..." Jesus clearly used ordinary people to accomplish the mission.

[131] M. HENGEL, *The Charismatic Leader and His Followers*, pp. 50-51. Hengel also observes that the 'following after' has been recorded in Rabbinical sources. However, the act of 'following after' is to be understood in the sense of 'walking behind the teacher' on their journeys. The pupil is always in a subordinated position.

[132] I. M. ZEITLIN, *Jesus and the Judaism of His Time*, p. 101.

[133] V. K. ROBBINS, *Jesus the Teacher*, p. 101.

[134] *Ibid*. Robbins has also remarked on the exceptional case that is seen with regard to Rabbi Akiba's journeying from Babylon to Jerusalem to find a disciple like Hillel.

[135] R. RIESNER, *Jesus as Preacher and Teacher*, p. 197.

[136] V. K. ROBBINS, *Jesus the Teacher*, p. 101. According to tradition, the beginning of a master-disciple relationship is typically shown as a struggle of a young man to gain an acceptance by a Rabbi. It is never shown as an initiative coming from the master to the disciple, asking him to 'follow me'. This is something peculiar to the call stories in the Gospels.

[137] Raymond F. COLLINS, *These Things Have Been Written, Studies on the Fourth Gospel*, (LTPM, 2), Louvain & Grand Rapids, Peeters & Eerdmans, 1990, p.46.

[138] H. WEDER, *Disciple*, p. 207. The cost of discipleship of Jesus is very high: a willingness to "let go" of all worldly riches and total surrender to be a disciple of Jesus. The one who follows the commandments is detached from the riches of his world. For the rich man in the gospel, his earthly possessions were more important than his discipleship of Jesus. That is why it is said that he went away sad because he was a man of great wealth. Here Jesus does not condemn material riches, nor does he discourage us from possessing wealth for one's needs. It is not an attack on the riches of this world but definitely an attack on

one's undue attachment to the perishable things of this world that prevented the rich young man being a disciple of Jesus. Therefore, the real problem lies not in the riches of this world but in one's failure to possess a Christ-like attitude towards material possessions.

[139] *Ibid.*

[140] J. P. MEIER, *Reflections on Jesus-of-History Research Today*, p. 91.

[141] The master-disciple relationship was even more important in Jesus' times, when there were no books, and all wisdom was transmitted orally. Among artists and certain categories of professionals the name master, in whose school one has been trained, is one of the things of which one is most proud and it is put at the top of one's references. On one point, however, Jesus distanced himself from what was happening in his time between the master and the disciples. The latter paid for their studies, so to speak, by serving the master, doing small jobs for him and giving him the services that a disciple can do for his master, such as washing his feet. The opposite happens with Jesus and his disciples: It is he who serves the disciples and washes their feet. Jesus is not truly of the category of masters who "preach, but do not practise." He did not instruct his disciples to do anything that he would not have done himself. It is the opposite of the masters reproved in the passage of the Gospel who "bind heavy burdens, hard to bear, and lay them on men's shoulders; but they themselves will not move them with their finger."

[142] H. F. WEISS, διδάσκαλος and διδάσκω, p. 318.

[143] R. F. COLLINS, *John and His Witness*, p. 38. In the words of Collins, the 'follow me' formula is said to be an authoritative command. This is widely used in the synoptic Gospels. For example, it is extended to the man who wanted to bury his father (Mt 8:22; Lk 9:59), to the tax collector (Mt 9:9; Mk 2:14; Lk 5:27), and then to the rich young man (Mt 19:21; Mk 10:21; Lk 18:22).

[144] V. K. ROBBINS, *Jesus the Teacher*, p. 107. In Rabbinical literature, the 'master/disciple' relationship is the process where the potential disciple has to get the consent both from God and a Rabbi. Only then can he begin to sit at the feet of the Rabbi to learn. In Philostratus's *Appolonius*, the disciple has to consider the teacher as godlike and express his obeisance before him, whereas, in the Gospels, it is Jesus 'the Teacher and Master' who seeks, summons and commissions people to be his disciples.

[145] Bruce CHILTON, *A Galilean Rabbi And His Bible, Jesus' Own Interpretation of Isaiah*, London, SPCK, 1984.

[146] Following the customary Rabbinical pattern, he took up a scroll of the Hebrew Bible, read it, presumably provided an Aramaic translation- paraphrase of the text, and then commented on it. The words he read were from Isaiah 61:1-2: "The Spirit of the Lord is upon me, because he has anointed me to preach good news to the poor. He has sent me to proclaim release to the captives and recovering of sight to the blind, to set at liberty those who are oppressed, to

proclaim the acceptable year of the Lord." But instead of doing what a Rabbi would normally do, apply the text to the hearers by comparing and contrasting earlier interpretations, he declared: "Today this text is being fulfilled today, even as you listen." Although the initial reaction to this audacious declaration was said to be wonderment 'at the gracious words, which proceeded out of his mouth' (Lk 4:22) his further explanation produced the opposite reaction, and everyone was filled with anger. See, James D. G. DUNN, *A New Perspective on Jesus: What the Quest for the Historical Jesus Missed*, Acadia Studies in Bible and Theology, Grand Rapids, Baker, 2005; James D. G. DUNN & Scot MCKNIGHT, *The Historical Jesus in Recent Research*, Winona Lake, IN, Eisenbrauns, 2006.

[147] When Riesner calls the style of Jesus preaching 'memorizable', it is to be properly understood. Riesner is totally opposed to the view (taken by some scholars) of assuming that Jesus encouraged his disciples to learn, some of his carefully formulated teaching summaries. Riesner names such a hypothesis as improbable. Cf. RIESNER, *Jesus as Preacher and Teacher*, p. 203. Herald Riesenfeld agrees that Jesus, in his teachings, followed the rabbinical method of teaching and forming his disciples, but adds that 'what was essential to his message he taught his disciples, that is, he made them learn by heart." See, Harald RIESENFELD, *The Gospel Tradition and Its Beginnings* (2nd ed.), London, Mowbray, 1961, p. 24. Also cf. P. H. DAVIDS, "The Gospels and Jewish Tradition: Twenty Years After Gerhardsson", *Gospel Perspectives I*, 75–99. A. Schlatter says that "The means by which he facilitated their work consisted merely of the free and continual access he granted them. The accounts know nothing of a formal preparation for their work, any more than they imply that Jesus used some 'method' of conversion. Therefore we do not hear anything of lessons, of sentences he had them memorize, of religious activities he drilled them in, or any other methods." A. SCHLATTER, *The History of the Christ,* trans. A. J. Köstenberger, Grand Rapids, Baker, 1997.

[148] R. RIESNER, *Jesus as Preacher and Teacher*, p. 192. Ed Tenhor's opinions are in agreement with Riesner when he says that "Jesus preached plainly about the human condition. He used a lot of illustrations and comparisons. In his sermons, Jesus used everyday objects and items to enable people to understand serious truths. He used illustrations called parables to make things clear, and perhaps to confuse those who did not want to understand. There were many short stories, extended stories, metaphors, and comparisons- and, for the initiates, exciting explosive revelations that helped them understand their relationship to God and others. The parables were often used to assist in explaining what the "God movement," or the "reign of God" was all about." E. TENHOR, *That Rabbi from Nazareth: A Quest for Historical Jesus*, p. 66. Read also, Martin KÄHLER, *The So-Called Historical Jesus and the Historical, Biblical Christ,* Philadelphia, Fortress, 1964.

[149] R. RIESNER, *Jesus as Preacher and Teacher*, p. 201.

[150] *Ibid.*, p. 189. Riesner notes the following synoptic passages, where it is said that Jesus taught in the synagogues (Cf. Mk 1:21; Mk 6:2//Mt 13:54; Mt 4:23; 9:35; Lk 4:15. 31; 6:6; 13:10).

[151] *Ibid.*, p. 192.

[152] E. TENHOR, *That Rabbi from Nazareth: A Quest for Historical Jesus*, p. 41. Ed Tenhor notes, that from the very beginning of his ministry, Jesus often taught in synagogues, a traditional teaching location, but he also taught by the seaside and on the hillside, and even on one occasion (Mk 4:1) from a boat, in order to teach a large crowd on the shore. (cf. Ed Tenhor, p.42). Jesus also taught in towns (cf. Ed Tenhor, pp.44-45) but he considers that Jesus probably preferred open air meetings such as desert places, rural places, along the sea shore, on the roads, in villages, hillsides, fields, and out on the plains. In p.65, Ed Tenhor affirms that it is clear from the first three gospels that Jesus entered the synagogues and preached there, but he also preached the Sermon on the Mount, the Sermon on the Plain, the sermons on the seashore.

[153] R. H. STEIN, *The Method and Message of Jesus' Teachings*, p. 7. In p.8, Stein asserts that it was not only *what* he taught but also *who* he was that attracted people to hear him. Closely related to this was the authority with which Jesus taught (cf. Mk 1: 21-28).

[154] Cf. JOSEPHUS, *Jewish Antiquities*, 18:63.

[155] E. TENHOR, *That Rabbi from Nazareth: A Quest for Historical Jesus*, p. 39. Tenhor affirms that Jesus in his time was a great teacher for many people. He observes that one of the most frequent titles to describe Jesus in the Gospels is "Teacher", used some forty-five times. Jaroslav Pelikan in his *Jesus Through the Centuries* notes that "It was as a rabbi that Jesus was known and addressed by his immediate followers and others." Cf. Jaroslav PELIKAN, *"Jesus Through the Centuries"*, New Haven, CT, Yale University Press, 1985. The closest parallel to Jesus' role as teacher and master is found in the man identified in the Qumran sectarian writings only as "the Teacher of Righteousness." Like Jesus, he functioned as an authoritative teacher, and adherence to him as such was a criterion of final judgment. In the Damascus Document an account of the origins of the community is provided. The earliest history of the community is broken into two periods: before the arrival of the Teacher of Righteousness and after his arrival. Whereas "for twenty years they were like blind men groping for the way," with the arrival of the Teacher of Righteousness, the members of the Qumran community were now able to understand how to obey God: "And God observed their deeds, that they sought Him with a whole heart, and He raised for them a Teacher of Righteousness to guide them in the way of His heart" (CD 1.11). Likewise, 4Q171 (Psalms Pesher) 1.3.15-16, Ps 37:23-24 is said to be about "the Priest, the Teacher of Righteousness, whom God chose to stand before Himself, whom God established to build for Him a community." The Teacher of Righteousness claimed to have the proper of understanding of the Torah, being the one through whom God would reveal to the community "the

hidden things in which Israel had gone astray" (CD 3.12-15). He also claimed
to be an inspired interpreter of the prophets, as the one "to whom God made
known all the mysteries of the words of His servants the Prophets" (1QpHab
7.5). In other words, the Teacher claimed to find inspired new applications of
prophecy for the final generation before the *eschaton*. At the final judgment,
the apostates from the community, those who initially accepted the halakic
instruction of the Teacher of Righteousness, but later rejected it and, therefore,
disobeyed the Torah, will stand condemned before God. Conversely, those who
"listened to the voice of the Teacher," and adhered to his instruction will inherit
salvation (CD 20.27-32; see also 1QpHab 2.1-3). Similarly, in 1QH 4[12].18a,
the Teacher of Righteousness founder says about his opponents: "Because they
said of the vision of knowledge: 'It is not true'; and of the path of your heart: It
is not that." In other words, the teacher's opponents rejected his halakic views,
as revealed to him by God; because of this they have rejected the path of God's
heart or the true way of obedience, which the teacher has made known. In
contrast, those who walk on the path of God's heart will find life (4.21). Finally,
members of the community are instructed to wait for the end, and reassured that
"all the ages of God come according to their fixed rule, as He has decreed for
them in the mysteries of His discernment" (7.10-14). The community, in other
words, understands itself as alone obedient to God, waiting for the end, when
God would bring judgment and vindication. This is borne out by 1QpHab 8.1-
3, where it is said of the community, identified as "those who observe the law in
the house of Judah", that God will exempt its members from final judgment,
"because of their deeds and their loyalty to the teacher of righteousness" (8.1-3).
The two criteria that God will use at the final judgment will be works and one's
relationship to the Teacher of Righteousness.

[156] E. TENHOR, *That Rabbi from Nazareth: A Quest for Historical Jesus*, p. 43.

[157] A. FINKEL, *The Pharisees and the Teacher of Nazareth*, p. 134.

[158] S. BYRSKOG, *Jesus the Only Teacher, Didactic Authority and Transmission in Ancient Israel*, p. 207.

[159] R. H. STEIN, *The Method and Message of Jesus' Teachings*, p. 8. Cf. Mt
5:21-22. 27-28. 31-32. 33-35. 38-39. 43-45. While explaining the temple action
in Mk 11: 27-33, Stein in p. 113 observes that the question of the opponents
during the cleansing involved not only Jesus' claim of authority to cleanse the
Temple but his other actions as well. This authority differed from that of his
contemporaries not only in degree but in kind.

[160] See, B. CHILTON, *Rabbi Jesus, An Intimate Biography: The Jewish Life
and Teachings that Inspired Christianity*, p. 149. The New Testament depicts
Jesus preaching with a prophetic authority. "When Jesus had finished saying
these things, the crowds were amazed at his teaching, because he taught as one
who had authority, and not as their teachers of the law. When he came down from
the mountainside, large crowds followed him." Mt 7:28-29. The Old Testament
prophets frequently introduce their proclamation with 'Thus says the Lord.'
Although this formula is not found in the gospels, 'I say to you' is very common

on the lips of Jesus and has been seen by some writers as a parallel expression. However, it is now clear that at the time of Jesus 'I say to you' was used in a wide variety of contexts. Although Jesus certainly used the formula as an expression of his authority, it is not necessarily an indication of his prophetic consciousness. In some passages in the gospels 'I say to you' is preceded by the Hebrew and Aramaic word *amen*, which is usually translated as 'truly' in some of the translations. The word *Amen* is used as an introduction which is attested in Judaism; the 'Amen, I say to you' sayings of Jesus do not differ significantly from the more frequent sayings introduced by 'I say to you'. See, Graham N. STANTON, *The Gospels and Jesus*, The Oxford Bible Series, 1989, p. 181. Jesus uses the word "Verily" or "Truly" in his preaching. This is not a translation of a Greek word, but the transliteration of an Aramaic (or Hebrew) word, namely *Amen*. It is the participle of a verb meaning 'to confirm,' and it was used to give one's assent. For example, it was (and still is) the response of the congregation to a prayer uttered by him who leads their worship. In this way they make it their own (1 Cor. 14:16). Very occasionally it is the conclusion to one's own prayer (*e.g.* Tobit 8:7f.), when it has the nature of a wish. Characteristically it is one's assent to words uttered by another. In the Gospels it is used only by Jesus, and always as a prefix to significant statements. Presumably this is to mark them out as solemn and true and important. This use of Amen to introduce one's own words appears to be Jesus' own, no real Jewish parallel being adduced. Cf. Leon MORRIS, *The Gospel of John*, *NICNT*, Grand Rapids, MI, Eerdmans, 1971, p. 169. Some seventy-five times throughout the four Gospels, Amen introduces an authoritative pronouncement by Jesus. As the one who had the authority to make such pronouncements, Jesus was the Prophet. The word prophet here means chiefly not one who foretells, although the sayings of Jesus do contain many predictions, but one who is authorized to speak on behalf of another and to tell forth. Cf. Jaroslav Pelikan, *Jesus Through the Centuries*. "A prophet is a messenger of Yahweh sent to declare to king or people 'the word of Yahweh.' Not so Jesus. In the synoptics he does not represent himself as a messenger, he never claims to declare 'the word of Yahweh,' and he is distinguished from the Old Testament prophets by many other traits." See, Morton SMITH, *Jesus the Magician: Charlatan or Son of God?*, 1978, p. 49. Jesus as an inspired prophet reflects the tradition that he was raised in, that of Galilean holy men who served directly as intermediaries between men and God. Jesus and his predecessors thus obviated the need for a Temple and priesthood as was practised in Jerusalem. The prophets Elijah and Elisha "both bypassed those in need in Israel in favour of non-Jews. Here Luke anticipates one of the major theses of his two volumes: as a result of Israel's rejection of Jesus, God's word is taken to the Gentiles." Graham N. STANTON, *The Gospels and Jesus*, *The Oxford Bible Series*, 1989, p. 94. Morton Smith disagrees and argues that Jesus was more a magician than a traditional prophet. "Jesus' fundamental activities - exorcism and cures - are either unknown (exorcisms) or rare (cures) in the stories of the prophets. See, M. SMITH, *Jesus the Magician: Charlatan or Son of God?*, pp. 218-219.

[161] Joseph KLAUSNER, *Jesus of Nazareth*, New York, Beacon Press, 1925, p.414. Joseph Klausner, a Jewish scholar, adds that in the ethical code of Jesus, there is sublimity, a distinctiveness and originality in form unparalleled in any other Hebrew ethical code; neither is there any parallel to the remarkable art of his parables. While Klausner names this as a new ethics for Israel for all time, Albert Schweitzer calls that an "interim ethic" implying that Jesus' basic ethic is meant only for a short interval. See, Albert SCHWEITZER, *The Quest of the Historical Jesus*, NY, 1968, pp. 365-366; Scot MCKNIGHT, "Jesus of Nazareth", Scot MCKNIGHT & Grant R. OSBORNE, eds., *The Face of New Testament Students*, Grand Rapids, Baker Book House / Leicester, Apollos, 2004.

[162] G. THEISSEN & A. MERZ, *The Historical Jesus*, p. 358. Certainly, Jesus has something different and original, such as his choosing the disciples rather than the other way around, and even the choice itself, of working men rather than orthodox students. Unlike the other *Rabbis* of Israel, Jesus *chooses his disciples.* It is the exact opposite of what the *rabbis* were doing. They began speaking in the squares and those who were convinced followed him. Jesus does the opposite. Scholars speak of a "break" by the historical Jesus from the world/environment and the culture wherein he was a part. In his Last Supper speech, Jesus told the disciples: "You did not choose me, I chose you" (Jn 15:16). See, Alister E. MCGRATH, "In What Way Can Jesus be a Moral Example for Christians?", *Journal of the Evangelical Theological Society* 34.3 (1991) 289-298; Craig A. EVANS, "Jesus' Ethic of Humility", *Trinity Journal* 13.2 (1992) 127-138.

[163] E. TENHOR, *That Rabbi from Nazareth: A Quest for Historical Jesus*, p. 55. Giving direction to this new attitude of New Ethics of Jesus is the love commandment. The law of God is important, but fulfilled in actually loving one's neighbour and doing good to those who hate you.

[164] See, R. W. STEIN, *The Method and Message of Jesus' Teaching*, pp. 112-114.

[165] *Ibid.*, p. 114.

[166] J. P. MEIER, *Reflections on Jesus-of-History Research Today*, p. 93.

[167] C. H. DODD, *The Founder of Christianity*, New York, Macmillan Company, 1970, p. 100.

[168] J. BALDET, *Jesus the Rabbi Prophet, A New Light on the Gospel Message*, p. 77.

[169] *Ibid.*, p. 136.

[170] J. P. MEIER, *Reflections on Jesus-of-History Research Today*, p. 93. E. P. Sanders also holds the same view in saying that Jesus no doubt shocked the pious by offering salvation to these outcasts without demanding the usual Jewish mechanism of repentance. See, E. P. SANDERS, *Jesus and Judaism*, pp. 200-211.

[171] D. COHN- SHERBOK, *The Jewish Messiah*, pp. 72-73.

[172] *Ibid.*, p. 77.

[173] *Ibid.*, p. 78. According to Sherbok, there are ample occasions on which one can see that Jesus of Nazareth was like any other ordinary Jew. But when it comes to his public ministry, Jesus faces a great deal of confrontations with the authorities of both politics and religion. For example, when he was confronted with Jewish religious leaders Sherbok writes, "From the start of Jesus ministry, his presence created divisions within the Jewish populace." See, D. COHN-SHERBOK, *The Jewish Messiah*, p. 64. Thus Sherbok points out that Jesus' teaching and stand brought a division among the Jews. "Although Jesus is portrayed as spending short periods of time in remote areas teaching his disciples, the Gospels suggest that there was a particular moment when he decided the time had come to confront the leaders in Jerusalem." See, *Ibid.*, p. 65. This confrontation is well explained by both his teachings and his condemnations of the teachings and practices of those very same leaders. Thus, Sherbok concludes that for many first century Jews, "Jesus was regarded simply as one preacher among many and a false Messiah." See, *Ibid.*, p. 79; Read, Douglas S. HUFFMAN, "The Historical Jesus of Ancient Unbelief", *Journal of the Evangelical Theological Society* 40.4 (1997) 551-564; Luke Timothy JOHNSON, *The Real Jesus: The Misguided Quest for the Historical Jesus and Truth of the Traditional Gospels*, Harper San Francisco, 1997; Dennis INGOLFSLAND, "The Historical Jesus According to John Dominic Crossan's First Strata Sources: A Critical Comment", *Journal of the Evangelical Theological Society* 45.3 (September 2002) 405-414.

[174] J. P. MEIER, *Reflections on Jesus-of-History Research Today*, p. 95. Meier explains that it was the unheard-of claim to authority over the Mosaic Law and over people's lives, more than any title Jesus may or may not have used of himself, that disturbed pious Jews and the Jewish authorities.

[175] Cf. Carl ARMERDING, "Moses, the Man of God", *Bibliotheca Sacra* 116: 464 (1959) 350-356. Moses taught Israel the statutes, the commandments, and the ordinances (Dt 4:1,5,14; 5:31; 6:1; 11:19). Parents, in turn, were instructed to teach these to their children (Dt 4:10; 11:19). The Levitical Order was to teach Israel all the statutes, ordinances, and the Law of Yahweh (Lev 10:11; Dt 33:10). Mention is made of the ministry of a teaching priest (2Ch 15:3; cf. Mal 2:6-7). The song of Moses was to be taught to the people (Dt 31:19, 22). David taught the people of Judah the lament over Saul and Jonathan (2Sa 1:18, NASB; cf. Jer 9:20 and Ps. 60 title). The judges were to teach the instructions concerning decisions (Dt 17:11). In his valedictorian address before turning over the reins of governing the people to young King Saul, Samuel promised to continue to teach Israel in the good and right way (1Sa 12:23). Jehoshaphat commanded the Levites to teach the law in the cities of Judah (2Ch 17:7,9), while Ezra taught the people the statutes and ordinances of the Lord (Ezr 7:10). The Assyrian king requested of the Judean monarch that one of the Israelitic priests might teach the Assyrian immigrants in Samaria the law of the God of the land (2Kgs 17:27 f.). David invited his children to listen to him as he taught them the fear

of the Lord (Ps 34:11); later he vowed that if Yahweh would bestow upon him moral renewal, he would teach transgressors the ways of God (Ps 51:13). He also proposed to teach the penitent the way they should go (Ps 32:8). Cf. Simon J. DE VRIES, "Moses and David as Cult Founders in Chronicles", *Journal of Biblical Literature* 107 (1988) 119-139; C. BEGG, "Josephus' Portrayal of the Disappearance of Enoch, Elijah, and Moses: Some Observations", *Journal of Biblical Literature* 109 (1990) 691-693; U. CASSUTO, "The Suffering Servant and Moses", *Church Quarterly Review* 165 (1964) 152-163. In the Wisdom Literature the preacher taught the people knowledge, weighing and studying and arranging proverbs with great care (Ecc 12:9). Solomon disclosed that his father had taught him adherence to paternal instruction (Pro 4:4), while in another place the writer asserts that he has taught his son or disciple the way of wisdom (Pro 4:11). Job petitioned his friends to teach him his error (Job 6:24). Bildad commended to Job the experience of former ages as a source of authoritative teaching (Job 8:10). Job indicated that even the fauna and flora join to instruct man (Job 12:7-8), and proposed to teach his friends the hand of God (Job 27:11). Jeremiah prophesied that the knowledge of Yahweh would not be taught in the days of the new covenant because all would know him personally (Jer 31:34; cf. Heb 6:11 and Isa 54:13). Cf. T. F. GLASSON, "*Moses and the Fourth Gospel*", Studies in Biblical Theology 40, London, SCM Press, 1963; J. D. CROSSAN, "From Moses to Jesus: Parallel Themes", *Bible Review* II/2 (1986) 18-27; Dale C. ALLISON, Jr., "Jesus and Moses (Mt 5:1-2)", *Expository Times* 98 (1987) 203-205; D. M. HAY, "Moses Through New Testament Spectacles", *Interpretation* 44 (1990) 240- 252; R. T. O'TOOLE, "The Parallels Between Jesus and Moses", *Biblical Theological Bulletin* 20 (1990) 22-29.

[176] J. NEUSNER & W. S. GREEN (eds.), *Rabbi*, p. 517. When Judaism speaks of rabbis, it always holds that Moses is the first rabbi in history. By Hebrew tradition Moses was the first rabbi among the people of Israel. To this day he is known to most Jews as *Moshe Rabbeinu* which means Moses our Teacher. Moses is also considered the greatest prophet in Israelite history and in the Hebrew Bible. In the Book of Numbers, Moses passed his leadership on to Joshua as commanded by God. Also, in that context is *semicha* which denotes ordination by the laying on of hands. Again this is first mentioned in Torah in the book of Numbers 27:15-23 and in Deuteronomy 34:9. By Jewish tradition, the authority granted by semicha has been passed from rabbi to rabbi from Moses to the present day. The governments of the Kingdoms of Israel and Judah were based on a system of Jewish kings, prophets, the legal authority of the court of the Sanhedrin and the ritual authority of priesthood. Members of the Sanhedrin all had to have been awarded their *semicha* which is ordination derived in an uninterrupted line of transmission from Moses; yet they were more frequently referred to as judges (*dayanim*) akin to the *Shoftim* or Judges rather than rabbis. Cf. Carl ARMERDING, "The Last Words of Moses: Deuteronomy 33", *Bibliotheca Sacra* 114: 455 (1957) 225-234; S. A. NIGOSIAN, "Moses as They Saw Him", *Vetus Testamentum* 43 (1993) 339-350.

[177] This is illustrated by an important teaching of King David in *Ethics of the Father* which is called *Pirkei Avot* of the Mishnah. Cf. *Ethics of the Fathers* 6:3. "He who learns from his fellowman a single chapter, a single halakha, a single verse, a single Torah statement, or even a single letter, must treat him with honour. For so we find with David King of Israel, who learned nothing from Ahitophel except two things, yet called him his teacher, his rabbi, his guide, his intimate, as it is said: You are a man of my measure, my guide, my intimate" Cf. Ps.55:14. One can derive from this the following: If David King of Israel who learned nothing from Ahitophel except for two things, called him his teacher his rabbi, his guide, his intimate, one who learns from his fellowman a single chapter, a single halakha, a single verse, a single statement, or even a single letter, how much more must he treat him with honour. And honour is due only for Torah, as it is said: "The wise shall inherit honour (Prov3:35), "and the perfect shall inherit good" (Prov 28:10). And only Torah is truly good, as it is said: "I have given you a good teaching, do not forsake My Torah" (Ps 128:2)." Cf. Barnabas LINDARS, "The Image of Moses in the Synoptic Gospels", *Theology* 58 (1955) 78-83; P. SHULER, "Philo's Moses and Matthew's Jesus: A Comparative Study in Ancient Literature", *The Studia Philonica Annual* 2 (1990) 86-103; Dale C. ALLISON, *The New Moses, A Matthean Typology*, Edinburgh, T & T Clark, 1993; Wayne S. BAXTER, "Mosaic Imagery in the Gospel of Matthew", *Trinity Journal* 20:1 (Spring 1999) 69-83; Linda L. BELLEVILLE, Reflections of Glory: Paul's Use of the Moses-Doxa Tradition in 2 Corinthians 3:1-18, *Journal for the Study of the New Testament Supplementary Series* 52, Sheffield, JSOT, 1991.

[178] G. VERMES, *Jesus the Jew*, p. 26. Cf. W. A. MEEKS, *The Prophet- King: Moses Traditions and the Johannine Christology*, SNT 14, Leiden, E. J. Brill, 1967. M.-É. BOISMARD, *Moses or Jesus: An Essay in Johannine Christology*, B. T. VIVIANO, trans., Philadelphia, Fortress, 1993, pp. 1–68.

[179] S. BYRSKOG, *Jesus the Only Teacher*, p. 204.

[180] J. P. MEIER, *Reflections on Jesus-of-History Research Today*, p. 95.

[181] R. H. STEIN, *The Method and Message of Jesus' Teachings*, p. 116. In p. 117, Stein, speaking of the words of Jesus "I say to you", affirms that Jesus claimed therefore to speak with an even greater authority than Moses, who received the stone tablets from the hand of God, for Jesus believed himself to possess authority. The Rabbis of his day might seek to twist the Law to fit their own interpretative scheme, but Jesus saw no such necessity. He simply placed his personal authority above it. To read more on the authority of Jesus, see, Eduard SCHWEIZER, *Jesus*, trans., David E. GREEN, John Knox Press, 1972, p. 14; Fred L. FISHER, *Jesus and His Teaching*, The Broadman Press, 1972, p. 85; Archibald M. HUNTER, *The Work and Words of Jesus*, The Westminster Press, 1950, pp. 87-88.

[182] D. SENIOR, *Jesus*, p. 98. According to Senior, there are more than 50 occurrences of 'Teacher' in the Gospels of which 30 are applied directly to Jesus.

[183] *Ibid.*

[184] *Ibid.*

[185] *Ibid.*, p. 99.

[186] W. D. DAVIES, *The Setting of the Sermon on the Mount*, p. 134.

[187] *Ibid.*, p. 132. Davies observes that Jesus not only taught in synagogues, but also in the open air by the sea and on the hills. Those who listened to him consisted not only of his disciples but also the general public, including publicans, 'sinners' and even members of the Sanhedrin.

[188] *Ibid.*, p. 131. The word Ἀμήν was the formula of affirmation to end a prayer, as in the farewell charge of Moses to the people of Israel, where each verse concludes 'and all the people shall say: Amen' (Dt. 27:14-26). In the New Testament an extension of the meaning of Ἀμήν becomes evident in the Sermon on the Mount: ἀμὴν γὰρ λέγω ὑμῖν·, occurs some seventy-five times throughout the four Gospels. Here Ἀμήν introduces an authoritative pronouncement by Jesus. He speaks as the one who had the authority to make such a pronouncement. Read, James D. G. DUNN, "Prophetic 'I' Sayings and the Jesus Tradition: The Importance of Testing Prophetic Utterances Within Early Christianity," *New Testament Studies* 24 (1978) 175-198.

[189] *Ibid.*, p. 132.

[190] I. M. ZEITLIN, *Jesus and the Judaism of His Time*, p. 100.

[191] *Ibid.*, p. 101.

[192] R. RIESNER, *Jesus as Preacher and Teacher*, p. 208. H. F. Weiss says that the manner in which Jesus is portrayed in the Gospels is evidence enough for one to say that Jesus acted like a Jewish teacher or Scribe. At the same time, Weiss observes that "the Evangelists emphasize, however, each in his own way, the uniqueness of Jesus' teaching in contrast to that of the Jewish teachers." See, H. F. WEISS, διδάσκαλος and διδάσκω, in *EDNT* 1 (1990) 317-319, p. 318. The corresponding differentiation from the other Rabbis is noted here as indicative of the authority Jesus manifested in his preaching (cf. Mk 1:22).

[193] *Ibid.*, p. 208. Hans Schwarz agrees with other writers who note that Jesus made a big impression on his contemporaries in so far as he acted like a scribe. However, he feels there are significant differences which makes Jesus distinct from other Rabbis (or scribes) of his time. He notes that Jesus "accompanied his teachings with miracles (cf. Mk 2:9), something which Rabbis usually did not do." See, H. SCHWARZ, *Christology*, p. 99. Furthermore, people also remarked that "he taught them as one who had authority and not as the scribes" (Mk 1:22). Read, Robert H. STEIN, "Authentic or Authoritative? What is the Difference?", *Journal of the Evangelical Theological Society*, 24.2 (1981) 126-130.

[194] *Ibid.* Riesner quotes from Mk 1:22 and says that it may be a redactional statement but the evangelist summarises correctly that Jesus claimed an authority- at least a prophetical authority. Irving M. Zeitlin insists that the quotations from the

OT are evidences of his knowledge of the Hebrew Scriptures to be both extensive and profound. Though Jesus is presented teaching in their synagogues, Zeitlin states that Jesus' teaching differed from that of the Scribes. See, I. M. ZEITLIN, *Jesus and the Judaism of His Time*, p. 48. Köstenberger asserts that "Jesus adapted this model in a number of ways and even broke common convention in his actions as well as in his teaching." See, A. J. KÖSTENBERGER, *Studies on John and Gender*, p. 72. Köstenberger observes that Jesus interpreted the OT messianic interpretations with reference to himself, something no other Rabbi of his day would have dared to do. See, Stephen J. PATTERSON, *The God of Jesus: The Historical Jesus and the Search for Meaning*, Harrisburg, PA, Continuum International Publishing Group - Trinity, 1998.

[195] *Ibid.*, p. 209.

[196] M. HENGEL, *The Charismatic Leader and His Followers*, p. 46. For Hengel, there is no 'prophetic call' present in the gospel narratives with regard to the actions of Jesus. He also notes the event of the Baptism of Jesus, but other than that there are no clear pointers to visions, ecstatic experiences and the like. But how can he explain the end of the Temptation in the wilderness and how about the Transfiguration? How can Hengel interpret the event in the Garden of Gethsemane? Are they not examples of the visions and ecstatic experiences of Jesus?

[197] In the Sermon on the Mount, Jesus says: "Think not that I have come to abolish the law and the prophets; I have come not to abolish them but to fulfil them. For truly (amen), I say to you, till heaven and earth pass away, not an iota, not a dot, will pass from the law until all is accomplished." (Mt. 5:17-18) That affirmation of the permanent validity of the law of Moses is followed by a series of specific quotations from the law, each introduced with the formula "You have heard that it was said to the men of old." Each such quotation is then followed by a commentary opening with the magisterial formula "But I say to you" (Mt. 5:21-48). The commentary is an intensification of the commandment, to include not only its outward observance but the inward spirit and motivation of the heart. All these commentaries are an elaboration of the warning that the righteousness of the followers of Jesus must exceed that of those who followed other doctors of the law (Mt. 5:20).

[198] M. HENGEL, *The Charismatic Leader and His Followers*, p. 45.

[199] Rabbi and Prophet yielded to two other categories, each of them likewise expressed in an Aramaic word and then in its Greek translation: *Messias*, the Aramaic form of "Messiah," translated as "Christ," the Anointed One (Jn 1:41, 4:25); and *Marana*, "our Lord" in the liturgical formula *Maranatha*, "Our Lord, come!" translated into Greek as *Kyrios* (1 Cor 16:22). The future belonged to these titles and to the identification of him as the Son of God and second person of the Trinity. But in the process of establishing themselves, the terms Christ and Lord as well as Rabbi and Prophet, often lost much of their Semitic content. To the Christian disciples of the first century the conception of Jesus as Rabbi was

self-evident; to the Christian disciples of the second century it was embarrassing; to the Christian disciples of the third century and beyond it was obscure. See, William R. HERZOG II, *Prophet and Teacher, An Introduction to the Historical Jesus*, Westminster/John Knox Press, 2005.

[200] R. H. STEIN, *The Method and Message of Jesus' Teachings*, p. 3. Stein observes from the New Testament that the people attributed the role of prophet to Jesus for several reasons such as that he worked miracles and signs (Lk 7:16; cf. Jn 3:2), and that Jesus; as any other prophet, claimed the possession of the Spirit (Mt 12:18; Mk 3:28-30; Lk 4: 16-30; cf. Jn 14:17) by which he was aware that he possessed a divine calling and anointing (Lk 4:18f.; 10:21).

[201] In Dt 18:20-22 God gave strict rules to prophets who were only to speak God's word to the people and not to add or take away from the message. A false prophet and his prophecies were to be rejected: "But the prophet, which shall presume to speak a word in my name, which I have not commanded him to speak that prophet shall die." Jesus, of whom it was said, "A great Prophet is risen up among us" (Lk 7:16), spoke only the Father's words: "For I have not spoken of myself; but the Father who sent me, he gave me a commandment, what I should say, and what I should speak. And I know that his commandment is life everlasting: whatsoever I speak therefore, even as the Father said unto me, so I speak" (Jn 12:49-50; see also Jn 17:8). Read, Scot MCKNIGHT, "Jesus and Prophetic Actions", *Bulletin for Biblical Research* 10.2 (2000) 197-232.

[202] V. TAYLOR, *The Names of Jesus*, p. 15. From the Synoptic narratives, it is made clear that Jesus was either thought to be John the Baptist risen from the dead, or 'a prophet, as one of the prophets' (Mk 6:15; Lk 9:8/ Mk 8:28; Mt 16:14; Lk 9:19). Jesus himself implied that he was esteemed as a prophet (Mk 6: 4; Mt 13:57) when he declared that a prophet is without honour in his own country.

[203] *Ibid.*, p. 17.

[204] Rudolf Bultmann was convinced that many of the sayings of Jesus in the gospels are actually later prophetic writings. He wrote that "The Church drew no distinction between such utterances by Christian prophets ascribed to the ascended Christ and the sayings of Jesus in the tradition for the reason that even the dominical sayings in the tradition were not the pronouncement of past authority, but sayings of the risen Lord, who is always a contemporary for the Church." See, R. BULTMANN, *History of the Synoptic Tradition*, p. 127. When the roles of Jesus as Rabbi are described and attribute to him a new and unique authority, an understanding of the title προφήτης is necessary. The word προφήτης chiefly means not one who foretells, although the sayings of Jesus do contain many predictions, but one who is authorised to speak on behalf of another and to 'tell forth'. In the NT, Jesus is viewed, by some, as a prophet (Mt 21:11; Jn 4:19; 9:17; see Mk 8:28). It is seen that in a self-referential way, Jesus saw himself as a prophet (Mt 13:57).

[205] Rudolf BULTMANN, *Theology of the New Testament*, Vol. 1, New York, NY, Charles Scribner's Sons, 1951, p. 34.

[206] See, B. CHILTON, *Rabbi Jesus,* p. 149.

[207] G. KITTEL, διδάσκαλος, p. 156. The teachings of Jesus contain quotations from the prophets. He sometimes made statements about current situations in his society, and at the same time he preached about the kingdom of God. This was in complete accord with the expectations of the people of his time. His prediction of future events and his teaching on 'the Kingdom of God' has led many scholars to conclude that he is an eschatological prophet. A question that has been around from the very beginning of Christianity is about the offence that Jesus had committed. Just what was its nature? Scholars have spoken much about the claim of Jesus to be "the Messiah." In fact, the gospels do not hold evidence that Jesus made such a claim, or even that his disciples had made such a claim at the time that the Pharisees were in conversation with Jesus. Very little, if anything is known about Jesus before he begins his ministry, and the first event recorded on which all of the gospels have something to say is his meeting with John the Baptist. It is clear that something profound happened. The synoptics speak of the "voice from heaven", and show Jesus withdrawing for a time, no doubt to make some kind of sense of this experience. The experience itself - described as heaven being opened, and in Matthew as lightning coming down on Jesus has similarities to the call of Ezekiel, in which a cloud and lightning are described.

[208] As Riesner contends, the role of teacher and the working of miracles may complement each other rather than stand in conflict." Cf. R. RIESNER, *Jesus als Lehrer*, p. 252. Hengel likewise notes that "prophet" and "teacher" should in no way be regarded as opposites. Cf. HENGEL, *Charismatic Leader and His Followers*, p. 45.

[209] E. TENHOR, *That Rabbi from Nazareth: A Quest for Historical Jesus*, p. 13. Ed Tenhor notes that many texts in the gospels affirm that Jesus was thought of as a prophet by many people of his day. For Tenhor, many well-meaning people of other faiths say that Jesus was just a prophet and nothing more. However, in the idea of Ed Tenhor, it seems that Jesus was first, a prophet in the tradition of the Jewish prophets. Even if Jesus is more than a prophet, nonetheless he was still a prophet.

[210] *Ibid*, p. 14. In p. 15, according to Tenhor, Jesus was projected or expected to be a messianic prophet. There was emerging, as can be seen in some documents of the Dead Sea Scrolls and other places within Judaism, an idea of a "messianic prophet" (Ac 3:17-26; 7:37), a returned Elijah, or Elijah-like figure. In p.18, Tenhor states that "Besides quoting Isaiah and other prophets, Jesus did take on the role of a prophet. He did this when he criticised the elitist leaders both in the religious world and in the political and economic world. He was often in conflict with authorities, proclaiming an alternative social vision, a vision that was not apocalyptic or eschatological alone, but a vision of the reign of God already taking place among the people.

[211] Cf. Albert SCHWEITZER, *The Quest of the Historical Jesus*, London, England, A. C. Black Ltd., 1931.

[212] Willem S. VORSTER, *Speaking of Jesus, Essays on Biblical Language, Gospel Narrative and the Historical Jesus*, Leiden, Boston et al., Brill, 1999, p. 310. This book is not at all concerned with the question of whether Jesus ever considered himself to be the eschatological prophet who would come at the end of times (cf. Mt 21:11; Jn 6:14; 7:40; Ac 3:22-26). To read more on Jesus the eschatological prophet, read, Oscar CULLMANN, *The Christology of the New Testament*, trans., Shirley C. GUTHRIE and Charles A. M. HALL, The Westminster Press, 1959, pp. 13-50

[213] *Ibid.*, p. 301.

[214] *Ibid.*

[215] *Ibid.*, p. 304. Whoever would characterise Jesus on the basis of his eschatological message alone would call him "prophet," the title given to the Baptist (Mk 11:32; Mt 11: 9). Actually, Jesus himself is several times called prophet, even though his followers, who believed him to be the Messiah, considered that too limited a title for him. (Mk 8: 28; Mt. 21: 11, 46; Lk 7: 16, 39; 13: 33; 24: 19; Mt, 12: 39).

[216] *Ibid.*, p. 306.

[217] Apart from this portrayal of the eschatological Davidic king as endued with the spirit of Yahweh, thereby receiving wisdom, understanding and knowledge, there is no strong expectation that the eschatological Davidic king would be a religious teacher. It seems that second- Temple Jews could not conceive the coming Davidic king as engaged in religious teaching to any significant extent. Since Jews of the second-Temple period perceived the need for an eschatological figure who would teach the people the ways of God, there arose the expectation of an eschatological priest whose function would be that of a teacher. Because Aaron was anointed when he became high priest, the eschatological priest is referred to sometimes as another "Messiah" (anointed one) to appear along side of the Davidic Messiah. The Davidic Messiah, on the other hand, assumes the role of military leader and king. Contrary to popular expectation, Jesus assumes the title of Davidic Messiah and the role of religious teacher but not that of a military leader/ king. Cf. Steven M. BRYAN, "Jesus and Israel's traditions of judgment and restoration", *Tyndale Bulletin* 51.2 (2000) 309-312.

[218] M. HENGEL, *The Charismatic Leader and His Followers*, p. 49.

[219] *Ibid.*, p. 50.

[220] *Ibid.*, p. 42.

[221] *Ibid.*, p. 45.

[222] *Ibid.*, p. 47. For Hengel, even the immediacy of Jesus' vision of life that is expressed in his preaching distinguishes him from the Rabbinical wise men or sages. He considers, it is not possible to assign Jesus within the development of any contemporary Jewish traditions.

Part - III

Jesus as ʽΡαββί in John's Christology and Holistic Theology

T he previous chapters have helped set the stage for a proper understanding of the meaning of the term ῥαββί in John's Gospel. The previous chapters have attempted to make clear that the term ῥαββί in the time of Jesus did not necessarily refer to a specific office or occupation. John's Gospel contains eight instances where Jesus is addressed as ῥαββί. This constitutes over half of the references in the four Gospels combined. The address is attributed to Jesus' first followers (1:38), Nathanael (1:49), Nicodemus (3:2), his disciples (4:31; 9:2: 11:8), the multitudes (6:25), and Mary Magdalene (20:16) The references to Jesus as Rabbi in John's Gospel present a consistent picture of the perception of Jesus as a religious teacher. The Fourth Gospel seems to indicate that Jesus was customarily perceived by his contemporaries as a religious teacher, a ῥαββί. This perception is not only confined to the circle of Jesus' immediate followers, but also to the crowds (6:25; cf. 7:15, 35), other Jewish teachers such as Nicodemus (3:2), and those who were friends of Jesus (11:28: ὁ διδάσκαλος). When groups or individuals in the Fourth Gospel use the title ῥαββί in addressing Jesus, why do others either avoid or replace the title ῥαββί with another title? Is there any theological motivation for John's use of the title ῥαββί from some while avoiding the same title from other people or disciples? These are important questions addressed in the following two chapters. This is the focus of this part of this book and will also be the culmination of this study.

Recent studies have neglected one important aspect of John's presentation of Jesus, namely Jesus' role as Rabbi. This study will provide a basis for Jesus as a Jewish teacher through John's presentations. In this context, the question is whether there is any special significance in each of the instances where Jesus was addressed as ῥαββί. Chapter one begins by looking at the context in which the term ῥαββί is used in the Gospel of John as well as the contemporary use of the term ῥαββί in relation to John the Baptist's "Lamb of God." Then this study notes how the evangelist introduces a shift from the term "Lamb of God" to ῥαββί and explores its significance. In the Fourth Gospel it is not only in 1:38, presentations. In this context, the question is whether there is any special significance in each of the instances where Jesus was addressed as ῥαββί. Chapter one begins by looking at the context in which the term ῥαββί is used in the Gospel of John as well as the contemporary use of the term ῥαββί in relation to John the Baptist's "Lamb of God." Then this study notes how the evangelist introduces a shift from the term "Lamb of God" to ῥαββί and explores its significance. In the Fourth Gospel it is not only in 1:38, but on various other occasions, that Jesus is addressed with the title ῥαββί. It is noted that the translation of ῥαββί with διδάσκαλε both in the beginning of the gospel (1:38) and again at the end of the gospel (20:16) may denote a special intention to present the Johannine Jesus specifically as a teacher in that community.[1] The question is whether the first ῥαββί reference in the Fourth Gospel (1:38) has any relation to Mary Magdalene's addressing Jesus as ῥαββουνί. Can it be inferred that the author of the Fourth Gospel is trying to present a unified Jesus, both of history and the Exalted, by presenting him as διδάσκαλος both at the beginning and end of the Gospel? This will be the focus in chapter one. The results of this study may also contribute to a further rehabilitation of John's historical reliability.[2] Scholars such as Rudolf Bultmann and C. H. Dodd, who deal extensively with 'Historical Jesus'[3] in the area of Johannine scholarship, have emphasized that Jesus must most of all be understood in terms of his Jewish cultural context.[4] This is greatly stressed by recent discoveries that have revealed an affinity between the Fourth Gospel and the Qumran writings.[5] The present study is intended to contribute to the study of the historical Jesus and the notion that Jesus was perceived by his contemporaries primarily as a Jewish religious teacher. In Johannine studies, Jesus' role as a ῥαββί constitutes the historical starting point for the fourth evangelist's presentation of Jesus, a fact that has generally been overlooked owing to a focus on John's "high" Christology and on Johannine theology rather than the historical Jesus. The second chapter will explore how the term ῥαββί fits into the evangelist's Christology in the light of the Resurrection and the faith development of his disciples.

Endnotes

[1] Cf. W. D. DAVIES, "Reflections on Aspects of the Jewish Background of the Gospel of John", in *Exploring the Gospel of John. In Honor of D. Moody Smith,* (ed.) R. A. CULPEPPER and C. C. BLACK, Westminster/John Knox, 1996, pp. 43–64. Cf. also J. D. G. DUNN, "John and the Oral Gospel Tradition", in *Jesus and the Oral Gospel Tradition,* ed. H. WANSBROUGH, *JSNTSS* 64, Sheffield, JSOT, 1991, pp. 351–379.

[2] Read, Everett F. HARRISON, "Historical Problems in the Fourth Gospel", *Bibliotheca Sacra* 116: 463 (1959) 205-211; Read also, Angus J. B. HIGGINS, *The Historicity of the Fourth Gospel,* London, Lutterworth, 1960; R. E. BROWN, "The Problem of Historicity in John", in *New Testament Essays,* Garden City, NY, Doubleday, 1965, pp. 187–217; Franz MUSSNER, *The Historical Jesus in the Gospel of St. John,* New York, Herder & Herder / London, Burns & Oates, 1967; KARRER, Der lehrende Jesus, p. 19 n. 100. Cf. Stewart C. GOETZ & Craig L. BLOMBERG, "The Burden of Proof", *Journal for the Study of the New Testament* 11 (1981) 39-63; C. L. BLOMBERG, *The Historical Reliability of the Gospels,* Downers Grove, IVP, 1987, pp. 188–189.

[3] Cf. Angus J. B. HIGGINS, *The Historicity of the Fourth Gospel,* London, Lutterworth, 1960; Stephen S. SMALLEY, "New Light on the Fourth Gospel", *Tyndale Bulletin* 17 (1966) 35-62; Leo G. COX, "John's Witness To The Historical Jesus", *Bulletin of the Evangelical Theological Society,* 9.4 (1966) 173-178. Cf. D. A. CARSON, "Current Source Criticism of the Fourth Gospel: Some Methodological Questions", *Journal of Biblical Literature* 97 (1978) 411-429; See, Klaus SCHOLTISSEK, "Johannine Studies: A Survey of Recent Research with Special Regard to German Contributions", *Currents in Research: Biblical Studies* 6 (1998) 227-259; David WENHAM, "A Historical View of John's Gospel", *Themelios* 23.2 (1998) 5-21; Klaus SCHOLTISSEK, "Johannine Studies: A Survey of Recent Research with Special Regard to German Contributions II", *Currents in Research, Biblical Studies* 9 (2001) 277-305.

[4] Cf. Francis J. MOLONEY, "The Fourth Gospel and the Jesus of History", *New Testament Studies* 46.1 (2000) 42-58; Cf. B. Chilton, *Galilean Rabbi,* pp. 32–33. Chilton concurs, "The Judaism of the rabbis is comparable to a great deal in the New Testament, especially when we set Jesus' teaching and ministry alongside the views and actions attributed to first century rabbis." Chilton also points out that the rabbis did not invent Judaism *de novo*: "Methodologically, they were traditionalists who handed on the views of predecessors." The verdict of M. HENGEL, "The Old Testament in the Fourth Gospel", in *The Gospels and the Scriptures of Israel,* (ed.) C. A. EVANS and W. R. STEGNER, JSNTSS 104, Sheffield, Sheffield Academic Press, 1994, p. 395, echoes these sentiments: "One thing remains certain: . . . the Fourth Gospel is to be understood primarily from the Jewish sources of its period." See, G. D. KILPATRICK, "The Religious Background of the Fourth Gospel", F. L. CROSS, ed., *Studies in the Fourth*

Gospel, London, Mowbray, 1957, pp. 36-44; F. F. BRUCE, "An Expository Study of St. John's Gospel", *The Bible Student* 24 (1953); 25 (1954); 26 (1955); 27 (1956); 28 (1957); 29 (1958); 30 (1959); John A. T. ROBINSON, "The New Look at the Fourth Gospel", *Texte und Untersuchungen* 73 (1959) 338-350; Barnabas LINDARS, "Traditions Behind the Fourth Gospel", Marinus DE JONGE, ed., *L'Évangile de Jean: Sources, rédaction, théologie*, Leuven, Louvain University Press and Peeters, 1977, pp. 107-124.

⁵ L. T. WITKAMP, "The Use of the Traditions in John 5.1-18", *Journal for the Study of the New Testament* 25 (1985) 19-47; Margaret DAVIES, *Rhetoric and Reference in the Fourth Gospel*, Journal for the Study of the New Testament Supplement, Sheffield, Continuum International Publishing Group, Sheffield Academic Press, 1992; Peter W. ENSOR, *Jesus and His Works: The Johannine Sayings in Historical Perspective*, Wissunt Zum Neuen Testament 2/85, Tubingen, Mohr, 1996.

Chapter - 1

Jesus as ʽΡαββί in John: The Role of a Teacher

Introduction

The purpose of this chapter is to look at those passages in which Jesus receives the title "Rabbi" in order to establish the proposition that John portrays Jesus primarily as a religious teacher with the title ῥαββί. Thus, this chapter is an investigation of the instances where Jesus is addressed or referred to as ῥαββί or "teacher" in the Fourth Gospel (Cf. Jn1: 38. 49; 3:2; 4:31; 6:25; 9:2; 11:8; and 20:16 (ῥαββουνί). When John uses the term ῥαββί with reference to Jesus, what he means in any particular context will be more closely explored, in particular when he uses it on different occasions in the Gospel. It is interesting to note that in the first 12 chapters Jesus is called a ῥαββί but he never receives that title in the final nine chapters of the same Gospel except when he is called ῥαββουνί by Mary Magdalene in the resurrection appearance narratives. The correspondence between the first and the last reference to Jesus as teacher in the Fourth Gospel (1:38 and 20:16) provides evidence of the unified perspective with which the Fourth Gospel views both the earthly and the resurrected Jesus. This draws attention to the relationship between the title ῥαββί and the 'Public Jesus' of John's Gospel.[1] When the Johannine way of addressing Jesus as 'Rabbi' is looked at closely, it can be seen that each instance may have a special significance,[2] although the use of the term ῥαββί always implies that Jesus was fundamentally perceived as a teacher.

This chapter will briefly analyse whether the various ραββί occurrences in John have the same meaning in addressing Jesus as teacher. Hence the particular Johannine portrayal of Jesus as a Rabbi in the course of his public ministry is analysed using the different texts where the title ραββί occurs in that Gospel. Thus, the various times the term is used in the Fourth Gospel are noted as well as whether it is used predominantly to mean 'teacher' or has any other connotation. Other aspects of Jesus' public ministry in John will be evaluated, in particular the 'master/disciple' relationship that John portrays as existing between Jesus and disciples, and other followers.

1.   'Ραββί (ὃ λέγεται μεθερμηνευόμενον Διδάσκαλε), ποῦ μένεις;

The first instance of the title ραββί addressed to Jesus in the Gospel according to John is found in Jn 1:38 where the two disciples of John the Baptist address Jesus in this manner in their first encounter with him (Jn 1:38b). In Jn 1:35, John the Baptist draws the attention of his disciples by pointing out Jesus saying ῎Ιδε ὁ ἀμνὸς τοῦ θεοῦ "Behold the Lamb of God". John the Baptist has already mentioned the same term "Behold the Lamb of God" for Jesus in Jn 1: 29.[3] Shortly afterwards, Jesus walks by John and two of John's disciples. As Jesus walks away, John tells his two disciples that Jesus is the 'Lamb of God' (verse 35). In the following section, the attribution of the term 'Lamb of God' to Jesus and the significance of referring to Jesus "Lamb" will be discussed.

Jesus as "Lamb of God"

The two disciples leave John's side and set out after Jesus. As they begin to draw near to Jesus, he turns around, seeing that they are following him and asks "What do you seek?" John the Baptist points to Jesus and identifies Jesus using two titles - the *Lamb* of God, and the *Son* of God. John witnesses very clearly that Jesus is of God.[4] The term 'Lamb of God' is seen as a special term in reference to Jesus and exists only in Johannine literature. Addressing Jesus as the 'Lamb of God' is seen twice in the first chapter. Indeed the Johannine term "Lamb of God" which was attributed to Jesus is a subject which can be discussed in much more detail. We explore the depth of meaning in that expression. For instance, could the Lamb spoken of in Isaiah possibly be the Paschal Lamb? Could it be the innocent Lamb of Jeremiah, going to its slaughter, or be the Lamb of Exodus sacrificed for the welfare of the people, as with the sacrifice on the cross? Again, could it be the Lamb of Leviticus which dies for the remission of the offerer's sins just as Christ dies for our sins? Which of these are the key to unlock the meaning of Lamb of God? Every one of these provides a richness of meaning as that expressed on John the Baptist's, "There is God's Lamb." Finally, the Lamb of God does powerfully call to mind the Paschal Lamb, so that is the way the expression is interpreted in this book.

Jesus – The Passover Lamb

In the New Testament, only in the Gospel of John is Jesus referred to as the 'Lamb of God.'[5] But note that in the book of Revelation (cf. Rev. 5:6.9; 7:14) he is referred to as a ram. Ferdinand Hahn, in his discussion on the address ῥαββί as applied to Jesus in this particular context, raises a question, "In 1:38 it may be asked to what degree we have the echo of its use as a title of distinction, since in John 1:35ff the most varied predicates are deliberately ascribed to Jesus and "Rabbi" is included among them."[6] For Du Plessis, the title "Lamb of God" in the fourth gospel is "a Messianic one and *terminus gloriae*. Like the other titles it expresses, from a different angle, the Divine Sonship of Jesus."[7] Geza Vermes observes that "the introduction of the title 'Lamb of God' is a landmark in John's creative contribution to the portrayal of his Jesus."[8] Vermes further adds "according to the evangelist, a divinely intended task of the Baptist was publicly to proclaim Jesus to the Jews as 'the Lamb of God who takes away the sins of the world' (Jn 1:29)."[9] Vermes further states, "For the Palestinian Jew, all sacrificed lambs, and especially the Passover lamb and the Tamid offering, were a memorial of the Akedah with its effects of deliverance, the forgiveness of sin and messianic salvation."[10] The Tamid is the continual burnt offering of a male lamb morning and evening (See Ex 29:38-42). The lamb has rich symbolism in Jewish thought. In the levitical purity system, a lamb is sacrificed for the atonement of sin while the Passover lamb is seen as the symbol of deliverance from evil. Here the question is whether "atonement of sin" and "deliverance from evil" are being equated?

The concepts of the Suffering Servant and the Passover Lamb are conceivably equivalent. The Passover Lamb symbolism appears to be foremost, but there is no reason why John might not also wish to bring to mind the rich imagery of the Suffering Servant in Isaiah 53. The other important passage to consider is Gen 22:7-8.[11] In Jewish thought, this was held to be a supremely important sacrifice. The title Lamb of God as used by John the Baptist is open to a number of interpretations. Some think it may be a reference to the Passover Lamb, but this lamb was not a sacrifice for sin. It is possible that as more is learnt about the first century through the Dead Sea scrolls, other early Jewish literature and archaeology, a clearer understanding may emerge of what this term means. According to A. Jaubert, a Midrashic tradition known at the time of the NT also has the image of a liberating lamb.[12] According to C. K. Barrett, the image of the Lamb of God refers to the paschal lamb's blood, which protected the children of Israel.[13] In the book of Isaiah, the lamb is used as an image of the suffering servant (Is 53:7). In the opinion of Barrett, 'Lamb of God' is seen as the Passover Lamb. The Passover Lamb is a real lamb. In the Servant motif, the "lamb" idea is only an isolated, incidental element. (Cf. 1Cor 5:7), "Christ our Passover has been sacrificed." But Isaiah 53:7 places πρόβατον καὶ ἀμνὸς in parallel; And 1 Pet 1:18-19 speaks of the blood of an unblemished and spotless lamb, using the term ἀμνὸς.

Passover symbolism is present in the Fourth Gospel, especially in relation to the death of Jesus. Jesus is condemned at noon on the day before the Passover (Jn 19:14) at the very time the priests begin to slay the lambs in the Temple. Cf. Hyssop was used to hold a wine-soaked sponge, during the crucifixion (19:29) and Hyssop was also used to smear blood on the doorposts in the Passover ritual (cf. Ex 12:22.) Jn 19:36 sees a fulfilment of Scripture in that none of Jesus' bones were broken. (cf. Ex 12:46): "No bone of the Passover lamb was to be broken." The problem with this view is that the Passover Lamb was not a sacrifice per se. But probably by Jesus' time the sacrificial context began to merge with the symbol of deliverance, which was the Passover.[14] With this historical background, the Evangelist portrays Jesus as the 'Lamb of God,' the one who brings the eschatological judgement and deliverance by sacrificing himself (cf. Jn 19: 14) for the redemption of sin. According to C. H. Dodd, Jesus as the 'Lamb of God' refers to an Apocalyptic Lamb.[15] Also, in the Jewish Apocalyptic writings, 'Messiah' is depicted as a horned lamb and used as an image of judgement and salvation. The book of Henoch narrates a story of the Hebrew people using animals to designate the actors. In 1Henock 89 the image of the lamb is used for David who will crush the enemy.[16] According to P. J. Du Plessis, "it is apparent that the word *lamb* immediately and almost automatically conjures up the vision of an animal being slaughtered for the remission of sin."[17] So it is possible that John would have taken advantage of the Hebrew tradition and referred to it to designate the Messiah as the Lamb of God. Still, the emphasis lies more with redemption and salvation.

From "Lamb of God" to "Rabbi"- A Shift

It is interesting to note that John the Baptist does not use the title ῥαββί (Jn 1:35) when he points out Jesus to his two disciples, but rather 'Lamb of God.' Now the question is why John made a shift from "Lamb of God" to "Rabbi. In Jn 1: 35 the Baptist, pointing to Jesus, uses the same words he uttered previously (Jn 1: 29) "Behold the Lamb of God." Plummer notes the repetition of the same title Ἴδε ὁ ἀμνὸς τοῦ θεοῦ and opines that "These disciples were probably present the previous day"[18] and that's why the explanatory clause in Jn 1:29 is omitted here. Westcott's observation also holds the same idea. "The words are not at this time a new revelation and, therefore, the explanatory clause is omitted."[19] This implies that the two disciples could have been present when John gave his first testimony. According to C. K. Barrett, "The testimony of the Baptist is repeated in order to furnish a motive for the action of the two disciples."[20] Beasley-Murray observes that "The cry, 'Look, the Lamb of God,' is a directive to the two disciples of John to follow Jesus."[21] Can it be considered a direct invitation to the disciples to follow Jesus? Francis J. Moloney observes that "for the Fourth Evangelist, as the Prologue (1:1-18) has already instructed the reader, the determining principle is that Jesus is the 'Lamb of God' (vv. 29, 34) and the 'Son of God' (v. 34). Never do these first disciples approach such belief."[22] So, for Moloney, the first two disciples who came from the camp of the Baptist did not follow Jesus as the Lamb of God.

2. Addressing Jesus as 'Rabbi' in John: A Deliberate Plan?

It is useful to ascertain whether the author had a deliberate plan to present Jesus as a ῥαββί when he switched from the term "Lamb of God" to "Rabbi." Raymond Brown opines that "in John the frequency of the terms "rabbi" and "teacher" used by the disciples in addressing Jesus, seems to follow a deliberate plan."[23] Hence, in agreement with Brown, the following section will deal with that specific and deliberate Johannine plan. It is worthy of note that the former disciples of the Baptist did not use the term 'Lamb of God' in addressing Jesus but rather ῥαββί. Lenski ventures the opinion that, "The two disciples of the Baptist do not venture to use a title derived from their own master's designation of Jesus as "the Lamb of God" or "the Son of God," v.34. These designations certainly had their illuminating effect upon them and yet were not of a kind to lend themselves to personal address in conversation."[24] Barnabas Lindars, referring to the word ῥαββί when attributed to Jesus by the disciples in Jn1: 38, asks whether "they are not yet ready to commit themselves to the implications of the title used by the Baptist."[25] Alan Culpepper takes a slightly different position in asking his readers to note that the two disciples of the Baptist have not yet fully become the disciples of Jesus. "John has pointed out Jesus as the Lamb of God; the disciples want to know where they can find him."[26] And so they use the title ῥαββί to address Jesus and want to know whether they can stay with him and learn from him. This strongly suggests that the author of the Gospel does have a purpose in placing the title ῥαββί in the story of the first disciples of Jesus.

A Movement: *From the Baptist (Witness) to* Jesus (Master)

The first chapter of the Fourth Gospel seems to say that John the Baptist had his own school of disciples and that Jesus' first disciples came from that camp. The Fourth Gospel notes that the disciples of John the Baptist addressed the Baptist as ῥαββί (cf. Jn 3:26). The Gospel notes that the Baptist's two former disciples also used the same term ῥαββί in their first encounter with Jesus (Jn 1:38). Could it be that they used that term out of force or habit, or could they have actually perceived Jesus at that moment as a Rabbi? In this passage, while there is no indication as to the place where they stayed, the main point is that their *allegiance* to Jesus is given immediately. However, there is no explicit mention of them both becoming disciples of Jesus at that period. So Bultmann concludes that their instant discipleship "is made indirectly."[27] Köstenberger points out that only the evangelist John notes that, "some of Jesus' first followers had previously been followers of the Baptist and that the Baptist himself has pointed them to Jesus."[28] One thing is clear from the Fourth Gospel: the first disciples of Jesus were once numbered among the disciples of the Baptist (cf. Jn 1:35-37).

The first people Jesus meets (after John the Baptist) and summons are those who turn out to be numbered among his closest disciples, perhaps to be thought of as the Twelve. All of those named in John 1 (Simon, Philip, Andrew, and Nathanael) appear in later gospel passages, and the "sons of Zebedee" also mentioned later. In Jn 1:35-42, the first meeting of the two disciples with Jesus is generally understood as the call to discipleship. However, one should bear that in mind that except in the case of call to Philip, there is no direct calling of Jesus in the Fourth Gospel. There are frequent stories of "following Jesus." Note the theme of "following Jesus" in Jn 1:37 marks true discipleship. It is mentioned in 1:37, 38, 40, 43 and later in 8:12, 10:4, 27, 12:26, 13:36, 21:19, 22. Jn 1:37 suggests that the disciples of the Baptist are about to become his disciples. It is also clear that the Baptist, after his mission is complete, disappears from the scene and his followers become followers of Jesus. In his observation on the title Rabbi as attributed to Jesus in Jn 1:38b, Raymond F. Collins states that when "the pursuers call upon Jesus as "Rabbi", the evangelist seems to intimate that they have switched allegiance. They are no longer disciples of John; they have become disciples of Jesus."[29]

Moloney looks at this movement or change in another way. For Moloney it is definitely a movement from the witness to the master. But there are various kinds of movements (motion) in Jn 1:35-39. First it is the movement of Jesus as he walks by (Jn 1: 35-36). When the Baptist pointed his disciples towards Jesus, they also began to walk (move) or, in the words of the evangelist, they 'followed' Jesus. The following of Jesus by the disciples implies "movement *away* from the Baptist and *toward* Jesus."[30] Thus, the witness of the Baptist brings the disciples towards Jesus. The two disciples leave one and start to follow the other. Subsequently, those who come out of the camp of the Baptist give the title Rabbi to Jesus in their first encounter and conversation with him. J. P. Meier observes that "A number of John's disciples (at least Andrew and Philip; probably Peter and Nathaniel are to be considered his disciples as well) transfer their allegiance to Jesus."[31] Andreas J. Köstenberger makes the same point when he concludes that "the first followers transferred their allegiance from one religious teacher, the Baptist, to another, Jesus, who was more, but not less than a ῥαββί."[32] Thus, John the Baptist is presented as a ῥαββί and the first two disciples who followed Jesus (Jn 1:35-38) are portrayed as having changed their allegiance from one ῥαββί to another ῥαββί. When this book says that Jesus was perceived by the disciples as ῥαββί in the sense of a teacher or master, it does not conclude that this refers to the historical Jesus. What is intended simply is that John, the author of the Fourth Gospel, presents Jesus as a teacher. It is not certain whether John is presenting even the historical Jesus as a teacher. This question requires further research.

Alfred Plummer observes that "there was strong antecedent probability that the first followers of Christ would be disciples of the Baptist."[33] It is reasonable to agree with Plummer when he says that the first disciples of Jesus were previously the disciples of the Baptist. But it is not clear whether all John's disciples followed Jesus when he initially pointed out the 'Lamb of God'. There is no evidence of that in the Fourth Gospel. It is necessary to note that there is a textual reference that John had his own disciples up to the point of his death (Mt14:12) and it is 'Gospel proof' that not all of the Baptist's disciples followed Jesus. When the Baptist was in prison he had access to his disciples (Mt 11:2), and when he was murdered his disciples came and buried his body (Mk 6:29). Again in the ministry of Jesus, based on the report of the disciples, that there was a kind of rivalry between John's disciples and those of Jesus (cf. Jn 3:22-25; 4:1). There is also some evidence in the book of the *Acts of the Apostles* that the group of the Baptist was still in existence in the time of the early Church (cf. Ac: 18:24; 19:7). It can also be presumed that, even after the departure of a certain number of disciples from the group of John the Baptist, there remained a separate school with all its distinctive features.

Two Enthusiastic Pupils after a Teacher

John, the author of the Fourth Gospel, puts the term ραββί in the mouth of the first disciples who both follow and question Jesus (cf. Jn 1:38b). In Jn 1:38b, John does not translate ραββί as 'my master' (a term of honour), but as teacher (διδάσκαλος) which meant the disciples considered him a teacher who can expound scriptures and include them in his company of disciples. C. K. Barrett says that John has put this term in the mouth of "imperfect or mistaken disciples."[34] T. L. Brodie is in agreement with this idea and states that, "in this case, it indicates that even though the disciples are receptive, ready to be taught, their appreciation of Jesus is still quite limited."[35] The following will evaluate whether the address ραββί by the two disciples is a mistaken address. Was it really intended to express their respect for him as a teacher? Is the understanding of Jesus as ραββί by the two disciples imperfect?

As Moody Smith explains, for those first disciples, "Jesus was truly a rabbi or a teacher (1:38)."[36] Scott points out, it is not only the first disciples in Jn 1:38 but "on the other occasions he is called διδάσκαλος, a direct equivalent of ραββί (Jn1:38), by his disciples (Jn1:38; 3:2; 11:28; 20:16), an appellation with which Jesus agrees (Jn 13:13.14)."[37] Rudolf Bultmann opines that the mode of address in Jn 1:38, calling Jesus a ραββί "is in no way intended as disrespectful, and thus as betraying a still imperfect understanding."[38] R.Bultmann observes regarding the two disciples that the way they follow Jesus and question him about his abode is an indication that they are "two enthusiastic pupils after a teacher."[39] Here it is necessary to understand the dialogue between Jesus and the two disciples. Jesus does not ask them, *"Whom* do you seek?" but *"What* do you seek?" This is not an unfriendly question, intended to put them off. Rather the question seems designed to encourage them to verbalize what they want from him and to crystallize just what they are doing. These two men respond, "Rabbi, where are you staying?" They may be politely asking Jesus to be his disciples. "Come and see" (Jn 1:39) is the response. It is a very different answer from the one Jesus gives to another man: "As they were walking along the road, someone said to him, 'I will follow you wherever you go.' But Jesus said to him, 'Foxes have holes and birds of the air have nests, but the Son of Man has nowhere to lay his head'" (Lk 9:57-58). There is no contradiction between the text in John 1:39 and that found in Lk 9:57-58.

Early-on in his ministry Jesus did have a place to stay (see Jn 2:12), but as this ministry grew and he became more dispersed, he had no permanent place of residence. If being a disciple literally means following one's master, then one would stay with that master. Jesus telling this potential disciple that there was nowhere to stay may have been a polite way for Jesus to decline the offer to become his "Rabbi." When Jesus encourages John's two disciples to come and see where he is staying, he seems to be inviting them to follow him as disciples. Thus, these two men spend the night at his house. This also expresses the eagerness and longing of the two to share an abode with him. They wanted, it seems, to have a conversation with him, not just on the way to the abode, but to spend some quality time with him in the place where he was residing. This would reflect the normal rabbinical practice of preaching to the disciples, seated in a place with the disciples around him, unlike the practice of 'wandering' preachers.

"Rabbi": A Customary Address of a Disciple to His Master

Schnackenburg observes the use of the term ῥαββί in Jn 1:38b and says that this is "the usual way for a disciple to address his master."[40] So, in the words of Schnackenburg, calling Jesus a ῥαββί is in accordance with Jewish custom of that time. Hence it is right and fitting that the disciples address Jesus as their master with the title Rabbi. Leon Morris discusses the title ῥαββί attributed to Jesus in Jn 1:38b and says "they address Him as "Rabbi", the customary form of address for disciples speaking to their teacher."[41] When Barnabas Lindars discusses Jn 1:38, he opines that ῥαββί is the usual way of addressing a religious teacher after 70 A.D. Lindars goes further in maintaining that the use of the term Rabbi occurred "as early as the lifetimes of Jesus."[42] Francis J. Moloney basically agrees that "the ex-disciples of the Baptist address Jesus as a respected teacher."[43] Moloney also makes a critical comment when he says "the narrator makes clear to the implied reader that these disciples are approaching Jesus as teacher, and no more."[44] So, according to Moloney, the term ῥαββί when attributed to Jesus is just to portray him as a teacher and nothing more than that. However, Howard-Brook commenting on Jn 1:38 says that the address ῥαββί given to Jesus is "ambiguous and indirect."[45] He also adds that both disciples "are willing to see Jesus as a holy teacher but want to know to what or whom Jesus is bonded."[46] Thus Howard-Brook accepts that the disciples saw Jesus as a teacher, but he adds the adjective 'holy' to the word 'teacher'. D. Moody Smith seems to agree with Schnackenburg on the term ῥαββί attributed to Jesus in Jn 1:38b and also portrays him as a teacher. But Moody Smith has a little different explanation when he says that "The translation of "Rabbi" as teacher is functional rather than literal, and tells something about the regard for teachers in ancient Judaism."[47] Thus, the Johannine Jesus, in Jn 1:38, is portrayed as a ῥαββί in the sense of a teacher. Is it true that the disciples of the Baptist considered Jesus only as a teacher? With this in mind, this book will now look into the next occurrence of the term ῥαββί in the Fourth Gospel. The second instance is to be found in Jn 1: 49 and is spoken by Nathanael.

3. 'Ραββί, σὺ εἶ ὁ υἱὸς τοῦ θεοῦ

In the first chapter of John's Gospel, (1:38 and 49), it is Jesus' first followers who approach him by addressing him as ῥαββί. When Jesus reaches Galilee, he first encounters Philip and calls him to follow him.[48] In 1:43 Jesus calls Philip, saying 'Follow me,' the very same words found in the story of the call of the first disciples when they are out fishing (Mk 1:16-20; Mt 4:18-22). It was, of course, common for a Rabbi like Jesus to develop a following of disciples; however, according to the Talmud (Mishnah 'Abot 1.6, 16) it was expected that disciples would seek out their own teachers. Thus Jesus' call 'Follow me' reverses the usual order; as is also seen elsewhere (Mk 2:14; Matthew 9:9, Lk 5:10, 27), Jesus summons others directly to be his disciples.

"Follow Me": Johannine Call to Testimony

The closing verses of chapter 1 in the Fourth Gospel contain the only description of how Jesus obtained any of his disciples. From chapter 2 on, we read of "Jesus and his disciples" (2:2),[49] or just "his disciples." The disciples play a very significant role in the New Testament Gospels. Each of the three Synoptic Gospels has two "callings." (Cf. Mt 4:18-21; Mk 1:16-20; Lk 5:1-10; Mt 10:1-4; Mk 3:13-19; Lk 6:12-16). The first "calling" is preliminary, comes very early in Jesus' ministry and does not seem to be permanent. The "call" is only for two sets of brothers: James and John, the sons of Zebedee, and Simon and Andrew. In Matthew and Mark, the calling of the four fishermen is briefly described. A more expanded account of the first calling is found in Luke Chapter 5, which goes a long way in explaining the terse accounts of Matthew and Mark. Immediately following their calling, Jesus challenges these men to follow him, because from now on they "will be catching people" (Lk 5:10). Luke then relates that they left their boats and everything to follow Jesus. John does not even mention this first "calling." We know that it was not until the second "calling" that Jesus appointed the twelve to be his disciples. This later calling is recorded in the Synoptic Gospels but is not found in the Gospel of John. When the 'call' stories are read in the presentation of the synoptic authors and John, the first difference noted is that in the synoptic Gospels Jesus is coming to Galilee after his baptism by John the Baptist and then meets and calls his first four disciples. In the Markan narrative, this call of the four in Galilee takes place once Jesus comes out of the desert where he has fasted and prayed for forty days. So the call narrative in Mark takes place at the start of Jesus' public ministry (Mk 1:16-20) and after the arrest of the Baptist (Mk 1:14), to which there is no reference in the Fourth Gospel.

The "Call Stories" in the Fourth Gospel, which takes place before the imprisonment of John the Baptist plays an important witnessing role. In John, it is the disciples of the Baptist (Jn 1:35-51) who have the initial encounter with Jesus and later become his disciples. In the Synoptic Gospels there is no similar account of the Baptist's disciples becoming the disciples of Jesus.[50] If the Fourth Gospel can be called the Gospel of testimonies,[51] the story of testimony begins with the role of the Baptist. The role of witnessing is being fulfilled here in all these events, and the testimony of the Baptist draws others towards Jesus to whom he was sent to testify. The same is especially true of his two disciples who, on hearing the testimony, start following Jesus (Jn 1:35-36). In fact, there is no "calling" of disciples in John except for the "calling" of Philip. In John, it is to Philip alone that Jesus speaks the words, "Follow Me" (John 1:43). The others are certainly encouraged to follow Jesus, but they are not "called" in the strict sense. There is not even a listing of the names of the twelve disciples in John's Gospel. There are only four references to "the twelve," three found in the same chapter (Jn 6:67, 70, 71), and the final one found in chapter 20, verse 24. In John, the most extensive listing of our Lord's disciples is found in the final chapter: "After this Jesus revealed himself again to the disciples by the Sea of Tiberius. Now this is how he revealed himself. Simon Peter, Thomas (called Didymus), Nathanael (who was from Cana in Galilee), the sons of Zebedee, and two other disciples of his were together" (Jn 21:1-2). Here, three disciples are named: Simon Peter, Thomas, and Nathanael. James and John are referred to indirectly as the "sons of Zebedee," and two other disciples are mentioned as present but not identified. There is no mention of James by name in John's Gospel, no mention of the inner three (Peter, James, and John). In the Synoptic Gospels, there are other callings to discipleship, as has been discussed.

From Doubt to Belief: Nathanael as a Representative Figure

"Now Philip was from Bethsaida, the city of Andrew and Peter. Philip found Nathanael[52] and said to him, "We have found the one Moses wrote about in the law, and the prophets also wrote about—Jesus of Nazareth, the son of Joseph (Jn 1:44-45)." In Jn 1:49, we see Nathanael approaching Jesus, calling him Rabbi (ἀπεκρίθη αὐτῷ Ναθαναήλ·ῥαββί…). Besides the term ῥαββί, John also puts some other titles in the mouth of Nathanael such as "Son of God" and "King of Israel."[53] Craig Koester sees Nathanael as a representative figure - the first of others within Judaism who will come to Jesus, hesitantly at first, but who will then see in Jesus a new revelation of God.[54] When Nathanael heard Philip's claims about Jesus he was dubious but went to see for himself. Jesus greeted him as "a true Israelite," a descendant of Jacob whose willingness to come despite his initial reservations showed that he had "no guile" (1:47). As Nathanael approaches, Jesus speaks of him to others, so that Nathanael overhears these words: "Look, a true Israelite in whom there is no deceit!" He has not yet met Jesus, nor even talked with him, and yet Jesus describes his heart and his character accurately. Nathanael accepts Jesus' words as the truth, and so he responds, "How do you know me?" In other words, "How do you know that I am an Israelite without deceit?" Nathanael soon recognises that Jesus was the royal Son of God and King of Israel foretold in the Scriptures. Jesus accepts his confession, then shifts to the plural to promise Nathanael that "you will see heaven opened and the angels of God ascending and descending upon the Son of Man (v. 51),"[55] In the dialogue with Nathanael, Jesus makes a major promise to these first disciples and hints at his true identity. Thus, Nathanael has an important representative role in the Gospel of John. The next chapter will deal with the aspect of "Rabbi" in Johannine Christology.

4.   A Meeting: 'Teacher of Israel' and 'Teacher from God'

John records the well-known dialogue between Jesus and Nicodemus in chapter 3. Nicodemus[56] in Jn 3:2 is a Pharisee and teacher, and it is remarkable that he addresses Jesus by the title ῥαββί. He is a member of the religious party, opposed to the teaching of Jesus. Nicodemus, described as "Teacher of Israel" Σὺ εἶ ὁ διδάσκαλος τοῦ Ἰσραὴλ 3:10), addresses Jesus as Rabbi "ῥαββί, we know that you are a teacher."(διδάσκαλος) come from God; no one can do the signs you are doing unless God is with him." Though a Pharisee steeped in Judaism, Nicodemus was perceptive enough to acknowledge "God's work through Jesus (Jn. 3:1-2)."[57] In the words of Köstenberger, "Apparently, this represents an effort by Nicodemus, the Pharisee and member of the Sanhedrin, to award Jesus similar status as a religious teacher...This must surely have been considered a gesture of goodwill and benevolence on the part of Nicodemus, since it was commonly recognized that Jesus lacked rabbinic credentials (cf. 7:15: μὴ μεμαθηκώς). Being addressed as ῥαββί also confirms that Jesus' assumption of the identity of a Jewish religious teacher provided him with common ground on which to interact with other Jewish rabbis such as Nicodemus."[58] Jn 3:2 introduces the question of knowledge at the outset of this narrative. This is pointed out by Neyrey, who draws attention to the fact that Nicodemus' statement (we know...) in v. 2 is challenged by Jesus' response in v. 3 (unless...). "Nicodemus' claim to know is replaced by his questions to Jesus."[59] His description of Jesus as a "teacher" is simply a repetition in Greek of the Aramaic ῥαββί" The construction of the Greek text suggests that emphasis be placed on the words, "from God." Thus Nicodemus understood Jesus to be more than a typical or ordinary teacher. Clearly Nicodemus considered Jesus to be a great teacher.

H. F. Weiss' research shows that the title ῥαββί attributed to Jesus has been translated as διδάσκαλος to present Jesus as a teacher. He further observes that in Jn 3: 2, the title "ῥαββί and διδάσκαλος are attributed to Jesus interchangeably."[60] Nicodemus politely addresses Jesus as a rabbi in God's service (3:2). In this instance Nicodemus says ῥαββί, οἴδαμεν ὅτι ἀπὸ θεοῦ ἐλήλυθας διδάσκαλος which translates in English as "Rabbi, we know that you are a teacher." Nicodemus begins by addressing Jesus as ῥαββί the Hebrew name used by the Jews as a term of respect for their teachers. Note that Nicodemus says, "We know." The use of the first person plural means that Nicodemus is including the members of the Sanhedrin in the praise of Jesus which he is about to give. Nicodemus functions here both as an individual and as a representative. In fact, in chapter 12, the summary statement says that it was Nicodemus' own group, the Pharisees, which prejudiced the authorities against acknowledging Jesus. Jesus was not an official rabbi among the Jews, but his prominence as a religious teacher gained him a certain respect even among his enemies, and they therefore gave him that title.

4.1 Use of Irony, Metaphor and Imagery: Traits of a Teacher

Even when Nicodemus acknowledges Jesus to be a teacher and someone who is from God, Jesus does not respond to what Nicodemus says. Instead he chooses to engage him in a seemingly unrelated topic of conversation.[61] The dialogue between Jesus and Nicodemus continues the contrast between Jesus and Judaism which was begun in chapter two. There is irony in Jesus' question here: "You are the teacher of Israel (a spiritual leader) and don't know these things?"[62] This carries the implication (at least) that Nicodemus had enough information at his disposal from the Old Testament Scriptures to have understood Jesus' statements about the necessity of being born from above by the regenerating work of the Spirit. To the question of what passages Nicodemus might have known which would have given him insight into Jesus' words, the answer could be Isa 44:3-5 and Ezek 37:9-10. But a more surprising answer is the passage proposed by Z. C. Hodges as the "seed-bed" for the ideas in Jesus' dialogue with Nicodemus: Prov 30:4-5. The discussion of the new birth prov es incomprehensible to a leading Jewish teacher, and Jesus' explanation of the kingdom of God breaks with the Jewish expectation of the kingdom. Here we see a discussion of the term "born again." John uses the word five times, in 3:3, 7; 3:31; 19:11 and 23. In the latter three cases the context makes clear that it means "from above". The word has a double meaning, as pointed out by Z. C. Hodges.[63] For Nicodemus, the term must surely have brought to mind the messianic kingdom, which the Messiah was supposed to inaugurate. The concepts of water and wind are linked to ἄνωθεν (v.3), because water and wind come from above.[64] Isa 44:3-5 and Ezek 37:9-10 are pertinent examples of water and wind as life-giving symbols of the Spirit of God[65] in his work among men. Both occur in contexts that deal with the future restoration of Israel as a nation prior to the establishment of the messianic Kingdom. It is therefore particularly appropriate that Jesus should introduce them in a conversation about entering the kingdom of God. It is not suggested that πνεύματος in the verse should be read as a direct reference to the Holy Spirit, but that both water and wind are figures which represent the regenerating work of the Spirit in the lives of men and women, a truth pointed to in the OT passages mentioned above. These were passages which should have been familiar to Nicodemus as "the teacher of Israel" (cf. 3:10). But Nicodemus had missed *precisely* this point about *who* Jesus was.

Understanding Misunderstandings in the Fourth Gospel

In chapter 3, it is quite clear that Nicodemus misunderstood Jesus' words. He over-literalised them, and thought Jesus was talking about a second physical birth, when Jesus was referring to a spiritual re-birth. In the dialogue, the statement in Jn 3: 5-8 brings a misunderstanding in 3:9 and it is clarified in 3:10-12. Jesus says that re-birth is necessary to enter the realm of God (3:3). Nicodemus misunderstands and takes the allegory literally.[66] Jesus adds v. 6 to clarify that what he has been talking about is, again, not physical but spiritual through the allegory of water and wind being indicative of the regenerating work of the Holy Spirit. In Jn 3:9, Nicodemus gives his response. It is clear that at this time he still has not grasped what Jesus is saying. Note also that this is the last appearance of Nicodemus in the dialogue. Of course, since Nicodemus the Pharisee has already found religion, he thinks that Jesus must be referring to physical re-birth (3:4). No, Jesus responds, someone who is re-born spiritually knows the experience as surely as one who has been refreshed by an invisible breeze (3:5-8). John uses the contemporary evangelical terminology of being "born again." John uses the phrase five times, in 3:3, 7; 3:31; 19:11 and 23. In the latter three cases the context makes clear that it means "from above." In 3:3, 7 it could mean either, but it seems that the primary meaning intended by Jesus is "from above." Thus, it is important to show that being "born again" and being "born of water and the Spirit" are one and the same idea. The latter expression echoes OT phraseology and might have been calculated to ring a bell in Nicodemus' mind, so whatever Jesus meant by the expression "born of water and the Spirit" must also be true of the expression "born again." The characters have to discover that their first impressions and usual trains of thought processes cannot help them understand the meaning of Jesus. They must move beyond what they have always known to come into his light. And the reader must make this move with them whenever these episodes are read. We can agree with Professor O'Brien when she says that it is necessary to identify with the initial confusion, uncertainty, and misunderstandings of the characters in John's Gospel. But they must learn from their misperceptions. As O'Brien summarises, "The Fourth Gospel presents Jesus as Other, the one who descends from above, the one whom the world does not know, the one who is radically disorienting. In this context, misunderstanding is an essential step toward enlightenment, and belief is characterized less by correctness than by acceptance of the enigma and persistence in following."[67] How can a respected ῥαββί among the Jews not know this (3:10)? The passages Nicodemus might have known which would have given him insight into

Jesus' words include: Prov 30:4-5; Isa 44:3-5 and Ezek 37:9-10. These passages should have been familiar to Nicodemus as "the teacher of Israel" (cf. 3:10), but he misunderstood everything, so Jesus made him understand through his dialogue and teaching.

Enlightenment through Initial Misunderstanding

In the Gospel of John, people are often depicted as being dull, or misunderstanding Jesus, or finding his teaching difficult or not understandable, for instance: (Nicodemus in 3:1-15; the Samaritan woman in 4:1-26; the disciples (14:5-9; 16:17-18; 20:9; 6:60; 10:6). In two instances in the conversation between Jesus and Nicodemus there is misunderstanding on the part of Nicodemus and Jesus explains to him.[68] Consider the episode of Jesus' demonstration in the temple (Jn 2:18-22), when the Jews appear in the story. They ask Jesus: "What sign do you show us for doing this?" (v.18). The Jews have a clear reason for posing this question, but Jesus does not answer it directly. He begins by speaking about the destruction and the raising up of the temple: "Destroy this temple, and in three days I will raise it up (v. 19)." Jesus uses expressions that, understandably, the Jews misunderstand. They heighten the readers' awareness of another level of the meaning of these words. The verbs "destroy" and "raise" can refer either to a building or to the body of Jesus. And indeed the narrator later explains that Jesus is not speaking of the material temple but of the temple of his body (v. 21). As many scholars have observed, Jesus' body is presented as a substitute for the Jerusalem temple. In fact, the story of Jesus in the temple and the teaching of Jesus' body as the new temple are inter-connected.

In 6:55, many disciples leave Jesus after he tells them that his "flesh is true food" and his "blood is true drink." In 11:27, Martha confesses her belief that Jesus is the "Messiah, the Son of God, the one who is coming into the world." But in 11:40, when Jesus commands that the stone of her brother's grave be taken away, she protests, "Lord, by now there will be a stench; he has been dead for four days." The twentieth chapter of the Gospel of John "succeeds" insofar as the reader really takes part in this "enlightenment through initial misunderstanding." Others blatantly reject Jesus because their eyes are blinded and their hearts are hardened, i.e., their minds are closed to true understanding (12: 39-40; cf. 1: 10-11). From this it follows that a teacher of Israel like Nicodemus is supposed to have proper knowledge. But his knowledge seems to stop at acknowledging Jesus as 'a teacher come from God' (Jn 3:2). His knowledge falls short of the truth because Nicodemus fails to see that Jesus is from above.[69] Three times in vv. 3-9 Nicodemus asks questions which reveal him as an outsider to the true knowledge of Jesus and his ministry.[70] Jesus says to him: ταῦτα οὐ γινῶσκεις; (v. 10). This is contrasted with v. 11, where the knowledge of the insiders is emphasized.

Nicodemus' incomplete understanding is also revealed by his appeal to the signs of Jesus. In chapter two the signs lead the disciples to believe in Jesus whereas, in chapter three, Nicodemus simply talks about the signs, but does not come to believe. In fact, Nicodemus is suspended in the text between Nathanael, the true Israelite who immediately abandoned his scepticism and confessed Jesus as ῥαββί (or teacher), "Son of God," and "King of Israel" (1:49), and the Samaritan Woman, the heretic Jew who comes to believe in Jesus as "the Christ" (4:29) and brings her fellow townspeople to him by her testimony (4:39). At the beginning of the pericope, Nicodemus is one of those Jews who believe in Jesus because of the signs he does, but whose faith Jesus finds inadequate (2:23-25).[71] At the end of the dialogue, Jesus ironically salutes him as a "teacher of Israel" who does not understand even the basics of Old Testament revelation, much less what Jesus has come to reveal (vv. 10, 12). But, if the reader perseveres through the text, it becomes clear that Jesus' irony is not so much a condemnation as a challenge.

Teaching Authority: Difference between Jesus and Nicodemus

Nicodemus is probably a member of the Sanhedrin, the Jewish ruling council. He is also said to be from the Pharisees and a 'ruler' of the Jews. In verse 10 Jesus identifies Nicodemus as 'the teacher of Israel.' Thus as a Pharisee, a ruler, and probably as a member of the Sanhedrin and teacher, Nicodemus represents the essence of Judaism at that time. In fact, in chapter 12, the summary statement says that it was Nicodemus' own group, the Pharisees, who intimidated the authorities to not acknowledge Jesus to be more than a potential trouble-maker. Despite the cordial titles with which he addressed Jesus as ῥαββί (teacher), it seems that Nicodemus did not go far enough in his conclusion about who Jesus really was. Jesus' initial response was abrupt and, no doubt, took Nicodemus by surprise (Jn. 3:3). In the NT, this represents an inadequate, though common, first impression of Jesus.

In the context of Jn 3:2, Köstenberger opines, "this address of Jesus as ῥαββί also confirms that Jesus' assumption of the identity of a Jewish religious teacher provided him with common ground on which to interact

with other Jewish rabbis such as Nicodemus."[72] Köstenberger agrees that
Jesus lacked rabbinic credentials. When it is said that as a teacher himself,
Jesus could argue with the teachers and scribes, there is a difference. It
is the difference between acclaimed and recognised rabbis and Jesus. As
previously stated, unlike the Jewish rabbis who had rabbinic authority,
Jesus relied entirely on his spiritual authority.

Jesus' assertive stance toward Nicodemus strikingly demonstrates
for John's readers that Jesus, while falling short of Nicodemus' rabbinic
credentials, commanded spiritual authority far exceeding that of
Nicodemus. In the opinion of Geza Vermes, "the best outline of Jesus as
a preacher in the Fourth Gospel is formulated in the words of Nicodemus:
"Jesus was a teacher commissioned by God, for no one can perform the works
that he does unless God is with him."[73] Köstenberger states, "The difference
between Jesus and other Jewish rabbis is also highlighted: unlike the Jewish
scribes, Jesus relied on his consciousness of having been sent by God and
his resultant spiritual authority rather than on rabbinic training. Also, in
breaking with Jewish custom, he apparently never attached himself to a
particular Jewish Rabbi, to follow him and learn from him. Jesus does not
return Nicodemus' courtesy. Rather than engaging in polite platitudes, he
lectures the "Teacher of Israel" on his need for regeneration."[74] Scott is of
a similar opinion. He observes that there is a contrast made here between
Jesus, the teacher who comes from God (Jn 3:2), and Nicodemus who
himself is the teacher of Israel (Jn 3:10). In the observation of Scott, the
authority of Jesus' teaching always comes from God whereas in the case
of Nicodemus, it is not so. Scott opines here that "in this sequence Jesus
places the authority for his teaching upon the fact that he has 'seen' these
things of which he speaks, he has come from heaven to reveal them.[75]
Thus, it is observed that the Johannine Jesus, the teacher, is not like other
teachers, for the authority for both his teaching and mighty deeds comes
from God and not simply from the worldly authorities.

As has been noted already many times, the terms ραββί and
διδάσκαλος attributed to Jesus "present him as a teacher" and that is once
again established in the conversation between Jesus and Nicodemus. For
the rest of the conversation it is Jesus who speaks. Though the account of
Nicodemus' visit to Jesus is relatively short, it includes some of the most
profound of Jesus' teachings. One of these is the concept of re-birth via
water and the Spirit (John 3:3-8). The conversation between Jesus and
Nicodemus, who is a high-ranking Jew, is very unusual when compared
to the typical relationship between Jesus and Jewish leaders described

in the gospels in general. In this conversation Nicodemus talks to Jesus as one teacher to another.[76] Nicodemus is a teacher himself. Jesus agrees with that in Jn 3:10 saying ὁ διδάσκαλος τοῦ Ἰσραήλ. Nicodemus is the first of what might be called 'the officials' with whom Jesus has personal engagement or conversation. In this instance, one cannot help but notice some of "the argumentation and questioning" which happens in the circles of great teachers and scholars of all times.

Geza Vermes in his *The Changing Faces of Jesus* speaks about the Johannine presentation of Jesus as a teacher. Vermes is faithful to history when he says that to understand John's terminology "ῥαββί" attributed to Jesus, "we must first inquire into the various connotations of 'teacher' in the first-century Judaism, which is the period of the beginning of Christianity?"[77] According to the current understanding of the address ῥαββί as 'Teacher' in the first century Judaism, the term could point to an official instructor, who would normally be a priest, a scribe or a Pharisee. In the interpretation of Vermes, Nicodemus, who is spoken of as a 'teacher of Israel' in Jn 3:10, and possibly a member of the Sanhedrin (Jn 7:50), belonged to the upper echelon of this category. However when the Johannine Jesus is called 'teacher', as Vermes points out, "clearly, Jesus did not belong to this stratum of Jewish society. Nor was he a ῥαββί in the technical sense, despite being repeatedly addressed as such in John (1:38; 3:2; 20:16), since he was not an expert in Jewish traditional law and Bible interpretation."[78] Thus Vermes agrees that the Johannine Jesus was called a ῥαββί in the sense of a teacher but not in the technical sense of having strict Jewish credentials.

5. ῥαββί, φάγε (4:31): Imparting of Knowledge to the Disciples
On three occasions, in Jn 4:31; 9:2; and 11:8, the term ῥαββί is used by the disciples to address Jesus. It should be kept in mind that the first two instances (Jn 1:38, 49) were by those who initially joined him, when Jesus was in the process of making disciples. In the discussion with the disciples (Jn 4:27-42), which takes place while the Samaritan woman (at the well) has gone into the city, a misunderstanding occurs. This is a perfect example of John's use of misunderstanding as a literary technique. Jesus is speaking of "living water" which is spiritual (ultimately this is a Johannine figure for the Holy Spirit, cf. 7:38-39) while the woman thinks he means physical water of some sort, which will satisfy thirst. Raymond Brown observes that "misunderstanding (vs. 11), irony (vs.12), the quick changing of an embarrassing subject (vs. 19), the front and back stage (vs. 29), the Greek

chorus effect of the villagers (v. 42) all these dramatic touches have been skilfully applied to make this one of the most vivid scenes in the Gospel and to give the magnificent doctrine of living water a perfect setting.[79] It has been pointed out that the disciples could have been seen even from a distance as they made their way through the fields to the well. The disciples think Jesus refers to physical food, while he is really speaking figuratively and spiritually again. Thus Jesus is forced to explain what he means, and that his "food" is his mission, to do the will of God and accomplish his work. This leads naturally into the metaphor of the harvest. The fruit of his mission is represented by the Samaritans who are coming to him.

In Jn 4:31, Jesus' disciples address their teacher as ῥαββί when returning from getting food (ῥαββί, φάγε). The disciples' address stands in marked contrast with the Samaritan woman's consistent address of Jesus as κύριος. Commenting on this, Köstenberger states that "the disciples, on the other hand, address Jesus as ῥαββί indicating their perception of him as their teacher."[80] In the narrative of the Samaritan woman, the disciples of Jesus still address him as ῥαββί whereas the Samaritan woman uses the title κύριος several times in the respectful sense of meaning 'Sir.'[81] Köstenberger thinks that the (equivalent of the) term κύριος may also have been used by the Samaritan woman to indicate respect while remaining distant, owing to the ethnic, social, and gender barriers separating her and Jesus.

'Salvation from Jews': Is it an Emphasis on Jesus' Jewishness?
The roles of Jesus as teacher and his followers as disciples is in keeping with contemporary Jewish practice and draws attention to an important theological feature of John's portrayal of Jesus. The Fourth Gospel offers a perfect case-study of the relationship between the portrayal of Jesus as a Jew and the criticism of the Jews and their religion in the New Testament. On the one hand, the Fourth Gospel is often described as the most anti-Jewish writing of the New Testament (See, Jn 8:44). On the other hand, Jesus is presented pointedly as a Jew in the narrative, and Jesus the Jew even states that "salvation is from the Jews" (4:22). Jesus' Jewishness is an important theme in this discussion. Jesus speaks here as a Jew, and he evaluates the religion of the Samaritans from a Jewish point of view. "In ch. 4, John presents Jesus judging Samaritanism from a Jewish point of view."[82] Jesus admits that the Jews have knowledge of the content of their worship, even though he frequently states elsewhere in the gospel that the Jews lack even a very basic knowledge of his Father (5:37–38; 7:28–29; 8:55).

Franz Mussner has tried to answer this question in a book whose subtitle is, "The Significance of Judaism for Christian Faith."[83] According to Mussner, the saying "salvation is from the Jews" (4:22) is an ancient statement of conviction emphasizing "that the eschatological salvation of the world remains with Judaism." The saying corresponds to the faith conviction of the evangelist who, through his positive reception of the saying, confessed the Jewish roots of the Church. Hartwig Thyen sees in the saying "salvation is from the Jews" a counterbalance to those passages of the Fourth Gospel where the Jews seem to be presented in a hostile light. According to Thyen, the saying is not a logical part of the dialogue in ch. 4, which shows that it has a fundamental significance[84] for the gospel and its relationship to Judaism. The saying also shows that the Johannine Christians did not deny their roots, although they were excommunicated violently from the synagogue. It is learnt from the saying that together with some other passages in the gospel, that the Jews have not ceased to be God's own people for the evangelist, even though certain people have rejected their own king in an incomprehensible way.[85]

A similar interpretation was recently formulated by Thomas Söding, who called the saying "the heart (Kernsatz) of the Johannine soteriology."[86] According to Söding, the Jewishness of Jesus is an application of the incarnation Christology of the gospel, because the fact that Jesus is a Jew is an expression of his humanity. Thus the words "salvation is from the Jews" are well in line with the emphasis on Jesus' Jewishness.[87] In this story, Jesus' Jewishness is closely connected to his teaching that shows how the salvation he offers supersedes the earlier ways to worship God.[88] This analysis thus has revealed that the controversial saying "salvation is from the Jews" is not necessarily contradictory to the portrayal of the Jews in the rest of the gospel as God's own people. Thus the emphasis on Jesus' Jewishness lays a foundation for his teaching on the true form of worship. The words "salvation is from the Jews" should also be seen in light of what Jesus says just before uttering these words. In the controversy over the right place of worship, Jesus seems to adopt the point of view of the Jews as he says to the Samaritan woman, "you worship what you do not know, we worship what we know." According to some scholars, "we"[89] in Jesus' mouth refers to Jesus and all the believers who share his teaching of God (cf. Jn 3:11). It is thus clear in the Johannine theology that the words "we know what we worship, for salvation is from the Jews" do not refer to the continuing priority of the Jews over the non-Jews. Because salvation is connected closely to Jesus' person in the gospel, the words "salvation is from the Jews" should be interpreted as a veiled messianic claim. This shows that Jesus' Jewishness is an important part of the Fourth Gospel's portrayal of Jesus. Jesus is indeed in many respects more Jewish than his Jewish contemporaries in the gospel. He is zealous in his defence of the purity of the temple, and he is a better teacher of the law than his opponents.

6.   Jesus a ῥαββί: With Supernatural Knowledge and Power

In Jn 6:25 the crowd addresses Jesus ῥαββί (ῥαββί, πότε ὧδε γέγονας). For Scott, ῥαββί is "the most common way in which people address Jesus in the Fourth Gospel."[90] After the miracle of the multiplication of loaves and fish, the multitude in 6:25 call him ῥαββί. This address is significant, for it comes from the crowd as an expression of their amazement. For Köstenberger, this is an indication that "the Jewish crowd continued to perceive Jesus first and foremost as a religious teacher."[91] The people who followed in the boats ask, "Teacher, when did you get here?" Jesus does not answer their direct question, but the implication here again is of supernatural knowledge on Jesus' part. Jesus knows their true motivation for following him and that distinguishes him from his contemporaries as someone with supernatural knowledge and power. While the ordinary crowd understand him just as a teacher, in the same chapter there is a development in the understanding of Jesus on the part of the disciples.

There is also a struggle and conflict on the part of some other disciples and Jews in understanding the teaching of Jesus. In Jn 6: 24-41, there are indications that Jesus was addressing a crowd of people and some of the "Jews". In Jn 6:60-66, it is evident that some of his own disciples were present and listening as well. And they did not like what they were hearing. Some of them were annoyed regarding Jesus' preaching, as being both "hard" and "harsh." In this context it is not so much "hard to understand" as "difficult to accept." It became apparent to some of Jesus' followers that there would be a cost involved in following him. In Jn 6:32-34, note that the crowd still misunderstands the nature of the true bread from heaven: "Lord, give us this bread." If they conceive of it as something that Jesus himself gives, they still have missed it. They take offence at some of Jesus' teaching, namely the imagery of "eating his flesh" and "drinking his blood." Jesus warns them that, if they thought this was a problem, there was an even worse cause for stumbling in store for them; his impending crucifixion in Jn 6:61b-62. Jesus asks, in effect, "Has what I just taught caused you to stumble? What will you do, then, if you see the Son of Man ascending to where he was before?" In Jn 6:67-71, in contrast to the response of some of his disciples, there is the response of the Twelve, whom Jesus questions concerning their loyalty to him. The confession of Peter differs considerably from the Synoptic accounts (Matt 16:16, Mark 8:29, and Luke 9:20) and directly concerns the disciples' personal loyalty to Jesus, in contrast to those other disciples (Jn 6:66) who had deserted him. Thus, there is a difference and also a considerable amount of progress noted in the understanding of the disciples. Looking at the passage in Jn 9:2 of the healing of the man born blind, there is another illustration of Jesus teaching his disciples as a Rabbi. The disciples question Jesus using the title ῥαββί and ask him about the cause of the blindness (ῥαββί, τίς ἥμαρτεν ...). It appears that their address and subsequent question to him is a further indication of their perception of Jesus 'as a teacher.' The question is followed by a religious instruction by Jesus. This, would have been just another incident in the public life of Jesus where Jesus would use a 'teachable moment' to impart knowledge to his disciples or others. However, as Köstenberger notes, "in this case, Jesus' answer transcended the wisdom of his scribal contemporaries",[92] who customarily attributed suffering to a person's sin whereas, for Jesus the ῥαββί, this was an occasion for the revelation of God's glory. That is, he gives them a correct understanding of the cause of the man's blindness.

The next occurrence of Jesus being addressed as ῥαββί occurs in Jn 11:8 where, once again, the disciples express their concern for their master Jesus. They say ῥαββί (ῥαββί, νῦν ἐζήτουν σε λιθάσαι οἱ Ἰουδαῖοι). The disciples express their concern for the life of their master and try to stop him from going to Bethany. And when Jesus insists on going there (Jn 11:16), Thomas expresses his real concern for the master. In the words of Köstenberger both in 4:31 and 11:8 "the disciples here express concern for the well-being of their teacher."[93] Thus, it could definitely be said that the disciples addressing Jesus as ῥαββί in John explains their understanding of Jesus as a teacher and master.

7. Women Disciples Addressing Jesus as ῥαββί

In the incident in Jn 11:28, the word ῥαββί is not applied directly to Jesus. Instead the Greek equivalent of διδάσκαλος is spoken by Martha to her sister when she says ὁ διδάσκαλος πάρεστιν καὶ φωνεῖ σε. Although there is no direct confirmation, it can be assumed from Martha's statement that Jesus was addressed even by his closest circle of friends as a teacher. But the sign of raising his friend Lazarus from the dead, as Köstenberger

notes, "explodes narrow notions of the role of a religious teacher."[94] Notice
that the image of Johannine Jesus as a teacher is put into question when he
performs such signs and wonders. Later in this chapter the role of "Rabbi"
in Johannine theology, and whether there is a connection between the
teaching of Jesus and his activities will be analysed. But in the episode
of Lazarus, this book will show that even within his closer circle, Jesus
has been understood and addressed as a teacher.

In a post-Resurrection narrative, Mary of Magdala addresses the risen
Jesus as ῥαββουνί (Jn 20:16). It is note worthy that, in both occurrences of
the term 'Rabbi' in Jn 1:38 and Jn 20:16, the terms ῥαββί and ῥαββουνί are
translated as διδάσκαλε. For Dalman, the Johannine address of ῥαββουνί
found in Jn 20:16, could not have been materially distinguished from the
form of address ῥαββί and, therefore, "John is right in interpreting it as
διδάσκαλε"[95] This particular instance of ῥαββουνί in Jn 20:16, in the words
of Köstenberger, "is no real exception"[96] in the presentation of Jesus
as ῥαββί meaning teacher. Furthermore, as if to emphasize the point,
John (once again) translates the term ῥαββουνί as διδάσκαλε. For Lapin,
"It is important to note that in John the terms 'rabbi' and 'rabbouni' are
each glossed as διδασκαλοσ, "teacher" (John 1:38; 20:16, respectively); it
seems to have taken on this meaning exclusively."[97] This adds weight to
the understanding that the Johannine Jesus is primarily perceived as ῥαββί
in the sense of a διδάσκαλος even after his death. Again, it is not only the
first disciples (Jn 1:38) that call Jesus ῥαββί in the sense of a διδάσκαλος
but also the women disciple who do so (Jn 20:16). The first disciples
(i.e. men) address Jesus (Jn 1:38) ῥαββί in the sense of a διδάσκαλος, and
the first disciple who saw the Risen Jesus (i.e. a woman) also recognises
Jesus as ῥαββουνί in the sense of διδάσκαλος. In the beginning (Jn 1:38)
and at the end after the resurrection (Jn 20:16), the author of the Gospel
presents Jesus as ῥαββί and as ῥαββουνί. As may be seen, the terms ῥαββί
and διδάσκαλος are used synonymously by John to refer to Jesus as a *teacher*.
Thus, this book holds that the Johannine Jesus, with all his mighty deeds,
is still a teacher.

Mary Magdalene and Her ῥαββουνί in the Fourth Gospel
In John's Gospel women seem to have an important place in their
encounters[98] with Jesus. As Seim opines, although Christ's relationship
with the women is stressed in Luke, it is even more evident in John. "Even
more than in Luke, women are main actors in scenes that are quantitatively
dominating and of great theological importance."[99] The Apostles are

invariably men but it is a clear that in John's Gospel the relationship of Jesus with women is exclusive and significant. Referring to the dialogue of Jesus with the Samaritan woman, Seim comments on the reaction of the disciples. The very fact that his disciples "were surprised to find him talking with a woman" (Jn 4:27) indicates something of the cultural perspective. Seim states that "their criticism is not voiced because it implies a criticism of Jesus."[100] However, Jesus did more than just converse with the Samaritan woman, he 'confided in her his greatest truth'[101] that he was the promised Messiah (v.26). As Seim observes, the dialogue with the women, and the way Jesus entrusted the task of witnessing to the women, suggests that it implies a "new role pattern for men and women."[102] In the episode of the adulterous woman (Jn 8), it is Jesus who remained and gave her peace and pardon, but 'no word of condemnation.'[103]

Jesus stays often in the house of Martha and Mary, and indeed has a fraternal relationship with the two sisters and their brother Lazarus. Jesus is never shown intimately participating in the feelings of the male apostles, but he participates in the grief of those two sisters at the death of their brother Lazarus. The intimate relationship with Mary and Martha at Bethany is recounted in the story of the Resurrection of Lazarus. However, among the women mentioned in the Fourth Gospel, it is clear that the role given to Mary Magdalene is particularly noteworthy.

In John's account of the resurrection of Jesus, his primary focus was on a woman, Mary Magdalene. She was the first person to see Christ after the resurrection and the person selected by Christ to tell all the other disciples. The fact that a woman was selected for this task is significant and raises a few fundamental questions. Why did John recount his version of the resurrection of Christ with Magdalene as the main, and only, character besides Christ? Constructive arguments should be made in a historical-critical method in order to substantiate Mary Magdalene's role as a disciple of Jesus, whom she called "Rabbouni" even after the resurrection.

Mary Magdalene in the Gospels

Mary Magdalene is mentioned in all four Gospels twelve times in total (Mt 27:56. 61; 28:1; Mk 15:40.47; 16:1.9; Lk 8:2; 23:49. 50-56; 24:10; John 19:25; 20:1.18). As a way of interpreting Jn 20:17, a comparison will be made of Mary Magdalene with the sinful woman of Luke 7. In looking for other possible parallels to Jesus' appearances to Mary Magdalene, a study will also be made of the other NT appearance stories (Mt 28; Lk 24; Jn 20- 21). Mary Magdalene's presence is marked at both great events of the Crucifixion and at the Empty Tomb on the early morning of the day of Resurrection, which is the core of the Paschal event. John tells the story in a way that is very different from the other versions. He puts the story in present tense, a literary device that adds a dramatic tension to the story.[104] John also simplifies the story. He does this in two ways. First, he has only two characters, Christ and Magdalene and second, he presents a simple and very realistic dialogue. By doing this, the reader focuses upon the content, not the secondary characters.

For Eisen, "In the ancient Church's interpretations of the Gospels and during the early Middle Ages, women were regarded as apostles even though they were not so entitled *expressis verbis* in the gospels themselves."[105] According to Karris,[106] women's roles in the early church were enhanced by their religious involvement, giving and sharing equal opportunities in service and leadership. Mckenzie[107] lists all seven women of the NT in his dictionary of the Bible. "Four women in the New Testament named Mary are important."[108] Coming to the same problem in the Fourth Gospel, Collins observes that Mary Magdalene "ought not to be identified with Mary of Bethany, the sister of Martha and Lazarus, since it is highly unlikely that the author of the Fourth Gospel would have identified a single individual by the use of two different place locations."[109] The brief outline below shows the place and presence of Mary Magdalene and the other women in the four Gospels.

Events	Matthew	Mark	Luke	John
Serving women	-	16:9	8:1-3	-
Crucifixion	27:55-56	15:40-41	23:49	19:25-27
Burial	27:57-61	15:42-47	23:50-56	19:38-42 (no direct mention of women)
Empty Tomb	28:1-10	16:1-8, 9-20	24:1-11	20:1-2
Appearance & commission	28:9-10	16:9-11	-	20:11-18

When the historical, religious and social background in the time of the historical Jesus is analysed, it shows that women were oppressed from antiquity through the time of the historical Jesus. Even the disciples of Jesus had the attitudes found in Jewish society. In the Fourth Gospel (Jn 4:27), the disciples are shown as being astonished at Jesus' conversation with a Samaritan woman. It could be that the disciples marvelled because the woman with whom Jesus was conversing was a Samaritan. It is a question whether Jesus' disciples had the same thinking pattern as any other Jew in this regard. Knowingly or unknowingly, the male disciples might have looked down upon women followers who wanted to follow and be in the company of Jesus. By his extended relationship, and including women in his company, Jesus proved himself to be a radical Jew. His radical way of relating with women might have disturbed the expectation of the disciples looking at Jesus as the Jewish Messiah, their Ραββί. Seim supports this argument thus; "The focus is solely on the female sex of the Samaritan as the essential point of difference and scandal." It would seem that the gender issue has dominated the way that we have approached the Gospels.[110] The Gospel of Luke opens with the annunciation to Mary (Lk 1:26-38) and closes, in effect, with the appearance of the Risen Jesus to Mary Magdalene (Lk 24:1-12). The group of 'women disciples' Luke mentions includes those 'healed from evil spirits.' In Luke, Mary Magdalene is known as one from whom Jesus had driven seven demons. "In Jewish thought, to be possessed of seven devils was to be lost, abandoned. Mary for that reason, is said to have been the harlot whom the Lord rescued."[111] But Luke never explicitly identifies her with the Sinful Woman of the previous chapter (Lk 7). Luke introduces her as the one who had been freed from evil spirits and never as a sinner. Mark's Gospel[112] also speaks of this group of women[113] who followed Jesus and even there this image of a sinner is not attributed to her. Even in the Fourth Gospel, the author does not make any link between Mary Magdalene and the image of the public prostitute (Jn 8). According to Seim, "Next to the Gospel of Luke, the Gospel of John offers rich material, both in quality and quantity, for examining the roles of women in early Christianity."[114] When an exegetical study is made of the person of Mary Magdalene, it is clear that even in the NT writings she does not appear among the list of the apostles.

Mary Magdalene a Disciple: Discoveries at Nag Hammadi

This section deals with Mary Magdalene as an ardent disciple of Jesus as shown in the NT writings and particularly in the Fourth Gospel. Here, the arguments are based on biblical assertions, particularly the textual evidence from the Fourth Gospel and the recent findings of some of the apocryphal Gospels, which the Church has named as extra-canonical literature. It would appear that the stories of Mary Magdalene as a disciple and an apostle have been intentionally ignored, as happened invariably to the majority of women in line with the historical and religious tradition of Judaism. As Raymond Brown observes, "The tradition that Jesus appeared first to Mary Magdalene has a good chance of being historical."[115] Among the newly discovered texts 'The Gospel of Mary' discovered at Nag Hammadi[116] in Egypt more than a half-century ago is an important text. Most scholars cite the mid-second century as the earliest plausible date of composition for these documents. However, according to Haskins,[117] a few of the documents are said to have been written as early as the late first century, making them contemporary with the New Testament Gospels. Among the newly discovered texts "The Gospel of Mary," discovered at Nag Hammadi testifies to this thesis in favour of her discipleship with Jesus. For example, in the Gospel of Mary, Mary Magdalene receives secret revelations from Jesus to the point of earning the jealousy of Peter.

The Gospel of Mary portrays "Peter as being jealous of the revelations that the Magdalene got from the Risen Christ."[118] Further, "The Gospel of Thomas" has Peter saying the following about the Magdalene: "Let Mary leave us, for women are not worthy of life."[119] Brown notes "it was probably John's portrait of Mary Magdalene that sparked the Gnostic Gospels to make her the chief recipient of post-resurrection revelation and a rival of Peter."[120] "The Gospel of Philip,"[121] also discovered at Nag Hammadi, shows another understanding of Mary's relationship as a companion of Jesus. In the Gospel of Philip, the "relationship between Jesus and Mary Magdalene is contrasted with Jesus' relationship with the rest of the disciples."[122] Brown's explanation[123] for all these arguments is that the Gnostic writers had been somehow influenced by the Fourth Gospel into making Mary Magdalene the disciple whom Jesus loved the most. This portrait of Mary Magdalene sparked the Gnostic writers to make her the disciple whom Jesus "loved most and the chief recipient of post-resurrectional revelation."[124]

In this scenario, the canonical Fourth Gospel predates the traditions revealed in the writings of Nag Hammadi. As Brown observes, the conclusions of this study do not come from "overly imaginative deductions about ecclesiastical history."[125] Though, in the Fourth Gospel, Mary Magdalene is the essential witness to the Risen Christ, she has not acquired the prominence of the early male apostles. Schneiders[126] thinks that the biblical text is not innocent, and has an attitude as if "the bible was written by men for men." Among the women mentioned in the Fourth Gospel, Jesus' Resurrection appearance to Mary Magdalene (Jn 20:11-

18) testifies to the vital role of witness and mission. The appearance, narrated in the event of the Resurrection, emerges as a demand to witness and to announce. As Seim opines, "In John men are very rarely addressed at all and never correspondingly. This happens to a woman for the first time in 20:11-18."[127] Further Mary Magdalene, a woman, represents the powerless (20:1-18) and the voiceless of the society. Bearing this in mind, it is astounding that Jesus chose to first reveal the truth of his resurrection to women as is evident in all four Gospels (Mt 28:1–7, Mk 16:1–7, Lk 24:10, Jn 20:10–18).

In John's resurrection account, Jesus appears first to Mary Magdalene. In John, her importance is shown through her call to witness the Resurrection of Jesus, a call that she receives personally from Jesus. In the words of Malina, "this most well- known female protagonist is not an isolated figure of importance among the women of the Gospels."[128] However, the text in Jn 21 may suggest that the first appearance to Mary Magdalene is either of no importance or that Mary Magdalene has been purposely ignored. From another view, the text may mean that Mary Magdalene is not included in the group of the eleven. But note the words of Howard-Brook on the later appearances, "this seaside experience is marked as the third revelation to the disciples but keeping the appearance to Mary Magdalene in a privileged category by itself."[129] We can be convinced that the second and the third appearances are never meant to minimise the appearance and commission to Mary Magdalene, but rather needs to be approached as strengthening the faith of the eleven. Collins observes that, "Mary can be counted among those who are truly believers and disciples for she can announce, "I have seen the Lord."[130] When the act of proclamation in the Fourth Gospel, "I have seen the Lord", is analysed, it is clear that it is she, not Peter, who is the first to see the risen Jesus. All of these aspects of an apostle are perfectly seen in the life of Mary Magdalene. If this is the criteria, it can be said that Mary was qualified to be not only an apostle, but to have a special role among the apostles based on being chosen to see him first at his resurrection.

8.   Johannine Jesus as Διδάσκαλος

Pursuing John's portrayal of Jesus as a teacher, this study will proceed with the relationship between Jesus and his closest followers in terms of the customary teacher-disciple relationship in the first-century Judaism. The Johannine address of ῥαββί to Jesus portrays Jesus not only as a teacher (a Jewish teacher) but one who, at the same time, was a master with his own disciples. The following section will analyse that aspect of the Johannine portrayal of Jesus *as Master* and the significance of holding others to discipleship.[131] According to Köstenberger, "John's Gospel clearly indicates that Jesus' contemporaries customarily perceived him as a religious teacher and that his relationship with his disciples largely conformed to the pattern of Jewish teacher-disciple relationships of his day."[132] Köstenberger explains the teachings of Jesus to his disciples, which substantiate that Jesus was following the rabbinic way of training them through questions and interpretations as well as "mystifying gesture."[133] He refers to Daube, who deals with the event of "foot-washing" as an example of the teacher-disciple relationship between Jesus and his disciples. Daube notes that the unfolding of Jesus' last extended time with his disciples at the footwashing (13:1–17) follows the rabbinic pattern of "mystifying gesture – question - interpretation."[134]

Köstenberger asserts that Jesus was the master of his disciples exactly in the Jewish sense. Looking at some of the features of the Johannine portrait of Jesus' disciples in light of their Jewish background, one important difference between contemporary rabbinic practice and Jesus is that Jesus chose his disciples, while generally disciples chose to attach themselves to a particular ῥαββί (cf. 15:16).[135] In keeping with this, Jesus frequently issued warnings to his disciples regarding the pervasive negative influence of the Jewish religious leadership. These issues come particularly to the fore in Jesus' shepherd allegory (chap. 10). There, in allusion to Ezekiel 34 and utilizing the familiar motif of God as Israel's shepherd, Jesus identifies the Jews' current leadership as faithless (cf. Zech 11:15–17), in contrast to himself, who is the "good shepherd." Here the image of shepherd and the role of ῥαββί merge because Jesus, the shepherd-teacher, takes great care to nurture a close, trusting relationship with his followers in order to protect them from any spiritual harm resulting from their exposure to false teaching. Sometimes Jesus is seen in debate with the Scribes and/ or the Pharisees.

Johannine Jesus: A Rabbi in the Company of Μαθηταί

John states that the disciples moved from their former individual life-styles to full identification with the master. For example, Peter accepted a name change, indicating that he had received a totally new course for his life (Jn 1:42). The disciples in John's gospel are portrayed as accepting identification with Jesus: like him, they also were questioned and put on trial; they feared for their lives because of this close affiliation with the master teacher (Jn 20:19); and they hid for several days after his death (Jn 20:26). They were present when Jesus performed signs, as when he turned the water into wine at a wedding (Jn 2). They learnt from what Jesus did, how he lived, and from what he said to them. They listened as Jesus used parables and figures of speech to teach them about his mission and destiny. After his resurrection the full impact of what they heard was realised as the Holy Spirit revealed all that Jesus had taught them. Sometimes their questions appear to have been for theological instruction (Jn 9:2). At other times their questions evoked advice and instruction from Jesus. Sometimes their questions were unspoken. They also tried to recall Hebrew Scriptures to make sense of what they were seeing in the life of Jesus (Jn 2:17), and after his death they continued to remember his own words. They baptized (Jn 4:2); they performed menial tasks for him such as buying food (John 4:8) and cleaning up after the meals (Jn 6:12). Thus, there are many examples of how Jesus' choice of disciples as well as the purpose of his group is different from a typical group of disciples of a typical Rabbi of that time.

In many instances, when Jesus has been addressed as ῥαββί it has come from his disciples (Jn 3:26; 4:31; 9:2; 11:8). The term μαθητής which means 'disciples' occurs nowhere else in the NT except for the Gospels and the Acts of the Apostles. Köstenberger adds that "the term customarily used for Jesus' followers in the Fourth Gospel, as in the Synoptics, is μαθητής."[136] However, Scott has a different opinion and, for him, the whole issue of discipleship in the Fourth Gospel is quite a complex matter. "Unlike the Synoptic tradition, we do not have here an individually named set of disciples who follow Jesus around and interact with him in the various stages and individual acts of his ministry."[137] The word μαθητής is important in the terminology of the Fourth Gospel as the evangelist gives a particular nuance to this term. So, it is possible that the Johannine Jesus was, in fact, seen as a 'master' in the eyes of his immediate disciples.

Köstenberger notes that the term μαθητής in John indicates that "the early church tied the term inextricably to the historical followers of the earthly Jesus."[138] The disciples' duty to care for their master's various needs even transcends his death. Thus, "the disciple whom Jesus loved" is given the responsibility of caring for Jesus' mother (19:26–27), while Joseph of Arimathea and Nicodemus, two secret followers of Jesus from among the Pharisees, assume responsibility for Jesus' burial, as was customary for disciples.[139] This suggests that the term μαθητής is part and parcel of the teacher-disciple relationship Jesus had with his followers during his earthly ministry. Thus the Fourth Gospel provides ample evidence to sustain the second part of this book: Jesus is depicted in terms of first-century Jewish teacher-disciple relationships. According to John's Gospel, Jesus exercised his role by way of verbal instruction, didactic actions, provision and protection of his followers, and teaching by example.[140] In all of this, Jesus is cast as operating within a paradigm used by the Jewish religious teachers of his day. Jesus' earthly pattern of a rabbi gathering around himself a circle of close followers thus is shown to serve the preparatory purpose of instructing God's new messianic community. As has been shown, this pattern is further substantiated by the Fourth Gospel's portrayal of the disciples' relationship with Jesus in terms of contemporary rabbi-disciple relationships.

For Köstenberger, John clearly depicts Jesus in a normal Jewish setting, having a typical 'master-disciple' relationship with his followers. This is expressed in the Fourth Gospel by both the oral teaching and actions of Jesus. However, in some other exegetes, the picture of 'discipleship' that is given by the author of the Fourth Gospel is different from that of the normal Jewish tradition of discipleship. Collins notes that the faith commitment of the first two disciples "gave them an identity distinct from that of the Jews and of John's disciples."[141] In the Johannine understanding of discipleship, personal faith commitment is very important. The disciples represent those who are made believers by Jesus through his words and signs. Both the word and sign in the Fourth Gospel invite the hearers to believe in Jesus. One who believes starts following Jesus as his/her master and becomes a disciple. Then the disciple is entrusted with a mission of witnessing to the master. This becomes a distinctive feature of Johannine discipleship, which differs from the synoptic descriptions on the call of the disciples.

In the Fourth Gospel the disciples are made by witnessing. The witnessing of a disciple leads another one to become a disciple of Jesus. While direct calls from Jesus dominate the Synoptics' call narratives, according to the Fourth Gospel the disciples are made by witnessing and believing. John the Baptist's witnessing has the implication to his disciples to follow Jesus. Thus the witnessing of one man leads to another testimony from Andrew as the fruit of his remaining with Jesus. Koester also notes "Johannine Christians neither derived a pattern of discipleship from the Mosaic Law and Jewish tradition nor accepted lawlessness (1 Jn 3: 4); they followed alternative norms."[142] Scott points out the basic differences that are seen in Jesus' call to discipleship. "Firstly we may note the way in which the Johannine Jesus calls disciples: he seeks them out in public places, be it in the men of ch. 1 or the Samaritan woman of ch. 4."[143] Thus the Johannine portrayal of the discipleship required by Jesus also differs from the traditional understanding of Jewish discipleship. In his book *The Mission of Jesus and the Disciples according to the Fourth Gospel*, Köstenberger notes that in the Fourth Gospel, there is "an increasing widening of the designation 'disciples' that transcends the followers of the historical Jesus."[144] Thus, in the Johannine understanding of discipleship, the Greek term μαθητής clearly explains the relationship of Jesus with the disciples on a wider level.

Johannine Jesus: A Revelatory Teacher

Martin Scott observes that "John, the author of the Fourth Gospel used this term ῥαββί eight times (Jn 1:38, 49; 3:2; 4:31; 6:25; 9:2; 11:8 and in 20:16, it is ῥαββουνί). Among the cluster of ῥαββί occurrences in John, Jesus "is called ῥαββί by his disciples, or potential disciples (Jn 1:38. 49; 3:2; 4:31; 9:2; 11:8), as well as by the people generally (Jn 6:25)."[145] In *Sophia and the Johannine Jesus*, Scott asserts that the Johannine Jesus had the primary mission of revealing what was known to him about God and "part of this revelation is carried out through his role as teacher."[146] Cornelis Bennema observes that "Jesus' main activity in the Fourth Gospel is teaching (cf. the use of διδάσκω in 6,59; 7,14-17.28.35; 8,2.20; 18,19-20) and he is frequently addressed as "Teacher" (1,38; 3,2; 8,4; 11,28; 13,13-14; 20,16)."[147] The Johannine presentations of Jesus' teaching are essentially in the public discourses of John 1-12 and the private discourses to the disciples in John 13-17. This teaching is revelatory in that it comes from God and is about God whom no one has seen (1:18; 3:34; 7:16-17). In fact, Jesus' revelation and teaching are identical, i.e., Jesus reveals through his teaching and he teaches through revelation.[148] The aim of his revelatory teaching is to reveal the identity and work of the Father and Son and the nature of their relationship (1:18; 3:11-13:31-36; 8:19; 14:9-11; 15:15; 17:6-8. 26).

Jesus encounters people with his revelatory teaching, which carries an intrinsic demand for a response; he confronts people with the choice of accepting or rejecting him and his revelation. Moreover, this revelation/ teaching leads to life/salvation if accepted but to judgement and death if rejected (e.g., 3:15-18:36; 5:24; 6:35; 9:41). Besides a revelatory aspect, Jesus' teaching also has a cleansing dimension. Jesus declares to his disciples in 15:3 that they are already clean (καθαροί) by or because of his revelatory word (cf. Jesus' statement in 13:10 that the disciples are clean (καθαροί). In 17:17 the idea is presented of God's Word, given by Jesus to the disciples (17:8.14), purifying the disciples. Both evoke the imagery of cleansing. More particularly, Jesus' word can cleanse people because it contains truth, which sanctifies and sets people free from sin (8:31-36; 17:17). Thus, the picture that emerges is of Jesus cleansing people by means of his word/teaching because it contains life-giving, liberating, purifying truth.

Jesus' revelatory teaching is essentially the communication of what he has seen and heard from the Father (3:12-13.31-34; 5:19-20; 8:26-28.38; 14:24; 15:15). Jesus can bring this revelation from and about God precisely because Jesus is endowed with the Spirit. [149] Jn 1:32-34 alludes to Isaiah 11:2 and signifies endowment of Jesus with the Spirit of wisdom, knowledge and might. The implication is that the Spirit provides Jesus with revelatory wisdom and knowledge, which would naturally form the basis for revelatory teaching. This agrees with 3:34, which indicates that Jesus can speak the words of God, i.e., bring God's revelation, because God gives Jesus the Spirit without measure. Thus, Jesus can be the Revealer of God, and as such provide revelatory teaching, precisely because he is endowed with the Spirit of wisdom, knowledge and power.

The Temple Episode: Teaching and Action

According to K. Wegenast, the work of the διδάσκαλος is "to teach or instruct, though the purpose and content of the teaching can be determined only from each individual context."[150] At the beginning of the temple episode, Jesus acts like any other pious Jew: as the Passover is at hand he goes up to Jerusalem (2:13). As Jesus comes to the temple, he finds people who are selling oxen, sheep, and pigeons, and he also encounters the money changers (v. 14). The Johannine narrator is the only one of the four evangelists who says that there were oxen and sheep in the temple area, and that Jesus drove them and the sellers out of the temple using the whip needed to control the animals. John's description may not be based on historical facts, but it is clear that the reaction of the Johannine Jesus to the arrangements in the temple was reasonable for a pious Jew.[151] Jesus is presented thus far in the story as a keen reformer of the religion who is upset by the corruption of the present temple and wants to restore its sanctity.[152] In the first part of the story, Jesus is portrayed as being furious at the ongoing defilement of the temple.[153] In his zealous defence of the temple and its sanctity Jesus stands in the best Jewish tradition. As a matter of fact, he is more Jewish than his Jewish contemporaries who profaned the temple.[154] From the Johannine point of view, it is only natural that Jesus' body is presented as a substitute for the material temple. The portrayal of Jesus as being more loyal to Jewish traditions than his fellow Jews lays a foundation for a teaching that shows Jesus as a substitute for the old temple.

Moving to Jn 7:15, we see Jesus in a teaching role. On this occasion Jesus is not directly addressed as Rabbi. In fact, the question πῶς οὗτος γράμματα οἶδεν μὴ μεμαθηκώς; implies that Jesus was considered to be lacking in his religious education or rabbinical training. As stated in the previous chapter, Jesus may not have had any formal Jewish training. It was also noted that Jesus should not be considered as being an 'ordained' rabbi. Bearing this in mind, the question in Jn 7:15 still implies that Jesus was considered a teacher but not in the same way as the usual teachers or scribes. Köstenberger opines, "Nevertheless, while the people's comment is derogatory, the statement confirms the common perception of Jesus as a religious teacher."[155] Thus, in the presentation of John, it is not only the disciples, but also the common people who understood Jesus to be a teacher.

Martha's statement to her sister Mary in 11:28 that "the Teacher [Jesus] is here" once again reinforces the notion that Jesus' contemporaries customarily perceived him as a religious teacher. In Jn 18:19-20 when the arrested Jesus is summoned before the high priest, the context refers to the teaching action of Jesus. When it is intimated that Jesus' teaching was characterised by subversiveness, secretiveness, and exclusivism, Jesus maintains, "I have spoken openly to the world; I always taught in synagogues and in the Temple, where all the Jews come together; and I spoke nothing in secret" (18:20). This is the only place where Jesus maintains that he taught and thus played the role of a teacher (ἐγὼ πάντοτε ἐδίδαξα ἐν συναγωγῇ καὶ ἐν τῷ ἱερῷ, ὅπου πάντες οἱ Ἰουδαῖοι συνέρχονται, καὶ ἐν κρυπτῷ ἐλάλησα οὐδέν). Note that neither the title ῥαββί or διδάσκαλος is attributed to Jesus. Nevertheless, Jesus does acknowledge that he taught in the synagogues. Later in this chapter the role of "Rabbi" in Johannine theology will be addressed and the question of whether there is a connection between the teaching of Jesus and his activities will be analysed.

Johannine Jesus and His Views on Jewish Sabbath

In Chapter 7, Jesus returns to a discussion that began in chapter 5, where he healed the lame man and was accused by the Jews of breaking the Sabbath. Jesus defended himself by referring to the practise of the Jews in performing circumcisions on the Sabbath (Jn 7:22).[156] The axiom "circumcision overrides the Sabbath" was accepted widely during the very end of the first century A.D. There is a discussion in *m. Shabb.* 19: 1-3 about what one may do in connection with circumcision on the Sabbath. R. Eliezer has the most liberal view, according to which one may do anything at all in connection with circumcision on the Sabbath. According to R. Aqiba, however, only those things which cannot be prepared in advance on the eve of the Sabbath can be done on the Sabbath.

For Jesus this practise exemplifies the claim he made earlier in v. 19: "Did not Moses give you the law? And yet no one of you keeps the law. Why do you seek to kill me?" It is not likely that the willingness of the Jews to kill Jesus is presented as a proof that they do not keep the law, even though this is claimed by some scholars.[157] Rather, the claim that "no one of you keeps the law" is as an introduction to the question "why do they seek to kill me." The statement "no one of you keeps the law" can be taken as a general thesis that is shown to be correct by the following discussion of how the Jews perform circumcisions even on the Sabbath (vv. 22–23).[158] Note that a close parallel to this Johannine passage can be found in Justin Martyr's writings. "Or did He [God] wish that they who received or performed circumcision on that day [on the Sabbath] be guilty of sin, since it is His command that circumcision be given on the eighth day after birth, even though that day may fall on the Sabbath? If He knew it would be sinful to perform that act on a Sabbath, could He not have decreed that infants be circumcised either a day before or a day after the Sabbath? And why did He not instruct those persons who lived before the time of Moses and Abraham to observe these same precepts; men, who are called just and were pleasing to God, even though they were not circumcised in the flesh, and did not keep the Sabbath?"[159] For Justin, the contradiction between the observance of the Sabbath and the commandment to circumcise on the eighth day provides justification to criticise both circumcision and the Sabbath. Both the Johannine Jesus and Justin see the conflict between the Sabbath observance and the practise of circumcision on the eighth day. They both use this conflict to undermine the claims of their opponents. The way in which these two principal pillars of Jewish identity are contrasted with each other betrays the separation of both the Johannine Jesus and Justin from these institutions.

According to C. K. Barrett, this was perhaps the meaning of the passage in the source used by the evangelist who, somehow, connects the transgression of the law with the attempt to kill Jesus.[160] Jesus refers to circumcision here because it seems to serve as a precedent for breaking the Sabbath in certain cases.[161] He accuses the Jews of acting in an inconsistent way: the Jews regard Jesus' action on the Sabbath as a transgression of the law although they do not regard what they do in connection with the rite of circumcision as such. They apply to their own actions different standards than those in judgement of Jesus, which means that their judgment is incorrect (v. 24). Jesus' reasoning here resembles an argument used in certain rabbinic texts. The sages argue that if circumcision, which concerns only one limb of the body, is performed on the Sabbath, all the more should the Sabbath be ignored if the whole body is in danger.

There is a notable difference, however, between Jesus' reasoning in John and the argument made by the sages. The rabbis refer to circumcision on the Sabbath in passages that deal with the question whether it is permitted to save life on the Sabbath or not. The situation, however, is quite different in John, where the man healed by Jesus had been ill for 38 years. This was clearly not an emergency.[162] In order for Jesus' argument to be persuasive, circumcision and the miraculous healing of the lame man should be comparable acts. "Rules, whether derived from the written or the oral law, can be developed in this way to fill a gap in information about rules; and this is acceptable because inference from one situation to another like it is known from daily life. ... In our case circumcision, though it enables a Jew to live by other commandments (Lev. 18:5 etc.), is neither more important than, nor less important than miraculous healing of paralysis, for the two are not comparable."[163] As this is, however, not the case, Jesus' reasoning in John is hardly compelling; his argument sounds like a cogent defence of his action, but if taken as such, it is not persuasive. This is the reason why Pancaro seeks for a more profound interpretation of the passage. According to him, "Jesus is presented here as the fulfilment of the purpose of circumcision. Circumcision is not, however, the main theme here, and it would be surprising if Jesus' allusion to it should contain a subtle teaching regarding the original purpose of this practise. [164] "The reference to circumcision on the Sabbath forms part of Jesus' justification of his own practice, but it is not a very convincing argument. Both circumcision on the eight day and Sabbath observance were required by the Law, whereas Jesus' healings, which did not prevent death, could easily have been postponed to the following day. The argument would therefore have convinced no Jew."[165] This suggests that the *Sitz im Leben* of Jesus' argument is not an intra-Jewish debate on what is and what is not permissible on the Sabbath.[166] Rather, Sabbath and circumcision are viewed from the standpoint of an outsider in order to show that Jesus' opponents do not follow their law because it is not consistent.[167] Jesus' way of using second person plural forms, when speaking of the law and circumcision confirms this conclusion.

Johannine Jesus: In Accordance with OT Prophets

According to John, Jesus' interpretation of the Hebrew Scriptures illustrates features that transcend the common interpretation of his day. Jesus' messianic consciousness causes him to read the Old Testament with references to himself, a feature not found among contemporary Rabbis. Nevertheless, in keeping with contemporary custom, while there are differences between Jesus' teaching and the teaching of other Jewish teachers, the validity of the people's perception of Jesus as a religious teacher is not affected. It is also true that there were differences in the teaching of different Rabbis. But, in keeping with the presentation of the Synoptics, Jesus' "rabbinic rulings" are portrayed by John, as regularly transcending the wisdom of his contemporaries.[168] Köstenberger observes, "According to the Johannine Jesus, his teaching ministry is in accordance with the divine promise given through the Old Testament prophets."[169] C. Evans' discussion of rabbinic terms and methods, as well as Targumic and Midrashic traditions,[170] in John is most helpful. In many instances, Jesus is shown quoting from the Hebrew Scriptures[171] in his teaching, as any other ῥαββί of his time would. According to Andreas Köstenberger, John's Gospel portrays Jesus as providing instruction for his followers in a number of ways. "He does so by verbal instruction as well as action"[172] and personal example. Apart from assuming responsibility for providing instruction to his followers, Jesus is also shown to provide for other needs of his disciples.

According to Johannes Beutler "there are about nine instances in the Gospel of John where a reference to "Scripture" or to a prophet can more or less clearly be identified."[173] According to Beutler, the nine instances of the fourth gospel with reference to the OT are Jn 1:23; 2:17; 6:45; 10:34; 12:38; 12:39-41; 13:18; 19:24; and 19:37. John portrays Jesus as using the Hebrew Scriptures in five instances. In Jn 1:51, the Johannine Jesus alludes to Gen 28:12[174] and in Jn 3:14-15, although it is not a direct quotation, an incident that clearly refers to Nu 21:8-9. In his preaching on the "Bread from Heaven" Jesus refers to the OT, very specifically in Jn 6:45, where he refers to Is 54:13. And in Jn 10:34 Jesus quotes from Ps 82:6; again in Jn 13:18 he speaks quoting from Is 41:10. And finally in Jn 15:25 Jesus refers to Ps 35:19.

Köstenberger opines that Jesus' verbal instruction to his disciples and others is clearly consistent with his Jewish environment. "His use of Scriptures, his rabbinic rulings, his style of argumentation, and even language place him squarely within a Jewish rabbinic context."[175] But in all the OT instances in John's Gospel, Jesus' interpretation of the Hebrew Scriptures transcends the common interpretation of his time. In every instance, Jesus either observes that the Hebrew scripture is fulfilled in him or his teaching ministry is in accordance with the promises of the OT prophets. This marks the difference between Jesus' teaching and the teaching of other Jewish teachers. In the NT gospels, it is, of course, not only John who attributes Jesus with this kind of reading or speaking from the Hebrew Scriptures. But as previously mentioned, the synoptic authors present Jesus as transcending the wisdom of his contemporaries. In John, an element similar to the presentation of the Synoptics is seen where the evangelists portray the wisdom of Jesus as exceeding the wisdom of the contemporary Rabbis.

Johannine Jesus with Didactic and Prophetic Qualities

Jesus manifested his role as a ῥαββί in his relationship with his disciples. The Johannine Jesus is depicted as engaging himself in verbal instructions and didactic actions, and as having a close relationship with his followers. At another level, Köstenberger observes the Johannine instances where all the Jews sought confirmation of the divine call of Jesus as the prophet or Messiah. In all those instances the Johannine Jesus expresses his authority as a rabbi who has both didactic and prophetic qualities, as is expressed in both his actions and words. Even "Jesus' miraculous healings and other amazing acts may be viewed, among other things, as serving the purpose of attesting to his authority as a religious teacher."[176] The Jesus of John's Gospel is, therefore, "a religious teacher with a difference- issuing startling claims and performing powerful "signs"-but a religious teacher nonetheless."[177] G. Vermes raises the question of what kind of teacher Jesus was in the Fourth Gospel. Vermes observes, "John's narrative makes it plain that Jesus did not derive his doctrinal authority, as did the rabbis of the Mishnah and the Talmud, from years of study at the feet of an acknowledged master."[178] Jn 7:15 says 'How is it that this man knows letters when he has never studied?' From the authorities' amazement at Jesus' wisdom, it is implied that Jesus was not a trained teacher. For Vermes then, John has portrayed Jesus "as a charismatic master whose message was confirmed by his mighty deeds."[179] We can agree with Vermes that Jesus was not a trained teacher. Nevertheless the Johannine Jesus *as a teacher* certainly had authority derived from a profound knowledge of Scripture and Law.

The reference of Jn 7:15, quoted by Vermes himself, is an indication that Jesus was an expert in the Hebrew Scriptures and Jewish Law.

So far, in the above sections, it has been argued that in the Gospel according to John, it is not only the disciples who see Jesus as a ῥαββί in the sense of a teacher but also the crowds and the Jewish religious leadership such as Scribes and Pharisees. Even the great teacher Nicodemus perceived Jesus as a ῥαββί, at least in accordance with the Jewish understanding of the term. However, at times, Jesus transcends the role of a contemporary ῥαββί. At the same time the disciples of Jesus, as presented in the Fourth Gospel, do not perceive Jesus just as their ῥαββί or take him to be quite like any other ῥαββί of their time. The disciples of Jesus in the Fourth Gospel are not even presented as merely understanding Jesus as if he were a conventional rabbi. Indeed the Johannine Jesus, by his temple action in Jn 2, is portrayed as a reformer of religion. Jesus the Rabbi in Chapter 3 even goes to the level of instructing Nicodemus who is reputed to be a great teacher in Israel. He speaks of real worship in Jn 4. By his preaching and authoritative instructions, Jesus is portrayed as having new authority than Moses. Thus, the same Johannine Jesus, while accommodating himself to the cultural and religious role of a ῥαββί, transcends that role by his preaching and actions.

Summary and Conclusions

This chapter's review of the Fourth Gospel began with John the Baptist pointing out Jesus as 'The Lamb of God' to his disciples, who immediately left the Baptist to follow Jesus. The first two disciples who followed Jesus (Jn 1:35-38) are portrayed as having changed their allegiance from one ῥαββί to another ῥαββί. Then, how the Evangelist consistently portrays Jesus as a 'teacher' was reviewed. In this regard, various exegetical views were discussed on the significance of the term 'Rabbi' meaning *teacher*. Also, the works of many authors were referenced, specifically Rudolf Schnackenburg whose review initiated the discussion of whether the term ῥαββί, which is applied to Jesus in Jn 1:38b, presents him as a teacher. However, there are many more authors who have evaluated the same question and agree that the Evangelist uses the term ῥαββί to mean 'teacher.' Hence the various instances in the Fourth Gospel were reviewed where this seems to be the case. This led to exploring whether or not the title 'Rabbi' was, in fact, used to address Jesus in his lifetime or whether it is a gloss used at the time when the Gospel was written, some decades after the resurrection of Jesus.

The contention that Jesus assumed the role of a Jewish religious teacher in keeping with Jewish practices, and that he was so viewed by his contemporaries was tested. It is not argued here that ῥαββί is the only Johannine category for Jesus, or even the most important. Rather, it is merely contended that John reflects the fact that this was the way Jesus was primarily perceived by his contemporaries. On the basis of this common perception, speculation arose as to whether Jesus was a prophet like Moses or the Messianic king. But if the historical starting point for John's presentation of Jesus is lost, there no longer remains any common ground on the basis of which the historical Jesus conducted the interchange with his Jewish interlocutors and the locus from which the evangelist seeks to lead his readers into a deeper understanding of Jesus' full and true identity. This study's focus on John's presentation of Jesus as a rabbi should in no way be viewed as an effort to diminish John's portrayal of Jesus in apocalyptic-prophetic terms. However, these elements are, in fact, incompatible with John's basic presentation of Jesus as a religious teacher.

For many authors, the Johannine Jesus is depicted as ῥαββί in terms of the first century Jewish teacher-disciple relationship. When Taylor observes the different instances of ῥαββί or ῥαββουνί in John's Gospel, he concludes that "in using ῥαββί eight times and 'Rabboni' once, his terminology seems more primitive."[180] Hahn suggests that "the earthly Jesus was recognised as a teacher and master, and even the later church preserved this."[181] Riesner considers the address ῥαββί as historical when given to Jesus. "We can safely say that in the four gospels the title of rabbi with its implicit characterisation of Jesus as a teacher was not introduced for secondary theological motives; it is rather Palestinian and historical."[182] For Riesner, if Jesus was seen and addressed as a teacher, then it can be further concluded that he also acted in some ways like a Jewish teacher.

Also note that Hershel Shanks, on his observation of the appearances of the term ῥαββί in the Gospels, raises an interesting question. "Why would the Gospel writers or later editors insert a Jewish title for Jesus when, at the time they wrote, the principal missionary activities of the new religion were already directed to the Gentiles?"[183] In answer to this question, Shanks himself gives a detailed explanation in which he attempts to substantiate that the title ῥαββί was "part of the authentic Jesus tradition at the time when John wrote his Gospel."[184] Furthermore, on two occasions when John attributes the titles ῥαββί and ῥαββουνί to Jesus, he translates those titles into διδάσκαλε so as to facilitate the proper understanding of his use of the title ῥαββί. Therefore, it seems evident that Jesus was, indeed, given that form of address in his lifetime.

S. Zeitlin takes a different view from Shanks and says it is a historical fact that John's Gospel was composed not earlier than the middle of the second century and was written for Gentile Christians. For Zeitlin, "At the time of its composition, the term rabbi was already in usage among the Jews."[185] But the question is whether or not, at that period, this term had the connotation of teacher. On this point, Zeitlin concludes, "it is possible that John in writing for the pagans, who were unacquainted with the term rabbi, interpreted it as meaning teacher."[186] When Vermes[187] observes the address ῥαββί to Jesus, he asserts that it is even questionable whether the term 'rabbi' in the gospel (in the specialized meaning) was current in the early decades of the first century Judaism. Again, Vermes referring to historical writing, notes that the great Jewish masters like Hillel, Shammai, and Gamaliel who lived in the age of Jesus are all called 'elders' and not 'rabbis.' Thus, Vermes maintains his independent position from others. After much review and discussion, it concludes that the title ῥαββί, when attributed to the Johannine Jesus, is very meaningful even if it is not truly historical to the authentic Jesus' time.

Endnotes

[1] Bultmann states, "Yet in face of the entire content of the Tradition it can hardly be doubted that Jesus did teach as a Rabbi, gather disciples and engage in disputations." Cf. R. BULTMANN, *The History of the Synoptic Tradition* (trans.), J. MARSH, Oxford, Basil Blackwell, 1963, p. 50. See also M. KARRER, "*Der lehrende Jesus: Neutestamentliche Erwägungen,*" ZNW 83 (1992) 1–2, who also refers to a similar quote in Rudolf BULTMANN, *Jesus,* Berlin, Deutsche Bibliothek, 1926, p. 2, n. 5. Presenting Jesus as a Rabbi also testifies to the Jewishness of the Fourth Gospel. Jewishness of John's Gospel is well presented by A. SCHLATTER, *Die Sprache und Heimat des vierten, Evangelisten, BFCT* 6, Gütersloh, C. Bertelsmann, 1902; and A. SCHLATTER *Der Evangelist Johannes,* Stuttgart, Calwer, 1930.

[2] See, Andreas J. KÖSTENBERGER, "Jesus as Rabbi in the Fourth Gospel", *Bulletin for Biblical Research* 8 (1998) 97-128.

[3] Cf. S. Lewis JOHNSON, Jr., "The Message of John the Baptist", *Bibliotheca Sacra* 113: 449 (1956) 30-36; Knox CHAMBLIN, "Gospel and Judgment in the Preaching of John the Baptist", *Tyndale Bulletin* 13 (1963) 7-15: Knox CHAMBLIN, "John the Baptist and the Kingdom of God", *Tyndale Bulletin* 15 (1964) 10-16; F. F. BRUCE, "John the Forerunner", *Faith and Thought* 94 (1965) 182-190; David R. CATCHPOLE, "John the Baptist, Jesus and the Parable of the Tares", *Scottish Journal of Theology* 31 (1978) 557;

Michael CLEARY, "The Baptist of History of Kerygma", *Irish Theological Quarterly* 54 (1988) 211-227.

[4] Read, Jerome MURPHY-O'CONNOR, "John the Baptist and Jesus: History and Hypotheses", *New Testament Studies* 36 (1990) 359-374; William B. BADKE, "Was Jesus a Disciple of John?", *Evangelical Quarterly* 62 (1990) 195-204; J. Ramsey MICHAELS, "Paul and John the Baptist: an odd couple?", *Tyndale Bulletin* 42.2 (1991) 245-260; Robert L. WEBB, *John the Baptiser and the Prophet,* Sheffield, JSOT Press, 1991; John W. PRYOR, "John the Baptist and Jesus: Tradition and Text in John 3:25", *Journal for the Study of the New Testament* 66 (1997) 15-26; Joan E. TAYLOR, *The Immerser, John the Baptist within Second Temple Judaism,* Studying the Historical Jesus, Grand Rapids, Eerdmans, 1997; Walter WINK, *John the Baptist in the Gospel Tradition*, Eugene, OR, Wipf & Stock Publishers, 1997; Colin BROWN, "What Was the John the Baptist Doing?", *Bulletin for Biblical Research* 7 (1997) 37-50.

[5] D. Brent SANDY, "John the Baptist's 'Lamb of God': Affirmation in Its Canonical and Apocalyptic Milieu", *Journal of the Evangelical Theological Society* 34.4 (1991) 447-459. Conceptually, the 'Lamb of God' is seen as the Suffering Servant. In this case the symbolism is picked up from Is. 53:7—"Like a lamb that is led to the slaughter, and like a sheep that is silent before its shearers, so he did not open his mouth." This is said of the suffering servant in Isaiah. This text (Is. 53:7) applied to Jesus in Acts 8:32. All the Servant-Songs occur in the second section of Isaiah (40-55). The New Testament associates this part of Isaiah with John the Baptist (Jn 1:23 and Is 40:3). Jesus is related to the Suffering Servant elsewhere in the Fourth Gospel (12:38 and Is. 53:1).

[6] F. HAHN, *The Titles of Jesus in Christology*, p. 74.

[7] P. J. DU PLESSIS, *"The Lamb of God in the Fourth Gospel"*, in J. H. PETZER & P. J. HARTIN (eds.), *A South African Perspective on the New Testament*: Essays by South African New Testament Scholars presented to B. M. Metzger during his Visit to South Africa in 1985, Leiden, Brill, 1986, p. 147.

[8] G. VERMES, *The Changing Faces of Jesus*, p. 35.

[9] *Ibid.*, pp. 35-36. Further, it is noted that Jeremiah at one point speaks of himself as a lamb, as a sheep undergoing serious threat, about to be slaughtered, but innocently. And of course that could connect very easily with Christ, total innocence put to death not for any crime, but on completely trumped up charges. So that would be a possibility construing Jesus as a lamb in that sense. In Exodus the law is laid down that each day at the temple two lambs are to be sacrificed, one at daybreak and one later on in the day, on behalf of the people for the welfare of God's people. That links up with Christ because his death was in the interest of the human race. Another reference to lambs that is found in the old Testament in Leviticus (4:32-34), where the reference is to the sin offering. If a lamb is brought as an offering for sin, it must be a perfect female. The one who offers must lay his hand on the head of the sin-offering victim, and slaughter it

as a sin-offering at the place where the burnt offering victims are slaughtered. Whereupon the priest shall take some of the blood of the sin offering with his finger and put it on the horns of the altar for burnt offerings, while all the rest of the blood he shall pour out at the base of the altar. Here what acts as a bridge between this and Christ is that Jesus' sacrifice could very well be defined, and in fact is so spoken of, in Ruth particularly, as achieving the forgiveness of sins.

[10] Geza VERMES, *Scripture and Tradition in Judaism,* Leiden, Brill, 1961, p. 225.

[11] Cf. E. W. BURROWS, "Did John the Baptist Call Jesus 'The Lamb of God'?", *Expository Times* 85 (1974) 245-249. Gen 22 is a familiar account of the attempted sacrifice of Isaac by his father, Abraham. There something is presented that suggests the Lamb of God. Would God ever be so brutal as to ask this kind of a sacrifice of a human being, of a father, that he slaughter his only son? The answer to that is very easily and quickly given. No. But this is a question of a test of Abraham's faith. Throughout Genesis Abraham is presented as a profoundly faithful man. It carries over into our liturgy where to this day Abraham is spoken of as our father in faith. The point to take from this account is simply this, that there is nothing that God could ever ask of Abraham that he would not do, that he would not accede to. Cf. Gen 22: 1-5. Notice the irony of what is written. Abraham does not want to terrify his attendants by saying "I am just going up there to kill my son." And so he lies. That is, after having worshipped God, Abraham and his son will return to the servants. When Abraham says this, he does not think that will be so, but in fact it is. Cf. Gen 22: 6-14. He can not say to his son, "I am going to kill you: you are the sacrifice." But indeed this is almost the way it works out. God provides a substitute for his son Isaac. The possibilities of linking this with the questions about John's Gospel are clear. The analogy is very strong. First, Jesus may be thought of as that ram. However, the ram caught in the bush substitutes for Isaac just as Christ in his death on the cross substitutes for us, for the human race. But in its place there is Jesus, the Lamb of God. That is one possible understanding of Lamb of God as John employs the term. Going back to that incident in the story of Abraham, there is a twofold distinction. There is only the parallel of the ram being the stand-in for Isaac as Jesus is the stand-in for us, but also the parallel between God and Abraham. Abraham was willing to sacrifice his son; God was willing to sacrifice his son (the difference being that Abraham does not end up having to sacrifice his son whereas God does). There are analogies for every one of these Old Testament references that have been looked at. But there may be a problem: The Lamb is said to take away the sin of the world; the Servant takes on or bears the sins of many. But early Christians would probably not have drawn a sharp distinction as to whether in his death Jesus took away sin or took it on himself. Thus the end result is the same, which means the world has its sin taken away.

[12] Cf. A. JAUBERT, *Approches de l'Evangile de Jean, Parole de Dieu*, Paris, 1976, pp. 137-138.

[13] See, C. K. BARRETT, "The Lamb of God", in *NTS* 1 (1954-55) 210-218.

[14] Cf. R. SMITH, "Exodus Typology in the Fourth Gospel", *Journal of Biblical Literature* 81 (1962) 329-342.

[15] C. H. DODD, *The Interpretation of the Fourth Gospel*, pp. 230-238.

[16] Cf. J. T. MILIK, *The Book of Enoch: Aramaic Fragments of Qumran Cave 4, With the Collaboration of M. Black*, Oxford, 1976, pp 222-224; 240-244.

[17] See, P. J. DU PLESSIS, *The Lamb of God in the Fourth Gospel*, p. 139. Probably the concept of the apocalyptic Lamb is not to be found in John's Gospel. There appears in Jewish Apocalyptic literature the figure of a conquering Lamb who will destroy evil in the world. Cf. Testament of Joseph 19:8 (Testaments of the Twelve Patriarchs) tells of the lamb that overcomes the evil beasts and crushes them underfoot. Cf. Enoch 90:38 refers to the end, when a horned bull that turns into a lamb with black horns will appear. Cf. Rev 7:17 and 17:14. This fits well with the Baptist's eschatological preaching as portrayed in the Synoptics. Cf. Mt 3:12, Lk 3:17 ("His winnowing fork is in his hand to clear his threshing floor. He will gather the wheat into his barn, but the chaff he will burn up with unquenchable fire." However, there are problems with this view. The words used for lamb in John and Revelation are different: John 1:29 employs ἀμνὸς; Revelation uses ἀμνὸν. Revelation may simply be using a standard apocalyptic term for Lamb, whereas ἀμνὸς has a broader connotation. The descriptive phrase Ἴδε ὁ ἀμνὸς τοῦ θεοῦ does not seem to fit an apocalyptic picture.

[18] Alfred PLUMMER, *The Gospel According to John* (Thornapple Commentaries), Grand Rapids, MI, Baker Book House, 1981, p. 83.

[19] Brooke Foss WESTCOTT, *Gospel According to John. The Greek Text with Introduction and Notes*, Grand Rapids, MI, Baker, 1958, p. 47.

[20] C. K. BARRETT, *The Gospel According to John. An Introduction with Commentary and Notes on the Greek Text,* London, SPCK, 1955, p. 150.

[21] George R. BEASLEY-MURRAY, *John* (*WBC* 36), Nashville, Thomas Nelson, 1999, p. 26.

[22] Francis J. MOLONEY, *The Fourth Gospel and the Jesus of History*, NTS 46 (2000) 42-58, p. 52.

[23] R. E. BROWN, *John*, p. 75.

[24] LENSKI, *Interpretation of St. John's Gospel*, Columbus, OH, Lutheran Book Concern, 1942, p. 147.

[25] B. LINDARS, *The Gospel of John* (NCB), London, Oliphants, 1972, p.113.

[26] R. A. CULPEPPER, *The Gospel and Letters of John* (IBT), Nashville, Abingdon, 1998, p. 122.

[27] Rudolf BULTMANN, *The Gospel of John*, Philadelphia, PA, The Westminster Press, 1971, p. 100, n. 6.

[28] A. J. KÖSTENBERGER, *Studies on John and Gender*, p. 76.

[29] R. F. COLLINS, *John and His Witness*, p. 38.

[30] Francis J. MOLONEY, *Belief in the Word. Reading John 1-4*, Minneapolis, Fortress Press, 1993, p. 67.

[31] J. P. MEIER, *A Marginal Jew*, Vol. 2, p. 120.

[32] A. J. KÖSTENBERGER, *Studies on John and Gender*, p. 77.

[33] Alfred PLUMMER, *St. John's Gospel* (Cambridge Bible), Cambridge, University Press, 1923, p. 77.

[34] C. K. BARRETT, *John*, p. 150.

[35] Thomas L. BRODIE, *The Gospel according to John*, Oxford, N. Y., Oxford University Press, 1993, p. 160.

[36] D. MOODY SMITH, *The Theology of the Gospel of John*, Cambridge, Cambridge University Press, 1995, p. 125. See also, Arthur H. MAYNARD (Review author), *"St. John's Gospel"*, in Walter LUTHI & Kurt SCHOENENBERGER, in *Journal of Bible and Religion*, Vol. 29, No. 2 (Apr., 1961), pp. 172-173.

[37] M. SCOTT, *Sophia and the Johannine Jesus*, p. 152.

[38] R. BULTMANN, *John*, p. 100, n. 5.

[39] *Ibid.* Lenski opines that the disciples' addressing Jesus as ραββί and their further question about his abode expresses "the desire to have a private, undisturbed conversation with Jesus regarding the high thoughts and hopes which had begun to stir their hearts." See. LENSKI, *Interpretation of St. John's Gospel*, p. 147.

[40] R. SCHNACKENBURG, *The Gospel according to John*, p. 308. There are some others who agree with the idea of calling a master ραββί as it was the customary way for a disciple to address his master. Lenski writes that by using the title ραββί the disciples "address Jesus with the usual respectful title given to Jewish teachers." See. LENSKI, *John*, p. 146. Melvyn M. Hillmer has the same idea as Schnackenburg and says "they address him as Rabbi, translated "teacher," which was the usual way for a disciple to address his master." See, Melvyn R. HILLMER, "They Believed in Him: Discipleship in the Johannine Tradition", in, Richard N. LONGERECKER (ed.), *Patterns of Discipleship in the New Testament*, Grand Rapids, MI, Eerdmans/ Cambridge, 1996, p. 79.

[41] Leon MORRIS, *The Gospel of John*, NICNT, Grand Rapids, MI, Eerdmans, 1971, p. 157. McKenzie goes back into history and says "Rabbi was the address given by a student of the scribes to his teacher." See, J. L. MCKENZIE, *Rabbi*, p. 718. According to McKenzie, the term "a rabbi" or "the rabbi" in the Gospels is used as a form of address to Jesus. Thomas L. Brodie agrees that "it was a respectful title, usually addressed to a religious teacher." See, T. L. BRODIE, *John*, p. 160.

[42] B. LINDARS, *John*, p. 113; Read also, Hartwig THYEN, "Das Heil kommt von den Juden", *Kirche: Festschrift für Günther Bornkamm zum 75, Geburtstag* (eds.) D. LÜHRMANN and G. STRECKER; Tübingen, Mohr-Siebeck, 1980, pp. 163–184, esp. pp. 169–170; .

[43] F. J. MOLONEY, *Belief in the Word*, pp. 67-68.

[44] *Ibid.*

[45] HOWARD-BROOK, *Becoming Children of God, John's Gospel and Radical Discipleship*, Maryknoll, NY, Orbis, 1994, p. 70.

[46] Ibid.

[47] D. MOODY SMITH, John, Abingdon New Testament Commentaries, Nashville TN, Abingdon, 1999, p. 72.

[48] Cf. D. A. CARSON, Gospel of John, p. 154. According to Carson, in the Gospel of John, the term "follow" usually refers to more than just "trailing along after" someone. It is Jesus' way of speaking of someone becoming his disciple. This is not always the case, but it is usually so. Here, there may be a little of both senses implied. Jesus invites Philip to come along and to join with him as a disciple. In the Synoptic Gospels, Philip is included once in each Gospel, and this is when Jesus appoints and names the twelve men as his disciples. Nothing else is said of him as an individual in the Synoptics. Based upon the Synoptics, we would not know what kind of person Philip was. As Philip's name appears 12 times in the Gospel of John, several incidents are depicted telling us something about him. (Cf. Jn 6:4-7; 12:20-23; 14:6-11). There is a question as to whether the pronoun "he" in Jn 1:43 actually refers to Jesus in Jn 1:43. In the Greek version of Jn 1:43, the pronoun "he" is not used as a subject. We are not sure about the subject of the verb. "On the next day Jesus wanted to depart for Galilee. 'He' found Philip and said to him, "Follow me." Disciples responded to a directed summons from Jesus, as seen when Philip simply followed when Jesus said, "Follow me" (Jn 1:43). Yet others responded to Jesus when given encouragement to do so by friends or family members. For example, Nathanael responded because of Philip's encouragement. Note that the author of the Fourth Gospel never uses the term 'call of the disciples' in his presentation of the first disciples. In the Synoptic perspective, this event is narrated always as a call from Jesus. The synoptic disciples receive the call from Jesus. The 'follow me' formula is applied in the Fourth Gospel to Philip (Jn 1:43) and then to Peter in the Post Resurrection narratives (Jn 21:19.22). It is agreed that the call extended to Philip in the Fourth Gospel seems to reflect the synoptic way of calling with the call formula of 'follow me.' Just as the disciples chose to follow Jesus, they also chose to change their minds. Some of Jesus' disciples also freely chose to leave after choosing to follow. The teaching became too burdensome (Jn 6:66). Judas betrayed Jesus (Jn 12:4; 13:26) and Peter denied him (Jn 18:17.25.27). Yet those who remained were true disciples (Jn 8:31). The disciples were always on the move. John's Gospel reveals that they attended a wedding (Jn 2:2), went

to Judea (Jn 3:22), climbed a mountain (Jn 6:3), went down to the sea (Jn 6:16), journeyed to a small wilderness town called Ephraim (Jn 11:54), and went over to a garden in the Kidron Valley (Jn 18:1). Peter and another disciple followed Jesus to the high priest for the trial, and the Beloved Disciple followed Jesus all the way to the place of the cross. Joseph of Arimathea followed the body of Jesus to the tomb (Jn 19:38). The disciples were not only in motion physically, but their life orientation also changed.

[49] The disciples believed in Jesus because of the signs he performed at Cana (cf. Jn 2). See, Carl ARMERDING, "The Marriage in Cana", *Bibliotheca Sacra* 118: 472 (1961) 320-326; J. Duncan M. DERRETT, "Water into Wine", *Biblische Zeitschrift* 7 (1963) 80-98; Calum CARMICHAEL, "The Marriage at Cana of Galilee", John DAVIES, Graham HARVEY & Wilfred G. E. WATSON, eds., *Words Remembered, Texts Renewed: Essays in Honour of John F. A.Sawyer*, Journal for the Study of the Old Testament Supplement No. 195, Sheffield, Continuum International Publishing Group - Sheffield Academic Press, 1995; Ronny REICH, "6 Stone Water Jars", *Jerusalem Perspective* 48 (1995) 30-33; See also, Ritva H. WILLIAMS, "The Mother of Jesus at Cana: A Social-Science Interpretation of John 2:1-12", *Catholic Biblical Quarterly* 59 (1997) 679-692; Debbie HUNN, "The Believers Jesus Doubted: John 2:23-25", *Trinity Journal* 25.1 (2004) 15-25.

[50] Cf. Majella FRANZMANN & Michael KLINGER, "The Call Stories of John 1 and 21", *Saint Vladimir's Theological Quarterly* 36 (1992) 7-15. Cf. Thomas DOWELL, "Jews and Christians in Conflict: Why the Fourth Gospel Changed the Synoptic Tradition", *Louvain Studies* 15 (1990) 19-37; Francis E. WILLIAMS, "The Fourth Gospel and the Synoptic Tradition: Two Johannine Passages", *Journal of Biblical Literature* 86 (1967) 311-319; Edward F. SIEGMAN, "St. John's Use of the Synoptic Material", *Catholic Biblical Quarterly* 30 (1968) 182-198; Cf. Barnabas LINDARS, "John and the Synoptic Gospels: A Test Case", *New Testament Studies* 27 (1981) 287-294; M. E. GLASSWELL, "The Relationship Between John and Mark", *Journal for the Study of the New Testament* 23 (1983) 99-115.

[51] See, Cf. J. C. HINDLEY, "Witness in the Fourth Gospel", *Scottish Journal of Theology* 18 (1965) 319. See also, Merrill C. TENNEY, "Topics from the Gospel of John: Part III: The Meaning of "Witness" in John", *Bibliotheca Sacra* 132 (July 1975) 229-241; See also, Urban C. VON WAHLDE, "The Witnesses to Jesus in John 5:31-40 and Belief in the Fourth Gospel", *Catholic Biblical Quarterly* 43 (1981) 385-404; Urban C. VON WAHLDE, "The Witnesses to Jesus in John 5:31-40 and Belief in the Fourth Gospel", *Catholic Biblical Quarterly* 43 (1981) 385-404; Stephen BARTON, "The Believer, the Historian and the Fourth Gospel", *Theology* 96 (1993) 289-302; Andrew T. LINCOLN, "The Beloved Disciple as Eyewitness and the Fourth Gospel as Witness", *Journal for the Study of the New Testament* 24.3 (2002) 3-26; Luc DEVILLERS, "Les trios témoins: Une Structure pour la quatrième évangile", *Revue Biblique* 104 (1997)

40-87; Edouard COTHENET, *La Chaîne des témoins dans l'évangile de Jean. De Jean-Baptiste au disciples bien-aimé*, Lire la Bible n. 142, Cerf, Paris, 2005.

[52] Cf. Charles E. HILL, "The Identity of John's Nathaniel", *Journal for the Study of the New Testament* 67 (1997) 45-61. Nathanael's name is found only in the Gospel of John, five times in chapter 1 and once in chapter 21. He is never mentioned in the other Gospels or anywhere else in the New Testament. Nathanael comes across quite differently in John than Philip. If Philip is a man who seems "out of his depth," Nathanael appears to be a man of great spiritual depth, greater than the others. Cf. L. MORRIS, *Gospel of John*, p. 166. It seems probable that Nathanael had had some outstanding experience of communion with God in the privacy of his own home, and that it is this to which Jesus refers. Whatever it was, Nathanael was able to recognize the allusion. Cf. L. MORRIS, *Gospel of John*, p. 169. Some Scholars suggest that Nathanael is to be identified with Bartholomew, an apostle who is never mentioned in John, just as Nathanael is never mentioned in the Synoptists. There are good reasons for supposing that Nathanael is "Bartholomew" in the Synoptic Gospels. Bartholomew is coupled with Philip in all three Synoptists (Matt. 10:3; Mark 3:18; Luke 6:14), while another link is that he is mentioned immediately after Thomas in Acts 1:13 and Nathanael is in the same position in John 21:2. Moreover Bartholomew is not really a personal name, but a patronymic meaning 'son of Tolmai'. It is possible that he had another name. The other disciples mentioned in this chapter all became apostles, and it is suggested that Nathanael is, accordingly, likely to have done so too. If he is to be identified with one of the apostles, Bartholomew is probably the one. Cf. L. MORRIS, Gospel of John, p. 164. Carson seems more convinced than Leon Morris: "The most likely suggestion is that Nathanael is the personal name of 'Bartholomew,' which is then understood to be an Aramaic patronymic (*i.e.* identifying the person as the son of someone: 'the son of Tholomaeus' or the like)." Cf. D. A. CARSON, *Gospel of John*, p. 159.

[53] Craig R. KOESTER, "Messianic Exegesis and the Call of Nathanael", *Journal for the Study of the New Testament* 39 (1990) 23-34. The words spoken by Philip to Nathanael reveal Jewish expectations about a coming one. "Him whom Moses in the law and also the prophets wrote" (1:45); but Philip then names Jesus in terms of human perceptions as the son of Joseph of Nazareth (1:45). Philip proclaims to Nathanael that Jesus is the one of whom Moses and the prophets wrote (1:45). Since Moses was regarded as the author of the Pentateuch this must be a reference to the 'Law and the Prophets,' a way of referring to the Hebrew Scriptures (Mt 5:17, 7:12; 11:13, Lk 16:16, Rom 3:21). Philip is confessing that the Scriptures point to Jesus, that the prophecies and promises of the Bible are all fulfilled in him. This is a common notion in the Gospel of John (2:17,22; 6:45; 7:37-39; 12:14-16; 20:9). Philip's confession to Nathanael in 1:45 is structurally parallel to Andrew's earlier confession that Jesus is the Messiah in 1:41. These confessions of faith in Jesus will come to a

climax in Nathanael's confession made directly to Jesus, Rabbi, you are the Son of God! You are the King of Israel!' (1:49). Note that Philip describes Jesus as the 'son of Joseph from Nazareth' (1:45, cf. 6:42). Nathanael, who comes from the village of Cana (21:2) near Nazareth, scorns these lowly origins. "Can anything good come out of Nazareth?" (Jn1: 46). The characters try to understand Jesus' identity in terms of his origins. As long as people fail to accept Jesus' origins with the Father they will never perceive Jesus' true identity. After Philip finds Nathanael and tells him they have found the Messiah, the one who was promised in the Law of Moses and the Prophets, Nathanael makes his way to see Jesus. See, T. SÖDING, "Was kann aus Nazareth schon gutes kommen?' (Joh 1.46), Die Bedeutung des Judeseins Jesu im Johannesevangelium", *NTS* 46 (2000) 21–41, esp. pp. 39–40.

[54] Craig KOESTER, *Symbolism in the fourth Gospel: Meaning, mystery, community,* Minneapolis, Fortress, 1995, p. 68. For more on the idea of representative figures see R. COLLINS, *These things have been written: Studies on the Fourth Gospel,* Louvain, Peeters Press, 1990, pp. 2-45 (esp. 11-14). Nathanael's famous response 'Can anything good come out of Nazareth?' has puzzled many readers. It is most likely a sharp comment but there is also a note of contempt in Nathanael's words. In John 7:52 it is understandable that Jesus' enemies (who are Judean) say 'no prophet is to rise from Galilee' but why does Nathanael, himself a Galilean, take offence at the fact that Jesus is from Galilee? Perhaps this is another example of how people were reluctant to accept that one of their own could be the promised One sent by God; as Jesus says elsewhere, prophets are not without honour except in their own country (Jn 4:44; Mt 13:54-57; Lk 4:24). Another contrast between Nathanael and the Judean leadership in Chapter 7 is that while in 7:10-52 extensive argument fails to convince the leadership that Jesus is to be believed because of his Galilean origins, Nathanael comes to believe through a personal encounter with Jesus. Jesus' divine insight (cf. 2:24-25) into Nathanael's character is expressed in 1:47 'Here is truly an Israelite in whom there is no deceit!' In the Gospel of John, just as Jesus is the Truth (Jn 1:9; 6:32, 55; 7:18; 15:1) so Nathanael is a 'true' Israelite, implicitly contrasted with 'the Jews' who oppose Jesus in the Gospel of John. It is important to remember that Jesus himself was one of 'the Jews' and so it is anachronistic to portray 'the Jews' as a whole in opposition to him. This negative portrayal of 'the Jews' in the Gospel of John is not historical but reflects a later situation of alienation between the Johannine community and the Jews at the time of the Gospel's writing around the end of the first century. On this topic, see, Robert KYSAR, *The Fourth Evangelist and His Gospel,* Minneapolis, Augsburg, 1975, pp. 131-137; Adele REINHARTZ, *Befriending the Beloved Disciple,* New York, Continuum, 2001.

[55] See, Marianne Meye THOMPSON, "Signs and Faith in the Fourth Gospel", *Bulletin for Biblical Research* 1 (1991) 89-108; Loren L. JOHNS & Douglas B.MILLER, "The Signs as Witnesses in the Fourth Gospel: Re-examining the

Evidence", *Catholic Biblical Quarterly* 56.3 (1994) 519-535; See Kikuo MATSUNAGA, "Is John's Gospel Anti-Sacramental? - A New Solution in the Light of the Evangelist's Milieu", *NTS* 27 (1980-81) 518. Jesus replies with a promise that Nathanael will see 'greater things than these' (Jn 1:50) and then follows (1:51) one of the 'Very truly I say to you' (ἀμήν, ἀμήν λέγω ὑμιν) statements that are only found in the Gospel of John (25 times). Such statements are authoritative and are directed not just to the individual Jesus is speaking to (in this case, Nathanael) but to us as readers of the Gospel as well (the pronoun 'to you' is plural). As with the confessions of Philip and Nathanael, the point of Jesus' words in 1:51 is Christological: he identifies himself as the 'Son of Man' upon whom the angels will ascend and descend. The title 'Son of Man' is common in the Synoptic Gospels, and is likely a messianic reference. Here in Jn 1:51 it seems to express the notion that the Son of Man bridges heaven and earth by coming from heaven to earth (Jn 3:13); the opening of the heavens also occurred at Jesus' baptism (Mt 3:16, Mk 1:10, Lk 3:21). And of course the image of angels ascending and descending recalls Jacob's dream of the ladder in Gen 28:10-17, except that in Jn 1:51 Jesus himself takes the place of the ladder: Jesus is the bridge between heaven and earth, the divine and human come together in and through him. Robert T. FORTNA, *The Gospel of Signs,* Society of New Testament Studies Monograph Series 11, Cambridge, Cambridge University Press, 1970; Merrill C. TENNEY, "Topics from the Gospel of John: Part II: The Meaning of the Signs", *Bibliotheca Sacra* 132 (April 1975) 145-60; Loren L. JOHNS & Douglas B. MILLER, "The Signs as Witnesses in the Fourth Gospel: Reexamining the Evidence", *Catholic Biblical Quarterly* 56.3 (1994) 519-535.

[56] Nicodemus appears only in John's Gospel (see, Jn 7:50, 19:39). According to John 3:1, Nicodemus was "a ruler of the Jews" and hence probably a member of the Sanhedrin. The Babylonian Talmud and the *Midrash Rabbah* name one Nakdimon, son of Gorion as one of the richest men in Jerusalem at the time the Romans destroyed the temple in A.D. 70. *Ta'anit* 19b-20a; *Ketubot* 65a, 66b-67a; *Gittim* 56a; *Abodah Zarah* 25a. Lamentations 1:31; Ecclesiastes 7:19. He may be the Nicodemus of John's account or his grandson. Read, Michael D. GOULDER, "Nicodemus", *Scottish Journal of Theology* 44 (1991) 153ff; See, Richard J. BAUCKHAM, "Nicodemus and the Gurion Family", *Journal of Theological Studies* 46 (1996) 1-37. *Nicodemus* is also named in several medieval Syriac and Armenian texts as one of the Seventy chosen by Christ, as described in Luke 10. These are the lists prepared by Jacob bar Salibi (also called Dionysus, died A.D. 1171), Michael the Syrian (A.D. 1126-1199), and Solomon of Basra (early 13th century A.D.) in his *Book of the Bee*. Nicodemus is not included in the lists of the Seventy prepared by Hippolytus and Dorotheus. John Chrysostom (A.D. 347-407), bishop of Constantinople, in his *Homily 85* on John 19:38, suggested that Joseph of Arimathea, who joined with Nicodemus to bury Christ after his crucifixion, was "not one of the twelve, but perhaps one of the seventy."

[57] Cf. M. MICHEL, "Nicodème ou le non-lieu de la vérité", *Revue des Sciences Religieuses* 55 (1981) 236 ; Jouette M. BASSLER, Mixed Signals: Nicodemus in the Fourth Gospel, *Journal of Biblical Literature*, Vol. 108, No. 4 (Winter, 1989), pp. 635-646. Nicodemus came, it seems, as a private investigator, to satisfy himself regarding the claims of Jesus. To open the conversation, he makes a statement, "We know that from God you are come a teacher." The words "from God" are in an emphatic position in the Greek text, the idea of Nicodemus being that Jesus was not a teacher who came from man, but from God. Nicodemus says, "We know that from God you are come a teacher." In reporting this statement, John uses the perfect tense, which in Greek refers to an action completed in past time having present results. By the use of this tense, John is telling us that Nicodemus not only spoke of the coming of Jesus as a teacher to Jerusalem, but that Jesus had established himself there as a teacher. He had taken root, so to speak, in their affections and respect. The Jewish leaders were losing the crowds, and they were following the new Teacher who was causing such excitement in Jerusalem. After that the Sanhedrin agreed that Jesus had come from God as a teacher, and that he had already established a reputation for himself among the people. Nicodemus tells Jesus why the members of the Sanhedrin had come to this conclusion. The reason was that they were convinced that no one was able to perform the signs, which Jesus was doing, unless God was with him. The Greek text here emphasizes the fact that it was the constant performance of signs which proved to the Sanhedrin that Jesus was from God, the idea being that, had he performed one or a few signs, there might have been a possibility that they were mere impositions and not true signs. So the proof for the divine source of Jesus' teaching was absolute. To read more, See, B. LINDARS, "*Two Parables in John*", *New Testament Studies* 16 (1969/70) 318-324; W. A. MEEKS, "The Man from Heaven", *Journal of Biblical Literature* 91 (1972) 53-54.

[58] A. J. KÖSTENBERGER, *Studies on John and Gender*, p. 77. Köstenberger states that in this Nicodemus contrasts with the increasingly hostile reaction to Jesus on the part of the Pharisees in general (cf. 1:24; 4:1; 7:32–52; 8:3–11; 9:13–41; 11:46–57; 12:19, 42; 18:3). One Pharisaic attitude reflected in the Fourth Gospel that can be corroborated from rabbinic sources is their contempt of the scripture- illiterate masses. cf. 7:49). Read also, J. M. AUWERS, "La Nuit de Nicodème comme Figure de Nouvelle Naissance", *Etudes Théologique et Religieuse* 79 (2004) 563-573; C. A. EVANS, *Word and Glory*, p. 166 calls this "a typical attitude toward the common people" in Jesus' day, referring also to statements attributed to Hillel ("An ignorant man cannot be holy," *m. 'Abot* 2:6) and Hanina ben Dosa (*m. 'Abot* 3:11).

[59] J. H. NEYREY, "John III – A Debate over Johannine Epistemology and Christology", *NT* 23 (1981) 115-127. See also C. S. KEENER, *The Gospel of John*, A Commentary, Peabody, MA, 2003, I, pp. 234-247.

[60] H. F. WEISS, διδάσκαλος and διδάσκω, in *EDNT* 1 (1990) 317-319, p. 318.

[61] See, Paul D. DUKE, *Irony in the Fourth Gospel*, Atlanta, John Knox, 1985; Leonhard Goppelt states, "The Gospel of John passed on the words of Jesus predominantly in another genre than the synoptics; it did not do so in sayings, parables, and controversy dialogues, but in connected or dialogical discourses." See, Leonhard GOPPELT, *Theology of the New Testament*, trans. J. E. ALSUP, Grand Rapids, Eerdmans, 1982, p. 293; D. Dale ELLENBURG, "The Relationship Between John and the Synoptic Gospels", *Journal of the Evangelical Theological Society* 38.2 (June 1995) 171-180; James D. DVORAK, "The Relationship Between John And The Synoptic Gospels", *Journal of the Evangelical Theological Society*, 41.2 (1998) 201-213; See also, Barnabas LINDARS, "Discourse and Tradition: The Use of the Sayings of Jesus in the Discourses of the Fourth Gospel", *Journal for the Study of the New Testament* 13 (1981) 83-101.

[62] See, Sandra SCHNEIDERS, *"Born Anew"*, *Theology Today*, Vol. 44, No. 2 (July 1987) 189-196, p. 193. What Jesus said should have been clear to Nicodemus against the background of the Old Testament. Yet he is being challenged to recognize the arrival of the New Covenant in the person of Jesus whose signs are meant to draw him into relationship with this Teacher-Revealer who surpasses Moses. Instead, Nicodemus, who begins with a confident assumption of spiritual wisdom expressed in his "we *know* who you are and whence you come," regresses through literal misunderstanding into total confusion. His final words are a defeated, "How can these things be?" Jesus, with supreme irony, then turns back on him his opening recognition. He who called Jesus "Teacher," an address which the reader recognizes as the perfect title on the lips of a disciple (because the Johannine Jesus is the ultimate Teacher-Revealer) but which Nicodemus did not really understand, is now gently mocked as a "teacher in Israel" who does not understand even "earthly things" such as the literal meaning of Jesus' discourse and thus is totally incapable of believing in the "heavenly things" Jesus is about to reveal. NICHOLSON, in his *Death as Departure*, p. 104 says that John 3:1-10 "revolves around the question of who Jesus is and what must happen before a person can adequately understand him." See also, G. R. O'DAY, *Revelation in the Fourth Gospel: Narrative Mode and Theological Claim*, Philadelphia, Fortress Press, 1986, p. 70

[63] Zane C. HODGES, "Problem Passages in the Gospel of John—Part 3: Water and Spirit—John 3:5", *Bibliotheca Sacra* 135 (1978) 206-220. Ezekiel speaks of an eschatological cleansing and renewal by God's Spirit that refers to the Jewish people. The context suggests a national revival of Israel. And, whatever applied to the nation of Israel necessarily applies to individuals of that nation. Cf. Ez 36:25, Is 44:3-4; Joel 2:28. Therefore, it is quite possible that "born of water and Spirit" is signalling a new begetting or birth that cleanses and purifies Jewish nationals. If John's readers were primarily, though not exclusively, Jews (cf., Jn 20:30-31 where his overarching purpose may very well be to identify Jesus as

the Messiah), then this reading of the dialogue between Jesus and Nicodemus would not only have been an effective evangelistic maneuver to the Jews, but also the communication of a hope realized, viz., the fulfilment of God's Old Testament promises anticipated in the spiritual renewal of his chosen people. This hope had never been fully understood nor realized before in Jewish history. But now, through faith in Jesus the Messiah, hope becomes reality. On the one hand, John is saying an individual's Jewish credentials were unimportant to this spiritual renewal. Yet, on the other hand, John intimates one's Jewish credentials significantly enhance this spiritual renewal, in that God faithfully and fully completes the promises he makes to his specially chosen people.

[64] See, Linda L. BELLEVILLE, "Born of Water and Spirit: John 3:5", *Trinity Journal* 1.2 (1980) 125-141. See also, G. JOHNSTON, *The Spirit-Paraclete in the Gospel of John*, Society of New Testament Studies Monograph Series 12, Cambridge, Cambridge University Press, 1970; James SWETNAM, "The Bestowal of the Spirit in the Fourth Gospel", *Biblica* 74 (1993) 556-576. Cf. P. JULIAN, *Jesus and Nicodemus, A Literary and Narrative Exegesis of Jn. 2,23–3,36*, European University Studies, Series XXIII Theology 711, Frankfurt am Main etc., 2000, p. 66; WAI- YEE NG, *Water Symbolism in John. An Eschatological Interpretation*, *Studies in Biblical Literature* 15, New York, 2001, pp. 78-81; D. A. LEE, *The Symbolic Narratives of the Fourth Gospel, The Interplay of Form and Meaning*, JSNTSS 95, Sheffield, 1994, pp. 170. 179; U. SCHNELLE, *Antidoketische Christologie im Johannesevangelium. Eine Untersuchung zur Stellung des vierten Evangeliums in der johanneischen Schule*, FRLANT 144, Göttingen, 1987, p. 201; see also U. SCHNELLE, *Das Evangelium nach Johannes*, THNT 4, Leipzig, 2000, p. 69; W. C. GREESE, "'Unless One is Born Again': The Use of a Heavenly Journey in John 3", *JBL* 107 (1988) 677-693, p. 689 similarly speaks of "becoming like Christ". The replacement of "born a!nwqen" by "born of water and Spirit" militates against the meaning "born again", since "born of water and Spirit" implies more than a second physical birth. Thus also T. G. BROWN, *Spirit in the Writings of John*, JSNTSS 253, London – New York, 2003, p. 119. According to Cornelis Bennema, the metaphorical birth of water-and-Spirit denotes the cleansing and transformation of people by means of the Spirit, which is based on a Spirit-provided understanding of the significance of Jesus' revelation culminating on the cross. Second, the "living water" that Jesus offers denotes the cleansing and life-giving qualities of Jesus' Spirit-imbued revelation. Third, according to John 3 and 6, Jesus' revelatory teaching is life-giving if its significance is understood, which is possible because the Spirit is actively reaching out to people through Jesus' teaching and revealing to people the significance of Jesus' revelation, especially the event on the cross. Cf. Cornelis BENNEMA, *Spirit Baptism in the Fourth Gospel, A Messianic Reading of John 1, 33*, *Biblica* 84 (2003) 35-60, pp. 53-56; T. G. BROWN, *Spirit in the Writings of John*, JSNTSS 253, London – New York, 2003, p. 119. OT expectations of spiritual renewal in terms

of water and Spirit (e.g. Ez 36: 25-27; Zech 13: 1; Joel 3: 1-2) accord with the narrative itself. In a narrative perspective it hardly makes sense for Jesus to blame Nicodemus for not understanding a rite that never appears in the story. From a narrative perspective the question of baptism has been overemphasized in the exegesis of birth. See, O. HOFIUS, "Das Wunder der Wiedergeburt, Jesu Gespräch mit Nicodemus Joh 3,1-21", *Johannesstudien,* Untersuchungen zur Theologie des vierten Evangeliums, (eds.) O. HOFIUS & H-C. KAMMLER, Tübingen (1996) 33-80, esp. 41-43.

[65] Cf. W. A. MEEKS, "The Man from Heaven in Johannine Sectarianism", *JBL* 91 (1972) 44-72, esp. 60-63; G. C. NICHOLSON, *Death as Departure,* The Johannine Descent-Ascent Schema, SBLDS

63, Chico, CA, 1983, pp. 10-12, 21-23. The Fourth Gospel envisages the time after Jesus' departure to be a continuation of Jesus' earthly ministry, in that there is a strong continuity between Jesus' earthly mission and the mission of the Paraclete and the disciples. First, the Paraclete is modelled on Jesus and will take over Jesus' functions after his departure (14:16). Second, as a revelatory Teacher, the Paraclete will enable the disciples to recall Jesus' revelatory words/ teaching and reveal to them their meaning and significance (14:26; 16:12-15), which will inform and prepare the disciples' witness to the world (15:26-27). Third, connecting 16:8-11 with 16:12-15, the Paraclete will convict the world of sin, righteousness and judgement precisely by revealing and teaching the significance of Jesus' historical revelation to and through the disciples because the world cannot see or know the Paraclete (14:17). The Paraclete's conviction of the world, on the basis of the proclamation of Jesus' words through the disciples, also results in either salvation or judgement, dependent on whether one accepts or rejects the correlated witness of the Paraclete and the disciples (15:18 – 16:4; 16:8-11; 17:14.20). Fourth, Jesus' mission is paradigmatic for the mission of the disciples (17:18; 20:21). Cf. D. A. CARSON, "The Function of the Paraclete in John 16:7-11", *JBL 98* (1979) 547-66.

[66] D. A. CARSON, "Understanding Misunderstandings in the Fourth Gospel", *Tyndale Bulletin* 33 (1982) 59-89.

[67] Cf. Kelli S. O'BRIEN, "Written That You May Believe: John 20 and Narrative Rhetoric", *Catholic Biblical Quarterly,* April 2005.

[68] Cf. F. F. BRUCE, *The Gospel of John,* Grand Rapids, Eerdmans, 1983, p. 84; Cf. Karl Olav SANDNES, "Whence and Wither, A Narrative Perspective on Birth a! nwqen (Jn 3. 3-8)", *Biblica* 85 (2004) 153-173; Read also, Barnabas LINDARS, "Word and Sacraments in the Fourth Gospel", *Scottish Journal of Theology* 29 (1976) 49.

[69] Cf. D. SPRIGGS, "Meaning of 'Water' in John 3:5", *Expository Times* 85 (1974) 149-150; M. PAMMENT, "John 3:5: 'Unless One Is Born of Water and the Spirit, He Cannot Enter the Kingdom of God'", *Novum Testamentum* 25 (1983) 190. Nicodemus, it seems, understood the teachings of Jesus the other

way, which explains his reply, "How can a man be born when he is old? He can not enter his mother's womb a second time and be born, can he?" John the Evangelist often uses the technique of the "misunderstood question" to bring out a particularly important point: Jesus says something which is misunderstood by the disciples or as here by Nicodemus, which then gives Jesus the opportunity to explain more fully and in more detail what he really meant. A number of modern exegetes insist that *anothen* should be translated as born "from above." They base their interpretation either on the sacramental practice of the early church or on the biblical theology of John regarding Jesus' origin. See, Linda BELLEVILLE, "Born of Water and Spirit: John 3:5", *Trinity Journal* [N.S.] 1 (1980) 138, n. 75. Belleville clearly shows that this makes no sense at the textual level. Ben Witherington in his, "The Waters of Birth: John 3.5 and I John 5.6-8", summarizes the arguments from Old Testament and comparative literature. See also Merrill C. TENNEY, "Literary Keys to the Fourth Gospel: The Imagery of John", *Bibliotheca Sacra* 121 (Jan. 1964) 13-21; R. FOWLER, "Born of Water and the Spirit (Jn. 3:5)", *Expository Times* 82 (1971) 159.

[70] M. DE JONGE, "Nicodemus and Jesus: Some Observations on Misunderstanding and Understanding in the Fourth Gospel", *Bulletin of the John Rylands Library* 53 (1971) 337-359. To read more, L. L. BELLEVILLE, "Born of Water and Spirit: John 3:5", Trinity Journal (1981) 125-141. C. K. Barrett in his St John's "Literary formula of enlightenment through initial misunderstanding", points out that Nicodemus learns that being born *anothen* does not mean literally re- entering his mother's womb and the Samaritan woman comes to realize that "living water" is not merely a matter of unending physical sustenance. The dialogue between Jesus and Nicodemus stands in marked contrast to Jesus' compassionate treatment of the Samaritan woman. Cf. C. L. BLOMBERG, "The Globalization of Biblical Interpretation: A Test Case—John 3–4", *BBR* 5 (1995) 1–15.

[71] Charles H. GIBLIN, "Suggestion, Negative Response and Positive Action in St. John's Portrayal of Jesus (John 2.1-11; 4.46-54; 7.2-14; 11.1-44)", *New Testament Studies* 26 (1980) 197-211. Nicodemus might have seen the signs even before he came to Jesus. But for Nicodemus, all the signs might only mean that Jesus is a great teacher sent from God. His approach to Jesus is well-intentioned but seems to be theologically inadequate. He rather seems to have failed to grasp the messianic implications of the sign-miracles. Read, Donald GUTHRIE, *"The Importance of Signs in the Fourth Gospel"*, *Vox evangelica* 5 (1967) 72-83; Gilbert VAN BELLE, *The Signs Source of the Fourth Gospel, Historical Survey and Critical Evaluation of the Semeia Hypothesis*, Leuven, Louvain University Press and Peeters, 1994.

[72] A. J. KÖSTENBERGER, *Studies on John and Gender*, p. 78. In pp. 82-84, Köstenberger demonstrates how Jesus interpreted the Hebrew Scripture and how he exceeds his Jewish counterparts. See also, Michael D. GOULDER, "Nicodemus", *Scottish Journal of Theology* 44 (1991) 153ff.

[73] G. VERMES, *The Changing Faces of Jesus*, p. 26. Read also, Stephen J. CASSELLI, "Jesus as Eschatological Torah", *Trinity Journal* 18.1 (1997) 15-41; Jey J. KANAGARAJ, "The Implied Ethics of the Fourth Gospel: A Reinterpretation of the Decalogue", *Tyndale Bulletin* 52.1 (2001) 33-60.

[74] See, A. J. KÖSTENBERGER, *Studies on John and Gender*, p. 77.

[75] M. SCOTT, *Sophia and the Johannine Jesus*, p. 152.

[76] F. Peter COTTERELL, "The Nicodemus Conversation: A Fresh Appraisal", *Expository Times* 96 (1985) 237-242. Nicodemus seeks Jesus out surreptitiously in the dead of the night. Even though no explanation for the timing of the interview is given by the Evangelist, in this conversation, the timing here in John is significant in terms of the light/darkness motif. Cf. Jn 9:4, 11:10, 13:30, 19:39, and 21:3. Out of the darkness, Nicodemus came to the Light of the World. See J. H. CHARLESWORTH, "*A Critical Comparison of the Dualism in 1QS 3:13-4:26 and the 'Dualism' Contained in the Gospel of John*", in *John and the Dead Sea Scrolls*, ed. J. H. CHARLESWORTH, New York, Crossroad, 1990. Cf. Zane C. HODGES, "*Problem Passages in the Gospel of John—Part 3: Water and Spirit—John 3:5*", *Bibliotheca Sacra* 135 (1978) 206-220.

[77] G. VERMES, *The Changing Faces of Jesus*, p. 26.

[78] *Ibid.*

[79] R. BROWN, *The Gospel According to John*, p. 176.

[80] A. J. KÖSTENBERGER, *Studies on John and Gender*, p. 78. Here, the getting of food for their Rabbi on the part of the disciples, and addressing Jesus as ῥαββί, is consistent with the pattern of a typical ῥαββί disciple relationship. Their getting food for him as well as questioning their teacher's talking with a Samaritan woman are entirely consistent with the pattern of Jewish teacher-disciple relationships.

[81] See, Kevin J. VANHOOZER, "Worship at the Well: From Dogmatics to Doxology (and Back Again)", *Trinity Journal* 23.1 (2002) 3-16. The Samaritan woman calls Jesus κύριος. The author of the Fourth Gospel presents Jesus as ῥαββί a total of eight times. Another important title that is given to the Johannine Jesus is κύριος. Later in this chapter the word κύριος will be compared with ῥαββί. Κύριος is translated "sir" in the NIV and NASB versions; Cf. Jn 4:11, 15, 19. If it is true that Samaritans at that time addressed God as Rabbi, the woman may have wanted to avoid any such connotation with regard to Jesus, at least early in the conversation. Cf. LOHSE, ῥαββί, p. 961, referring also to G. DALMAN, Die *Worte Jesu*, p. 275

[82] Cf. D. DAUBE, "Jesus and the Samaritan Woman", *Journal of Biblical Literature* 69 (1950) 137-47; R. D. POTTER, "Topology and Archaeology in the Fourth Gospel", in *Studia Evangelica* 1, *Texte und Untersuchungen zur Geschichte der altchristlichen Literatur* 73, Berlin, Akademie-Verlag, 1959, pp. 329-337; R. J. BULL, "An Archaeological Context for Understanding John

4:20", *Biblical Archaeologist* 38 (1975) 54-59. Samaritans are descendants of two groups. One is the remnant of native Israelites who were not deported after the fall of the Northern Kingdom in 722 BC and the other is foreign colonists brought in from Babylonia and Media by the Assyrian conquerors to settle the land with inhabitants who would be loyal to Assyria. There was theological opposition between the Samaritans and the Jews because the former refused to worship in Jerusalem. After the exile the Samaritans put obstacles in the way of the Jewish restoration of Jerusalem, and in the 2nd century BC the Samaritans helped the Syrians in their wars against the Jews. In 128 BC the Jewish high priest retaliated and burned the Samaritan temple on Mount Gerazim. See, M. PAMMEL, "Is There Convincing Evidence of Samaritan Influence on the Fourth Gospel", *ZNW* 73 (1982) 221–230, esp. p. 223. From a Jewish point of view shared by the Johannine Jesus, the Samaritans were ignorant as late-born servants of God, whereas the Jews worshipped the true God right from the beginning. They are the original recipients of God's statutes and laws, and all of God's promises were made for them. As the bearers of God's promises they have the knowledge of what they worship. If interpreted in this way, Jesus' words to the Samaritan woman are genuinely Johannine, as noted by Ferdinand Hahn. See Ferdinand HAHN, "'Das Heil Kommt von den Juden': Erwägungen zu Joh 4.22b", *Die Verwurzelung des Christentums im Judentum: Exegetische Beiträge zum christlich- jüdischen Gespräch*, Neukirchen-Vluyn: Neukirchener Verlag, 1996, pp. 99–118, esp. p. 115. According to the Johannine view, Jesus should be the fulfilment of the knowledge the Jews have; the scriptures of the Jews point to him, although the Jews in Jesus' time do not understand this (cf. 5:36–47; 8:37–59). Thus Jesus' words that the Jews "know what they worship for salvation is from the Jews" have to do more with the Jews as the historical people of God than with the unbelieving and even hostile contemporaries of Jesus. Cf. I. DE LA POTTERIE, "Histoire de l'exégèse", p. 92. From the Johannine point of view, the Jews are privileged as the people of God compared to the Samaritans and other non-Jews, but they may lose their privileged position. If they do not accept Jesus as their Messiah, they miss the hour of salvation that has already come with Jesus. Cf. F. HAHN, "Das Heil", p. 116. See, LEIDIG, *Jesu Gespräch*, p. 119; Cf. B. OLSSON *Structure and Meaning in the Fourth Gospel: A Text-Linguistic Analysis of John 2:1–11 and 4:1–42*, ConNT 6, Lund, CWK Kleerup, 1974, p. 187; J. E. BOTHA, *Jesus and the Samaritan Woman: A Speech Act Reading of John 4:1–42,* NovTSup 65, Leiden, E. J. Brill, 1991, pp. 146–147.

[83] Franz MUSSNER, *Tractate on the Jews: The Significance of Judaism for Christian Faith*, Philadelphia and London, Fortress Press and SPCK, 1984, pp. 26–28.

[84] Hartwig THYEN, "Das Heil kommt von den Juden", *Kirche: Festschrift für Günther Bornkamm zum 75, Geburtstag,* (eds.) D. LÜHRMANN and G. STRECKER, Tübingen, Mohr-Siebeck, 1980, pp. 163–184, esp. pp. 169–170.

[85] *Ibid., p. 183.*

[86] Thomas SÖDING, "Was kann aus Nazareth schon gutes kommen?' (J o h 1 . 4 6) , Die Bedeutung des Judeseins Jesu im Johannesevangelium", *NTS* 46 (2000) 21–41, esp. pp. 39–40.

[87] J. E. BOTHA, *Jesus and the Samaritan Woman: A Speech Act Reading of John 4:1–42,* NovTSup 65, Leiden, E. J. Brill, 1991, pp. 146–147. See also, J. BLIGH, "Jesus in Samaria", *Heythrop Journal* 3 (1962) 329-346; J. BOWMAN, "Early Samaritan Eschatology", *Journal of Jewish Studies* 6 (1955) 63-72; J. BOWMAN, "Samaritan Studies", *Bulletin of the John Rylands Library* 40 (1957/58) 298-329. Jesus' attitude towards the Samaritans in John is well in line with 2 Kgs 17:24–41, according to which the Samaritans practised syncretism. This view was also expressed in later Jewish tradition according to which the Samaritans were ignorant (Cf. *Sir* 50:26 speaks of "the foolish people that dwell in Shechem") and liable to syncretism. In *Ant.* XII, 257–264, Josephus tells how during the persecutions of Antiochus Epiphanes the Samaritans approached Antiochus and denied their kinship with the Jews and wanted their unnamed temple to be known as that of Zeus Hellenios. From the point of view of Josephus, the action of the Samaritans was dubious and totally unacceptable to any true Jew. See R. J. COGGINS, "The Samaritans in Josephus," in *Josephus, Judaism, and Christianity*, (eds.) L. H. FELDMAN and G. HATA, Leiden, E. J. Brill, 1987, pp. 257–273, esp. pp. 265–266. According to Coggins, Josephus emphasized the culpability of the Samaritans on purpose. According to 2 Mac 6:2, the dedication of the temple on Mt. Gerizim was to Zeus Xenios. This title meant "the protector of the rights of the strangers" and was probably less offensive than the one mentioned by Josephus. See also J. A. GOLDSTEIN, *II Maccabees*, AB 41a, Garden City, New York, Doubleday, 1983, p. 272. Goldstein notes that the naming of the temple would have been inconsequential to most of the Jews; different Hellenistic designations for God were not alien to the Jews of the second century BCE. See J. A. GOLDSTEIN, *I Maccabees*, AB 41, Garden City, New York, Doubleday, Goldstein 1976, pp. 137, 142.

[88] Although Josephus implies that there were syncrenistic tendencies among the Samaritans in the second century B.C, he is not able to present any clear evidence of these tendencies in his own time. It is not until in post-tannaitic rabbinic tradition that the explicit accusation that the Samaritans practised idolatry is encountered. Rabbis took as their starting point the story that tells how Jacob hid all the images of the foreign gods in his family under the oak near Shechem (Gen 35:4); according to them, the Samaritans lusted for these images and, therefore, regarded Mt. Gerizim as their holy place. See *Gen. Rab.* 81; *y. Abod. Zar.* 5:4. It should be noted that this view does not correspond to the nature of the Samaritan religion in the first centuries A.D. In spite of his anti-Samaritan feelings, Josephus is not able to mention any examples of the Samaritans serving other gods than "the most high God." B. HALL, *Samaritan Religion*, p. 166. According to Hall, it is "quite unlikely that Josephus ... believed that the worship of any other god than "the most high God" existed among the

Samaritans of the first century AD, for had he believed that such worship existed, he would almost certainly … have made a statement to this effect." See also F. DEXINGER, "Limits of Tolerance in Judaism: The Samaritan Example", *Jewish and Christian Self-Definition, vol 2: Aspects of Judaism in the Graeco-Roman Period*, eds. E. P. SANDERS, A. I. BAUMGARTEN and Alan MENDELSON, Philadelphia, Fortress Press, 1981, pp. 88–114, esp. p. 106: "The Samaritans of his (Josephus') time were definitely not syncretists." It is interesting also that earlier rabbinic traditions represented in the Mishnah do not mention any idolatry among the Samaritans. Cf. HALL, *Samaritan Religion*, p. 208. Hall notes that the Samaritans do not receive a single mention in the tractate devoted to idolatry (*Aboda Zara*), although this is what one would expect had the practise of idolatry existed among the Samaritans of Palestine. It seems, therefore, that the implicit reference of the Johannine Jesus to idolatrous tendencies among the Samaritans is based more on a reading of 2 Kgs 17:24–41 than on the religion of the Samaritans in the first century CE. From the point of view of mainstream Judaism, the Samaritans were late-comers as the worshippers of the God of Israel; therefore, they lacked the right knowledge of what they worshipped. Cf. D. R. HALL, "The Meaning of *synchraomai* in John 4:9", *Expository Times* 83 (1971/72) 56-57; I. H., MARSHALL, "The Problem of New Testament Exegesis [John 4:1-45]", *Journal of the Evangelical Theological Society* 17 (1974) 67-73; T. OKURE, *The Johannine Approach to Mission: A Contextual Study of John 4:1–42*, WUNT 31, Tübingen, Mohr-Siebeck, 1988, p. 109.

[89] P. J. CAHILL, "Narrative Art in John IV", *Religious Studies Bulletin* 2 (1982) 41-48; C. R. KOESTER, "'The Savior of the World' (John 4:42)", *JBL* 109 (1990) 665–680, esp. pp. 672–673; ODEBERG, *The Fourth Gospel*, pp. 170–71; OLSSON, *Structure and Meaning*, p. 197. Jesus' words about the Jews who know what they worship should be understood in light of what he says of the ignorance of the Samaritans. Jesus' words that the Samaritans do not know what they worship reflect a Jewish anti-Samaritan tradition that is based on a reading of 2 Kgs 17:24–41. This passage tells how the nations that were brought to Samaria and that were later identified with the Samaritans did not at first fear the Lord, and so the Lord punished them (v. 25). Cf. Ignace DE LA POTTERIE, "'*Nous adorons, nous, ce que nous connaissons, car le salut vient des Juifs'*, Histoire de l'exégèse et interprétation de Jn 4, 22*", *Bib* 64 (1983) 74–115, esp. p. 96 n. 37; O. BETZ, "To Worship", p. 423. The words in 2 Kings, "they do not know the statutes of the law of the god of the land" (vv. 17-26) come very close to the words of Jesus in John, "you do not know what you worship" I. DE LA POTTERIE, "Histoire de l'exégèse," p. 96. In the scriptural story, the new residents in Samaria are instructed how to fear the Lord. They indeed begin to worship the God of Israel but, at the same time, continue to make their own gods and serve them. The Samaritans are thus presented as worshipping both the Lord and their own gods which means, from a Jewish point of view, that they have not understood what it means to worship the only God of Israel. In John, this is expressed by the words "you worship what you do not know."

This formulation also recalls those scriptural passages that speak of gentiles who do not know the God of Israel. Jesus' words in John, therefore, contain an implicit reference to the idolatrous tendencies among the Samaritans. B. HALL, *Samaritan Religion from John Hyrcanus to Baba Rabba: A Critical Examination of the Relevant Material in Contemporary Christian Literature, the Writings of Josephus, and the Mishnah*, Studies in Judaica 3, Sydney, Mandelbaum Trust, University of Sydney, 1987, p. 232. According to Hall, Jn 4:21–22 in no way suggests that the worship of any other gods than the God of Israel existed among the Samaritans. Hall is quite right in denying the worship of idols among the first century Samaritans, but this is no ground for saying that John does not refer to syncretism among the Samaritans. What John writes about the ignorant Samaritans reflects rather the scriptural story than the contemporary situation of the Samaritans. See J. A. T. ROBINSON, "The 'Others' of John 4, 38: A Test of Exegetical Method", *Studia Evangelica* 1, *Texte und Untersuchungen zur Geschichte der altchristlichen Literatur* 73, Berlin, Akademie-Verlag, 1959, pp. 510-515; See, C. KOESTER, *The Saviour of the World*, p. 674.

[90] M. SCOTT, *Sophia and the Johannine Jesus*, p. 152.

[91] A. J. KÖSTENBERGER, *Studies on John and Gender*, p. 79. For Köstenberger, the address of Jesus as ῥαββί in 6:25 is significant because it is issued by the crowds. The timing, shortly after the feeding of the multitude, is important as well, since it balances the passage in 6:14–15 where Jesus, on account of his messianic sign, is called "the Prophet" and some intend to make him king. The passage makes clear that the Jewish crowds continued to perceive Jesus first and foremost as a religious teacher, albeit one who performed remarkable feats and who taught with unusual authority. Cf. Paul W. BARNETT, "The Feeding of the Multitude in Mark 6/John 6", David WENHAM & Craig BLOMBERG, eds., *Gospel Perspectives*, Vol. 6., Sheffield, JSOT Press, 1986, pp. 273-293; David GIBSON, "Eating is Believing? On Midrash and the Mixing of Metaphors in John 6", *Themelios* 27.2 (2002) 5-15.

[92] *Ibid.*, p. 79. Köstenberger states that the disciples' interrogation of Jesus with regard to the cause of a man's blindness in 9:2 while addressing their master as ῥαββί fits into the pattern which by now has become a familiar one for the reader of John's Gospel (cf. 1:38, 49; 4:31). The closeness of their relationship and its purpose of providing a framework for religious instruction allow Jesus' followers to inquire regarding a matter that puzzled them. As they accompanied their master and associated closely with him, teachable moments often arose that allowed a teacher to impart his knowledge and insight to his disciples.

[93] *Ibid.*, p. 80. In Jn 4:31, the disciples urge their master to eat, knowing that he had not had food for an extended period of time. As a characteristic feature of first-century Jewish disciples, in 11:8, Jesus' disciples fear for their master's life. When Jesus insists that he must go, Thomas, reflecting genuine concern, remarks to his fellow disciples, "Let us also go, that we may die with him" (11:16).

[94] *Ibid.*, p. 80.

[95] G. DALMAN, Die *Worte Jesu*, p. 340.

[96] A. KÖSTENBERGER, *Studies on John and Gender*, p. 76.

[97] H. LAPIN, *Rabbi*, p. 602.

[98] In the Fourth Gospel, the following passages testify how rich the Gospel is in its perspective of women. In these passages, the roles of women genuinely coincide with the purpose and interest of the author of the Gospel and the Johannine community in its view of women proclaimers. Jn 2:1-12 (Mother of Jesus at the wedding feast at Cana); 4:4-42 (the Samaritan woman in dialogue with Jesus); 11:1-44 (Martha and Mary with Jesus); 12:1-8 (Jesus at the house of Mary and Martha at Bethany); 19:25-27 (the mother of Jesus, her sister Mary the wife of Clopas, and Mary of Magdala at the foot of the Cross); 20:1-18 (Mary Magdalene on the day of Resurrection).

[99] T. K. SEIM, *Roles of Women in the Gospel of John*, in Lars Hartman & Birger Olsson (ed.), *Aspects on the Johannine Literature* (Papers presented at a conference of Scandinavian New Testament Exegetes at Uppsala June 16-19, 1986, CB New Testament Series 18, Almqvist and Wiksell International, (1987) 56-70, p. 57.

[100] *Ibid.*, p. 59.

[101] According to the Fourth Gospel, this was the only occasion before his passion in which Jesus explicitly discloses that he was the Christ. Here the concern is with Jesus' relationship with women, but it is surely significant that he discloses this to a woman, whose testimony is later supported by others, both men and women.

[102] T. K. SEIM, *Roles of Women in the Gospel of John*, p. 59.

[103] It is certainly significant that no woman is rejected and condemned by Jesus. He condemns and rejects the scribes and the Pharisees in harsh words, but not the Sinful Woman, for whom he has words of pardon and peace. Though the reliability of this account has been questioned, it serves as a perfect expression of Jesus' way of looking at women and opting for their liberation. Jesus challenges the woman's accusers to execute their death sentence if they can justify themselves as having never committed a sin. The attitude of Jesus and his response to this sinful act is astonishing. There is no condemnation, only a warning.

[104] Leon MORRIS, *The Gospel According to John*, *The New International Commentary on the New Testament*, Michigan, Eerdmans Publishing Co., 1971, pp. 836-837.

[105] U. E. EISEN, *Women office holders in Early Christianity: Epigraphical and Literary Studies*, trans. Linda M. MALONEY, Collegeville MN, Liturgical Press, 2000, p. 50.

[106] R. J. KARRIS, *Jesus and the Marginalized in St. John's Gospel*, Collegeville, Liturgical Press, 1990, pp. 75-8. The reality was that the Johannine community itself had its involvement with Samaritans and women in ministry and service.

Service and ministry of the women were in practice in the Johannine church. It is also possible that the relationship with the Samaritans and the role of the women in the Johannine church might have brought a tension between the Christians in Galilee and the apostolic Christians in Jerusalem. John includes many narratives which feature women, incidentally and intentionally, and that would have affected a scandal in rabbinical circles.

[107] J. L. MCKENZIE, *Dictionary of the Bible*, New York-London, Macmillan, 1965, pp. 551-3. According to Mckenzie, the seven women listed in the NT are Mary, the mother of Jesus, Mary Magdalene, Mary the sister of Martha and Lazarus (Lk 10:39-42, Jn 11; 12:1-8), Mary, the mother of James and Joses (Mk 15:40.47; 16:1; Lk 24:10), Mary, the wife of Clopas (Jn 19:25), Mary the mother of John Mark (Ac 12:2), Mary, a woman who worked hard in Rome (Rom 16: 6).

[108] G. M. ALEXANDER, *The Handbook of Biblical Personalities*, New York, NY, Seabury Press, 1981, pp. 186-8. Mary, the mother of Jesus is mentioned in Mt 1:16, 18-24; 2:11; 13:55; Mk 6:3; Lk 1:26-2:34; Jn 2:1-12; Ac 1:14. The other Mary, the mother of James the less and Joses, is a follower of Jesus from Galilee. She was probably the wife of Clopas, and probably one among the women at the foot of the cross and at the empty tomb Mt 27:56, 61; 28:1; Mk 15:40, 47; 16:1 Lk 24:10. Then comes Mary Magdalene Mt 27:56, 61; 28:1; Mk 15:40, 47; 16:1, 9; Lk 8:2; 24:10; Jn 19:25; 20:1, 11, 16, 18. She is identifies as Mary from whom seven demons had gone out. Then comes Mary of Bethany in Lk 10:38-42; Jn 11; 1-46; 12:1-11 who is said to be the Mary under the Lord's feet. Then there comes another Mary, the mother of John Mark, a Jewess of Jerusalem who is mentioned in Mk 14:51. It is probably at her house that, Jesus had the last supper with his disciples. Cf. Ac 12: 12-17.

[109] R. F. COLLINS, *These Things have been written. Studies on the Fourth Gospel*, *LTPM* 2, Louvain, Peeters, Eerdmans, 1990, p. 33.

[110] T. K. SEIM, *Roles of Women in the Gospel of John*, p. 59.

[111] G. M. ALEXANDER, *The Handbook of Biblical Personalities*, p. 187.

[112] In Mark's Gospel Mary Magdalene is named (Mk 15.40), then Mary, mother of James follows, and Salome, but these are joined by many others who came up with him to Jerusalem. So it is clear that they started accompanying Jesus and remained with him as his disciples from Galilee to Jerusalem. It is also evident that many women supported him out of their means and would not be drawn away from him even at the Passion. This is said expressly in the Gospel, which stresses their presence even at the Deposition of Jesus in the Tomb. When Mark speaks of them in the passion narratives, it underlines their faithfulness to Christ, even when the male disciples had abandoned him.

[113] See, Grant R. OSBORNE, "Women in Jesus' Ministry", *Westminster Theological Journal* 51.2 (1989) 259-291. The list of the women disciples seems to introduce the name of Mary Magdalene as one of the women disciples whose conversion is of so much of importance in Luke's view. Once Jesus had

welcomed her in his immense goodness, she could not stay away from him and so she began to follow and serve Jesus and his disciples. It is said that these women followed Jesus from Galilee. Luke gives some of their names as Joanna, wife to Chouza, Herod's steward, Susanna, and many others who helped Jesus and the Twelve.

[114] T. K. SEIM, *Roles of Women in the Gospel of John*, p. 56.

[115] R. E. BROWN, *The Community of the Beloved Disciple*, p. 190. From the fact that John and Matthew present the first appearance to a woman or women and the later appearances to the male apostles, probably reflect the fact that women did not serve as official preachers of the church.

[116] Nag Hammadi library was discovered in 1945 in the area of Nag Hammadi in Egypt. This library consists of 4th century Coptic manuscripts, which are copies of manuscripts originally written in Greek. These manuscripts belonged to Gnostic Christians.

[117] S. HASKINS, *Mary Magdalene: Myth and Metaphor*, p. 34.

[118] J. M. ROBINSON (Gen. Ed.), *The Nag Hammidi Library in English* (Revised Edition), San Francisco, CA, Harper & Row, 1988, pp. 526-527.

[119] *Ibid.*, p. 138. Similar examples of Peter being upstaged by Mary Magdalene occur in the Gospel of the Egyptians and Pistis Sophia, which are Gnostic documents found prior to the discovery of the Nag Hammadi Library.

[120] R. E. BROWN, *The Community of the Beloved Disciple*, pp. 154-155. He notes further that in the Gospel of Philip she has become the disciple whom Jesus loved most. As in the Gospel of Mary, Peter becomes jealous of Mary Magdalene. Furthermore, Brown argues that the Gnostics made Mary Magdalene into the Beloved Disciple in response to her portrayal in the Fourth Gospel.

[121] The Gospel of Philip makes reference to the same group of women that are standing by the cross in the Fourth Gospel. However, the Gospel of Philip clearly cites Mary Magdalene as the 'companion' of Jesus.

[122] J. M. ROBINSON, *The Nag Hammidi Library in English*, p. 148.

[123] R. E. BROWN, *The Community of the Beloved Disciple*, p. 154. In other words, Brown argues that what is in these Gospels is a reaction to what is written in the canonical Fourth Gospel with regard to the place of Mary Magdalene. For Brown, the writers of the Gnostic gospels were influenced by the Fourth Gospel where they find the portrait of Mary Magdalene as an extraordinary proclaimer of the Resurrected Christ.

[124] *Ibid.*, p. 154.

[125] R. E. BROWN, *The Community of the Beloved Disciple*, p. 19.

[126] J. ASHTON (ed.), *The Interpretation of John*, p. 236. The woman in the Hebrew society; characteristically the women in scripture are mostly portrayed as unwanted and downtrodden present a clear picture of women as inferiors. Women certainly were oppressed from the beginning and there was no liberation

for them even after the great Exodus event, which is said to be the epicentre of the OT history of salvation. They were marginalized in history. This is explicitly clear when certain narratives of the Gospel are analysed.

[127] T. K. SEIM, *Roles of Women in the Gospel of John*, p. 59.

[128] B. J. MALINA & R. L. ROHRBAUGH, *Social Science Commentary on the Gospel of John*, Minneapolis, Fortress, 1998, p. 288.

[129] W. HOWARD- BROOK, *Becoming Children of God: John's Gospel and Radical Discipleship*, Mary knoll, NY, Orbis, 1999, p. 475.

[130] R. F. COLLINS, *These Things have been written*, p. 35.

[131] See R. T. FRANCE, "Mark and the Teaching of Jesus", in *Gospel Perspectives: Studies of History and Tradition in the Four Gospels,* (ed.) R. T. FRANCE and D. WENHAM, Sheffield, JSOT, 1980, pp. 101–136; R. P. MEYE, *Jesus and the Twelve,* Grand Rapids, Eerdmans, 1968, pp. 30–87; E. F. SEIGMAN, "St. John's Use of the Synoptic Material", *Catholic Biblical Quarterly* 30 (1968) 182-198. Francis E. WILLIAMS, "The Fourth Gospel and the Synoptic Tradition: Two Johannine Passages", *Journal of Biblical Literature* 86 (1967) 311-319. R. P. MEYE, "Jesus as Preacher and Teacher", in *Jesus and the Oral Gospel Traditions*, ed. Henry WANSBOROUGH, Sheffield, JSOT, 1991, pp. 185–210. C. H. DODD, *"Jesus als Lehrer und Prophet"* in *Mysterium Christi: Christological Studies by British and German Theologians*, (ed.) G. K. A. BELL and A. DEISSMANN, London, Longmans & Green, 1930, pp. 67–86; E. FASCHER, *"Jesus der Lehrer"*, *TLZ* 79 (1954) 325–342; H. RIESENFELD, *The Gospel Tradition and its Beginnings. A Study in the Limits of "Formgeschichte",* London, Mowbray, 1957; and F. HAHN, *Christologische Hoheitstitel*, FRLANT 83, Göttingen, Vandenhoeck & Ruprecht, 1963, pp. 74–95; C. L. BLOMBERG, "Where Do We Start Studying Jesus?", in *Jesus Under Fire,* (ed.) M. J. WILKINS and J. P. MORELAND, Grand Rapids, Zondervan, 1995, pp. 30–36.

[132] A. KÖSTENBERGER, *Studies on John and Gender*, p. 94. In p. 87, Köstenberger observes that among other things, the role of rabbi entailed the provision for his disciples' various other needs and the protection of his disciples from false teaching and any harm. Cf. R. T. FRANCE, *Jesus and the Old Testament,* London, Tyndale, 1971, pp. 208–209; D. A. CARSON, *"John and Johannine Epistles,"* p. 255. Jesus' actions in the Upper Room thus dramatically run counter to contemporary Jewish convention: Jesus the teacher renders a service to his pupils rather than vice versa, and the specific task performed exceeds that from which even pupils in contemporary Judaism were exempt. Owing to its startling nature and the power of personal example, Jesus' "mystifying gesture" constitutes an extremely effective teaching method. As the Johannine Jesus remarks, "Do you know what I have done to you? You call me Teacher and Lord, and you are right, for so I am. If I then, the Lord and the Teacher, washed your feet, you also ought to wash one another's feet.

For I gave you an example that you also should do as I did to you. Truly, truly, I say to you, a slave is not greater than his master; neither is one who is sent greater than the one who sent him. If you know these things, you are blessed if you do them" (13:12b–17). Cf. Mt 10:24–25; Lk 6:40. Cf. the discussion by R. RIESNER, *Jesus als Lehrer*, pp. 256–259. Köstenberger, when he speaks about the teacher-pupil relationship between Jesus and his disciples in pp.88-89, observes the occasion of the disciples' commissioning and states that Jesus as the sent Son of the Father, modeled absolute dependence, obedience, and faithfulness to his sender (cf. e.g. 4:34; 5:23, 30, 36, 38; 6:38–39; 7:16, 18, 28; 8:26; 9:4; 12:44–45, 49; 13:20; 14:10b, 24).

[133] A. KÖSTENBERGER, *Studies on John and Gender*, pp. 86-87; Cf. M. M. THOMPSON, *Historical Jesus and Johannine Christ*, p. 41, n. 47. In accordance with contemporary Jewish belief, the presence of a messenger was equivalent to the presence of the sender himself (cf. 13:20.) See, BÜHNER, *Der Gesandte und sein Weg*, 209, n. 1. Cf. also Mt 10:40; Mk 9:37; Lk 10:16. How much more was this true if the one sent was the son, particularly the first-born son, of a Father. Cf. esp. A. E. HARVEY, *Christ as Agent, The Glory of the Christ*, in the *New Testament Studies in Christology in Memory of George Bradford Caird*, (ed.) L. D. HURST and N. T. WRIGHT, Oxford, Clarendon, 1987, pp. 239–250. At the occasion of the disciples' commissioning, Jesus charged his followers to emulate the same characteristics he had displayed during his earthly sojourn as the paradigmatic Sent One: "As the Father has sent me, I also send you" (20:21; cf. 9:7). Generally, Jesus and his disciples share a relationship characterized by openness that allows Jesus' followers to inquire regarding the significance of their teacher's actions or even to challenge him. An example of this is Peter's initial refusal to permit Jesus to wash his feet in the upper room (13:6–10). Throughout the Farewell Discourse, the disciples address various questions to their teacher whenever they fail to grasp an aspect of his teaching (Peter: 13:36–38; Thomas: 14:5; Philip: 14:8; and Judas, not Iscariot: 14:22). This coheres with contemporary Jewish practice. As Aberbach notes, "Students would not hesitate to question their teacher when his actions seemed to contradict his teachings or when his behaviour appeared unseemly (cf. *m. Ber.* 2:6–7; *y. Sot.* 1:4)." Cf. ABERBACH, *Relations*, p. 20. *M. Ber.* 2:6–7 is attributed to Rabban Gamaliel (possibly, Paul's teacher: CE 30–40); *y. Sot.* 1:4 is attributed to R. Meir, student of R. Ishmael and R. Aqiba and among the third generation of Tannaites (ca. CE 130–160). Cf. Str-St 73, 83–84. Pupils were not supposed to ask questions irrelevant to the subject under discussion lest the teacher be put to shame (cf. *b. Shab.* 3b). In *b. Šhbb.* 3b, R. H. iyya is quoted as saying to Rab (both ca. CE 200), "When Rabbi is occupied with one tractate, do not ask him a question relating to another." It was the mark of a wise disciple to confine himself to relevant questions, while the uncultured *Golem* would do precisely the opposite. cf. *m. Abot.* 5:7, reads: There are seven marks of the clod and seven of the wise man. The wise man does not speak before one that is greater than he in wisdom; and he does not break in upon

the words of his fellow; and he is not hasty in making answer; he asks what is relevant and makes answer according to the *Halakah*; and he speaks on the first point first and on the last point last; and of what he has heard no tradition he says, 'I have not heard'; and he agrees to the other hand, students were not only permitted but encouraged to ask the master to explain whatever they had failed to grasp during the discourse. It was a well-known principle that "a shame-faced person cannot learn." Cf. also, *Der. Ez. Zut.*. 1:1–2 reads: "The characteristics of a scholar are that he is meek, humble, alert, filled [with a desire for learning], modest, beloved by all, humble to the members of his household and sin-fearing. He judges a man according to his deeds, and says 'I have no desire for all the things of this world because this world is not for me.' He sits and studies, soiling his cloak at the feet of the scholars. In him no one sees any evil. He questions according to the subject-matter and answers to the point. The style and content permit a date in the early Amoraic period (CE 250). Ginsberg notes that there may even have been an independent collection already in existence in the time of the Tannaim, as the book contains material "which is old and often quoted as Baraithoth (Tannaitic sayings outside the Mishnah) by the early authorities." See, M. GINSBERG, Der. Ez. Zut.. in *Hebrew-English Edition of the Babylonian Talmud: Minor Tractates*, ed. Abraham COHEN, London, Soncino, 1984.

[134] See, DAUBE, *NT and Rabbinic Judaism*, pp. 182–183. Daube cites the parallel of Yohanan ben Zakkai (CE 80), who sobbed on his death bed in order that his followers might inquire about the cause of his grief, thus providing the opportunity for an explanation. Similarly, Jesus performs the footwashing to teach his disciples about the need for mutual service. He gets up, girds his loins with a towel, and begins to wash the feet of his followers, a task commonly reserved in that day for household slaves. According to Jewish belief, "All manner of service that a slave must render to his master, the *pupil* must render to his *teacher*—except that of taking off his shoe" (*b.Ketub.* 96a). This saying is attributed to R. Joshua b. Levi (third century CE). Only a Canaanite slave performed this menial service, and a student performing it might be mistaken for such a slave. Cf. M. ABERBACH, *Relations Between Master and Disciple, Essays* presented to Chief Rabbi Israel Brodie, London, Soncino, 1967, p. 5.

[135] A. KÖSTENBERGER, *Studies on John and Gender*, pp. 88-90; Cf. R.

RIESNER, *Jesus as Preacher and Teacher*, p. 197; RENGSTORF, "ìáèçôç̀ð, êô̈ë.," pp. 444, 447. "Provide yourself with a teacher and get yourself a fellow-disciple" (*m. 'Abot* 1:6). Cf. E. LOHSE, *Rabbi*, p. 962; R. RIESNER, *Jesus als Lehrer*, p. 269.

[136] A. J. KÖSTENBERGER, *Studies on John and Gender*, p. 88. The word μαθητής occurs in the Fourth Gospel a total of seventy-eight times of which seventy-four are with reference to the followers of Jesus. Exceptionally, in three instances, the word μαθητής refers to the disciples of John the Baptist in Jn 1:35. 37; 3:25, while in 9:28, it refers to the disciples of Moses. A synoptic comparison of the term μαθητής shows that in Mt it is found 72 times, Mk 42

times and Luke 35 times. In Acts, it occurs 28 times. So, of 255 instances of
the occurrence of the word μαθητής both in the gospels and Acts, it is John that
has the most examples. In pp. 89-91, Köstenberger, in his *Studies on John and
Gender* observes how the disciples of a certain rabbi would often follow their
teacher wherever he went (*b. Ber.*23a,b, 24a, 60a; *b. Shab.* 12b, 108b, 112a; *b.
'Erub.* 30a; *b. Rosh Hash* 34b; *y. Mag.* 2:1; *y. B. Mes.* 2:3). *B. Ber.* 23a–b, 24a
mentions Rabbah b. Bar Hana (first- generation Amoraim; cf. Str-St 94) following
R. Yohanan (d. 279; Str- St 95) and Raba (d. 352) following R. Nahman (third-
generation Amoraim); *b. Ber.* 60a refers to a disciple following R. Ishmael son of
R. Jose; *b. Šabb.* 12b mentions Rabbah b. Bar Hanah (first generation Amoraim)
following R. Eleazar (130–160); *b. Shab.* 108b refers to Rabin walking behind R.
Jeremiah, and *b. Shab.* 112a to R. Jeremiah walking behind R. Abbahu (c. 309); *b.
'Erub.* 30a mentions Rabban b. Bar Hana (first-generation Amoraim) following R.
YohAnan (d. 279); *b. Rosh Hash.* 34b discusses R. Abbahu following R. Yohanan;
y. Hag. 2:1 refers to R. Eleazar ben Arakh walking behind Rabban Yoh. anan
ben Zakkai (c. CE 70; Eleazar ben Arakh is mentioned as one of Yohanan b.
Zakkai's five most important students); and *y. B. Mes.* 2:3 mentions someone
walking behind R. H. alafta (c. 330.) and Simeon walking behind R. Eleazar.
Köstenberger further comments on the earlier rabbinic method of learning. He
cites, "He who abases himself (i.e. exposes his ignorance by asking questions)
for the (sake of learning the) words of the Torah will eventually be exalted, but
he who muzzles himself (i.e. refrains from asking questions) will have to put his
hand to his mouth" (viz., when he, in turn, will be asked to answer questions;
b. Ber. 63b). This saying is attributed to R. Samuel bar Nahman, a third-
generation Amoraim (second half of third century CE). Students could also
argue freely with their teachers during discussions, which formed the essence
of instruction at all higher educational institutions; but they were expected to
do so not in a contentious spirit but reverently and with due restraint. This
open interchange did not diminish the disciples' respect for their teacher. Rather,
respect grew into love, loyalty, and deep devotion. As Aberbach continues, "In
spite of the extraordinary reverence in which rabbis were held by their students,
the relations between them were usually very close and far from formal. It was
. . . essentially a paternal filial relationship transcended and surpassed by the
intense love master and disciple bore to each other (*Cant. Rab.* 8:7; *b. Ber.*
5b; *b. Sanh.*101a)." *Cant. Rab.* was composed around CE 650–750; *b. Ber.* 5b is
placed at the death of R. Yohanan (d. CE 279); *b. Sanh.* 101a is attributed to
Rabban b. Bar Hana, a first-generation Amoraim (ca. CE 250). Citing the above
references, Köstenberger attempts to present the Johannine portrayal of Jesus as
a teacher with his group of disciples. For Köstenberger, John portrays Jesus'
disciples as accompanying their teacher at a large variety of occasions. They
lived with him (e.g., 1:39; 3:22). They joined him at a wedding together with his
mother and brothers (2:1–12; on Jesus' relationship with his brothers, see 7:1–10).
They were the witnesses and beneficiaries of his teaching. They accompanied
him when he healed the sick (4:43–54; 5:1–15; chaps. 9 and 11) and fed the

multitudes (6:1–13). In this, the Johannine portrayal concurs impressively with that of the Synoptics, where the disciples' major characteristic likewise is their "following" (ἀκολουθοῦντας) of Jesus, that is, their close fellowship with him. Cf. Anselm SCHULZ, *Nachfolgen und Nachahmen, Studien über das Verhältnis der neutestamentlichen Jüngerschaft zur urchristlichen Vorbildethik*, SANT VI, München, Kösel, 1962, p. 137. The word ἀκολουθέω is also used in John in 1:37, 38, 40, 43; 6:2; 8:12; 10:4, 5, 27; 11:31; 12:26; 13:36, 37; 18:15; 20:6; 21:19, 20, 22. Read, Scot MCKNIGHT, "Jesus and the Twelve", *Bulletin for Biblical Research* 11.2 (2001) 203-232.

[137] M. SCOTT, *Sophia and the Johannine Jesus*, p. 155. Scott classifies the Johannine concept of μαθητής into three categories of followers: 1. The μαθηταί who appear as a group at various points but whose role is never quite clearly defined. 2. The Beloved disciple, who appears only in the second half of the gospel from Ch.13 but holds a special position as a witness to the Jesus tradition. 3. The various individuals, mostly unnamed, specifically women who interact with Jesus more than any other category at the crucial Christological points or events in the gospel.

[138] A. J. KÖSTENBERGER, *Studies on John and Gender*, p. 88. In pp. 92-94, Köstenberger explains the duties of the disciples for their masters in the Jewish society and he compares that to the relations between Jesus and his disciples in the Fourth Gospel. One of the characteristics of Jesus' disciples according to the Fourth Gospel is their rendering of service to their teacher. They are sent to buy bread (4:8) and are asked to help provide food for the multitudes (6:5). At the feeding of the multitude, Jesus instructs them to have the people sit down, to distribute the food, and later to gather up leftovers (6:10, 12). In this, they conform to the customary pattern expected of disciples in their day. Shopping, together with the preparation and cooking of food and waiting at tables were considered duties of the followers of a rabbi (*y. Sheb.* 9:9; *Lam. Rab.* 3:17; *y.Ber.* 8:5; *t. Ber.* 6:4–5). Cf. ABERBACH, *Relations*, p. 21. *y. Sheb.* 9:9 contains Talmudic commentary on the Mishnaic tractate by the same name; among the teachers mentioned is R. Joshua b. Levi. *Lam. Rab.* was compiled ca. CE 450 (Str-St 310); among the rabbis listed is R. Yehudah ben Bathyra, dated either 20/30–90 or ca. 100–160 (Str-St 83); and *y. Ber.* 8:5 provides commentary on the dispute between the houses of Hillel and Shammai regarding the order of a meal. *t. Ber.* 6:4–5 is framed in terms of contrasting rulings of Hillel and Shammai (first century CE). Notably, as in the case of the foot washing, Jesus' preparing of breakfast for his disciples subsequent to his resurrection reverses the common pattern of teacher-disciple relationships in his day (21:9–13).

[139] As Aberbach notes, "The death of a teacher was a major disaster for his students. It was a matter of course for disciples to attend their master's funeral or even to bury him themselves" (cf. *y. Ber.* 3:1; *y.*Mo'ed Qat.. 3:5; b. Ber. 42b; b. Sanh. 68a; end of Semahot 11). See, ABERBACH, *Relations*, p. 21. The passage in *y. Ber.* 3:1 is attributed to R. Yannai the younger, grandson of R. Yannai "the

Elder," Yohanan's teacher, and R. Yose, one of the redactors of the Babylonian Talmud; *y. Mo'ed Qat.* 3:5 comments on the Mishnaic tractate *Mo'ed Qatan*, which deals with "lesser holy days" (cf. Str-St 127); *b. Ber.* 42b is placed at the death of Rab (d. CE 247; see Str-St 93); the passage in *b. Sanh.* 68a is attributed to the time of R. Aqiba (c. CE 135); and the end of *Semahot* 11 recounts the death of Rabban Gamaliel the Elder, Paul's teacher, and the words of his student and brother-in-law R. Eliezer (CE 90–130). Also, disciples were responsible to honor their deceased teacher by following his teaching closely. "After completing their course of studies, disciples were expected, as far as possible, to follow and propagate their master's teaching. The perfect scholar was one who... had 'fully absorbed his master's teaching' and 'was drawing on it to spread it abroad' (*b. Yoma* 28a)." Ibid., 18. The saying is attributed to R. Eleazar (CE 130–160). The reference is to R. Eleazar's explanation of Gen 24:2, where it is said that Eliezer, Abraham's servant, "ruled over all" his master had, which Eleazar takes to means that Eliezer ruled over [knew, controlled] the Torah of his master. The faithful witness borne by "the disciple whom Jesus loved" to his master's teaching in form of a written Gospel can be seen as a discharge of this responsibility. It is not possible here to discuss at length the degree to which Johannine style flavors the Fourth Gospel's presentation of Jesus' teachings. But note the interesting suggestion by Gerhardsson that John, by reproducing Jesus' statements in his [John's] own words rather than verbatim, may have followed a Hellenistic rather than Jewish approach. See, GERHARDSSON, *Memory & Manuscript*, p. 130; Cf. also D. A. CARSON, "Historical Tradition in the Fourth Gospel: After Dodd, What?", in *Gospel Perspectives II*, ed. R. T. FRANCE and D. WENHAM, Sheffield, JSOT, 1981, pp. 122–123.

[140] Cf. A. J. KÖSTENBERGER, *Studies on John and Gender*, pp. 93-94. Köstenberger observes that the fourth evangelist concludes, "This is the disciple who bears witness of these things, and wrote these things; and we know that his witness is true. And there are many other things which Jesus did, which if they were written in detail, I suppose that even the world itself would not contain the books which were written" (Jn 21:24–25). See, A. J. KÖSTENBERGER, The *Mission of Jesus and the Disciples according to the Fourth Gospel*, Grand Rapids, MI & Cambridge, UK, Eerdmans, 1998, pp. 158-161. Here he argues that the Fourth Gospel establishes an explicit link between the witnessing roles of Jesus and the "disciple whom Jesus loved" by the parallel phraseology of 1:18 and 13:25. By virtue of their close proximity to the fount of revelation (the Father or Jesus respectively), Jesus and the "disciple whom Jesus loved" are able to communicate to others the true meaning and inner substance of God's and Jesus' words. Jesus' word, in turn, is put by the fourth evangelist on the same level as Scripture in 2:22. Gerhardsson in his *Memory and Manuscript*, p. 330 comments in this regard, "They [apostolic eyewitnesses] taught in the name of their Master, and bore witness to the words and works of their Teacher in a way which recalled—at least formally— the witness borne by other Jewish

disciples to the words and actions of their teachers." Cf. REIM, *Targum und Johannesevangelium*, p. 10. This refers to *Tg. Isa* 53:8: "And the wondrous things that shall be wrought for us in his days who shall be able to recount?" cite the parallel in Rabban Yohanan b. Zakkai (c. CE 80). In pp. 95-96, Köstenberger observes the rabbinical images in the Johannine Farewell Discourses. The farewell discourse (Jn 13–16) is reminiscent of Moses' parting instructions to his fellow- Israelites regarding their imminent entrance into the Promised Land in Deuteronomy. Cf. A. LACOMARA, "Deuteronomy and the Farewell Discourse (Jn 13:31–16:33)", *CBQ* 36 (1974) 65–84. Jesus is here presented as the one who accomplishes God's giving of the Law through Moses (cf. 1:17). Thus he issues a "new commandment" for his disciples to love one another the way he loved them, that is, by giving his life for them (13:34–35; cf. 15:13). In the overall theological context of the Fourth Gospel, the discourse functions as one among several links between Israel, the old covenant community, and the followers of Jesus the Messiah, God's new covenant people. Cf. esp. J. W. PRYOR, *John: Evangelist of the Covenant People*, Downers Grove, IL, Intervarsity, 1992.

[141] R. F. COLLINS, *John and His Witness*, p. 45. On the first level of witnessing it is John the Baptist, whereas the later witnessing is by the disciples themselves. In the case of the first disciples, "they were referred by the Baptist, they came and stayed with Jesus and had convincing experience that he was the Messiah." See, F. JOHN, *The Vision of Discipleship*, p. 63. The author has presented the key words of hearing, following, seeing, staying and witnessing as the marks of the discipleship of Jesus. As Cullen I. K. Story quotes, the result of the stay of the first disciples with Jesus brought conviction and led them to the mission of witnessing. "Conviction, however was born out of that brief sojourn since Andrew, with no hesitation, not only informed his brother of their finding the Messiah but brought him to Jesus." See, Cullen I. K. STORY, *The Fourth Gospel, Its Pattern and Power*, Shippensburg PA, Ragged Edge Press, 1997, pp. 52-53.

[142] Craig R KOESTER, *Symbolism in the Fourth Gospel, Meaning Mystery Community*, Minneapolis, Fortress, 1995, p. 239. The image of discipleship given in this Gospel takes a different picture from that of the Jewish frame of law. Yet it is evident that the Johannine community also considered laws as indispensable to witness to Jesus (Jn 5:39). The Johannine discipleship invites the disciples to embrace the new law that is love. This love commandment, which has its root in Torah, is rightly interpreted and lived by Jesus.

[143] M. SCOTT, *Sophia and the Johannine Jesus*, p. 156. In the course of the final farewell, in Jn 15:16, Jesus makes this point clear that those who have been chosen by him are chosen only by his initiative.

[144] A. J. KÖSTENBERGER, The *Mission of Jesus and the Disciples according to the Fourth Gospel*, p. 144. In all these instances, the term μαθητής occurs in Jn not only for the immediate followers of Jesus but also in a wider perspective. Nevertheless, the term μαθητής also occurs in the Fourth Gospel in relation to the

disciples in a wider sense. (See, J n 1 : 3 5 . 3 7 ; 2 : 2 . 1 1 . 1 2 . 1 7 . 2 2 ; 3 : 2 2 . 2 5 ; 4 : 1 . 2 . 8 . 2 7 ; 6:3.8.12.16.22.24.60.61.66; 12:4.16; 13:5.22.23.35; 19:26.27.38). The term μαθητής occurs some 74 times with reference to followers of Jesus in every chapter but 5, 10, 14, and 17, the first instance being 2:2 at the wedding in Cana. The fact that the term occurs nowhere else in the New Testament outside of the Gospels and the book of Acts indicates that the early church tied the term inextricably to the historical followers of the earthly Jesus. This suggests that the term μαθητής is part and parcel of the teacher-disciple relationship Jesus had with his followers during his earthly ministry. Cf. RENGSTORF, "μαθητής", p. 442. Daube points out that the relationship of master and disciples was similar to that of parents and children. However, while the parent-child relationship was based on nature, the master-disciple relationship was a matter of choice. See, D. DAUBE, "Responsibilities of Master and Disciples in the Gospels", *NTS* 19 (1972–73) 3. Like family members, master and disciples had responsibilities, not just *to*, but also *for* one another in the outside world. This identification in the eyes of the world came into sharper focus toward the end of Jesus' ministry, when it became clear that his disciples would be held responsible for his teaching. Thus the Johannine Jesus prepares his disciples, "If the world hates you, you know that it has hated me before it hated you . . . Remember the word that I said to you, 'A slave is not greater than his master.' If they persecuted me, they will also persecute you . . . But all these things they will do to you for my name's sake, because they do not know the One who sent me" (15:18–21).

[145] Martin SCOTT, *Sophia and the Johannine Jesus*, JSNT 71, Sheffield, Sheffield Academic Press, 1992, p. 152.

[146] *Ibid.*

[147] Cornelis BENNEMA, *Spirit Baptism in the Fourth Gospel, A Messianic Reading of John 1, 33*, Biblica 84 (2003) 35-60, pp. 50-52. The 'acceptance' of Jesus' revelatory teaching in order to receive life/salvation is based on an adequate belief-response that recognizes and understands the true identity and work of the Father and Son, and their relationship. People, however, by themselves cannot come to such belief-response, and cannot "hear"/understand the words of Jesus/God because they do not know God and are not from God (1:18; 7:28; 8:19, 43, 47, 55; 16:3; 17:3). In short, some people are not from God and so unable of themselves to grasp the meaning and significance of Jesus' life-giving teaching because they lack understanding. The Spirit is, according to the Fourth Gospel, instrumental in the process of bringing people to understanding belief and hence salvation. First, those people who accept, i.e., believe in Jesus, are born from God (1: 12-13). Jn 3: 3-5 subsequently elucidates this birth from God as a birth from the Spirit, which alludes to the eschatological cleansing and transformation of Israel that God will bring about by means of his Spirit (Ez 36:25-27; 37: 1-14). This new birth is accomplished through looking in belief at the one lifted up on the cross (3:14-15). However, 3:9-13 points out that Nicodemus is not able to grasp Jesus' revelation and to respond in belief,

and implies that a birth of the Spirit is accomplished through some sort of understanding of Jesus' revelation, especially that of the cross. Second, the Spirit is actively reaching out to people through Jesus' teaching. In John 4, Jesus is depicted as the source of "living water" (4:10.14), which is a metaphor for Jesus' Spirit- imbued revelatory teaching that cleanses and purifies, and which leads to eternal life/salvation if it is accepted (4:41-42). In John 6, Jesus states that his words are life-and-Spirit (6:63), i.e., the Spirit gives life (6:63a) precisely in and through Jesus' life-giving words (6:63c). This coheres with the concept of the Spirit of truth in John 13-17. After Jesus' departure, the Spirit will mediate or reveal to people the life-giving truth present in Jesus' teaching (16:13), and, in fact, the disciples already "know", i.e., have experienced, this Spirit as such (14:17). In summary, the Spirit provides Jesus with revelatory wisdom and knowledge that is the basis for his revelatory teaching, which cleanses and gives life because it contains liberating and purifying truth/wisdom. People need to know God through an understanding and acceptance of Jesus' teaching, and subsequently become from God through a new birth. The Spirit functions in this process as the facilitator of true understanding, in that the Spirit mediates to people the life-giving truth present in Jesus' word so that people may come to true understanding and belief, and to a subsequent birth in the Spirit. Thus Jesus performs activities of revelation and cleansing (through his teaching) by means of the Spirit.

[148] Cf. C. BENNEMA, *Spirit Baptism in the Fourth Gospel,* pp. 53-56. Jesus' main activity in the Fourth Gospel is to provide Spirit-imbued revelatory teaching that cleanses and restores people, in that it brings life/salvation to those who accept Jesus and his revelation. To put it differently, Jesus cleanses and transforms people, and hence gives them eternal life through his revelatory teaching by means of the Spirit, in that the Spirit empowers Jesus and is active in and through Jesus' life- giving revelation. Jesus reveals God by means of his Spirit-imbued teaching, which, if accepted, cleanses the person and brings life/ salvation, or, if rejected, brings judgement and condemnation. This concept could then be an expression or interpretation of Jesus' baptizing with the Holy Spirit. Hence, according to the Fourth Evangelist, Jesus' confronting of people with his Spirit-imbued revelatory life-giving teaching is essentially an actualisation of Jesus' baptizing with the Holy Spirit. Spirit-baptism then denotes the concept of cleansing through revelation; through Jesus' Spirit-imbued word/teaching, which reveals God; people are cleansed (cf. 13: 10; 15:3; 17:17). All people who encounter Jesus' teaching, then, undergo this baptism with the Holy Spirit, but the effect it has on people depends on one's response to Jesus; those who accept Jesus' teaching experience the baptism as cleansing and salvific, whereas those who reject it experience this same baptism as causing judgement.

[149] The strong continuity between Jesus' earthly ministry and the ministry of the Paraclete and the disciples invites the question of how the latter ministry may be related to Jesus' Spirit-baptism, i.e., the question of how the mission of the

Paraclete and the disciples will then be one of revelation and cleansing. If the disciples were cleansed by Jesus' revelatory word (15:3; 17:17), then further revelation of Jesus' teaching (provided by the Paraclete) will be expected to result in further cleansing (cf. "truth" being the cleansing content of Jesus' word [17:17] that is mediated to people by the Spirit of truth [16:13]). Moreover, the disciples' witness is informed by and based on Jesus' words as the result of the Paraclete's revelatory teaching activity. Hence, if other people may believe in Jesus through the disciples' Paraclete-imbued words (15:26-27; 17:20), then they will also be cleansed by these words. People who are confronted with the combined witness of the Paraclete and the disciples are essentially confronted with the revelatory life-giving teaching of Jesus himself. In fact, the disciples' words are 'Paraclete' and 'life' (cf. 6:63), and therefore are expected to have the same revelatory and cleansing quality/effect as Jesus' words. Thus, the glorified Jesus will continue his work of revelation and cleansing by means of the Spirit-Paraclete through the disciples, and hence Jesus will continue to baptize people with the Holy Spirit, in that people will be confronted with the disciples' Paraclete-imbued witness. The final text to be looked at is 20:22, concerning the giving of the Spirit. This book has argued elsewhere that the 'giving' of the Spirit in 20:22 denotes the disciples' reception or experience of a new relationship with the Spirit that secures and sustains their salvation. Further, and that the coming of the Spirit as Paraclete refers to an event beyond the chronological horizon of the Fourth Gospel. If "to baptize with the Holy Spirit" refers to Jesus' confrontation of, for instance, his disciples with his life-giving teaching (in and through which the Spirit is active), and if the giving of the Spirit by Jesus secures and sustains the disciples' saving relationship with Jesus, then the disciples' reception of the Spirit in 20:22 should probably also be included in the concept of Jesus baptizing with the Holy Spirit. Moreover, if "to baptize with the Holy Spirit" also refers to Jesus' continuous ministry of revelation and cleansing after his glorification through the disciples by means of the Spirit-Paraclete, then it is likely that the coming of the Spirit-Paraclete would also come under the heading "to baptize with the Holy Spirit". Hence, both the giving of the Spirit in 20:22 and the awaited coming of the Spirit-Paraclete can be included in the concept "to baptize with the Holy Spirit". Cf. C. BENNEMA, *The Power of Saving Wisdom*, An Investigation of Spirit and Wisdom in Relation to the Soteriology of the Fourth Gospel, WUNT II/148, Tübingen, 2002, pp. 117-120; Cf. TURNER, *Spirit*, pp. 68-69; C. BENNEMA, *Power*, pp. 168-181; C. BENNEMA, "The Giving of the Spirit in John's Gospel — A New Proposal?", *EvQ* 74 (2002) 195-213; J. R. MICHAELS, "Baptism and Conversion in John: A Particular Baptist Reading", *Baptism, the New Testament and the Church, Historical and Contemporary Studies in Honour of R. E. O. White*, eds. S. E. PORTER & A. R. CROSS, JSNTSS 171, Sheffield, 1999, pp. 136 - 140.

[150] K. WEGENAST, διδάσκω in *NIDNTT*, Vol. 3 (1975) 759-765, p. 761. The word διδάσκω which means "to teach" occurs 95 times in the NT. There are 48 occurrences in the Synoptics (14 in Mt; 17 in Mk; and 17 in Lk). In John, one

finds it 9 times. Whenever Jesus is portrayed as a Rabbi and perceived as teacher (διδάσκαλος), we see Jesus teaching his disciples or the people in general. ῥαββί 1:38, 49; 3:2; 4;31; 6:25; 9:2; 11:8 (translated as διδάσκαλε in 1:38 and 20:16); κύριος: 4:11, 15, 19, 49; 5:7; 6:34, 68; (8:11); 9:36, 38; 11:3, 12, 21, 27, 32, 34, 39; 12:21, 38; 13:6, 9, 25, 36, 37; 14:5, 8, 22; 20:15, 28; 21:15, 16, 17, 20, 21. Cf. also the references to Jesus' teaching activity διδάσκω in 6:59; 7:14, 28, 35; (8:2;) 8:20; 9:34; 18:20. Most references are to Jesus teaching in synagogues or the Temple; moreover, the Fourth Gospel contains one reference each to the teaching activities of the Father (8:28) and the Spirit (14:26). Wegenast observes that the teaching activity (διδάσκω) of Jesus occurs more often in John. Apart from Jn 8:28; 14:26 Jesus himself is the subject of the verb διδάσκω and the theme of the teaching is always the message of Jesus as the one who reveals God. Besides these references, Jn 8:28 refers to the teaching of the Father and Jn 14:26 denotes the teaching of the Spirit. It is noteworthy that the disciples of Jesus portrayed in the Fourth Gospel are never shown teaching.

[151] See E. P. SANDERS, *Judaism: Practise and Belief 63 BCE – 66 CE*, London/Philadelphia, SCM Press/Trinity Press, 1992, pp. 87–88. Many scholars note with good reasons that John's description of the conditions in the temple betrays ignorance of the circumstances in the first century temple. S. MENDNER, "Die Tempelreinigung,", *ZNW* 47 (1956) 93–112, esp. p. 104; J. D. M. DERRETT, "The Zeal of the House and the Cleansing of the Temple", *The Downside Review* 95 (1977) 79–94, esp. p. 83; E. W. STEGEMANN, "Zur Tempelreinigung im Johannesevangelium", *Die Hebräische Bibel und ihre zweifache Nachgeschichte: Festschrift für Rolf Rendtorff zum 65, Geburtstag*, ed. E. BLUM, C. MACHOLZ and E. W. STEGEMANN, Neukirchen- Vluyn, Neukirchener Verlag, 1990, pp. 503–516, esp. pp. 507–508; M. DAVIES, *Rhetoric and Reference in the Fourth Gospel,* JSNTS 69, Sheffield, JSOT Press, 1992, p. 277. *Had* the quadrupeds been brought inside the temple area, every devout Jew would have had a reason to protest. As Ekkehard W. Stegemann notes, "The mere presence (of oxen and sheep in the temple) is so provocative that it does not need a particularly strong aspiration for the purity of the temple to understand Jesus' action. Every Jew at every time should consider this action appropriate." See, E. W. STEGEMANN, *Tempelreinigung*, p. 510. See also E. P. SANDERS, *Judaism*, pp. 87–88: "Everyone would have seen the pasturing of herds and flocks in the temple as a profanation. The citation of the psalm, "Zeal for your house will consume me" emphasizes that Jesus' furious attack against the vendors of the animals and the money-changers is an expression of his zeal for the temple and its holiness.

[152] See, R. J. MCKELVEY, *The New Temple: The Church in the New Testament*, Oxford Theological Monographs, Oxford, University Press, 1969, pp. 77–78: "Jesus' words in v. 16, if taken by themselves, might convey the impression that nothing more than a reform of the cult is in mind; but clearly John's understanding of the cleansing is much more far-reaching." DAVIES,

Rhetoric and Reference, 233: "[V. 17] could imply that Jesus will be concerned about the safeguarding the Temple itself. This possible interpretation is corrected by what follows." T. SÖDING, "Die Tempelaktion Jesu", *TTZ* 101 (1992) 36–64, esp. p. 47.

[153] Victor EPPSTEIN, "The Historicity of the Gospel Account of the Cleansing of the Temple", *Zeitschrift für die neutesamentliche Wissenschaft* 55 (1964) 42-58; Read also, R. J. CAMPBELL, "Evidence for the Historicity of the Fourth Gospel in John 2:13-22", in Elizabeth A. LIVINGSTONE, ed., *Studia Evangelica*, Vol. 7, Berlin, Akademie, 1982, pp. 101-120.

[154] See C. H. DODD, *The Interpretation of the Fourth Gospel,* Cambridge, University Press, 1953, pp. 301–302; R. E. BROWN, *The Gospel According to John,* AncB 29, Garden City, New York, Doubleday, 1966, pp. 124–125; C. K. BARRETT, *The Gospel According to St. John: An Introduction with Commentary and Notes on the Greek Text,* 2nd ed., London, SPCK, 1978, p. 195; L. HARTMAN, "'He spoke of the Temple of his Body' (Jn 2:13–22)", *Svensk Exegetisk Årsbok* 54 (1989) 70–79.

[155] *Ibid.* In Jn 7:15, reference is made to Jesus' lack of rabbinic training (Πῶς οὗτος γράμματα οἶδεν μὴ μεμαθηκώς;). In Jesus' case, people "marvelled" (ἐθαύμαζον.) cf. Jn 7:15 and Ac 4:13). In Acts 4:13 Peter and John are called "unschooled, ordinary men" who nevertheless spoke with spiritual insight and authority. Another evidence is provided in 7:35, "Where does this man intend to go that we shall not find him? He is not intending to go to the dispersion and *teach* the Greeks, is he?"

[156] For this discussion see J. NEUSNER, *A History of the Mishnaic Law of Appointed Times, Part One: Shabbat,* SJLA 34, Leiden, E. J. Brill, 1981, pp. 169–173.

[157] Cf. R. BROWN, *John,* p. 316; B. LINDARS, *John,* p. 289; C. K. BARRETT, *John,* p. 319.

[158] See, J. H. BERNARD, *The Gospel According to St. John,* 2 Vols., ICC, Edinburgh, T. T. Clark, 1928, p. 261; M. KOTILA, *Umstrittener Zeuge, Studien zur Stellung des Gesetzes in der johanneishen Theologiegeschichte,* Annales Academiae Scientiarum Fennicae, D i s s e r t a t i o n e s H u m a n o r u m L i t t e r a r u m 4 8, S u o m a l a i n e n tiedeakatemia, Helsinki, 1988, p. 40.

[159] Justin Martyr's *Dialogue with Trypho, Dial.* 27.5, Translated by Thomas B. FALLS, in *The Fathers of the Church* 6.

[160] See C. K. BARRETT, *John,* p. 319.

[161] B. LINDARS, *John,* p. 291; J. H. NEYREY, "The Trials (Forensic) and Tribulations (Honor Challenges) of Jesus: John 7 in Social Science Perspective", *BTB* 26 (1996) 107–124, esp. p. 112.

[162] Cf. R. E. BROWN, *John,* p. 313; C. K. BARRETT, *John,* p. 320; S. PANCARO, *The Law in the Fourth Gospel: The Torah and the Gospel, Moses*

and *Jesus, Judaism and Christianity according to John*, NovTSup 42, Leiden, E. J. Brill, 1975, p. 163; KOTILA, Umstrittener Zeuge, 1991, p. 41; J. D. M. DERRETT, "Circumcision and Perfection: A Johannine Equation (John 7:22–23)", *EvQ* 63 (1991) 221–224, esp. p. 219.

163 Cf. J. D. M. DERRETT, *Circumcision*, pp. 220–221.

164 Cf. PANCARO, *Law*, p. 167.

165 Cf. DAVIES, *Rhetoric and Reference*, p. 308.

166 See, KOTILA, *Umstrittener Zeuge*, p. 42; H. WEISS, "The Sabbath in the Fourth Gospel", *JBL* 110 (1991) 311–321, esp. p. 314; M. LABAHN, *Jesus als Lebensspender: Untersuchungen zu einer G e s c h i c h t e d e r j o h a n n e i s c h e n Tr a d i t i o n a n h a n d i h re r Wundergeschichten*, BZNW 98, Berlin, W. de Gruyter, 1999, p. 254.

167 Cf. I. DUNDERBERG, *Johannes und die Synoptiker: Studien zu Joh 1–9,* Annales Academiae Scientiarum Fennicae, Dissertationes Humanorum Litterarum 69, Suomalainen tiedeakatemia, Helsinki, 1994, pp. 106-107. The function of the Johannine discussion about circumcision and the Sabbath is closely connected to the present narrative context of this discussion. The section where Jesus refers to the practise of circumcision on the Sabbath is preceded by a section dealing with Jesus' teaching (7:14–18). The Jews call the authority of Jesus' teaching into question because he has not received a proper education to become a teacher. In his answer, Jesus states that he has derived his teaching directly from God. He does not need any human permission for his teaching, which makes him unlike any other teacher. In light of this, the following scene, where Jesus develops a halakhic- like argument, is interesting. Jesus has just declared his independence from the categories of human learning, but he still uses these very categories to refute the claims made against him. He is presented as a sovereign master of scriptural interpretation. He may not have received any formal education, but he is nevertheless a better teacher than his opponents. Jesus' treatment of the Sabbath theme serves to show that he is superior to the Jews even according to the very standards of the Jews. Jesus' paradoxical attitude toward the teaching of the Jews is another example of how Jesus is portrayed in the gospel both as the one who cherishes Jewish traditions in a superior way and as the one who follows these traditions.

168 A. J. KÖSTENBERGER, *Studies on John and Gender*, pp. 82-83. Circumcision was done in order to fulfill the commandment. Cf. Lev 12:3. See, J. C. THOMAS, "*The Fourth Gospel and Rabbinic Judaism*", *ZNW* 82 (1991) 173–174; C. A. EVANS, *Word and Glory*, p. 154. Evans notes that the question of the cause of people's suffering was of interest to rabbis. Evans also points to the parallel between Jesus' saying in 9:4, "We must work the deeds of the one who sent me while it is day," and R. Simeon b. Eleazar's admonition to work while one has opportunity and life (CE 200). Cf. also R. Tarphon's statement, "the day is short and the task is great" (*m. 'Abot* 2:15; c. CE 50–120); cf. J.

NEUSNER, "A Life of Rabbi Tarfon ca. 50–120 CE", *Judaica* 17, 1961, pp. 141–167. It may further be noted that Jesus' claim of God as his witness (Jn 5:32) and his comments regarding the lack of validity of self-witness (5:31–47) are both consistent with contemporaneous rabbinic discussion. See, C. A. EVANS, *Word and Glory*, p. 154. Evans refers to the parallels in *m. 'Abot* 4:22 and *Exod. Rab.* 1:15 on Ex 1:17. See also, T. THOMAS, *Fourth Gospel and Rabbinic Judaism*, pp. 174–77; M. HENGEL, *Old Testament in the Fourth Gospel*, p. 386.

[169] A. J. KÖSTENBERGER, *Studies on John and Gender*, pp. 82-83. In Jn 10:34–36, Jesus establishes the legitimacy of his claim to deity by referring to Ps 82:6 where God extends the designation "gods" even to Israel. The reference to Isa 41:10 in 13:18 ("He who eats my bread has lifted up his heel against me") reveals that Jesus viewed even Judas' betrayal as in accordance with Scripture (cf. 17:12). Similarly, Jesus in 15:25 acknowledges that people's rejection of him fulfilled Old Testament prophecy ("They hated me without a cause"; cf. 19:28). Moreover, Jesus occasionally refers to Old Testament types, such as when making mention of the "serpent in the wilderness" in 3:14–15 (cf. Num 21:8–9). The latter instance is particularly interesting. Jesus here evidences a reading of the Old Testament in light of his messianic calling, in particular the substitutionary nature of his death. Another instance of Jesus' elaborating on antecedent Old Testament types is his discourse on the "Bread of Heaven" (6:30–59). Responding to the Jews' challenge for a sign of similar proportions as God's provision of manna in the wilderness through Moses (cf. 2:18 for a similar request), Jesus points to the fruit of his own mission, again in terms of substitutionary atonement. cf. P. BORGEN, *Bread from Heaven: An Exegetical Study of the Concept of Manna in the Gospel of John and the Writings of Philo*, NovTSup 10, Leiden, E. J. Brill, 1965. Borgen emphasizes the midrashic character of the discourse. See the critique by D. A. CARSON, *Gospel According to John*, pp. 287–288. Carson charges that Borgen "does not sufficiently allow for the revelatory stance that Jesus adopts in this chapter, quite unlike any of the teachers in the Jewish parallels that are commonly adduced." Cf. also R. SCHNACKENBURG, "*Das Brot des Lebens (John 6)*", in *Das Johannesevangelium IV*, Teil, Ergänzende Auslegungen und Exkurse, HTKNT, Freiburg/Basel/Wien, Herder, 1984, pp. 119–131.

[170] Cf. C. A. EVANS, *Word & Glory*, pp. 146–186; J.-A. BÜHNER, *Der Gesandte und sein Weg im Evangelium*, WUNT 2/2, Tübingen, Mohr- Siebeck, 1977, p. 428; J. A. T. ROBINSON, "The New Look on the Fourth Gospel", in *Twelve New Testament Studies,* SBT 34, London, SCM, 1962, pp. 94–106.

[171] Cf. C. K. BARRETT, *The Old Testament in the Fourth Gospel*, in *JTS* 48 (1947) 155-168; J. W. WENHAM, *Our Lord's View of the Old Testament*, London, The Tyndale Press, 1953, pp. 32ff. According to C. K. Barrett, the number of direct quotations from the OT given in the fourth gospel is small when compared with those of the other Gospels although from the use of the O. T. quotations in the Fourth Gospel Barrett concludes that the evangelist had a wide

knowledge of the O. T. For more details in this regard, Cf. D. A. CARSON, "*John and Johannine Epistles*", in *It Is Written: Scripture Citing Scripture,* (ed.), D. A. CARSON and H. G. M. WILLIAMSON, Cambridge, Cambridge University Press, 1988, p. 246; C. A. EVANS, *Word and Glory*, pp. 174–175. *Jesus'* use of the Hebrew Scriptures according to John is well explained in many instances. All of the uses of the Old Testament in John are subsumed under "Johannine theology." Cf. G. REIM, *Studien zum alttestamentlichen Hintergrund des Johannesevangeliums*, SNTMS 22, Cambridge, Cambridge University Press, 1974. See also, Edwin D. FREED, *Old Testament Quotations in the Gospel of John*, Supplements to Novum Testamentum 11, Leiden, E. J. Brill, 1965, pp. 126-129. Among the Old Testament quotations in the Fourth Gospel, Freed observes that seven quotations are given on the lips of Jesus: 6:45; 7:37f.; 10:34; 13:18; 15:25; 17:12; 19:28; six in the words of the writer: 12:15; 12:38; 12:39f.; 19:24; 19:36; 19:37; three on the lips of the crowd: 6:31; 7:42; 12:13; one in the words of the Baptist: 1:23; and one is put in the minds of Jesus' disciples: 2:17. Freed also gives some more details in this regard. Regarding Jesus' reference to the Hebrew Scriptures, one notes five instances of particular quotations in John: in 1:51, to Gen 28:12; in 6:45, to Isa 54:13; in 10:34, to Ps 82:6; in 13:18, to Isa 41:10; and in 15:25, to Ps 35:19 or 69:5. In 1:51, Jesus claims that he transcends God's revelation to Jacob as the new, greater revelation of God. Jesus' reference in 6:45 to Isa 54:13, "And they shall all be taught of God" (cf. Jer 31:31–34; Ezek 36:24–26), is remarkable for the purpose of the present study in that the saying emphasizes Jesus' (and later the Spirit's) teaching role of God's new messianic community (cf. 7:37–39). The following passages in John have some sort of parallel in the Synoptics, either as quotations from the same O. T. passage or allusions to the same passage or are in some other way related to Synoptic passage: 1:23; 7:42; 12:13; 12:15; 12:39f.; 19:24. At least five other places (2:17; 13:18; 19:28f; 19:36; 19:37) reveal an interesting and important light on the problem of John's relationship to the Synoptics. Freed concludes that when John was quoting a passage of O. T. scripture, he was bound by no rule or fixed text, testimony or other. In every instance his quoted texts appears to be adapted to its immediate context, to his literary style, and to the whole plan of the composition of his gospel. Cf. also B. D. CHILTON, *A Galilean Rabbi and His Bible: Jesus' Use of the Interpreted Scripture of His Time*, GNS 8, Wilmington, DE: Michael Glazier, 1984; Cf. also, Glenn BALFOUR, "The Jewishness of John's Use of the Scriptures in John 6:31 and 7:37-38", *Tyndale Bulletin* 46.2 (1995) 357-380; Craig L. BLOMBERG, "John and Jesus", Scot MCKNIGHT & Grant R. OSBORNE, eds., *The Face of New Testament Students*, Grand Rapids, Baker Book House/ Leicster, Appollos, 2004.

[172] A. J. KÖSTENBERGER, *Studies on John and Gender*, pp. 82-83. Köstenberger refers to a number of works to prove that Johannine Jesus functioned like a Jewish teacher. On Jesus' teaching techniques, see esp. R. RIESNER, *Jesus as Preacher and Teacher*, pp. 201–208. The study of Jesus' verbal instruction entails an investigation of his use of Scripture, his "rabbinic rulings," and his style

of argumentation. Jesus also uses rabbinic style, particularly arguments from the lesser to the greater. In 3:12, he asks Nicodemus: "If I told you earthly things and you do not believe, how shall you believe if I tell you heavenly things?" In 5:46, he asks: "But if you do not believe his (Moses') writings, how will you believe my words?" In 6:27, he exhorts his audience, "Do not work for the food which perishes, but for the food which endures to eternal life." In 7:23, Jesus queries, "If a man receives circumcision on the Sabbath that the Law of Moses may not be broken, are you angry with me because I made an entire man well on the Sabbath?" And in 10:34–36, he refers to Ps 82:6 in order to legitimate his claim to deity. If in Psalm 82 God extends the designation of "gods" even to Israel, Jesus contends, how can the one chosen and sent by God be accused of blasphemy when he claims to be the Son of God?

[173] Johannes BEUTLER, *"The Use of "Scripture" in the Gospel of John"*, in R. Alan CULPEPPER & C. Clifton BLACK (eds.), *Exploring the Gospel of John*, Kentucky, Louisville, Westminster John Knox Press, 1996, p. 148. According to Maarten J. J. Menken, in John's gospel, there are seventeen passages, which qualify as OT quotations. But Menken observes that the majority of John's quotations do not precisely agree with a known version of the OT (Hebrew Text, LXX, or another of the Greek versions); sometimes it is even unclear from which OT passage the evangelist wishes to quote. But when he summarises his findings concerning the OT text of the fourth evangelist and his redaction of the quotations, Menken opines that it is evident that the LXX is the Bible of the fourth evangelist. The Greek translation is the source of the large majority of John's OT quotations. For more details in this study, see, Maarten J. J. MENKEN, *Old Testament Quotations in the Fourth Gospel: Studies in Textual Form*, Kampen, Kok, 1996, pp. 11-15. 205-212; W. A. MEEKS, *The Prophet-King: Moses Traditions and the Johannine Christology*, Novum Testamentum Supplements, Leiden, E.J. Brill, 1967.

[174] To set the scene, go all the way back to the Old Testament Book of Genesis and read the following incident in the life of Jacob, whom God renamed "Israel." (Cf. Gen 28:10-17.) Describing Nathanael as one 'in whom there is no deceit' may be an implicit contrast with the father of the people of Israel, Jacob, who cheated his brother Esau out of his birthright (Genesis 25:29-34). The image of Nathanael beneath a fig tree (1:48) is unclear. The fig tree may stand for Judaism, and Nathanael may represent those to whom John the Baptist said Jesus would be revealed (1:31). The point of 1:48 is that Jesus already knows Nathanael even before they meet face to face. When Nathanael hears this he comes to faith in Jesus, confessing this faith in 1:49. Nathanael doubted that anything good could come from Nazareth. He questioned Philip's recommendation of Jesus, solely on the basis of the place of origin of Jesus. Yet, a moment later, Nathanael recognised Jesus as "Son of God; King of Israel!" It is worth considering just what it is that so quickly and thoroughly changes Nathanael's mind. Jesus promises Nathanael that he and the other disciples will see what

Jacob saw. They will see a new Bethel (house of God), a new place where the
divine and human meet. Jacob was a man in whom there was much deceit.
Most of his life he schemed and manipulated to get ahead at the expense of
others. Jacob was also the first "Israelite," in that God would soon rename him
"Israel" (Gen 32:28). Jacob was a schemer and a deceiver. He managed to take
advantage of his older brother and his father, depriving Esau of his birthright
(Gen 25) and Esau of a blessing (Gen 27). He fled from Canaan, and especially
from Esau on the (partially true) pretext that he was seeking a wife among his
relatives in Paddan-aram. On his way to Paddan-aram, Jacob spent the night under
the stars. He had a dream in which he saw a ladder extending from the earth
into heaven. On this ladder, angels were ascending and descending. God then
spoke to Jacob, reiterating the covenant He had made with Jacob's forefathers,
Abraham and Isaac. God promised to make a great nation of Jacob and also to
bring him safely back to this land which he was leaving. In the morning when
Jacob awoke, he vividly recalled the dream he had during the night. His response
is most interesting in terms of what elements of the dream he perceived to be
important and impressive. Jacob's mind fixed upon the place where this dream
was given (Gen 28:16-17). He was awestruck that God was in that place, and
yet he did not know it (until after his dream). He fixed upon that place as the
place of God's presence and dwelling, as the place where heaven and earth, God
and man, meet. In Jacob's words, it was the gateway to heaven. This dream
was a reiteration of the Abrahamic Covenant, only this time it was Jacob
through whom these blessings would be bestowed. Perhaps of more importance
to Jacob (at that point in time), it provided a very real incentive for Jacob to
return to Israel. How easy it would have been for Jacob to flee to Paddan-aram
and never return to the promised land. Jacob now realized not only that God
had promised to bless him, but that ultimately He would bless him in this
place. The allusions to Jacob's dream in Jn 1:51 provide a powerful symbol
of Jesus' identity. Jacob is able to glimpse a meeting place between heaven and
earth. He sees the divine messengers who mediate between God and humanity.
The character of Nathanael is disclosed through allusions to his ancestor Jacob,
who was noted for his guile because he stole the birthright from his brother
Esau but who was later the first to bear the name "Israel" (Gen 27:35; 32:28).
He himself is the new meeting point between heaven and earth, the place where
God is to be revealed. As Jacob caught a glimpse of the divine presence at
Bethel (Jn1: 51; Gen 28:12), Jesus' promise is confirmed when the disciples
together see his divine glory manifest at Cana, Nathanael's hometown (Cf. Jn
2:11; 21:2). See, Christopher ROWLAND, "John 1.51, Jewish Apocalyptic and
Targumic Tradition", *New Testament Studies* 30 (1984) 498-507. See, Bruce W.
LONGENECKER, "The Unbroken Messiah: A Johannine Feature and Its Social
Functions", *New Testament Studies* 41 (1995) 428-441. Most likely, while under a
fig tree, Nathanael had been reading and meditating about Jacob and particularly
this text in Genesis. The fig tree was almost a symbol of home (cf. Isa. 36:16;
Mic. 4:4; Zech. 3:10). In later times, its shade was definitely used as a place for

prayer, meditation, and study, and there is no reason to think the practice does not go back to Jesus' time. Some believe this was the place where Nathanael, like other Israelites, went to meditate and pray. There is also a good possibility that Nathanael was meditating on the Messiah who was to come since the fig tree was used as shade for teaching or studying by the later Rabbis (Cf. *Midrash Rabbah on Eccles.* 5:11). Also, the fig tree was symbolic for messianic peace and plenty - Mic 4:4, Zech 3:10. But there is a radical change of mind when he meets with Jesus. Nathanael's confession is thorough and complete: "Rabbi, you are the Son of God; you are the King of Israel!" (verse 49). There is a significance in the confession of Nathanael. It is a confession of Jesus' messiahship and its strong allusions to Ps 2:6-7, is a well-known Messianic Psalm. See, Merrill C. TENNEY, "Literary Keys to the Fourth Gospel: The Old Testament and the Fourth Gospel", *Bibliotheca Sacra* 120 (Oct. 1963) 300-308.

[175] A. J. KÖSTENBERGER, *Studies on John and Gender*, p. 84. Some of Jesus' sayings recorded in John's Gospel appear to reflect Targumic language and tradition, such as his statement "Abraham your father rejoiced to see my day" (8:56) and his words to Thomas that they are blessed who do not see but believe (20:29). Cf. G. REIM, "*Targum und Johannesevangelium*", *BZ* 27 (1983) 6–7; C. A. EVANS, *Word and Glory*, pp. 154-162. Evans refers to R. Yohanan's rebuke of a skeptical student: "Had you not seen, would you not have believed?" (*b. B. Bat.*75a; cf. *b. Sanh.* 100a). Köstenberger holds the view that the teaching of Jesus is geared to establishing the messianic claims on the basis of the OT expectations. This, of course, does not mean that Jesus merely conformed to the pattern of teaching used by others rabbis of his day. Rather, his teaching is devoted to establishing his messianic claims on the basis of Old Testament expectations. W. A. MEEKS, *The Prophet-King: Moses Traditions and the Johannine Christology*, Novum Testamentum Supplements, Leiden, E.J. Brill, 1967; Stan HARSTINE, *Moses as a Character in the Fourth Gospel*, Continuum International Publishing Group, Sheffield Academic Press, 2002.

[176] A. J. KÖSTENBERGER, *Studies on John and Gender*, p. 85. Köstenberger quotes from Gerhardsson who calls this kind of rabbinic teaching method as "the Rabbi's didactic symbolic actions," "concrete, visible measures whereby they capture the attention of their pupils, after which they either explain what they have done or leave it to the pupils to work it out for themselves." Cf. GERHARDSSON, *Memory and Manuscript*, p. 185. To prove this, Köstenberger brings in two instances in the Gospel of John as direct evidence. The two examples are Jesus' cleansing of the Temple and the foot washing, interestingly placed by the fourth evangelist at the beginning and at the end of Jesus' ministry. Jesus' cleansing of the Temple (2:13–22) is cast by the fourth evangelist as a deliberate action designed to provoke discussion and to provide Jesus with an opportunity to present himself as the fulfillment of the symbolism represented by the Temple. Cf. C. A. EVANS, *Word and Glory*, pp. 159–160. He points out that

Jesus' statement that he will build the "Temple" may represent an adaptation of the targumic tradition that Messiah will build the Temple. Cf. *Tg. Isa.* 53:3; *Tg. Zech.* 6:12–13; cf. also G. REIM, *Targum und Johannesevangelium*, p. 10; W. D. DAVIES, *The Gospel and the Land: Early Christian and Jewish Territorial Doctrine*, Sheffield, JSOT, 1994, pp. 288–335. Jesus' explanation of the act of destruction and rebuilding of the Temple comes as a prophetic sign which points out the meaning of his death and resurrection. Only much later do the disciples understand, as the fourth evangelist duly notes in 2:22; cf. 12:16. Cf. D. A. CARSON, *"Understanding Misunderstandings in the Fourth Gospel,"* *TynB* 33 (1982) 59–89. In p. 88, Köstenberger notes that Jesus also taught by example. Reference has already been made to Jesus' statement in 13:13–15, "You call me Teacher and Lord; and you are right, for so I am. If I then, the Lord and the Teacher, washed your feet, you also ought to wash one another's feet. For *I gave you an example* that you also should do as I did to you." The use of example also comes to the fore in 5:20, where Jesus claims that "the Father loves the Son, and shows him all things that he himself is doing" (cf. 1:18). Jesus' teaching by example is emphasized by verbally instructing to emulate him: "Truly, truly, I say to you, he who believes in me, the works that I do shall he do also; and greater works than these shall he do; because I go to the Father" (14:12). Cf. Andreas KÖSTENBERGER, *"The 'Greater Works' of the Believer According to John 14:12"*, *Didaskalia* 6 (1995) 36–45.

[177] *Ibid.*, p. 98. In pp. 85-86, Köstenberger observes that people's challenge of Jesus' authority in reaction to his startling act of overthrowing the tables of the moneychangers did not seek evidence of the usual type. Cf. D. DAUBE, *The New Testament and Rabbinic Judaism*, New York, Arno, 1973, p. 211. Rather, the Jews sought confirmation of Jesus' special, divine call as the Prophet or Messiah. A rabbi's authority included both didactic and prophetic functions and was manifested by both words and actions. Jesus' miraculous healings and other amazing acts thus may be viewed, among other things, as serving the purpose of attesting to his authority as a religious teacher. In this particular instance, however, Jesus does not acquiesce to the Jews' demand for a sign. Rather, he elaborates on the significance of the act he has just done, the temple cleansing. See, Andreas KÖSTENBERGER, *"The Seventh Johannine Sign: A Study in John's Christology"*, *BBR* 5 (1995) 87–103.

[178] G. VERMES, *The Changing Faces of Jesus*, p. 26.

[179] *Ibid.*

[180] V. TAYLOR, *The Names of Jesus*, p. 13.

[181] F. HAHN, *The Titles of Jesus in Christology*, p. 75.

[182] R. RIESNER, *Jesus as Preacher and Teacher*, p. 188.

[183] H. SHANKS, *Is the Title "Rabbi" Anachronistic in the Gospels?*, p.342.

[184] *Ibid.* Moreover, the appearance of the title ραββί in the Synoptic Gospels needs to be considered here. Yet, this book does not address the historicity of the term ραββί that is attributed to the synoptic Jesus. That is left open for further study.

[185] S. ZEITLIN, *A Reply "Is the Title "Rabbi" Anachronistic in the Gospels?"*, p. 342.

[186] *Ibid.*

[187] G. VERMES, *The Changing Faces of Jesus*, p. 26. See also, Glenn BALFOUR, "Is John's Gospel Anti-Semitic?", *Tyndale Bulletin* 48.2 (1997) 369-372; David D. C. BRAINE, "The Inner Jewishness of John's Gospel as a Clue to the Inner Jewishness of Jesus", *Studien zum Neuen Testamen und seiner Umwelt* 13 (1989) 101-155.

Chapter - 2

Jesus as Rabbi Johannine Development of Christology

Introduction

The preceding chapter sought to establish that John's Gospel bears witness that Jesus was perceived by his contemporaries primarily as a Jewish teacher. First of all, "Rabbi" or "teacher" is the customary address of Jesus in the Fourth Gospel. Also, John portrays the relationship between Jesus and his closest followers in terms of the customary teacher-disciple relationship in t h e first-century Judaism.[1] This portrays Jesus' assuming the role of teacher by instructing his disciples through word and action, protecting them from harm and providing for their needs. The disciples assumed the role of faithful followers, including the performance of menial tasks and the perpetuation of their Master's teaching. Before proceeding further, there is a general remark to be made about Johannine scholarship. The Johannine Christology has hitherto paid little attention to the role of Jesus as "Rabbi and Teacher"[2] which is one title given to Jesus in the Fourth Gospel which cannot be ignored. Thus this chapter will explore whether the term ῥαββί can contribute anything towards the presentation of Johannine Christology. Does the Johannine use of the term ῥαββί refer only to the earthly Jesus? When persons address Jesus as ῥαββί in the Fourth Gospel, are they qualifying themselves as believers by doing so? If Jesus is perceived as ῥαββί in the sense of a teacher, is there any significant role that fact can play in Johannine Christology? For John, is the term ῥαββί acceptable as a Christological category? What is the meaning of "Jesus the Rabbi" in the presentation of the Johannine Theology and Christology?

1. The Johannine Jesus as Rabbi: A Paradox?

In writing his Gospel, John uses a distinctive style which is in part a blend of the past, present and future. Yet, there are also debates regarding usage of various aspects of Jewish/Greek, past/present and human/divine.[3] When Riesner considers that the application of the term ῥαββί to Jesus is rather Palestinian and historical, he says that "in the four gospels the address rabbi with its implicit characterisation of Jesus as a teacher was not introduced by secondary theological motives."[4] So it seems that, for Riesner, calling Jesus a Rabbi does not have any Christological implication but D. Moody Smith states that "before Jesus is ever named in the Gospel he is identified with the word (*logos*) of God in the prologue, and before he is addressed as the Messiah he is called first of all 'rabbi.'"[5] Moody Smith is convinced that the two terms of *Logos* and Rabbi "nicely bracket Johannine Christology, in the sense that everything else falls between them."[6] Hence the question is whether the title ῥαββί given to the Johannine Jesus has any Christological implications. Further, the author of the gospel has any implicit or explicit Christological motives in presenting Jesus as ῥαββί in the sense of a Jewish teacher.

Köstenberger states that "the Johannine Christology is not a projection onto the life of Jesus but that John's "high Christology" is rooted in Jesus' earthly life and ministry."[7] D. Moody Smith states that "before Jesus is addressed as the Messiah in the fourth gospel he is called first of all R*abbi*."[8] Thus Moody Smith is convinced, as noted above, that the two terms of *Logos* and Rabbi nicely bracket Johannine Christology. Moody Smith asserts that as *logos*, Jesus Christ is anchored in God, whereas as Rabbi, he appears as a man among other human beings and other Rabbis such as John the Baptist (3:26). It is true that the earthly title of Rabbi addressed to Jesus leads to the disappearance of *logos*. Nevertheless, it is also true that the earthly title of Jesus as ῥαββί does not diminish Jesus' God-given role and authority. Hence, in agreement with Moody Smith, understanding Jesus as Rabbi in the Fourth Gospel is necessary to comprehending the term Messiah given to the Johannine Jesus. Nevertheless, there are others who suggest that the application of ῥαββί to the Johannine Jesus presents a paradox to the image of Jesus' incarnation and Son of God in the Fourth Gospel. The following section will discuss whether or not there is a paradox.

2. Rabbi and Son of God: A Paradox of the Incarnation

The following references are noted in the Johannine Christological titles. Jesus, the Son of God: Jn 1:34, 39; 5:25; 10:36; 11:4, 27; 20:31. Jesus, the

Son of Man: Jn 1:51; 3:13, 14; 5;27; 6:27, 53, 62; 8:28; 9:35; 12:23, 24; 13:31. Jesus is portrayed as Christ in Jn 1:17, 20, 25, 41; 3:28; 4:25, 29; 7:26, 27, 31, 41, 42; 9:22; 10:24; 11:27; 12:34; 17:3; 20:31. But the title ῥαββί is found in eight places: Jn 1:38, 49; 3:2; 4:31; 6:25; 9:2; 11:8 and in 20:16, it is ῥαββουνί. In these citations, Jn 1:38 and 20:16, it is translated as διδάσκαλε. Again Jn 6:59; 7:14, 28, 35; (8:2); 8:20; 9:34; 18:20, refer to Jesus as a Teacher. Also, the term Κύριος occurs in 4:11, 15, 19, 49; 5:7; 6:34, 68; (8:11); 9:36, 38; 11:3, 12, 21, 27, 32, 34, 39; 12:21, 38; 13:6, 9, 25, 36, 37; 14:5, 8, 22; 20:15, 28; 21:15, 16, 17, 20, 21. Thus, one can see these later occurrences also dominating in the Johannine expressions of Jesus. The pre-dominant aspects of John's portrayal of Jesus are as follows; Jesus is portrayed as Son of God (1:34, 39; 5:25; 10:36; 11:4, 27; 20:31), the eschatological Son of Man (1:51; 3:13, 14; 5:27; 6:27, 53, 62; 8:28; 9:35; 12:23, 24; 13:31), and the Christ (1:17, 20, 25, 41; 3:28; 4:25, 29; 7:26, 27, 31, 41, 42; 9:22; 10:24; 11:27; 12:34; 17:3; 20:31). No one calls him Son of Man in the Gospel.[9] Only Jesus so identifies himself. In the Old Testament, in one of the last books of the canon, the image of Son of Man is found. The scene is found in the Book of Daniel (7:1-14). The "Ancient of Days" (God) is seated apart from every other heavenly creature, and no one except "one like a son of man" can approach him. To this "Son of man" figure is given all authority.

Though the Bible describes many prophets and teachers who have come down from God and a select few (Enoch and Elijah) who have gone up to God, the unique claim of Jesus is that he is the Son of Man who has both come down and up (cf. Jn 3:13). The divine origin and divine destiny of the Son of Man are thus a central claim to divine status in this Gospel. He allows others to call him what they like, but his own designation in the first 12 chapters is almost always Son or Son of Man. Twelve times he calls himself Son of Man in the first half of the Gospel and only once in the second half (13:31-32). Implicit in the title is the whole scope of Jesus' earthly ministry and heavenly authority. Encountering the Son of Man in history cannot be divorced from encountering his exalted position before God. It is no wonder that Jesus would draw disciples to himself by claiming the title Son of Man in his public dialogues (3:13-14; 8:28; 12:23,32-34). Son of Man is also used variously in the other Gospels. When it refers to Jesus' identity, it is in three senses: earthly ministry, death-resurrection, and future exaltation- judgment. John does not distinguish these senses when he uses the title. Rather he seems to blur the categories so that they are all applicable whenever Jesus cites Son of Man as his identity. However, it is noteworthy that the only way Jesus is *addressed* in the Fourth Gospel is as ῥαββί, Teacher (in Greek διδάσκαλος) and Lord or Master (κύριος), terms largely synonymous in John.[10] While the evangelist's portrayal of Jesus transcends that of Rabbi/Teacher/Master, enlarging the scope of his Christology to include terms such as Son of God, Son of Man, or Christ, his account makes clear that Jesus' contemporaries perceived and addressed Jesus primarily as a religious teacher, a ῥαββί.

For Sanders and Mastin, the title ῥαββί in Jn 1:38 is a paradox of the incarnation. Interpreting Jn 1:38b, where Jesus is addressed with the title ῥαββί, Sanders and Mastin suggest that the term Rabbi in Jn 1:38 "subtly emphasises the paradox of the incarnation. It is intended to show reverence, yet fails utterly to express the true dignity of him to whom it is addressed."[11] But Moody Smith, commenting on the same verse, suggests that "to human eyes, even friendly ones, Jesus appears as rabbi, that is, a teacher (as the term is translated in 1:38)."[12] When Moody Smith observes the term ῥαββί as attributed to Jesus, in comparison to the Johannine concept of *Logos*, he asserts that "this teacher seen from the side of God is the *logos*, the agent of God in creation as well as redemption, so that he can himself be called *theos*, God (1:1. 18; 20:28)."[13] And from this perspective, Moody Smith concludes, "by juxtaposing logos and "rabbi", we establish a framework within which to understand Johannine Christology, because the terms represent two poles, divine and human."[14] This interpretation of the Johannine portrayal of Jesus as a ῥαββί would solve the paradox that Sanders and Mastin perceive.

R. Bultmann commenting on the term ῥαββί that is given to Jesus by his disciples, calls it "a paradox between Jesus as Son of God and a Jewish Rabbi."[15] Even when Nathanael recognises Jesus as 'the Son of God', he addresses him as ῥαββί, and thereafter the disciples in the Fourth Gospel address Jesus with the same designation in Jn 4:31; Jn 9:2; Jn 11: 8. Bultmann says that in John "the form of address brings out the paradox that the Son of God appears as a Jewish Rabbi."[16] In other words, he considers that the term ῥαββί is meant only to apply to the earthly Jesus, and so, for Bultmann, such a designation is in contradiction with the Johannine presentation of Jesus as Son of God. However, Scott makes a link between Jesus' role *as a teacher* and his relationship to God. For Scott, "Jesus' authority as teacher rests upon his relationship to God."[17] The Johannine Jesus is presented as declaring that his teaching is not his own, but is from the one who sent him (Jn 7: 16-17). Scott observes, "Jesus also makes it known to his disciples that the Spirit, whom he will send, will continue in the same tradition as Teacher (14:26)."[18] So, for Scott the address of the Johannine Jesus *as a teacher* does not present a paradox to the image of Son of God. The reasoning by Scott is the one accepted in this book. Namely, there is no paradox in the application of rabbi to the Johannine Jesus and the image of Jesus incarnation and Son of God in the Fourth Gospel.

3. "High Christology" & "Historical Jesus": Conflict in John?

It is important to remember that the Fourth Gospel was written (at least in part) to specifically clarify the divinity of the person of Jesus Christ.[19] The Johannine Jesus is often understood in terms of the Fourth Gospel's emphasis on Christ's divinity. Many scholars agree that the Johannine Gospel emphasizes Christ's deity, especially as portrayed in the Prologue.[20] However, when one speaks of Johannine Christology or of the research over Johannine Christological titles, the title ῥαββί has often been ignored. Can it be argued that because of the so- called "high Christology on Johannine Theology" the aspect of Jesus as a Rabbi has been neglected? Will it be relevant to argue that Jesus was basically perceived as a Rabbi in the sense of a teacher and that from there it grew to other Johannine Christological titles? Works, such as Marianne Thompson's "The Humanity of Jesus in the Fourth Gospel", have countered the arguments of Käsemann and others that John portrays Jesus in docetic terms, that is, as a divine rather than an earthly human figure.[21] The question is whether, in John, the understanding of Jesus with the title ῥαββί in the sense of "teacher" has its own significance in the wider Christological and theological understanding of the Gospel. So, in this second chapter, moving from the exegetical study of Johannine attribution of Rabbi to Jesus, attention will be focused on the question of the relevance and significance of addressing Jesus as ῥαββί in Johannine Christology.

The Gospel of John presents the ministry of Jesus in two segments. First, there is the "public Jesus" who interacts with the world, performs "signs" and makes speeches to crowds and various individuals about who he is. This is the Jesus of the first 12 chapters. Second, there is the "private Jesus" who gives his final address to an exclusive group the night before he dies. The announcement of his death and resurrection follow but the speech resumes afterwards. The last eight chapters of the Gospel cover this material. Scholars often find the clue for this two-part schema in the introduction to the Gospel, often called the Prologue. There it is stated, "He came unto his own, and his own people did not accept him (cf. chaps. 1-12). But to all who accepted him, who believed in his name, he gave power to become children of God (cf. chaps. 13-21)" (Jn 1:11-12). The following three roles of Jesus are discerned in John's presentation: Jesus as the Sent Son; Jesus as the one who came into the world and returned to the Father (descent-ascent); and Jesus as the eschatological Shepherd-teacher.[22] D. Moody Smith in his *The Theology of the Gospel of John* says that "among traditional Jewish titles applied to Jesus in John we find also rabbi."[23] When the Fourth Gospel is read, most of the Christological titles have been used to designate Jesus but not to address him. On the other hand, the term ῥαββί has always been used as one of the major terms in addressing the Johannine Jesus. J. Ashton's work on "*Understanding the Fourth Gospel*"[24] gives much attention to the aspects of Jesus the Messiah, Son of God, Son of Man and the Christ, but not to Jesus as Rabbi.[25] Similarly, the work of Schnackenburg[26] in his "*Jesus in the Gospels*", pays no attention to the aspect of Jesus as a Jewish teacher. Thus, the emphasis of study has been on the Christology of the Gospel and has largely neglected the aspect of Jesus in his role as ῥαββί. This could be precisely because many exegetes think that the aspect of Jesus' ministry as 'a religious teacher' is not co-related to the notion of Johannine Christology.

4. A Change in Christological Titles: A Progression in Faith

In presenting Jesus as a Rabbi in the sense of "a teacher", in no way is John minimising the role of Jesus. There is a gradual development of faith in the life of the believers in John. There is also a holistic approach in his presentation of Jesus. Hence, the presentation of the earthly Jesus as a Rabbi is not in conflict with the Jesus who receives the final acclamation as "Lord and God" (cf. Jn 20: 28). Based on the above, what is needed is to be clear about the proper understanding of Johannine Christology. From the perception of the historical Jesus as ῥαββί, John leads his readers towards an understanding of the exalted Lord. To portray the gradual development of the Johannine Christology, from Jesus as ῥαββί to Jesus as the Lord and God, a chart is included to briefly explain the Johannine presentation of Jesus in a holistic understanding. The intention of this chart is to illustrate how the term ῥαββί serves as a basis for the development of a Johannine Christology. Wherever John portrays Jesus as a teacher, one can observe that he also

ῥαββί 1:38	Εὑρήκαμεν τὸν Μεσσίαν (ὅ ἐστιν μεθερμηνευόμενον Χριστός) Jn 1:41
ῥαββί 1:49	σὺ εἶ ὁ υἱὸς τοῦ θεοῦ, σὺ βα σιλεὺς εἶ τοῦ Ἰσραήλ. 1:49
ῥαββί 3:2	οἴδαμεν ὅτι ἀπὸ θεοῦ ἐλήλυθας διδάσκαλος·οὐδεὶς γὰρ δύναται ταῦτα τὰ σημεῖα ποιεῖν ἃ σὺ ποιεῖς, ἐὰν μὴ ᾖ ὁ θεὸς μετ' αὐτοῦ. Jn 3:2
ῥαββί 4:31	οἴδαμεν ὅτι οὗτός ἐστιν ἀλή θῶς ὁ σωτὴρ τοῦ κόσμου. Jn 4:42
ῥαββί 6:25	σὺ εἶ ὁ ἅγιος τοῦ θεοῦ. Jn 6:69
ῥαββί 9:2	Σὺ πιστεύεις εἰς τὸν υἱὸν τοῦ ἀνθρ ώπου; (Jn 9: 35) Πιστεύω, κύριε·καὶ προσεκύνησεν αὐτῷ. Jn 9:38.
ῥαββί 11:8	σὺ εἶ ὁ Χριστὸς ὁ υἱὸς τοῦ θεοῦ ὁ εἰς τὸν κόσμον ἐρχόμενος. Jn 11:27
ῥαββουνί 20:16	Ἑώρακα τὸν κύριον, καὶ ταῦτα εἶπεν αὐτῇ. (Jn 20:18) Ὁ κύριός μου καὶ ὁ θεός μου. Jn 20:28

presents, in the same passage, some other Christological titles as well. He does not stop with the simple presentation of Jesus as a teacher but takes him beyond time and space to eventually portray him as Lord and God. In another way, the chart highlights the gradual faith development of the believers wherever Jesus is given the title ῥαββί in the gospel. It also shows how the application of the term ῥαββί to Jesus in the Fourth Gospel witnesses to the divinity or exalted status of Jesus by the expression of some other Christological categories in the same passage or episode.

In the chart, the first column shows the occurrence of the title "Rabbi" in the fourth gospel and the second column the Christological titles that follow. It is to be noted that each Christological title that is given is not what precedes the address "Rabbi" but what proceeds. This supports the book that in the fourth gospel the progression in Christological titles points to the progression in faith. The chart is used to defend our position, that in the Fourth Gospel, the progression in Christological titles points to apply the Christological title to Jesus. If "Rabbi" refers to the human Jesus, then the Christological title that follows presents a divine Jesus. Hence, it may be said that the title "Rabbi" functions as the face value for the identification of Jesus, but later when the Christological title is expressed. It says specifically about who Jesus is. Thus, it becomes clear that when the author of the gospel presents the development of titles, he projects the progression of faith professed by the believers. For example, in Jn 1:35-38, the Baptist introduced Jesus as the "lamb of God", but the two disciples did not believe that immediately. However, after staying with Jesus (Jn 1:39) Andrew tells his brother Simon Peter that "we have seen the Messiah" (Jn 1:41). The use of Jewish titles suggests an early stage in the composition of the gospel when the community members were mainly Palestinian Jews. The term Messiah is a transliteration of the Hebrew term, meaning, "anointed." In the Old Testament, this ("Christos," "the Christ") term became one of the names by which the promised Messiah (Dan 9:25-26) was known. Only twice is the term "Messiah" found in the New Testament, and both times it is in the Gospel of John. In each case, this Hebrew term is translated Χριστος in the Greek translation of the Old Testament (the Septuagint). The title "Messiah" presents the conversion that took place in those two disciples. The image of Messiah has a Christological depth as well as a Christological uplifting. The statement "we have seen the Messiah" is a proof that by "following and staying" with Jesus they have progressed in their faith. Thus the explanation of the above chart follows which shows how the author of the gospel presents the progression in Christological titles and portrays the progression in faith. gospel when the community members were mainly Palestinian Jews. The term Messiah is a transliteration of the Hebrew term, meaning, "anointed." In the Old Testament, this ("Christos," "the Christ") term became one of the names by which the promised Messiah (Dan 9:25-26) was known. Only twice is the term "Messiah" found in the New Testament, and both times it is in the Gospel of John. In each case, this Hebrew term is translated ×ñéóôoò in the Greek translation of the Old Testament (the Septuagint). The title "Messiah" presents the conversion that took place in those two disciples. The image of Messiah has a Christological depth as well as a Christological uplifting.

The statement "we have seen the Messiah" is a proof that by "following and staying" with Jesus they have progressed in their faith. Thus the explanation of the above chart follows which shows how the author of the gospel presents the progression in Christological titles and portrays the progression in faith.[27] Though the disciples of the Baptist address Jesus as ῥαββί (Jn 1:38), the climax of that episode is different. Jn 1: 39-41 explains the stages of their faith development. λέγει αὐτοῖς, Ἔρχεσθε καὶ ὄψεσθε. ἦλθαν οὖν καὶ εἶδαν ποῦ μένει καὶ παρ᾽ αὐτῷ ἔμειναν τὴν ἡμέραν ἐκείνην·Andrew, one of the two disciples of the Baptist, who approaches Jesus as ῥαββί, reports to his brother Simon Peter that they have "found the messiah" which is translated the Christ (Jn 1:41) Εὑρήκαμεν τὸν Μεσσίαν (ὅ ἐστιν μεθερμηνευόμενον Χριστός). In the first episode itself a progression is seen in the faith of the disciples which John presents by introducing the Christological title "Messiah".

5. From "Rabbi" to "Messiah": A Transition or a Progression?

According to Kevin Quast,"An eschatological messianic interpretation is the dominant one in the context of Jn 1."[28] First of all, the identity of Jesus as the Messiah is revealed to John at Jesus' baptism [29] (Cf. 1:31-34). John begins to declare that Jesus is the one of whom he has been speaking. John was speaking of the one who is somewhere in Israel, among his people but not yet recognized (1:26-27. 30-31), and then in 1: 26-27. 30-31 proclaims Jesus as the promised Messiah (1:29-30).

John the Baptist: A Messianic Message

As for the Baptist, he was insistent in placing before his disciples and the people the Messianic message[30] of Scripture. The idea that repentance ought to occur prior to water baptism is precisely what John the Baptist put forth to the Pharisees and Sadducees (Mt 3:7-9). In spite of the numerous speculations of John the Baptist's supposed relationship with Qumran (if he even had one at all), a glance at the "*Manual of Discipline*"[31] indicates that the people at Qumran did administer some type of purification with water. The text of 1QS 3:4-9 demonstrates that a changed lifestyle, or repentance from sin and obedient commitment to Torah was the necessary prerequisite before one could enter into the Qumran community. It remains possible that John adapted the Qumranian practice of daily ritual cleansing to a single, unrepeatable and eschatological rite (cf., Mt 3:2; 3:11, 12). Furthermore, the fact that a dispute arose over John's baptism and "the matter of ceremonial washing" (Jn 3:25) strongly suggests some degree of continuity between John's water baptism and Jewish purification rites. Many Old Testament passages allude to a moral purification that utilizes water as the chief agent of cleansing (Is 1:16; Jer. 4:14; Ez 36:25;

Zech 13:1). The significant point of difference for John's baptism is that it was meant for Jews as well as Gentiles. No longer could the children of Abraham insist that their heritage alone was sufficient for entry into the kingdom of God (Mt 3:9). They too, needed to manifest true repentance and submit to water baptism. Though the ethical element regarding repentance is present in all three types of baptism (Jewish, Qumranian, Baptistic), it was John's baptism alone that inaugurated God's coming reign in Jesus of Nazareth.

Development in the Understanding of Jesus as Messiah

In the opinion of Schnackenburg, the request of the disciples to Jesus in Jn 1:38 probably indicates "a desire to hear Jesus expounding the Scriptures, on the all-decisive question of the Messiah."[32] The disciples, when addressing Jesus as ῥαββί, show their desire to listen to Jesus expounding the Scriptures. In doing this, they appear to identify Jesus as the promised Messiah. Schnackenburg holds the view that the sources for this argument are not revealed here in the Gospel but in the Qumran writings. Although the approaches to Messianism were different from the Qumran community (and others), there was a common thirst, found in all such groups, for an intensive study of the Scriptures. When Andrew comes to his brother Peter, he informs him that they have found "the Messiah," "the Christ."

The perception of Rabbi as a religious teacher (Jn 1: 38) evolves into the understanding of Jesus as Μεσσία (Jn 1:41).[33] The Jewish title - Messiah - is translated into Greek as Χριστος. This is not Jesus' surname. Χριστος is not a name but a title which means "anointed". By the time that Jesus started his public ministry, many Jews were expecting the ultimate Messiah, perhaps a priest, a king or even a military figure, one who was specially anointed by God to intervene decisively to change history. Priests (Ex 28:41; 40:15; etc.), prophets (1 Kgs 19:16) and kings (1 Sam 9:16; 16:3; 2 Sam 12:7) were anointed with oil to consecrate them for their office and duties. "Therefore God, your God, has anointed you with the oil of gladness more than your companions" (Ps 45:7). Most of the time the expected Messiah (to use the transliteration of the Hebrew term for "the Anointed One") is called "the Christ." This expression occurs 56 times in the New Testament, 17 of which are in John's Gospel. (cf. Jn 1:20, 25, 41; 3:28; 4:29, 42; 6:69; 7:26, 27, 31, 41 (2x), 42; 10:24; 11:27; 12:34; 20:31). John's purpose in writing this Gospel is to convince his readers that Jesus of Nazareth is "the Christ": "But these are written that you may believe that Jesus is the Christ, the Son of God, and that believing you may have life in His name" (Jn 20:31).

Andrew found first his own brother Simon and said to him, "We have found the Messiah" (which is translated Christ) (Jn 1:41). The woman said to him, "I know that Messiah is coming (the one called Christ). Whenever he comes, he will tell us everything" (Jn 4:25). Andrew is certainly right in saying "they have found "the Messiah", but he is saying far more than he realizes at this point in his life. What he and all the other disciples need to learn is what it means to be "the Messiah." Their understanding of this is limited and at times distorted. So it is that when Peter makes his "great confession" that Jesus is "the Christ" (Mt 16:16), he almost immediately thereafter rebukes "the Christ" for talking about his imminent suffering and death on the cross (Mt 16:21-23).

The following discussion investigates the various aspects of Jesus' assumption of the role of teacher according to John's Gospel. It is well substantiated in this section that the first disciples basically approached Jesus as a teacher; however, when the title ῥαββί is used for the Johannine Jesus, it should not be concluded that Jesus was purely perceived as a teacher and nothing more. If this is so, then as Schnackenburg says, the two disciples of John found in Jesus something more than a master of exegesis; they gradually came to the conviction that he was the Messiah promised in Scripture (cf. Jn 1: 41). This particular form of address, "ῥαββί" should be seen as the initial stage in a growth process of their faith understanding of who Jesus really is.

"Rabbi" to Messianic Revelation: A Theological Progression

Jesus revealed his glory in Cana and the disciples believed in him (Jn 2:11). The narrator makes this comment on the incident and thus turns it into a story about knowing Jesus and his ministry. In the episode of Nathanael in Jn 1:49, although Philip introduced Jesus to Nathanael (Jn 1:45) as someone "of whom Moses in the law, and also the prophets wrote- Jesus of Nazareth, the Son of Joseph", Nathanael first addresses Jesus as Rabbi. Moreover, some other titles like Son of God and King of Israel are also used by Nathanael. According to D. A. Carson,[34] if Nathanael's expression of the Christological titles such as "Son of God" and "King of Israel" is historical, it may well reflect an initial perception that still required growth in understanding as a result of a committed following of Jesus as ῥαββί. It seems that Nathanael gives these titles as the result of his awe-stricken state over the supernatural vision of Jesus (Jn 1: 48). Nathanael's use of *"Son of God"* shows that Nathanael apparently does not fully comprehend Jesus' identity. In Jn 1:49, when the titles such as "Son of God" and "King of Israel" are given to Jesus soon after addressing him as "ῥαββί", they seem to be inconsistent terms.

The question is whether John has any plan in doing so. In the first two instances of "Rabbi" in John, Köstenberger maintains that "The use of ῥαββί as address for Jesus in 1:38 and 49 clearly indicates that Jesus' first followers conceived of their relationship with Jesus in terms of a teacher-disciple relationship."[35] Indeed, the first two disciples start to follow Jesus after hearing the acclamation of the Baptist, "Behold the Lamb of God" (Jn 1:36). However, it is noteworthy that they both address Jesus with the term ῥαββί and not "Lamb of God." Nathanael first addresses Jesus as ῥαββί before he acclaims, "You are the Son of God" (Jn 1:49). C. K. Barrett refers to the address of Jesus as ῥαββί in Jn 1: 49 and says, "It is apparently inconsistent with the titles 'Son of God' and 'King of Israel.'"[36] 'Son of God' and 'King of Israel' are two Jewish messianic titles, which show that Nathanael understands Jesus within his Jewish frame of context. Nathanael's statement, "ῥαββί you are the Son of God. You are the king of Israel" (1:49), if historical, may well reflect an initial perception that still required growth in understanding "as a result of a committed following of this ῥαββί."[37] Accordingly, "They expressed their perception of him as a religious teacher by addressing him as such."[38] It is clear that the first two episodes, which deal with the "first disciples" (Jn 1: 35-51), are not exactly parallels of each other. However, the important point is that the disciples are shown by the author of the gospel perceiving Jesus as a ῥαββί in the sense of a teacher, but they do not stop with that. The story about Jesus calling disciples (1:35-51) closes as follows: "You will see heaven opened and the angels of God ascending and descending upon the Son of Man" (v. 51). This closing is anticipated by references in the immediate context to "seeing", "finding" and "believing" the Messiah. V. 51 makes an explicit reference to Jacob's theophany in Gen 28:12. "All disciples are promised a vision like Jacob's. They will thereby truly become Israelites like Nathanael (v. 47)."[39] In the light of Philo's well-known etymological explanation of the meaning of Israel (Gen 32:28-30) as "the one who sees God",[40] the epistemological interest of John's text becomes even more apparent.

Jacob never saw God, although he had a genuine theophany. In one sense the promise is never literally fulfilled in John's gospel; there is no theophany of ascending/descending angels. But Thomas, for example, received an apparition of the risen Jesus and acknowledges that figure to be *Kyrios* and *Theos*. The gospel of John absolutely maintains that "no one has ever seen God" (1:18; 6:46) except the Son, of course. Nor has anyone ever ascended the heaven to see God or receive revelations (3:13) except the Son. The Israelites neither saw God's shape nor heard his voice (5:37). No, neither Abraham nor Moses nor Elijah nor any of Israel's prophets or visionaries has ever seen God. Abraham, for example, saw Jesus' day (8:56). As has been shown, this refers to an experience of Abraham during his life on earth, such as the theophany at the Covenant of the Pieces (Gen 15) or his reception of the three heavenly visitors (Gen 18). Although Abraham is credited with prophetic visions of the future, John's text is not referring to a vision of Jesus-who-is-to- come-as-the-Messiah, for the text continues with the extraordinary claim that Jesus was not a mere future figure revealed to Abraham but rather a contemporary of Abraham, nay an eternal divine figure: "before Abraham came into being, I AM" (8:58). John's gospel argues in several places that the appearing deity was not God whom no one has ever seen but Jesus.[41] Although the Johannine text insists that Abraham did not see God, he had theophanies nonetheless. Abraham saw Jesus in his visions as the appearing deity, as the one who bears the name of God, "I AM." Likewise in John 12:41 it is stated that Isaiah "saw his glory." Although Isaiah prophesied about future events (see. Sir 48:24-25), it is commonly argued that John's text refers to a time in the prophet's life when he saw his glory during the vision in the temple (Cf. Isa 6). Isaiah did not see God, but since the theophany was genuine, he must have seen the heavenly Jesus, the glory of God, the true Shekinah who pitched his tent there.

Textual Nicodemus – Becoming a Potential Disciple of Jesus

Among the various occurrences of the term ῥαββί, one of the remarkable instances is found in Jn 3: 2 where the title is given to Jesus by Nicodemus, the Pharisee. Nicodemus, besides addressing Jesus as ῥαββί, also added another title such as "a teacher comes from God." When Nicodemus gave the title ῥαββί as a respectful compliment to Jesus, it is certain that, both from hearing about Jesus from others and now through his personal contacts with him, he is convinced that Jesus was a Rabbi in the sense of a teacher. But the question is whether he was convinced that Jesus was indeed a ῥαββί, in the original sense of a Jewish religious teacher. It seems that in the understanding of Nicodemus, who comes from the learned circle of that society, Jesus deserves honour and distinction embodied in the title ῥαββί.

There are certain scholars who regard Nicodemus as a representative figure. According to Raymond F. Collins, the "textual Nicodemus" is a "type" or "representative" figure in the Fourth Gospel."[42] He maintains that "The textual Nicodemus is actually a type of the true Israelite who progresses in faith from seeing the signs, to accepting the truth according to the Scriptures, to finally confessing Jesus openly"[43] as the one in whom the Old Testament finds its fulfilment. Jesus goes on speaking to Nicodemus, and through him to the reader, about his own identity and mission. And Nicodemus, who seems to vanish from the stage at this point, will reappear twice more in the course of the Gospel."[44] Another way of saying this is that John deals with those who are potential disciples as he deals with actual disciples.

Potential disciples in the Gospel of John are those individuals who gave a positive response to the call of Jesus. Among these people are John's most well known and loved characters: Nicodemus, the Samaritan woman at the well, the paralytic at the spring, the man born blind. These persons appeal to us because they have faith and depth. Jesus encounters these people individually and addresses each one personally. They respond honestly and realistically. Lazarus' sister Mary, the official with the sick boy, Nicodemus, the Samaritan woman, the paralytic, and the blind man give a varied responses to the call of discipleship. If Jn 1:11-12 lists the table of contents for this book on discipleship, then Jn 12 also records a summary of how effective the 'public Jesus' was. "Although he had performed so many signs in their presence, they did not believe him" (12:37). In general, the signs and the speeches did not win the masses, the crowds. John 12 also stresses that Jesus did not expect that his work would be popular among the people (12:38-43). Rather the focus of his ministry was on individuals who in some way responded. "The one who believes in me believes not in me but in the one who sent me. The one who sees me sees him who sent me" (12: 44-45).

It was doubtlessly impressive to many of John's original readers that Nicodemus later in the Gospel ends up as a follower of Jesus (cf. 7:50–52; 19:38–42). In chapter 7, the Gospel portrays Nicodemus as a defender of Jesus' right to a fair trial (7:50-51); in chapter 19, Nicodemus helps to bury Jesus with honour. Is this a hint that Nicodemus has taken Jesus' words to heart after his conversation that night? In 7:50-52, Nicodemus appeals to the Law of Moses to defend Jesus to his fellows in the Sanhedrin: "Does our law judge a person without giving him a hearing and learning what he does?" The Jewish leaders immediately identify Nicodemus with Jesus and his followers by asking, "Are you also a Galilean?" In the words of Sandra Schneiders, "In other words, Nicodemus in this scene, although still dependent on the Old Testament, "does the truth" according to the Law (3:21).[45] We are not told how Nicodemus responds to the taunt, but the evangelist, in 7:50, is at pains to remind the reader that this is the same Nicodemus who had come to Jesus before."[46] Finally, in 19:39-42, Nicodemus aligns himself publicly with Jesus in his "lifting up" by joining Joseph of Arimathea in removing Jesus' body from the cross and burying him with an enormous outlay of spices that reminds the reader of Mary of Bethany's action in 12:3. The evangelist reminds the reader that this now public disciple is the same Nicodemus who first came to Jesus "by night" (19:39). By doing the truth, Nicodemus has finally come to the Light and it "is manifest that his works are done in God" (cf. 3:21).

For Nicodemus the Pharisee, Jesus is indeed a Rabbi who teaches the ways of God. Hence, in the presentation of Jesus as ῥαββί, in the episode of Nicodemus, the progress is evident in the Christological titles saying that Jesus is a teacher from God and who teaches the ways of God. Again the Johannine characteristic of presenting a faith development in a potential believer (disciple), is seen in Nicodemus, who begins his dialogue by addressing Jesus ῥαββί. Lapin thinks, "even in John 3:2, where Jesus is called 'a teacher come from God' in addition to ῥαββί, the use of the term ῥαββί is explained on the basis of Jesus' ability to perform signs."[47] Köstenberger thinks that "difficulty for Jesus' earthly ministry seemed to arise precisely at the point where his role of ῥαββί was transcended, be it in terms of his implicit or explicit claims of deity, his "signs" resulting in significant popular acclaim or other messianic manifestations."[48] Here the question is whether the term Rabbi explicitly implies someone who had the power to perform signs. Even if the term ῥαββί is linked to someone who can perform signs, in the case of Johannine Jesus, it cannot be a paradox. When Jesus was challenged about his miraculous work on the Sabbath (5:1-15), Scott observes that the truth which Jesus delivers "is based on his relationship with the Father, whose work he does and without whom he can do nothing (Cf. Jn 5:19-24)."[49] So the power to perform signs (or miraculous works), far from separating the human person of Jesus, serves to confirm his relationship with his Father. Hence, in the contexts when his role of ῥαββί transcends and when some other acclamations are given to Jesus, it may be said that there is a gradual development of faith.

Progression from κύριος (Jew) – Prophet – Messiah (Universal)

The narrator explains that Jews have no dealings with Samaritans (4:9). The Samaritan woman wonders how Jesus as a Jew can ask her, a

Samaritan woman, for a drink. This information is crucial to the whole meeting. The previous chapter discussed how a representative of the Jews, Nicodemus, failed to understand that God had sent Jesus to save the world. In the beginning of chapter 4, Jesus leaves the land of the Jews and starts to Galilee through the land of the Samaritans. The conclusion of Jesus' meeting with the Samaritans stands in contrast to his meeting with Nicodemus. After Jesus has stayed for two days in Samaria, the Samaritans from the woman's village recognize him as the saviour of the world (4: 42). The Samaritan woman and her fellow townspeople had met a Jew who turns out to be the Messiah and the saviour of the world. If the story of Nicodemus in chapter 3 is perhaps the best-known story in the Gospel (because, among other things, of 3:16), then the story of the woman at the well must be the second best known. Among other things, it challenges our preconceived notions about social and ethnic barriers. Jesus was clearly not bound by such conventions in his offer of the free gift of "living water" to the woman in this story.

Raymond Brown has an excellent statement to explain this event and messianic revelation of Jesus in this episode. "John is too good a dramatist to leave the story without a conclusion that would bring together the themes of the two scenes. The woman who was so important in Scene 1 is recalled because it is on her word that the townspeople believe. But the completion of the Father's work (vs. 34), the harvest of the Samaritans, is to have greater durability; for the townspeople come to believe on Jesus' own word that he is the Savior of the world. If our story in 4: 4, particularly in Scene 1, has portrayed the steps by which a soul comes to believe in Jesus, it also portrays the history of the apostolate, for the harvest comes outside of Judea among foreigners. We can scarcely believe that the evangelist did not mean for us to contrast the unsatisfactory faith of the Jews in 2:23-25 based on a superficial admiration of miracles with the deeper faith of the Samaritans based on the word of Jesus. Nicodemus, the rabbi of Jerusalem, could not understand Jesus' message that God had sent the Son into the world so that the world might be saved through him (3: 17); yet the peasants of Samaria readily come to know that Jesus is really the Savior of the world."[50] In the bigger picture, the incident also serves to illustrate Jesus' greater purpose in coming into the world (cf. the Prologue), with its statements about the Light coming into the world. Jesus' purpose went beyond simply being the Messiah of the Jewish people. He came to be the Saviour of the entire world.

A Jew seen as the Messiah of the Samaritans

The immediate narrative context of the saying "salvation is from the Jews" shows that Jesus' Jewishness is also an important theme for his teaching of the true worship of God. In this context, for Gail R. O'Day, the saying has an ironic undertone.[51] The Samaritans, who are not full members of God's people from a Jewish point of view, receive Jesus whereas the Jews reject their own Messiah. As Wayne A. Meeks notes, "salvation is *from* the Jews; they are God's 'own' people. But it is the non-Jews, the Samaritans, who recognise and accept it."[52] The whole story in chapter 4 illustrates how Jesus moves away from the Jews to the non-Jews who welcome him. The Samaritan woman recognizes Jesus as a Jewish prophet[53] after Jesus has revealed the secrets of her previous marital life. There is a clear progression in the woman's attitude toward Jesus: at first she is suspicious of Jesus and regards him only as "a Jew" (4: 9) but later she is ready to accept Jesus as a prophet.[54] This progression is important to the following teaching of true worship. A non-Jew, who at first was sceptical of Jesus, finds that she is speaking with a Jewish prophet, and asks a question a prophet should be able to answer.

The question of the right place of worship, an age-long matter of controversy between the Jews and the Samaritans, is closely connected to the woman's confession that Jesus is a prophet. The woman begins to realize that Jesus is the fulfilment of what has been promised. Because Jesus is presented as the fulfilment of past promises, he can be presented also as the one who surpasses these promises. On the basis of the prologue of the gospel it is known that Jesus is more than was expected: he is God's eternal word who became flesh. But because Jesus also fulfils the expectations of a prophet and the Messiah,[55] he can determine in a new way how God should be worshipped. And as the emissary of salvation he can teach with all authority that the previous ways to worship God have to give way to the true worship of the Father in spirit and truth. These words imply that Jesus, who is presented pointedly as a Jew in the story, is the one whom the woman is expecting.[56] That salvation is from the Jews creates a possibility that Jesus, the Jew, can indeed be the bringer of salvation.

Rabbi of "The People" (6:24) – A Giver of Life

Again in 6: 24-25, "the people" call Jesus Rabbi. We meet this address in the context of the multiplication of loaves and fish, a sign performed by Jesus. When the people gave this title to Jesus, they wanted to make him their leader. However, Jesus' answer to them shows that they sought him, not because they saw the signs, but because they ate the loaves and were filled. But here the title ῥαββί comes from the mouth of the people and that is in the context of the performance of signs. This still raises a question of whether the Johannine term rabbi is connected to Jesus' performance of signs and supernatural power. In the Bread of Life discourse, Scott finds Jesus' claim to be based on the fact that God has placed his seal on him. Scott concludes, "This pattern continues in every instance where Jesus sets out to teach - his authority is clearly God-given."[57] Moody Smith, discussing the Johannine theology, asserts that the miracles in John have a specific role. "Those miracles as signs are intended to play a distinct and definite role in interpreting Jesus' life- giving work, which was the effect of his entire ministry and glorification."[58] Moody Smith thus underscores that the miraculous works in John should not lead one to conclude that "in the Fourth Gospel we are dealing with some sort of naïve, superhuman Christology." [59] It can, therefore, be said that there is always continuity in the Johannine presentation of Jesus as a teacher and in his activities. The continuity exists between the God-given foundation of the teaching and the Son's delivery of it. From what has been discussed above, as regards the relationship between Jesus and God his Father, it can be asserted that the teaching of Jesus and the authority for his teaching emerges from the intimacy and the relationship that he had with his Father. Hence the Johannine presentation of Jesus as ῥαββί is in no way a contradiction either to the 'incarnation' or to the 'Son of God' image of Jesus. Further, the Johannine presentation of Jesus as teacher lays the foundation for the Johannine Christology, which combines the two sides of Jesus, human and divine.

6. Seeking the Human Jesus ῥαββουνί and Recognising the Christ

In the Synoptic Gospels there is a portrayal of several women, whereas in the Fourth Gospel it is only Mary Magdalene who approached the tomb. Collins on his observation of this comparison comments that, "A comparison of the traditions would thus incline us to the belief that the Johannine form of the visit to the tomb tradition has reduced the Galilean women to the single figure of Mary Magdalene."[60] Indeed, she has been called "the apostle to the apostles" because she was the first one to see the Risen Lord even before Peter. As Eisen observes, "they are not explicitly called apostles, but they are the first to receive the message of Jesus' Resurrection, and they are commissioned by angels to hand on the news."[61] Indeed, in recognition of the fact that Mary Magdalene was the first to proclaim the Resurrection of Christ, the Church has honoured her with the title *"apostola apostolorum."*[62] In the story of the appearance, the angels and then Jesus himself asks Magdalene, who weeps by the tomb, why she is weeping. "She offers what appears to be the only logical explanation to the data: someone has taken Jesus' body out of the tomb and cannot be found,"[63] She replies to the angels that "they have taken away my Lord, and I do not know where they have laid him." Turning around, she sees Jesus standing there, but mistakes him for the gardener.

John gives Magdalene the role to communicate to all the other disciples the fact that Christ has risen. John gives this role to a woman and this seems very significant. "The greeting 'woman' is the same word that was used by Jesus to address his mother in 2:4 and 19:26 and will be used by the risen Jesus to address Mary in 20:15."[64] Jesus seems very comfortable with Magdalene. When Jesus calls to her by her name, she immediately recognizes his voice. "It needed no more than the utterance of her name, in the way that Jesus used to speak to her."[65] She saw Jesus before any other apostle and indeed she was given the first commission by our Lord to spread the Good News of Resurrection (Jn 20:17). According to the Johannine appearance narratives (20:1-18), the Risen Jesus appears first to Mary Magdalene. The account of the appearance, as narrated by the author of the Gospel, presents a unique and fundamental facet of women in leadership. She is well presented as a woman leader representing all other women disciples of Galilee and of the Fourth Gospel. As Collins opines, "we must look to Mary Magdalene as being the representative of the Galilean woman within the Fourth Gospel."[66] Though the male apostles, according to the NT, were the ones to proclaim, in the Gospel of John it will be Mary Magdalene who will carry to the Apostles this Good News of Resurrection.

In Luke, Peter's importance is shown in that he was the first to see the risen Jesus (Lk 24:34). Brown says that "John revises this tradition by having it be a woman, Mary Magdalene, to whom Jesus first appears (20:14), instructing her to go and tell his 'brothers' the disciples (20:17-18) of his ascension to the Father."[67] In John, Mary Magdalene is sent by the risen Lord himself and she proclaims the apostolic announcement of the resurrection. Seim observes that "in John's version Mary of Magdala is the first to have 'seen the Lord', and she is the first to be entrusted with the proclamation of the Risen Lord."[68] Qualifications to become an apostle according to Acts required knowledge of Jesus' ministry from the beginning and a personal witness of his resurrection (Ref. Ac 1:21-22). In Johannine perspective, coming to Jesus and believing in him is also seen in

Mary Magdalene. Again in Pauline perspective, having seen the Lord and bearing witness to that is an excellent mark of discipleship. Both of these aspects are seen in the life of Mary Magdalene and she is portrayed as an apostle of Christ. Based on her observation of the Gospel traditions, on the appearance of the Risen Jesus to Mary Magdalene, and the commission that she received from Jesus, Eisen opines that, "Mary and the other women can be interpreted as apostles, in line with Pauline definition of an apostle (1Cor 9:1)."[69] She reports to the disciples "I have seen the Lord," the same words used by Paul to claim his Apostleship (1Cor 9:1; 15:8-9). So the author of the Fourth Gospel presents as if she is commissioned to preach (20:17), which she does faithfully well (20:18).

Jesus asking Mary Magdalene (Jn 20: 17-18) to go and tell the other disciples he was risen shows that this woman has a complementary role in the mission. Mary Magdalene's relationship with Jesus, despite Christ sending her to the Apostles to announce the Resurrection, also has indeed an entirely personal aspect of leadership. Thus Mary Magdalene represents a woman's call to discipleship and leadership. The Magdalene's services of proclamation and witness are roles really challenging to the then current attitude of gender discrimination. According to Setzer,[70] the prominent role of female disciples was an early and firmly recognised tradition, which quickly became an embarrassment to the male leaders of the emerging institutional church. As Seim notes in the Johannine story of the empty tomb, three persons are equally involved: Simon Peter, the Beloved disciple and Mary Magdalene. "Each of them is given some priority, and only when their various pieces of evidence are gathered together does the witness become complete."[71] One needs to note carefully that in the Gospel of John, the women "are not presented as dependent on or subordinate to men's authority, but as acting on their own."[72] The unique place given to "women as proclaimers"[73] in the Fourth Gospel was quite different from that of other first-century Christian churches. Seim continues to say that "authority, witness and proclamation were shared responsibilities including both women and men (Peter as well as Mary Magdalene)."[74] Brown notes that "the Johannine attitude toward women was quite different from that attested in other first-century Christian churches." He adds, "The unique place given to women as proclaimers in the Fourth Gospel reflects the history, the theology, and the values of the Johannine community."[75] As Seim observes, "like everyone else in the Gospel they (the women) stand back for Jesus only, as he is the ultimate authority for all"[76] and are never under the domination of men. The aspect of 'witness of Mary Magdalene' is very relevant today if, Jesus' resurrection is to be proclaimed as a 'passage of liberation.'[77] When the Risen Jesus calls Mary Magdalene by her name in the gospel (Jn 20:17), "she recognized him" as the risen Christ, and she was called as a disciple. Schneiders observes that Jesus' first words in the Gospel to his first disciples[78] are 'What do you seek?'(1:38). That is consistent with his question to Mary Magdalene on the morning of the resurrection 'Whom do you seek?'(20:15).

As Beasley-Murray observes, the synoptic women (Mk 16:6; Matt 28:5; Lk 24:5) are in search at the empty tomb. In the narrative, Mary Magdalene is asked why she is crying "to elucidate the same quest for Jesus."[79] But this is a search of the disciples for Jesus, their master. Culpepper, in his analysis of Mary Magdalene's search, says the following. "Mary Magdalene's understanding is limited. Jesus is her friend and teacher, she sees how he dies, discovers the tomb empty, sees the angels, sees the risen Lord, but is unenlightened, wondering only where they have taken the Lord's body."[80] Though Culpepper says that Mary Magdalene did not recognise the Risen Christ, his position makes clear that she was a disciple of Jesus in his lifetime. According to Beasley-Murray, this understanding and recognition reached its perfection when Jesus addressed her as Mary, as he had always addressed her. Mary in turn addressed him *Rabbouni*. "All the love and faith and joy of which her illuminated heart and mind were capable were poured into the word: Teacher!"[81] Collins says that Mary's faith is inadequate as indicated in the form of address, which Mary directs to the Risen Lord. "She calls him Teacher (20:16) as did the first two disciples (Jn 1:38)"[82] On the other hand, Raymond Brown comments that, "In the Good Shepherd parable (Jn 10:11-18), the shepherd's own sheep recognise him by his voice when he calls them by name. In the resurrection appearance of Jesus to Mary Magdalene she recognises him only when he calls her by her name 'Mary' (Jn 20:16). She is thus recognised as one of his own, as one he loved to the end (Jn 13:1)."[83] Beasley-Murray holds the same opinion as Brown in saying that "the shepherd had called his sheep by name, and the sheep heard and joyfully responded (Jn 10:3). Jesus thereby re- established the personal relationship that Mary thought she had forever lost."[84] This presupposes that Mary Magdalene is a disciple; that she hears his voice and responds (10:3-4) to her master.

In John, Mary Magdalene's role somewhat parallels that of the Samaritan Woman (Jn 4). Both of them are called to be evangelisers and leaders of a community, yet each one's mission context is different. "The Samaritan woman has also been honoured by some church fathers as an apostle to

Samaria."[85] Mary Magdalene differs in being sent. Jesus instituted Mary
Magdalene as apostle to the apostles. Schneiders observes that "What
experience within the Johannine community would have suggested to
the evangelist to make a woman the central character of two such major
missionary texts as the story of the evangelisation of Samaria (4:1-42)
and the commission to announce the resurrection (20:1-18)?"[86] Mary
Magdalene evangelised her co-apostles with the news of the resurrection
of the Messiah. Raymond Brown called this "the supreme Christological
pronouncement of the Fourth Gospel." He interprets Jesus' command to
"Stop holding onto me" (Jn 20:17) as nothing more than a reminder to Mary
of her commission, suggesting that it might even be rendered, "Don't
just stand there! Go tell my brothers!" One can see much appreciation in
Howard-Brook's writings regarding the role of Mary Magdalene in Jn 20,
when he says that, "For all time, the news of the resurrection is brought
to the community by the word of a woman, the first apostle of the risen
Christ... Both her experience and her apostleship remain privileged,
unassailable, and apart from the experience of all later believers."[87] It is
really astonishing that this woman was given a prominent place in scripture
right from the beginning of the early church and at the time the gospels
were written. As Eisen opines, "this finding reveals that these interpreters
maintained a broader concept of apostolicity, and it also shows that the title,
apostolos was closely associated with primary missionary activity."[88] The
textual evidences and the arguments have revealed that Mary Magdalene
has been a disciple of Jesus.

In Brown's research on the *Johannine Community and the Beloved
Disciple*[89] he clearly asserts the position of the Beloved disciple as the
author of the Gospel. Brown in his work on the beloved disciple suggests
that the Johannine picture becomes more understandable in its reference
to an eyewitness. In such a case, the question is whether the position
taken by some scholars who argue for Mary Magdalene to be the beloved
disciple could be a valid argument. As this question does not fall in our area
of research, we are not exploring further in that regard.

7. Johannine Jesus : ῥαββί and κύριος

As has been stressed in many preceding pages, in the Fourth Gospel, the
disciples (and various other people) are portrayed as addressing Jesus as
ῥαββί. The question arises as to whether the Johannine address of ῥαββί
when attributed to Jesus was historically accurate (that is to say, the title
ῥαββί was actually given to Jesus in his day), or was just something the

Johannine community used in retrospect, when the gospel of John was actually written some decades after the event. According to Brooke Foss Westcott, "The fresh recollection of the incident seems to bring back the original terms which had almost grown to be foreign words."[90] This draws attention to the fact that, in the Fourth Gospel, Jesus was called ῥαββί meaning 'Master' or 'Teacher' (Jn 1:38). Hence, if one concludes that the title "teacher" was intended as a translation of the Aramaic/ Hebrew name *Rab*, the question is: was the earthly Jesus known and addressed as ῥαββί? Can it be inferred that the address ῥαββί given to Jesus explicitly shows that he was seen as a religious leader and addressed as a teacher in that community?

Howard-Brook observes that the narrator's translation of the word ῥαββί into teacher "provides the social implication that at least some of the audience was not Jewish, or at least not Hebrew-speaking."[91] Barnabas Lindars observes the translation of the term ῥαββί into διδάσκαλε and states, "John is usually careful to translate his Jewish terms for the benefit of his Greek readers."[92] Recently, taking the same issue for discussion, Köstenberger opines that "it is significant that the address of Jesus as ῥαββί in John is confined to the time of Jesus' earthly ministry."[93] The one instance in 20:16 where Jesus is addressed as ῥαββουνί by Mary Magdalene is no real exception. John may indicate the inappropriateness[94] of such an address subsequent to Jesus' resurrection by translating the term and following it in short order with Thomas' confession of Jesus as "Lord and God" Ὁ κύριός μου καὶ ὁ θεός μου (20:28). By this John draws a very important distinction in identity between the earthly and the exalted Jesus. From the address ῥαββί given to Jesus, one may conclude that John, the author of the Fourth Gospel, consciously presents the historical Jesus as a *teacher* of that time. On the other hand, when John uses the title ῥαββί meaning 'teacher', with reference to Jesus, should it be considered as a retrospective portrayal, by John, in the latter part of first century Christianity? So, it remains inconclusive whether or not the designation 'Rabbi' given to Jesus is historical or not. Although scholars like Shanks and Riesner hold that the address ῥαββί was authentic and given to the historical Jesus, it seems to remain questionable. Since it belongs to a wider area of discussion, that question is left open for further study. Even if it is agreed that the term ῥαββί was authentically addressed to Jesus of Nazareth, the role of ῥαββί with regard to Jesus in John should never be considered merely a title.

The previous discussion has shown that John's Gospel clearly indicates that Jesus' contemporaries customarily perceived him as a religious teacher and that his relationship with his disciples largely conformed to the pattern of Jewish teacher-disciple relationships of his day. It has also been noted that references to Jesus as ῥαββί are, with the exception of 20:16, confined to the phase of Jesus' earthly ministry in John depicted in chs.1–12. Thereafter, Jesus is addressed by his disciples as "Lord" (Farewell discourse: 13:6, 9, 25, 36, 37; 14:5, 8, 22; Peter and the "disciple whom Jesus loved" in the epilogue: 21:15, 16, 17, 20, 21), a sufficiently ambiguous term to accommodate both notions of "master" (teacher) and "Lord" (including God worthy of worship; 20:28). This shift in terminology suggests that, beginning in John 13, Jesus' role as religious teacher is transcended by his anticipation of his return to heaven. While this fact was already hinted at in the first part of John's Gospel (cf., e.g., 8:31), it now takes center stage. Jesus' relationship with his disciples is elevated above their physical life with him and following of him, to a spiritual association and discipleship that transcends mere physical realities, including Jesus' physical departure from his followers and reaches into eternity (cf. esp. 14:2–3).[95] Therefore Jesus' assumption of the role of rabbi during his earthly public ministry now gives way to his role as the exalted Lord. This is insufficiently recognized by contemporary patterns of discipleship that seek to duplicate Jesus' culture-related pattern of gathering around himself a circle of close disciples as the primary paradigm for discipleship.[96] In this role, Jesus will be the recipient of prayer and worship while remaining involved in the disciples' ministry (cf. esp. 14:12). The Spirit will provide continuity with Jesus' ministry by serving as the disciples' teacher on behalf of Jesus (14:26; 16:13–15).

In the opinion of Köstenberger, "John's Gospel shows an organic development from the earthly Jesus' instruction of his followers to their belief that Jesus continued to be present in his community by his Spirit as the exalted Lord."[97] From the observations of Köstenberger on the subject of organic development in the Johannine Christology, an important question arises. This question centres around the dual understanding (or addressing) of Jesus such as ῥαββί and κύριος. The following paragraphs will attempt to present a proper understanding of these two terms as they are addressed to the Johannine Jesus. The significance that these titles have with regard to Johannine Christology will also be addressed. The question is: just how far is the synoptic view being reflected in the Johannine use of the term κύριος when it is attributed to Jesus? Furthermore, why does John use the two terms ῥαββί and κύριος in reference to Jesus? Indeed, how does John himself interpret these terms in a variety of contexts? In the following section, the gradual development of these terms from ῥαββί to κύριος in the Fourth Gospel will be addressed in the light of Johannine Christology.

The Johannine Jesus: A Shift from ῥαββί to κύριος

In the Fourth Gospel, Jesus is addressed with both the terms ῥαββί and κύριος. There are many texts[98] where these two important terms are both used with reference to Jesus. As has already been noted, the references to Jesus as ῥαββί are usually confined to the phase of Jesus' earthly ministry, to show him as a teacher. Since John in his Gospel has used the terms ῥαββί and κύριος in a complex way, the relationship of one with the other needs to be looked at. At the same time, the distinctive 'meaning' of each term needs particular attention.

Use of the Title κύριος to the Johannine Jesus: An Overview

Vermes says that a scrutiny of John, with regard to addressing Jesus as κύριος discloses no established pattern. Vermes in his *Jesus the Jew* analyses the use of the title κύριος in the Fourth Gospel and asserts, "The Fourth Gospel, theologically the most developed of the New Testament writings and an exemplary mixture of Jewish and Hellenistic elements, mirrors to perfection the full extent of the evolution of the use and significance of 'lord.'"[99] Vermes, in his later work, observes that "Lord (*kyrios*) is the most frequently used title of Jesus in the Gospel of John."[100] In the Fourth Gospel, the title κύριος occurs more than 30 times and, like its parallels in Jewish literature of the intertestamental period, it exhibits a great diversity of meanings. In the lowest semantic level of a polite form of address as 'sir', it is used with regard to a variety of persons in John. For example, in Jn 12:21, Philip is addressed as "sir." Whether this "sir" denotes διδάσκαλε or κύριε remains a question. But in the translations of the Fourth Gospel, κύριος is more accurately rendered with the term "Lord."

In the Fourth Gospel there are many examples[101] where the term κύριος is used as designation for Jesus. Jesus is addressed as "sir" even by a total stranger like the Samaritan Woman (Jn 4:11), the royal official (Jn 4:49), and people who sympathised with him (Jn 6:34). However, when κύριε comes from the mouth of the apostles, it mostly means the respected address, 'sir' or 'master' (i.e. teacher). Very significantly, Jesus is addressed as κύριε in the Fourth Gospel when one expresses faith in Jesus.[102] Köstenberger observes that Jesus is addressed by his disciples as "Lord", a somewhat ambiguous term which encompasses both "master" (teacher) and "Lord."[103] For Vermes, the title κύριε "primarily links Jesus to his dual role of charismatic Hasid and teacher, and if the stress is greater in the earlier strata of tradition, this is no doubt due to the fact that his impact as a holy man preceded that of teacher and founder of a religious community."[104] In the Johannine passages where κύριος is attributed to Jesus, Jn 13:13 seems to be a significant passage, where Jesus himself agrees that he is both a teacher as well as Lord. ὑμεῖς φωνεῖ τέ με Ὁ διδάσκαλος καὶ Ὁ κύριος, καὶ καλῶς λέγετε, εἰμὶ γάρ. Vermes agrees that this reference (Jn 13: 13-14; cf. Jn 13:16; 15:15.20) where "Jesus of John refers to himself as 'Lord', it is in the sense of teacher or Master."[105] How is this double title of 'master' and 'Lord' given to Jesus in the Johannine Gospel to be interpreted?

The Johannine Jesus as κύριος: *Gradual Faith Development*

The common understanding is that, according to the writings in the Fourth Gospel, during the early days of the disciples' association with Jesus, they generally called him ῥαββί. But in the development of the Gospel in the later chapters, the disciples mostly address Jesus as κύριος (Lord). It is true that the Johannine use of the title ῥαββί, in reference to Jesus, is dominant in John 1-12. However, what is significant here is that the Johannine Jesus also receives the address κύριος in the first 12 chapters in John. When Jesus is addressed as Rabbi in the fourth gospel, the question arises whether it is an attempt by the author to capture the growth in the disciples' understanding and the development of their faith in Jesus. What is the significance of κύριος being used by the evangelist more frequently in Jn13-21? Does John refer to the Risen Christ here, or is this an expression of the faith development of the disciples? The following section will attempt to answer these questions.

For Köstenberger, the title κύριος given to Jesus is an indication of his role as the exalted Lord. "Jesus' assumption of the role of Rabbi during his earthly public ministry now gives way to his role as the exalted Lord."[106] Does this mean when Jesus is given the title κύριος he can no longer be called ῥαββί? Is it that when Jesus is given the title κύριος in John, he is seen as the exalted and glorified Lord? Hence to be considered are how the use of the term ῥαββί which later became κύριος or how the earthly Jesus who was addressed as ῥαββί is presented later on in the Fourth Gospel as κύριος in the sense of meaning the 'exalted Lord.' Besides, the significant role that the term κύριος plays in the Johannine Christology is to be looked into. But before that it must be determined whether the earthly (historical) Johannine Jesus was addressed at all as κύριος.

Κύριος *Applied to the Earthly Jesus*

Before proceeding, the Greek term κύριος is the definite equivalent of the Hebrew/Aramaic term and the Greek ῥαββί is the equivalent of the Hebrew/Aramaic term רבי. In the Palestinian context of Jesus' time, Hahn says that *Mar* was the universal application of the term 'Lord' as was the way that the term was applied. So for Hahn both titles refer to the human Jesus. Hahn maintains,"the latter was very soon confined in application to the scribes"[107] whereas *Mar* retained its wider meaning. Hahn also agrees that in the New Testament, both *Mar* and *Rab* were currently used as a formal address to superiors. However, *Mar* was also used for equals. Therefore the word took on the character of an expression of courtesy. Hahn further says "in any case we must reckon with the indiscriminate use of *Mari* and *Rabbi* in the time of Jesus."[108] If the term ῥαββί was preferred in addressing a teacher of the law, the term κύριε might equally be used in similar circumstances. Hahn concludes that Jesus was addressed not only as ῥαββί but also as κύριε. Under no circumstances, he says, may it be assumed that the address of κύριε given to Jesus implied the transference to him of a 'divine title'. For Hahn, in the Palestinian context, addressing Jesus with title κύριε refers only to his earthly activity, in so far as "it was not absorbed into eschatological contexts."[109] In the understanding of Hahn, in the Jewish context, when κύριε refers to the Jewish teacher, it is inappropriate to transfer that title to the eschatological level and apply it to the ultimate authority and activity of Jesus.

However, D. Moody Smith in his *The Theology of the Gospel of John* states, "Lord (Greek *kyrios*) is seldom applied to Jesus during his public ministry but is reserved for the period of resurrection, although the vocative *kyrie*, with the meaning "sir," appears frequently."[110] Yet Hahn is clear that the title κύριος when applied to Jesus as a Jewish teacher (with his pupils), indicates that it is not absorbed into any eschatological context. However, once the term κύριος emerges in an eschatological context (or implied exalted status), it shows an organic evolution in the presentation of Johannine Christology.

Κύριος *Applied to the Exalted (Risen) Jesus*

According to Hahn, the title κύριος when attributed to Jesus in the context of the early Church, also referred to the perceived exalted rank of Jesus. This was a developed understanding. He observes that the description κύριε stood for "Jesus as Lord not only in view of His earthly activity, but above all to express the exalted rank and authority of the One who was to return."[111] Here κύριος depicts Jesus as a 'judge of the world' whose return is expected and is invoked by the Church with the call "*Maranatha*." These two terms have eschatological overtones in the liturgy of the early Church. "With this description the earthly church forged a Christological conception quite independently of any traditional concept of a saviour, and was able to include it in both the earthly and the ultimate activity of Jesus."[112] For Hahn, in the gradual development of the title κύριος as given to Jesus, "it becomes clear that the concept of exaltation cannot stand at the beginning of development, and expresses rather a basic and far-reaching new Christological interpretation attained by the early church."[113] Vincent Taylor suggests that "the Fourth Gospel supplies an impressive confirmation of the view that κύριος is a post-Resurrection title."[114] He observes that the title κύριος was given to Jesus in the post-Easter context. He concludes that it is clear that the Evangelist feels it appropriate to speak of 'the Lord' in these contexts but does not feel at liberty to use the title in connection with the earlier ministry. Here, Taylor takes the position that the title κύριος is applicable only to the Risen Lord. "From this evidence we must conclude that it is highly improbable that this title was in use in the lifetime of Jesus. It is as the Risen and Ascended Lord that He is κύριος."[115] Leopold Sabourin asserts that, more than the synoptic writers, "it is even more evident in the Fourth Gospel, where κύριος is always used to designate the Risen Jesus."[116] Sabourin holds the view that several previous uses of the word κύριος (Jn 4: 1; 6: 23) "do not belong to the primitive text."[117] Thus according to Sabourin, "certainly a greater dignity than that of *rabbi* underlies the name "Lord" in this remark of Jesus to His Apostles."[118] Thus, Taylor and Sabourin see a gradual development in the address of Jesus as κύριος in John.

Κύριος *Applied to the Johannine Jesus: Coming to Belief in Jesus*
Richard J. Cassidy observes that, within John's Gospel, κύριος is the pre-eminent title of address used, particularly by those who truly believe in Jesus. This pattern of applying the title κύριος to Jesus is seen both in the time of Jesus' public ministry and after his resurrection. It is used both by the disciples and others within the Gospel, particularly by those "who are in the process of coming to belief in Jesus."[119] Cassidy also observes that the title κύριος is given to Jesus at the washing of the feet, in Martha and Mary's interactions with Jesus during Lazarus' death, and in the resurrection and post-resurrection scenes of John 20 (where we see the acclamation of Thomas). In all the above instances, the term κύριος "serve

unmistakably to convey and enhance the meaning that Jesus is a figure of exalted standing, someone whose sovereign power extends even to the limits of death and life."[120] According to Cassidy, when the title κύριος is given to the Risen Jesus in John 20, it denotes "Jesus, the one who has risen to a glorified state, Jesus, the one who is now sovereign beyond the limits of space and time, is consistently addressed and referred to as 'Lord.'"[121] Geza Vermes in *The Changing Faces of Jesus* discusses the episode of Mary Magdalene's designation of κύριος in the post-Easter narratives. He states that "The 'Lord', signifying Jesus, is endowed with a more elevated spiritual meaning in post-resurrection accounts. For example 'I have seen the Lord'(Jn 20:18), or 'It is the Lord'(Jn 21:17). Indeed, in the highly charged atmosphere of John's Gospel, 'Lord' imperceptibly rises from 'Sir' to greater heights."[122] Thus the above ideas support the view that the title κύριος can be applied to Jesus in the context of persons coming to believe in Jesus' resurrection. In the Johannine context, this view may not be totally supportable as the title κύριος is also given to Jesus even before his resurrection. Thus, it can be maintained that in the mind of the author of the Fourth Gospel, the term κύριος has a very significant role with regard to the faith development of the disciples.

Κύριος *to Jesus: Faith Development of the Disciples*

For Raymond Brown, the disciples' address to Jesus as ῥαββί marks the initial stage in their relationship. Calling Jesus by the title κύριος marks a growth in their faith and understanding of Jesus. The term ῥαββί appears "almost exclusively in the Book of Signs, while in the Book of Glory the disciples address Jesus as κύριος. In these forms of address John may be attempting to capture the growth of understanding on the disciples' part."[123] It certainly seems that there is a close link between these two titles given to the Johannine Jesus. Not only that, but a development is also seen from ῥαββί to κύριος with regard to the faith development of the disciples. In doing that, the context of the post-Easter narratives in Chapter 20 of the Fourth Gospel is examined to see how the faith development of the disciples is portrayed through the persons of Mary Magdalene and Thomas. This section will also endeavour to show the significant role that the term ῥαββί plays in Johannine Christology.

8. Calling Risen Christ as ῥαββουνί: Is it Inappropriate?

According to the author of the Fourth Gospel, during the early days of the disciples' association with Jesus, they apparently called him ῥαββί. Then later, more particularly in the Johannine post-Resurrection narratives, they use the title κύριος when addressing Jesus. In other words, after the resurrection, the title κύριος is always used for Jesus, and not Rabbi. She uses the term κύριος totally three times in reference to Jesus in this context of appearance and announcement: Jn 20: 2. 13. 18. However, in the episode of Jesus' appearance to Mary Magdalene, before calling Jesus ῥαββουνί, Mary uses the title κύριος (20:15) "Sir" in her mistaken belief that she was talking to the gardener.

Subsequent to Jesus' resurrection, the appellation ῥαββουνί in Jn 20:16 may be deemed inappropriate by the fourth evangelist. As Lapin observes "when she realised that he was indeed the risen Jesus, she called him *rabbouni*."[124] Dalman notes the context of Jn 20:16 implies that "Mary desires to resume the old attitude towards the "Master" which is not permitted by Jesus."[125] Here there is an agreement on the level of *translation* of ῥαββουνί into διδάσκαλε, but there is disagreement on the level of *identity* of the risen Jesus by still addressing him as ῥαββουνί. In the words of Moody Smith, when it is fully understood who Jesus is and his role is truly recognised, "he is no longer called a rabbi, for even when his disciples call him ῥαββί, they thereby signal that they do not really understand him."[126] For Köstenberger, the translation of ῥαββουνί, which is διδάσκαλε, is an indication of inappropriateness of such an address subsequent to the resurrection of Jesus. In this respect, this study agrees with Dalman, Moody Smith and Köstenberger in saying that using the term ῥαββουνί for the Risen Christ is inappropriate because the Risen Lord cannot resume his earlier role of διδάσκαλε in the sense of being a mere teacher.

Mary to Thomas: Culmination of Johannine Theology
Professor O'Brien observes that Chapter 20 in the Gospel of John is a memorable chapter indeed, in which a weeping Mary Magdalene turns to see her resurrected "Rabbouni", and Thomas moves from doubt to confession. This very important chapter even takes the relatively unusual step of directly addressing its reader at its end, "These are written that you may (come to) believe that Jesus is the Messiah, the Son of God, and that through this belief you may have life in his name."[127] The story of Thomas is about the failure to be convinced of the resurrection through the testimony of others and the consequent need for personal experience of the Risen Christ. This brings to mind the testimony of the Samaritans, "We no longer believe because of your word; for we have heard for ourselves, and we know that this is truly the saviour of the world" (Jn 4:42).

A disciple of Jesus calls him "Lord and God" (20:28; see 1:1-2), while his opponents charge that Jesus "makes himself equal to God" (5:18) and "makes himself God" (10:34). What is the scope of these remarks about Jesus, in particular in the context of a transition from Mary Magdalene's attribution of ῥαββουνί to Thomas' cry of "Lord and God? What meaning goes into the confession of Jesus as "Lord and God" and what is meant by claiming that Jesus is "equal to God"?[128] In what ways is Jesus properly called "God"? In the gospel prologue, Jesus is called *Theos* (1:1-3). Chapter 5 deals with Jesus' creative "working," in which context Jesus is alleged to be "equal to God" (5:18). *Theos*, then, is the appropriate name for Jesus when he exercises creative power. Creative power is not only claimed but demonstrated (1:1-18; 5:1-9, 19-20) and so Jesus is rightly called *Theos*. *Kyrios*, however, is much more difficult to deal with, for while Jesus is often acclaimed *Kyrios* in John, this title is constantly open to the minimalist interpretation of "sir" or "master." There is, however, one climactic confession in the gospel in which Jesus is acclaimed "My Lord (*Kyrios*) and my God (*Theos*)" (20:28). Surely at this point κύριος should be treated as a cultic title, its full force acclaiming Jesus as a divine figure. But what is intended by acclaiming Jesus as κύριος after his resurrection?

Proclamation of Thomas: A Realisation of the Identity of Jesus

With the proclamation by Thomas, it is difficult to see how any more profound analysis of Jesus' person could be given. Jn 20:28 echoes 1:1 and 1:14 both: the Word was God and the Word became flesh. As noted in previous sections, the Fourth Gospel uses many other titles for Jesus: the Lamb of God (1:29, 36), the Son of God (1:34, 49), Rabbi (1:38), Messiah (1:41), the King of Israel (1:49), the Son of Man (1:51). Now the climax is reached with the proclamation by Thomas, "My Lord and my God." Thus the Gospel has come full circle from 1:1, where the Evangelist had introduced the reader to who Jesus was, to 20:28, where the last of the disciples has come to the full realization of who Jesus was. Jesus does ask Thomas, "Have you believed because you have seen me?" It is even similar to his earlier question to Nathanael, "Do you believe because I told you that I saw you under the fig tree?" (Jn 1:50).

What Jesus had predicted in 8:28 had come to pass: "When you lift up the Son of Man, then you will know that I AM..." By being lifted up in crucifixion, which led in turn to death, resurrection and exaltation with the Father, Jesus revealed his true identity as both Lord and God. It is also noted that the Thomas' pericope in the same context has its own significant place in presenting the Risen Jesus not as διδάσκαλε but as Ὁ κύριός μου καὶ ὁ θεός μου. For Köstenberger, the purpose of Thomas' confession of Jesus as "Lord and God" is to draw "a very important distinction in identity between the earthly and the exalted Jesus."[129] Indeed it is an exalted confessional title quite different from the exclamation of Mary Magdelene (Jn 20:13) τὸν κύριόν μου, essentially little more than a respectful reference. Geza Vermes agrees that it is "in the words that Thomas addressed to Jesus that the climax is reached: 'My Lord and my God!'"[130] According to Sabourin, Thomas' confession, 'my Lord and my God,' "expresses perfectly the faith of the primitive community for which Jesus of Nazareth is the glorified Christ and the divine κύριος, sovereign of all created beings, visible and invisible."[131] Above all, as Cassidy notes, "Thomas' confession unmistakably conveys an unsurpassed Christological meaning and thus serves as a fitting summit point a Gospel that's so manifestly concerned with Jesus' exalted status."[132] C. H. Dodd argues that this confession of Thomas is "an attempt to identify the Jesus of faith with the incarnated Λογος (1:1, 18)."[133] Marianne Meye Thompson observes "in confessing Jesus as "God" the Fourth Gospel never denies Jesus' humanity."[134] For M. M. Thompson, John, the author of the Fourth Gospel, "does accept Jesus' humanity; but he also confesses that he who became flesh is the word of God, that he who performed signs is the light of the world and bread from heaven and that he who died on the cross is the resurrection and the life."[135] So M. M. Thompson correctly concludes that the Christology of the fourth gospel functions within theology. Vermes asserts that this acclamation of the Johannine Thomas in 20:28 is not just a slip of the tongue of the evangelist but "it may have been the subconscious upsurge of the essence of his theology which is cleverly intimated in the opening verse of the Prologue, where Jesus, 'the Word', is clearly identified as 'God.'"[136] It is concluded by stating that the Johannine address of 'My Lord and my God!' to the Risen Jesus is not an accident but rather an acclamation that brings the culmination of Johannine Christology.

Christological Confessions: Expression of the Ideology of Revolt

The content of the high Christological confession of the Johannine community can now be spelled out in detail. Jesus is truly and fully "equal to God" because he has God's two basic and comprehensive powers, creative and eschatological. Jesus is correctly called "God" because he exercises creative power, and "Lord" because he has full eschatological power. Jesus validly bears the name "I AM," and as "I AM," Jesus shares the two attributes of a genuine deity, for he is eternal-in-the-past and imperishable-in-the-future. God demands, moreover, that Jesus receives honour equal to that accorded God himself. Moreover, he is a unique and heavenly figure. He is face to face with God (1:1-2), is in the bosom of God (1:18) and reveals the presence of God (1:51). Yet this confession developed and came to maturity as the creed of a group distinguishing itself from synagogue and church, even in revolt against the hostility found in these groups. The confession itself became a criterion (8:24), which separated authentic Johannine Christians from all other people, a differentiation according to which the world itself was divided into two spheres as human and divine, heaven and earth, or spirit and flesh. The high Christological confession replicates this perspective and becomes the chief expression of this ideology of "revolt." Thus Johannine Christology is a blend of both the humanity and the divinity of Jesus. Likewise, the terms ῥαββί and κύριος when attributed to Jesus can never be contradictory. That is simply the way the author of the Fourth Gospel presents the faith development of those who come to believe in Jesus. F. J. Moloney in his recent article "The Fourth Gospel and the Jesus of History" speaks of the Johannine presentation of the first disciples (Jn 1: 35-51). For Moloney, "It is a misreading of the Johannine point of view in this passage to see the disciples as rapidly moving to expressions of correct messianic understanding of Jesus."[137] Moloney is saying that the disciples did not move rapidly to Jesus. It is true that an external overview of the text gives the impression that the first disciples are led rapidly to confess that they saw the Messiah (cf. Jn 1:41. 45. 49); but the intention of the author of the fourth gospel could not have been so. The experience by the first disciples of Jesus as Messiah is shown as an organic development of their faith in Jesus. They begin with the basic level of looking at Jesus as a teacher but as they stay with him and listen to him they gradually grow in their faith and that culminates in recognising him as 'Messiah' (Cf. Jn 1: 41) and 'Lord and God' (Cf. Jn 20:28).

As Murphey states, "The fourth gospel is written in a simple style with common words, brief statements, picturesque language, and frequent repetition; the effect is profound."[138] It allows the reader to focus upon a few points. It is mostly agreed that the authorship of the fourth gospel is anonymous.[139] "Tradition has held that it was Jesus' disciple John, son of Zebedee, talked about in other Gospels and in the Acts of the Apostles, who authored what we call the Fourth Gospel."[140] Yet, there is no hard evidence suggesting that John wrote this Gospel. The Gospel of John was originally written in Greek.[141] It is thought to have been written around 90-100 AD.

Originally, early Christian historians said that the Gospel was written to fill in some of the holes in the other three gospels. Other interpreters have suggested that it was a "way of holding Judaism together after the terrible destruction of all Israel in 67- 73 AD. The Pharisees insisted that "all who were not thoroughly Jewish should not be allowed into the synagogues of Palestine."[142] The Gospel of John attempts to provide an answer to this and tries to allow the reader of the Gospel an opportunity to discover Jesus for himself or herself. This is a very distinctive literary style of John.[143] Professor O'Brien explains the episode of Thomas in chapter 20 as follows. "[T]he Fourth Gospel speaks to people precisely in Thomas' situation, to people who were not there on Easter and who did not see or touch Jesus' wounds, and its purpose is to proclaim to them that very same witness so that they may believe."[144] Thus, we come to a conclusion that in the presentation of an ascending Christology, John's portrayal of Jesus as ῥαββί in the sense of a teacher has a greater significance in a holistic understanding of the Johannine Jesus.

Summary and Conclusions

In sum, John's Gospel provides unmistakable evidence that Jesus was perceived as a ῥαββί, a Jewish religious teacher, by his contemporaries. While the disciples came to know Jesus as more than just a ῥαββί, and while Jesus' own messianic self- consciousness transcended the role of teacher, the Jewish religious leadership, the crowds and the disciples perceived Jesus in accordance with the accepted cultural role of ῥαββί. Jesus, in turn, used this role as common ground with other religious teachers, be it hostile ("the Jews") or open (Nicodemus) and conducted his relationship with his disciples within the framework of a religious teacher's dealings with his students. What is the significance and the implications of the present study's finding that Jesus, according to John, assumed the role of ῥαββί and was first of all perceived as such by his contemporaries? First, this conclusion suggests that Johannine Christology is not a projection onto the life of Jesus but that John's "high Christology" is rooted in Jesus' earthly life and ministry.

An extreme skepticism regarding the ability of current interpreters to learn anything about the historical Jesus from the Gospels is unwarranted. John's Gospel shows an organic development from the earthly Jesus' instruction of his followers to their belief that Jesus continued to be present in his community through his Spirit as the exalted Lord. The relationship between the "historical Jesus" and the "Christ of faith" is not one of radical disjunction, but one of a gradually emerging realization that the disciples' relationship with their rabbi, Jesus, was to be transcended by their spiritual communion with the ascended Messiah.[145] Moreover, a needed corrective to a conventional understanding of Johannine Christology has been presented. Far from reflecting a docetic or otherwise idealized Christ, John's Gospel is found to reflect, in accordance with the Synoptics, Jesus' thoroughly human and cultural pattern of living and relating. As mentioned, this does not mean that Jesus was reduced to a merely human figure. It does, however, imply that Jesus' messianic claims and his disciples' understanding of Jesus as the Christ grew from his assumption of the accepted cultural role of a Jewish religious teacher.[146] As argued, the Fourth Gospel does not present Jesus merely as a conventional Rabbi.

As E. P. Sanders asks, echoing Joseph Klausner: "How was it that Jesus lived totally within Judaism, and yet was the origin of a movement that separated from Judaism?" The answer, at least in part, may be seen in the fact that Jesus, while accommodating himself to the cultural role of ῥαββί, at the same time transcended this role by virtue of his unique personal identity. The difficulty for Jesus' earthly ministry seemed to arise precisely at the point where his role of ῥαββί was transcended, be it in terms of his implicit or explicit claims of deity, his "signs" resulting in significant popular acclaim, or other messianic manifestations. Finally, as previously mentioned, by pointing to John's casting of Jesus in terms of a first-century Jewish Rabbi, Jesus is in no way limited to being a mere marginal Galilean Jew. On the contrary, as was presented, that Jesus' followers came to believe that their teacher was the Son of God (e.g., 1:49; 20:28). The Jesus of John's Gospel is therefore a religious teacher with a distinction. The question was then asked whether, in the Fourth Gospel, the term 'Rabbi' has any connotation or link with the term 'Lord' (κύριος). Raymond Brown's idea on the Johannine terms of ῥαββί and κύριος applied to the Johannine Jesus was the starting point of a review. This led first to an in-depth review of how the synoptic Gospels use the term κύριος in order to see how the term can be understood in a wider context. The Johannine meaning of the term κύριος as applied to Jesus was explored from the synoptic perspective. Finally, there was a discussion of how the term ῥαββί is used in the light of Johannine Christology and the faith development of his disciples. Also, the progression was traced back to the use of the term ῥαββί to its culmination: 'Messiah' (Jn 1:41) and 'Lord and God' (Jn 20:28).

Thus, Part III chapter two of this book concludes that in John, "the term ῥαββί applied to the Johannine Jesus" provides unmistakable evidence that Jesus was indeed basically perceived as a Rabbi. It is not only his disciples, but also the people and even Jesus' opponents who address Jesus as ῥαββί in the sense of teacher. Again, it is concluded that the application of the title ῥαββί to the Johannine Jesus also has a role to play in the Christology of the Fourth Gospel. This aspect of looking at the Johannine Jesus basically as a teacher in no way minimises his exalted status, of one who is acclaimed as Messiah or Lord and God. Thus, the image of "Jesus the teacher" serves as a starting point to build up the Johannine Christology, which is seen to be both ascending and holistic.

Endnotes

[1] Cf. Francis J. MOLONEY, "The Fourth Gospel and the Jesus of History", *New Testament Studies* 46.1 (2000) 42-58; See, J. Armitage ROBINSON, *The Historical Character of St. John's Gospel*, London, Longmans-Green, 1908; Franz MUSSNER, *The Historical Jesus in the Gospel of St. John*, New York, Herder & Herder / London, Burns & Oates, 1967; Everett F. HARRISON, "Historical Problems in the Fourth Gospel", *Bibliotheca Sacra* 116: 463 (1959) 205-211.

[2] It is well documented that the human and historical aspect of Johannine Christology has not been given much attention. See, E. EARLE ELLIS, "Background and Christology of John's Gospel: Selected Motifs", *South western Journal of Theology* 31 (1988) 24-31; Kimberly D. BOOSER, "The Literary Structure of John 1-18: Examination of Its Theological Implications Concerning God's Saving Plan Through Jesus Christ", *Evangelical Journal* 16 (1998) 13-29; G. Van BEKKE, H. G. VAN DER WATT & P. MARITZ, *Theology and Christology in the Fourth Gospel*, Essays by the Members of the SNTS Johannine Writings Seminar, Peeters Publishers, 2005.

[3] Everett F. HARRISON, "Historical Problems in the Fourth Gospel", *Bibliotheca Sacra* 116: 463 (1959) 205-211; See, Leo G. COX, "John's Witness to The Historical Jesus", *Bulletin of the Evangelical Theological Society*, 9.4 (1966) 173-178; Andreas J. KÖSTENBERGER, "The Seventh Johannine Sign: A Study in John's Christology", *Bulletin for Biblical Research* 5 (1995) 87-104.

[4] R. RIESNER, *Jesus as Preacher and Teacher*, p. 188.

[5] D. MOODY SMITH, *The Theology of the Gospel of John*, p. 91.

[6] *Ibid.*

[7] A. KÖSTENBERGER, *Studies on John and Gender*, p. 96.

[8] D. MOODY SMITH, *The Theology of the Gospel of John*, p. 91.

[9] Jesus never calls himself "Messiah" or "Son of God" in the Gospel of John. The Son of Man title is especially significant in the Gospel of John. It is Jesus'

own way of referring to himself. See, Peder BORGEN, "Some Jewish Exegetical Traditions as Background for Son of Man Sayings in John's Gospel (Jn 3,13-14 and Context)", Marinus DE JONGE, ed., *L'Évangile de Jean: Sources, rédaction, théologie*, Gembloux, Duculot, Leuven, Louvain University Press and Peeters, 1977, pp. 243-258; Cf. D. Francois TOLMIE, "The Characterization of God in the Fourth Gospel", *Journal for the Study of the New Testament* 69 (1998) 57-75; Jakob VAN BRUGGEN, *Jesus the Son of God: The Gospel Narratives as Message*, Grand Rapids, Baker, 1999.

[10] See, H. H. ROWDON, ed., *Christ the Lord, Essays in Honour of Donald Guthrie*, Leicester, IVP, 1982; Sydney TEMPLE, "A Key to the Composition of the Fourth Gospel", *Journal of Biblical Literature* 80 (1961) 220-232; Cf. W. H. Griffith THOMAS, "The Purpose of the Fourth Gospel, Part I", *Bibliotheca Sacra* 125: 499 (1968) 254-262; Bruce E. SCHEIN, *Following the Way: The Setting of John's Gospel*, Minneapolis, Augsburg, 1980. See also, M. M. THOMPSON, *The Humanity of Jesus in the Fourth Gospel*, Philadelphia, Fortress, 1988; John ASHTON, *Understanding the Fourth Gospel*, Oxford, Clarendon, 1991. Ashton discusses Jesus according to John primarily as Messiah, Son of God, and Son of Man, but not as a Jewish religious teacher. Read also, Rudolf SCHNACKENBURG, *Jesus in the Gospels*, (trans.) O. C. DEAN, Jr., Louisville, Westminster/John Knox, 1995. Schnackenburg does not refer to Jesus as a Jewish religious teacher in his discussion of Johannine Christology. Cf also, M. HENGEL, *Die johanneische Frage,* WUNT 67, Tübingen, MohrSiebeck, 1993; R. G. MACCINI, *Her Testimony is True: Women as Witnesses according to John, JSNTSS* 125, Sheffield, Sheffield Academic Press, 1996, pp. 144. 240-241; R. BAUCKHAM, (ed.), *The Gospels for All Christians: Rethinking the Gospel Audiences,* Grand Rapids, Eerdmans, 1997, pp. 9-48.

[11] J. N. SANDERS & B. A. MASTIN, *A Commentary on the Gospel according to John*, Black New Testament Commentaries, London, Adam And Charles, 1968, p. 98.

[12] D. MOODY SMITH, *The Theology of the Gospel of John*, p. 91.

[13] *Ibid.*

[14] *Ibid.*

[15] R. BULTMANN, *John*, p. 100, n.5.

[16] *Ibid.*

[17] M. SCOTT, *Sophia and the Johannine Jesus*, p. 152. The Johannine Jesus is not teaching in secret like the group of gnostics; He teaches openly to all who wish to listen to him (cf. Jn 18: 20). The places of his teaching include the synagogue (cf. Jn 6: 59) and the Temple court (cf. Jn 7:14. 28; 8:20; 18:20).

[18] *Ibid.*

[19] Cf. Martinus C. DE BOER, *From Jesus to John: Essays on Jesus and New Testament Christology in Honour of Marinus De Jonge*, Sheffield, Continuum

International Publishing Group - Sheffield Academic Press, 1993; See also, H. KOESTER, "History and Cult in the Gospel of John and in Ignatius of Antioch", *Journal of Theology and the Church* 1 (1965) 111-123; D. M. DAVEY, "Justin Martyr and the Fourth Gospel", *Scripture* 17 (1965) 117-122; Raymond E. BROWN, *The Community of the Beloved Disciple*, New York, Paulist, 1978; M. DE JONGE, "The Beloved Disciple and the Date of the Gospel of John", E. BEST & R. M. WILSON, eds., *Text and Interpretation, Essays in Honour of Matthew Black,* Cambridge, Cambridge University Press, 1979, pp. 99-114; James D. G. DUNN, "Let John Be John", Peter STUHLMACHER, ed., *Das Evangelium und die Evangelien,* Tübingen, Mohr, 1983, pp. 309-339; Brendan BYRNE, "The Faith of the Beloved Disciple and the Community in John 20", *Journal for the Study of the New Testament* 23 (1985) 83-97; D. Moody SMITH, *Johannine Christianity: Essays on Its Setting, Sources, and Theology*, Columbia, University of South Carolina Press, 1989; Thomas L. BRODIE, *The Quest for the Origin of John's Gospel: A Source Oriented Approach*, New York, Oxford University Press INC., 1994; Andreas KÖSTENBERGER, "The Destruction of the Second Temple and the Composition of the Fourth Gospel", *Trinity Journal* 26.2 (Fall 2005) 205-242.

[20] Craig E. EVANS, *Word* and Glory: On the Exegetical and Theological Background of John's Prologue, JSNTSS 89, Sheffield, JSOT, 1993, pp. 13–17; Robert KYSAR, "The Background of the Prologue of John's Gospel: Critique of Historical Methods", *Canadian Journal of Theology* 16 (1970) 250-255; David R. CARNEGIE, "The Kerygma in the Fourth Gospel", *Vox Evangelica* 7 (1971) 39-74; Merrill C. TENNEY, "Topics from the Gospel of John: Part I: The Person of the Father", *Bibliotheca Sacra* 132 (Jan. 1975) 37-46; C. T. R. HAYWARD, "The Holy Name of the God of Moses and the Prologue of St John's Gospel", *New Testament Studies* 25 (1978) 16-32; Edwin D. FREED, "Theological Prelude to the Prologue of John's Gospel", *Scottish Journal of Theology* 32 (1979) 257ff; R. A. CULPEPPER, "The Pivot of John's Prologue", *New Testament Studies* 27 (1980) 1-31; Jeff STALEY, "The Structure of John's Prologue", *Catholic Biblical Quarterly* 48 (1986) 241-264; John ASHTON, "The Transformation of Wisdom: A Study of the Prologue of John's Gospel", *New Testament Studies* 32 (1986) 161-186;. Jeffrey Lloyd STALEY, "The Structure of John's Prologue: Its Implications for the Gospel's Narrative Structure", *Catholic Biblical Quarterly* 48 (1986) 241-263; Thomas H. TOBIN, "The Prologue of John and Hellenistic Jewish Speculation", *Catholic Biblical Quarterly* 52 (1990) 252-269; Jan G. VAN DER WATT, "The Composition of the Prologue of John's Gospel: The Historical Jesus Introducing Divine Grace", *Westminster Theological Journal* 57 (1995) 311-332; Simon R. VALENTINE, "The Johannine Prologue - A Microcosm of the Gospel", *Evangelicals Quarterly* 68 (1996) 291-304; Gordon D. KIRCHHEVEL, "The Children of God and the Glory that John 1:14 Saw", *Bulletin for Biblical Research* 6 (1996) 87-94; Mary COLOE, "The Structure of the Johannine Prologue and Genesis 1", *Australian Biblical Review*

45 (1997) 40-55; Benedict T. VIVIANO, "The Structure of the Prologue of John (1:1-18): A Note", *Revue Biblique* 105 (1998) 176-184; Stephen VOORWINDE, "John's Prologue: Beyond Some Impasses of Twentieth Century Scholarship", *Westminster Theological Journal* 64.1 (2002) 15-44.

[21] Cf. M. M. THOMPSON, *"The Historical Jesus and the Johannine Christ"*, in *Exploring the Gospel of John, In Honor of D. Moody Smith*, (ed.) R. A. CULPEPPER and C. C. BLACK, Louisville, KY, Westminster/John Knox, 1996, p. 21. Thompson helpfully contrasts the respective contents of Jesus' teaching in the Synoptics and in John on pp. 22–25 and 29–31; Cf. R. A. CULPEPPER, *Anatomy of the Fourth Gospel*, Philadelphia, Fortress, 1983; J. L. MARTYN, *History and Theology in the Fourth Gospel* (rev. ed.), Nashville, Abingdon, 1979. For recent trends in Johannine scholarship, see, F. F. SEGOVIA (ed.), *"What is John?" Readers and Readings of the Fourth Gospel*, SBL Symposium Series 3, Atlanta, Scholars Press, 1996. The Fourth Gospel provides a historically reliable portrait of Jesus. While it is true that the fourth gospel is given to more theologizing than the Synoptics, this does not mean that history in the fourth gospel is treated lightly. Cf. Andreas ROSENBERGER, *"Frühe Zweifel an der johanneischen Verfasserschaft des vierten Evangeliums in der modernen Interpretations geschichte"*, *European Journal of Theology* 5 (1996) 37–46.

[22] See, Andreas KÖSTENBERGER, *The Missions of Jesus and the Disciples According to the Fourth Gospel,* Grand Rapids, Eerdmans, 1998. A survey of the history of interpretation of John's Gospel shows that while the first two aspects of Johannine Christology have been adequately recognized, the third role has often reflected the common perception of Jesus among his contemporaries, friends and foes alike: that Jesus was perhaps more, but certainly no less, than a rabbi.

[23] D. MOODY SMITH, *The Theology of the Gospel of John*, p. 125. To read more about the affinity between John's Gospel and Jewishness, read; James S. ACKERMAN, "The Rabbinic Interpretation of Psalm 82 and the Gospel of John (John 10:34)", *Harvard Theological Review* 59 (1966) 186-191; R. G. BRATCHER, *"The Jews in the Gospel of John"*, *Bible Translator* 26 (1975) 401-409; David D. C. BRAINE, "The Inner Jewishness of John's Gospel as a Clue to the Inner Jewishness of Jesus", *Studien zum Neuen Testamen und seiner Umwelt* 13 (1989) 101-155; Aileen GUILDING, *The Fourth Gospel and Jewish Worship,* Oxford, Clarendon Press, 1960; Bruce GRIGSBY, "If Any Man Thirsts...": Observations on the Rabbinic Background of John 7,37-39", *Biblica* 67 (1986) 101-108; Cf. also *John and the Dead Sea Scrolls*, (ed.) J. H. CHARLESWORTH, New York, Crossroad, 1990; R. BAUCKHAM, *"The Qumran Community and the Gospel of John"*, Presentation at the Annual Meeting of the Society of Biblical Literature, November 24, 1997 argues persuasively that the Fourth Gospel does not depend directly on the Qumran writings but that both are indebted to a common Jewish theological and interpretive milieu. Read, John Christopher THOMAS, "The Fourth Gospel and Rabbinic Judaism", *Zeitschrift für die neutesamentliche Wissenschaft* 82 (1991) 159-182.

[24] John ASHTON, *Understanding the Fourth Gospel*, Oxford, Clarendon, 1991.

[25] Cf., C. H. DODD, *Historical Tradition in the Fourth Gospel*, Cambridge, Cambridge University Press, 1963; Leon MORRIS, "*History and Theology in the Fourth Gospel*", in *Studies in the Fourth Gospel*, Grand Rapids, Eerdmans, 1969, pp. 65–138; M. M. THOMPSON, "*Historical Jesus and Johannine Christ*", pp. 25–26 and 32–35.

[26] Rudolf SCHNACKENBURG, *Jesus in the Gospels*, Louisville- Westminster, John Knox, 1995.

[27] Read, D. NEALE, "Was Jesus a Messiah? Public response to Jesus and his ministry", *Tyndale Bulletin* 44.1 (1993) 89-101; Edward P. MEADORS, *Jesus the Messianic Herald of Salvation*, Peabody, MA, Hendrickson Publishers, 1997; Lidija NOVAKOVIC, "Jesus as the Davidic Messiah in Matthew", *Horizons in Biblical Theology* 19.2 (1997) 148-191.

[28] See, Kevin QUAST, *Reading the Gospel of John. An Introduction*, New York, NY, Mahwah, NJ, Paulist, 1991, p. 15.

[29] Archie W. D. HUI, "John the Baptist and Spirit-Baptism", *Evangelical Quarterly* 71.2 (1999) 99-115; Robert L. WEBB, "Jesus' Baptism: Its Historicity and Implications", *Bulletin for Biblical Research* 10.2 (2000) 261-310.

[30] Read, Torleif ELGVIN, "The Messiah who was Cursed on the Tree", *Themelios* 22.3 (1997) 14-21.

[31] Cf. L. F. BADIA, *The Qumran Baptism and John the Baptist's Baptism*, Lanham, University Press of America, 1980, 52-53. Qumran ceremonial activities are assumed to have been known at least among the Pharisees and Sadducees, include the Jewish practices of ceremonial washings. It is said that one period in which the Qumran sect occupied the area near the Dead Sea was ca. 4 B.C.- 68 A.D. Cf. Aileen GUILDING, *The Fourth Gospel and Jewish Worship*, Oxford, Clarendon Press, 1960; Barnabas LINDARS, "Word and Sacraments in the Fourth Gospel", *Scottish Journal of Theology* 29 (1976) 49ff; See, Rainer RIESNER, "Bethany Beyond the Jordan (John 1:28) Topography, Theology and History in the Fourth Gospel", *Tyndale Bulletin* 38 (1987) 29-63.

[32] Rudolf SCHNACKENBURG, *The Gospel according to John*, Vol.1, NY, Cross Road, 1987, pp. 308-309; Also, J. CALVIN, *St. John*, Calvin New Testament Commentaries, T. H. L. PARKER (trans.), Grand Rapids, MI, Eerdmans, 1961, p. 36. According to Calvin, the title Rabbi was commonly given to men of high rank or with any kind of honour. But here the Evangelist records another contemporary use of it. Calvin thinks, "by this name they addressed teachers and expounders of the Word of God." As regards the address of the two disciples, Jesus as ῥαββί, R. F. Collins writes that "the use of the title "Rabbi" implies that the disciples looked upon Jesus as a teacher and interpreter of the Law. It is not unlikely that the disciples sought out Jesus precisely because he was one who could interpret the Scriptures." See, R. F. COLLINS, *These Things Have been Written*, p. 103.

[33] Cf. Gerald F. HAWTHORNE, "The Concept of Faith in the Fourth Gospel", *Bibliotheca Sacra* 116: 462 (1959) 117-126. We know from Jn 1: 40 that Andrew, Simon's brother, was one of the two disciples who followed Jesus home. Andrew wasted no time finding his brother Simon and telling him, "We have found the Messiah" (verse 41). Peter accompanies Andrew and they make their way to Jesus. When Jesus looks upon Peter, he gives him a new name: Cephas, the Aramaic equivalent to *Petros* (Peter), meaning "rock." It is interesting that Jesus does not "call" Peter here. Instead, Jesus renames Simon, Peter "the Rock." Cf. Leon MORRIS, *The Gospel According to John*, Grand Rapids, Westminster, B. Eerdmans Publishing Co., 1971, p.160. This scene, while placed in a different context to the Synoptic scenes, follows the Markan sequence of Baptism, then the calling of disciples at the beginning of Jesus' ministry. In the Synoptic Gospels, it is never said how or when Simon was given the name Peter. It is simply written that his name was Peter. Throughout these Gospels he is either called Simon or Peter or Simon Peter. John alone supplies us with the story of how Peter got his name. Simon is far from a "rock" when Jesus first meets him. He begins to evidence some rock-like traits at the "great confession" (Mt 16:15- 19), but not until after the resurrection of Jesus and Pentecost does Peter truly become a "rock." Jesus' naming of Simon is therefore prophetic. This was the case in other instances of renaming in the Bible. God did not rename an individual after the changes took place, but before they came about. Abram (meaning "exalted father") was renamed Abraham ("father of a multitude") before Isaac was born (Genesis 17:5). Giving a name to someone implies much in the Bible. Adam named the animals God created, reflecting the fact that God had appointed him to "rule" over his creation. Besides Abraham, God renamed a number of other people, including Sarai (to Sarah), and Jacob (to Israel). In each case, it reflects God's plan to change the destiny of the one whose name he has changed. The giving of a new name when done by men is an assertion of the authority of the giver (e.g. II Kings 23:34; 24:17). When done by God it speaks of a new character in which the man henceforth appears (e.g. Gen. 32:28).

[34] D. A. CARSON, *John*, pp. 147-148. Cf. Peter is also given special epiphanies (Mk 5:37-43; 9:2-8; 13:3-37 and 14:33-42), special revelations (Mt 16:17; 17:24-27), special instruction (Lk 12:41-48); see also 2 Peter 1:16-21. Thus epiphanies or revelations are given to individual disciples so that this revelation may help that disciple to play the role of witnessing.

[35] A. J. KÖSTENBERGER, *Studies on John and Gender*, p. 77.

[36] C. K. BARRETT, *John*, p. 150. For Nathanael, at least, coming from Nazareth is not in Jesus' favour, so far as any claim to being Messiah is concerned. John shows that Nathanael is sceptical about Jesus. From what little he knows of him, Nathanael is not predisposed to accept him as the Messiah. Despite his dubiousness about Jesus' origins, Nathanael does go to Jesus. This presents Nathanael as a believer in Jesus when he enthusiastically responds, "You are the Son of God; You are the King of Israel." Nathanael recognises

the Rabbi as 'The Son of God' and 'The King of Israel' (v. 49). Also, W. A. MEEKS, *The Prophet-King: Moses Traditions and the Johannine Christology,* NovTSup 14, Leiden, E. J. Brill, 1967, p. 41 n. 2; Günther BORNKAMM, "Zur Interpretationdes Johannesevangeliums", *EvT* 28 (1968) 8-25.

[37] D. A. CARSON, *Gospel According to John,* Grand Rapids, Eerdmans, 1991, pp. 147–148.

[38] A. J. KÖSTENBERGER, *Studies on John and Gender*, pp. 76-77

[39] Cf. B. E. GÄRTNER, "The Pauline and Johannine Idea of 'To Know God' Against the Hellenistic Background", *NTS* 14 (1967-8) 209-231; See Peder BORGEN, "God's Agent in the Fourth Gospel", *Religions in Antiquity*, (ed.) Jacob NEUSNER, Leiden, Brill, 1968, pp. 137-147. J. H. NEYREY, "John III – A Debate over Johannine Epistemology and Christology", *NT* 23 (1981) 115-127; Karl Olav SANDNES, "Whence and Wither, A narrative Perspective on Birth a! nwqen (Jn 3. 3-8)", *Biblica* 85 (2004) 153-173, p. 155.

[40] See J. H. NEYREY, "The Jacob Allusions in John 1:51", *CBQ* 44 (1982) 586-605, esp. 592, n. 30; Philo argues that the theophanies in the Hebrew Scriptures were not visions of God (material persons cannot see the immaterial God). Therefore, they were revelations of God's Logos or of a Power of God. In Gen 17:1, for example, Abraham did not see God but only a Power of God (*Mut.* 15, 17). Despite his request to God to "show me Thyself" (Ex 33:13 LXX), Moses saw only "the back of God," which is one of "the powers that keep guard around you" (*Sp. Leg.* I. 45-46). In Gen 28:12, Jacob saw one of the powers of God (*Somn.* I. 70). But in another theophany (Gen 31:13), Jacob is told that the appearing figure is *not* God but "god who appeared to you *in place of God*" (*Somn.* I. 228). Are there two gods? No, Philo can distinguish between *no theos and theos*. Accordingly the holy word in the present instance has indicated Him who is truly God by means of the article saying "I am the God" (Gen 31:13) while it omits the article when mentioning him who is improperly so called, saying "Who appeared to you in one place" not "of the God," but simply "of God" (*Somn.* I.229). For Philo references, see *Plant.* 86-87, *Abr.* 124-125, *Somn.* I.160, 163 and *Q. Ex.* II.62. See also, *Det.* 160; *Mut.* 11; *Somn.* I.230-31; *Mos.* I.66, 74-76; PHILO, *Cher.* 88-89; *Leg. All.* I.5; *Gen. R.* 11.10 and *Ex. R.* 30.6. See also, Alan SEGAL and Nils DAHL, "Philo and the Rabbis on the Names of God", *JSJ* 9 (1978) 1-28. See also A. MARMORSTEIN, "Philo and the Names of God", *JQR* 22 (1931-32) 295-306; Morton SMITH, "The Image of God, Notes on the Hellenization of Judaism with Especial Reference to Goodenough's Work on Jewish Symbols", *BJRL* 40 (1957-58) 473-512.

[41] Cf. Justin Martyr, *Dialogue with Trypho*, Dial. 56- 127. For example, Justin Martyr employed it in his *Dialogue with Trypho*, when he argued with his Jewish opponent that it was Jesus who appeared to the Patriarchs. After systematically demonstrating that Jesus appeared to Abraham (*Dial.* 56, 59), to Moses (*Dial.* 56, 59, 60, 120), and to Jacob (*Dial.* 58, 60, 86, 126), Justin

summarized his claim to have shown that neither Abraham nor Isaac nor Jacob nor any other man saw the Father and ineffable Lord of all and of Christ, but (saw) him, who was according to his will, his Son, being God, and the Angel because he ministered to his will (*Dial.* 127). The structure of Justin's argument, moreover, is like that of John: 1) no one has ever seen God, 2) therefore the Patriarchs, who received genuine theophanies according to the Scriptures, saw Jesus, 3) who is properly called God.

[42] See Raymond F. COLLINS, "*The Representative Figures of the Fourth Gospel*-I", *Downside Review* 94 (1976), pp. 16-46. Here Collins gives a good explanation of the concept of representation as well as a specific treatment of Nicodemus as a type.

[43] J. N. SUGGIT, "*Nicodemus-the True Jew. The Relationship Between the Old and New Testament*", *Neotestamentica* 141, Republic of South Africa, 1981, pp. 100- 101. According to Schneiders, there is no doubt Nicodemus functioned in *John's community* as the hero of its Jewish Christian members, but his primary function in the *Gospel* is to catch the conscience of the reader. Nicodemus is the very type of the truly religious person who is, on the one hand, utterly sincere and, on the other, complacent about his or her knowledge of God and God's will. Such people are basically closed to divine revelation. Like Nicodemus, they "know" who Jesus is, what his message means (cf. 3:2). And like Nicodemus, it is only after they have been reduced to the futility of their own ignorance that they can begin the process of coming to the light not by argument or reasoning but by accepting the truth, a process which gradually opens them to the true meaning of the Scriptures. To read more, Cf. D. MOODY SMITH, "'*God's Only Son': The Translation of John iii 16 in the RSV*", *Journal of Biblical Literature* 72 (1953) 213-219; P. BORGEN, "*Some Jewish Exegetical Traditions as Background for Son of Man Sayings in John's Gospel* (Jn 3,13-14 and context)", in *L'Evangile de Jean: Sources, rédaction, théologie*, ed. M. DE JONGE, Louvain, University Press, 1977, pp. 243-258.

[44] Sandra SCHNEIDERS, "*Born Anew*", *Theology Today*, Vol. 44, No. 2 (July 1987) 189-196, p. 190. In p. 195 Schneiders notes that in the Nicodemus passage, the reader experiences both identification with and distance from Nicodemus, and comes to recognize in him or herself the disciple who comes to the light only through an ongoing recognition of the truth. We are caught up in the textual reversals: Nicodemus who claims to know is played off against Jesus who truly knows; the one whom Nicodemus blindly calls "teacher" reveals that the self-confident scribe is not truly a teacher; the "signs" that brought Nicodemus to Jesus are revelatory only in the light of the new birth which he cannot understand, and thus his "coming to Jesus," the Light, is really a remaining in darkness, and so on. See, Dennis SYLVA, "Nicodemus and His Spices (John 19.39)", *New Testament Studies* 34 (1988) 148-151.

[45] To read more on this subject of actual disciples and potential disciples in the Gospel of John, See, Marinus DE JONGE, "Jewish Expectations about

the Messiah according to the Fourth Gospel", *New Testament Studies* 19 (1973) 246-270.

⁴⁶ S. SCHNEIDERS, "*Born Anew*", p. 191.

⁴⁷ H. LAPIN, *Rabbi*, p. 602.

⁴⁸ A. J. KÖSTENBERGER, *Studies on John and Gender*, pp. 76-77.

⁴⁹ M. SCOTT, *Sophia and the Johannine Jesus*, p. 153.

⁵⁰ R. BROWN, *The Gospel According to John*, pp. 184-185

⁵¹ For the implied irony, see, Gail R. O'DAY, *Revelation in the Fourth Gospel: Narrative Mode and Theological Claim,* Philadelphia, Fortress Press, 1986, p. 70; E. C. HOSKYNS, *The Fourth Gospel,* (ed.) F. N. DAVEY, 2nd edition, London, Faber and Faber, 1947, p. 244; Barnabas LINDARS, *The Gospel of John,* NCB, London, Oliphants, 1972, p. 189. For the messianic interpretation of these words see also O. BETZ, "To Worship in Spirit and in Truth: Reflections on John 4, 20–26", *Jesus, der Messias Israels: Aufsätze zur biblischen Theologie,* WUNT 42, Tübingen, Mohr-Siebeck, 1987, pp. 420–438, esp. pp. 433–435.

⁵² W. A. MEEKS, *The Prophet-King: Moses Traditions and the Johannine Christology,* NovTSup 14, Leiden, E. J. Brill, 1967, 41 n.2.

⁵³ Cf. G. O'DAY, *Revelation in the Fourth Gospel,* p. 67; T. OKURE, The Johannine Approach to Mission: A Contextual Study of John *4:1–42,* WUNT 31, Tübingen, Mohr-Siebeck, 1988, p. 109.

⁵⁴ Cf. B. OLSSON, *Structure and Meaning in the Fourth Gospel: A Text-Linguistic Analysis of John 2:1–11 and 4:1–42,* ConNT 6, Lund, CWK Kleerup, 1974, p. 187; Gail O'DAY, *Revelation in the Fourth Gospel,* 67–68; T. OKURE, *The Johannine Approach to Mission,* pp. 114–115

⁵⁵ Cf. E. LEIDIG, *Jesu Gespräch mit der Samaritanerin und weitere Gespräche im Johannesevangelium,* Theologische Dissertationen 15, Basel, Friedrich Reinhardt, 1981, p. 126: "Als Messias, der die Verheissung Gottes er füllte, konnte Jesus Zäune und Trennungsvorschriften zwischen Juden und Samaritanern aufheben.

⁵⁶ Cf. E. C. HOSKYNS, *The Fourth Gospel,* (ed.) F. N. DAVEY, 2nd edition, London, Faber and Faber, 1947, p. 244; Barnabas LINDARS, *The Gospel of John,* NCB, London, Oliphants, 1972, p. 189; O. BETZ, "To Worship in Spirit and in Truth: Reflections on John 4, 20–26," *Jesus, der Messias Israels: Aufsätze zur biblischen Theologie*, WUNT 42, Tübingen, Mohr-Siebeck, 1987, pp. 420–438, esp. pp. 433–435.

⁵⁷ M. SCOTT, *Sophia and the Johannine Jesus*, p. 153.

⁵⁸ D. MOODY SMITH, *The Theology of the Gospel of John*, p. 166.

⁵⁹ *Ibid.*

⁶⁰ R. F. COLLINS, *These Things have been written. Studies on the Fourth Gospel*, p. 33.

[61] U. E. EISEN, *Women officeholders in Early Christianity*, p. 50; Read also, Barnabas LINDARS, "The Composition of John XX", *New Testament Studies* 7 (1961) 142-147; Gerd LÜDEMANN, *Resurrection of Jesus: History, Experience, Theology*, Fortress Press, 1995.

[62] Raymond E. BROWN, Roles of Women in the Fourth Gospel, in *TS* 36 (1975) 688-699, p. 693. Though Brown uses this phrase here, it is Rhabanus Maurus who named Mary Magdalene as the apostle of apostles. If you directly take this to the Gospel of John, that will be irrelevant because the author of the Gospel has never used the term Apostle in the Gospel.

[63] Gail R. O'DAY, "The Gospel According to John", *The Women's Biblical Commentary*, Kentucky, Westminster/John Knox, 1992, pp. 293-294, 300-301.

[64] *Ibid.*, p. 301.

[65] George R. BEASLEY-MURRAY, *John, World Biblical Commentary Volume 36*, Texas, Word Books Publisher, 1987, p. 375.

[66] R. F. COLLINS, *These Things have been written*, p. 34.

[67] R. E. BROWN, *The Community of the Beloved Disciple*, New York, Paulist, 1979, p. 189.

[68] T. K. SEIM, *Roles of Women in the Gospel of John*, p. 61.

[69] U. E. EISEN, *Women officeholders in Early Christianity*, pp. 50-51.

[70] C. SETZER, *Excellent Women: Female Witness to the Resurrection*, JBL 116 (1997) 259-272, p. 259; P. S. MINEAR, "'We don't know where...' John 20, 2," *Interpretation* 30 (1976) 125-139. There are arguments today that argue for the physical presence of Mary Magdalene at the Last Supper. The question here is why women are not portrayed as part of the Twelve in the Gospels and are referred to only peripherally. As some scholars opine, men wrote the Gospels in the context of a male dominated Jewish society. Feminist scholars today see Mary Magdalene as indicative of what happened to women in general in the early church.

[71] T. K. SEIM, *Roles of Women in the Gospel of John*, p. 61.

[72] E.S. FIORENZA, *In Memory of Her. A Feminist Theological Reconstruction of Christian Origins*, New York, 1983, p. 323.

[73] R. E. BROWN, *The Community of the Beloved Disciple*, New York, Paulist, 1979, p. 183.

[74] T. K. SEIM, *Roles of Women in the Gospel of John*, p. 61.

[75] R. E. BROWN, *The Community of the Beloved Disciple*, p. 183.

[76] T. K. SEIM, *Roles of Women in the Gospel of John*, p. 58.

[77] See, Barnabas LINDARS, "The Composition of John XX", *New Testament Studies* 7 (1961) 142-147; E. L. BODE, *The First Easter Morning: The Gospel Accounts of the Women's Visit to the Tomb of Jesus*, Analecta Biblica 45, Rome, Pontifical Biblical Institute, 1970; K. P. G. CURTIS, "Three Points of Contact

Between Matthew and John in the Burial and Resurrection Narratives", *Journal of Theological Studies* 23 (1972) 440-444; D. C. FOWLER, "The Meaning of 'Touch Me Not' in John 20:17", *Evangelical Quarterly* 47 (1975) 16-25; Cf. Dorothy A. LEE, "Partnership in Easter Faith: The Role of Mary Magdelene and Thomas in John 20", *Journal for the Study of the New Testament* 58 (1995) 37-49. Mary Magdalene had the honour to bear and announce a message to the apostles who once considered this woman a demoniac. Now she has become a preacher to preachers and a witness to the others. Apostolic preaching could have carried to the world the announcement of the redemption that had come, but the redemption and liberation in fact was first revealed in its true greatness in the appearance to Mary Magdalene. In Risen Christ, there is no discrimination or oppression and this is the good news which Jesus used Mary of Magdalene to announce. The intention of Jesus is to communicate and remind his male disciples that there is no discrimination in the act of witness and proclamation. Cf. Sandra M. SCHNEIDERS, "Because of the Woman's Testimony... Re-examining the Issue of Authorship in the Fourth Gospel", *New Testament Studies* 44 (1998) 513-535.

[78] John ASHTON (ed.), *The Interpretation of John*, Edinburgh, T & T Clark, 1997, p. 250. The Greek word for 'to seek' expresses deep desire that finalises religiously significant attitudes and actions. Jesus asks, "whom do you seek?" which approximates the question posed in calling the first disciples (1:38). This expression equates to Jesus considering Mary Magdalene a disciple.

[79] G. R. BEASLEY-MURRAY, *John*, WBC, vol. 36, 2nd Nashville, Thomas Nelson Publishers, 1999, p. 374. Edition,

[80] R. A. CULPEPPER, *The Anatomy of the Fourth Gospel: A Study of Literary Design*, Philadelphia, Fortress, 1987, p. 144.

[81] G. R. BEASLEY-MURRAY, *John*, p. 375.

[82] R. F. COLLINS, *These Things have been written*, p. 34.

[83] R. E. BROWN, *The Community of the Beloved Disciple*, p. 192.

[84] G. R. BEASLEY-MURRAY, *John*, p. 375.

[85] T. K. SEIM, *Roles of Women in the Gospel of John*, p. 61.

[86] J. ASHTON, *The Interpretation of John*, pp. 241-242. The argument here is whether such stories related to women in the Fourth Gospel would have been acceptable in a community that restricted the apostolic identity and missionary activity of women. The question here is whether a male writer would be allowed by other males to write about women if his community were particularly, exclusively or predominantly led by males. As shown, the author of the Fourth Gospel explicitly portrays the active roles of women in the Johannine community. Also, the identification of the author himself/ herself is an important question to be explored. Thus, the intention of the author is clear, narrating the events of Jesus with women and bringing out the openness in relating to them, crossing the boundaries of Jewish society and its religious barriers.

[87] W. HOWARD- BROOK, *John,* p. 453.

[88] U. E. EISEN, *Women officeholders in Early Christianity*, p. 50. When the ancient interpretations of the Gospels and commentaries are examined closely, it is clear that women have been considered as apostles even if not explicitly.

[89] R. E. BROWN, *The Community of the Beloved Disciple*, pp. 31-33. At one time Brown was of the opinion that John, son of Zebedee, was the author of the Fourth Gospel but later he realised that there was little evidence to prove that. Brown's work in 1966 on 'The Gospel according to John', p. xcviii presents his earlier position on the authorship of the Gospel. But when Brown released his work on 'The Community of the Beloved Disciple' in 1979 he argued that the Beloved disciple was the author. The question is whether Mary Magdalene could be considered as the Beloved Disciple. According to Brown, the Fourth Gospel was authored by an anonymous follower of Jesus referred to in the Gospel text as the Beloved Disciple. He adds that this Beloved Disciple knew Jesus personally and was in the originating group of the Johannine Community. If the author of the Fourth Gospel had to be an eyewitness (Jn 21:24), then the possibility that Mary Magdalene was that eyewitness should be explored.

[90] B. F. WESTCOTT, *John,* p. 48. Though authors such as Westcott conclude that ῥαββί was the original term given to Jesus by the first two disciples, there are still others who think differently. Alfred Plummer opines that when John wrote his Gospel ῥαββί is a comparatively modern word and therefore ῥαββί translated into διδάσκαλε is "all the more requiring explanation to Gentile readers." For Plummer, John often interprets between Hebrew and Greek; thrice in this section (Jn 1:38. 42. 43). See, A. PLUMMER, *John,* pp. 83-84.

[91] See, HOWARD-BROOK, *Becoming Children of God,* p. 70. D. Moody Smith also accepts this position and states that "of course, the translation also implies that the intended reader, or hearer, might not understand Hebrew." D. MOODY SMITH, *John,* p. 72. Thus, when the Hebrew terms are translated in John, the question is whether it is for the benefit of the readers of the Johannine community or for today's readers. To place the question very explicitly, is it due to Hellenistic influence in the Fourth Gospel that Jesus who is called ῥαββί is translated as διδάσκαλε? This book mantanins that it is not due to the Hellenistic influence alone. It is also possible that John gives the title ῥαββί and translates it as διδάσκαλε to show that this was a term used for the authentic Jesus of history. Since his readers are Gentiles, he translates the original Aramaic term into Greek.

[92] B. LINDARS, *John,* p. 113. It is interesting to note the use of the term Rabbi in some of the English translations. Basically, the Hebrew and Aramaic word *Rab* was taken into Greek New Testament as a foreign word. Translations from the Greek texts into English differ greatly in the different versions. Both Jerusalem Bible and the New American Bible use the word Rabbi in the English consistently. The Revised Standard Version uses Rabbi in John's Gospel, but for Matthew and Mark it is usually translated as Master and rabbi is presented in

a footnote. The Good News Bible avoids the term Rabbi in almost all cases. Lenski observes that "John himself interprets the Hebrew title for his Greek readers and retains the vocative διδάσκαλε." See, LENSKI, *Interpretation of St. John's Gospel*, p. 146. Leon Morris opines that "the evangelist explains the Aramaic word for the benefit of his Jewish readers." See. L. MORRIS, *John*, p. 157. Coulot opines that it is the custom of the redactor to translate the Semitic terms. "Elle correspond à l'habitude chez un rédacteur de traduire les termes sémitiques." See, C. COULOT, *Jésus et le disciple*, p. 203. Collins expresses the same opinion, "As is his custom, the evangelist translates the transliterated Hebrew term for the benefit of his readers." See, R. F. COLLINS, *John and His Witness*, p. 37. Collins notes the different occurrences in the Gospel of John where, the Hebrew or Aramaic terms have been translated. (See. Jn 1:38, 41, 42; 4:25; 5:2; 9:7; 11:16; 19:13, 17; 20:16, 24; 21:2 and Cf. 19:20.) In another work, Collins says the translations of John are due to "definite tendency to translate Semitisms." See, R. F. COLLINS, *These Things Have Been Written*, p. 103. But Collins' opinion differs from the interpretation by Lindars on the concept of 'Greek readers.' This issue of translating the Semitic terms for the Greek readers also has an indirect message: that the readers of the Johannine community were in need of all these translations and interpretations of the terms originated in a Semitic context.

[93] A. KÖSTENBERGER, *Studies on John and Gender*, p. 76.

[94] C. EVANS, *Word and Glory*, p. 151. Evans believes that John mistakenly attributes this reference to Jesus in 20:16.

[95] Cf. C. A. EVANS, *Word and Glory*, p. 158. Evans notes that Jesus' statement that "there are many dwelling places in my Father's house" probably reflects Targumic language. He particularly refers to *Tg. Neof.* Ex 33:13–14: "The glory of my Shekinah will accompany among you and will prepare a resting place for you." Cf. also REIM, "*Targum und Johannesevangelium*," p. 10. In p. 96, Köstenberger observes the growth in faith by the followers of Jesus. He also notes how the Rabbi is presented as an exalted Christ in the development of the Gospel. Köstenberger says that the disciples are enjoined to move from a physical following of Jesus during his earthly ministry to a vital spiritual connection with him by the study of his word and prayer (cf. esp. chaps. 14–16).

[96] Cf. PRYOR, *John: Evangelist of the Covenant People*, p. 55. For important missiological implications, see "Challenge of a Systematized Biblical Theology of Mission: Missiological Insights from the Gospel of John", *Missiology* 23 (1995) 445–464.

[97] A. KÖSTENBERGER, *Studies on John and Gender*, p. 96.

[98] ῥαββί: 1:38, 49; 3:2; 4:31; 6:25; 9:2; 11:8; 20:16. In 1:38 and 20:16, ῥαββί is translated as διδάσκαλε. Κύριος occurs in 4:11. 15. 19. 49; 5:7; 6:34, 68; (8:11); 9:36. 38; 11:3. 12. 21. 27. 32. 34. 39; 12:21. 38; 13:6. 9. 25. 36. 37; 14:5. 8. 22; 20:15. 28; 21:15. 16. 17. 20. 21. Apart from ῥαββί and διδάσκαλος, the title

κύριος is also used with regard to Jesus in NT. Also the title κύριος occurs more often in the synoptic passages than the Fourth Gospel. But the titles ῥαββί and ῥαββουνί occur more in the Fourth Gospel. It is noted that the title κύριος is apt in the sense of a "master" who is considered a superior in that community. But this book does not fully agree that the title κύριος is always equivalent to expressing the sense of a teacher or master (superior) of a group or community. And Jesus has a special role of more than teacher in the Johannine theology.

⁹⁹ G. VERMES, *Jesus the Jew*, p. 126. In the observation of Vermes, "the meaning of the Johannine 'lord' mostly varies between a quite prosaic 'sir' and 'teacher.'" Vermes agrees that the story of the miraculous cure of the son of the royal official from Capernaum, parallel to that of the centurion in the earlier Gospels, is reminiscent of the Synoptic style in addressing Jesus as κύριε. Vermes also observes that, in the episode of Lazarus, Martha gives the title κύριε to Jesus. By this, according to Vermes, the evangelist affirms that Jesus is patently the Messiah. Read also, G. M. STYLER, "Stages in Christology in the Synoptic Gospels", *New Testament Studies* 10 (1963-64) 398-409; Royce Gordon GRUENLER, *New Approaches in Jesus and the Gospels: A Phenomenological and Exegetical Study of Synoptic Christology*, Grand Rapids, Baker, 1982.

¹⁰⁰ G. VERMES, *The Changing Faces of Jesus*, p. 34; F. F. BRUCE, "The Humanity of Jesus Christ", *Journal of the Christian Brethren Research Fellowship* 24 (1973) 5-15.

¹⁰¹ See, Jn 4:11, 15, 19, 49; 5:7; 6:34; 8:11; 9:36, 38; 20:15.

¹⁰² See, Jn 6:68; 11:3. 12. 21. 27. 32. 34. 39; 13:6. 9. 25. 36. 37; 14:5. 8. 22; 21:15. 16. 17. 20. 21.

¹⁰³ A. KÖSTENBERGER, *Studies on John and Gender*, pp. 94-95. Jesus is given this title "κύριος" mostly after Chap.12, and in the Farewell discourse: Jn 13:6. 9. 25. 36. 37; 14: 5. 8. 22. In 20:28, Thomas addresses the Risen Jesus as Lord and God. And in the epilogue, Peter and the Beloved disciple give this title to Jesus (Jn 21:15. 16. 17. 20. 21). Read, John A. WITMER, "Did Jesus Claim to Be God", *Bibliotheca Sacra* 125: 498 (1968) 147-156.

¹⁰⁴ G. VERMES, *Jesus the Jew*, p. 127.

¹⁰⁵ *Ibid.*, p. 35.

¹⁰⁶ A. KÖSTENBERGER, *Studies on John and Gender*, p. 95.

¹⁰⁷ F. HAHN, *The Titles of Jesus in Christology*, p. 79.

¹⁰⁸ *Ibid.*

¹⁰⁹ *Ibid.*, p. 102.

¹¹⁰ D. MOODY SMITH, *The Theology of the Gospel of John*, p. 90. Moody Smith maintains that there is a contradiction. He says that Jesus is 'seldom' referred to as 'Lord' in his earthly ministry, but goes on to say that the word is used only after his death.

[111] F. HAHN, *The Titles of Jesus in Christology*, p. 103.

[112] *Ibid.*

[113] *Ibid.*, Only from Ps. 110: 1 as a point of departure the title κύριός arose with the motive of exaltation.

[114] V. TAYLOR, *The Names of Jesus*, p. 43. Though Taylor calls the term Κύριός as a post-Resurrection title to Jesus, he also notes other earlier places where Jesus has been given this title 4:1; 6:23; 11:2; 13: 32 (twice). In contrast, in the Easter and post-Easter narratives, there are nine examples of Κύριός: Jn 20:2. 12. 13. 18. 20. 25. 28; 21:7a. 7b.

[115] *Ibid.*

[116] Leopold SABOURIN, *The Names and Titles of Jesus, Themes of Biblical Theology*, New York, Macmillan Company, 1967, p. 257.

[117] *Ibid.*

[118] *Ibid.*

[119] Richard J. CASSIDY, *John's Gospel in New Perspective, Christology and the Realities of Roman Power*, Mary knoll, NY, Orbis, 1992, p. 36. Cassidy points out that the title κύριος is given to Jesus even after the resurrection. For Cassidy, κύριος in John is a term expressing faith in Jesus, especially by those who witness Jesus' healing.

[120] *Ibid.*

[121] *Ibid.*, p. 37.

[122] G. VERMES, *The Changing Faces of Jesus*, p. 35.

[123] R. E. BROWN, *John*, p. 75. Lenski puts forward the idea that "Jesus accepts this title ῥαββί even to the last, as we see in 10:13, although κύριος, "Lord" soon came to be used more frequently by his disciples." See, LENSKI, *Interpretation of St. John's Gospel*, p. 146. On the contrary, Coulot, in his exegetical study on "*Jésus et le Disciple*" observes that the addressing of Jesus as ῥαββί and κύριος occurs alternatively in the first 11 chapters. C. COULOT, *Jésus et le Disciple*, p. 203. "*Cependant en Jn, "rhabbi" est utilisé en alternance avec "kurios" dans les onze premiers chapitres...L'appellation est aussi une caractéristique johannique.*" Mark W. G. Stibbe agrees with Raymond Brown and opines that "the narrator frequently portrays the disciples addressing Jesus as 'Rabbi' (Master) in the first part of the Gospel (chs. 1-12), while he most frequently has them calling Jesus 'Kurios' (Lord) in the second part." See. Mark W. G. STIBBE, *John, Readings; A New Biblical Commentary*, Sheffield, England, 1993, p. 37.

[124] H. LAPIN, *Rabbi*, p. 602.

[125] G. DALMAN, *The Words of Jesus*, p. 340.

[126] D. MOODY SMITH, *The Theology of the Gospel of John*, p. 91.

[127] Kelli S. O'BRIEN, "Written That You May Believe: John 20 and Narrative Rhetoric", *Catholic Biblical Quarterly*, April 2005.

[128] Cf. J. Louis MARTYN, "Glimpses into the History of the Johannine Community", *L'Evangile de Jean: Sources, rédaction, et théologie*, (ed.) M. DE JONGE, BETL 44, Gembloux, Duculot, 1977, pp. 149-175; Nils DAHL, "The Johannine Church and History", *Jesus in the Memory of the Early Church*, Minneapolis, Augsburg, 1976, pp. 108- 109; L. URBAN and P. HENRY, "Before Abraham Was I AM, Does Philo Explain John 8:56-58?", *Studia Philonica* 6 (1979-80) 166-193;

[129] A. KÖSTENBERGER, *Studies on John and Gender*, p. 76.

[130] G. VERMES, *Jesus the Jew*, p. 126. Vermes names the incident of Thomas' touching the body of the risen Jesus and his exclamation of 'My Lord and My God (20:28) as an "intense spiritual excitement." See, G. VERMES, *The Changing Faces of Jesus*, p. 35. Read also, Murray J. HARRIS, *Jesus as God: The New Testament Use of Theos in Reference to Jesus*, Grand Rapids, Baker 1952; T. SURIANO, "Doubting Thomas: An Invitation to Belief", *Bible Today* 53 (1971) 309-315; Douglas MCCREADY, "He Came Down From Heaven: The Preexistence of Christ Revisited", *Journal of the Evangelical Theological Society* 40.3 (1997) 419-432.

[131] L. SABOURIN, *The Names and Titles of Jesus*, p. 257.

[132] R. J. CASSIDY, *John's Gospel in New Perspective*, p. 38.

[133] C. H. DODD, *Interpretation of the Fourth Gospel, Historical Tradition in the Fourth Gospel*, Cambridge, UK, Cambridge University Press, 1963, pp. 430-431.

[134] Marianne Meye THOMPSON, *The Humanity of Jesus in the Fourth Gospel*, Philadelphia, Fortress Press, 1988, p. 127; To read more in this perspective, see, A. MARMORSTEIN, *The Old Rabbinic Doctrine of God*, New York, KTAV, 1969, pp. 41-53; E. E. URBACH, *The Sages*, Jerusalem, Magnes Press, 1975, pp. 448-461; See also R. RIESNER, "Der Ursprung der Jesus-Überlieferung," *TZ* 38 (1982) 493–513.

[135] *Ibid.*, p. 128.

[136] G. VERMES, *The Changing Faces of Jesus*, p. 35; Read also, E. P. GROENEWALD, "The Christological Meaning of John 20:31", *Neotestamentica* 2 (1968) 131-140; T. C. DE KRUIJF, "'Hold the Faith' or, 'Come to Believe'? A Note on John 20, 31", *Bijdragen: Tijdschrift voor philosophie en theologie* 36 (1975) 439-49.

[137] F. J. MOLONEY, *The Fourth Gospel and the Jesus of History*, pp. 51-52.

[138] Cecil. B. MURPHEY (compiled.), *Dictionary of Biblical Literacy*, Tennessee, Oliver-Nelson Publishers, 1989, p. 83.

[139] G. R. O'Day, *John*, p. 293.

[140] John J. KILGALLEN, *A Brief Commentary on the Gospel of John,* New York, Mellen Biblical Press, 1992, pp. Introduction i-iv.

[141] G. O'DAY, *John,* p. 293.

[142] J. J. KILGALLEN, *Gospel of John*, pp. vii-viii.

[143] G. O'DAY, *John,* p. 293.

[144] See, Kelli S O'BRIEN, "Written That You May Believe: John 20 and Narrative Rhetoric", *Catholic Biblical Quarterly*, April 2005. This book maintains, it is true that, in contrast to Mary Magdalene and Thomas, the Beloved Disciple seems to immediately believe, but the Beloved Disciple's belief gives no confession, no "My Lord and my God!" Only in 21:24 does the Beloved Disciple really witness at the end of the Gospel. "It is this disciple who testifies to these things and has written them ..." Hence, the presence of the Beloved Disciple should not cast a negative light on the experiences of Mary and Thomas.

[145] Cf. M. M. THOMPSON, *Historical Jesus and Johannine Christ*, pp. 21–42. See also C. S. EVANS, *The Historical Christ and the Jesus of Faith: The Incarnational Narrative as History,* Oxford, Clarendon, 1996. This is the message of John's Gospel. If these observations are correct, they confirm the emerging consensus that Jesus can only be adequately understood within a Jewish framework. Cf. W. R. TELFORD, "Major Trends and Interpretive Issues in the Study of Jesus", in *Studying the Historical Jesus, Evaluations of the State of Current Research,* ed. B. CHILTON and C. A. EVANS, Leiden, E. J. Brill, 1994, pp. 70-71.

[146] As R. RIESNER, *Jesus als Lehrer*, p. 254 points out against the views of F. HAHN, *Christologische Hoheitstitel*, pp. 80–81 and in agreement with C. H. DODD, *Jesus als Lehrer und Prophet*, p. 69, the term ῥαββί should not be understood as a Christological title. As Riesner contends, the early church preserved reminiscences of Jesus' being addressed as ῥαββί during his earthly ministry because he in fact lived as a religious teacher. Rather, among other things, the Johannine Jesus is cast as the true reformer of Jewish religion. Jesus cleanses the Temple (2:13–22), instructs the "Teacher of Israel" regarding his need for spiritual regeneration (3:3–8), teaches that true worship is spiritual (4:21–24), points to the true significance of Jewish religious feasts (7:37–38; 8:12; 9:5) or invests them with new meaning (e.g., the Passover), and supersedes Moses, through whom God had given the Law (1:17; 5:45–46) and Abraham, the Jewish patriarch (8:58). Yet Jesus was even more than a reformer of Judaism.

General Summary and Conclusions

After the prologue (Jn 1:1-18), in the Fourth Gospel, attention is focused on John the Baptist. To the delegation that came from Jerusalem, John the Baptist said that he was not the Messiah (cf. Jn 1:19-28) and announced that the Messiah was in their midst (cf. Jn 1: 29-34). The day after he met Jesus by the River Jordan, John the Baptist was with two of his disciples when he saw Jesus passing by. The Baptist stares and then exclaims "Look there is the Lamb of God." Upon hearing this, his two disciples leave their leader and immediately follow Jesus. (cf. 1: 35-37). Becoming aware of their following, Jesus turns and asks them "What do you seek?" They answer "Rabbi where do you live?" (cf. Jn 1: 38).

Now, what did the evangelist mean by calling Jesus 'Rabbi' at that moment? Did the evangelist mean, for example, that the two disciples saw Jesus as a Rabbi similar to any of the many Rabbis in Jerusalem at that time, or did the disciples assume Jesus must be a Rabbi because of the exalted way John the Baptist had spoken about him? Could there also be some other reason altogether? In fact, the meaning of the term 'Rabbi' in the context of John 1:38b forms the basis of this book. First, the historical antecedents of the term were explored. Second, the contemporary use of the term during the public ministry of Jesus was reviewed. Finally, the particular way the evangelist John used the term in the Fourth Gospel was discussed.

In part I chapter one, the question was in what ways and in what contexts has the title 'Ραββί, been used in the time before the historical Jesus? The findings can be summarised as follows. Rabbi in its adjective form "rab" derives from the Hebrew רבי and means "many" "great" or "master." In biblical Hebrew, this means "great" or "distinguished". Rabbi in classical Hebrew and in modern Israel means teacher or, more literally, great one. The term רבי expresses authority in five areas. The five areas are classified as vocational, cultic, judicial, military and governmental. Among the five, the vocational area stands for a supervisor, foreman or chief. In the cultic area, it points to the chief priest, and in the judicial area it designates the authority of chief magistrate. In the military area, this title stands for an officer, captain or commander and, finally, in the governmental line, it is used for a royal official or for a ruler. רבי was used to refer to the master of a slave or of a disciple. Thus, r`abbi, literally meant "my master" and was a term of respect used by slaves in addressing their owners and by disciples in addressing their teachers. In the ancient Judean schools, the sages were addressed as 'Ραββί,. This term of respectful address gradually came to be used as a title, the pronominal suffix "i" ("my") losing its significance with the frequent use of the term.

The role of Rabbis within Jewish communities has been, and continues to be, multifaceted. In ancient times, Rabbi was a Hebrew term used as a title for those who were distinguished for learning, were the authoritative teachers of the Law, or were the appointed religious leaders of their community. It was also seen that there existed in ancient Israel and ancient Judaism several texts confirming the existence of several schools that promoted the learning which formed the teacher-pupil relationship. They appear in the OT in the narratives of the Elijah/Elisha relationship, the writings of the later prophets, the wisdom writings and later in the Rabbinic literature. Though it is difficult to ascertain the teacher-pupil relationship in the prophetical books, the correlation with the existence of groups of learners or followers adhering to the prophets indicate that this kind of relationship existed. People like Ben Sira and other prominent Rabbis provided individuals and groups of pupils with the basic formation for the learning of scripture. It was also noted that the existence of elementary scribal schools were responsible for imparting knowledge and providing formation for Jewish pupils in Israel. Finally, the development of the more organised sort of schools, which were also influenced by the Greek-Hellenistic culture and world were noted.

In part I chapter two, a detailed study was undertaken of the various occurrences in the New Testament where the title 'Ραββί, occurs with particular reference to the gospels. The study found that the title 'Ραββί, most likely predates the earliest Gospel of Mark although it is not used at all in the Gospel of Luke. Furthermore, John appears to use the term interchangeably with the title διδάσκαλος, and the question being why. And finally the significance of the title 'Ραββί, in the post resurrection era was analysed, especially from the time of the destruction of the Temple in 70 A.D. It is accepted by most scholars that the use of the title rabbi for ordained scholars does not appear in any Jewish sources before 70 A.D.

Hershel Shanks, for example warns the reader very strongly to avoid any claim that the OT uses of Rab is authentic evidence for the use of Rabbi in the Gospels. He affirms that currently available materials do not show a use of the term Rabbi as a title for ordained scholars prior to the Roman destruction of the Temple. Hence, Shanks agrees, the title Rabbi for ordained scholars does not appear in Jewish sources until 70 A.D. But this does not mean that the title Rab, Rabbi or Rabban never existed before the time of the destruction of the Temple. This study has a problem with the position of Solomon Zeitlin in his simplification of the frequent occurrence of the title rabbi in the Gospels. If this title does not exist, how is it that the term rabbi occurs at least fourteen times in three of the four Gospels? Then, using observations based on the occurrence of the term 'Ραββί, in the gospels, a detailed study was made as to whether the use of the title 'Ραββί, in the gospels is anachronistic. In this regard, the opposing views of Shanks and Zeitlin were reviewed in depth. While Shanks holds the view that the use of the title 'Ραββί, in the gospels is not anachronistic, Zeitlin rejects this point of view and says that the title 'Ραββί, in the gospels is purely anachronistic. After much review and reflection on these opposing views, Shanks' conclusion was adopted. The point (proffered by many scholars) that the title may be a gloss used retrospectively only after the destruction of the second Temple in 70 A.D., was not ignored. Rather, in response to that view, it is agreed with Shanks, who holds that if the title 'Ραββί, was in use 'officially' after 70 A.D. it is also probable that it was 'unofficially' used in the time of Jesus.

Part II investigated whether Jesus can be called a 'Rabbi', and if so, how to understand that title with reference to his person and mission. In the first chapter of part II, a detailed study was made of the various equivalent terms used by the synoptic authors in addressing Jesus as 'Rabbi' in different circumstances. It was noted that the term 'Ραββί, in the sense of a teacher, occurs in all the gospels with the exception of the gospel according to Luke. It was further noted that it is not only the title 'Rabbi' that is used by the synoptic writers, who often preferred to use some equivalent terms to express the notion of a 'teacher.' Based on the works of authors such as R. Riesner, G. Dalman, H. Lapin and J. Donaldson, it was found that both the common terms διδάσκαλος (*Didaskalos* as transliteration) which occurs invariably in all three gospels and Luke's ἐπιστάτα (*Epistata* as transliteration) with reference to Jesus, could be traced back to the Aramaic term ῥαββί (*Rabbi* as transliteration) -but not in every case. After much review, we can agree with the stand of Donaldson that the adaptation or avoidance of the term ῥαββί, in the synoptic gospels is precisely for Christological reasons and not due to any reluctance to use the term. Thus the possibility remains that many of these terms were inserted when the gospels were eventually written some decades after the event. This would have been done, no doubt, in the light of the faith experience of first generation Christianity.

Clearly, the title 'Rabbi' in the first century AD was attributed to any charismatic religious leader, like Jesus. It was certainly used in the sense of being seen as a 'teacher' or a dispenser of wisdom. Whether this should be understood in a technical or formal sense of being an 'ordained' official or in an honorific sense, in which the high esteem of their disciples or followers is expressed, was looked at in greater depth. To this end Jesus as a 'Rabbi' in the sense of a Jewish teacher was reviewed from three different angles. First, the position of Martin Hengel was discussed. He holds the view that Jesus was not a mere teacher but a Charismatic leader and eschatological prophet. Second, a number of scholarly works were looked at to see whether Jesus could be seen as a Rabbi in the sense of a teacher like any other teacher of his day. To put this in context, an analysis was made of the way Jesus began and continued his public ministry in Palestine. As I. M. Zeitlin (and others) note, Jesus was steeped in the Jewish faith and tradition from the outset. His knowledge of the Hebrew Scripture and of his Jewish heritage was such that, as Kittel noted, Jesus lived as a Jewish Rabbi of his time. Therefore, those who followed him naturally accepted him as such. Nevertheless, as Davies and Hengel have noted, Jesus did not fit completely into the mould of a typical Rabbi. This raised the possibility that the term 'Rabbi' could have been used both in a formal and honorific sense with reference to Jesus. This book has expressed partial agreement with this position. However, this book does not maintain that Jesus was just like any other contemporary Rabbi.

The idea that Jesus was more than a teacher was then reviewed. The Gospel accounts of Jesus quite clearly demonstrate that it was the 'content' of his teaching that distinguished him from all other Rabbis of his day. In fact, it was the uniqueness of his message, the way he claimed to justify his teaching by his own authority, and not depending on either Scripture or past Rabbinical sources, that ultimately brought him into conflict with the Sanhedrin. It was often the way he spoke that made him appear more of a prophet than a mere teacher. This was a striking difference noted between Jesus and other Rabbis.

The relationship that Jesus had with his most intimate followers, his disciples, was also different. First of all, he 'called' (chose) them rather than the other way round. They remained close to him throughout his ministry, which was not confined to the synagogue or temple but included travelling in the countryside and towns and speaking to large crowds. Jesus called them to discipleship but not for a mere increase of knowledge in the Law and the prophets. The conclusion is that Jesus was not a formal 'ordained' Rabbi in the ordinary accepted sense of the term, but acted and proved to be more than an ordinary teacher. This is not to say that Jesus was not perceived as 'one who teaches.' Indeed he was given, by his disciples and others, all the respect and honour due to a Rabbi of his time.

With the historical and contemporary understanding of the term 'Rabbi' covered in parts I and II, this study was prepared to look at the way the term was used in the Gospel of John. This was done in part III and began by looking at the context in which the term 'Ραββί, was first used in Jn 1:38b. The significance of how the evangelist introduced a shift from the term 'Lamb of God' to the term 'Rabbi' was explored. The particular Johannine portrayal of Jesus as a Rabbi in the course of his public ministry was then reviewed. In this regard, the various uses of the term ῥαββί (*Rabbi* as transliteration) in the Fourth Gospel were noted and clearly show that it is used predominantly to mean 'teacher'. To give greater depth to that insight, other aspects of the Johannine Jesus' public ministry were explored, in particular, the 'teacher/disciple' relationship that John portrays as existing between Jesus and his disciples (and other followers).

Then, a study was done of how the evangelist consistently portrays Jesus as a 'teacher.' In this regard, various exegetical views were discussed on the significance of the term 'Rabbi' meaning teacher. The works of many authors were referred to, especially Rudolf Schnackenburg whose idea initiated the discussion of whether the term ῥαββί (*Rabbi* as transliteration) which is applied to Jesus in Jn 1:38b, presents him as a teacher. There are many other authors who have expressed the same idea and agree that the evangelist uses the term 'Rabbi' to mean 'teacher.' Various instances were noted in the fourth gospel where this dimension is in evidence. This led to exploring whether or not the title 'Rabbi' was, in fact, used to address Jesus in his lifetime or as a gloss used at the time when the gospel was written.

It is important to remember that, unlike the synoptic gospels, John uses a distinctive style, which is in part a blend of the past, present, and future. Hence how the term fits into the evangelist's Christology was explored in the light of the resurrection and the faith development of his disciples and the early Christian community. The study centred on the question of whether the term 'Ραββί, in John's gospel referred only to the earthly Jesus or had other connotations. In this regard what Riesner stated was noted, namely that, when the authors of the four gospels use the address 'Rabbi' in reference to Jesus, with its implicit characterisation of Jesus as a teacher, it was not introduced by secondary theological motives. Riesner convincingly argues that the term rabbi attributed to Jesus of Nazareth is Palestinian and historical. Hence, for Riesner, Jesus was not only seen and addressed as a teacher but also acted in some ways like a Jewish teacher. Part III chapter one of this book maintains that, when Jesus is addressed as 'Ραββί, in the gospels, the evangelists have their own theological motives for using the title. Thus, this book disagrees with Riesner that addressing Jesus as a Rabbi in the sense of a teacher has nothing to do with the theology of each gospel.

Along with many Johannine scholars, chapter two of part III agrees that John is presenting an ascending Christology. In that respect, this study suggested that, by presenting Jesus as a 'Ραββί, John considered this address as the historical starting point of his Christology. And this study agrees with Köstenberger that, by calling Jesus primarily 'Ραββί, John's so-called 'high Christology' reveals it to be basically rooted in the earthly life and ministry of Jesus. Hence it is concluded and affirmed that addressing the Johannine Jesus as 'Ραββί, is in no way a contradiction either to the Johannine theme of incarnation, or Jesus as Son of God.

The next question explored was whether in the Fourth Gospel the term 'Ραββί, has any connotation or link with the term κύριος. Raymond Brown's views on the Johannine terms of 'Ραββί, and κύριος applied to the Johannine Jesus was the starting point of this discussion. This led to an in-depth study of how the synoptic gospels use the term κύριος to see how the term can be understood in a wider context. The Johannine meaning of the term κύριος was then looked at as applied to Jesus from the synoptic perspective. Then, how the term Ραββι, is used was explored in the light of Johannine Christology and the faith development of Jesus' disciples. As was discussed, the first chapter of John begins by calling Jesus 'Rabbi' (Jn 1:38b) and ends by calling him 'Messiah' (Jn 1:41) and 'Lord and God' (Jn 20:28).

In fact the followers of Jesus, who primarily perceived him as a teacher, are led to believe that their teacher was Lord and God (as the Son of God). we can agree with Raymond Brown that looking at Jesus basically as a 'Ραββί, and finally acclaiming him as Lord and God, is not a contradiction, but is the typical Johannine portrayal of the faith development of the immediate disciples of Jesus. Similarly, with Köstenberger, it is agreed that John's gospel shows an organic development from the earthly Jesus' instruction of his followers as a 'Ραββί, and later their belief that Jesus continued to be present in their community as the exalted Lord. Thus, in calling Jesus 'Ραββί, and applying other Christological titles, John presents a gradual growth in faith from the 'call of the first disciples' to the acclamation of the 'ascended Messiah'.

Thus in part III it is seen that in Jn 1:38b the term 'Rabbi', attributed by the Baptist's two disciples to the Johannine Jesus, provides unmistakable evidence that Jesus was indeed perceived as a Rabbi. Not only his disciples, but also the people and even opponents addressed Jesus as 'Rabbi' in the sense of teacher. Again it is convincing that the application of the title 'Ραββί, to the Johannine Jesus also has a role to play in the Christology of the Fourth Gospel. This aspect of looking at the Johannine Jesus as a teacher in no way minimises the exalted status of he who was acclaimed as 'Messiah' or 'Lord and God'. The title "Rabbouni" given by Mary Magdalene to Jesus and the response Jesus gave to her acclamation at the Resurrection episode present both an aspect of Jesus' humanity (His Incarnation) and also his divinity (His Ascension and Glory). Jesus does not deny that he was still the Master yet he is not just a master after the Resurrection, he is Lord and God. This is the Christological development that is well developed and presented in the Johannine Gospel when John has used the titles of both 'Ραββί, and ῥαββουνί, in attribution to Jesus. Thus, the image of Rabbi in the sense of "Jesus the teacher or Master" serves as a launch pad to build up a Johannine Christology, which this book asserts to be both ascending and holistic.

Epilogue and Future Research

In this concluding section, it is realised that the subject of this book is a vast area and what has been done in this work is just one part of it. Indeed, the present study has led to numerous discussions focusing on this particular aspect of looking at Jesus as ʽΡαββί, in the sense of a teacher. The Historical-Critical method of this study has helped in observing critically the texts and evaluating them exegetically. The perusal of the scholarly works which have been used in this regard have been invaluable in shaping this book. It is also realised that the present work is not a comprehensive one, but reveals new avenues for further discussion and research. As a result of this study of the Johannine Jesus as ʽΡαββί, some of the areas which are considered important for further study can be specified.

This study covered the historical background for the term ῥαββί (*Rabbi* as transliteration) in which the focus was on etymology, different interpretations and the use of the term both in the contexts of usage in ancient Palestine and Babylon. Further research in Johannine studies might take up questions such as, from where did John get the term ʽΡαββί? Did John take that word from the synoptic gospels? Did John refer to the works of the synoptic gospels when he wrote his gospel? In the New Testament gospels, it is evident that it is Mark who has mostly used the term ʽΡαββί among the synoptic gospels. Thus, could John have taken it from the Markan source? Or is it from the tradition of John? Did John use his own sources to present Jesus as a Rabbi? The hypothesis of John's dependence on the synoptic gospels was not discussed in detail in this book, which is also open to a prospective further research.

To a certain extent, the present study has contributed to the study of the historical Jesus. For example, the works of authors such as John P. Meier, who deal with this particular aspect of study regarding the historical Jesus, have been used. But this study has not gone deeply into that specific area. Now at this point it is realised that the Johannine understanding of Jesus as a "Rabbi" in the sense of a teacher constitutes the historical starting point for the fourth evangelist's presentation of the historical Jesus. While it is a common opinion that 'Historical Jesus Research' is more doable in the Synoptic Gospels than in the Fourth Gospel, the question centres on whether or not the study of the Johannine Jesus as a ῾Ραββί, in the Jewish and Hellenistic context contributes anything to the area of historical Jesus research.

Bibliography

Texts and Tools

ALAND, B., ALAND, K., KARAVIDOPOULOS, J., MARTINI, C. M. & METZGER, B. M (eds.), *Greek-English New* Testament, 27th ed. 8th Printing, Stuttgart, Deutsche Bibelgesellschaft, 1998.

ALAND, K. & ALAND, B., *The Text of the New Testament An Introduction to the Critical Editions and to the Theory and Practice of Modern Textual Criticism,* RHODES, E. F. (trad.), Leiden, Brill, 1989.

ALAND, K. (ed.), *Synopsis Quattuor Evangeliorurn,* Stuttgart, Deutsche Bibelgesellschaft, 1965.

ALAND, K., *Synopsis of the Four Gospels: Completely Revised on the Basis of the Greek Text of the Nestle Aland (English-Only Text)*, United Bible Societies, 1982.

ALAND, K., *Vollständige Konkordanz zum griechischen Neuen Testament,* Vol. I, Part 2, Berlin, NewYork, Walter De Gruyter, 1983.

ALAND, N., *Novum Testamentum Graece,* Post Eberhard et Erwin Nestle editione vicesima septima revisa conmmuniter ediderunt Barbara et Kurt Aland, Johannes Karavidopoulous, Carlo M. Martini, Bruce M. Metzger, Apparatum criticum nov curs elaboraverunt Barbara et Kurt Aland una cum Instituto Studiorum Textus Novi Testamenti Monasterii Wesrphaliae, Stuttgart, Deutsche Bibelgesellschaft, 2001.

ALLEN, H. J., *New Testament Greek: A Beginning and Intermediate Grammar*, Peabody, MA, Hendrikson, 1986.

ANDERSON, F. I. & FORBES A. D., *The Vocabulary of the Old Testament*, Pontifical Biblical Institute, Rome, 1989.

ARNDT, W. F. and GINGRICH, F. W. (eds.), *A Greek-English Lexicon of the New Testament and Other Early Christian Literature*, Chicago, University of Chicago Press, 1957.

BACHMANN, H. & SLABY, W. A., *Concordance to the Novum Testamentum Graece of Nestle-Aland*, 26th edition, and to the Greek New Testament, 3rd edition, Berlin & New York, Walter de Gruyter, 1987.

BAIRD, W., *History of New Testament Research*, 2 vol., Minneapolis, Fortress Press, 2002, Vol. 1: *From Deism to Tubingen*, 1991, Vol. 2: *From Jonathan Edwards to Rudolf Bultmann* 2002.

BALZ, H. & SCHNEIDER, G. (eds.), *Exegetical Dictionary of the New Testament*, *EDNT*, 3 vols. Grand Rapids, Eerdmans, 1990-93.

BARRETT, C. K. (ed.), *The New Testament Background: Writings from Ancient Greece and the Roman Empire That Illuminate Christian Origins*, rev. ed., San Francisco, Harper, 1995.

BARTON, J. & MUDDIMAN, J., (eds.), *Oxford Biblical Commentary*, New York, Oxford University Press, 2001.

BARTON, J. (ed.), *The Cambridge Companion to Biblical Interpretation*, Cambridge, Cambridge University Press, 1998.

BARTON, J., (ed.), *The Biblical World*, New York, Routledge, 2002.

BARTON, J., *Reading the Old Testament Methodology in Biblical Study*, London, Darton Longman & Todd, 1984.

BAUER, J. B. (ed.), *Bauer Encyclopaedia of Biblical Theology*, London, UK, Sheed and Ward, 1978.

BAUER, W. (ed.), *A Greek- English Lexicon of the New Testament and Other Early Christian Literature* (*BDAG*), third edition, based on W. Bauer's *Griechisch-deutsches Wörterbuch zu den Schriften des Neuen Testaments und der frühchristlichen Literatur*, sixth edition, ed. Kurt Aland and Barbara Aland, with Viktor Reichmann and on previous English editions by W. F. Arndt, F. W. Gingrich, and F. W. Danker, Chicago & London, Chicago University Press, 2000.

BEAUCHAMP, P., *L'Un et l'autre Testament, tome 1. Essai de lecture* (PDD), Paris, Seull, 1976.

BEAUCHAMP, P., *L'Un et l'autre Testament, tome 2. Accomplir les Ecritures*, PDD, Paris, Seull, 1990.

BERGANT, D., & KARRIS, R. L., *The Collegeville Bible Commentary*, Collegeville, MN, Liturgical Press, 1989.

BERLIN, A., BRETTLER, M. Z., & FISHBANE, M., (eds.), *The Jewish Study Bible*, New York, Oxford University Press, 2003.

BERRY, G. R., *Interlinear Greek-English New Testament*, 1897, repr., Grand Rapids, Michigan, Baker Book House, 1981.

Biblia Hebraica Stuttgartensia BHS, 5th rev. ed. by W. Rudolph, H. P. Rüger, et al., Stuttgart, Deutsche Bibelgesellschaft, 1997.

BLASS, F. & DEBRUNNER, A., *A Greek Grammar of the New Testament and Other Early Christian Literature: A Translation and Revision of the Nineteenth*

German edition incorporating supplementary notes of A. Debrunner, FUNK, R. F. (trad.), Chicago & London, University Press of Chicago, 1961.

BLENKINSOPP, J., *A History of Prophecy in Israel: From the Settlement in the Land to the Hellinistic Period,* Philadelphia, Westminster Press, 1983.

BLOWERS, P. M., *The Bible in Greek Christian Antiquity*, Notre Dame, University of Notre Dame Press, 1997.

BOARDMAN, J., GRIFFIN, J., MURRAY, O. (ed.), *The Roman World*, Oxford History of the Classical World, New York, Oxford University Press, 1986.

BOISMARD, M. E., & LAMOUILLE, A., *Synopsis Greaca Quattuor Evangeliorum*, Leuven & Paris, Peeters, 1986.

BOTTERWECK, G. J. & RINGGREN, H. (eds.), *Theological Dictionary of the Old Testament*, Trans. by John T. Willis, Grand Rapids, Eerdmans, 1974ff.

BRIGHT, J., *A History of Israel,* London/Louisville, Westminster/John Knox Press, 2000.

BROMILEY, G. W. et al. (eds.), *The International Standard Bible Encyclopedia*, Grand Rapids, MI, William B. Eerdmans, 1988.

BROWN, (ed.), *The New International Dictionary of New Testament Theology*, Grand Rapids, Michigan, Zondervan Publishing House, 1975.

BROWN, C. (ed.), *New International Dictionary of New Testament Theology*, Exeter, Devon, UK, Paternoster, 1975.

BROWN, F., DRIVER, S. R. & BRIGGS, C. A., *The New Brown-Driver-Briggs Hebrew and English Lexicon with an Appendix Containing the Biblical Aramaic*, 1906, repr., Peabody, Hendrickson Publishers, 1979.

BROWN, R. E., FITZMYER, J. A. & MURPHY, R. E., (ed.), *The New Jerome Biblical Commentary*, revised edition, Englewood Cliffs, NJ, Prentice-Hall, 1990.

BROWN, R. E., *The Critical Meaning of the Bible*, New York, Paulist Press, 1981.

BROWN, R. K. & Comfort, P. W. (trans.), DOUGLAS, J. D., *The New Greek-English Interlinear New Testament*, NRSV translation, 4th ed., Tyndale House, 1993.

BROWNING, W. R. F., *A Dictionary of the Bible*, rev. ed., New York, Oxford University Press, 2004.

BURNEY, C. F., *Notes on the Hebrew Text of the Books of Kings, With an Introduction and Appendix,* Oxford, Clarendon Press, 1903.

BURRIDGE, R., *What Are the Gospels? A Comparison with Greco-Roman Biography*, Society for New Testament Studies Monograph 70, Cambridge, Cambridge University Press, 1992. 501

BUTTRICK, G. A. (ed.), *The New Interpreter's Dictionary of the Bible* (4 vols.), Nashville, Abingdon Press, 1995.

CARTLIDGE, D. R. & DUNGAN, D. (eds.), *Documents for the Study of the Gospels*, Minneapolis, Fortress Press, 1993.

CASSIDY, R. J., *Christians and Roman Rule in the New Testament: New Perspectives*, Companions to the New Testament Series, New York, Crossroads, 2001.

CHILDS, B. S., *Biblical Theology of the Old and New Testaments Theological Reflections on the Christian Bible,* London, SCM Press, 1992.

CHILDS, B. S., *Introduction to the Old Testament as Scripture,* Philadelphia, Fortress Press, 1979.

CLARKE, K. D., *Textual Optimism: A Critique of the United Bible Societies' Greek New Testament,* JSNTSup 138, Sheffield, Sheffield Academic Press, 1997.

COLLINS, R. F., *Introduction to the New Testament,* New York, Image Books, 1987.

COMFORT, P. W. & BARRETT, D. P., *The Complete Text of the Earliest New Testament Manuscripts*, Grand Rapids, MI, Baker, 1999.

COOGAN, M. D., BRETTLER, M. Z., NEWSOM, C. A. & PERKINS, P., (eds.), *The New Oxford Annotated Bible with Apocrypha, 3rd Edition, New Revised Standard Version,* New York, Oxford University Press, 2001.

COUNTRYMAN, L. W., *Read It In Greek: An Introduction to New Testament Greek*, Grand Rapids, MI, Wm. B. Eerdmans, 1999.

COURT, J. M., *Reading the New Testament,* New Testament Readings 67, London, Roufledge, 1997.

DANKER, F. W. & ARNDT, W. (ed.), *A Greek-English Lexicon of the New Testament and Other Christian Literature*, 4th edition, Chicago, University of Chicago Press, 2000.

DAVIES, B. (ed.), *A Compendious and Complete Hebrew and Chaldee Lexicon to the Old Testament*, 2nd ed. Boston: Ira Bradley & Co., 1875.

DE MARGERIE, B., *An Introduction to the History of Exegesis*, 3 volumes, Petersham, MA, St. Bede's, 1995.

DOCNIEZ, C. & HARL, M., *La Bible des Septante: Le Pentateuque d'Alexandrie,* Texte grec et traduction, Paris, Cerf, 2001.

DORIVAL, G. (trad.), *La Bible d'Alexandrie, LXXX, 4 Les Nombres,* Traduction du texte grec de La Septant, Introduction et Notes, Paris, Cerf, 1994.

DOTAN, A. (ed.), *Biblia Hebraica Lenin gradensia,* Prepared According to the Vocalisation Accents and Masora of Aaron ben Moses ben Asher in the Leningrad Codex, Peabody, Hendrickson Publishers, 2001.

DRIVER, S. R., *The Use of Tenses in Hebrew and Some Syntactical Questions*, Oxford, Clarendon Press, 1892.

DUNGAN, D. L., *A History of the Synoptic Problem*, Anchor Bible Reference Library, New York, Doubleday, 1999.

EFIRD, J. M., *A Grammar for New Testament Greek*, Nashville, Abingdon Press, 1990.

EHRMAN, B. D., *The New Testament and Other Early Christian Writings: A Reader*, 2nd ed., New York, Oxford University Press, 2003.

ELDON, J. E., "Textual Critism (NT)", *The Anchor Bible Dictionary,* New York, Doubleday, 1992.

ELLIOT, J. K., *The Principles and Practice of New Testament Textual Criticism,* Leuven, Leuven University Press, 1990.

ELLIOTT, K. & MOIR, I., *Manuscripts and the Text of the New Testament: An Introduction for English Readers,* Edinburgh, T&T Clark, 1985.

EVANS, C. & PORTER, S. E. (ed.), *Dictionary of New Testament Background,* Downers Grove, IL, Intervarsity Press, 2000.

FARMER, W. R., *The International Biblel Commentary: A Catholic and Ecumenical Commentary for the 21st Century,* Collegeville, MN, Liturgical Press, 1998.

FERGUSON, E., *Backgrounds of Early Christianity,* 2nd ed., Grand Rapids, Wm. B. Eerdmans, 1993.

FIORENZA, E. S., *Bread Not Stone: The Challenge of Feminist Biblical Interpretation,* Boston, Beacon Press, 1995.

FISCHER, B., GRIBOMONT, J., SPARKS, H. F. D. & THIELE, W. (ed.), *Biblia Sacra Juxta VulgatamVersionem,* Adiuvantibus, Recensuit et brevi apparatu critico instruxit Robertus Weber, Editionem quartam emendatwn cum sociis, B. Fischer, H. I. Frede, H. F. D. Sparks, Preparavit Roger Gryson, Stuttgart, Deutsche Bibelgesellschaft, 1994.

FITZMYER, J. A., *The Biblical Commission's Document The Interpretation of the Bible in the Church,* Text and Commentary (SubBi 18), Rome, Pontificio Istituto Biblico, 1995.

FITZMYER, J. A., *The Semitic Background of the New Testament,* rev. ed., Grand Rapids, MI, Wm. B. Eerdmans, 1997.

FREEDMAN, D. N., *et al.* (ed.), *The Leningrad Codex, A Facsimile Edition,* Grand Rapids, Eerdmans, 1998.

FREEDMAN, D. N., *The Anchor Bible Dictionary,* 6 vol., New York, Doubleday, 1992.

GAMBLE, H. Y., *Books and Readers in the Early Church: A History of Early Christian Texts,* New Haven, Yale, 1995.

GEORFFREY, Dr. W., (ed.), *The New Standard Jewish Encyclopedia,* Encyclopedia Publishing Co., 1992. 504

GINGRICH, F. W., *Shorter Lexicon of the Greek New Testament,* (2nd ed. rev.), DANKER, F. W., Chicago, University of Chicago Press, 1983.

GOODRICK, E. & KOHLENBERGER, J. R., *The NIV Exhaustive Concordance,* Grand Rapids, MI, Zondervan, 1990.

GREEN, J. B., *Hearing the New Testament: Strategies for Interpretation,* Grand Rapids, MI, Wm. B. Eerdmans, 1995.

GREEN, J., MCKNIGHT, S. & MARSHALL, L. H. (eds.), *Dictionary of Jesus and the Gospels,* Downers Grove, IL, Intervarsity Press, 1992.

HarperCollins Bible Commentary, MAYS, J. L. (ed.), San Francisco, Harper San Francisco, 2000.

HATCH, E. & REDPATH, H. A., *Concordance to the Septuagint,* Edinburgh, T & T Clark, 1998.

HAYES, J. H. (ed.), *New Testament: History of Interpretation,* Nashville, TN, Abingdon, 2005.

HENRY, M., *Commentary On The Whole Bible,* Grand Rapids, Michigan, Zondervan Publishing House, 1961.

HOFFMANN, P. & HIEKE, T. et al., *Synoptic Concordance,* Vols. 1&2, Berlin & New York, Walter de Gruyter, 2000.

JOHNSON, L. T. & KURZ, W. S., *The Future of Catholic Biblical Scholarship: A Constructive Conversation,* Grand Rapids, MI, Wm. B. Eerdmans, 2002.

JOÜON, P. & MURAOKA, T., *A Grammar of Biblical Hebrew, Part One, Orthography and Phonetics, Part Two, Morphology,* SubBi 14/I, Rome, Pontificio Istituto Biblico 1991.

JOÜON, P. & MURAOKA, T., *A Grammar of Biblical Hebrew,* Part Three, *Syntax,* SubBi 14/TI, Rome, Pontificio Istituto Biblico, 1991.

JOÜON, P., *Grammaire de l'hébreu biblique,* Rome, Institut Biblique Pontifical, 1923.

KITTEL, G. & FRIEDRICH, G. (eds.), *Theological Dictionary of the New Testament,* 10 vols. Trans. by BROMILEY, G. W., Grand Rapids, Eerdmans, 1964-76.

KOEHLER, L. & BAUMGARTNER, W., *The Hebrew and Aramaic Lexicon of the Old Testament* 3, Leiden & New York, E. J. Brill, 1996.

KOHLENBERGER, J. R. & SWANSON, J. A., *The Hebrew-English Concordance to the Old Testament, with the New International Version,* Grand Rapids, Zondervan, 1998.

KOHLENBERGER, J. R. (ed.), *The Concise Concordance to the New Revised Standard Version,* New York, Oxford University Press, 1993.

KOHLENBERGER, J. R. (ed.), *The New American Bible Concise Concordance,* New York, Oxford University Press, 2003.

KOHLENBERGER, J. R. (ed.), *The NRSV Concordance: Unabridged,* Grand Rapids, Zondervan, 1991.

KOHLENBERGER, J. R., GOODRICK, E. W. & SWANSON, J. A. (eds.), *The Exhaustive Concordance to the Greek New Testament,* Grand Rapids, MI, Zondervan, 1995.

KRENTZ, E., *The Historical-Critical Method,* Guides to Biblical Scholarship, reprint of 1975 edition, Wift, 2002.

KUBO, S., *A Reader's Greek-English Lexicon to the New Testament,* Grand Rapids, Zondervan, 1975.

LACOCQUE, A. & RICOEUR, P., *Thinking Biblically: Exegetical and Hermeneutical Studies,* Chicago, University of Chicago Press, 1998.

LAMPE, G. W. H., *Patristic Greek Lexicon,* New York, Oxford University Press, 1961.

LIDDELL, A. G. & SCOTT, R., *Greek-English Lexicon with a Revised Supplement*, 9th ed. by Stuart Jones & McKenzie, New York, Clarendon / Oxford University Press, 1996.

LIENHARD, J. T., *The Bible, the Church, and Authority: the Canon of the Christian Bible in History and Theology*, Collegeville, MN, Liturgical Press, 1995.

LISOWSKY, G. (ed.), *Konkordanz zum Hebraischen Alten Testament, Concordance to the Hebrew OT)*, 3rd ed. Stuttgart, Deutsche Bibelgesellschaft, 1993.

LIVINGSTONE, E. A., *The Oxford Dictionary of the Christian Church*, 3rd ed., New York, Oxford University Press, 1997.

LOUW, J. P. & NIDA, E. A., *A Greek-English Lexicon of the New Testament, Based on Semantic Domains*, 2 vols. 2nd ed., New York, United Bible Societies, 1989.

MARSHALL, A., (ed.), *The Interlinear NIV Parallel New Testament in Greek and English*, Grand Rapids, Zondervan, 1998.

MARTIN, R. P. & DAVIDS, P. H. (eds.), *Dictionary of the Later New Testament and Its Developments*, Downer Grove, IL, Intervarsity Press, 1998.

MAYS, J. L. & BLENKINSOPP, J. (ed.), *HarperCollin's Bible Commentary*, rev. ed., San Francisco, HarperCollins, 2000.

MCCARTER, P. K., *Textual Criticism Recovering the Text of the Hebrew Bible* (GBSOTS), Philadephia, Fortress Press, 1986.

MCKAY, K. L., *A New Syntax of the Verb in New Testament Greek An Aspectual Approach*, Studies in Biblical Greek, 5, New York-San Francisco-Bern, Lang, 1994.

MCKENZIE, J. L., *Dictionary of the Bible*, London, Geoffrey Chapman, 1978.

MCKNIGHT, E., *What is Form Criticism?*, Guides to Biblical Scholarship, Philadelphia, Fortress Press, 1969.

METZGER, B. M. & COOGAN, M. D. (eds.), *The Oxford Guide to Ideas & Issues of the Bible*, New York, Oxford University Press, 2001.

METZGER, B. M. & EHRMAN, B. D., *The Text of the Testament: Its Transmission, Corruption, and Restoration*, 4th ed., New York, Oxford University Press, 2005.

METZGER, B. M., *A Textual Commentary on the Greek New Testament: A Companion Volume to the United Bible Societies' Greek New Testament* (Fourth Revised Edition), Münster, Deutsche Bibelgesellschaft, 1993.

METZGER, B., *The Canon of the New Testament: Its Origin, Development, and Significance*, New York, Clarendon / Oxford University Press, 1987.

METZGER, B., *The Early Versions of the New Testament: Their Origins, Transmission, and Limitations*, Oxford, Clarendon Press, 1977.

MORGAN, R. & BARTON, J., *Biblical Interpretation*, Oxford Bible Series, New York, Oxford University Press, 1988.

MOULTON, W. F., *A Concordance to the Greek Testament*, 5th ed. Edinburgh, T&T Clark, 1978.

MOUNCE, W. D., *A Graded Reader of Biblical Greek,* Grand Rapids, Zondervan, 1996.

MOUNCE, W. D., *Basics of Greek Grammar*, rev. ed., Grand Rapids, Zondervan, 2003.

MOUNCE, W. D., *The Analytical Lexicon to the Greek New Testament*, Grand Rapids, Zondervan, 1993.

MOUNCE, W. D., *The Morphology of Biblical Greek,* Grand Rapids, Zondervan, 1994.

MURPHY-O'CONNOR, J., *The Holy Land: An Oxford Archaeological Guide from Earliest times to 1700,* 4th ed., Oxford Archaeological Guides, New York, Oxford University Press, 1998.

NEILL, S. & WRIGHT, T., *The Interpretation of the New Testament, 1861-1986,* New York, Oxford University Press, 1988.

NEIRYNCK, F., *Q – Parallels, Q Synopsis and IQP/ CritEd Parallels*, Leuven, Peeters, 2001.

NEWMAN, Jr. B. M., *A Concise Greek-English Dictionary of the New Testament*, New York, United Bible Societies, 1993.

O'KEEFE, J. & RENO, R. R., *Sanctified Vision: An Introduction to Early Christian Interpretation of the Bible*, Baltimore, Johns Hopkins University Press, 2005.

OSIEK, C., *What are they saying about the Social Setting of the New Testament?*, New York, Paulist Press, 1992.

PATTE, D., *What is Structural Exegesis?*, Guides to Biblical Scholarship, Philadelphia, Fortress Press, 1976.

PERRIN, N., *What is Redaction Criticism?*, Guides to Biblical Scholarship, reprint of 1969 edition, Fortress Press, 2002.

PILCH, J. J. & MALINA, B. (eds.), *Handbook of Biblical Social Values,* Peabody, MA, Hendrickson, 1998.

PILCH, J. J., *The Cultural Dictionary of the Bible*, Collegeville, MN, Liturgical Press, 1998.

PORTER, S. E., *Handbook to Exegesis of the New Testament*, Leiden, Brill, 1997.

POWELL, M. A., *What is Narrative Criticism?*, Guides to Biblical Scholarship, New Testament Series, Minneapolis, Fortress Press, 1991.

PRICKETT, S., *Reading the Text: Biblical Criticism and Literary Theory*, Cambridge, MA, Blackwell, 1991.

RAGON, E., *Grammaire complète de la langue grecque*, Paris, J. de Girord, 1929.

REHKOPF, F., *Septuaginta - Vokabular,* Göttingen, Vandenhoeck & Ruprecht, 1989.

RICHES, J., *The World of Jesus: First-Century Judaism in Crisis*, Understanding Jesus Today, Cambridge, Cambridge University Press, 1990.

ROBINSON, J. M. & HOFFMANN, P. et al., *The Sayings Gospel Q in Greek and English with parallels from the Gospels of Mark and Thomas*, Leuven & Paris et al., Peeters, 2001.

ROBINSON, T. A., *Mastering Greek Vocabulary*, 2nd ed., Peabody, MA, Hendrikson, 1990.

RUDOLPH W. & RÜGER H. P. (ed.), *Biblia Hebraica Stuttgartensia* quae antea cooperantibus A. Alt, O. Eissfeldt, P. Kahie ediderat R. Kittel, Editio funditus renovata adjuvantibus H. Bardtke, et al. Cooperatibus H. P. Rüger et J. Zielgier ediderunt K. Elliger et W. Rudolph. Textum Mosoreticum curavit H. P. Rüger Masorem elaboravit G. E. Weil, editio quinta emendata opera A. Schenker, Stuttgart, Deutsche Bibelgesellschaft, 1997.

SANDERS, J., *Canon and Community: A Guide to Canonical Criticism*, Guides to Biblical Scholarship, Philadelphia, Fortress Press, 1984.

SCHNEIDERS, S., *The Revelatory Text: Interpreting the New Testament as Sacred Scripture*, Collegeville, MN, Liturgical Press, 1999.

SCOTT, W. R., *A Simplified Guide to* Biblia Hebraica Stuttgartensia, *A Critical Apparatus, Massora, Accents, Unusual Letters & Other Markings*, Berkeley, Bibal Press, 1990.

SENIOR, D., (ed.), *The Catholic Study Bible: New American Bible*, New York, Oxford University Press, 1990.

SINGER, I., *The Jewish encyclopedia: A descriptive record of the history, religion, literature, and customs of the Jewish people from the earliest times to the present day*, New York, Funk and Wagnalls, 1901-1906.

STRONG, J., *The Exhaustive Concordance of the Bible*, New York, Abingdon Press, 1965.

STUHLMUELLER, C., *The Collegeville Pastoral Dictionary of Biblical Theology*, Collegeville, MN, Liturgical Press, 1996.

SWANSON, R. J., *New Testament Greek manuscripts, Variant Readings Arranged in Horizontal Lines against Codex Vaticanus*, Sheffield, England, Sheffield Academic press, 1995.

SWETNAM, J., *An Introduction to the Study of New Testament Greek: Part One, Morphology*, 2 vols. Rome, Pontifical Biblical Institute, 1998.

THAYER, J. H., *A Greek-English Lexicon of the New Testament*, New York, American Book Company, 1889.

THROCKMORTON, B. H., *Gospel Parallels: A Comparison of the Synoptic Gospels*, 5th Nashville, Thomas Nelson, 1993.

edition, NRSV translation, TOV, E., *Textual Criticism of the Hebrew Bible*, Assen/Maastricht, Van Gorcum, 1981, 1992.

TOV, E., *The Text-Critical Use of the Septuagint in Biblical Research*, Jerusalem, Simor Ltd., 1997.

TRENCHARD, W. C., *Complete Vocabulary Guide to the Greek New Testament*, rev. ed., Grand Rapids, Zondervan, 1998.

ULRICH, E., *The Text of the Hebrew Scriptuies at the Time of Hillel and Jesus*, in A. LEMAIRE (ed.), *Congress Volume*, (VTSup. 92), Leiden & Boston, Brill, 2002, pp. 85-108.

VAN NESS GOETCHIUS, E., *The Language of the New Testament,* reprint of 1965 edition, Prentice-Hall, 1997.

VAN VOORST, R. E., *Building Your New Testament Greek Vocabulary,* Grand Rapids, MI, Eerdmans, 1990.

VANGEMEREN, W. A. et al. (eds.), *New International Dictionary of Old Testament Theology and Exegesis,* Carlisle, Cumbria, Paternoster, 1997.

VIA, D. O., *What is New Testament Theology?,* Guides to Biblical Scholarship, New Testament Series, Minneapolis, Fortress Press, 2002.

VINE, W. E., *An Expository Dictionary of New Testament Words,* Old Tappan, N. J., Fleming H. Revell Co., 1940.

WALLACE, D. B., *Greek Grammar Beyond the Basics,* Grand Rapids, Zondervan, 1997.

WALTKE, B. K. & O'CONNOR, M. P., *An Introduction to Biblical Hebrew Syntax,* Winona Lake, Eisenbrauns, 1990.

WATSON, W. G. E., *Traditional Techniques in Classical Hebrew Verse,* JSOTSup 170, Sheffield, Sheffield Academic Press, 1994.

WENHAM, J. W., PENNINGTON, J. & YOUNG, N., *Elements of New Testament Greek,* rev. ed., Cambridge, Cambridge University Press, 2002.

WERBLOWSKY, R. J. Z. & WIGODER, G., *The Oxford Dictionary of Jewish Religion,* New York & Oxford, Oxford University Press, 1997.

WHITAKER, R. E. & KOHLENBERGER, J. R. (ed.), *The Analytical Concordance to the Revised Standard Version of the New Testament,* Grand Rapids, Wm. B. Eerdmans, 2000.

WHITE, L. M. & YARBROUGH, O. L., *The Social World of the First Christians: Essays in Honor of Wayne A. Meeks,* Minneapolis, Fortress Press, 1995.

WONNENBERGER, R, *Understanding BHS, A Manual for the Users of the Biblia Hebraica Stuttgartensia (SB* 8) Roma, Pontificio Istituto Biblico, 1990.

WÜRTHWEIN, E., *The Text of the Old Testament: An Introduction to the* Biblia Hebraica, RHODES, E. F. (trans.), Grand Rapids, Eerdmans, 1995.

YOUNG, R., *Analytical Concordance to the Bible,* Grand Rapids, Michigan, Wm. B. Eerdmans Publishing Co., 1970.

ZERWICK, M. & GROSVENOR, M., *A Grammatical Analysis of the Greek New Testament,* 5th rev. ed., Rome, Editrice Pontificio Instituto Biblia, 1996.

2. Reference Works

BACHER, W., *"Gamaliel I",* in *The Jewish Encyclopedia* 5 (1903) 558-559.

BAUER, W., *Iesus, BDAG* (2000) 471-472.

BOGAERT, P. M., Les etudes sur la Septante : Bilan et perspectives, *RTL* 16 (1985) 174-200.

BROWN F. & DRIVER S. R. et al., 'Rab', *A Hebrew And English Lexicon of the Old Testament with an Appendix Containing the Biblical Aramaic,* Oxford, Clarendon Press, 1952, p. 912.

BROYDÉ, I., "*Rabbi*", in *JE* (1905) 294-295.

CHILTON, B. D., "Judaism", *Dictionary of Jesus and the Gospels*, pp. 402-405.

COMFORT, P. W. & BARRETT, D. P., *The Complete Text of the Earliest New Testament Manuscripts*, Grand Rapids, MI, Baker, 1999.

EISENSTEIN, J. D., "*Rabbi*", in *JE* 10 (1905) 294-297. ELLISON, H. L., "*Rabbi*", in BROWN, C. (ed.), *NIDNTT* 3 (1978) 115-116.

ERHARTER H., *Lexikon fur Theologie und Kirche*, HOFER, J. and RAHNER, K. (ed.), Friberg, 1957-65.

EVANS, C. A., *Messianism*, in C. A. EVANS, S. E. PORTER (ed.), *Dictionary of New Testament Background,* Leicester, Inter-Varsity Press, 2000, pp. 698-707.

EVANS, C. A., SANDERS, J. A., *Early Christian Interpretation of the Scriptures of Israel, Investigations and Proposals,* JSNTSup 148, Sheffield, Sheffield Acadenuc Press, 1997.

FISHBANE, M., *Biblial Interpretation in Ancient Israel,* Oxford, Clarendon Press, 1985.

FOKKELMAN, J. P., *Comment lire le Recit Biblique. Une Introduction Pratique,* Cistercierines de l'abbaye Notre-Dame de Clairefontaine, LLR 13, Bruxelles, Lessius, 2002.

FOKKELMAN, J. P., *Narrative Art in Genesis: Specimens of stylistic and Structural Analysis,* Sheffield, Sheffield Academic Press, 1991.

FOKKELMAN, J. P., *Reading Biblical Narrative A Practical Guide,* Leiden, Deo Publishing, 1999.

GOULD, G. P., "*Disciples*", in *Dictionary of Jesus and the Gospels*, Downers Grove, IL, Leicester, UK, Intervarsity Press, (1992) 176.

GRABBE, L. L., *Priests, Prophets, Diviners, Sages: A Socio- historical Study of Religious Specialists in Ancient Israel,* Valley Forge, Trinity, 1995.

GUTSTEIN, M. A. "*Rabbi*", in HARSEY, W. D. et al., (eds.), *Collier's Encyclopedia with Bibliography and Index*, New York, Macmillian Educational Company, (1988) 580.

HERTZ, R., "*Rabbi, Rabbinate*" in JOHN, B. (ed.), *The Oxford Dictionary of World Religions*, N.Y., Oxford University Press, 1997, p. 788.

HIMELSTEIN, S., " *Rabbai and Rabbinate* ", in WERBLOWSKY, R. J. Z. & WIGODER, G. (eds.), *The Oxford Dictionary of Jewish Religion*, New York, (1997) 567-568.

HITCHCOCK, R. D., "*Rabbi*", "*An Interpreting Dictionary of Scripture Proper Names*", New York, N.Y., 1869.

JONATHAN, Z. (ed.), *The Harper Collins Dictionary of Religion*, HarperCollins Publishers Inc., 1995.

KANARFOGEL, E., "*Rabbinate*", in JONES, L., et al. (ed.), *Encyclopedia of Religion* (2nd ed.), Vol II. (Pius IX – Rivers), Thomsan Gale, (2005) 7578-81.

KECK, L. E., *Jesus in New Testament Christology* in *ABR* (1980) 1-21.

KITTEL, G., Διδάσκαλος in *TDNT* 2 (1964) 152-159.

KOEHLER, L. & BAUMGARTNER, W., et al., *Rab*, *HALOT* 3, Leiden & New York, E. J. Brill, 1996, 1172-1174.

KREDEL, E. M., *"Disciple"*, in *Bauer Encyclopaedia of Biblical Theology* (1978) 209-213.

LAPIN, H., *"Rabbi"* in *ABD*, Vol.5 (1992) 600-602.

LAPIN, H., *"Rabbi"* in FREEDMAN, D. N., *The Anchor Bible Dictionary*, Vol. 5, O-Sh, N.Y., Double day, (1992) 600- 602.

LOHSE, E., 'Ραββί & 'Ραββουνί, *TDNT* 6 (1968) 961- 965. MACARTHUR, J. (ed.), *The MacArthur Study Bible*, Nashville, Word Publishing, 1997.

MALINA, B. J., *The New Testament World: Insights from Cultural Anthropology*, 3rd John Knox, 2001. ed., Louisville, KY, Westminster

MALINA, B. J., *The Social World of Jesus and the Gospels*, New York, Routledge, 1996.

MALINA, B. J., *Windows on the World of Jesus: Time Travel to Ancient Judea*, Louisville, KY, Westminster John Knox, 1993.

MCKENZIE, J. L., *"Rabbi"*, *Dictionary of the Bible*, London, Geoffrey Chapman, 1978.

MCKENZIE, J. L., *Dictionary of the Bible*, New York-London, Macmillan, 1965.

MEYER, R., *"Saddoukaios"*, *Theological Dictionary of the New Testament* (TDNT), 7:35-54.

MÜLLER, D., μαθητὴς, *NIDNT* (1975) 483-490.

NEIRYNCK, F., *Q – Parallels, Q Synopsis and IQP/ CritEd Parallels*, Leuven, Peeters, 2001.

NEPPER-CHRISTENSEN, P., μαθητὴς, *EDNT* 2 (1991) 372-374.

NEUSNER, J. & GREEN, W. S., (eds.), *"Rabbi"*, *Dictionary of Judaism in the Biblical Period*, Vol. 2., NY, Simon & Schuster Macmillan, (1996) 516-18.

NEUSNER, J. & SCOTT, G. W. (eds.), *"Rabbi"*, in *Dictionary of Judaism in the Biblical Period*, Vol. 2., NY, Simon & Schuster Macmillan, (1996) 516-18.

NEUSNER, J., *"Rabbinic Judaism in Late Antiquity"*, in JONES, L. et al. (ed.), *Encyclopedia of Religion* (2nd ed.), Vol. II. (Pius IX – Rivers), Thomsan Gale, (2005) 7583-7590.

PATAI, R., *"Rabbi"*, *Encyclopaedia Americana*, Vol. 23 (Pumps to Russell), International Edition, Grolier, Danbury – Connecticut, 2000, p. 108.

RABBINOUITZ, L. I., *"Rabbi, Rabbinate"* in *Encyclopaedia Judaica* 13 (1971) 1447-1458.

RENGSTORF, K. H., μαθητὴς, in *TDNT* 4 (1967) 439. RENGSTORF, K. H., μαθητὴς, in *TDNT* 4 (1967) 439.

SAFRA, J. E. (ed.), *"rabbi"*, in *The New Encyclopaedia Britannica*, Vol. 9, (15th ed.), Chicago, IL, 2002, p. 871.

SAFRA, J. E. (ed.), *"rabbi"*, *The New Encyclopaedia Britannica*, Vol. 9, (15th ed.), Chicago, 2002, p. 871.

SALDARINI, A. J., *Pharisees, Scribes, and Sadducees in Palestinian Society: A Sociological Approach*, Grand Rapids, MI, Wm. B. Eerdmans, 2001.

SCHNEIDER, G., 'Ραββί **&** 'Ραββουνί, *EDNT* 3 (1990) 205-206.

SHULER, P. L., Disciple, in *Harper's Bible Dictionary* (1990) 222.

SKA, J. L., La nouvelle critique et l'exegese anglo-saxonne, *RSR* 80 (1992) 29-53.

SNYDER, H. G., *Teachers and Texts in the Ancient World: Philosophers, Jews, and Christians*, Religion in the First Christian Centuries, New York, Routledge, 2000.

STAMBAUGH, J. E. & BALCH, D. L., *The New Testament in Its Social Environment*, Library of Early Christianity 2, Philadelphia, Westminster John Knox, 1986.

STEGEMANN, W., MALINA, B. & THEISSEN, G. (eds.), *The Social Setting of Jesus and the Gospels*, Minneapolis, Fortress Press, 2002.

TATE, R. W., *Biblical Interpretation: an Integrated Approach*, Peabody, MA, Hendrickson, 1991.

THEISSEN, G., *Social Reality and the Early Christians: Theology, Ethics, and the World of the New Testament*, Edinburgh, T&T Clark, 1999.

THEISSEN, G., *Sociology of Early Palestinian Christianity*, BOWDEN, J. (trans.), Philadelphia, Fortress Press.

TUCKER, W. D. Jr., "*Rabbi, Rabboni*" in FREEDMAN, D. N. (ed.), *Dictionary of the Bible*, Grand Rapids, M. I., Cambridge, U.K., William B. Eerdmans Publishing Company, (2000) 1105-1106.

TURRO, J. C., "*Rabbi*", in MARTHALER, B. L. et al (ed.), *New Catholic Encyclopedia* (2nd ed.), Pau- Red (Vol. 2),

Washington D.C., Thomson Gale in association with the Catholic University of America, (2003) 882-883.

TWELFTREE, G. H., "Scribes", *Dictionary of Jesus and the Gospels*, pp. 732-735.

WEDER, H., "*Disciple, Discipleship*", *ABD* 2 (1992) 207-210. WEGENAST, K., Διδάσκαλος, *NIDNTT* (1975) 766.

WEISS, H. F., Διδάσκαλος & Διδάσκω, *EDNT* 1 (1990) 317-319.

WESTERHOLM, S., "Pharisees", *Dictionary of Jesus and the Gospels*, DJG, pp. 609-614.

WESTERMANN, C., *Basic Forms of Prophetic Speech*, Louisville, Westminster/ John Knox Press, 1991.

WILSON, M. R., "*Rabbi*", in *ISBE* 4 (1998) 30.

3. Commentaries on Johannine Literature

ABBOTT, E. A., *Johannine Grammar*, London, A & C Black, 1906, repr. 1968.

ABBOTT, E. A., *Johannine Vocabulary: A Comparison of the Words of the Fourth Gospel with Those of the Three*, London, A & C Black, 1905, repr. 1968.

BARCLAY, W., *The Gospel of John*, 2 vols., Daily Study Bible, Edinburgh, Saint Andrew Press, Philadelphia, Westminster, 1956, rev. ed., 1975.

BARRETT, C. K., *The Gospel according to John: An Introduction with Commentary and Notes on the Greek Text*, 2nd ed., London, S.P.C.K., Philadelphia, Westminster, 1978.

BAUER, W., *Das Johannesevangelium*, HKNT 6, Tübingen, J. C. B. Mohr P. Siebeck, 1912, 2nd ed. 1925, 3rd ed. 1933.

BEASLEY- MURRAY, G. R., *John*, WBC 36, Nashville, Thomas Nelson, 1999.

BECKER, J., *Das Evangelium nach Johannes*, 2 vols., ÖTK 4.1-2. Gütersloh, Mohn, Würzburg, Echter, 1979-1981, 2nd ed. 1984-1985.

BERNARD, J. H., *A Critical and Exegetical Commentary on the Gospel according to St. John*, 2 vols. International Critical Commentary 29, Alan Hugh MCNEILE (ed.), Edinburgh, T&T Clark, 1928, repr. 1953, 1969, 1976.

BOISMARD, M.-E., & A. LAMOUILLE, *L'Evangile de Jean*, Synopse des Quatre Evangiles en Français III, Paris, Cerf, 1977.

BOISMARD, M.-E., *Du baptême a Cana (Jean I, 19-II, 11)*, Paris, Éditions du Cerf, 1956.

BOISMARD, M.-E., *St. John's Prologue*, London, BlackFriars, Westminster, MD, Newman, 1957.

BRODIE, T. L., *The Gospel according to John: A Literary and Theological Commentary*, New York, Oxford University Press, 1993.

BROWN, R. E., *The Gospel & Epistles of John: A Concise Commentary*, Collegeville, MN, Liturgical Press, 1988.

BROWN, R. E., *The Gospel According to John I-XII & XIII- XXI: A New Translation with Introduction and Commentary*, 2 vols. Anchor Bible 29 & 29A. Garden City, NY, Doubleday, 1966-70.

BROWN, R. E., *The Gospel and Epistles of John: A Concise Commentary*, Collegeville, MN, Liturgical Press, 1988.

BROWN, R., *The Community of the Beloved Disciple: The Life, Loves, and Hates of an Individual Church in New Testament Times*, Mahwah, NJ, Paulist, 1979.

BRUCE, F. F., *The Gospel according to John*, Grand Rapids, Eerdmans, 1971; rev. ed. with new title: *The Gospel of John*, 1983.

BULTMANN, R. K., *Das Evangelium des Johannes*, Meyer's Kommentar, Göttingen, Vandenhoeck & Ruprecht, 1941, repr. 1950-1986.

BULTMANN, R., *The Gospel of John. A Commentary*, (trans.), G.R.BEASLEY-MURRAY et al., Philadelphia, Westminster Press, 1971.

CALLOUD, J. & GENUYT, F., *L'Evangile de Jean: Lecture sémiotique des chapitres...*, 4 vols. Lyon, Centre Thomas More, 1985-91.

CALVIN, J., *St. John*, trans. PARKER, T. H. L., Grand Rapids, MI, Eerdmans, 1961.

CARSON, D. A., *The Gospel according to John*, Leicester, England, InterVarsity Press, Grand Rapids, Eerdmans, 1991; repr. 2000.

CHARAN SINGH, M., *St. John, The Great Mystic*, Punjab, India, Radha Soami Satsang Beas, 1967; 2nd ed. 1978; changed title in 6th edition, *Light on Saint John*, 1994.

CULLMANN, O., *Early Christian Worship,* Studies in Biblical Theology 10, Trans., by A. Stewart Todd & James B. Torrance, London, SCM Press, 1953; repr. 1959, 1966.

CULPEPPER, R. A. & BLACK, C. C., *Exploring the Gospel of John: In Honor of D. Moody Smith,* Louisville, Westminster John Knox, 1996.

CULPEPPER, R. A. (ed.), *The Johannine Literature,* Sheffield New Testament Guides, Sheffield, Sheffield Academic Press, 2000.

CULPEPPER, R. A., *The Anatomy of the Fourth Gospel: A Study in Literary Design,* Minneapolis, Fortress, 1983.

CULPEPPER, R. A., *The Gospel and Letters of John, IBT,* Nashville, Abingdon, 1998.

DELEBECQUE, E., *Evangile de Jean, Texte Traduit et Annoté, CahRB* 23, Paris, Gabalda, 1987.

EDWARDS, M. J., *John,* Blackwell Bible Commentaries, Malden, MA, Blackwell, 2004.

EISENBEIS, W., *A Translation of the Greek Expressions in the Text of "The Gospel of John, A Commentary by Rudolf Bultmann",* Lanham, MD, University Press of America, 1982.

ELLIOTT, W. J. & PARKER, D. C. (eds.), *The Gospel according to St. John,* The NT in Greek, IV, Leiden, New York, E. J. Brill, 1995.

ELLIS, P. F., *The Genius of John: A Composition-Critical Commentary on the Fourth Gospel,* Collegeville, MN, Liturgical Press, 1984.

ERDMAN, C. R., *The Gospel of John: An Exposition,* Philadelphia, Westminster, 1944.

FENTON, J. C., *The Gospel according to John in the Revised Standard Version,* Oxford University Press, Clarendon, 1970.

FILSON, F. V., *The Gospel according to John,* Layman's Bible Commentary, Richmond, VA, John Knox, 1963; alternate title: *Saint John,* London, SCM Press, 1963.

GANGEL, K. O., *John,* Holman New Testament Commentary, Nashville, Broadman & Holman, 2000.

GROSSOUW, W. K. M., *Revelation and Redemption: A Sketch of the Theology of St. John,* (Trans.), SCHOENBERG, M. W., Westminster, MD, Newman, 1955; London, Chapman, 1958.

HARRINGTON, D. J., *John's Thought and Theology: An Introduction,* Good News Studies, 33, Wilmington, DE, Michael Glazier, 1990.

HARRINGTON, D. J., *Sacra Pagina* series, 13 vol. to date, Collegeville, MN, Liturgical Press, 1991-.

HOSKYNS, E. C., *The Fourth Gospel, by the Late Edwyn Clement Hoskyns,* 2 vols., 2nd ed., by F. N. DAVEY, London, Faber & Faber, 1961, repr. 1967.

HOWARD-BROOK, W., *Becoming Children of God. John's Gospel and Radical Discipleship,* Maryknoll, NY, Orbis, 1994.

JEREMIAS, J., *Der Prolog des Johannesevangeliums (Johannes 1, 1-18)*, Stuttgart, Calwer, 1967.

JOANNES, S. E., *Commentaire sur l'Évangile de Jean*, (ed.), JEAUNEAU, E., Paris, Éditions du Cerf, 1972.

KECK, L. (ed.), *The New Interpreter's Bible*, 6 vol., Nashville, Abingdon, 1994-.

KEENER, C. S, *The Gospel of John: A Commentary*, 2 vols. Peabody, MA, Hendrickson, 2003.

KÖSTENBERGER, A. J., *Encountering John: The Gospel in Historical, Literary, and Theological Perspective*, Encountering Biblical Studies, Grand Rapids, Baker, 2000.

KÖSTENBERGER, A. J., *John*, Baker Exegetical Commentary on the NT, Grand Rapids, Baker, 2004.

KRUSE, C. G., *The Gospel according to John: An Introduction and Commentary*, Tyndale NT Commentaries, Grand Rapids, Eerdmans, 2004.

KYSAR, R., *John*, Augsburg Commentary on the NT, Minneapolis, Augsburg, 1986.

KYSAR, R., *John, the Maverick Gospel*, Rev. ed. Louisville, Westminster John Knox, 1993.

KYSAR, R., *Preaching John*, Fortress Resources for Preaching, Minneapolis, Fortress, 2002.

LAGRANGE, M-J., *Évangile selon Saint Jean*, 5th ed. Études bibliques, Paris, Librairie V, Lecoffre, J. Gabalda, 1936.

LENSKI, R. C. H., *The Interpretation of St. John's Gospel*, Columbus, OH, Lutheran Book Concern - Wartburg, 1942, repr. Minneapolis, Augsburg, 1961.

LÉON-DUFOUR, X., *Lecture de l'Evangile selon Jean*, 3 vols. Parole de Dieu, Paris, Seuil, 1988, 1990, 1993.

LIGHTFOOT, R. H., *St. John's Gospel: A Commentary*, (ed.), EVANS, C. F., Oxford, Clarendon, 1956, repr. 1983, London, Oxford University Press, 1960.

LINDARS, B., *The Gospel of John: Based on the Revised Standard Version*, New Century Bible, London, Oliphants, 1972; repr. Grand Rapids, Eerdmans, 1981.

MALATESTA, E., *St. John's Gospel, 1920-1965, A Cumulative and Classified Bibliography of Books and Periodical Literature on the Fourth Gospel*, Rome, Pontifical Biblical Institute, 1967.

MALINA, B. & ROHRBAUGH, R. L., *Social-Science Commentary on the Gospel of John*, Minneapolis, Fortress, 1998.

MARTYN, J. L., *History & Theology in the Fourth Gospel*, rev. ed., Nashville, Abingdon, 1979.

MAYS, J. L., MILLER, P. D. & ACHTEMEIER, P. J., *Interpretation: A Bible Commentary for Teaching and Preaching*, 33 volumes to date, Louisville, KY, Westminster John Knox, 1980s.

MCPOLIN, J., *John,* NT Message 6, Wilmington, DE, Michael Glazier, 1979, rev. ed. 1990.

MICHAELS, J. R., *John,* Good News Commentary, Cambridge – Hagerstown, Harper & Row, 1984.

MICHAELS, J. R., *John,* New International Biblical Commentary, 4. Peabody, MA, Hendrickson, 1989, repr. 1995.

MICHAELS, J. R., *John,* NIBC 4, Peabody, MA, Hendrickson, 1989.

MILLS, W. E., *The Gospel of John,* Bibliographies for Biblical Research, NT Series, Lewiston, NY, Edwin Mellen, 1995.

MOLONEY, F. J., *Belief in the Word, Reading John 1-4*, Minneapolis, Fortress, 1993.

MOLONEY, F. J., *Glory Not Dishonor, Reading John 13-21*, Minneapolis, Fortress, 1998.

MOLONEY, F. J., *Reading John: Introducing the Johannine Gospel and Letters,* Melbourne, Collins Dove, 1995.

MOLONEY, F. J., *Signs and Shadows: Reading John 5-12,* Minneapolis, Fortress, 1996.

MOLONEY, F. J., *The Gospel of John,* Sacra Pagina Series 4, Collegeville, MI, Liturgical Press, 1998.

MOODY SMITH, D., *John,* Abingdon New Testament Commentaries, Nashville, TN, Abingdon, 1999.

MORGAN, G. C., *The Gospel according to John,* London, Marshall Morgan & Scott, 1933, 2nd edition Westwood, NJ, Los Angeles, Fleming H. Revell, 1934.

MORRIS, L., *The Gospel according to John: The English Text with Introduction, Exposition and Note,* New International Commentary on the NT, Grand Rapids, Eerdmans, 1971, rev. ed. 1995.

MURRAY, J. O. F., *Jesus according to St. John,* London NY, Toronto, Longmans, Green & Co, 1938.

ODEN, T. C. & HALL, C. H. (ed.), *The Ancient Christian Commentary on Scripture,* Downers Grove, IL, Intervarsity Press, 1998-.

PERKINS, P., "The Gospel according to John", *New Jerome Biblical Commentary,* (ed.), BROWN, R., FITZMYER, J. & MURPHY, R., Englewood Cliffs, NJ, Prentice Hall, 1990, 942-985.

PLUMMER, A., *The Gospel according to John,* Thornapple Commentaries, Grand Rapids, MI, Baker Book House, 1981.

QUAST, K., *Reading the Gospel of John: An Introduction,* New York, Paulist, 1991.

RENSBERGER, D., *Johannine Faith and Liberating Community,* Louisville, KY, Westminster John Knox, 1988.

RICHARDSON, A., *The Gospel according to Saint John: Introduction and Commentary,* Torch Bible Commentaries, London, SCM Press, 1959.

SANDERS, J. N., *A Commentary on the Gospel according to St. John*, (ed.), MASTIN, B. A., Harper's NT Commentaries, New York, Harper & Row, 1968, repr. London, Black, 1975.

SCHNACKENBURG, R., *Das Johannesevangelium*, Freiburg– Basel – Wien, Herder, 1965-1984, 4th edition, 1985-1986.

SCHNACKENBURG, R., *The Gospel according to St John*, Part I, (trans.), SMYTH, K., Herder's Theological Commentary on the New Testament, NY, Crossroad, 1987.

SCHNACKENBURG, R., *The Gospel according to St. John,* 2 vols. (Trans.), HASTINGS, C., New York, Seabury, 1980.

SCHNACKENBURG, R., *The Gospel according to St. John*, 3 vols., New York, Crossroad, 1982.

SCHNEIDER, J., *Das Evangelium nach Johannes*, Theologischer Handkommentar zum Neuen Testament 4, (ed.), FASCHER, E., Berlin, Evangelische Verlagsanstalt, 1976.

SCHNELLE, U., *Das Evangelium nach Johannes*, Leipzig, Evangelische Verlagsanstalt, 1998.

SEGOVIA, F. F. (ed.), *"What is John?" Vol. I: Readers and Readings of the Fourth Gospel,* Atlanta, Scholars Press, 1996.

SEGOVIA, F. F. (ed.), *"What is John?" Vol. II: LIterary and Social Reading of the Fourth Gospel*, Atlanta, Scholars Press, 1998.

SLOYAN, G. S., *What Are They Saying about John?* New York, Paulist, 1991.

SMITH, D. E., *John, The Storyteller's Companion to the Bible*, vol. 10., WILLIAMS, M. E. (ed.), Nashville, Abingdon, 1996.

SMITH, D. M., *John among the Gospels: The Relationship in Twentieth Century Research*, Minneapolis, Fortress, 1992.

SMITH, D. M., *John*, Abingdon NT Commentaries, Nashville, Abingdon, 1999.

SMITH, D. M., *John,* Proclamation Commentaries, Philadelphia, Fortress, 1976, 2nd edition, 1986.

SMITH, D. M., *The Theology of the Gospel of John*, Cambridge & New York, Cambridge University Press, 1995.

STIBBE, M. W. G., *John, Readings; A New Biblical Commentary*, Sheffield, England, JSOT, 1993.

STORY, C. I., *The Fourth Gospel, the Book of John: Its Purpose, Pattern, & Power*, Shippensburg, White Mane, 1996.

TALBERT, C. H., *Reading John: A Literary and Theological Commentary on the Fourth Gospel and the Johannine Epistles,* Reading the NT, New York, Crossroad, 1992.

TASKER, R. V. G., *The Gospel according to St. John: An Introduction and Commentary*, Tyndale NT Commentaries, Grand Rapids, Eerdmans, 1960, repr. 1965, 1994.

TAYLOR, M. J., *John, The Different Gospel: A Reflective Commentary*, Staten Island, NY, Alba House, 1983.

TEMPLE, W., *Readings in St. John's Gospel*, 2 vols., London, Macmillan, 1939-1940.

TENNEY, M. C., *John: The Gospel of Belief: An Analytic Study of the Text*, Grand Rapids, Eerdmans, 1948.

TURNER, G. A., & MANTEY, J. R., *The Gospel according to John*, Evangelical Commentary on the Bible, 4, Grand Rapids, Eerdmans, 1964.

VAN BELLE, G., *Johannine Bibliography 1966-1985: A Cumulative Bibliography on the Fourth Gospel*, Louvain, Leuven University Press - Uitgeverij Peters, 1988.

VAN DEN BUSSCHE, H., *Jean: Commentaire de l'évangile spirituel*, Paris-Bruges, Desclée de Brouwer, 1967.

VANBELLE, G. (ed.), *Johannine Bibliography 1966-1985: A Cumulative Bibliography of the Fourth Gospel* (BETL, 82), Leuven, University Press, 1988.

WAGNER, G., *An Exegetical Bibliography on the Gospel of John and the Epistles of John; 2nd Series*, Rüschlikon-Zürich, Baptist Theological Seminary, 1983.

WENGST, K., *Das Johannesevangelium*, 2 vols., Theologischer Kommentar zum NT, 4. Stuttgart, W. Kohlhammer, 2000-2001.

WESTCOTT, B. F., *The Gospel according to John*, Volume 1, London, W. C. I, James Clarke & Co Ltd, 1980, 1989.

WESTCOTT, B. F., *The Gospel according to St. John: The Greek Text with Introduction and Notes, by the Late Brooke Foss Westcott*, 2 vols. in 1, (ed.), WESTCOTT, A., Grand Rapids, Eerdmans, 1954, repr., Grand Rapids, Baker, 1980.

WIJNGAARDS, J., *The Gospel of John and His Letters*, Message of Biblical Spirituality, 11, Wilmington, DE, Michael Glazier, 1986.

WITHERINGTON, B., *John's Wisdom: A Commentary on the Fourth Gospel*, Louisville, KY, Westmionster / John Knox, 1995.

WRIGHT, N. T., *John for Everyone*, 2 vols, Louisville, KY, Westminster John Knox Press, 2004.

4. Studies (Secondary Literature)

ABRAHAMS, I., *Studies in Pharisaism and the Gospels*, 2nd edn, 2 vol., Cambridge, Cambridge University Press, 1923.

ABRAMS, M. H., *A Glossary of Literary Terms*, Chicago, Holt Rinehart and Winston, 1988.

AGNEW, P. W., "The Two-Gospel Hypothesis and a Biographical Genre for the Gospels, *in* FARMER, W. R., (ed.), *New Synoptic Studies, The Cambridge Gospel Confrrence and Beyond*, Macon, Mercer University Press, 1983, pp.481-499.

ALAN, D. & BECK, D. R., *Rethinking the Synoptic Problem,* Grand Rapids, Baker Books, 2001.

ALEXANDER, G. M., *The Handbook of Biblical Personalities*, New York, NY, Seabury Press, 1981.

ALISON, D. C., *Jesus of Nazareth: Millennarian Prophet*, Minneapolis, Fortress Press, 1998.

ALLEN, C., *The Human Christ: The Search for the Historical Jesus*, New York, The Free Press, 1998.

ALLISON, D. C. *Jesus of Nazareth: Millenarian Prophet*. Minneapolis, Fortress, 1998.

ALLISON, D. C., *The New Moses: A Matthean Typology*, T&T Clark, Edinburgh, 1993.

ALLISON, D. C., *The Sermon on the Mount: Inspiring the Moral Imagination*, Companions to the New Testament, New York, Crossroad, 1999.

ALONSO-SCHOKEL, L., "Trends: Plurality of Methods, Priority of Issues ", in EMERTON, J.A. (ed.), *Congress Volume Jerusalem 1986,* VTSup 40, Leiden, Brill, 1986, pp. 285-298.

ANDERSON, J. C. & MOORE, S. D., *Mark and Method New Approaches in Biblical Studies,* Minneapolis, Fortress Press, 1992.

ANDERSON, P. N., *The Christology of the Fourth Gospel: Its Unity and Disunity in the Light of John 6, Wissenschaftliche Untersuchungen zum Neuen Testament* 2.78, Tübingen, Mohr, 1996, Harrisburg, PA, Trinity, 1999.

ANDRÉ, L., *Earliest Archaeological Evidence of Jesus Found in Jerusalem*, in *Biblical Archeology* 28/6 (2002), 24-33, 70-71.

APPASAMY, A. J., *Christianity as Bhakti Marga: A Study of the Johannine Doctrine of Love,* Madras, Christian Literature Society for India, 1926; repr. 1991.

APPOLD, M. L., *The Oneness Motif in the Fourth Gospel: Motif Analysis and Exegetical Probe into the Theology of John, WUNT* 2, Reihe 1, Tübingen, Mohr, 1976.

ASHTON, J. (ed.), *The Interpretation of John, Issues in Religion and Theology* 9, Philadelphia, Fortress, London, SPCK, 1986, Second Edition: Studies in New Testament Interpretation, Edinburgh, T&T Clark, 1997.

ASHTON, J., *Studying John: Approaches to the Fourth Gospel*, New York, Oxford University Press, 1995.

ASHTON, J., *Understanding the Fourth Gospel*, Oxford, Oxford University Press, 1993.

ASKWITH, E. H., *The Historical Value of the Fourth Gospel,* London, Hodder & Stoughton, 1910.

BAARDA, T., *The Gospel Quotations of Aphrahat, the Persian Sage: Aphrahat's Text of the Fourth Gospel*, Amsterdam, Vrije Universiteit, 1975.

BACON, B. W. & KRAELING, C. H., *The Gospel of the Hellenists,* New York, H. Holt & Co., 1933.

BACON, B. W., *The Fourth Gospel in Research and Debate: A Series of Essays on Problems Concerning the Origin and Value of the Anonymous Writings Attributed to the Apostle John,* New York, Moffat, Yard & Co., 1910.

BAILEY, J. A., *The Traditions Common to the Gospels of Luke and John,* Leiden, E.J. Brill, 1963.

BAILEY, J. L. & VANDER BROEK, L. D., *Literary Forms in the New Testament: A Handbook,* Louisville, Westminster/John Knox Press, 1992.

BALL, D. M., *'I AM' in John's Gospel: Literary Function, Background, and Theological Implications,* Sheffield, Sheffield Academic Press, 1996.

BANERJEE, B. N., *Jesus My Teacher,* Delhi, India, The Christian Institute for the Study of Religion and Society, 2000.

BARR, J., *The Concept of Biblical Theology, An Old Testament Perspective,* London, SCM *Press,* 1999.

BARR, J., *The Semantics of Biblical Language,* London, SCM Press, 1961.

BARR, J., The Synchronic, the Diachronic and the Historical: A Triangular Relationship?" in DE MOOR, J. C. (ed.), *Synchrony or Diachrony? A Debate on Method in Old Testament Exegesis,* Kampen 1994; *Oudtestamentische Studiën* 34 (1995) 1-14.

BARRETT, C. K. *Essays on John,* London, *SPCK,* Philadelphia, Westminster, 1982.

BARRETT, C. K., *The Gospel of John and Judaism,* Philadelphia, Fortress, 1975.

BARRETT, C. K., *The Lamb of God,* in *NTS* 1 (1954-55) 210-218.

BARRETT, C. K., *The Old Testament in the Fourth Gospel,* in *JTS* 48 (1947) 155-168.

BARTON, J., Historical Criticism and Literary Interpretation: Is There Any Common Ground? ", in. PORTER, S. E., JOYCE, P. & ORTON, D. E. (ed.), *Crossing the Boundaries Essays in Biblical interpretation,* F. S Michael D. Goulder, Leiden, Brill, 1994, pp. 3-16.

BARTON, J., MORGAN R, *Biblical Interpretation,* Oxford, Oxford University Press, 1988.

BAUMGARTNER, W., *Die Literarischen Gattungen in der Weisheit des Jesus Sirach,* ZAW 34 (1914) 161-198.

BEASLEY-MURRAY, G. R., *Gospel of Life: Theology in the Fourth Gospel,* Peabody, MA, Hendrickson, 1991.

BEASLEY-MURRAY, G. R., *Jesus and the Kingdom of God,* Exeter, Paternoster, Eerdmans, 1986.

BEASLEY-MURRAY, G. R., *John,* WBC, vol. 36, 2nd Edition, Nashville, Thomas Nelson Publishers, 1999.

BEAUDE, P. M., *L'Accomplissenrent des Ecritures,* CF 104, Paris, Cerf, 1980.

BECK, D. R., *The Discipleship Paradigm: Readers and Anonymous Characters in the Fourth Gospel,* Leiden, New York, E. J. Brill, 1997.

BECKER, J., *Messianic Expectation in the Old Testament,* trad. D. E. Green, Edinburgh, T&T Clark, 1980.

BEINERT, W. & FIORENZA, F. S. (ed.), *Handbook of Catholic Theology,* New York, Herder & Herder, 1995.

BEIRNE, M., *Women and Men in the Fourth Gospel: A Discipleship of Equals, JSNT* Supp. 242, Sheffield, Sheffield Academic Press, 2003.

BELLEVILLE, L. L., "Born of Water and Spirit: John 3:5," *Trinity Journal* (1981) 125-141.

BELLINGER, W. H. & FARMER, W. R. (ed.), *Jesus and the Suffering Servant: Isaiah 53 and Christian Origins*, Philadelphia, Trinity Press International, 1998.

BEN-CHORIN, S., *Brother Jesus; The Nazarene through Jewish Eyes,* (trans.), KLEIN, J. S. & REINHART, M., Athens and London, University of Georgia Press, 2001.

BERTELS, T. M., *"His Witness is True": John and His Interpreters,* New York, P. Lang, 1989.

BETZ, H. C., *The Sermon on the Mount: A Commentary*, Hermeneia Series, Minneapolis, Fortress Press, 1995.

BETZ, O., The Kerygma of Jesus, *Interp* 2 (1968) 131-146. BIERINGER, R., *Leadership in the New Testament*, Unpublished Course material for the summer course in the Faculty of Theology, KU Leuven, Leuven, 2002.

BIERINGER, R., POLLEFEYT, D. & VANDECASTEELE- VANNEUVILLE, F. (eds.), *Anti-Judaism and the Fourth Gospel: Papers from the Leuven Colloquium, January 2000,* JCH, 1, Assen, Van Gorcum, 2001.

BITTLESTON, K., *The Gospel of John,* Hudson, Anthroposophic Press, 1990.

BIVIN, D. & BLIZZARD, R. B., *Understanding the Difficult Words of Jesus*, 2nd rev. ed., Shippensburg, PA, Destiny Image Publishers, 1994.

BIVIN, D. (ed.), "Jerusalem Synoptic Commentary Preview: The Rich Young Ruler Story", *Jerusalem Perspective* 38 & 39 (1993) 3-28, 30-31.

BIVIN, D., "A New Solution to the Synoptic Problem", *Jerusalem Perspective* 32 (1991) 3-5.

BIVIN, D., "Counting the Cost of Discipleship: Lindsey's Reconstruction of the Rich Young Ruler Complex", *Jerusalem Perspective* 42, 43 & 44 (1994) 23-35.

BIVIN, D., "Matthew 16:18: The Petros-petra Wordplay - Greek, Aramaic, or Hebrew?", *Jerusalem Perspective* 46 & 47 (1994) 32-38.

BLACK, M., *An Aramaic Approach to the Gospels and Acts*, 3rd ed., Peabody, Massachusetts, Hendrickson Publishers Inc, 1967.

BLOMBERG, C. L., *The Historical Reliability of John's Gospel: Issues and Commentary*, Downers Grove, IL, InterVarsity Press, 2001.

BOCCACCINI, G., "Multiple Judaisms: A New Understanding of the Context of Earliest Christianity" *Bible Review* 11:1 (1995) 38-46.

BOCHLER, A., The Reading of the Law and the Prophets in A Trennial Cycle, *JQR 6* (1893-1894) 11-13.

BOCK, D. L., *Luke*, Baker Exegetical Commentary on the New Testament 3, 2 vol., Baker Book House, 1994 & 1996.

BOERS, H., *What is New Testament Theology, The Rise of Criticism and the Problem of a Theology of the New Testament,* Philadelphia, Fortress Press, 1979.

BOISMARD, M-E., *Comment Luc a remanié l'évangile de Jean, Cahiers de la Revue biblique* 51, Paris, J. Gabalda, 2001.

BOISMARD, M-E., *Moses or Jesus: An Essay in Johannine Christology,* Minneapolis, Fortress, Leuven, Peeters, 1993.

BORG, M. J. & WRIGHT, N. T., *The Meaning of Jesus: Two Visions*, Harper SanFrancisco, 1999.

BORG, M. J., *Jesus: a New Vision: Spirit, Culture, and the Life of Discipleship*, San Francisco, HarperSan Francisco, 1991.

BORG, M. J., *Meeting Jesus Again for the First Time: the Historical Jesus and the Heart of Contemporary Faith*, San Francisco, HarperCollins, 1994.

BORG, M. J., *The Lost Gospel Q: Original Sayings of Jesus*, Berkely, CA, Ulysses Press, 1999.

BORGEN, P., "Some Jewish Exegetical Traditions as Background for Son of Man Sayings in John's Gospel (Jn 3,13-14 and context)," in *L'Evangile de Jean: Sources, rdaction, thologie*, DE JONGE, M. (ed.), Louvain, University Press, 1977, pp. 243-258.

BORGEN, P., *Philo, John, and Paul: New Perspectives on Judaism and Early Christianity,* Atlanta, Scholars Press, 1987.

BORING, M. E., *The Continuing Voice of Jesus: Christian Prophecy and the Gospel Tradition*, Louisville, Westminster/John Knox, 1991.

BORNKAMM, G., *Jesus of Nazareth,* (reprint of 1960 edition), Minneapolis, Fortress Press, 1994.

BOUSSET, W., *Kyrios Christos: A History of the Belief in Christ from the Beginning of Christianity to Irenaeus,* ET, German Original 1913, 1921, Nashville, Abington, 1970.

BOWKER, J., *Jesus and the Pharisees*, Cambridge, Cambridge University Press, 1973.

BOWMAN, J., *The Fourth Gospel and the Jews: A Study in R. Akiba, Esther, and the Gospel of John,* Pittsburgh, Pickwick, 1975.

BOYARIN, D., *Intertextuality and Reading of Midrash*, ISBL, Bloomington, Indiana University Press, 1990.

BRADBY, E. L., In Defence of Q, *ExpT* 68 (1956-1957) 315-318.

BRENNER, A., FONTAINE C., *A Feminist Companion to Reading the Bible Approaches, Methods and Strategies* (A Feminist Companion to the Bible 10), Sheffield, Sheffield Academic Press, 1997.

BRES, J., *La narrativité* (Champs linguistiques), Louvain-la- Neuve, Duculot, 1994.

BREWER, D. I., *Techniques and Assumptions in Jewish Exegesis Before 70 CE* (TSAJ 30), Tübingen, J. C. B. Mohr Siebeck, 1992.

BRIDGES, J. J., *Structure and History in John 11: A Methodological Study Comparing Structuralist and Historical Critical Approaches*, San Francisco, Mellen, 1991.

BROCK, C., *John, Behold the Lamb: A Bible Study Guide,* Neosho, Church Growth International, 1994.

BRODIE, T. L., *The Gospel According to John: A Literary and Theological Commentary*, New York, Oxford University Press, 1997.

BRODIE, T. O. P., *The Quest for the Origin of John's Gospel: A Source-Oriented Approach,* New York, Oxford University Press, 1993.

BROOKE, G. J., KAESTLI, J. D. (ed.), *Narrativity in the Bible and Related Texts,* (BETL 149), Leuven, Leuven University Press, 2000.

BROWN, R. E. &, CHARLESWORTH, J. H. et al., *John and Qumran,* London, Geoffrey Chapman, 1972.

BROWN, R. E., *A Once-and-Coming Spirit at Pentecost: Essays on the Liturgical Readings between Easter and Pentecost, Taken from the Acts of the Apostles and from the Gospel according to John,* Collegeville, MN, Liturgical Press, 1994.

BROWN, R. E., *A Retreat with John the Evangelist: That You May Have Life,* Cincinnati, St. Anthony Messenger Press, 1998.

BROWN, R. E., *An Introduction to New Testament Christology*, New York, Paulist Press, 1994.

BROWN, R. E., *An Introduction to the Gospel of John*, New York, NY, Doubleday, 2003.

BROWN, R. E., *Roles of Women in the Fourth Gospel*, in *TS* 36 (1975) 688-699.

BROWN, R. E., *The Community of the Beloved Disciple*, New York, Paulist Press, 1979.

BROWN, R. E., *The Gospel of John*, Anchor Bible 29-29A, 2 vol., New York, Doubleday, 1966.

BRUMBERG-KRAUS, J. D., 'A Jewish Ideological Perspective on the Study of Christian Scripture' in *Jewish Social Studies*, vol. 4, no.1, 1997.

BRUTEAU, Beatrice, *Jesus Through Jewish Eyes: Rabbis and Scholars Engage an Ancient Brother in a New Conversation*, Maryknoll, Orbis, 2001.

BUCHANAN, G., *Introduction to Intertextuality*, Lewiston, New York, Edwin Mellen Press, 1994.

BUCKWALTER, H. D., *The Character and Purpose of Luke's Christology,* Cambridge, CambridgeUniversity Press, 1996.

BULTMANN, R., *Jesus and the Word*, London & Glasgow, Fontana Books, 1958.

BULTMANN, R., *The Gospel of John: A Commentary*, Philadelphia, PA, Westminster Press, 1998.

BULTMANN, R., *Theology of the New Testament, ET* 2 vols., New York, Scribner, 1951-1955.

BURGE, G. M., *Interpreting the Fourth Gospel*, Grand Rapids, Baker, 1992, Repr., *Interpreting the Gospel of John,* Guides to NT Exegesis, Grand Rapids, Baker, 1998.

BURKETT, D. R., *The Son of Man in the Gospel of John, JSNTSup* 56, Ithaca, CUP Services, Sheffield, Sheffield Academic Press, 1991.

BURNEN, F. W., "Characterization and Reader Construction of Characters in the Gospels", *Serneia*, 63 (1993) 1-28.

BURNEY, C. F., *The Aramaic Origin of the Fourth Gospel*, Oxford, England, Clarendon Press, 1922.

BURRIDGE, R. A., *What Are the Gospels?* Cambridge, Cambridge University Press, 1992.

BUSSE, U., *Das Johannesevangelium: Bildlichkeit, Diskurs und Ritual, Bibl. Ephem. Theol. Lovan.* 162, Louvain, Peeters, 2002.

BUTLER, T. C., Narrative Form Criticism: Dead or Alive? in E. CARPENTER (ed.), *A Biblical Itinerary In Search of Method, Form and Content, Essays in Honour of George W. Coats,* JSOTSup. 240, Sheffield, Sheffield Academic Press, 1997, pp.39-59.

BYRSKOG, S., *Jesus the Only Teacher, Didactic Authority and Transmission in Ancient Israel, Ancient Judaism and the Matthean Community*, CB, New Testament Series 24, Stockholm, Almqvist & Wiksell International, 1994.

CALOUD, J., "Le texte *à* lire" in L. PANIER (éd), *Le temps de la lecture. Exégèse biblique et sémiotique,* FS Jean Delorme (LD 155), Paris, Cerf, 1993, pp. 31-63.

CARMICHAEL, C. M., *The Story of Creation: Its Origin and its Interpretation in Philo and the Fourth Gospel,* Ithaca, Cornell University Press, 1996.

CARMIGNAC, J., *La naissance des Evangiles Synoptiques,* Paris, O.E.I.L., 1984.

CARROLL, R. P., *The Elijah-Elisha Sagas: Some remarks on Prophetic Succession in Ancient Israel, VT* 19 (1969) 400-415.

CARSON, D. A., *The Gospel According to John*, Grand Rapids, MI, Leicester, Inter-Varsity Press, 1991.

CARTER, W., *What Are They Saying About Matthew's Sermon on the Mount?*, New York, Paulist Press, 1994.

CASEY, M., *An Aramaic Approach to Q*, Cambridge, United Kingdom, Cambridge University Press, 2002.

CASSIDY, R. J., *John's Gospel in New Perspective, Christology and the Realities of Roman Power*, Maryknoll, NY, Orbis, 1992.

CAVADINI, J. C. (ed.), *Miracles in Jewish and Christian Antiquity: Imaging Truth*, Notre Dame, 1999.

CHANCE, B. J. & HORNE, M. P., *Rereading the Bible: An Introduction to the Biblical Story,* Upper Saddle River, Prentice Hall, 2000.

CHARLES, C. H. *Apocrypha*, Oxford University Press, Oxford, 1913.

CHARLESWORTH, J. H. & BROWN, R., *John and Qumran*, Chapman, London, 1972.

CHARLESWORTH, J. H. & JOHN, L. L. (ed.), *Hillel and Jesus*, Fortress Press, Minneapolis, 1977.

CHARLESWORTH, J. H. & Walter P. W. (eds.), *Jesus Two Thousand Years Later*, Harrisburg, Trinity Press International, 2000 .

CHARLESWORTH, J. H. (ed.), *Jesus' Jewishness: Exploring the Place of Jesus within Early Judaism*, New York, Crossroad, 1991.

CHARLESWORTH, J. H. (ed.), *Jews and Christians*, Crossroads, NY, 1994.

CHARLESWORTH, J. H. (ed.), *The Messiah, Developments in Earliest Judaism and Christianity: The First Princeton Symposium on Judaism and Christian Origins,* Minneapolis, Fortress, 1992.

CHARLESWORTH, J. H. (ed.), *The Messiah*, Fortress Press, Minneapolis, 1992.

CHARLESWORTH, J. H., (ed.), *Jesus and the Dead Sea Scrolls*, Doubleday, NY, 1992.

CHARLESWORTH, J. H., "*From Barren Mazes to Gentle Rappings: The Emergence of' Jesus Research*," Princeton Seminary Bulletin 7 (1986).

CHARLESWORTH, J. H., *Critical Reflections on the Odes of Solomon: Literary Setting, Textual Studies, Gnosticism, The Dead Sea Scrolls & the Gospel of John, JSPS* 22, Ithaca, CUP Services, 1998.

CHARLESWORTH, J. H., *Jesus Within Judaism: New Light from Exciting Archeological Discoveries*, Anchor Bible Reference, New York, Doubleday, 1988.

CHARLESWORTH, J. H., *The Beloved Disciple: Whose Witness Validates the Gospel of John,* Valley Forge, PA, Trinity Press International, 1995.

CHILDS, B. S., *Introduction to the Old Testament as Scripture,* Philadelphia, Fortress Press, 1979.

CHILTON, B. & CRAIG, A. E., *Studying the Historical Jesus*: *Evaluations of the Current State of Research*, Leiden, Brill, 1994.

CHILTON, B. D. & EVANS C. A., *Jesus in Context: Temple, Purity, and Restoration,* AGJU 39, Leiden & New York & Cologne, Brill, 1997.

CHILTON, B. D. & EVANS, C. A., *Studying the Historical Jesus, Evaluations of the State of Current Research, NNTS* 19, Leiden, Brill, 1994.

CHILTON, B. D., *A Galilean Rabbi and his Bible: Jesus' own Interpretation of Isaiah,* London, SPCK, 1984.

CHILTON, B., "The Son of Man - Who Was He?" *Bible Review* 12:4 (1996) 34-39, 45-47.

CHILTON, B., *A Feast of Meanings: Eucharistic Theologies from Jesus through Johannine Circles, NovTest Supp* 72. Leiden, New York, E. J. Brill, 1994.

CHILTON, B., *A Galilean Rabbi, Jesus and His Bible*, SPCK, London, 1984.

CHILTON, B., *Profiles of a Rabbi*, Scholars Press, Atlanta, GA, 1989.

CHILTON, B., *Rabbi Jesus: An Intimate Biography*, New York, New York, Image Books, 2000.

CHILTON, B., *Rabbi Paul: An Intellectual Biography*, New York, New York, Doubleday, 2004.CHOPP, R. S., *The Power to Speak: Feminism, Language, God,* New York, Crossroad, 1989.

CLARK, E. A., 'Ideology, History, and the Construction of "Women" in Late Ancient Christianity', *Journal of Early Christian Studies* 2 (1994) 155-84.

COHEN, S. J. D., *Epigraphical Rabbis*, in *JQR* 72 (1981) 1-17. COHN-SHERBOK, D., *The Jewish Messaiah*, Edinburgh, T & T Clark, 1997.

COLLINS, J. J., *Between Athens and Jerusalem: Jewish Identity in the Hellenistic Diaspora*, 2nd ed., Grand Rapids, MI, Wm. B. Eerdmans, 1999.

COLLINS, R. F., *John and His Witness*, Zacchaeus Studies: NT, Collegeville, MN, Liturgical Press, 1991.

COLLINS, R. F., *These Things Have Been Written: Studies on the Fourth Gospel*, Louvain, Peeters, Grand Rapids, Eerdmans, 1990.

COLSON, F. H. & WHITAKER, G. H., *Philo,* ten volumes, Loeb edition, Cambridge, MA, Harvard University Press, 1958.

COLWELL, E. C., *The Greek of the Fourth Gospel: A Study of its Armaisms in the Light of Hellenistic Greek,* Chicago, University of Chicago Press, 1931.

COMBET-GALLAND, C., HOUZIAUX, A., MORDILLAT, G. & QUESNEL, M., *Jésus-Christ, de quoi est-on sûr ?*, Broché, Editions de l'Atelier, 2006.

COMBET-GALLAND, C., « L'évangile selon Marc », in MARGUERAT, D. éd., *Introduction au Nouveau Testament, Son histoire, son écriture, sa théologie*, Genève, Labor et Fides, 2000, pp. 35-61.

CONWAY, C. M., *Men and Women in the Fourth Gospel: Gender and Johannine Characterization, SBLDS* 167, Atlanta, Society of Biblical Literature, 1999.

CONZELMANN, H., *The Theology of St. Luke*, Philadelphia, Fortress Press, 1981.

COOKE, G., *Who Wrote the Fourth Gospel?: A Short Summary of the Evidence,* Bognor Regis, Sussex, New Horizon, 1981.

COTTER, W. (ed.), *Miracles in Graeco-Roman Antiquity: A Sourcebook*, Context of Early Christianity, New York, Routledge, 1999.

COTTERELL, P., TYRNER, M., *Linguistics & Biblical Interpretation*, London, SPCK, 1989.

COULOT, C., *Jésus et le Disciple. Etude sur L'autorité messianique de Jésus*, (*Etudes Biblique*. 8), Paris, Libraire Lecoffre, 1987.

COUNET, P. C., *John, a Postmodern Gospel: Introduction to Deconstructive Exegesis Applied to the Fourth Gospel, Biblical Interpretation* 44, Leiden, Boston, MA, Brill, 2000.

CRANE, A. M., *Knowing the Master through John: An Interpretation in the Light of Modern Thought and Understanding,* Boston, Lothrop, Lee & Shepard, 1926.

CROSSAN, J. D., "Why Christians Must Search for the Historical Jesus", *Bible Review* 12:2 (1996) 35-38, 42-45.

CROSSAN, J. D., *Excavating Jesus: Beneath the Stones, Behind the Texts,* San Francisco, Harper San Francisco, 2001.

CROSSAN, J. D., *In Parables: The Challenge of the Historical Jesus,* New York, Harper & Row, 1973.

CROSSAN, J. D., *Jesus: A Radical Biography,* San Francisco, HarperCollins, 1994.

CROSSAN, J. D., *The Essential Jesus- Original Sayings and Earliest Images,* New York, NY, HarperCollins Publishers, 1998.

CROSSAN, J. D., *The Gospel of Eternal Life: Reflections on the Theology of St. John,* Milwaukee, Bruce, 1967.

CROSSAN, J. D., *The Historical Jesus,* New York, NY, HarperCollins Publishers, 1992.

CROSSAN, J. D., *The Historical Jesus: The Life of a Mediteranean Jewish Peasant,* Edinburgh, T&T Clark, 1991.

CROSSAN, J. D., *Who Killed Jesus? Exposing the Roots of Anti-Semitism in the Gospel Story of the Death of Jesus,* San Francisco, Harper Collins, 1996.

CULLMAN, O., *The Christology of the New Testament,* rev. ed., Philadelphia, Westminster John Knox, 1963.

CULLMANN, O., *Early Christian Worship,* Philadelphia, Westminster, 1978.

CULLMANN, O., *The Johannine Circle: Its Place in Judaism, Among the Disciples of Jesus and in Early Christianity: A Study in the Origin of the Gospel of John,* London, S.C.M. Press, Philadephia, Westminster, 1976.

CULPEPPER, P. A. & SEGOVIA, F. F. (ed.), *The Fourth Gospel from a Literary Perspective,* Atlanta, Scholar's Press, 1991.

CULPEPPER, R. A. & BLACK, C. C. (eds.), *Exploring the Gospel of John: In Honor of D. Moody Smith,* Louisville, KY, Westminster/John Knox, 1996.

CULPEPPER, R. A. (ed.), *Critical Readings of John 6,* Leiden; New York, E. J. Brill, 1997.

CULPEPPER, R. A. (ed.), *The Johannine Literature: With an Introduction by R. A. Culpepper,* Sheffield New Testament Guides, Sheffield, Sheffield Academic Press, 2000.

CULPEPPER, R. A., *Anatomy of the Fourth Gospel: A Study in Literary Design,* Foundation and Facets, Philadelphia, Fortress, 1983, repr. 1987.

CULPEPPER, R. A., *John, the Son of Zebedee: The Life of a Legend,* Columbia, University of South Carolina Press, 1993, Minneapolis, Augsburg Fortress, 2000.

CULPEPPER, R. A., *The Johannine School: An Evaluation of the Johannine-School Hypothesis Based on an Investigation of the Nature of Ancient Schools,* Missoula, MT, Scholars Press, 1975.

D'SOUZA, J., *The Lamb of God in the Johannine Writings*, Allahabad, St. Paul Publ., 1968.

DAHL, N. A., *Jesus the Christ: The Historical Origins of Christological Doctrine*, ed. Donald H. JUEL, Minneapolis, Fortress, 1991.

DALMAN, G. H., *The Words of Jesus: Considered in the Light of Post-Biblical Jewish Writings and Aramaic Language*, Edinburgh, Clark, 1902.

DAUBE, D., *The New Testament and Rabbinic Judaism,* University of London, Athlone Press, 1956.

DAVEY, J. E., *The Jesus of St. John: Historical and Christological Studies in the Fourth Gospel,* London, Lutterworth, 1956.

DAVIES, M., *Rhetoric and Reference in the Fourth Gospel*, JSNTSup 69, Sheffield, Sheffield Academic Press, 1992.

DAVIES, S., Women in the Third Gospel and the New Testament Apoocrypha, in A. J. LEVINE, in *'Women Like This' New Perspectives on Jewish Women in the Greco-Roman World,* SBLEJL 1, Atlanta, Scholars Press, 1991.

DAVIES, W. D., *The Setting of the Sermon on the Mount*, Cambridge, Cambridge University Press, 1964.

DAVIS, P. G., "*Divine Agents, Mediators, and New Testament Christology,*" *JThS* 45 (1994) 479-503.

DAWES, G. W. (ed.), *The Historical Jesus Quest: Landmarks in the Search for the Jesus of History*, Louisville, Kentucky, Westminster John Knox Press, 2000.

DAWES, G. W. (ed.), *The Historical Jesus Question: The Challenge of History to Religious Authority*, Nashville, Westminister John Knox, 2001.

DE BOER, M. C. (ed.), *From Jesus to John: Essays on Jesus & the New Testament Christology in Honour of Marinus de Jonge*, JSNTSup 84, Sheffield, JSOT Press, Ithaca, CUP Services, 1993.

DE JONGE, M. "Nicodemus and Jesus: Some Observations on Misunderstanding and Understanding in the Fourth Gospel", *Bulletin of the John Rylands Library* 53 (1971) 337-359.

DE JONGE, M., *Christology in Context: The Earliest Christian Response to Jesus*, Philadelphia, Westminster, 1988.

DE JONGE, M., *Jesus, Stranger from Heaven and Son of God: Jesus Christ and the Christians in Johannine Perspective*, Missoula, MT, Scholars Press, 1977.

DE JONGE, M., *Jesus, the Servant Messiah*, New Haven- London, Yale University Press, 1991.

DEAN-OTTING, M. & ROBBINS, V. K., "Biblical Sources for Pronouncement Stories in the Gospels", *Semeia* 63 (1993) 93-113.

DECONICK, A. D., *Voices of the Mystics: Early Christian Discourse in the Gospels of John and Thomas and Other Ancient Christians Literature, JSNTSup* 157, Sheffield, Sheffield Academic Press, 2001.

DENAUX, A., *John and the Synoptics*, Leuven, Leuven, Uitgeverij Peeters, 1992.

Dictionary of Judaism in the Biblical period, Vol. 2., NY, Simon & Schuster Macmillian, 1996 (516-18).

DIEL, P. & SOLOTAREFF, J., *Symbolism in the Gospel of John*, San Francisco, Harper & Row, 1988.

DODD, C. H., *"Iesous ho didaskalos kai prophetes," Theology,* 17 (1928) 205-208; "Jesus as Teacher and Prophet," in *Mysterium Christi,* (ed.), BELL, G. K. A. & DEISSMANN, D. A., London, Longmans, Green and Company, 1931, pp. 53-66.

DODD, C. H., *Historical Tradition in the Fourth Gospel*, Cambridge, England, University Press, 1963.

DODD, C. H., *The Founder of Christianity*, London, Collins, 1971.

DODD, C. H., *The Interpretation of the Fourth Gospel*, Cambridge, England, University Press, 1953, repr. 1968.

DONAHUE, J. R., *The Gospel in Parable: Metaphor, Narrative, and Theology in the Synoptic Gospels*, Philadelphia, Fortress Press, 1990.

DONALDSON, J., *The Title Rabbi in the Gospels- Some Reflections on the Evidence of the Synoptics*, in *JQR* 63 (1972/73) 287- 291.

DRAISMA, S. (ed.), *Intertextuality in Biblical Writings. Essays in Honour of Bas van Iersel,* Kampen, Kok Press, 1989.

DRUMMOND, J., *An Inquiry into the Character and Authorship of the Fourth Gospel*, London, Williams & Norgate, 1903, New York, Charles Scribner, 1986.

DU PLESSIS, P. J., *The Lamb of God in the Fourth Gospel*, in J. H. PETZER & P. J. HARTIN (eds.), *A South African Perspective on the New Testament*: Essays by South African New Testament Scholars presented to B.M. Metzger during his Visit to South Africa in 1985, Leiden, Brill, 1986, pp. 136-148.

DUBE, M. W. & STALEY, J. L. (eds.), *John and Postcolonialism: Travel, Space and Power*. Bible and Postcolonialism 7, London, Continuum, 2002.

DULING, D. C., 'Insights from Sociology for New Testament Christology:A Test Case', *SBLSP (1985)* 351-368.

DUMAIS, M., "Sens de l'Ecriture. Réexamen a La lumière de l'herméneutiques philosophique et des approches littéraires récentes", *NTZ*45(1999)310-331.

DUMM, D., *A Mystical Portrait of Jesus: New Perspectives on John's Gospel*, Collegeville, MN, The Liturgical Press, 2001.

DUNN, J. D. G., *Christology in the Making: A New Testament Inquiry into the Origins of the Doctrine of the Incarnation*, 2nd ed., Grand Rapids, Wm. B. Eerdmans, 1996.

DUNN, J. D. G., *Jesus and the Spirit: A Study of the Religious and Charismatic Experience of Jesus and the First Christians as Reflected in the New Testament*, Grand Rapids, Wm. B. Eerdmans, 1997.

DURAISINGH, C. & HARGREAVES, C., *India's Search for Reality and the Relevance of the Gospel of John Papers from a Conference Held in Pune in February 1974*, Delhi, I.S.P.C.K., 1975.

EATON, J., *The Origin of the Book of Isaiah, VT* 9 (1959) 138-157.

EDWARDS, D. L., *The Real Jesus*, San Francisco, Harper Collins, 1992.

EDWARDS, H. E., *The Disciple Who Wrote These Things: A New Inquiry into the Origins and Historical Value of the Gospel according to St. John*, London, J. Clarke, 1953.

EDWARDS, R. A., *The Gospel according to St. John: Its Criticism and Interpretation*, London, Eyre & Spottiswoode, 1954.

EHRMAN, B. D., FEE, G. D. & HOLMES, M. W., *The Text of the Fourth Gospel in the Writings of Origin*, Atlanta, Scholars Press, 1992.

EHRMAN, B. D., *Jesus: Apocalyptic Prophet of the New Millenium*, New York, NY, Oxford University Press, 2000.

EHRMAN, B. D., *The New Testament: A Historical Introduction to the Early Christian Writings*, New York, NY, Oxford University Press, 2000.

EHRMAN, B., *The Orthodox Corruption of Scripture: The* Effect of Early Christological Controversies on the Texts of *the New Testament*, Oxford and New York, Oxford University Press, 1993.

EISEN, U. E., *Women officeholders in Early Christianity: Epigraphical and Literary Studies*, (trans.), L. M. MALONEY, Collegeville MN, Liturgical Press, 2000.

ELLER, V., *The Beloved Disciple. His Name His Story His Thought*, Grand Rapids, MI, Eerdmans, 1987.

ELLIGER, K., *Der Prophet Tritojesaja, ZAW* 49 (1931) 112-141.

ELLIS, P. F., *The Genius of John: a Composition-Critical Commentary on the Fourth Gospel*, Collegeville, MN, Liturgical Press, 1984.

ENSOR, P. W., *Jesus and His Works: The Johannine Sayings in Historical Perspective*, Tübingen, J. C. B. Mohr, Paul Siebeck, 1996.

EVANS, C. A., *Jesus and His Contemporaries: Comparative Studies*, Leiden, Brill Academic, 2001.

EVANS, C. A., *Life of Jesus Research: An Annotated Bibliography*, rev. ed., New Testament Tools and Studies 24, Leiden, E. J. Brill, 1996.

EVANS, C. A., *Word and Glory: On the Exegetical and Theological Background of John's Prologue, JSNTSup* 89, Sheffield, Sheffield Academic Press, 1993.

EVANS, C. S., *The Historical Christ and the Jesus of Faith: the Incarnational Narrative as History*, New York, Oxford University Press, 1996.

FALK, R. H., *Jesus the Pharisee: A New look at the Jewishness of Jesus*, NY, Paulist Press, 1985.

FEDDMAN, A. J., *The Rabbi and His Early Ministry*, New York, 1941.

FERREIRA, J., *Johannine Ecclesiology, JSNTSup* 160, Sheffield, Sheffield Academic Press, 1998.

FEUILLET, A., *Johannine Studies*, Staten Island, NY, Alba House, 1965.

FINKEL, A., *The Pharisees and the Teacher of Nazareth, A Study of Their Background, Their Halachic and Midrashic Teachings, The Similarities and Differences*, Leiden, Köln, E. J. Brill, 1964.

FIORENZA, E. S. (ed.), *Aspects of Religious Propaganda in Judaism and Early Christianity*, Notre Dame – London, University of Notre Dame Press, 1976.

FIORENZA, E. S., *In Memory of Her, A Feminist Theological Reconstruction of Christian Origins*, New York, 1983.

FISHBANE, M., *Biblical Interpretation in Ancient Israel,* Oxford, Clarendon Press, 1985.

FISHBANE, M., *'Inner Biblical Exegesis: Types and Strategies of Interpretation in Ancient Israel'*, in HARTMAN, G. H. & SANFORD, B. (eds.), *Midrash and Literature,* New Haven, Yale University Press, 1986, pp. 19-37.

FITZMYER, J. A., *A Wandering Aramean, Collected Aramaic Essays*, MI, USA, Scholars Press, 1979.

FITZMYER, J. A., *Luke the Theologian: Aspects of His Theology*, New York, Paulist Press, 1989.

FITZMYER, J. A., *Whose Name is This*, in *America* 187 (2002) 9-13.

Fitzmyer, Joseph A., *A Christological Catechism: New Testament Answers*, Mahwah, NJ, Paulist, 1992.

FLUSSER, D., "Jesus", In *Encyclopaedia Judaica*, 10: 0-14, Jerusalem, Keter Publishing House, 1972.

FLUSSER, D., "Jesus, His Ancestry, and the Commandment of Love", In *Jesus' Jewishness: Exploring the Place of Jesus in Early Judaism*, James H. Charlesworth, ed., 153-174, New York, Crossroad Publishing Co., 1991.

FLUSSER, D., 'Jesus, his Ancestry and the Commandments of Love' in CHARLESWORTH, J. H. (ed.), *Jesus' Jewishness; Exploring the Place of Jesus in Early Judaism*, New York: Crossroad Publishing, 1991.

FLUSSER, D., *Jesus*, Jerusalem, Magnes Press, 1997. FLUSSER, D., *Judaism and the Origins of Christianity*, Jerusalem, Magnes Press, 1988.

FORD, R. Q., *The Parables of Jesus*, Minneapolis, Fortress Press, 1997.

FORTNA, R. T., and THATCHER, T. (eds.), *Jesus in Johannine Tradition,* Louisville, Westminster, John Knox, 2001.

FORTNA, R. T., *The Fourth Gospel and Its Predecessor: From Narrative Source to Present Gospel*, Philadelphia, Fortress, 1988.

FORTNA, R. T., *The Gospel of Signs: A Reconstruction of the Narrative Source Underlying the Fourth Gospel*, London, Cambridge University Press, 1970.

FOSDICK, H. E., *The Man from Nazareth: As His Contemporaries Saw Him*, London, SCM Press Ltd., 1950.

FOSSUM, J., "Understanding Jesus' Miracles", *Bible Review* 10:2(1994)16-23,50.

FOWLER, R.W., "Characterizing Character in Biblical Narrative", *Semeia* 63 (1993) 97-104.

FRANCE, R. T., *The Evidence for Jesus*, London, Hodder & Stoughton, 1986.

FREDRIKSEN, P., "Did Jesus Oppose the Purity Laws?" *Bible Review* 11:3 (1995) 19-25, 42-45.

FREDRIKSEN, P., *From Jesus to Christ: The Origin of the New Testament Images of Jesus*, rev. ed., New Haven, Yale University Press, 2000, original edition, 1988.

FREDRIKSEN, P., *Jesus of Nazareth King of the Jews: A Jewish Life and the Emergence of Christianity*, New York, Knopf, 1999.

FREED, E. D., *Old Testament Quotations in the Gospel of John*, *NovTSupp* 11. Leiden, E. J. Brill, 1965.

FREY, J. & SCHNELLE, U. (eds.), *Kontexte des Johannesevangeliums: Das vierte Evangelium in religions- und traditionsgeschichtlicher Perspektive*, Tübingen: Mohr Siebeck, 2004.

FREYNE, S., *Jesus, A Jewish Galilean: A New Reading of the Jesus Story*, New York, T&T Clark, 2004.

FRIEDLANDER, G., *The Jewish Sources of the Sermon on the Mount*, London, Routledge, 1911.

FRY, H., *Christian-Jewish Dialogue; a Reader*, Exeter, University of Exeter, 1996.

FULLER, R., *The Foundations of New Testament Christology*, New York, Scribner, 1965.

FUNK, R. W. & HOOVER, R. W., *The Five Gospels: What Did Jesus Really Say?*, San Francisco, CA, Harper Collins, 1997.

FUNK, R. W. (ed.), *The Acts of Jesus: The Search for the Authentic Deeds of Jesus,* Polebridge Press, 1998.

GAEBELEIN, A. C., *The Gospel of John: A Complete Analytical Exposition of the Gospel of John*, New York, Our Hope, 1925.

GARDNER-SMITH, P., *Saint John and the Synoptic Gospels,* Cambridge, England, University Press, 1938.

GARLAND, D. E., *Reading Matthew: A Literary and Theological Commentary on the First Gospel*, Reading the New Testament Series, New York, Crossroad, 1999.

GEIGER, A., *Judaism and Its History*, vol. I., New York, Thalmessinger & Cahn, 1866.

GEORGE, L. D., *Reading the Tapestry: A Literary-Rhetorical Analysis of the Johannine Resurrection Narrative (John 20-21)*, Studies in Biblical Literature 14, New York, Peter Lang, 2000.

GETTY-SULLIVAN, M. A., *Women in the New Testament,* Collegeville, MN, Liturgical Press, 2001.

GEVARYAHU , H . M . I . , *Privathäuserals Versammlungsstätten von Meister und Jüngern, ASTI* 12 (1983) 5-12.

GEVARYAHU, H. M. I., *The School of Isaiah, Biography and Transmission in the Book of Isaiah, JBQ* 18 (1989-90) 62-68.

GLASSON, T. F., *Moses in the Fourth Gospel,* London, SCM Press, 1963.

GOERGEN, D., *The Mission and Ministry of* Jesus, Wilmington, Michael Glazier, 1986.

GOLDIN, J., *Studies in Midrash and Related Literature,* Philadelphia - New York - Jerusalem, The Jewish Publication Society, 1988.

GOLDIN, J., *The Magic of Magic and Superstition,* Elisabeth SCHUESSLER FIORENZA (ed.), *Aspects of Religious Propaganda in Judaism and Early Christianity,* London, University of Notre Dame Press, 1976.

GOLDSTEIN, M., *Jesus Within the Jewish Tradition,* New York, Macmillan, 1950.

GOLKA, F. W., *Die israelitische Weisheitsschule oder 'des Kaisers neue Kleider', VT* 33 (1983) 257-270.

GOWLER, D. B., 'Characterization in Luke: A Socio- Narratological Approach', *Biblical Theology Bulletin* 19 (1989) 54-62.

GOWLER, D. B., 'Hospitality and Characterization in Luke 11:37-54: A Socio-Narratological Approach', *Semeia* 64 (1993) 213-251.

GOWLER, D. B., *Host, Guest, Enemy, and Friend: Portraits of the Pharisees in Luke and Acts,* Emory Studies in Early Christianity 1, New York, Peter Lang Press, 1991.

GRAETZ, H., *History of the Jews; From the Earliest Times to the Present Day,* ed. by & trans. from German original of 1853-1870 by Bella Lowy, London, Jewish Chronicle, 1901.

GRAFFY, A., *Trustworthy and True: The Gospels beyond 2000,* Blackrock, Co. Dublin, Columba Press, 2001.

GREEN, J. B. & TURNER, M. (ed.), *Jesus of Nazareth: Lord and Christ: Essays on the Historical Jesus and New Testament Christology,* Grand Rapids, Eerdmans, 1994.

GREEN, J. B., "In Quest of the Historical: Jesus, the Gospels, and Historicisms Old and New," *New Scholar's Review* 28 (1999) 544-560.

GREEN, J. B., *The Theology of the Gospel of Luke,* Cambridge, Cambridge University Press, 1995.

GROLLENBERG, L., *Unexpected Messiah,* London, SCM, 1988.

GRÜNWALD, I., SHAKED, S. & STROUMSA, G. (ed.), *Messiah and Christos: Studies in the Jewish Origins of Christianity,* Festschrift David Flusser, Tübingen, Mohr, 1992.

GUILDING, A., *The Fourth Gospel and Jewish Worship: A Study of the Relation of St. John's Gospel to the Ancient Jewish Lectionary System*, Oxford, Clarendon, 1960. 552

GUNDRY, R. H., *Jesus the Word according to John the Sectarian : A Paleofund amentalist Manifesto for Contemporary Evangelicalism, Especially Its Elites, in North America*, Grand Rapids, Eerdmans, 2001.

GUTHRIE, D., "The Importance of Signs in the Fourth Gospel," *Vox evangelica* 5 (1967) 72-83.

HAENCHEN, E., *John*, Hermeneia, 2 vol., trans. Robert W. Funk, Philadelphia, Fortress Press, 1984.

HAGNER, D., *The Jewish Reclamation of Jesus; an Analysis and Critique of the Modern Jewish Study of Jesus*, Grand Rapids, Michigan, Zondervan, 1984.

HAHN, F., *The Titles of Jesus in Christology, Their History in Early Christianity*, London, Lutterworth, 1969.

HALDIMANN, K., *Rekonstruktion und Entfaltung: Exegetische Untersuchungen zu Joh 15 und 16,* Beihefte zur Zeitschrift für die Neutestamentliche Wissenschaft und die Kunde der Ältern Kirche, Berlin, Walter de Gruyter, 2000.

HAMID-KAHNI, S., *Revelation and Concealment of Christ: A Theological Enquiry into the Elusive Language of the Fourth Gospel*, WUNT 2.120., Tübingen, Mohr/ Siebeck, 2000.

HANSON, A. T., *The Prophetic Gospel: A Study of John and the Old Testament*, Edinburgh, T & T Clark, 1991.

HARNER, P. B., *Relation Analysis of the Fourth Gospel: A Study in Reader-Response Criticism*, Lewiston, NY, Edwin Mellen, 1993.

HARRINGTON, D. J., *Gospel of Matthew*, Sacra Pagina 1, Collegeville, MN, Liturgical Press, 1991.

HARRIS, ELIZABETH, *Prologue and Gospel: The Theology of the Fourth Evangelist*, JSNTSup 107, Sheffield, Sheffiled Academic Press, 1994.

HARRISON, E. F., "Historical Problems in the Fourth Gospel," *Bibliotheca Sacra* 116: 463 (1959) 205-211.

HARSTINE, S., *Moses as a Character in the Fourth Gospel: A Study of Ancient Reading Techniques, JSNTSS* 229, London, New York, Sheffield Academic Press, 2002.

HARTMAN, L. F., "Synoptic Question," *Encyclopedic Dictionary of the Bible,* 2nd rev. ed., New York, McGraw-Hill Book Company, Inc., 1963, col. 2376.

HARTMAN, L., & OLSSON, B. (ed.), *Aspects on the Johannine Literature* (Papers presented at a conference of Scandinavian New Testament Exegetes at Uppsala June 16-19,

1986, CB New Testament Series 18, Stolkhom, Almqvist and Wiksell International, 1987.

HARVEY, A. E., *Jesus and the Constraints of History*, Philadelphia, Westminster, 1982.

HASKINS, S., *Mary Magdalene: Myth and Metaphor*, NY, Harper Collins, 1993.

HAWKIN, D. J., *The Johannine World: Reflections on the Theology of the Fourth Gospel and Contemporary Society*, Albany, State University of New York Press, 1996.

HENGEL, M., *Between Jesus and Paul: Studies in the Earliest History of Christianity*, *ET*, Philadelphia, Fortress, 1983.

HENGEL, M., *Judaism and Hellenism*, 2 vol., Philadelphia, Fortress Press, 1974.

HENGEL, M., *The Charismatic Teacher and His Followers*, Edinburgh, UK, T & T Clark, 1981.

HENGEL, M., *The Four Gospels and the One Gospel of Jesus Christ: An Investigation of the Collection and Origin of the Canonical Gospels*, London, SCM Press, 2000.

HENGEL, M., *The Son of God: The Origin of Christology and the History of Jewish- Hellenistic Religion*, Philadelphia, Fortress, 1976.

HICK, J., *The Metaphor of God Incarnate*, London, SCM, 1993.

HIGGINS, A. J. B., *Jesus and the Son of Man*, London, Lutterworth, 1964.

HIGGINS, A. J. B., *The Historicity of the Fourth Gospel*, London, Lutterworth, 1960.

HIGGINS, A. J. B., *The Tradition about Jesus: Three Studies*, Edinburgh, Oliver & Boyd, 1969.

HILL, C. E., *The Johannine Corpus in the Early Church*, Oxford, Oxford University Press, 2004.

HILL, R. A., *An Examination and Critique of the Understanding of the Relationship between Apocalypticism and Gnosticism in Johannine Studies*, Lewiston, NY, Edwin Mellen, 1997.

HILLMER, M. R., *Gospel of John in the Second Century*, Th. D. Thesis, Harvard University Divinity School, 1966.

HILTON, M., *The Christian Effect on Jewish Life*, London, SCM Press, 1994.

HOARE, F. R., *The Original Order and Chapters of St. John's Gospel*, London, Burns, Oates & Washbourne, 1944.

HODGES, Z. C., "Problem Passages in the Gospel of John, Part 3: Water and Spirit—John 3:5" *Bibliotheca Sacra* 135 (1978) 206-220.

HOLLENBACH, P. W., 'Jesus, Demoniacs, and Public Authorities: A Socio-Historical Study', *JAAR* 49 (1981) 567-588.

HOLLENBACH, P. W., 'Recent Historical Jesus Studies and the Social Sciences', *SBLSP* (1983) 61-78.

HOLLENBACH, P. W., 'The Historical Jesus Question in North America Today', *BTB* 19 (1989) 11-22.

HOLTZMAN, H., *Die synoptischen Evangelien: Ihr Ursprung und geschichtlicher Charakter*, The Synoptic Gospels, Their origin and historical character, Leipzig, Engelmann, 1863.

HOOVER, R. W. (ed.), *Profiles of Jesus*, Santa Rosa, CA, Polebridge Press, 2002.

HORSELEY, R. A., *Galilee: History, Politics, People*, Valley Forge, PA, Trinity Press International, 1995.

HORSELEY, R. A., *Jesus and Empire: The Kingdom of God and the New World Disorder*, Minneapolis, Fortress Press, 2002.

HORSLEY, R. A. & HANSON, J., *Bandits, Prophets, and Messiahs: Popular Movements at the Time of Jesus*, San Francisco, Harper Collins, 1985.

HOWARD- BROOK, W., *Becoming Children of God: John's Gospel and Radical Discipleship*, Mary knoll, NY, Orbis, 1999.

HOWARD, W. F., *The Fourth Gospel in Recent Criticism and Interpretation*, London, Epworth, 1931, repr. 1935.

JACOBSON, A., *The First Gospel: An Introduction to Q*, Sonoma, CA, Polebridge Press, 1992.

JASPER, A., *The Shining Garment of the Text: Gendered Readings of John's Gospel, JSNTSup* 165, Sheffield, Sheffield Academic Press, 1998.

JAUBERT, A., *Approaches de l'Evangile de Jean, Parole de Dieu*, Paris, 1976.

JENKINS, P., *Hidden Gospels: How the Search for Jesus Lost Its Way*, New York, Oxford University Press, 2001.

JEREMIAS, J., *Jerusalem in the Time of Jesus*, Minneapolis, Fortress Press, 1975.

JEREMIAS, J., *Jesus and the Message of the New Testament*, Fortress Classics in Biblical Studies, (ed.), HANSON, K. C., Minneapolis, MN, Fortress Press, 2002.

JEREMIAS, J., *New Testament Theology I: The Proclamation of Jesus*, London, SCM Press, 1971.

JEREMIAS, J., *The Problem of the Historical Jesus*, Fortress Press, 1964.

JEWETT, R. (ed.), *Christology and Exegesis: New Approaches, Semeia* 30, Society of Biblical Literature, Decatur, GA, Scholars Press, 1985.

JOBLING, D. & PIPPIN, T. (eds.), *Ideological Criticism of Biblical Texts, Semeia* 59, Atlanta, Scholars Press, 1992.

JOHN, F., *The Vision of Discipleship According to John*, Rome, Pontifical University of Urbania, 1997.

JOHNSON, L. T., "The Search for (the Wrong) Jesus." *Bible Review* 11:6 (1995) 20-25, 44.

JOHNSON, L. T., *The Living Jesus: Learning the Heart of the Gospel*, San Francisco, Harper San Francisco, 2000.

JOHNSON, L. T., *The Real Jesus: the Misguided Quest for the Historical Jesus and the Truth of the Traditional Gospels*, San Francisco, HarperSanFrancisco, 1995.

JOHNSON, L. T., *The Real Jesus: The Misguided Quest for the Historical Jesus and the Truth of the Traditional Gospels*, San Francisco, HarperCollins, 1996.

JOHNSON, L. T., *The Writings of the New Testament: An Interpretation*, Philadelphia, Fortress Press, 1986.

JONES, D., *The Traditions of the Oracles of Isaiah of Jerusalem*, ZAW 67 (1955) 226-246.

JONKER, L. C., *Exclusivity and Variety: Perspectives on Multidimensional Exegesis*, CEBT 19, Kempen, Kok Pharos Publishing House, 1996.

JOSEPH, F., *Les antiquités juives*. Texte, traduction, et notes, Cerf, 1990. 1995. 2001.

JUEL, D., *Messianic Exegesis. Christological Interpretation of the Old Testament in the Early Christianity*, Philadelphia, Fortress, 1987.

KÄHLER, M., *The So-Called Historical Jesus and the Historic Biblical Christ*, (trans.), BRAATEN, C. E., Philadelphia, Fortress Press, 1964.

KANAGARAJ, J. J., *'Mysticism' in the Gospel of John: An Inquiry into its Background*, JSNTSup 158, Sheffield, Sheffield Academic Press, 1998.

KARRIS, R. J., *Jesus and the Marginalized in St. John's Gospel*, Collegeville, Liturgical Press, 1990.

KÄSEMANN, E., "The Problem of the Historical Jesus," in *Essays on New Testament Themes*, trans. MONTAGUE, W. J., *Studies in Biblical Theology* 41, London, SCM, 1964, pp. 15-47.

KECK, L. E., *Jesus in New Testament Christology* in *ABR* (1980) 1-21.

KECK, L., *Who Is Jesus? History in Perfect Tense*, Studies on Personalities of the New Testament, University of South Carolina Press, 2000.

KEE, H. C. *Miracle in the Early Christian World*, New Haven and London, Yale University Press, 1983.

KEE, H. C., *Jesus in History: an Approach to the Study of the Gospels*, rev. ed., Fort Worth: Harcourt Brace, 1996.

KEE, H. C., *What Can We Know About Jesus*, Understanding Jesus Today, Cambridge, Cambridge University Press, 1995.

KELBER. W. H., "Récit et Révélation: voiler, dévoiler et revoiler", *RHPR* 69 (1989) 389-410.

KENNEY, G. C., *Leadership in John: An Analysis of the Situation and Strategy of the Gospel and Epistles of John*, Lanham, MD, University Press of America, 2000.

KINGSBURY, J. D. & BAUER, D. R. (eds.), *Who Do You Say That I Am? Essays on Christology*, Westminister John Knox, 1999.

KINGSBURY, J. D., *Conflict in Luke: Jesus, Authorities, Disciples*, Minneapolis, Fortress Press, 1991.

KINGSBURY, J. D., *Conflict in Mark: Jesus, Authorities, Disciples*, Minneapolis, Fortress Press, 1989.

KINGSBURY, J. D., *Jesus Christ in Matthew, Mark, and Luke*, rev. ed., Minneapolis, Fortress Press, 2002.

KINGSBURY, J. D., *Matthew: Structure, Christology, Kingdom*, Minneapolis, Fortress Press, 1989.

KINGSBURY, J. D., *The Christology of Mark's Gospel*, Philadelphia, Fortress Press, 1989.

KLAUSNER, J., *Jesus of Nazareth; His Life, Times, and Teaching*, New York, Macmillan, 1929.

KLOPPENBORG, J. S., '"Easter Faith" and the Sayings Gospel Q', *Semeia* 49 (1990) 71-99.

KLOPPENBORG, J. S., 'Alms, Debt and Divorce: Jesus' Ethics in their Mediterranean Context', *Toronto Journal of Theology* 6 (1990) 182-200.

KLOPPENBORG, J. S., 'Blessing and Marginality: The 'Persecution Beatitude' in Q, Thomas & Early Christianity', *Forum* 2/3 (1986) 36-56.

KLOPPENBORG, J. S., 'Nomos and Ethos in Q', in GOEHRING, J. E., SANDERS, J. T. & HEDRICK, C. W., in collaboration with BETZ, H. D. (eds.), *Gospel Origins and Christian Beginnings: In Honor of James M. Robinson,* Sonoma, CA, Polebridge Press, 1990, PP. 35-48.

KLOPPENBORG, J. S., *Q Parallels: Synopsis, Critical Notes & Concordance,* Sonoma, CA, Polebridge Press, 1988.

KLOPPENBORG, J. S., 'Symbolic Eschatology and the Apocalypticism of Q', *HTR* 30 (1987) 287-306.

KLOPPENBORG, J. S., *The Formation of Q: Trajectories in Ancient Wisdom Collections. Studies in Antiquity and Christianity,* Philadelphia, Fortress Press, 1987.

KOESTER, C. R., *Symbolism in the Fourth Gospel: Meaning, Mystery, Community*, Minneapolis, Fortress, 1995, 2nd ed., 2003.

KOESTER, C. R., *Symbolism in the Fourth Gospel: Meaning, Mystery, Community*, Minneapolis, Fortress Press, 1995.

KOESTER, H., "One Jesus and Four Primitive Gospels: The Problem of the 'Historical Jesus' and the Question of Primitive Gospel Forms", in *Trajectories through Early Christianity*, ROBINSON, J. M. & KOESTER, H. (eds.), Philadelphia, Fortress, 1971.

KOESTER, H., "*The Historical Jesus and the Historical Situation of the Quest: An Epilogue*" in CHILTON, B. D. & EVANS, C. A. (eds.), *Studying the Historical Jesus*, pp. 533-545.

KOHLER, K., *Abba , Father. Title of Spiritual Leader and Saint, JQR* 13 (1901) 567-580.

KORT W. A., *Story, Text, and Scripture Literary Interests in Biblical Narrative,* University Park & London, The Pennsylavania State University Press, 1988.

KÖSTENBERGER, A. J., *Encountering John: The Gospel in Historical, Literary, and Theological Perspective*, Encountering Biblical Studies, Grand Rapids, Baker, 2000.

KÖSTENBERGER, A. J., *Studies on John and Gender: A Decade of Scholarship*, Studies in Biblical Literature, 38, New York, Peter Lang, 2001.

KÖSTENBERGER, A. J., *The Missions of Jesus and the Disciples according to the Fourth Gospel: With Implications for the Fourth Gospel's Purpose and the Mission of the Contemporary Church*, Grand Rapids/Cambridge, U.K., Eerdmans, 1998.

KYSAR, R., *The Fourth Evangelist and His Gospel: An Examination of Contemporary Scholarship*, Minneapolis, Augsburg, 1975.

LAPIDE, P., *Israelis, Jews and Jesus*, trans. by Peter Heinegg, New York, Doubleday, 1979.

LAPIDE, P., *The Resurrection of Jesus; a Jewish Perspective*, London, S.P.C.K., 1983.

LARRY W. H., *Lord Jesus Christ: Devotion to Jesus in Earliest Christianity*, Grand Rapids, MI, Eerdmans, 2003.

LATEGAN, B. C. & VORSTER, W. S., *Text and Reality: Aspects of Reference in Biblical Texts,* Philadelphia, Fortress Press and Atlanta, Scholars Press, 1985.

LEE, D. A, *The Symbolic Narratives of the Fourth Gospel: The Interplay of Form and Meaning*, JSNTSup 95, Sheffield, Sheffield Academic Press, 1994.

LEE, D., *Flesh and Glory: Symbolism, Gender and Theology in the Gospel of John*, New York, Crossroad, 2002.

LEMAIRE, A., *Earliest Archaeological Evidence of Jesus Found in Jerusalem*, *Biblical Archaeology* 28/6 (2002) 24-33, 70-71.

LEMAIRE, A., *Education (Israel)*, ABD 2 (1992) 305-312. LEMAIRE, A., *Sagesse et écoles*, VT 34 (1984) 270-281.

LEON-DUFOUR, X. (éd.), *Exégèse et herméneutique,* Paris, Seuil, 1972.

LÉON-DUFOUR, X., *The Gospels and the Jesus of History*, Collins, 1968.

LEWIS, F. G., *The Irenaeus Testimony to the Fourth Gospel: Its Extent, Meaning, and Value*. Chicago, University of Chicago Press, 1908.

LIGHTSTONE, J. N., *The Commerce of the Sacred*, Scholars Press, Chico, California 1984.

LINDARS, B., "Two Parables in John", *New Testament Studies* 16 (1969/70) 318-324.

LINDARS, B., *Jesus, Son of Man: A fresh examination of the Son of Man sayings in the Gospels in the light of recent research*, Grand Rapids, MI, Eerdmans, 1983.

LINDARS, B., *The Gospel of John*, New Century Commentaries, Grand Rapids, Eerdmans, 1982.

LINDSEY, R. L. (ed.), *A Comparative Greek Concordance of the Synoptic Gospels*, 3 vols., Jerusalem, Dugith Publishers, 1985-1989.

LINDSEY, R. L., "A Modified Two-Document Theory of the Synoptic Dependence and Interdependence", *Novum Testamentum* 6 (1963) 239-263.

LINDSEY, R. L., "Paraphrastic Gospels", *Jerusalem Perspective* 51 (1996) 10-15.

LINDSEY, R. L., "Unlocking the Synoptic Problem: Four Keys for Better Understanding Jesus", *Jerusalem Perspective* 49 (1995) 10-17, 38.

LINDSEY, R. L., (ed.), *A Comparative Greek Concordance of the Synoptic Gospels*, 3 vols. Jerusalem, Dugith Publishers, 1985-1989.

LINDSEY, R. L., *A Hebrew Translation of the Gospel of Mark*, 2nd ed. Jerusalem, Dugith Publishers, 1973.

LINDSEY, R. L., A Modified Two-Document Theory of the Synoptic Dependence and Interdependence, *Novum Testamentum* 6 (1963) 239-263.

LINDSEY, R. L., *Jesus Rabbi & Lord: The Hebrew Story of Jesus Behind Our Gospels*, Oak Creek, WI, Cornerstone Publishing, 1990.

LOADER, W. R. G., *Jesus and the Fundamentalism of His Day: The Gospels, the Bible and Jesus,* Grand Rapids, Eerdmans, 2001.

LOADER, W. R. G., *The Christology of the Fourth Gospel: Structure and Issues*, *Beiträge zur biblischen Exegese und Theologie* 23, Frankfurt am Main, New York, P. Lang, 1989.

LOHFINK, N., *Glauben lernen in Israel, KatBl* 108 (1983) 84-99.

LOHFINK, N., *Gottesvolk als Lerngemeinschaft. Zur Kirchenwirklichkeit im Buch Deuteronominum, BK* 39 (1984) 90-100.

LONGENECKER, R. N. (ed.), *Patterns of Discipleship in the New Testament*, Grand Rapids, MI, Cambridge, UK, Eerdmans, 1996.

LONGMAN, T., *Literary Approaches to Biblical Interpretation,* Grand Rapids, Zondervan, 1987.

LÜDEMANN, G., *Jesus after Two Thousand Years: What He Really Said and Did*, BOWDEN, J. (trans.), London, SCM Press, 2000.

LUNDBOM, J. R., *Baruch, Seraiah, and Expanded Colophons in the Book of Jeremiah, JSOT* 36 (1986) 89-114.

LUZ, U., *The Theology of the Gospel of Matthew*, New Testament Theology, Cambridge, Cambridge University Press, 1995.

MACCINI, R. G., *Her Testimony Is True: Women as Witnesses according to John*, *JSNTSup* 125, Sheffield, Sheffield Academic press, 1996.

MACCOBY, H., *Early Rabbinic Writings*, Cambridge, University Press, 1998.

MACCOBY, H., *Revolution in Judaea; Jesus and the Jewish Resistance,* London, Ocean Books, 1973.

MACGREGOR, G. H. C. & MORTON, A. Q., *The Structure of the Fourth Gospel*, Edinburgh, Oliver & Boyd, 1961.

MACK, B. H., *A Myth of Innocence: Mark and Christian Origins,* Fortress Press, 1988.

MACK, B. L., *Rhetoric and the New Testament,* Minneapolis, Fortress Press, 1990.

MACK, B. L., *The Lost Gospel: The Book of Q and Christian Origins*, Reprint Editioned., New York, N Y, HarperSanFrancisco, 1997.

MACK, B., *A Myth of Innocence: Mark and Christian Origins*, Philadelphia, Fortress, 1988.

MAIER, P. L., *Josephus: The Essential Writings*, Grand Rapids, MI, Kregel Publications, 1988.

MALBON, E. S. & BERLIN, A. (eds.), *Characterization in Biblical Literature*, Semeia 63, Atlanta, Scholars Press, 1993.

MALHERBE, A. J. & MEEKS, W. A. (ed.), *The Future of Christology: Essays in Honor of Leander E. Keck*, Minneapolis, Fortress, 1993.

MALINA, B. J. & Jerome H. N., *Calling Jesus Names: The Social Value of Labels in Matthew*, Sonoma, CA, Polebridge Press, 1988.

MALINA, B. J. & WAETJEN, H. C., *The Gospel of John in Sociolinguistic Perspective: Protocol of the Forty-eighth Colloquy, 11 March 1984*, Berkeley, CA, Center for Hermeneutical Studies in Hellenistic and Modern Culture, 1985.

MALINA, B. J., & ROHRBAUGH, R. L., *Social Science Commentary on the Gospel of John*, Minneapolis, Fortress, 1998.

MALINA, B. J., 'Dealing with Biblical (Mediterranean) Characters, A Guide for U.S. Consumers', *BTB* 19 (1989) 127-141.

MALINA, B. J., 'Jesus as Charismatic Leader?', *BTB* 14 (1984) 55-62.

MALINA, B. J., *The Gospel of John in Sociolinguistic Perspective*, Colloquy of the Center for Hermeneutical Studies in Hellenistic and Modern Culture. Protocol Series 48, Berkeley, CA, 1985.

MALINA, B. J., *The Social Gospel of Jesus: The Kingdom of God in Mediterranean Perspective*, Minneapolis, Fortress Press, 2000.

MALLAU, H. H., *Baruch/Baruchschriften*, *TRE* 5 (1980) 269-276.

MANNS, F., *L'evangile de Jean et la sagesse*, Studium Biblicum Franciscanum, Analecta, 62, Jerusalem, Franciscan Printing Press, 2003.

MANSON, T. W., *The Sayings of Jesus*, Grand Rapids: Eerdmans, 1957.

MARTIN, B. L., *Christ and the Law in Paul*, NTS 62, Leiden, Brill, 1989.

MARTYN, J. L., *History and Theology in the Fourth Gospel*, New York, Harper & Row, 1968, 2nd ed., Nashville, Abingdon, 1979, 3rd ed., Louisville, Westminster John Knox Press, 2003.

MARTYN, J. L., *History and Theology in the Fourth Gospel*, New York, Harper & Row, 1968.

MAYOTTE, R. A., *The Complete Jesus*, South Royalton, VT, Steerforth Press, 1997.

MCARTHUR, H. K., *In Search of the Historical Jesus*, SPCK, 1970.

MCCULLOCH, L. A., *The Teachings of the Bhagavad Gita and the Teachings of the Fourth Gospel Compared and Contrasted*, India, C. H. Loehlin, 1950.

MCGRATH, J. F., *John's Apologetic Christology: Legitimation and Development in Johannine Christology*, SNTSMS 111, Cambridge, Cambridge University Press, 2001.

MCKENZIE, S. L., HAYNES, S. R. (ed.), *To Each Its Own Meaning: An Introduction to Biblical Criticism and their Application,* Louisville, Westminster & John Knox Press, 1993.

MCKNIGHT, E., *The Bible and the Reader: An Introduction to Literary Criticism,* Philadelphia, Fortress Press, 1985.

MEEKS, W. A., 'The Man from Heaven in Johannine Sectarianism', *JBL* 91 (1972) 44-72.

MEEKS, W. A., *The Prophet-King. Moses Traditions and the Johannine Christology, NovTSupp* 14, Leiden, E. J. Brill, 1967.

MEIER, J. P., "The Present State of the 'Third Quest' for the Historical Jesus: Loss and Gain," *Biblica* 80 (1999) 459-487.

MEIER, J. P., *A Marginal Jew, Rethinking the Historical Jesus,* Vol. 1, New York & London et al., Doubleday, 1991.

MEIER, J. P., *A Marginal Jew, Rethinking The Historical Jesus,* Vol. 2, New York & London et al., Doubleday, 1994.

MEIER, J. P., *A Marginal Jew, Rethinking The Historical Jesus,* Vol. 3, New York & London et al., Doubleday, 2001.

MEIER, J. P., *A Marginal Jew: Rethinking the Historical Jesus,* New York, Doubleday, 1991-2001.

MELBOURNE, B. L., *Slow to Understand: The Disciples in Synoptic Perspective,* Lanham/New York/London, University Press of America, 1988.

MENDENHALL, G. E., *Ancient Israel's Faith and History: An Introduction to the Bible in Context,* Westminster John Knox Press, 2001.

MENKEN, M. J. J., *Old Testament Quotations in the Fourth Gospel: Studies in Textual Form, CBET* 15, Kampen, the Netherlands, Kok Pharos, 1996.

METZGER, B. M., *The New Testament: Its Background, Growth, and Content,* Nashville, TN, Abingdon, 1989.

MEYER, M., *The Gospel of Thomas: The Hidden Sayings of Jesus,* 1st ed., San Francisco, California, Harper Collins, 1992.

MILIK, J. T., *The Book of Enoch: Aramaic Fragments of Qumran Cave 4, With the Colloboration of M. Black,* Oxford, 1976.

MILLARD, A., *Reading and Writing in the Time of Jesus* (JSNTSup), Sheffield, Sheffield Academic Press, 2000.

MILLER, R. J., "Battling over the Jesus Seminar: Why the Ugly Attacks?", *Bible Review* 13:2 (1997) 19-22, 47.

MLAKUZHYIL, G., *The Christocentric Literary Structure of the Fourth Gospel, AnBib* 117, Rome, Biblical Institute Press, 1987.

MOLONEY, F. J., *Glory Not Dishonor: Reading John 13-21,* Minneapolis, Fortress Press, 1998.

MOLONEY, F. J., *The Fourth Gospel and the Jesus of History,* in NTS 46 (2000) 42-58.

MOLONEY, F. J., *The Gospel of John*, Sacra Pagina, Collegeville, MN, Liturgical Press, 1998.

MOLONEY, F. J., *The Johannine Son of Man*, Biblioteca di scienze religiose 14. Rome, LAS, 1976, 1978.

MOLONEY, F. J., *The Word Became Flesh*, Butler, WI, Clergy Book Service, 1977.

MONTAGUE, G. T., *The Vision of the Beloved Disciple: Meeting Jesus in the Gospel of John*, New York, Alba House, 2000.

MONTEFIORE, C. G., *Rabbinic Literature and Gospel Teachings*, London, Macmillan, 1 9 3 0 . MONTEFIORE, C. G., *Some Elements in the Religious Teaching of Jesus*, London, Macmillan, 1910.

MONTEFIORE, C. G., 'The Originality of Jesus', in *Hibbert Journal*, vol. XXVIII, 1929.

MONTEFIORE, C. G., 'The Significance of Jesus for his Own Age', in *Hibbert Journal*, vol. X, 1911-1912.

MONTEFIORE, C. G., 'What a Jew Thinks About Jesus' in *Hibbert Journal*, vol. XXXIII, 1934-1935.

MOODY SMITH, D., *New Testament Theology, The Theology of the Gospel of John*, Cambridge, NY, Cambridge University Press, 1995.

MOODY, D., "'God's Only Son': The Translation of John iii 16 in the RSV", *Journal of Bibilcal Liturature* 72 (1953) 213-19.

MORRIS, L., *Jesus is the Christ: Studies in the Theology of John*, Grand Rapids, Eerdmans, Leicester, England, Inter Varsity Press, 1989.

MOULE, C. F. D., *The Origin of Christology*, Cambridge-New York, Cambridge University Press, 1977.

MOYISE, S., (ed.), *The Old Testament in the New Testament,* Sheffield, Sheffield Academic Press, 2000.

MUSSNER, F., *The Historical Jesus in the Gospel of St. John*, Freiburg, Herder, London, Burns & Oates, 1967.

NAMITHA, *A New Paradigm for Evangelisation in the Third Millennium: In the Light of Mission in the Gospel according to St. John and the Early Upanishads*, Bangalore, India, St. Peter's Pontifical Institute Publications, 2000.

NEIRYNCK, F., *Duality in Mark: Contributions to the Study of Markan Redaction,* BETL 31, Leuven, Leuven University Press, 1972, second edition in 1988.

NEUSNER, J. (ed.), *Christianity, Judaism, and Other Greco- Roman Cults*, Leiden, Brill, 1975.

NEUSNER, J. *The Mishnah*, New Haven and London, Yale UP, 1998.

NEUSNER, J., *A Rabbi Talks with Jesus*, New York, Doubleday, 1993.

NEUSNER, J., *Invitation to the Talmud*, San Francisco, Harper Collins, 1973, 1984.

NEUSNER, J., *The Incarnation of God: The Character of Divinity in Formative Judaism*, Philadelphia, Fortress, 1988.

NEYREY, J. H., *An Ideology of Revolt: John's Christology in Social-Science Perspective*. Philadelphia, Fortress, 1988.

NICKELSBURG, G. W. E., *Jewish Literature Between the Bible and the Mishnah*, Philadelphia, Fortress, 1981.

NICKLE, K. F., *"More about Jesus Would I Know," Theology Today* 49 (1992) 398-407.

NICOL, W, *Essays on the Jewish Background of the Fourth Gospel, Neotestamentica* 6, Pretoria, N.T.W.S.A., 1972.

NICOL, W, *The Semeia in the Fourth Gospel, Tradition and Redaction*, Leiden, E. J. Brill, 1972.

NOLAN, A., *Jesus Before Christianity*, rev. ed., Maryknoll, NY, Orbis Books, 1992.

NORRIS, R. A., *Understanding the Faith of the Church* (1979), pp. 159f.

NOTLEY, R. S., "Anti-Jewish Tendencies in the Synoptic Gospels",*Jerusalem Perspective* 51 (1996) 20-35, 38.

O'DAY, G. R., *Revelation in the Fourth Gospel: Narrative Mode and Theological Claim*, Philadelphia, Fortress, 1986.

O'DAY, G. R., *The Word Disclosed: John's Story and Narrative Preaching*, St. Louis, MO, CBP Press, 1987, revised 2002.

O'NEILL, J. C., *"The Silence of Jesus,"* in *NTS* 15 (1969) 153-167.

O'NEILL, J. C., *Jesus as Teacher, in Priests and People*, Vol. 13 (1999) 308-312.

ODEBERG, H., *The Fourth Gospel: Interpreted in Its Relation to Contemporaneous Religious Currents in Palestine and the Hellenistic-Oriental World*, Uppsala, Almquist & Wiksells, 1929, repr. Amsterdam, B. R. Grüner, Chicago, Argonaut, 1968.

OLSSON, B. & HARTMAN, L., *Aspects on the Johannine Literature: Papers Presented at a Conference of Scandinavian New Testament Exegetes at Uppsala, June 16-19, 1986*, Stockholm, Almqvist & Wiksell International, 1987.

ORTON, D. E. (ed.), *The Composition of John's Gospel: Selected Studies from "Novum Testamentum"*, Leiden, Boston, E. J. Brill, 1999.

OSCAR, C., *The Christology of the New Testament*, Philadelphia, Westminster, 1963.

PAGELS, E. H., *Beyond Belief: The Secret Gospel of Thomas*, New York, Random House, 2003.

PAGELS, E. H., *The Gnostic Gospels*, New York, NY, Vintage Books, 1989.

PAGELS, E. H., *The Johannine Gospel in Gnostic Exegesis: Heracleon's Commentary on John, SBLMS* 17, Nashville, Abingdon, 1973, repr. Atlanta, Scholars Press, 1989.

PAINTER, J. R., CULPEPPER, A. & SEGOVIA, F. F. (eds.), *Word, Theology, and Community in John*, Festschrift Robert Kysar, St. Louis, Chalice Press, 2002.

PAINTER, J., *Reading John's Gospel Today*, Atlanta, John Knox, 1980.

PAINTER, J., *The Quest for the Messiah: The History, Literature and Theology of the Johannine Community,* Edinburgh, T & T Clark, 1991, 2nd ed., Nashville, Abingdon, 1993.

PANCARO, S., *The Law in the Fourth Gospel:The Torah and the Gospel, Moses and Jesus Judaism and Christianity according to John, NovTSupp* 42, Leiden, E. J. Brill, 1975.

PATTE, D., *Discipleship According to the Sermon on the Mount*, Valley Forge, PA, Trinity Press International, 1996.

PATTE, D., *The Gospel According to Matthew: A Structural Commentary on Matthew's Faith*, Philadelphia, Fortress Press, 1987.

PAUL N. A., *The Christology of the Fourth Gospel*, Valley Forge, PN, Trinity Press International, 1996.

PAZDAN, M. M., *The Son of Man: A Metaphor for Jesus in the Fourth Gospel*, Zacchaeus Studies, NT, Collegeville, MN, Liturgical Press, 1991.

PELIKAN, J., *Jesus Through the Centuries: His Place in the History of Culture*, Yale University Press, 1985.

PERKINS, P., *Jesus as Teacher*, Understanding Jesus Today, Cambridge, Cambridge University Press, 1990.

PERRIN, N., *Jesus and the Language of the Kingdom*, Philadelphia, Fortress Press, 1976.

PERRIN, N., *What is Redaction Criticism* (GBSNTS), Philadelphia, Fortress Press, 1969.

PETER M. H., *Christology and the Synoptic Problem: An Argument for Markan Priority*, Society for New Testament Studies Monograph Series 94, New York, Cambridge University Press, 1997.

PETERSEN, N. R., 'Community Foundation in the New Testament',*New Catholic World* 226/1352 (1983) 63-65.

PETERSEN, N. R., 'Insights and Models for Understanding the Healing Activity of the Historical Jesus', *SBLSP (1993)* 154-177.

PETERSEN, N. R., *Introducing the Cultural Context of the New Testament,* Hear the Word, vol. 2, New York, Paulist Press, 1992.

PETERSEN, N. R., *Literary Criticism for New Testament Critics* (GBSNTS), Philadelphia, Fortress Press, 1978.

PETERSON, N. R., *The Gospel of John and the Sociology of Light: Language and Characterization in the Fourth Gospel*, Valley Forge, PA, Trinity Press International, 1993.

PHILLIPS, C. R., *In Search of the Occult: An Annotated Anthology*, Helios 15/2, 1988.

PHIPPS, W. E., *The Wisdom and Wit of Rabbi Jesus*, Louisville, Westminster/John Knox, 1993.

PORTER, J. R., *Jesus Christ: The Jesus of History, the Christ of Faith*, New York, Oxford University Press, 1999.

POWELL, E., *The Unfinished Gospel: Notes on the Quest for the Historical Jesus*, Westlake Village, CA, Symposium Books, 1994.

POWELL, M. A., *Jesus as a Figure in History*, Louisville, Kentucky, Westminster John Knox Press, 1998.

POWELL, M. A., *What Is Narrative Criticism?*, Minneapolis, Fortress Press, 1990.

PRIOR, J. G., *The Historical Critical Method in Catholic Exegesis*, Roma, Editrice Pontificà Università Gregoriana, 1999.

PUMMER, R., "The Samaritans - A Jewish Offshoot or a Pagan Cult?" *Bible Review* 7:5 (1991) 22-29, 40.

PUTHENKANDATHIL, E., *Philos: A Designation for the Jesus-Disciple Relationship: An Exegetico-Theological Investigation of the Term in the Fourth Gospel*, Frankfurt am Main; New York, P. Lang, 1993.

QUAST, K., *Reading the Gospel of John, An Introduction*, NY, Mahwah NJ, Paulist, 1991.

RÄISÄNEN, H., *Beyond New Testament Theology: A Story and A Programme*, Philadelphia, Trinity Press International, 1990.

RAUSCH, T. P., *Who is Jesus?: An Introduction to Christology*, Collegeville, Minnesota, Liturgical Press, 2003.

RAVINDRA, R., *Christ the Yogi: A Hindu Reflection on the Gospel of John*, Rochester, Inner Traditions International, 1998.

REINHARTZ, A., *Befriending the Beloved Disciple: A Jewish Reading of the Gospel of John*, New York, Continuum, 2001.

REMUS, H., *Jesus as Healer*, Understanding Jesus Today, Cambridge, Cambridge University Press, 1997.

RENDTORFF, R., *Erwägungen zur Frühgeschichte des Prophetentums in Israel*, *ZTK* 59 (1962) 145-167.

RESSEGUIE, J. L, *The Strange Gospel: Narrative Design and Point of View in John*, Biblical Interpretation 56., Leiden, Boston, Brill, 2001.

RICHMOND, W. J., *The Gospel of the Rejection: A Study in the Relation of the Fourth Gospel to the Three*, London, J. Murray, 1906.

RICO, C., "Contexte, autorité et mode de signification. De La linguistique à l'interprétation de la Bible", *RB* 108 (2001) 598- 613.

RIESENFELD, H., *The Gospel Tradition and Its Beginnings*, 2nd ed., London, Mowbray, 1961.

RIESNER, R., *Jesus as Preacher and Teacher in Jesus and the Oral Gospel Tradition*, Sheffield, Sheffield Academic Press, 1991.

RINGE, S. H., *Wisdom's Friends: Community and Christology in the Fourth Gospel*, Louisville, Westminster / John Knox, 1999.

ROBBINS, V. K., "Text and Context in Recent Studies of Mark," *Religious Studies Review* 17 (1991) 16-23.

ROBBINS, V. K., *Jesus the Teacher: A Socio-Rhetorical Interpretation of Mark*, Minneapolis, Fortress Press, 1992.

ROBINSON, J. A. T. & COAKLEY, J. F., *The Priority of John*, London, SCM Press, 1985.

ROBINSON, J. A., *The Historical Character of St. John's Gospel*, London, New York, Longmans, Green & Co., 1929.

ROBINSON, J. M., (Gen. ed.), *The Nag Hammidi Library in English* (Revised Edition), San Francisco, CA, Harper & Row, 1988.

ROBINSON, J. M., "*The Q Trajectory*," in PEARSON (ed.), *Future of Early Christianity* (*Essays in honor of Helmut Koester*), Minneapolis, Fortress, 1997.

ROBINSON, J. M., HOFFMAN, P., KLOPPENBORG, J. S., & MORELAND, M. C. (ed.), *The Sayings Gospel Q in Greek and English: With Parallels from the Gospels of Mark and Thomas*, Minneapolis, MN, Augsburg Fortress Publishers, 2002.

ROHRBAUGH, R. L., "Social Location of Thought as a Heuristic Construct in New Testament Study," *JSNT* 30 (1987) 103-19.

ROTHSCHILD, F. A. (ed.), *Jewish Perspectives on Christianity*, New York, Crossroad, 1990.

RUDERMAN, D. B., "*Rabbi and Teacher*", in COHEN, A. A. & MENDES-FLOHR, P. (eds.), *Contemporary Jewish Religious Thought*, NY, The Free Press, 1987, pp. 741-747.

SABOURIN, L., *The Names and Titles of Jesus, Themes of Biblical Theology*, New York, Macmillan, 1967.

SADANANDA, D., *The Johannine Exegesis of God: An Exploration into the Johannine Understanding of God*, New York, de Gruyter, 2004.

SAFRAI, C., "Jesus' Jewish Parents", *Jerusalem Perspective* 40 (1993), 10-11, 14-15.

SAFRAI, S. & STERN, M. (ed.), *The Jewish People in the First Century: Compendia Rerum Iudaicarum ad Novum Testamentum*, Philadelphia, Fortress, 1974, 1976.

SAFRAI, S., "Jesus and the Hasidim", *Jerusalem Perspective* 42, 43 & 44 (1994) 3-22.

SAFRAI, S., "Literary Languages in the Time of Jesus", *Jerusalem Perspective* 31 (1991) 3-8.

SAFRAI, S., "Spoken Languages in the Time of Jesus", *Jerusalem Perspective* 30 (1991) 3-8, 13.

SAFRAI, S., "Teaching of Pietists in Mishnaic Literature", *The Journal of Jewish Studies* 16 (1965) 15-33.

SAFRAI, S., "The Jewish Cultural Nature of Galilee in the First Century", *Immanuel* 24/25 (1990) 147-186.

SAFRAI, S., "The Place of Women in First-century Synagogues", *Jerusalem Perspective* 40 (1993) 3-6, 14.

SALIER, W. H., *The Rhetorical Impact of the Semeia in the Gospel of John: A Historical and Hermeneutical Perspective*, *WUNT* 2.186, Tübingen, Mohr/Siebeck, 2004.

SALMON, V., *The Fourth Gospel: A History of the Textual Tradition of the Original Greek Gospel*, Collegeville, MN, Liturgical Press, 1976.

SANDERS, E. P., *Jesus and Judaism*, Philadelphia, Fortress Press, 1985.

SANDERS, E. P., *Jesus and Judaism*, Philadelphia, Fortress, 1985.

SANDERS, E. P., *The Historical Figure of Jesus*, New York, Allen Lane/Penguin, 1993.

SANDERS, J. A., "Scripture as Canon for Post-Modern Times", *BTB* 25 (1995) 56-63.

SANDERS, J. N., *The Fourth Gospel in the Early Church: Its Origin & Influence on Christian Theology Up to Irenaeus*, Cambridge, University Press, 1943.

SANDMEL, S., *Judaism and Christian Beginnings*, New York, Oxford University Press, 1978.

SANDMEL, S., *We Jews and Jesus*, New York, Oxford University Press, 1965.

SCHAEFER, P., *The Aim and Purpose of Early Jewish Mysticism*, Oxford Center for Postgraduate Studies 1986.

SCHAFER-LICHTENBERGER, C., *'Josua' und 'Elischa' – eine biblische Argumentation zur Begründung der Autorität und Legitimität des Nachfolgers*, *ZAW* 101 (1989) 198-222.

SCHECHTER, S., *Aspects of Rabbinic Theology*, New York, Schocken Books, 1961.

SCHECHTER, S., 'Some Rabbinic Parallels to the New Testament' in *Jewish Quarterly Review*, vol. XII, 1900.

SCHEIN, B. E., *Following the Way: The Setting of John's Gospel*, Minneapolis, Augsburg, 1980.

SCHENK,, W., "The Roles of Readers or the Myth of the Reader", *Semeia* 48(1989) 55-80

SCHIFFMAN, L. H., "New Light on the Pharisees - Insights from the Dead Sea Scrolls", *Bible Review* 8:3 (1992) 30-33, 54.

SCHILLEBEECKX, E., *Christ: The Experience of Jesus as Lord, ET*, New York, Seabury, 1980.

SCHILLEBEECKX, E., *Jesus: An Experiment in Christology, ET*, New York, Seabury, 1979.

SCHMITT, H.-C., *Prophetie und Tradition, Beobachtungen zur Frühgeschichte des israelitischen Nabitums*, *ZTK* 74 (1977) 255-272.

SCHNACKENBURG, R., *Jesus in the Gospels: a Biblical Christology*, trans. O.C. Dean, Jr., Louisville, Westminster John Knox, 1995.

SCHNACKENBURG, R., *The Gospel According to St. John*, 2 vol., New York, Seabury Press, 1968, 1980.

SCHNEIDERS, S. M., *The Revelatory Text: Interpreting the New Testament as Scriptur e,* San Francisco , HarperSanFrancisco, 1991.

SCHNEIDERS, S. M., *Written That You Might Believe: Encountering Jesus in the Fourth Gospel*, New York, Crossroad, 1999, rev. ed. 2003.

SCHNELLE, U., *Antidocetic Christology in the Gospel of John: An Investigation of the Place of the Fourth Gospel in the Johannine School*, Minneapolis, Fortress, 1992.

SCHNELLE, U., *The Human Condition: Anthropology in the Teachings of Jesus, Paul, & John.* Minneapolis, Augsburg, Fortress, 1996.

SCHUCHARD, B. G., *Scripture Within Scripture: The Interrelationship of Form and Function in the Explicit Old Testament Citations in the Gospel of John, SBLDS* 133, Atlanta, Scholars Press, 1992.

SCHÜRER, E., *The History of the Jewish People in the Age of Jesus Christ (175 B.C.-A.D. 135),* rev. ed. VERMES, G. et al, (eds.), Edinburgh, T. & T. Clark, 1973.

SCHÜSSLER F. E., 'Remembering the Past in Creating the Future: Historical-Critical Scholarship and Feminist Biblical Interpretation', in COLLINS, A. E. (ed.), *Feminist Perspectives on Biblical Scholarship,* SBL Centennial Publications 10, Atlanta, Scholars Press, 1985, pp. 43-63.

SCHÜSSLER F., E., *Bread Not Stone: The Challenge of Feminist Biblical Interpretation,* Boston, Beacon Press, 1985.

SCHÜSSLER F., E., *In Memory of Her: A Feminist Theological Reconstruction of Christian Origins,* New York, Crossroad Press, 1983.

SCHWARZ, H., *Christology,* Grand Rapids, MI, Cambridge, UK, Eerdmans, 1998.

SCHWEITZER, A., *The Quest for the Historical Jesus*, (ed.), BOWDEN, J., Fortress Press, 2001.

SCHWEIZER, E., *Jesus Christ: The Man from Nazareth and the Exalted Lor*, ed. Hulitt GLOER, Macon, Georgia, Mercer University Press, 1987.

SCHWEIZER, E., *Jesus the Parable of God: What Do We Really Know About Jesus,* Allison Park, PA, Pickwick, 1994.

SCHWEIZER, E., *Lordship and Discipleship*, SBL 28, London, SCM Press, 1960.

SCHWEIZER, E., *The Good News According to Luke,* Atlanta, John Knox Press, 1984.

SCOTT, B. B. & DEAN, M. E., 'A Sound Map of the Sermon on the Mount', in *SBLSP* 32 (1993) 726-39.

SCOTT, B. B., *Hear Then the Parable: A Commentary on the Parables of Jesus,* Minneapolis, Fortress Press, 1991.

SCOTT, E. F., *The Fourth Gospel: Its Purpose and Theology,* Edinburgh, T& T Clark, 1906, repr. 1908, 1920, 1923, 1926.

SCOTT, E. F., *The Historical and Religious Value of the Fourth Gospel,* Boston and New York, Houghton Mifflin, 1909.

SCOTT, M., *Sophia and the Johannine Jesus, JSNTSup* 71, Sheffield, Sheffield Academic Press, 1992.

SCROGGS, R., *Christology in Paul and John: The Reality and Revelation of God* (Proclamation Commentaries), Philadelphia, Fortress, 1988.

SEELEY D., *Deconstructing the New Testament,* Leiden, Brill, 1994.

SEGOVIA, F. F. (ed.), *Discipleship in the New Testament,* Philadelphia, Fortress, 1985.

SEGOVIA, F. F. (ed.), *What is John? Readers and Readings of the Fourth Gospel,* SBL Symposium Series 3, Atlanta, GA, Scholar's Press, 1996.

SEGUNDO, J. L., *Jesus of Nazareth, Yesterday & Today,* 5 vol., Maryknoll, NY, Orbis, 1980.

SENIOR, D., *A Gospel Portrait of Jesus,* Cincinnati, OH, Pflaum Standard, 1975.

SERVOTTE, H., *According to John: A Literary Reading of the Fourth Gospel,* London, Darton, Longman & Todd, 1994.

SETZER, C., *Excellent Women: Female Witness to the Resurrection, JBL* 116, (1997) 259-272.

SHANKS, H., "*Is The Title 'Rabbi' Anachronistic in the Gospels?*" *JQR* 53 (1963) 337-345.

SHANKS, H., *Origins of the Title "Rabbi", JQR* 59 (1968) 152-57.

SHERWIN, B., 'Who Do You Say That I Am?' in *Journal of Ecumenical Studies,* vol. 31, 3-4, 1994.

SHUPAK, N., *The 'Sitz im Leben' of the Book of Proverbs in the Light of a Comparison of Biblical and Egyptian Wisdom Literature, RB* 94 (1987) 98-119.

SIDEBOTTOM, E. M., *The Christ of the Fourth Gospel, in the Light of First-Century Thought,* London, SPCK, 1961.

SLOAN, R. B. & PARSONS, M. C. (eds.), *Perspectives on John: Methods and Interpretation in the Fourth Gospel, NABPR* Special Studies, 11, Lewiston, NY, Edwin Mellen, SLOYAN, G., *John,* Interpretation Commentary, Atlanta, John Knox Press, 1988.

SLOYAN, G., *What are they saying about John?,* New York, Paulist Press, 1991.

SMITH, D. E. (ed.), *How Gospels Begin, Semeia* 52, Atlanta, Scholars Press, 1991.

SMITH, D. M., *Johannine Christianity: Essays on its Setting, Sources, and Theology,* Edinburgh, T&T. Clark, Columbia, SC, University of South Carolina Press, 1984.

SMITH, D. M., *Johannine Christianity: Essays on Its Setting, Sources, and Theology,* Columbia, SC, University of South Carolina Press, 1989.

SMITH, D. M., *John Among the Gospels: The Relationship in Twentieth-Century Research*, Minneapolis, Fortress, 1992, 2nd edition, 2001.

SMITH, D. M., *John*, Abingdon New Testament Commentary, Nashville, Abingdon, 1999.

SMITH, D. M., *The Composition and Order of the Fourth Gospel: Bultmann's Literary Theory*, New Haven, Yale University Press, 1965.

SMITH, D. M., *The Theology of the Gospel of John*, Cambridge, New York, Cambridge University Press, 1995.

SMITH, K., *The Amazing Structure of the Gospel of John*, Blackwood, South Australia, Sherwood Publications, 2000.

SMITH, M. H., *Jesus: A Sourcebook*, New Brunswick, NJ, Peaquod Press, 2000.

SMITH, M. H., *John: A Sourcebook*, New Brunswick, NJ, Peaquod Press, 2002.

SMITH, M., *Jesus the Magician*, San Francisco, Harper & Row, STANTON, G. N., *The Gospels and Jesus*, Oxford Bible Series, 2nd ed., New York, Oxford University Press, 2002.

STANTON, G., *Gospel Truth? Today's Quest for Jesus of Nazareth*, San Francisco, Harper Collins, 1995.

STEINER, R., *The Gospel of St. John and Its Relation to the* Other Gospels: Fourteen Lectures Delivered in Kassel, June *24-July 7, 1909*, New York, Anthroposophic Press, 1948, 2nd ed., Spring Valley, NY, Anthroposophic Press, 1982.

STEINER, R., *The Gospel of St. John: A Cycle of Twelve* Lectures, Unrevised by Author, Given at Hamburg from 18th to *31st of May, 1908*, Trans. by Maude Breckenridge Monges, New York, Anthroposophic Press, London, Rudolf Steiner, 1940, rev. ed. Spring Valley, NY, Anthroposophic Press, 1962, repr. 1984.

STIBBE, M. W. G. (ed.), *The Gospel of John as Literature: An Anthology of Twentieth-Century Perspectives,* NT Tools and Studies, 17, Leiden, New York, E. J. Brill, 1993.

STIBBE, M. W. G., *John as Storyteller: Narrative Criticism and the Fourth Gospel*, *SNTSMS* 73, Cambridge, England, New York, Cambridge University Press, 1992.

STOCK, A., *The Method and Message of Matthew*, Collegeville, MN, Liturgical Press, A Michael Glazier Book, 1995.

STONE, M. (ed.), *Jewish Writings of the Second Temple Period*, Philadelphia, Fortress, 1984.

STORY, C. I. K., *The Fourth Gospel. Its Purpose Pattern and Power*, Shippensburg PA, Ragged Edge Press, 1997.

STRACHAN, R. H., *The Fourth Gospel: Its Significance and Environment*, 3rd ed., London, SCM Press, 1941.

STRACK, H. L. & STEMBERGER, G., *Introduction to the Talmud and Midrash*, Edinburgh, T & T Clark, 1991.

STRAUSS, D. F., *The Christ of Faith and the Jesus of History: A Critique of Schleiermacher's The Life of Jesus*, (KECK, L. E. trans.), Philadelphia, Fortress Press, 1977.

SWANSON, R. J. (ed.), *New Testament Greek Manuscripts: John*, Sheffield, Sheffield Academic Press, 1995 & Pasadena, William Carey International University Press, 1998.

SWANSON, R. J., *John, New Testament Greek manuscripts, Variant Readings Arranged in Horizontal Lines against Codex Vaticanus*, Sheffield, England, Sheffield Academic press, 1995.

TALBERT, C. H., *Reading John: A Literary and Theological Commentary on the Fourth Gospel and the Johannine Epistles*, Reading the New Testament Series, New York, Crossroad, 1999.

TATUM, W. B., *In Quest of Jesus*, 'Revised and Enlarged' ed., Nashville, TN, Abingdon Press, 1999.

TAYLOR, V., *The Names of Jesus*, London, Macmillan, 1954. TAYLOR, V., *The Person of Christ in New Testament Teaching*, London, Macmillan, 1958.

TELFORD, W. R., *The Theology of the Gospel of Mark*, New Testament Theology, Cambridge, Cambridge University Press, 1999.

TEMPLE, S., *The Core of the Fourth Gospel*, Oxford & London, Mowbrays, 1975.

THATCHER, T., *The Riddles of Jesus in John: A Study in Tradition and Folklore, SBLMS* 53, Atlanta, Society of Biblical Literature, 2000.

THEISSEN, G. & MERZ, A., *The Historical Jesus: A Comprehensive Guide*, Fortress Press, 2003.

THEISSEN, G., *The Gospels in Context: Social and Political History in the Synoptic Tradition*, Minneapolis, Fortress, 1991.

THOMPSON, M. M., *The God of the Gospel of John*, Grand Rapids, Eerdmans, 2001.

THOMPSON, M. M., *The Humanity of Jesus in the Fourth Gospel*, Philadelphia, Fortress, 1988, republished as *Incarnate Word: Perspectives on Jesus in the Fourth Gospel*, Peabody, MA, Hendrickson, 1993.

TÖDT, H. E., *The Son of Man in the Synoptic Tradition*, London, SCM, 1965.

TOLBERT, M. A., *Sowing the Gospel: Mark's World in a Literary-Historical Perspective*, Minneapolis, Fortress Press, 1989.

TOVEY, D., *Narrative Art and Act in the Fourth Gospel,* JSNTSup 151, Sheffield, Sheffienld academic Press, 1997.

TRITES, A. A., *The New Testament Concept of Witness*, Cambridge &London et al., Cambridge University Press, 1977.

TROCME, E., *Jesus: As Seen by His Contemporaries,* (trans.), WILSON, R. A., Philadelphia, Westminster Press, 1973.

TUCKETT, C. M., *Christology and the New Testament, Jesus and His Earliest Followers*, Edinburgh, University Press, 2001.

TUCKETT, C. M., *Luke's Literary Achievement: Collected Essays*, Journal for the Study of the New Testament, Supplement 116, Sheffield, Sheffield Academic Press, 1995.

TWELFTREE, G. H., *Jesus the Exorcist: A Contribution to the Study of the Historical Jesus*, Peabody, MA, Hendrickson, 1997.

VAN BELLE, G., *The Signs Source in the Fourth Gospel: Historical Survey and Critical Evaluation of the Semeia Hypothesis*, BETL 116, Leuven, Leuven University Press, Uitgeverij Peeters, 1994.

VAN SEGBROECK, F. et al. (eds.), *The Four Gospels 1992: Festschrift Frans Neirynck*, 3 vols. BETL 100, Leuven, Leuven University Press, Uitgeverij Peeters, 1992.

VAN TILBORG, S., *Imaginative Love in John*, Biblical Interpretation Series 2, Leiden, Brill, 1993.

VAN TILBORG, S., *Reading John in Ephesus*, NovTSup 83, Leiden/New York/Cologne, E J Brll, 1996.

VAN VOORST, R. E., *Jesus Outside the New Testament: An Introduction to the Ancient Evidence*, Grand Rapids, MI, Wm. B. Eerdmans, 2000.

VANIER, J., *Drawn into the Mystery of Jesus through the Gospel of John*, London, Darton, Longman, Todd, 2004.

VAWTER, B., *This Man Jesus*: *An Essay Toward a New Testament Christology*, London, Geoffrey Chapman, 1975.

VERMES, G., *Dead Sea Scrolls, Forty Years On*, Oxford University Press, Oxford, 1987.

VERMES, G., *Essenes*, Sheffield University Press, Sheffield, 1989.

VERMES, G., *Jesus and the World of Judaism*, SCM Press, London, 1983.

VERMES, G., 'Jesus the Jew' in CHARLESWORTH, J. H. (ed.), *Jesus' Jewishness; Exploring the Place of Jesus in Early Judaism*, New York, Crossroad Publishing, 1991.

VERMES, G., *Jesus the Jew: a Historian's Reading of the Gospels*, Philadelphia, Fortress Press, 1981.

VERMES, G., *The Changing Face of Jesus*, New York, Penguin Books, 2001.

VERMES, G., *The Religion of Jesus the Jew*, Minneapolis, Fortress Press, 1993.

VERNON R. K., *Ancient Quotes and Anecdotes: From Crib to Crypt*, Sonoma, CA, Polebridge Press, 1989.

VERNON R. K., 'Interpreting the Gospel of Mark as a Jewish Document in a Graeco-Roman World', in FLESHER, P. V. M. (ed.), *New Perspectives on Ancient Judaism*, Lanham/ New York/London, University Press of America, 1990, pp. 47-72.

VERNON R. K., *Jesus the Teacher: A Socio-Rhetorical Interpretation of Mark*, Minneapolis, Fortress Press, 1992.

VERNON R. K., 'Pronouncement Stories from a Rhetorical Perspective', *Forum* 4/2 (1988) 3-32.

VIA, Jr., D. O., *The Parables: Their Literary and Existential Dimension*, Philadelphia, Fortress Press, 1967; Vol. 1: *The Roots of the Problem and the Person* (1991); Vol. 2: *Mentor, Message, Miracles* (1994); Vol. 3: *Companions and Competitors* (2001).

VORSTER, W. S., *Speaking of Jesus, Essays on Biblical Language, Gospel Narrative and the Historical Jesus*, Leiden, Boston et al., Brill, 1999.

WAETJEN, H. C., *The Gospel of the Beloved Disciple: A Work in Two Editions*, New York, T&T Clark, 2005.

WAGNER, W. F., *First Reader in New Testament Greek: An Inductive Study of the Gospel of John*, Falls Church, W. F. Wagner, 1992.

WALTHER, J. A., *New Testament Greek Workbook: An Inductive Study of the Complete Text of the Gospel of John*, Chicago, University of Chicago Press, 1966.

WALVOORD, J. F., *Jesus Christ Our Lord*, Moody Press, 1969. WATSON, A., *Jesus and the Jews: The Pharisaic Tradition in John*, Athens, University of Georgia press, 1995.

WATSON, E. G., *Wisdom's Daughters: Stories of Women around Jesus*, Cleveland, Pilgrim Press, 1997.

WEBB, V., *John's Message: Good News for the New Millennium*, Nashville, Abingdon, 2000.

WEISS, J., *Jesus' Proclamation of the Kingdom of God*, (trans.), HIERS, R. H. & HOLLAND, D. L., Philadelphia, Fortress Press, 1971.

WENDT, H. H. & LUMMIS, E. W., *The Gospel according to St. John: An Inquiry into its Genesis and Historical Value*, Edinburgh, T. & T. Clark, 1902.

WERNER H. K., *The Oral and Written Gospel*, reprint, Indiana University Press, 1997.

WESTCOTT, B. F., *The Revelation of the Father: Short Lectures on the Titles of the Lord in the Gospel of St. John*, London, Macmillan, 1904.

WESTERMAN, C., *The Parables of Jesus in the Light of the Old Testament*, Minneapolis, Fortress Press, 1990.

WESTERMANN, C., *The Gospel of John in the Light of the Old Testament*, Peabody, Hendrickson, 1998.

WHITACRE, R.A., *Johannine Polemic: The Role of Tradition and Theology*, Chico, CA, Scholars Press, 1982.

WILCOX, M., *Jesus in the Light of his Jewish Environment, Aufstieg und Niedergang der Römischen Welt* II, 25, 1, Berlin- New York, de Gruyter, 1982.

WILKINS, M. J., *Following The Master, A Biblical Theology of Discipleship*, Grand Rapids, MI, Zondervan, 1992.

WILLETT, M. E., *Wisdom Christology in the Fourth Gospel*, San Francisco, Mellen, 1992.

WILLIAMS, J. G., *The Prophetic "Father", A Brief Explanation of the Term "Sons of the Prophets," JBL* 85 (1966) 344-348.

WILSON, A., *Conceptual Glossary and Index to the Vulgate Translation of the Gospel according to John,* Alpha-Omega, A.211, Hildesheim & New York, Olms-Weidmann, 2000.

WILSON, R. R., *Prophecy and Society in Ancient Israel,* Phildephia, Fortress Press, 1980.

WITHERINGTON III, B., *Jesus the Sage: The Pilgrimage of Wisdom,* Minneapolis, Fortress Press, 2000.

WITHERINGTON III, B., *John's Wisdom: A Commentary on the Fourth Gospel,* Louisville, KY, Westminster John Knox, 1995.

WITHERINGTON III, B., *The Christology of Jesus,* Minneapolis, Fortress, 1990.

WITHERINGTON III, B., *The Jesus Quest: The Third Search for the Jew of Nazareth,* 2nd ed., Downers Grove, IL, Intervarsity Press, 1997.

WITHERINGTON III, B., *The Many Faces of the Christ: The Christologies of the New Testament and Beyond,* Companions to the New Testament, New York, Crossroad, 1998.

WRIGHT, N. T., "How Jesus Saw Himself", *Bible Review* 12:3 (1996) 22-29.

WRIGHT, N. T., *Christian Origins and the Question of God,* Minneapolis, Fortress Press, 1997.

WRIGHT, N. T., *The Challenge of Jesus: Rediscovering Who Jesus Was and Is,* Downers' Grove, IL, Intervarsity Press, 1999.

WYLEN, S., *The Jews in the Time of Jesus,* New York, Paulist, 1996.

YEE, G. A., *Jewish Feasts in John's Gospel,* Zacchaeus Studies, New Testament, Wilmington, DE, M. Glazier, 1988.

YOUNG, B. H. & FLUSSER, D., Messianic Blessings in Jewish and Christian Texts, In *Judaism and the Origins of Christianity,* FLUSSER, D. (ed.), Jerusalem, Magnes Press, 1988, pp. 280-300.

YOUNG, B. H., "'Save the Adulteress!' Ancient Jewish Responsa in the Gospels", *New Testament Studies* 41 (1995) 59-70.

YOUNG, B. H., "The Cross, Jesus and the Jewish People", *Immanuel* 24/25 (1990) 23-34.

YOUNG, B. H., *Jesus and His Jewish Parables: Rediscovering the Roots of Jesus' Teaching,* Mahwah, NJ, Paulist Press, 1989.

YOUNG, B. H., *Jesus the Jewish Theologian,* Peabody, MA, Hendrickson Publishers, 1995.

YOUNG, B. H., *The Jewish Background to the Lord's Prayer,* Dayton, OH, Center for Judaic-Christian Studies, 1984.

ZEITLIN, I. M., *Jesus and the Judaism of His Time,* Cambridge, UK, Polity Press, 1988.

ZEITLIN, S., *"Beginnings of Christianity and Judaism" JQR* 27 (1937) 385-398.

ZEITLIN, S., *"Is the Title "Rabbi" Anachronistic in the Gospels?"*, *JQR* 53 (1962-63) 345-349.

ZEITLIN, S., *"The Title Rabbi in the Gospels is Anachronistic"*, *JQR* 59 (1968) 158-160.

ZEITLIN, S., *Josephus on Jesus*, Philadelphia, JPS, 1931. ZEITLIN, S., *The Title Rabbi in the Gospels is Anachronistic*, *JQR* 51 (1961) 122.

ZIMMERLI, W., *Ezechiel/Ezechielbuch*, *TRE* 10 (1982) 766-781.

ZIMMERMAN, F., *The Aramaic Origin of the Four Gospels*, New York, Ktav Publishing House Inc, 1979.

www.ingramcontent.com/pod-product-compliance
Lightning Source LLC
Chambersburg PA
CBHW051550100726
47898CB00001B/46